D1516132

THE BEST KNOWN WORKS OF
EMILE ZOLA

THE
BEST KNOWN WORKS OF
EMILE ZOLA

Including *Nana, The Miller's Daughter*
and *Nantas*

THE BOOK LEAGUE OF AMERICA

New York

1941
BLUE RIBBON BOOKS

CONTENTS

NANA

CHAPTER I

AT NINE O'CLOCK in the evening the body of the house at the Théâtres des Variétés was still all but empty. A few individuals, it is true, were sitting quietly waiting in the balcony and stalls, but these were lost, as it were, among the ranges of seats whose coverings of cardinal velvet loomed in the subdued light of the dimly burning luster. A shadow enveloped the great red splash of the curtain, and not a sound came from the stage, the unlit footlights, the scattered desks of the orchestra. It was only high overhead in the third gallery, round the domed ceiling where nude females and children flew in heavens which had turned green in the gaslight, that calls and laughter were audible above a continuous hubbub of voices, and heads in women's and workmen's caps were ranged, row above row, under the wide-vaulted bays with their gilt-surrounding adornments. Every few seconds an attendant would make her appearance, bustling along with tickets in her hand and piloting in front of her a gentleman and a lady, who took their seats, he in his evening dress, she sitting slim and undulant beside him while her eyes wandered slowly round the house.

Two young men appeared in the stalls; they kept standing and looked about them.

"Didn't I say so, Hector?" cried the elder of the two, a tall fellow with little black mustaches. "We're too early! You might quite well have allowed me to finish my cigar."

An attendant was passing.

"Oh, Monsieur Faucfery," she said familiarly, "it won't begin for half an hour yet!"

"Then why do they advertise for nine o'clock?" muttered Hector, whose long thin face assumed an expression of vexation. "Only this morning Clarisse, who's in the piece, swore that they'd begin at nine o'clock punctually."

For a moment they remained silent and, looking upward, scanned the shadowy boxes. But the green paper with which these were hung rendered them more shadowy still. Down below, under the dress circle, the lower boxes were buried in utter night. In those on the second tier there was only one stout lady, who was stranded, as it were, on the velvet-covered balustrade in front of her. On the right hand and on the left, between lofty pilasters, the stage boxes, bedraped with long-fringed scalloped hangings, remained untenanted. The house with its white and gold, relieved by soft green tones, lay only half disclosed to view, as though full of a fine dust shed from the little jets of flame in the great glass luster.

"Did you get your stage box for Lucy?" asked Hector.

"Yes," replied his companion, "but I had some trouble to get it. Oh, there's no danger of Lucy coming too early!"

He stifled a slight yawn; then after a pause:

"You're in luck's way, you are, since you haven't been at a first night before. The *Blonde Venus* will be the event of the year. People have been talking about it for six months. Oh, such music, my dear boy! Such a sly dog,

Bordenave! He knows his business and has kept this for the exhibition season."

Hector was religiously attentive. He asked a question.

"And Nana, the new star who's going to play Venus, d'you know her?"

"There you are; you're beginning again!" cried Fauchery, casting up his arms. "Ever since this morning people have been dreeing me with Nana. I've met more than twenty people, and it's Nana here and Nana there! What do *I* know? Am I acquainted with all the light ladies in Paris? Nana is an invention of Bordenave's! It must be a fine one!"

He calmed himself, but the emptiness of the house, the dim light of the luster, the churchlike sense of self-absorption which the place inspired, full as it was of whispering voices and the sound of doors banging—all these got on his nerves.

"No, by Jove," he said all of a sudden, "one's hair turns gray here. I—I'm going out. Perhaps we shall find Bordenave downstairs. He'll give us information about things."

Downstairs in the great marble-paved entrance hall, where the box office was, the public were beginning to show themselves. Through the three open gates might have been observed, passing in, the ardent life of the boulevards, which were all astir and aflare under the fine April night. The sound of carriage wheels kept stopping suddenly; carriage doors were noisily shut again, and people began entering in small groups, taking their stand before the ticket bureau and climbing the double flight of stairs at the end of the hall, up which the women loitered with swaying hips. Under the crude gaslight, round the pale, naked walls of the entrance hall, which with its scanty First Empire decorations suggested the peristyle of a toy temple, there was a flaring display of lofty yellow posters bearing the name of "Nana" in great black letters. Gentlemen, who seemed to be glued to the entry, were reading them; others, standing about, were engaged in talk, barring the doors of the house in so doing, while hard by the box office a thickset man with an extensive, close-shaven visage was giving rough answers to such as pressed to engage seats.

"There's Bordenave," said Fauchery as he came down the stairs. But the manager had already seen him.

"Ah, ah! You're a nice fellow!" he shouted at him from a distance. "That's the way you give me a notice, is it? Why, I opened my *Figaro* this morning —never a word!"

"Wait a bit," replied Fauchery. "I certainly must make the acquaintance of your Nana before talking about her. Besides, I've made no promises."

Then to put an end to the discussion, he introduced his cousin, M. Hector de la Faloise, a young man who had come to finish his education in Paris. The manager took the young man's measure at a glance. But Hector returned his scrutiny with deep interest. This, then, was that Bordenave, that showman of the sex who treated women like a convict overseer, that clever fellow who was always at full steam over some advertising dodge, that shouting, spitting, thigh-slapping fellow, that cynic with the soul of a policeman! Hector was under the impression that he ought to discover some amiable observation for the occasion.

"Your theater——" he began in dulcet tones.

Bordenave interrupted him with a savage phrase, as becomes a man who dotes on frank situations.

"Call it my brothel!"

At this Fauchery laughed approvingly, while La Faloise stopped with his pretty speech strangled in his throat, feeling very much shocked and striving to appear as though he enjoyed the phrase. The manager had dashed off to shake hands with a dramatic critic whose column had considerable influence. When he returned La Faloise was recovering. He was afraid of being treated as a provincial if he showed himself too much nonplused.

"I have been told," he began again, longing positively to find something to say, "that Nana has a delicious voice."

"Nana?" cried the manager, shrugging his shoulders. "The voice of a squirt!"

The young man made haste to add:

"Besides being a first-rate comedian!"

"She? Why she's a lump! She has no notion what to do with her hands and feet."

La Faloise blushed a little. He had lost his bearings. He stammered:

"I wouldn't have missed this first representation tonight for the world. I was aware that your theater——"

"Call it my brothel," Bordenave again interpolated with the frigid obstinacy of a man convinced.

Meanwhile Fauchery, with extreme calmness, was looking at the women as they came in. He went to his cousin's rescue when he saw him all at sea and doubtful whether to laugh or to be angry.

"Do be pleasant to Bordenave—call his theater what he wishes you to, since it amuses him. And you, my dear fellow, don't keep us waiting about for nothing. If your Nana neither sings nor acts you'll find you've made a blunder, that's all. It's what I'm afraid of, if the truth be told."

"A blunder! A blunder!" shouted the manager, and his face grew purple. "Must a woman know how to act and sing? Oh, my chicken, you're too *stoopid*. Nana has other good points, by heaven!—something which is as good as all the other things put together. I've smelled it out; it's deuced pronounced with her, or I've got the scent of an idiot. You'll see, you'll see! She's only got to come on, and all the house will be gaping at her."

He had held up his big hands which were trembling under the influence of his eager enthusiasm, and now, having relieved his feelings, he lowered his voice and grumbled to himself:

"Yes, she'll go far! Oh yes, s'elp me, she'll go far! A skin—oh, what a skin she's got!"

Then as Fauchery began questioning him he consented to enter into a detailed explanation, couched in phraseology so crude that Hector de la Faloise felt slightly disgusted. He had been thick with Nana, and he was anxious to start her on the stage. Well, just about that time he was in search of a Venus. He—he never let a woman encumber him for any length of time; he preferred to let the public enjoy the benefit of her forthwith. But there was a deuce of a row going on in his shop, which had been turned topsy-turvy by that big damsel's advent. Rose Mignon, his star, a comic actress of much subtlety and an adorable singer, was daily threatening to leave him in the lurch, for she was furious and guessed the presence of a rival. And as for the bill, good God! What a noise there had been about it all! It had ended by his deciding to print the names of the two actresses in the same-sized type. But it wouldn't do to bother him. Whenever any of his little women, as he called them—Simonne or Clarisse, for instance—wouldn't go the way he wanted her to he just up with his foot and caught her one in the rear. Otherwise life was impossible. Oh yes, he sold 'em; *he* knew what they fetched, the wenches!

"Tut!" he cried, breaking off short. "Mignon and Steiner. Always together. You know, Steiner's getting sick of Rose; that's why the husband dogs his steps now for fear of his slipping away."

On the pavement outside, the row of gas jets flaring on the cornice of the theater cast a patch of brilliant light. Two small trees, violently green, stood sharply out against it, and a column gleamed in such vivid illumination that one could read the notices thereon at a distance, as though in broad daylight, while the dense night of the boulevard beyond was dotted with lights above the vague outline of an ever-moving crowd. Many men did not enter the theater at once but stayed outside to talk while finishing their cigars under the rays of the line of gas jets, which shed a sallow pallor on their faces and silhouetted their short black shadows on the asphalt. Mignon, a very tall, very broad fellow, with the square-shaped head of a strong man at a fair, was forcing a passage through the midst of the groups and dragging on his arm the banker Steiner, an exceedingly small man with a corporation already in evidence and a round face framed in a setting of beard which was already growing gray.

"Well," said Bordenave to the banker, "you met her yesterday in my office."

"Ah! It was she, was it?" ejaculated Steiner. "I suspected as much. Only I was coming out as she was going in, and I scarcely caught a glimpse of her."

Mignon was listening with half-closed eyelids and nervously twisting a great diamond ring round his finger. He had quite understood that Nana was in question. Then as Bordenave was drawing a portrait of his new star, which lit a flame in the eyes of the banker, he ended by joining in the conversation.

"Oh, let her alone, my dear fellow; she's a low lot! The public will show her the door in quick time. Steiner, my laddie, you know that my wife is waiting for you in her box."

He wanted to take possession of him again. But Steiner would not quit Bordenave. In front of them a stream of people was crowding and crushing against the ticket office, and there was a din of voices, in the midst of which the name of Nana sounded with all the melodious vivacity of its two syllables. The men who stood planted in front of the notices kept spelling it out loudly; others, in an interrogative tone, uttered it as they passed; while the women, at once restless and smiling, repeated it softly with an air of surprise. Nobody knew Nana. Whence had Nana fallen? And stories and jokes, whispered from ear to ear, went the round of the crowd. The name was a caress in itself; it was a pet name, the very familiarity of which suited every lip. Merely through enunciating it thus, the throng worked itself into a state of gaiety and became highly good natured. A fever of curiosity urged it forward, that kind of Parisian curiosity which is as violent as an access of positive unreason. Everybody wanted to see Nana. A lady had the flounce of her dress torn off; a man lost his hat.

"Oh, you're asking me too many questions about it!" cried Bordenave, whom a score of men were besieging with their queries. "You're going to see her, and I'm off; they want me."

He disappeared, enchanted at having fired his public. Mignon shrugged his shoulders, reminding Steiner that Rose was awaiting him in order to show him the costume she was about to wear in the first act.

"By Jove! There's Lucy out there, getting down from her carriage," said La Faloise to Fauchery.

It was, in fact, Lucy Stewart, a plain little woman, some forty years old, with a disproportionately long neck, a thin, drawn face, a heavy mouth, but withal of such brightness, such graciousness of manner, that she was really very charming. She was bringing with her Caroline Héquet and her mother—Caroline a woman of a cold type of beauty, the mother a person of a most worthy demeanor, who looked as if she were stuffed with straw.

"You're coming with us? I've kept a place for you," she said to Fauchery.

"Oh, decidedly not! To see nothing!" he made answer. "I've a stall; I prefer being in the stalls."

Lucy grew nettled. Did he not dare show himself in her company? Then, suddenly restraining herself and skipping to another topic:

"Why haven't you told me that you knew Nana?"

"Nana! I've never set eyes on her."

"Honor bright? I've been told that you've been to bed with her."

But Mignon, coming in front of them, his finger to his lips, made them a sign to be silent. And when Lucy questioned him he pointed out a young man who was passing and murmured:

"Nana's fancy man."

Everybody looked at him. He was a pretty fellow. Fauchery recognized him; it was Daguenet, a young man who had run through three hundred thousand francs in the pursuit of women and who now was dabbling in stocks, in order from time to time to treat them to bouquets and dinners. Lucy made the discovery that he had fine eyes.

"Ah, there's Blanche!" she cried. "It's she who told me that you had been to bed with Nana."

Blanche de Sivry, a great fair girl, whose good-looking face showed signs of growing fat, made her appearance in the company of a spare, sedulously well-groomed and extremely distinguished man.

"The Count Xavier de Vandeuvres," Fauchery whispered in his companion's ear.

The count and the journalist shook hands, while Blanche and Lucy entered into a brisk, mutual explanation. One of them in blue, the other in rose-pink, they stood blocking the way with their deeply flounced skirts, and Nana's name kept repeating itself so shrilly in their conversation that people began to listen to them. The Count de Vandeuvres carried Blanche off. But by this time Nana's name was echoing more loudly than ever round the four walls of the entrance hall amid yearnings sharpened by delay. Why didn't the play begin? The men pulled out their watches; late-comers sprang from their conveyances before these had fairly drawn up; the groups left the sidewalk, where the passers-by were crossing the now-vacant space of gaslit pavement, craning their necks, as they did so, in order to get a peep into the theater. A street boy came up whistling and planted himself before a notice at the door, then cried out, "Woa, Nana!" in the voice of a tipsy man and hied on his way with a rolling gait and a shuffling of his old boots. A laugh had arisen at this. Gentlemen of unimpeachable appearance repeated: "Nana, woa, Nana!" People were crushing; a dispute arose at the ticket office, and there was a growing clamor caused by the hum of voices calling on Nana, demanding Nana in one of those accesses of silly facetiousness and sheer animalism which pass over mobs.

But above all the din the bell that precedes the rise of the curtain became audible. "They've rung; they've rung!" The rumor reached the boulevard, and thereupon followed a stampede, everyone wanting to pass in, while the servants of the theater increased their forces. Mignon, with an anxious air, at last got hold of Steiner again, the latter not having been to see Rose's costume. At the very first tinkle of the bell La Faloise had cloven a way through the crowd, pulling Fauchery with him, so as not to miss the opening scene. But all this eagerness on the part of the public irritated Lucy Stewart. What brutes were these people to be pushing women like that! She stayed in the rear of them all with Caroline Héquet and her mother. The entrance hall was now empty, while beyond it was still heard the long-drawn rumble of the boulevard.

"As though they were always funny, those pieces of theirs!" Lucy kept repeating as she climbed the stair.

In the house Fauchery and La Faloise, in front of their stalls, were gazing about them anew. By this time the house was resplendent. High jets of gas illumined the great glass chandelier with a rustling of yellow and rosy flames, which rained down a stream of brilliant light from dome to floor. The cardinal velvets of the seats were shot with hues of lake, while all the gilding shone again, the soft green decorations chastening its effect beneath the too-decided paintings of the ceiling. The footlights were turned up and with a vivid flood of brilliance lit up the curtain, the heavy purple drapery of which had all the richness befitting a palace in a fairy tale and contrasted with the meanness of the proscenium, where cracks showed the plaster under the gilding. The place was already warm. At their music stands the orchestra were tuning their instruments amid a delicate trilling of flutes, a stifled tooting of horns, a singing of violin notes, which floated forth amid the increasing uproar of voices. All the spectators were talking, jostling, settling themselves in a general assault upon seats; and the hustling rush in the side passages was now so violent that every door into the house was laboriously admitting the inexhaustible flood of people. There were signals, rustlings of fabrics, a continual march past of skirts and head dresses, accentuated by the black hue of a dress coat or a sur-tout. Notwithstanding this, the rows of seats were little by little getting filled up, while here and there a light toilet stood out from its surroundings, a head with a delicate profile bent forward under its chignon, where flashed the lightning of a jewel. In one of the boxes the tip of a bare shoulder glim-mered like snowy silk. Other ladies, sitting at ease, languidly fanned them-selves, following with their gaze the pushing movements of the crowd, while young gentlemen, standing up in the stalls, their waistcoats cut very low, gar-denias in their buttonholes, pointed their opera glasses with gloved finger tips.

It was now that the two cousins began searching for the faces of those they knew. Mignon and Steiner were together in a lower box, sitting side by side with their arms leaning for support on the velvet balustrade. Blanche de Sivry seemed to be in sole possession of a stage box on the level of the stalls. But La Faloise examined Daguenet before anyone else, he being in occupation of a stall two rows in front of his own. Close to him, a very young man, seventeen years old at the outside, some truant from college, it may be, was straining wide a pair of fine eyes such as a cherub might have owned. Fauchery smiled when he looked at him.

"Who is that lady in the balcony?" La Faloise asked suddenly. "The lady with a young girl in blue beside her."

He pointed out a large woman who was excessively tight-laced, a woman who had been a blonde and had now become white and yellow of tint, her broad face, reddened with paint, looking puffy under a rain of little childish curls.

"It's Gaga," was Fauchery's simple reply, and as this name seemed to astound his cousin, he added:

"You don't know Gaga? She was the delight of the early years of Louis Philippe. Nowadays she drags her daughter about with her wherever she goes."

La Faloise never once glanced at the young girl. The sight of Gaga moved him; his eyes did not leave her again. He still found her very good looking but he dared not say so.

Meanwhile the conductor lifted his violin bow and the orchestra attacked the overture. People still kept coming in; the stir and noise were on the increase. Among that public, peculiar to first nights and never subject to change, there were little subsections composed of intimate friends, who smilingly forgathered again. Old first-nighters, hat on head, seemed familiar and quite at ease and kept exchanging salutations. All Paris was there, the Paris of literature, of finance and of pleasure. There were many journalists, several authors, a number of stock-exchange people and more courtesans than honest women. It was a singularly mixed world, composed, as it was, of all the talents and tarnished by all the vices, a world where the same fatigue and the same fever played over every face. Fauchery, whom his cousin was questioning, showed him the boxes devoted to the newspapers and to the clubs and then named the dramatic critics—a lean, dried-up individual with thin, spiteful lips and, chief of all, a big fellow with a good-natured expression, lolling on the shoulder of his neighbor, a young miss over whom he brooded with tender and paternal eyes.

But he interrupted himself on seeing La Faloise in the act of bowing to some persons who occupied the box opposite. He appeared surprised.

"What?" he queried. "You know the Count Muffat de Beuville?"

"Oh, for a long time back," replied Hector. "The Muffats had a property near us. I often go to their house. The count's with his wife and his father-in-law, the Marquis de Chouard."

And with some vanity—for he was happy in his cousin's astonishment—he entered into particulars. The marquis was a councilor of state; the count had recently been appointed chamberlain to the empress. Fauchery, who had caught up his opera glass, looked at the countess, a plump brunette with a white skin and fine dark eyes.

"You shall present me to them between the acts," he ended by saying. "I have already met the count, but I should like to go to them on their Tuesdays."

Energetic cries of "Hush" came from the upper galleries. The overture had begun, but people were still coming in. Late arrivals were obliging whole rows of spectators to rise; the doors of boxes were banging; loud voices were heard disputing in the passages. And there was no cessation of the sound of many conversations, a sound similar to the loud twittering of talkative sparrows at close of day. All was in confusion; the house was a medley of heads and arms which moved to and fro, their owners seating themselves or trying to make themselves comfortable or, on the other hand, excitedly endeavoring to remain standing so as to take a final look round. The cry of "Sit down, sit down!" came fiercely from the obscure depths of the pit. A shiver of expectation traversed the house: at last people were going to make the acquaintance of this famous Nana with whom Paris had been occupying itself for a whole week!

Little by little, however, the buzz of talk dwindled softly down among occasional fresh outbursts of rough speech. And amid this swooning murmur, these perishing sighs of sound, the orchestra struck up the small, lively notes of a waltz with a vagabond rhythm bubbling with roguish laughter. The public were titillated; they were already on the grin. But the gang of clappers in the foremost rows of the pit applauded furiously. The curtain rose.

"By George!" exclaimed La Faloise, still talking away. "There's a man with Lucy."

He was looking at the stage box on the second tier to his right, the front of which Caroline and Lucy were occupying. At the back of this box were observable the worthy countenance of Caroline's mother and the side face of a tall young man with a noble head of light hair and an irreproachable getup.

"Do look!" La Faloise again insisted. "There's a man there."

Fauchery decided to level his opera glass at the stage box. But he turned round again directly.

"Oh, it's Labordette," he muttered in a careless voice, as though that gentleman's presence ought to strike all the world as though both natural and immaterial.

Behind the cousins people shouted "Silence!" They had to cease talking. A motionless fit now seized the house, and great stretches of heads, all erect and attentive, sloped away from stalls to topmost gallery. The first act of the *Blonde Venus* took place in Olympus, a pasteboard Olympus, with clouds in the wings and the throne of Jupiter on the right of the stage. First of all Iris and Ganymede, aided by a troupe of celestial attendants, sang a chorus while they arranged the seats of the gods for the council. Once again the prearranged applause of the clappers alone burst forth; the public, a little out of their depth, sat waiting. Nevertheless, La Faloise had clapped Clarisse Besnus, one of Bordenave's little women, who played Iris in a soft blue dress with a great scarf of the seven colors of the rainbow looped round her waist.

"You know, she draws up her chemise to put that on," he said to Fauchery, loud enough to be heard by those around him. "We tried the trick this morning. It was all up under her arms and round the small of her back."

But a slight rustling movement ran through the house; Rose Mignon had just come on the stage as Diana. Now though she had neither the face nor the figure for the part, being thin and dark and of the adorable type of ugliness peculiar to a Parisian street child, she nonetheless appeared charming and as though she were a satire on the personage she represented. Her song at her entrance on the stage was full of lines quaint enough to make you cry with laughter and of complaints about Mars, who was getting ready to desert her for the companionship of Venus. She sang it with a chaste reserve so full of sprightly suggestiveness that the public warmed amain. The husband and Steiner, sitting side by side, were laughing complaisantly, and the whole house broke out in a roar when Prullière, that great favorite, appeared as a general, a masquerade Mars, decked with an enormous plume and dragging along a sword, the hilt of which reached to his shoulder. As for him, he had had enough of Diana; she had been a great deal too coy with him, he averred. Thereupon Diana promised to keep a sharp eye on him and to be revenged. The duet ended with a comic yodel which Prullière delivered very amusingly with the yell of an angry tomcat. He had about him all the entertaining fatuity of a young leading gentleman whose love affairs prosper, and he rolled around the most swaggering glances, which excited shrill feminine laughter in the boxes.

Then the public cooled again, for the ensuing scenes were found tiresome. Old Bosc, an imbecile Jupiter with head crushed beneath the weight of an immense crown, only just succeeded in raising a smile among his audience when he had a domestic altercation with Juno on the subject of the cook's accounts. The march past of the gods, Neptune, Pluto, Minerva and the rest, was well-nigh spoiling everything. People grew impatient; there was a restless, slowly growing murmur; the audience ceased to take an interest in the performance and looked round at the house. Lucy began laughing with Labordette; the Count de Vandeuvres was craning his neck in conversation behind Blanche's sturdy shoulders, while Fauchery, out of the corners of his eyes, took stock of the Muffats, of whom the count appeared very serious, as though he had not understood the allusions, and the countess smiled vaguely, her eyes lost in reverie. But on a sudden, in this uncomfortable state of things, the applause of the clapping contingent rattled out with the regularity of platoon firing. People turned toward the stage. Was it Nana at last? This Nana made one wait with a vengeance.

It was a deputation of mortals whom Ganymede and Iris had introduced, respectable middle-class persons, deceived husbands, all of them, and they came before the master of the gods to proffer a complaint against Venus, who was assuredly inflaming their good ladies with an excess of ardor. The chorus, in quaint, dolorous tones, broken by silences full of pantomimic admissions, caused great amusement. A neat phrase went the round of the house: "The cuckolds' chorus, the cuckolds' chorus," and it "caught on," for there was an encore. The singers' heads were droll; their faces were discovered to be in keeping with the phrase, especially that of a fat man which was as round as the moon. Meanwhile Vulcan arrived in a towering rage, demanding back his wife who had slipped away three days ago. The chorus resumed their plaint, calling on Vulcan, the god of the cuckolds. Vulcan's part was played by Fontan, a comic actor of talent, at once vulgar and original, and he had a role of the wildest whimsicality and was got up as a village blacksmith, fiery red wig, bare arms tattooed with arrow-pierced hearts and all the rest of it. A woman's voice cried in a very high key, "Oh, isn't he ugly?" and all the ladies laughed and applauded.

Then followed a scene which seemed interminable. Jupiter in the course of it seemed never to be going to finish assembling the Council of Gods in order to submit thereto the deceived husband's requests. And still no Nana! Was the management keeping Nana for the fall of the curtain then? So long a period of expectancy had ended by annoying the public. Their murmurings began again.

"It's going badly," said Mignon radiantly to Steiner. "She'll get a pretty reception; you'll see!"

At that very moment the clouds at the back of the stage were cloven apart and Venus appeared. Exceedingly tall, exceedingly strong, for her eighteen years, Nana, in her goddess's white tunic and with her light hair simply flowing unfastened over her shoulders, came down to the footlights with a quiet certainty of movement and a laugh of greeting for the public and struck up her grand ditty:

> *"When Venus roams at eventide."*

From the second verse onward people looked at each other all over the house. Was this some jest, some wager on Bordenave's part? Never had a more tuneless voice been heard or one managed with less art. Her manager judged of her excellently; she certainly sang like a squirt. Nay, more, she didn't even know how to deport herself on the stage: she thrust her arms in front of her while she swayed her whole body to and fro in a manner which struck the audience as unbecoming and disagreeable. Cries of "Oh, oh!" were already rising in the pit and the cheap places. There was a sound of whistling, too, when a voice in the stalls, suggestive of a molting cockerel, cried out with great conviction:

"That's very smart!"

All the house looked round. It was the cherub, the truant from the boardingschool, who sat with his fine eyes very wide open and his fair face glowing very hotly at sight of Nana. When he saw everybody turning toward him he grew extremely red at the thought of having thus unconsciously spoken aloud. Daguenet, his neighbor, smilingly examined him; the public laughed, as though disarmed and no longer anxious to hiss; while the young gentlemen in white gloves, fascinated in their turn by Nana's gracious contours, lolled back in their seats and applauded.

"That's it! Well done! Bravo!"

Nana, in the meantime, seeing the house laughing, began to laugh herself. The gaiety of all redoubled itself. She was an amusing creature, all the same, was that fine girl! Her laughter made a love of a little dimple appear in her chin. She stood there waiting, not bored in the least, familiar with her audience, falling into step with them at once, as though she herself were admitting with a wink that she had not two farthings' worth of talent but that it did not matter at all, that, in fact, she had other good points. And then after having made a sign to the conductor which plainly signified, "Go ahead, old boy!" she began her second verse:

" 'Tis Venus who at midnight passes——"

Still the same acidulated voice, only that now it tickled the public in the right quarter so deftly that momentarily it caused them to give a little shiver of pleasure. Nana still smiled her smile: it lit up her little red mouth and shone in her great eyes, which were of the clearest blue. When she came to certain rather lively verses a delicate sense of enjoyment made her tilt her nose, the rosy nostrils of which lifted and fell, while a bright flush suffused her cheeks. She still swung herself up and down, for she only knew how to do that. And the trick was no longer voted ugly; on the contrary, the men raised their opera glasses. When she came to the end of a verse her voice completely failed her, and she was well aware that she never would get through with it. Thereupon, rather than fret herself, she kicked up her leg, which forthwith was roundly outlined under her diaphanous tunic, bent sharply backward, so that her bosom was thrown upward and forward, and stretched her arms out. Applause burst forth on all sides. In the twinkling of an eye she had turned on her heel and was going up the stage, presenting the nape of her neck to the spectators' gaze, a neck where the red-gold hair showed like some animal's fell. Then the plaudits became frantic.

The close of the act was not so exciting. Vulcan wanted to slap Venus. The gods held a consultation and decided to go and hold an inquiry on earth before granting the deceived husband satisfaction. It was then that Diana surprised a tender conversation between Venus and Mars and vowed that she would not take her eyes off them during the whole of the voyage. There was also a scene where Love, played by a little twelve-year-old chit, answered every question put to her with "Yes, Mamma! No, Mamma!" in a winy-piny tone, her fingers in her nose. At last Jupiter, with the severity of a master who is growing cross, shut Love up in a dark closet, bidding her conjugate the verb "I love" twenty times. The finale was more appreciated: it was a chorus which both troupe and orchestra performed with great brilliancy. But the curtain once down, the clappers tried in vain to obtain a call, while the whole house was already up and making for the doors.

The crowd trampled and jostled, jammed, as it were, between the rows of seats, and in so doing exchanged expressions. One phrase only went round: "It's idiotic." A critic was saying that it would be one's duty to do a pretty bit of slashing. The piece, however, mattered very little, for people were talking about Nana before everything else. Fauchery and La Faloise, being among the earliest to emerge, met Steiner and Mignon in the passage outside the stalls. In this gaslit gut of a place, which was as narrow and circumscribed as a gallery in a mine, one was well-nigh suffocated. They stopped a moment at the foot of the stairs on the right of the house, protected by the final curve of the balusters. The audience from the cheap places were coming down the steps with a continuous tramp of heavy boots; a stream of black dress coats was passing, while an attendant was making every possible effort to protect a chair, on which she had piled up coats and cloaks, from the onward pushing of the crowd.

"Surely I know her," cried Steiner, the moment he perceived Fauchery. "I'm certain I've seen her somewhere—at the casino, I imagine, and she got herself taken up there—she was so drunk."

"As for me," said the journalist, "I don't quite know where it was. I am like you; I certainly have come across her."

He lowered his voice and asked, laughing:

"At the Tricons', perhaps."

"Egad, it was in a dirty place," Mignon declared. He seemed exasperated. "It's disgusting that the public give such a reception to the first trollop that comes by. There 'll soon be no more decent women on the stage. Yes, I shall end by forbidding Rose to play."

Fauchery could not restrain a smile. Meanwhile the downward shuffle of the heavy shoes on the steps did not cease, and a little man in a workman's cap was heard crying in a drawling voice:

"Oh my, she ain't no wopper! There's some pickings there!"

In the passage two young men, delicately curled and formally resplendent in turndown collars and the rest, were disputing together. One of them was repeating the words, "Beastly, beastly!" without stating any reasons; the other was replying with the words, "Stunning, stunning!" as though he, too, disdained all argument.

La Faloise declared her to be quite the thing; only he ventured to opine that she would be better still if she were to cultivate her voice. Steiner, who was no longer listening, seemed to awake with a start. Whatever happens, one must wait, he thought. Perhaps everything will be spoiled in the following acts. The public had shown complaisance, but it was certainly not yet taken by storm. Mignon swore that the piece would never finish, and when Fauchery and La Faloise left them in order to go up to the foyer he took Steiner's arm and, leaning hard against his shoulder, whispered in his ear:

"You're going to see my wife's costume for the second act, old fellow. It *is* just blackguardly."

Upstairs in the foyer three glass chandeliers burned with a brilliant light. The two cousins hesitated an instant before entering, for the widely opened glazed doors afforded a view right through the gallery—a view of a surging sea of heads, which two currents, as it were, kept in a continuous eddying movement. But they entered after all. Five or six groups of men, talking very loudly and gesticulating, were obstinately discussing the play amid these violent interruptions; others were filing round, their heels, as they turned, sounding sharply on the waxed floor. To right and left, between columns of variegated imitation marble, women were sitting on benches covered with red velvet and viewing the passing movement of the crowd with an air of fatigue as though the heat had rendered them languid. In the lofty mirrors behind them one saw the reflection of their chignons. At the end of the room, in front of the bar, a man with a huge corporation was drinking a glass of fruit syrup.

But Fauchery, in order to breathe more freely, had gone to the balcony. La Faloise, who was studying the photographs of actresses hung in frames alternating with the mirrors between the columns, ended by following him. They had extinguished the line of gas jets on the façade of the theater, and it was dark and very cool on the balcony, which seemed to them unoccupied. Solitary and enveloped in shadow, a young man was standing, leaning his arms on the stone balustrade, in the recess to the right. He was smoking a cigarette, of which the burning end shone redly. Fauchery recognized Daguenet. They shook hands warmly.

"What are you after there, my dear fellow?" asked the journalist. "You're hiding yourself in holes and crannies—you, a man who never leaves the stalls on a first night!"

"But I'm smoking, you see," replied Daguenet.

Then Fauchery, to put him out of countenance:

"Well, well! What's your opinion of the new actress? She's being roughly handled enough in the passages."

"Bah!" muttered Daguenet. "They're people whom she'll have had nothing to do with!"

That was the sum of his criticism of Nana's talent. La Faloise leaned forward and looked down at the boulevard. Over against them the windows of a hotel and of a club were brightly lit up, while on the pavement below a dark mass of customers occupied the tables of the Café de Madrid. Despite the lateness of the hour the crowd were still crushing and being crushed; people were advancing with shortened step; a throng was constantly emerging from the Passage Jouffroy; individuals stood waiting five or six minutes before they could cross the roadway, to such a distance did the string of carriages extend.

"What a moving mass! And what a noise!" La Faloise kept reiterating, for Paris still astonished him.

The bell rang for some time; the foyer emptied. There was a hurrying of people in the passages. The curtain was already up when whole bands of spectators re-entered the house amid the irritated expressions of those who were once more in their places. Everyone took his seat again with an animated look and renewed attention. La Faloise directed his first glance in Gaga's direction, but he was dumfounded at seeing by her side the tall fair man who but recently had been in Lucy's stage box.

"What *is* that man's name?" he asked.

Fauchery failed to observe him.

"Ah yes, it's Labordette," he said at last with the same careless movement.

The scenery of the second act came as a surprise. It represented a suburban Shrove Tuesday dance at the Boule Noire. Masqueraders were trolling a catch, the chorus of which was accompanied with a tapping of their heels. This 'Arryish departure, which nobody had in the least expected, caused so much amusement that the house encored the catch. And it was to this entertainment that the divine band, let astray by Iris, who falsely bragged that he knew the Earth well, were now come in order to proceed with their inquiry. They had put on disguises so as to preserve their incognito. Jupiter came on the stage as King Dagobert, with his breeches inside out and a huge tin crown on his head. Phoebus appeared as the Postillion of Lonjumeau and Minerva as a Norman nursemaid. Loud bursts of merriment greeted Mars, who wore an outrageous uniform, suggestive of an Alpine admiral. But the shouts of laughter became uproarious when Neptune came in view, clad in a blouse, a high, bulging workman's cap on his head, lovelocks glued to his temples. Shuffling along in slippers, he cried in a thick brogue:

"Well, I'm blessed! When ye're a masher it'll never do not to let 'em love yer!"

There were some shouts of "Oh! Oh!" while the ladies held their fans one degree higher. Lucy in her stage box laughed so obstreperously that Caroline Héquet silenced her with a tap of her fan.

From that moment forth the piece was saved—nay, more, promised a great success. This carnival of the gods, this dragging in the mud of their Olympus, this mock at a whole religion, a whole world of poetry, appeared in the light of a royal entertainment. The fever of irreverence gained the literary first-night world: legend was trampled underfoot; ancient images were shattered. Jupiter's make-up was capital. Mars was a success. Royalty became a farce and the army a thing of folly. When Jupiter, grown suddenly amorous of a little laundress, began to knock off a mad cancan, Simonne, who was playing the part of the laundress, launched a kick at the master of the immortals' nose and addressed him so drolly as "My big daddy!" that an immoderate fit of laughter shook the whole house. While they were dancing Phoebus treated Minerva to salad bowls of negus, and Neptune sat in state among seven or eight women who regaled him with cakes. Allusions were eagerly caught; indecent meanings were attached to them; harmless phrases were diverted from their proper significations in the light of exclamations issuing from the stalls. For a long time past the theatrical public had not wallowed in folly more irreverent. It rested them.

Nevertheless, the action of the piece advanced amid these fooleries. Vulcan, as an elegant young man clad, down to his gloves, entirely in yellow and with

an eyeglass stuck in his eye, was forever running after Venus, who at last
made her appearance as a fishwife, a kerchief on her head and her bosom,
covered with big gold trinkets, in great evidence. Nana was so white and
plump and looked so natural in a part demanding wide hips and a voluptuous
mouth that she straightway won the whole house. On her account Rose Mignon was forgotten, though she was made up as a delicious baby, with a wickerwork burlet on her head and a short muslin frock and had just sighed forth
Diana's plaints in a sweetly pretty voice. The other one, the big wench who
slapped her thighs and clucked like a hen, shed round her an odor of life, a
sovereign feminine charm, with which the public grew intoxicated. From the
second act onward everything was permitted her. She might hold herself
awkwardly; she might fail to sing some note in tune; she might forget her
words—it mattered not: she had only to turn and laugh to raise shouts of
applause. When she gave her famous kick from the hip the stalls were fired,
and a glow of passion rose upward, upward, from gallery to gallery, till it
reached the gods. It was a triumph, too, when she led the dance. She was at
home in that: hand on hip, she enthroned Venus in the gutter by the pavement side. And the music seemed made for her plebeian voice—shrill, piping
music, with reminiscences of Saint-Cloud Fair, wheezings of clarinets and
playful trills on the part of the little flutes.

Two numbers were again encored. The opening waltz, that waltz with the
naughty rhythmic beat, had returned and swept the gods with it. Juno, as a
peasant woman, caught Jupiter and his little laundress cleverly and boxed his
ears. Diana, surprising Venus in the act of making an assignation with Mars,
made haste to indicate hour and place to Vulcan, who cried, "I've hit on a
plan!" The rest of the act did not seem very clear. The inquiry ended in a final
galop after which Jupiter, breathless, streaming with perspiration and minus
his crown, declared that the little women of Earth were delicious and that
the men were all to blame.

The curtain was falling, when certain voices, rising above the storm of
bravos, cried uproariously:

"All! All!"

Thereupon the curtain rose again; the artistes reappeared hand in hand. In
the middle of the line Nana and Rose Mignon stood side by side, bowing and
curtsying. The audience applauded; the clappers shouted acclamations. Then
little by little the house emptied.

"I must go and pay my respects to the Countess Muffat," said La Faloise.

"Exactly so; you'll present me," replied Fauchery; "we'll go down afterward."

But it was not easy to get to the first-tier boxes. In the passage at the top
of the stairs there was a crush. In order to get forward at all among the various
groups you had to make yourself small and to slide along, using your elbows in
so doing. Leaning under a copper lamp, where a jet of gas was burning, the
bulky critic was sitting in judgment on the piece in presence of an attentive
circle. People in passing mentioned his name to each other in muttered tones.
He had laughed the whole act through—that was the humor going the round

of the passages—nevertheless, he was now very severe and spoke of taste and morals. Farther off the thin-lipped critic was brimming over with a benevolence which had an unpleasant aftertaste, as of milk turned sour.

Fauchery glanced along, scrutinizing the boxes through the round openings in each door. But the Count de Vandeuvres stopped him with a question, and when he was informed that the two cousins were going to pay their respects to the Muffats, he pointed out to them box seven, from which he had just emerged. Then bending down and whispering in the journalist's ear:

"Tell me, my dear fellow," he said, "this Nana—surely she's the girl we saw one evening at the corner of the Rue de Provence?"

"By Jove, you're right!" cried Fauchery. "I was saying that I had come across her!"

La Faloise presented his cousin to Count Muffat de Beuville, who appeared very frigid. But on hearing the name Fauchery the countess raised her head and with a certain reserve complimented the paragraphist on his articles in the *Figaro*. Leaning on the velvet-covered support in front of her, she turned half round with a pretty movement of the shoulders. They talked for a short time, and the Universal Exhibition was mentioned.

"It will be very fine," said the count, whose square-cut, regular-featured face retained a certain gravity.

"I visited the Champ de Mars today and returned thence truly astonished."

"They say that things won't be ready in time," La Faloise ventured to remark. "There's infinite confusion there——"

But the count interrupted him in his severe voice:

"Things will be ready. The emperor desires it."

Fauchery gaily recounted how one day, when he had gone down thither in search of a subject for an article, he had come near spending all his time in the aquarium, which was then in course of construction. The countess smiled. Now and again she glanced down at the body of the house, raising an arm which a white glove covered to the elbow and fanning herself with languid hand. The house dozed, almost deserted. Some gentlemen in the stalls had opened out newspapers, and ladies received visits quite comfortably, as though they were at their own homes. Only a well-bred whispering was audible under the great chandelier, the light of which was softened in the fine cloud of dust raised by the confused movements of the interval. At the different entrances men were crowding in order to talk to ladies who remained seated. They stood there motionless for a few seconds, craning forward somewhat and displaying the great white bosoms of their shirt fronts.

"We count on you next Tuesday," said the countess to La Faloise, and she invited Fauchery, who bowed.

Not a word was said of the play; Nana's name was not once mentioned. The count was so glacially dignified that he might have been supposed to be taking part at a sitting of the legislature. In order to explain their presence that evening he remarked simply that his father-in-law was fond of the theater. The door of the box must have remained open, for the Marquis de Chouard, who had gone out in order to leave his seat to the visitors, was back again. He was straightening up his tall, old figure. His face looked soft and white under a broad-brimmed hat, and with his restless eyes he followed the movements of the women who passed.

The moment the countess had given her invitation Fauchery took his leave, feeling that to talk about the play would not be quite the thing. La Faloise was the last to quit the box. He had just noticed the fair-haired Labordette, comfortably installed in the Count de Vandeuvres's stage box and chatting at very close quarters with Blanche de Sivry.

"Gad," he said after rejoining his cousin, "that Labordette knows all the girls then! He's with Blanche now."

"Doubtless he knows them all," replied Fauchery quietly. "What d'you want to be taken for, my friend?"

The passage was somewhat cleared of people, and Fauchery was just about to go downstairs when Lucy Stewart called him. She was quite at the other end of the corridor, at the door of her stage box. They were getting cooked in there, she said, and she took up the whole corridor in company with Caroline Héquet and her mother, all three nibbling burnt almonds. A box opener was chatting maternally with them. Lucy fell out with the journalist. He was a pretty fellow, to be sure! He went up to see other women and didn't even come and ask if they were thirsty! Then, changing the subject:

"You know, dear boy, I think Nana very nice."

She wanted him to stay in the stage box for the last act, but he made his escape, promising to catch them at the door afterward. Downstairs in front of the theater Fauchery and La Faloise lit cigarettes. A great gathering blocked the sidewalk, a stream of men who had come down from the theater steps and were inhaling the fresh night air in the boulevards, where the roar and battle had diminished.

Meanwhile Mignon had drawn Steiner away to the Café des Variétés. Seeing Nana's success, he had set to work to talk enthusiastically about her, all the while observing the banker out of the corners of his eyes. He knew him well; twice he had helped him to deceive Rose and then, the caprice being over, had brought him back to her, faithful and repentant. In the café the too-numerous crowd of customers were squeezing themselves round the marble-topped tables. Several were standing up, drinking in a great hurry. The tall mirrors reflected this thronging world of heads to infinity and magnified the narrow room beyond measure with its three chandeliers, its moleskin-covered seats and its winding staircase draped with red. Steiner went and seated himself at a table in the first saloon, which opened full on the boulevard, its doors having been removed rather early for the time of year. As Fauchery and La Faloise were passing the banker stopped them.

"Come and take a bock with us, eh?" they said.

But he was too preoccupied by an idea; he wanted to have a bouquet thrown to Nana. At last he called a waiter belonging to the café, whom he familiarly addressed as Auguste. Mignon, who was listening, looked at him so sharply that he lost countenance and stammered out:

"Two bouquets, Auguste, and deliver them to the attendant. A bouquet for each of these ladies! Happy thought, eh?"

At the other end of the saloon, her shoulders resting against the frame of a mirror, a girl, some eighteen years of age at the outside, was leaning motionless in front of her empty glass as though she had been benumbed by long and fruitless waiting. Under the natural curls of her beautiful gray-gold hair a virginal face looked out at you with velvety eyes, which were at once soft and candid.

She wore a dress of faded green silk and a round hat which blows had dinted. The cool air of the night made her look very pale.

"Egad, there's Satin," murmured Fauchery when his eye lit upon her.

La Faloise questioned him. Oh dear, yes, she was a streetwalker—she didn't count. But she was such a scandalous sort that people amused themselves by making her talk. And the journalist, raising his voice:

"What are you doing there, Satin?"

"I'm bogging," replied Satin quietly without changing position.

The four men were charmed and fell a-laughing. Mignon assured them that there was no need to hurry; it would take twenty minutes to set up the scenery for the third act. But the two cousins, having drunk their beer, wanted to go up into the theater again; the cold was making itself felt. Then Mignon remained alone with Steiner, put his elbows on the table and spoke to him at close quarters.

"It's an understood thing, eh? We are to go to her house, and I'm to introduce you. You know the thing's quite between ourselves—my wife needn't know."

Once more in their places, Fauchery and La Faloise noticed a pretty, quietly dressed woman in the second tier of boxes. She was with a serious-looking gentleman, a chief clerk at the office of the Ministry of the Interior, whom La Faloise knew, having met him at the Muffats'. As to Fauchery, he was under the impression that her name was Madame Robert, a lady of honorable repute who had a lover, only one, and that always a person of respectability.

But they had to turn round, for Daguenet was smiling at them. Now that Nana had had a success he no longer hid himself: indeed, he had just been scoring triumphs in the passages. By his side was the young truant schoolboy, who had not quitted his seat, so stupefying was the state of admiration into which Nana had plunged him. That was it, he thought; that was the woman! And he blushed as he thought so and dragged his gloves on and off mechanically. Then since his neighbor had spoken of Nana, he ventured to question him.

"Will you pardon me for asking you, sir, but that lady who is acting—do you know her?"

"Yes, I do a little," murmured Daguenet with some surprise and hesitation.

"Then you know her address?"

The question, addressed as it was to him, came so abruptly that he felt inclined to respond with a box on the ear.

"No," he said in a dry tone of voice.

And with that he turned his back. The fair lad knew that he had just been guilty of some breach of good manners. He blushed more hotly than ever and looked scared.

The traditional three knocks were given, and among the returning throng, attendants, laden with pelisses and overcoats, bustled about at a great rate in order to put away people's things. The clappers applauded the scenery, which represented a grotto on Mount Etna, hollowed out in a silver mine and with sides glittering like new money. In the background Vulcan's forge glowed like a setting star. Diana, since the second act, had come to a good understanding with the god, who was to pretend that he was on a journey, so as to leave the way clear for Venus and Mars. Then scarcely was Diana alone than Venus made her appearance. A shiver of delight ran round the house. Nana was nude. With quiet audacity she appeared in her nakedness, certain of the sovereign power of her flesh. Some gauze enveloped her, but her rounded shoulders, her Amazonian bosom, her wide hips, which swayed to and fro voluptuously, her whole body, in fact, could be divined, nay discerned, in all its foamlike whiteness of tint beneath the slight fabric she wore. It was Venus rising from the waves with no veil save her tresses. And when Nana lifted her arms the golden hairs in her armpits were observable in the glare of the footlights. There was no applause. Nobody laughed any more. The men strained forward with serious faces, sharp features, mouths irritated and parched. A wind seemed to have passed, a soft, soft wind, laden with a secret menace. Suddenly in the bouncing child the woman stood discovered, a woman full of restless suggestion, who brought with her the delirium of sex and opened the gates of the unknown world of desire. Nana was smiling still, but her smile was now bitter, as of a devourer of men.

"By God," said Fauchery quite simply to La Faloise.

Mars in the meantime, with his plume of feathers, came hurrying to the trysting place and found himself between the two goddesses. Then ensued a passage which Prullière played with great delicacy. Petted by Diana, who wanted to make a final attack upon his feelings before delivering him up to Vulcan, wheedled by Venus, whom the presence of her rival excited, he gave himself up to these tender delights with the beatified expression of a man in clover. Finally a grand trio brought the scene to a close, and it was then that an attendant appeared in Lucy Stewart's box and threw on the stage two immense bouquets of white lilacs. There was applause; Nana and Rose Mignon bowed, while Prullière picked up the bouquets. Many of the occupants of the stalls turned smilingly toward the ground-floor occupied by Steiner and Mignon. The banker, his face blood-red, was suffering from little convulsive twitchings of the chin, as though he had a stoppage in his throat.

What followed took the house by storm completely. Diana had gone off in a rage, and directly afterward, Venus, sitting on a moss-clad seat, called Mars to her. Never yet had a more glowing scene of seduction been ventured on. Nana, her arms round Prullière's neck, was drawing him toward her when Fontan, with comically furious mimicry and an exaggerated imitation of the face of an outraged husband who surprises his wife in *flagrante delicto*, appeared at the back of the grotto. He was holding the famous net with iron meshes. For an instant he poised and swung it, as a fisherman does when he is going to make a cast, and by an ingenious twist Venus and Mars were caught in the snare; the net wrapped itself round them and held them motionless in the attitude of happy lovers.

A murmur of applause swelled and swelled like a growing sigh. There was some hand clapping, and every opera glass was fixed on Venus. Little by little Nana had taken possession of the public, and now every man was her slave.

A wave of lust had flowed from her as from an excited animal, and its influence had spread and spread and spread till the whole house was possessed by it. At that moment her slightest movement blew the flame of desire: with her little finger she ruled men's flesh. Backs were arched and quivered as though unseen violin bows had been drawn across their muscles; upon men's shoulders appeared fugitive hairs, which flew in air, blown by warm and wandering breaths, breathed one knew not from what feminine mouth. In front of him Fauchery saw the truant schoolboy half lifted from his seat by passion. Curiosity led him to look at the Count de Vandeuvres—he was extremely pale, and his lips looked pinched—at fat Steiner, whose face was purple to the verge of apoplexy; at Labordette, ogling away with the highly astonished air of a horse dealer admiring a perfectly shaped mare; at Daguenet, whose ears were blood-red and twitching with enjoyment. Then a sudden idea made him glance behind, and he marveled at what he saw in the Muffats' box. Behind the countess, who was white and serious as usual, the count was sitting straight upright, with mouth agape and face mottled with red, while close by him, in the shadow, the restless eyes of the Marquis de Chouard had become catlike phosphorescent, full of golden sparkles. The house was suffocating; people's very hair grew heavy on their perspiring heads. For three hours back the breath of the multitude had filled and heated the atmosphere with a scent of crowded humanity. Under the swaying glare of the gas the dust clouds in mid-air had grown constantly denser as they hung motionless beneath the chandelier. The whole house seemed to be oscillating, to be lapsing toward dizziness in its fatigue and excitement, full, as it was, of those drowsy midnight desires which flutter in the recesses of the bed of passion. And Nana, in front of this languorous public, these fifteen hundred human beings thronged and smothered in the exhaustion and nervous exasperation which belong to the close of a spectacle, Nana still triumphed by right of her marble flesh and that sexual nature of hers, which was strong enough to destroy the whole crowd of her adorers and yet sustain no injury.

The piece drew to a close. In answer to Vulcan's triumphant summons all the Olympians defiled before the lovers with ohs and ahs of stupefaction and gaiety. Jupiter said, "I think it is light conduct on your part, my son, to summon us to see such a sight as this." Then a reaction took place in favor of Venus. The chorus of cuckolds was again ushered in by Iris and besought the master of the gods not to give effect to its petition, for since women had lived at home, domestic life was becoming impossible for the men: the latter preferred being deceived and happy. That was the moral of the play. Then

Venus was set at liberty, and Vulcan obtained a partial divorce from her.
Mars was reconciled with Diana, and Jove, for the sake of domestic peace,
packed his little laundress off into a constellation. And finally they extricated
Love from his black hole, where instead of conjugating the verb *amo* he had
been busy in the manufacture of "dollies." The curtain fell on an apotheosis,
wherein the cuckolds' chorus knelt and sang a hymn of gratitude to Venus,
who stood there with smiling lips, her stature enhanced by her sovereign
nudity.

The audience, already on their feet, were making for the exits. The authors
were mentioned, and amid a thunder of applause there were two calls before
the curtain. The shout of "Nana! Nana!" rang wildly forth. Then no sooner
was the house empty than it grew dark: the footlights went out; the chandelier was turned down; long strips of gray canvas slipped from the stage
boxes and swathed the gilt ornamentation of the galleries, and the house, lately
so full of heat and noise, lapsed suddenly into a heavy sleep, while a musty,
dusty odor began to pervade it. In the front of her box stood the Countess
Muffat. Very erect and closely wrapped up in her furs, she stared at the
gathering shadows and waited for the crowd to pass away.

In the passages the people were jostling the attendants, who hardly knew
what to do among the tumbled heaps of outdoor raiment. Fauchery and
La Faloise had hurried in order to see the crowd pass out. All along the entrance hall men formed a living hedge, while down the double staircase came
slowly and in regular, complete formation two interminable throngs of human
beings. Steiner, in tow of Mignon, had left the house among the foremost.
The Count de Vandeuvres took his departure with Blanche de Sivry on his
arm. For a moment or two Gaga and her daughter seemed doubtful how to
proceed, but Labordette made haste to go and fetch them a conveyance, the
door whereof he gallantly shut after them. Nobody saw Daguenet go by. As
the truant schoolboy, registering a mental vow to wait at the stage door, was
running with burning cheeks toward the Passage des Panoramas, of which he
found the gate closed, Satin, standing on the edge of the pavement, moved
forward and brushed him with her skirts, but he in his despair gave her a
savage refusal and vanished amid the crowd, tears of impotent desire in his
eyes. Members of the audience were lighting their cigars and walking off,
humming:

When Venus roams at eventide.

Satin had gone back in front of the Café des Variétés, where Auguste let her
eat the sugar that remained over from the customers' orders. A stout man, who
came out in a very heated condition, finally carried her off in the shadow of
the boulevard, which was now gradually going to sleep.

Still people kept coming downstairs. La Faloise was waiting for Clarisse;
Fauchery had promised to catch up Lucy Stewart with Caroline Héquet and
her mother. They came; they took up a whole corner of the entrance hall and
were laughing very loudly when the Muffats passed by them with an icy
expression. Bordenave had just then opened a little door and, peeping out, had

obtained from Fauchery the formal promise of an article. He was dripping with perspiration, his face blazed, as though he were drunk with success.

"You're good for two hundred nights," La Faloise said to him with civility. "The whole of Paris will visit your theater."

But Bordenave grew annoyed and, indicating with a jerk of his chin the public who filled the entrance hall—a herd of men with parched lips and ardent eyes, still burning with the enjoyment of Nana—he cried out violently:

"Say 'my brothel,' you obstinate devil!"

CHAPTER II

AT TEN O'CLOCK the next morning Nana was still asleep. She occupied the second floor of a large new house in the Boulevard Haussmann, the landlord of which let flats to single ladies in order by their means to dry the paint. A rich merchant from Moscow, who had come to pass a winter in Paris, had installed her there after paying six months' rent in advance. The rooms were too big for her and had never been completely furnished. The vulgar sumptuosity of gilded consoles and gilded chairs formed a crude contrast therein to the bric-a-brac of a secondhand furniture shop—to mahogany round tables, that is to say, and zinc candelabras, which sought to imitate Florentine bronze. All of which smacked of the courtesan too early deserted by her first serious protector and fallen back on shabby lovers, of a precarious first appearance of a bad start, handicapped by refusals of credit and threats of eviction.

Nana was sleeping on her face, hugging in her bare arms a pillow in which she was burying cheeks grown pale in sleep. The bedroom and the dressing room were the only two apartments which had been properly furnished by a neighboring upholsterer. A ray of light, gliding in under a curtain, rendered visible rosewood furniture and hangings and chairbacks of figured damask with a pattern of big blue flowers on a gray ground. But in the soft atmosphere of that slumbering chamber Nana suddenly awoke with a start, as though surprised to find an empty place at her side. She looked at the other pillow lying next to hers; there was the dint of a human head among its flounces: it was still warm. And groping with one hand, she pressed the knob of an electric bell by her bed's head.

"He's gone then?" she asked the maid who presented herself.

"Yes, madame, Monsieur Paul went away not ten minutes back. As Madame was tired, he did not wish to wake her. But he ordered me to tell Madame that he would come tomorrow."

As she spoke Zoé, the lady's maid, opened the outer shutter. A flood of daylight entered. Zoé, a dark brunette with hair in little plaits, had a long canine face, at once livid and full of seams, a snub nose, thick lips and two black eyes in continual movement.

"Tomorrow, tomorrow," repeated Nana, who was not yet wide awake, "is tomorrow the day?"

"Yes, madame, Monsieur Paul has always come on the Wednesday."

"No, now I remember," said the young woman, sitting up. "It's all changed. I wanted to tell him so this morning. He would run against the nigger! We should have a nice to-do!"

"Madame did not warn me; I couldn't be aware of it," murmured Zoé. "When Madame changes her days she will do well to tell me so that I may know. Then the old miser is no longer due on the Tuesday?"

Between themselves they were wont thus gravely to nickname as "old miser" and "nigger" their two paying visitors, one of whom was a tradesman of economical tendencies from the Faubourg Saint-Denis, while the other was a Walachian, a mock count, whose money, paid always at the most irregular intervals, never looked as though it had been honestly come by. Daguenet had made Nana give him the days subsequent to the old miser's visits, and as the trader had to be at home by eight o'clock in the morning, the young man would watch for his departure from Zoé's kitchen and would take his place, which was still quite warm, till ten o'clock. Then he, too, would go about his business. Nana and he were wont to think it a very comfortable arrangement.

"So much the worse," said Nana; "I'll write to him this afternoon. And if he doesn't receive my letter, then tomorrow you will stop him coming in."

In the meantime Zoé was walking softly about the room. She spoke of yesterday's great hit. Madame had shown such talent; she sang so well! Ah! Madame need not fret at all now!

Nana, her elbow dug into her pillow, only tossed her head in reply. Her nightdress had slipped down on her shoulders, and her hair, unfastened and entangled, flowed over them in masses.

"Without doubt," she murmured, becoming thoughtful; "but what's to be done to gain time? I'm going to have all sorts of bothers today. Now let's see, has the porter come upstairs yet this morning?"

Then both the women talked together seriously. Nana owed three quarters' rent; the landlord was talking of seizing the furniture. Then, too, there was a perfect downpour of creditors; there was a livery-stable man, a needlewoman, a ladies' tailor, a charcoal dealer and others besides, who came every day and settled themselves on a bench in the little hall. The charcoal dealer especially was a dreadful fellow—he shouted on the staircase. But Nana's greatest cause of distress was her little Louis, a child she had given birth to when she was sixteen and now left in charge of a nurse in a village in the neighborhood of Rambouillet. This woman was clamoring for the sum of three hundred francs before she would consent to give the little Louis back to her. Nana, since her last visit to the child, had been seized with a fit of maternal love and was desperate at the thought that she could not realize a project, which had now become a hobby with her. This was to pay off the nurse and to place the little man with his aunt, Mme Lerat, at the Batignolles, whither she could go and see him as often as she liked.

Meanwhile the lady's maid kept hinting that her mistress ought to have confided her necessities to the old miser.

"To be sure, I told him everything," cried Nana, "and he told me in answer that he had too many big liabilities. He won't go beyond his thousand francs a month. The nigger's beggared just at present; I expect he's lost at play. As to that poor Mimi, he stands in great need of a loan himself; a fall in stocks has cleaned him out—he can't even bring me flowers now."

She was speaking of Daguenet. In the self-abandonment of her awakening she had no secrets from Zoé, and the latter, inured to such confidences, received them with respectful sympathy. Since Madame condescended to speak to her of her affairs she would permit herself to say what she thought. Besides, she was very fond of Madame; she had left Mme Blanche for the express purpose of taking service with her, and heaven knew Mme Blanche was straining every nerve to have her again! Situations weren't lacking; she was pretty well known, but she would have stayed with Madame even in narrow circumstances, because she believed in Madame's future. And she concluded by stating her advice with precision. When one was young one often did silly things. But this time it was one's duty to look alive, for the men only thought of having their fun. Oh dear, yes! Things would right themselves. Madame had only to say one word in order to quiet her creditors and find the money she stood in need of.

"All that doesn't help me to three hundred francs," Nana kept repeating as she plunged her fingers into the vagrant convolutions of her back hair. "I must have three hundred francs today, at once! It's stupid not to know anyone who'll give you three hundred francs."

She racked her brains. She would have sent Mme Lerat, whom she was expecting that very morning, to Rambouillet. The counteraction of her sudden fancy spoiled for her the triumph of last night. Among all those men who had cheered her, to think that there wasn't one to bring her fifteen louis! And then one couldn't accept money in that way! Dear heaven, how unfortunate she was! And she kept harking back again to the subject of her baby—he had blue eyes like a cherub's; he could lisp "Mamma" in such a funny voice that you were ready to die of laughing!

But at this moment the electric bell at the outer door was heard to ring with its quick and tremulous vibration. Zoé returned, murmuring with a confidential air:

"It's a woman."

She had seen this woman a score of times, only she made believe never to recognize her and to be quite ignorant of the nature of her relations with ladies in difficulties.

"She has told me her name—Madame Tricon."

"The Tricon," cried Nana. "Dear me! That's true. I'd forgotten her. Show her in."

Zoé ushered in a tall old lady who wore ringlets and looked like a countess who haunts lawyers' offices. Then she effaced herself, disappearing noiselessly with the lithe, serpentine movement wherewith she was wont to withdraw from a room on the arrival of a gentleman. However, she might have stayed. The Tricon did not even sit down. Only a brief exchange of words took place.

"I have someone for you today. Do you care about it?"

"Yes. How much?"

"Twenty louis."

"At what o'clock?"

"At three. It's settled then?"

"It's settled."

Straightway the Tricon talked of the state of the weather. It was dry weather, pleasant for walking. She had still four or five persons to see. And she took her departure after consulting a small memorandum book. When she was once more alone Nana appeared comforted. A slight shiver agitated her shoulders, and she wrapped herself softly up again in her warm bedclothes with the lazy movements of a cat who is susceptible to cold. Little by little her eyes closed, and she lay smiling at the thought of dressing Louiset prettily on the following day, while in the slumber into which she once more sank last night's long, feverish dream of endlessly rolling applause returned like a sustained accompaniment to music and gently soothed her lassitude.

At eleven o'clock, when Zoé showed Mme Lerat into the room, Nana was still asleep. But she woke at the noise and cried out at once:

"It's you. You'll go to Rambouillet today?"

"That's what I've come for," said the aunt. "There's a train at twenty past twelve. I've got time to catch it."

"No, I shall only have the money by and by," replied the young woman, stretching herself and throwing out her bosom. "You'll have lunch, and then we'll see."

Zoé brought a dressing jacket.

"The hairdresser's here, madame," she murmured.

But Nana did not wish to go into the dressing room. And she herself cried out:

"Come in, Francis."

A well-dressed man pushed open the door and bowed. Just at that moment Nana was getting out of bed, her bare legs in full view. But she did not hurry and stretched her hands out so as to let Zoé draw on the sleeves of the dressing jacket. Francis, on his part, was quite at his ease and without turning away waited with a sober expression on his face.

"Perhaps Madame has not seen the papers. There's a very nice article in the *Figaro*."

He had brought the journal. Mme Lerat put on her spectacles and read the article aloud, standing in front of the window as she did so. She had the build of a policeman, and she drew herself up to her full height, while her nostrils seemed to compress themselves whenever she uttered a gallant epithet. It was a notice by Fauchery, written just after the performance, and it consisted of a couple of very glowing columns, full of witty sarcasm about the artist and of broad admiration for the woman.

"Excellent!" Francis kept repeating.

Nana laughed good-humoredly at his chaffing her about her voice! He was a nice fellow, was that Fauchery, and she would repay him for his charming style of writing. Mme Lerat, after having reread the notice, roundly declared that the men all had the devil in their shanks, and she refused to explain herself further, being fully satisfied with a brisk allusion of which she alone knew the meaning. Francis finished turning up and fastening Nana's hair. He bowed and said:

"I'll keep my eye on the evening papers. At half-past five as usual, eh?"

"Bring me a pot of pomade and a pound of burnt almonds from Boissier's," Nana cried to him across the drawing room just as he was shutting the door after him.

Then the two women, once more alone, recollected that they had not embraced, and they planted big kisses on each other's cheeks. The notice warmed their hearts. Nana, who up till now had been half asleep, was again seized with the fever of her triumph. Dear, dear, 'twas Rose Mignon that would be spending a pleasant morning! Her aunt having been unwilling to go to the theater because, as she averred, sudden emotions ruined her stomach, Nana set herself to describe the events of the evening and grew intoxicated at her own recital, as though all Paris had been shaken to the ground by the applause. Then suddenly interrupting herself, she asked with a laugh if one would ever have imagined it all when she used to go traipsing about the Rue de la Goutte-d'Or. Mme Lerat shook her head. No, no, one never could have foreseen it! And she began talking in her turn, assuming a serious air as she did so and calling Nana "daughter." Wasn't she a second mother to her since the first had gone to rejoin Papa and Grandmamma? Nana was greatly softened and on the verge of tears. But Mme Lerat declared that the past was the past—oh yes, to be sure, a dirty past with things in it which it was as well not to stir up every day. She had left off seeing her niece for a long time because among the family she was accused of ruining herself along with the little thing. Good God, as though that were possible! She didn't ask for confidences; she believed that Nana had always lived decently, and now it was enough for her to have found her again in a fine position and to observe her kind feelings toward her son. Virtue and hard work were still the only things worth anything in this world.

"Who is the baby's father?" she said, interrupting herself, her eyes lit up with an expression of acute curiosity.

Nana was taken by surprise and hesitated a moment.

"A gentleman," she replied.

"There now!" rejoined the aunt. "They declared that you had him by a stonemason who was in the habit of beating you. Indeed, you shall tell me all about it someday; you know I'm discreet! Tut, tut, I'll look after him as though he were a prince's son."

She had retired from business as a florist and was living on her savings, which she had got together sou by sou, till now they brought her in an income of six hundred francs a year. Nana promised to rent some pretty little lodgings for her and to give her a hundred francs a month besides. At the mention of this sum the aunt forgot herself and shrieked to her niece, bidding her squeeze their throats, since she had them in her grasp. She was meaning the men, of course. Then they both embraced again, but in the midst of her rejoicing Nana's face, as she led the talk back to the subject of Louiset, seemed to be overshadowed by a sudden recollection.

"Isn't it a bore I've got to go out at three o'clock?" she muttered. "It *is* a nuisance!"

Just then Zoé came in to say that lunch was on the table. They went into the dining room, where an old lady was already seated at table. She had not taken her hat off, and she wore a dark dress of an indecisive color midway between puce and goose dripping. Nana did not seem surprised at sight of her. She simply asked her why she hadn't come into the bedroom.

"I heard voices," replied the old lady. "I thought you had company."

Mme Maloir, a respectable-looking and mannerly woman, was Nana's old friend, chaperon and companion. Mme Lerat's presence seemed to fidget her at first. Afterward, when she became aware that it was Nana's aunt, she looked at her with a sweet expression and a die-away smile. In the meantime Nana, who averred that she was as hungry as a wolf, threw herself on the radishes and gobbled them up without bread. Mme Lerat had become ceremonious; she refused the radishes as provocative of phlegm. By and by when Zoé had brought in the cutlets Nana just chipped the meat and contented herself with sucking the bones. Now and again she scrutinized her old friend's hat out of the corners of her eyes.

"It's the new hat I gave you?" she ended by saying.

"Yes, I made it up," murmured Mme Maloir, her mouth full of meat.

The hat was smart to distraction. In front it was greatly exaggerated, and it was adorned with a lofty feather. Mme Maloir had a mania for doing up all her hats afresh; she alone knew what really became her, and with a few stitches she could manufacture a toque out of the most elegant headgear. Nana, who had bought her this very hat in order not to be ashamed of her when in her company out of doors, was very near being vexed.

"Push it up, at any rate," she cried.

"No, thank you," replied the old lady with dignity. "It doesn't get in my way; I can eat very comfortably as it is."

After the cutlets came cauliflowers and the remains of a cold chicken. But at the arrival of each successive dish Nana made a little face, hesitated, sniffed and left her plateful untouched. She finished her lunch with the help of preserve.

Dessert took a long time. Zoé did not remove the cloth before serving the coffee. Indeed, the ladies simply pushed back their plates before taking it. They talked continually of yesterday's charming evening. Nana kept rolling cigarettes, which she smoked, swinging up and down on her backward-tilted chair. And as Zoé had remained behind and was lounging idly against the sideboard, it came about that the company were favored with her history. She said she was the daughter of a midwife at Bercy who had failed in business. First of all she had taken service with a dentist and after that with an insurance agent, but neither place suited her, and she thereupon enumerated, not without a certain amount of pride, the names of the ladies with whom she had served as lady's maid. Zoé spoke of these ladies as one who had had the making of their fortunes. It was very certain that without her more than one would have had some queer tales to tell. Thus one day, when Mme Blanche was with M. Octave, in came the old gentleman. What did Zoé do? She made believe to tumble as she crossed the drawing room; the old boy rushed up to her assistance, flew to the kitchen to fetch her a glass of water, and M. Octave slipped away.

"Oh, she's a good girl, you bet!" said Nana, who was listening to her with tender interest and a sort of submissive admiration.

"Now I've had my troubles," began Mme Lerat. And edging up to Mme Maloir, she imparted to her certain confidential confessions. Both ladies took lumps of sugar dipped in cognac and sucked them. But Mme Maloir was wont to listen to other people's secrets without even confessing anything concerning herself. People said that she lived on a mysterious allowance in a room whither no one ever penetrated.

All of a sudden Nana grew excited.

"Don't play with the knives, Aunt. You know it gives me a turn!"

Without thinking about it Mme Lerat had crossed two knives on the table in front of her. Notwithstanding this, the young woman defended herself from the charge of superstition. Thus, if the salt were upset, it meant nothing, even on a Friday; but when it came to knives, that was too much of a good thing; that had never proved fallacious. There could be no doubt that something unpleasant was going to happen to her. She yawned, and then with an air of profound boredom:

"Two o'clock already. I must go out. What a nuisance!"

The two old ladies looked at one another. The three women shook their heads without speaking. To be sure, life was not always amusing. Nana had tilted her chair back anew and lit a cigarette, while the others sat pursing up their lips discreetly, thinking deeply philosophic thoughts.

"While waiting for you to return we'll play a game of bezique," said Mme Maloir after a short silence. "Does Madame play bezique?"

Certainly Mme Lerat played it, and that to perfection. It was no good troubling Zoé, who had vanished—a corner of the table would do quite well. And they pushed back the tablecloth over the dirty plates. But as Mme Maloir was herself going to take the cards out of a drawer in the sideboard, Nana remarked that before she sat down to her game it would be very nice of her if she would write her a letter. It bored Nana to write letters; besides, she was not sure of her spelling, while her old friend could turn out the most feeling epistles. She ran to fetch some good note paper in her bedroom. An inkstand consisting of a bottle of ink worth about three sous stood untidily on one of the pieces of furniture, with a pen deep in rust beside it. The letter was for Daguenet. Mme Maloir herself wrote in her bold English hand, "My darling little man," and then she told him not to come tomorrow because "that could not be" but hastened to add that "she was with him in thought at every moment of the day, whether she were near or far away."

"And I end with 'a thousand kisses,'" she murmured.

Mme Lerat had shown her approval of each phrase with an emphatic nod. Her eyes were sparkling; she loved to find herself in the midst of love affairs. Nay, she was seized with a desire to add some words of her own and, assuming a tender look and cooing like a dove, she suggested:

"A thousand kisses on thy beautiful eyes."

"That's the thing: 'a thousand kisses on thy beautiful eyes'!" Nana repeated, while the two old ladies assumed a beatified expression.

Zoé was rung for and told to take the letter down to a commissionaire. She had just been talking with the theater messenger, who had brought her mistress the day's playbill and rehearsal arrangements, which he had forgotten in the morning. Nana had this individual ushered in and got him to take the latter to Daguenet on his return. Then she put questions to him. Oh yes! M. Bordenave was very pleased; people had already taken seats for a week to come; Madame had no idea of the number of people who had been asking her address since morning. When the man had taken his departure Nana announced that at most she would only be out half an hour. If there were any visitors Zoé would make them wait. As she spoke the electric bell sounded. It was a creditor in the shape of the man of whom she jobbed her carriages. He had settled himself on the bench in the anteroom, and the fellow was free to twiddle his thumbs till night—there wasn't the least hurry now.

"Come, buck up!" said Nana, still torpid with laziness and yawning and stretching afresh. "I ought to be there now!"

Yet she did not budge but kept watching the play of her aunt, who had just announced four aces. Chin on hand, she grew quite engrossed in it but gave a violent start on hearing three o'clock strike.

"Good God!" she cried roughly.

Then Mme Maloir, who was counting the tricks she had won with her tens and aces, said cheeringly to her in her soft voice:

"It would be better, dearie, to give up your expedition at once."

"No, be quick about it," said Mme Lerat, shuffling the cards. "I shall take the half-past four o'clock train if you're back here with the money before four o'clock."

"Oh, there'll be no time lost," she murmured.

Ten minutes after Zoé helped her on with a dress and a hat. It didn't matter much if she were badly turned out. Just as she was about to go downstairs there was a new ring at the bell. This time it was the charcoal dealer. Very well, he might keep the livery-stable keeper company—it would amuse the fellows. Only, as she dreaded a scene, she crossed the kitchen and made her escape by the back stairs. She often went that way and in return had only to lift up her flounces.

"When one is a good mother anything's excusable," said Mme Maloir sententiously when left alone with Mme Lerat.

"Four kings," replied this lady, whom the play greatly excited.

And they both plunged into an interminable game.

The table had not been cleared. The smell of lunch and the cigarette smoke filled the room with an ambient, steamy vapor. The two ladies had again set to work dipping lumps of sugar in brandy and sucking the same. For twenty minutes at least they played and sucked simultaneously when, the electric bell having rung a third time, Zoé bustled into the room and roughly disturbed them, just as if they had been her own friends.

"Look here, that's another ring. You can't stay where you are. If many folks call I must have the whole flat. Now off you go, off you go!"

Mme Maloir was for finishing the game, but Zoé looked as if she was going to pounce down on the cards, and so she decided to carry them off without in any way altering their positions, while Mme Lerat undertook the removal of the brandy bottle, the glasses and the sugar. Then they both scudded to the kitchen, where they installed themselves at the table in an empty space between the dishcloths, which were spread out to dry, and the bowl still full of dishwater.

"We said it was three hundred and forty. It's your turn."

"I play hearts."

When Zoé returned she found them once again absorbed. After a silence, as Mme Lerat was shuffling, Mme Maloir asked who it was.

"Oh, nobody to speak of," replied the servant carelessly; "a slip of a lad! I wanted to send him away again, but he's such a pretty boy with never a hair on his chin and blue eyes and a girl's face! So I told him to wait after all. He's got an enormous bouquet in his hand, which he never once consented to put down. One would like to catch him one—a brat like that who ought to be at school still!"

Mme Lerat went to fetch a water bottle to mix herself some brandy and water, the lumps of sugar having rendered her thirsty. Zoé muttered something to the effect that she really didn't mind if she drank something too. Her mouth, she averred, was as bitter as gall.

"So you put him——?" continued Mme Maloir.

"Oh yes, I put him in the closet at the end of the room, the little unfurnished one. There's only one of my lady's trunks there and a table. It's there I stow the lubbers."

And she was putting plenty of sugar in her grog when the electric bell made her jump. Oh, drat it all! Wouldn't they let her have a drink in peace? If they were to have a peal of bells things promised well. Nevertheless, she ran off to open the door. Returning presently, she saw Mme Maloir questioning her with a glance.

"It's nothing," she said, "only a bouquet."

All three refreshed themselves, nodding to each other in token of salutation. Then while Zoé was at length busy clearing the table, bringing the plates out one by one and putting them in the sink, two other rings followed close upon one another. But they weren't serious, for while keeping the kitchen informed of what was going on she twice repeated her disdainful expression:

"Nothing, only a bouquet."

Notwithstanding which, the old ladies laughed between two of their tricks when they heard her describe the looks of the creditors in the anteroom after the flowers had arrived. Madame would find her bouquets on her toilet table. What a pity it was they cost such a lot and that you could only get ten sous for them! Oh dear, yes, plenty of money was wasted!

"For my part," said Mme Maloir, "I should be quite content if every day of my life I got what the men in Paris had spent on flowers for the women."

"Now, you know, you're not hard to please," murmured Mme Lerat. "Why, one would have only just enough to buy thread with. Four queens, my dear."

It was ten minutes to four. Zoé was astonished, could not understand why her mistress was out so long. Ordinarily when Madame found herself obliged to go out in the afternoons she got it over in double-quick time. But Mme Maloir declared that one didn't always manage things as one wished. Truly, life was beset with obstacles, averred Mme Lerat. The best course was to wait. If her niece was long in coming it was because her occupations detained her; wasn't it so? Besides, they weren't overworked—it was comfortable in the kitchen. And as hearts were out, Mme Lerat threw down diamonds.

The bell began again, and when Zoé reappeared she was burning with excitement.

"My children, it's fat Steiner!" she said in the doorway, lowering her voice as she spoke. "I've put *him* in the little sitting room."

Thereupon Mme Maloir spoke about the banker to Mme Lerat, who knew no such gentleman. Was he getting ready to give Rose Mignon the go-by? Zoé shook her head; she knew a thing or two. But once more she had to go and open the door.

"Here's bothers!" she murmured when she came back. "It's the nigger! 'Twasn't any good telling him that my lady's gone out, and so he's settled himself in the bedroom. We only expected him this evening."

At a quarter past four Nana was not in yet. What could she be after? It was silly of her! Two other bouquets were brought round, and Zoé, growing bored, looked to see if there were any coffee left. Yes, the ladies would willingly finish off the coffee; it would waken them up. Sitting hunched up on their chairs, they were beginning to fall asleep through dint of constantly taking their cards between their fingers with the accustomed movement. The half-hour sounded. Something must decidedly have happened to Madame. And they began whispering to each other.

Suddenly Mme Maloir forgot herself and in a ringing voice announced: "I've the five hundred! Trumps, Major Quint!"

"Oh, do be quiet!" said Zoé angrily. "What will all those gentlemen think?"

And in the silence which ensued and amid the whispered muttering of the two old women at strife over their game, the sound of rapid footsteps ascended from the back stairs. It was Nana at last. Before she had opened the door her breathlessness became audible. She bounced abruptly in, looking very red in the face. Her skirt, the string of which must have been broken, was trailing over the stairs, and her flounces had just been dipped in a puddle of something unpleasant which had oozed out on the landing of the first floor, where the servant girl was a regular slut.

"Here you are! It's lucky!" said Mme Lerat, pursing up her lips, for she was still vexed at Mme Maloir's "five hundred." "You may flatter yourself at the way you keep folks waiting."

"Madame isn't reasonable; indeed, she isn't!" added Zoé.

Nana was already harassed, and these reproaches exasperated her. Was that the way people received her after the worry she had gone through?

"Will you blooming well leave me alone, eh?" she cried.

"Hush, ma'am, there are people in there," said the maid.

Then in lower tones the young woman stuttered breathlessly:

"D'you suppose I've been having a good time? Why, there was no end to it. I should have liked to see you there! I was boiling with rage! I felt inclined to smack somebody. And never a cab to come home in! Luckily it's only a step from here, but never mind that; I did just run home."

"You have the money?" asked the aunt.

"Dear, dear! That question!" rejoined Nana.

She had sat herself down on a chair close up against the stove, for her legs had failed her after so much running, and without stopping to take breath she drew from behind her stays an envelope in which there were four hundred-franc notes. They were visible through a large rent she had torn with savage fingers in order to be sure of the contents. The three women round about her stared fixedly at the envelope, a big, crumpled, dirty receptacle, as it lay clasped in her small gloved hands.

It was too late now—Mme Lerat would not go to Rambouillet till tomorrow, and Nana entered into long explanations.

"There's company waiting for you," the lady's maid repeated.

But Nana grew excited again. The company might wait: she'd go to them all in good time when she'd finished. And as her aunt began putting her hand out for the money:

"Ah no! Not all of it," she said. "Three hundred francs for the nurse, fifty for your journey and expenses, that's three hundred and fifty. Fifty francs I keep."

The big difficulty was how to find change. There were not ten francs in the house. But they did not even address themselves to Mme Maloir who, never having more than a six-sou omnibus fair upon her, was listening in quite a disinterested manner. At length Zoé went out of the room, remarking that she would go and look in her box, and she brought back a hundred francs in hundred-sou pieces. They were counted out on a corner of the table, and Mme Lerat took her departure at once after having promised to bring Louiset back with her the following day.

"You say there's company there?" continued Nana, still sitting on the chair and resting herself.

"Yes, madame, three people."

And Zoé mentioned the banker first. Nana made a face. Did that man Steiner think she was going to let herself be bored because he had thrown her a bouquet yesterday evening?

"Besides, I've had enough of it," she declared. "I shan't receive today. Go and say you don't expect me now."

"Madame will think the matter over; Madame will receive Monsieur Steiner," murmured Zoé gravely, without budging from her place. She was annoyed to see her mistress on the verge of committing another foolish mistake.

Then she mentioned the Walachian, who ought by now to find time hanging heavy on his hands in the bedroom. Whereupon Nana grew furious and more obstinate than ever. No, she would see nobody, nobody! Who'd sent her such a blooming leech of a man?

"Chuck 'em all out! I—I'm going to play a game of bezique with Madame Maloir. I prefer doing that."

The bell interrupted her remarks. That was the last straw. Another of the beggars yet! She forbade Zoé to go and open the door, but the latter had left the kitchen without listening to her, and when she reappeared she brought back a couple of cards and said authoritatively:

"I told them that Madame was receiving visitors. The gentlemen are in the drawing room."

Nana had sprung up, raging, but the names of the Marquis de Chouard and of Count Muffat de Beuville, which were inscribed on the cards, calmed her down. For a moment or two she remained silent.

"Who are they?" she asked at last. "You know them?"

"I know the old fellow," replied Zoé, discreetly pursing up her lips.

And her mistress continuing to question her with her eyes, she added simply: "I've seen him somewhere."

This remark seemed to decide the young woman. Regretfully she left the kitchen, that asylum of steaming warmth, where you could talk and take your ease amid the pleasant fumes of the coffeepot which was being kept warm over a handful of glowing embers. She left Mme Maloir behind her. That lady was now busy reading her fortune by the cards; she had never yet taken her hat off, but now in order to be more at her ease she undid the strings and threw them back over her shoulders.

In the dressing room, where Zoé rapidly helped her on with a tea gown, Nana revenged herself for the way in which they were all boring her by muttering quiet curses upon the male sex. These big words caused the lady's maid not a little distress, for she saw with pain that her mistress was not rising superior to her origin as quickly as she could have desired. She even made bold to beg Madame to calm herself.

"You bet," was Nana's crude answer; "they're swine; they glory in that sort of thing."

Nevertheless, she assumed her princesslike manner, as she was wont to call it. But just when she was turning to go into the drawing room Zoé held her back and herself introduced the Marquis de Chouard and the Count Muffat into the dressing room. It was much better so.

"I regret having kept you waiting, gentlemen," said the young woman with studied politeness.

The two men bowed and seated themselves. A blind of embroidered tulle kept the little room in twilight. It was the most elegant chamber in the flat, for it was hung with some light-colored fabric and contained a cheval glass framed in inlaid wood, a lounge chair and some others with arms and blue satin upholsteries. On the toilet table the bouquets—roses, lilacs and hyacinths—appeared like a very ruin of flowers. Their perfume was strong and penetrating, while through the dampish air of the place, which was full of the spoiled exhalations of the washstand, came occasional whiffs of a more pungent scent, the scent of some grains of dry patchouli ground to fine powder at the bottom of a cup. And as she gathered herself together and drew up her dressing jacket, which had been ill fastened, Nana had all the appearance of having been surprised at her toilet: her skin was still damp; she smiled and looked quite startled amid her frills and laces.

"Madame, you will pardon our insistence," said the Count Muffat gravely. "We come on a quest. Monsieur and I are members of the Benevolent Organization of the district."

The Marquis de Chouard hastened gallantly to add:

"When we learned that a great artiste lived in this house we promised ourselves that we would put the claims of our poor people before her in a very special manner. Talent is never without a heart."

Nana pretended to be modest. She answered them with little assenting movements of her head, making rapid reflections at the same time. It must be the old man that had brought the other one: he had such wicked eyes. And yet the other was not to be trusted either: the veins near his temples were so queerly puffed up. He might quite well have come by himself. Ah, now that she thought of it, it was this way: the porter had given them her name, and they had egged one another on, each with his own ends in view.

"Most certainly, gentlemen, you were quite right to come up," she said with a very good grace.

But the electric bell made her tremble again. Another call, and that Zoé always opening the door! She went on:

"One is only too happy to be able to give."

At bottom she was flattered.

"Ah, madame," rejoined the marquis, "if only you knew about it! there's such misery! Our district has more than three thousand poor people in it, and yet it's one of the richest. You cannot picture to yourself anything like the present distress—children with no bread, women ill, utterly without assistance, perishing of the cold!"

"The poor souls!" cried Nana, very much moved.

Such was her feeling of compassion that tears flooded her fine eyes. No longer studying deportment, she leaned forward with a quick movement, and under her open dressing jacket her neck became visible, while the bent position of her knees served to outline the rounded contour of the thigh under the thin fabric of her skirt. A little flush of blood appeared in the marquis's cadaverous cheeks. Count Muffat, who was on the point of speaking, lowered his eyes. The air of that little room was too hot: it had the close, heavy warmth of a greenhouse. The roses were withering, and intoxicating odors floated up from the patchouli in the cup.

"One would like to be very rich on occasions like this," added Nana. "Well, well, we each do what we can. Believe me, gentlemen, if I had known——"

She was on the point of being guilty of a silly speech, so melted was she at heart. But she did not end her sentence and for a moment was worried at not being able to remember where she had put her fifty francs on changing her dress. But she recollected at last: they must be on the corner of her toilet tablⓔ

under an inverted pomatum pot. As she was in the act of rising the bell sounded for quite a long time. Capital! Another of them still! It would never end. The count and the marquis had both risen, too, and the ears of the latter seemed to be pricked up and, as it were, pointing toward the door; doubtless he knew that kind of ring. Muffat looked at him; then they averted their gaze mutually. They felt awkward and once more assumed their frigid bearing, the one looking square-set and solid with his thick head of hair, the other drawing back his lean shoulders, over which fell his fringe of thin white locks.

"My faith," said Nana, bringing the ten big silver pieces and quite determined to laugh about it, "I am going to entrust you with this, gentlemen. It is for the poor."

And the adorable little dimple in her chin became apparent. She assumed her favorite pose, her amiable baby expression, as she held the pile of five-franc pieces on her open palm and offered it to the men, as though she were saying to them, "Now then, who wants some?" The count was the sharper of the two. He took fifty francs but left one piece behind and, in order to gain possession of it, had to pick it off the young woman's very skin, a moist, supple skin, the touch of which sent a thrill through him. She was thoroughly merry and did not cease laughing.

"Come, gentlemen," she continued. "Another time I hope to give more."

The gentlemen no longer had any pretext for staying, and they bowed and went toward the door. But just as they were about to go out the bell rang anew. The marquis could not conceal a faint smile, while a frown made the count look more grave than before. Nana detained them some seconds so as to give Zoé time to find yet another corner for the newcomers. She did not relish meetings at her house. Only this time the whole place must be packed! She was therefore much relieved when she saw the drawing room empty and asked herself whether Zoé had really stuffed them into the cupboards.

"*Au revoir*, gentlemen," she said, pausing on the threshold of the drawing room.

It was as though she lapped them in her laughing smile and clear, unclouded glance. The Count Muffat bowed slightly. Despite his great social experience he felt that he had lost his equilibrium. He needed air; he was overcome with the dizzy feeling engendered in that dressing room with a scent of flowers, with a feminine essence which choked him. And behind his back, the Marquis de Chouard, who was sure that he could not be seen, made so bold as to wink at Nana, his whole face suddenly altering its expression as he did so, and his tongue nigh lolling from his mouth.

When the young woman re-entered the little room, where Zoé was awaiting her with letters and visiting cards, she cried out, laughing more heartily than ever:

"There are a pair of beggars for you! Why, they've got away with my fifty francs!"

She wasn't vexed. It struck her as a joke that *men* should have got money out of her. All the same, they were swine, for she hadn't a sou left. But at sight of the cards and the letters her bad temper returned. As to the letters, why, she said "pass" to them. They were from fellows who, after applauding her last night, were now making their declarations. And as to the callers, they might go about their business!

Zoé had stowed them all over the place, and she called attention to the great capabilities of the flat, every room in which opened on the corridor. That wasn't the case at Mme Blanche's, where people had all to go through the drawing room. Oh yes, Mme Blanche had had plenty of bothers over it!

"You will send them all away," continued Nana in pursuance of her idea. "Begin with the nigger."

"Oh, as to him, madame, I gave him his marching orders a while ago," said Zoé with a grin. "He only wanted to tell Madame that he couldn't come to-night."

There was vast joy at this announcement, and Nana clapped her hands. He wasn't coming, what good luck! She would be free then! And she emitted sighs of relief, as though she had been let off the most abominable of tortures. Her first thought was for Daguenet. Poor duck, why, she had just written to tell him to wait till Thursday! Quick, quick, Mme Maloir should write a second letter! But Zoé announced that Mme Maloir had slipped away unnoticed, according to her wont. Whereupon Nana, after talking of sending someone to him, began to hesitate. She was very tired. A long night's sleep— oh, it would be so jolly! The thought of such a treat overcame her at last. For once in a way she could allow herself that!

"I shall go to bed when I come back from the theater," she murmured greedily, "and you won't wake me before noon."

Then raising her voice:

"Now then, gee up! Shove the others downstairs!"

Zoé did not move. She would never have dreamed of giving her mistress overt advice, only now she made shift to give Madame the benefit of her experience when Madame seemed to be running her hot head against a wall.

"Monsieur Steiner as well?" she queried curtly.

"Why, certainly!" replied Nana. "Before all the rest."

The maid still waited, in order to give her mistress time for reflection. Would not Madame be proud to get such a rich gentleman away from her rival Rose Mignon—a man, moreover, who was known in all the theaters?

"Now make haste, my dear," rejoined Nana, who perfectly understood the situation, "and tell him he pesters me."

But suddenly there was a reversion of feeling. Tomorrow she might want him. Whereupon she laughed, winked once or twice and with a naughty little gesture cried out:

"After all's said and done, if I want him the best way even now is to kick him out of doors."

Zoé seemed much impressed. Struck with a sudden admiration, she gazed at her mistress and then went and chucked Steiner out of doors without further deliberation.

Meanwhile Nana waited patiently for a second or two in order to give her time to sweep the place out, as she phrased it. No one would ever have expected such a siege! She craned her head into the drawing room and found it empty. The dining room was empty too. But as she continued her visitation in a calmer frame of mind, feeling certain that nobody remained behind, she opened the door of a closet and came suddenly upon a very young man. He was sitting on the top of a trunk, holding a huge bouquet on his knees and looking exceedingly quiet and extremely well behaved.

"Goodness gracious me!" she cried. "There's one of 'em in there even now!"

The very young man had jumped down at sight of her and was blushing as red as a poppy. He did not know what to do with his bouquet, which he kept shifting from one hand to the other, while his looks betrayed the extreme of emotion. His youth, his embarrassment and the funny figure he cut in his struggles with his flowers melted Nana's heart, and she burst into a pretty peal of laughter. Well, now, the very children were coming, were they? Men were arriving in long clothes. So she gave up all airs and graces, became familiar and maternal, tapped her leg and asked for fun:

"You want me to wipe your nose; do you, baby?"

"Yes," replied the lad in a low, supplicating tone.

This answer made her merrier than ever. He was seventeen years old, he said. His name was Georges Hugon. He was at the Variétés last night and now he had come to see her.

"These flowers are for me?"

"Yes."

"Then give 'em to me, booby!"

But as she took the bouquet from him he sprang upon her hands and kissed them with all the gluttonous eagerness peculiar to his charming time of life. She had to beat him to make him let go. There was a dreadful little dribbling customer for you! But as she scolded him she flushed rosy-red and began smiling. And with that she sent him about his business, telling him that he might call again. He staggered away; he could not find the doors.

Nana went back into her dressing room, where Francis made his appearance almost simultaneously in order to dress her hair for the evening. Seated in front of her mirror and bending her head beneath the hairdresser's nimble hands, she stayed silently meditative. Presently, however, Zoé entered, remarking:

"There's one of them, madame, who refuses to go."

"Very well, he must be left alone," she answered quietly.

"If that comes to that they still keep arriving."

"Bah! Tell 'em to wait. When they begin to feel too hungry they'll be off."

Her humor had changed, and she was now delighted to make people wait about for nothing. A happy thought struck her as very amusing; she escaped from beneath Francis' hands and ran and bolted the doors. They might now crowd in there as much as they liked; they would probably refrain from making a hole through the wall. Zoé could come in and out through the little doorway leading to the kitchen. However, the electric bell rang more lustily than ever. Every five minutes a clear, lively little ting-ting recurred as regularly as if it had been produced by some well-adjusted piece of mechanism.

And Nana counted these rings to while the time away withal. But suddenly she remembered something.

"I say, where are my burnt almonds?"

Francis, too, was forgetting about the burnt almonds. But now he drew a paper bag from one of the pockets of his frock coat and presented it to her with the discreet gesture of a man who is offering a lady a present. Nevertheless, whenever his accounts came to be settled, he always put the burnt almonds down on his bill. Nana put the bag between her knees and set to work munching her sweetmeats, turning her head from time to time under the hairdresser's gently compelling touch.

"The deuce," she murmured after a silence, "there's a troop for you!"

Thrice, in quick succession, the bell had sounded. Its summonses became fast and furious. There were modest tintinnabulations which seemed to stutter and tremble like a first avowal; there were bold rings which vibrated under some rough touch and hasty rings which sounded through the house with shivering rapidity. It was a regular peal, as Zoé said, a peal loud enough to upset the neighborhood, seeing that a whole mob of men were jabbing at the ivory button, one after the other. That old joker Bordenave had really been far too lavish with her address. Why, the whole of yesterday's house was coming!

"By the by, Francis, have you five louis?" said Nana.

He drew back, looked carefully at her headdress and then quietly remarked: "Five louis, that's according!"

"Ah, you know if you want securities . . ." she continued.

And without finishing her sentence, she indicated the adjoining rooms with a sweeping gesture. Francis lent the five louis. Zoé, during each momentary respite, kept coming in to get Madame's things ready. Soon she came to dress her while the hairdresser lingered with the intention of giving some finishing touches to the headdress. But the bell kept continually disturbing the lady's maid, who left Madame with her stays half laced and only one shoe on. Despite her long experience, the maid was losing her head. After bringing every nook and corner into requisition and putting men pretty well everywhere, she had been driven to stow them away in threes and fours, which was a course of procedure entirely opposed to her principles. So much the worse for them if they ate each other up! It would afford more room! And Nana, sheltering behind her carefully bolted door, began laughing at them, declaring that she could hear them pant. They ought to be looking lovely in there with their tongues hanging out like a lot of bowwows sitting round on their behinds. Yesterday's success was not yet over, and this pack of men had followed up her scent.

"Provided they don't break anything," she murmured.

She began to feel some anxiety, for she fancied she felt their hot breath coming through chinks in the door. But Zoé ushered Labordette in, and the young woman gave a little shout of relief. He was anxious to tell her about an account he had settled for her at the justice of peace's court. But she did not attend and said:

"I'll take you along with me. We'll have dinner together, and afterward you shall escort me to the Variétés. I don't go on before half-past nine."

Good old Labordette, how lucky it was he had come! He was a fellow who never asked for any favors. He was only the friend of the women, whose little bits of business he arranged for them. Thus on his way in he had dismissed the creditors in the anteroom. Indeed, those good folks really didn't want to be paid. On the contrary, if they *had* been pressing for payment it was only for the sake of complimenting Madame and of personally renewing their offers of service after her grand success of yesterday.

"Let's be off, let's be off," said Nana, who was dressed by now.

But at that moment Zoé came in again, shouting:

"I refuse to open the door any more. They're waiting in a crowd all down the stairs."

A crowd all down the stairs! Francis himself, despite the English stolidity of manner which he was wont to affect, began laughing as he put up his combs. Nana, who had already taken Labordette's arm, pushed him into the kitchen and effected her escape. At last she was delivered from the men and felt happily conscious that she might now enjoy his society anywhere without fear of stupid interruptions.

"You shall see me back to my door," she said as they went down the kitchen stairs. "I shall feel safe, in that case. Just fancy, I want to sleep a whole night quite by myself—yes, a whole night! It's sort of infatuation, dear boy!"

CHAPTER III

THE COUNTESS SABINE, as it had become customary to call Mme Muffat de Beuville in order to distinguish her from the count's mother, who had died the year before, was wont to receive every Tuesday in her house in the Rue Miromesnil at the corner of the Rue de Pentièvre. It was a great square building, and the Muffats had lived in it for a hundred years or more. On the side of the street its frontage seemed to slumber, so lofty was it and dark, so sad and conventlike, with its great outer shutters, which were nearly always closed. And at the back in a little dark garden some trees had grown up and were straining toward the sunlight with such long slender branches that their tips were visible above the roof.

This particular Tuesday, toward ten o'clock in the evening, there were scarcely a dozen people in the drawing room. When she was only expecting intimate friends the countess opened neither the little drawing room nor the dining room. One felt more at home on such occasions and chatted round the fire. The drawing room was very large and very lofty; its four windows looked out upon the garden, from which, on this rainy evening of the close of April, issued a sensation of damp despite the great logs burning on the hearth. The sun never shone down into the room; in the daytime it was dimly lit up by a faint greenish light, but at night, when the lamps and the chandelier were burning, it looked merely a serious old chamber with its massive mahogany First Empire furniture, its hangings and chair coverings of yellow velvet, stamped with a large design. Entering it, one was in an atmosphere of cold dignity, of ancient manners, of a vanished age, the air of which seemed devotional.

Opposite the armchair, however, in which the count's mother had died—a square armchair of formal design and inhospitable padding, which stood by the hearthside—the Countess Sabine was seated in a deep and cozy lounge, the red silk upholsteries of which were soft as eider down. It was the only piece of modern furniture there, a fanciful item introduced amid the prevailing severity and clashing with it.

"So we shall have the shah of Persia," the young woman was saying.

They were talking of the crowned heads who were coming to Paris for the exhibition. Several ladies had formed a circle round the hearth, and Mme du Joncquoy, whose brother, a diplomat, had just fulfilled a mission in the East, was giving some details about the court of Nazr-ed-Din.

"Are you out of sorts, my dear?" asked Mme Chantereau, the wife of an ironmaster, seeing the countess shivering slightly and growing pale as she did so.

"Oh no, not at all," replied the latter, smiling. "I felt a little cold. This drawing room takes so long to warm."

And with that she raised her melancholy eyes and scanned the walls from floor to ceiling. Her daughter Estelle, a slight, insignificant-looking girl of sixteen, the thankless period of life, quitted the large footstool on which she was sitting and silently came and propped up one of the logs which had rolled from its place. But Mme de Chezelles, a convent friend of Sabine's and her junior by five years, exclaimed:

"Dear me, I would gladly be possessed of a drawing room such as yours! At any rate, you are able to receive visitors. They only build boxes nowadays. Oh, if I were in your place!"

She ran giddily on and with lively gestures explained how she would alter the hangings, the seats—everything, in fact. Then she would give balls to which all Paris should run. Behind her seat her husband, a magistrate, stood listening with serious air. It was rumored that she deceived him quite openly, but people pardoned her offense and received her just the same, because, they said, "she's not answerable for her actions."

"Oh that Léonide!" the Countess Sabine contented herself by murmuring, smiling her faint smile the while.

With a languid movement she eked out the thought that was in her. After having lived there seventeen years she certainly would not alter her drawing room now. It would henceforth remain just such as her mother-in-law had wished to preserve it during her lifetime. Then returning to the subject of conversation:

"I have been assured," she said, "that we shall also have the king of Prussia and the emperor of Russia."

"Yes, some very fine fetes are promised," said Mme du Joncquoy.

The banker Steiner, not long since introduced into this circle by Léonide de Chezelles, who was acquainted with the whole of Parisian society, was sitting chatting on a sofa between two of the windows. He was questioning a deputy, from whom he was endeavoring with much adroitness to elicit news about a movement on the stock exchange of which he had his suspicions, while the Count Muffat, standing in front of them, was silently listening to their talk, looking, as he did so, even grayer than was his wont.

Four or five young men formed another group near the door round the Count Xavier de Vandeuvres, who in a low tone was telling them an anecdote. It was doubtless a very risky one, for they were choking with laughter. Companionless in the center of the room, a stout man, a chief clerk at the Ministry of the Interior, sat heavily in an armchair, dozing with his eyes open. But when one of the young men appeared to doubt the truth of the anecdote Vandeuvres raised his voice.

"You are too much of a skeptic, Foucarmont; you'll spoil all your pleasures that way."

And he returned to the ladies with a laugh. Last scion of a great family, of feminine manners and witty tongue, he was at that time running through a fortune with a rage of life and appetite which nothing could appease. His racing stable, which was one of the best known in Paris, cost him a fabulous amount of money; his betting losses at the Imperial Club amounted monthly to an alarming number of pounds, while taking one year with another, his mistresses would be always devouring now a farm, now some acres of arable land or forest, which amounted, in fact, to quite a respectable slice of his vast estates in Picardy.

"I advise you to call other people skeptics! Why, you don't believe a thing yourself," said Léonide, making shift to find him a little space in which to sit down at her side.

"It's you who spoil your own pleasures."

"Exactly," he replied. "I wish to make others benefit by my experience."

But the company imposed silence on him: he was scandalizing M. Venot. And, the ladies having changed their positions, a little old man of sixty, with bad teeth and a subtle smile, became visible in the depths of an easy chair. There he sat as comfortably as in his own house, listening to everybody's remarks and making none himself. With a slight gesture he announced himself by no means scandalized. Vandeuvres once more assumed his dignified bearing and added gravely:

"Monsieur Venot is fully aware that I believe what it is one's duty to believe."

It was an act of faith, and even Léonide appeared satisfied. The young men at the end of the room no longer laughed; the company were old fogies, and amusement was not to be found there. A cold breath of wind had passed over them, and amid the ensuing silence Steiner's nasal voice became audible. The deputy's discreet answers were at last driving him to desperation. For a second or two the Countess Sabine looked at the fire; then she resumed the conversation.

"I saw the king of Prussia at Baden-Baden last year. He's still full of vigor for his age."

"Count Bismarck is to accompany him," said Mme du Joncquoy. "Do you know the count? I lunched with him at my brother's ages ago, when he was representative of Prussia in Paris. There's a man now whose latest successes I cannot in the least understand."

"But why?" asked Mme Chantereau.

"Good gracious, how am I to explain? He doesn't please me. His appearance is boorish and underbred. Besides, so far as I am concerned, I find him stupid."

With that the whole room spoke of Count Bismarck, and opinions differed considerably. Vandeuvres knew him and assured the company that he was great in his cups and at play. But when the discussion was at its height the door was opened, and Hector de la Falois made his appearance. Fauchery, who followed in his wake, approached the countess and, bowing:

"Madame," he said, "I have not forgotten your extremely kind invitation."

She smiled and made a pretty little speech. The journalist, after bowing to the count, stood for some moments in the middle of the drawing room. He only recognized Steiner and accordingly looked rather out of his element. But Vandeuvres turned and came and shook hands with him. And forthwith, in his delight at the meeting and with a sudden desire to be confidential, Fauchery buttonholed him and said in a low voice:

"It's tomorrow. Are you going?"

"Egad, yes."

"At midnight, at her house."

"I know, I know. I'm going with Blanche."

He wanted to escape and return to the ladies in order to urge yet another reason in M. de Bismarck's favor. But Fauchery detained him.

"You never will guess whom she has charged me to invite."

And with a slight nod he indicated Count Muffat, who was just then discussing a knotty point in the budget with Steiner and the deputy.

"It's impossible," said Vandeuvres, stupefaction and merriment in his tones.

"My word on it! I had to swear that I would bring him to her. Indeed, that's one of my reasons for coming here."

Both laughed silently, and Vandeuvres, hurriedly rejoining the circle of ladies, cried out:

"I declare that on the contrary Monsieur de Bismarck is exceedingly witty. For instance, one evening he said a charmingly epigrammatic thing in my presence."

La Faloise meanwhile had heard the few rapid sentences thus whisperingly interchanged, and he gazed at Fauchery in hopes of an explanation which was not vouchsafed him. Of whom were they talking, and what were they going to do at midnight tomorrow? He did not leave his cousin's side again. The latter had gone and seated himself. He was especially interested by the Countess Sabine. Her name had often been mentioned in his presence, and he knew that, having been married at the age of seventeen, she must now be thirty-four and that since her marriage she had passed a cloistered existence with her husband and her mother-in-law. In society some spoke of her as a woman of religious chastity, while others pitied her and recalled to memory her charming bursts of laughter and the burning glances of her great eyes in the days prior to her imprisonment in this old town house. Fauchery scrutinized her and yet hesitated. One of his friends, a captain who had recently died in Mexico, had, on the very eve of his departure, made him one of those gross postprandial confessions, of which even the most prudent among men are occasionally guilty. But of this he only retained a vague recollection; they had dined not wisely but too well that evening, and when he saw the countess, in her black dress and with her quiet smile, seated in that Old World drawing room, he certainly had his doubts. A lamp which had been placed behind her threw into clear relief her dark, delicate, plump side face, wherein a certain heaviness in the contours of the mouth alone indicated a species of imperious sensuality.

"What do they want with their Bismarck?" muttered La Faloise, whose constant pretense it was to be bored in good society. "One's ready to kick the bucket here. A pretty idea of yours it was to want to come!"

Fauchery questioned him abruptly.

"Now tell me, does the countess admit someone to her embraces?"

"Oh dear, no, no! My dear fellow!" he stammered, manifestly taken aback and quite forgetting his pose. "Where d'you think we are?"

After which he was conscious of a want of up-to-dateness in this outburst of indignation and, throwing himself back on a great sofa, he added:

"Gad! I say no! But I don't know much about it. There's a little chap out there, Foucarmont they call him, who's to be met with everywhere and at every turn. One's seen faster men than that, though, you bet. However, it doesn't concern me, and indeed, all I know is that if the countess indulges in high jinks she's still pretty sly about it, for the thing never gets about—nobody talks."

Then although Fauchery did not take the trouble to question him, he told him all he knew about the Muffats. Amid the conversation of the ladies, which still continued in front of the hearth, they both spoke in subdued tones, and, seeing them there with their white cravats and gloves, one might have supposed them to be discussing in chosen phraseology some really serious topic. Old Mme Muffat then, whom La Faloise had been well acquainted with, was an insufferable old lady, always hand in glove with the priests. She had the grand manner, besides, and an authoritative way of comporting herself, which bent everybody to her will. As to Muffat, he was an old man's child; his father, a general, had been created count by Napoleon I, and naturally he had found himself in favor after the second of December. He hadn't much gaiety of manner either, but he passed for a very honest man of straightforward intentions and understanding. Add to these a code of old aristocratic ideas and such a lofty conception of his duties at court, of his dignities and of his virtues, that he behaved like a god on wheels. It was the Mamma Muffat who had given him this precious education with its daily visits to the confessional, its complete absence of escapades and of all that is meant by youth. He was a practicing Christian and had attacks of faith of such fiery violence that they might be likened to accesses of burning fever. Finally, in order to add a last touch to the picture, La Faloise whispered something in his cousin's ear.

"You don't say so!" said the latter.

"On my word of honor, they swore it was true! He was still like that when he married."

Fauchery chuckled as he looked at the count, whose face, with its fringe of whiskers and absence of mustaches, seemed to have grown squarer and harder now that he was busy quoting figures to the writhing, struggling Steiner.

"My word, he's got a phiz for it!" murmured Fauchery. "A pretty present he made his wife! Poor little thing, how he must have bored her! She knows nothing about anything, I'll wager!"

Just then the Countess Sabine was saying something to him. But he did not hear her, so amusing and extraordinary did he esteem the Muffats' case. She repeated the question.

"Monsieur Fauchery, have you not published a sketch of Monsieur de Bismarck? You spoke with him once?"

He got up briskly and approached the circle of ladies, endeavoring to collect himself and soon with perfect ease of manner finding an answer:

"Dear me, madame, I assure you I wrote that 'portrait' with the help of biographies which had been published in Germany. I have never seen Monsieur de Bismarck."

He remained beside the countess and, while talking with her, continued his meditations. She did not look her age; one would have set her down as being twenty-eight at most, for her eyes, above all, which were filled with the dark blue shadow of her long eyelashes, retained the glowing light of youth. Bred in a divided family, so that she used to spend one month with the Marquis de Chouard, another with the marquise, she had been married very young, urged on, doubtless, by her father, whom she embarrassed after her mother's death. A terrible man was the marquis, a man about whom strange tales were beginning to be told, and that despite his lofty piety! Fauchery asked if he should have the honor of meeting him. Certainly her father was coming, but only very late; he had so much work on hand! The journalist thought he knew where the old gentleman passed his evenings and looked grave. But a mole, which he noticed close to her mouth on the countess's left cheek, surprised him. Nana had precisely the same mole. It was curious. Tiny hairs curled up on it, only they were golden in Nana's case, black as jet in this. Ah well, never mind! This woman enjoyed nobody's embraces.

"I have always felt a wish to know Queen Augusta," she said. "They say she is so good, so devout. Do you think she will accompany the king?"

"It is not thought that she will, madame," he replied.

She had no lovers: the thing was only too apparent. One had only to look at her there by the side of that daughter of hers, sitting so insignificant and constrained on her footstool. That sepulchral drawing room of hers, which exhaled odors suggestive of being in a church, spoke as plainly as words could of the iron hand, the austere mode of existence, that weighed her down. There was nothing suggestive of her own personality in that ancient abode, black with the damps of years. It was Muffat who made himself felt there, who dominated his surroundings with his devotional training, his penances and his fasts. But the sight of the little old gentleman with the black teeth and subtle smile whom he suddenly discovered in his armchair behind the group of ladies afforded him a yet more decisive argument. He knew the personage. It was Théophile Venot, a retired lawyer who had made a specialty of church cases. He had left off practice with a handsome fortune and was now leading a sufficiently mysterious existence, for he was received everywhere, treated with great deference and even somewhat feared, as though he had been the representative of a mighty force, an occult power, which was felt to be at his back. Nevertheless, his behavior was very humble. He was churchwarden at the Madeleine Church and had simply accepted the post of deputy mayor at the town house of the Ninth Arrondissement in order, as he said, to have something to do in his leisure time. Deuce take it, the countess was well guarded; there was nothing to be done in that quarter.

"You're right, it's enough to make one kick the bucket here," said Fauchery to his cousin when he had made good his escape from the circle of ladies. "We'll hook it!"

But Steiner, deserted at last by the Count Muffat and the deputy, came up in a fury. Drops of perspiration stood on his forehead, and he grumbled huskily:

"Gad! Let 'em tell me nothing, if nothing they want to tell me. I shall find people who will talk."

Then he pushed the journalist into a corner and, altering his tone, said in accents of victory:

"It's tomorrow, eh? I'm of the party, my bully!"

"Indeed!" muttered Fauchery with some astonishment.

"You didn't know about it. Oh, I had lots of bother to find her at home. Besides, Mignon never would leave me alone."

"But they're to be there, are the Mignons."

"Yes, she told me so. In fact, she did receive my visit, and she invited me. Midnight punctually, after the play."

The banker was beaming. He winked and added with a peculiar emphasis on the words:

"You've worked it, eh?"

"Eh, what?" said Fauchery, pretending not to understand him. "She wanted to thank me for my article, so she came and called on me."

"Yes, yes. You fellows are fortunate. You get rewarded. By the by, who pays the piper tomorrow?"

The journalist made a slight outward movement with his arms, as though he would intimate that no one had ever been able to find out. But Vandeuvres called to Steiner, who knew M. de Bismarck. Mme du Joncquoy had almost convinced herself of the truth of her suppositions; she concluded with these words:

"He gave me an unpleasant impression. I think his face is evil. But I am quite willing to believe that he has a deal of wit. It would account for his successes."

"Without doubt," said the banker with a faint smile. He was a Jew from Frankfort.

Meanwhile La Faloise at last made bold to question his cousin. He followed him up and got inside his guard:

"There's supper at a woman's tomorrow evening? With which of them, eh? With which of them?"

Fauchery motioned to him that they were overheard and must respect the conventions here. The door had just been opened anew, and an old lady had come in, followed by a young man in whom the journalist recognized the truant schoolboy, perpetrator of the famous and as yet unforgotten "*très chic*" of the *Blonde Venus* first night. This lady's arrival caused a stir among the company. The Countess Sabine had risen briskly from her seat in order to go and greet her, and she had taken both her hands in hers and addressed her as her "dear Madame Hugon." Seeing that his cousin viewed this little episode with some curiosity, La Faloise sought to arouse his interest and in a few brief phrases explained the position. Mme Hugon, widow of a notary, lived in retirement at Les Fondettes, an old estate of her family's in the neighborhood of Orleans, but she also kept up a small establishment in Paris in a house belonging to her in the Rue de Richelieu and was now passing some weeks there in order to settle her youngest son, who was reading the law and in his "first year." In old times she had been a dear friend of the Marquise de Chouard and had assisted at the birth of the countess, who, prior to her marriage, used to stay at her house for months at a time and even now was quite familiarly treated by her.

"I have brought Georges to see you," said Mme Hugon to Sabine. "He's grown, I trust."

The young man with his clear eyes and the fair curls which suggested a girl dressed up as a boy bowed easily to the countess and reminded her of a bout of battledore and shuttlecock they had had together two years ago at Les Fondettes.

"Philippe is not in Paris?" asked Count Muffat.

"Dear me, no!" replied the old lady. "He is always in garrison at Bourges." She had seated herself and began talking with considerable pride of her eldest son, a great big fellow who, after enlisting in a fit of waywardness, had of late very rapidly attained the rank of lieutenant. All the ladies behaved to her with respectful sympathy, and conversation was resumed in a tone at once more amiable and more refined. Fauchery, at sight of that respectable Mme Hugon, that motherly face lit up with such a kindly smile beneath its broad tresses of white hair, thought how foolish he had been to suspect the Countess Sabine even for an instant.

Nevertheless, the big chair with the red silk upholsteries in which the countess sat had attracted his attention. Its style struck him as crude, not to say fantastically suggestive, in that dim old drawing room. Certainly it was not the count who had inveigled thither that nest of voluptuous idleness. One might have described it as an experiment, marking the birth of an appetite and of an enjoyment. Then he forgot where he was, fell into brown study and in thought even harked back to that vague confidential announcement imparted to him one evening in the dining room of a restaurant. Impelled by a sort of sensuous curiosity, he had always wanted an introduction into the Muffats' circle, and now that his friend was in Mexico through all eternity, who could tell what might happen? "We shall see," he thought. It was a folly, doubtless, but the idea kept tormenting him; he felt himself drawn on and his animal nature aroused. The big chair had a rumpled look—its nether cushions had been tumbled, a fact which now amused him.

"Well, shall we be off?" asked La Faloise, mentally vowing that once outside he would find out the name of the woman with whom people were going to sup.

"All in good time," replied Fauchery.

But he was no longer in any hurry and excused himself on the score of the invitation he had been commissioned to give and had as yet not found a convenient opportunity to mention. The ladies were chatting about an assumption of the veil, a very touching ceremony by which the whole of Parisian society had for the last three days been greatly moved. It was the eldest daughter of the Baronne de Fougeray, who, under stress of an irresistible vocation, had just entered the Carmelite Convent. Mme Chantereau, a distant cousin of the Fougerays, told how the baroness had been obliged to take to her bed the day after the ceremony, so overdone was she with weeping.

"I had a very good place," declared Léonide. "I found it interesting."

Nevertheless, Mme Hugon pitied the poor mother. How sad to lose a daughter in such a way!

"I am accused of being overreligious," she said in her quiet, frank manner, "but that does not prevent me thinking the children very cruel who obstinately commit such suicide."

"Yes, it's a terrible thing," murmured the countess, shivering a little, as became a chilly person, and huddling herself anew in the depths of her big chair in front of the fire.

Then the ladies fell into a discussion. But their voices were discreetly attuned, while light trills of laughter now and again interrupted the gravity of their talk. The two lamps on the chimney piece, which had shades of rose-colored lace, cast a feeble light over them while on scattered pieces of furniture there burned but three other lamps, so that the great drawing room remained in soft shadow.

Steiner was getting bored. He was describing to Fauchery an escapade of that little Mme de Chezelles, whom he simply referred to as Léonide. "A blackguard woman," he said, lowering his voice behind the ladies' armchairs. Fauchery looked at her as she sat quaintly perched, in her voluminous ball dress of pale blue satin, on the corner of her armchair. She looked as slight and impudent as a boy, and he ended by feeling astonished at seeing her there. People comported themselves better at Caroline Héquet's, whose mother had arranged her house on serious principles. Here was a perfect subject for an article. What a strange world was this world of Paris! The most rigid circles found themselves invaded. Evidently that silent Théophile Venot, who contented himself by smiling and showing his ugly teeth, must have been a legacy from the late countess. So, too, must have been such ladies of mature age as Mme Chantereau and Mme du Joncquoy, besides four or five old gentlemen who sat motionless in corners. The Count Muffat attracted to the house a series of functionaries, distinguished by the immaculate personal appearance which was at that time required of the men at the Tuileries. Among others there was the chief clerk, who still sat solitary in the middle of the room with his closely shorn cheeks, his vacant glance and his coat so tight of fit that he could scarce venture to move. Almost all the young men and certain individuals with distinguished, aristocratic manners were the Marquis de Chouard's contribution to the circle, he having kept touch with the Legitimist party after making his peace with the empire on his entrance into the Council of State. There remained Léonide de Chezelles and Steiner, an ugly little knot against which Mme Hugon's elderly and amiable serenity stood out in strange contrast. And Fauchery, having sketched out his article, named this last group "Countess Sabine's little clique."

"On another occasion," continued Steiner in still lower tones, "Léonide got her tenor down to Montauban. She was living in the Château de Beaurecueil, two leagues farther off, and she used to come in daily in a carriage and pair in order to visit him at the Lion d'Or, where he had put up. The carriage used to wait at the door, and Lèonide would stay for hours in the house, while a crowd gathered round and looked at the horses."

There was a pause in the talk, and some solemn moments passed silently by in the lofty room. Two young men were whispering, but they ceased in their turn, and the hushed step of Count Muffat was alone audible as he crossed the floor. The lamps seemed to have paled; the fire was going out; a stern shadow fell athwart the old friends of the house where they sat in the chairs they had occupied there for forty years back. It was as though in a momentary pause of conversation the invited guests had become suddenly aware that the count's mother, in all her glacial stateliness, had returned among them.

But the Countess Sabine had once more resumed:

"Well, at last the news of it got about. The young man was likely to die, and that would explain the poor child's adoption of the religious life. Besides, they say that Monsieur de Fougeray would never have given his consent to the marriage."

"They say heaps of other things too," cried Léonide giddily.

She fell a-laughing; she refused to talk. Sabine was won over by this gaiety and put her handkerchief up to her lips. And in the vast and solemn room their laughter sounded a note which struck Fauchery strangely, the note of delicate glass breaking. Assuredly here was the first beginning of the "little rift." Everyone began talking again. Mme du Joncquoy demurred; Mme Chantereau knew for certain that a marriage had been projected but that matters had gone no further; the men even ventured to give their opinions. For some minutes the conversation was a babel of opinions, in which the divers elements of the circle, whether Bonapartist or Legitimist or merely worldly and skeptical, appeared to jostle one another simultaneously. Estelle had rung to order wood to be put on the fire; the footman turned up the lamps; the room seemed to wake from sleep. Fauchery began smiling, as though once more at his ease.

"Egad, they become the brides of God when they couldn't be their cousin's," said Vandeuvres between his teeth.

The subject bored him, and he had rejoined Fauchery.

"My dear fellow, have you ever seen a woman who was really loved become a nun?"

He did not wait for an answer, for he had had enough of the topic, and in a hushed voice:

"Tell me," he said, "how many of us will there be tomorrow? There 'll be the Mignons, Steiner, yourself, Blanche and I; who else?"

"Caroline, I believe, and Simonne and Gaga without doubt. One never knows exactly, does one? On such occasions one expects the party will number twenty, and you're really thirty."

Vandeuvres, who was looking at the ladies, passed abruptly to another subject:

"She must have been very nice-looking, that Du Joncquoy woman, some fifteen years ago. Poor Estelle has grown lankier than ever. What a nice lath to put into a bed!"

But interrupting himself, he returned to the subject of tomorrow's supper.

"What's so tiresome of those shows is that it's always the same set of women. One wants a novelty. Do try and invent a new girl. By Jove, happy thought! I'll go and beseech that stout man to bring the woman he was trotting about the other evening at the Variétés."

He referred to the chief clerk, sound asleep in the middle of the drawing room. Fauchery, afar off, amused himself by following this delicate negotiation. Vandeuvres had sat himself down by the stout man, who still looked very sedate. For some moments they both appeared to be discussing with much propriety the question before the house, which was, "How can one discover the exact state of feeling that urges a young girl to enter into the religious life?" Then the count returned with the remark:

"It's impossible. He swears she's straight. She'd refuse, and yet I would have wagered that I once saw her at Laure's."

"Eh, what? You go to Laure's?" murmured Fauchery with a chuckle. "You venture your reputation in places like that? I was under the impression that it was only we poor devils of outsiders who——"

"Ah, dear boy, one ought to see every side of life."

Then they sneered and with sparkling eyes they compared notes about the table d'hôte in the Rue des Martyrs, where big Laure Piédefer ran a dinner at three francs a head for little women in difficulties. A nice hole, where all the little women used to kiss Laure on the lips! And as the Countess Sabine, who had overheard a stray word or two, turned toward them, they started back, rubbing shoulders in excited merriment. They had not noticed that Georges Hugon was close by and that he was listening to them, blushing so hotly the while that a rosy flush had spread from his ears to his girlish throat. The infant was full of shame and of ecstasy. From the moment his mother had turned him loose in the room he had been hovering in the wake of Mme de Chezelles, the only woman present who struck him as being the thing. But after all is said and done, Nana licked her to fits!

"Yesterday evening," Mme Hugon was saying, "Georges took me to the play. Yes, we went to the Variétés, where I certainly had not set foot for the last ten years. That child adores music. As to me, I wasn't in the least amused, but he was so happy! They put extraordinary pieces on the stage nowadays. Besides, music delights me very little, I confess."

"What! You don't love music, madame?" cried Mme du Joncquoy, lifting her eyes to heaven. "Is it possible there should be people who don't love music?"

The exclamation of surprise was general. No one had dropped a single word concerning the performance at the Variétés, at which the good Mme Hugon had not understood any of the allusions. The ladies knew the piece but said nothing about it, and with that they plunged into the realm of sentiment and began discussing the masters in a tone of refined and ecstatical admiration. Mme du Joncquoy was not fond of any of them save Weber, while Mme Chantereau stood up for the Italians. The ladies' voices had turned soft and languishing, and in front of the hearth one might have fancied one's self listening in meditative, religious retirement to the faint, discreet music of a little chapel.

"Now let's see," murmured Vandeuvres, bringing Fauchery back into the middle of the drawing room, "notwithstanding it all, we must invent a woman for tomorrow. Shall we ask Steiner about it?"

"Oh, when Steiner's got hold of a woman," said the journalist, "it's because Paris has done with her."

Vandeuvres, however, was searching about on every side.

"Wait a bit," he continued, "the other day I met Foucarmont with a charming blonde. I'll go and tell him to bring her."

And he called to Foucarmont. They exchanged a few words rapidly. There must have been some sort of complication, for both of them, moving carefully forward and stepping over the dresses of the ladies, went off in quest of another young man with whom they continued the discussion in the embrasure of a window. Fauchery was left to himself and had just decided to proceed to the hearth, where Mme du Joncquoy was announcing that she never heard Weber played without at the same time seeing lakes, forests and sunrises over landscapes steeped in dew, when a hand touched his shoulder and a voice behind him remarked:

"It's not civil of you."

"What d'you mean?" he asked, turning round and recognizing La Faloise.

"Why, about that supper tomorrow. You might easily have got me invited."

Fauchery was at length about to state his reasons when Vandeuvres came back to tell him:

"It appears it isn't a girl of Foucarmont's. It's that man's flame out there. She won't be able to come. What a piece of bad luck! But all the same I've pressed Foucarmont into the service, and he's going to try to get Louise from the Palais-Royal."

"Is it not true, Monsieur de Vandeuvres," asked Mme Chantereau, raising her voice, "that Wagner's music was hissed last Sunday?"

"Oh, frightfully, madame," he made answer, coming forward with his usual exquisite politeness.

Then, as they did not detain him, he moved off and continued whispering in the journalist's ear:

"I'm going to press some more of them. These young fellows must know some little ladies."

With that he was observed to accost men and to engage them in conversation in his usual amiable and smiling way in every corner of the drawing room. He mixed with the various groups, said something confidently to everyone and walked away again with a sly wink and a secret signal or two. It looked as though he were giving out a watchword in that easy way of his. The news went round; the place of meeting was announced, while the ladies' sentimental dissertations on music served to conceal the small, feverish rumor of these recruiting operations.

"No, do not speak of your Germans," Mme Chantereau was saying. "Song is gaiety; song is light. Have you heard Patti in the *Barber of Seville?*"

"She was delicious!" murmured Léonide, who strummed none but operatic airs on her piano.

Meanwhile the Countess Sabine had rung. When on Tuesdays the number of visitors was small, tea was handed round the drawing room itself. While directing a footman to clear a round table the countess followed the Count de Vandeuvres with her eyes. She still smiled that vague smile which slightly disclosed her white teeth, and as the count passed she questioned him.

"What *are* you plotting, Monsieur de Vandeuvres?"

"What am I plotting, madame?" he answered quietly. "Nothing at all."

"Really! I saw you so busy. Pray, wait, you shall make yourself useful!"

She placed an album in his hands and asked him to put it on the piano. But he found means to inform Fauchery in a low whisper that they would have Tatan Néné, the most finely developed girl that winter, and Maria Blond, the same who had just made her first appearance at the Folies-Dramatiques. Meanwhile La Faloise stopped him at every step in hopes of receiving an invitation. He ended by offering himself, and Vandeuvres engaged him in the plot at once; only he made him promise to bring Clarisse with him, and when La Faloise pretended to scruple about certain points he quieted him by the remark:

"Since I invite you that's enough!"

Nevertheless, La Faloise would have much liked to know the name of the hostess. But the countess had recalled Vandeuvres and was questioning him as to the manner in which the English made tea. He often betook himself to England, where his horses ran. Then as though he had been inwardly following up quite a laborious train of thought during his remarks, he broke in with the question:

"And the marquis, by the by? Are we not to see him?"

"Oh, certainly you will! My father made me a formal promise that he would come," replied the countess. "But I'm beginning to be anxious. His duties will have kept him."

Vandeuvres smiled a discreet smile. He, too, seemed to have his doubts as to the exact nature of the Marquis de Chouard's duties. Indeed, he had been thinking of a pretty woman whom the marquis occasionally took into the country with him. Perhaps they could get her too.

In the meantime Fauchery decided that the moment had come in which to risk giving Count Muffat his invitation. The evening, in fact, was drawing to a close.

"Are you serious?" asked Vandeuvres, who thought a joke was intended.

"Extremely serious. If I don't execute my commission she'll tear my eyes out. It's a case of landing her fish, you know."

"Well then, I'll help you, dear boy."

Eleven o'clock struck. Assisted by her daughter, the countess was pouring out the tea, and as hardly any guests save intimate friends had come, the cups and the platefuls of little cakes were being circulated without ceremony. Even the ladies did not leave their armchairs in front of the fire and sat sipping their tea and nibbling cakes which they held between their finger tips. From music the talk had declined to purveyors. Boissier was the only person for sweetmeats and Catherine for ices. Mme Chantereau, however, was all for Latinville. Speech grew more and more indolent, and a sense of lassitude was lulling the room to sleep. Steiner had once more set himself secretly to undermine the deputy, whom he held in a state of blockade in the corner of a settee. M. Venot, whose teeth must have been ruined by sweet things, was eating little dry cakes, one after the other, with a small nibbling sound suggestive of a mouse, while the chief clerk, his nose in a teacup, seemed never to be going to finish its contents. As to the countess, she went in a leisurely way from one guest to another, never pressing them, indeed, only pausing a second or two before the gentlemen whom she viewed with an air of dumb interrogation before she smiled and passed on. The great fire had flushed all her face, and she looked as if she were the sister of her daughter, who appeared so withered and ungainly at her side. When she drew near Fauchery, who was chatting with her husband and Vandeuvres, she noticed that they grew suddenly silent; accordingly she did not stop but handed the cup of tea she was offering to Georges Hugon beyond them.

"It's a lady who desires your company at supper," the journalist gaily continued, addressing Count Muffat.

The last-named, whose face had worn its gray look all the evening, seemed very much surprised. What lady was it?

"Oh, Nana!" said Vandeuvres, by way of forcing the invitation.

The count became more grave than before. His eyelids trembled just perceptibly, while a look of discomfort, such as headache produces, hovered for a moment athwart his forehead.

"But I'm not acquainted with that lady," he murmured.

"Come, come, you went to her house," remarked Vandeuvres.

"What d'you say? I went to her house? Oh yes, the other day, in behalf of the Benevolent Organization. I had forgotten about it. But, no matter, I am not acquainted with her, and I cannot accept."

He had adopted an icy expression in order to make them understand that this jest did not appear to him to be in good taste. A man of his position did not sit down at tables of such women as that. Vandeuvres protested: it was to be a supper party of dramatic and artistic people, and talent excused everything. But without listening further to the arguments urged by Fauchery, who spoke of a dinner where the Prince of Scots, the son of a queen, had sat down beside an ex-music-hall singer, the count only emphasized his refusal. In so doing, he allowed himself, despite his great politeness, to be guilty of an irritated gesture.

Georges and La Faloise, standing in front of each other drinking their tea, had overheard the two or three phrases exchanged in their immediate neighborhood.

"Jove, it's at Nana's then," murmured La Faloise. "I might have expected as much!"

Georges said nothing, but he was all aflame. His fair hair was in disorder; his blue eyes shone like tapers, so fiercely had the vice, which for some days past had surrounded him, inflamed and stirred his blood. At last he was going to plunge into all that he had dreamed of!

"I don't know the address," La Faloise resumed.

"She lives on a third floor in the Boulevard Haussmann, between the Rue de l'Arcade and the Rue Pesquier," said Georges all in a breath.

And when the other looked at him in much astonishment, he added, turning very red and fit to sink into the ground with embarrassment and conceit:

"I'm of the party. She invited me this morning."

But there was a great stir in the drawing room, and Vandeuvres and Fauchery could not continue pressing the count. The Marquis de Chouard had just come in, and everyone was anxious to greet him. He had moved painfully forward, his legs failing under him, and he now stood in the middle of the room with pallid face and eyes blinking, as though he had just come out of some dark alley and were blinded by the brightness of the lamps.

"I scarcely hoped to see you tonight, Father," said the countess. "I should have been anxious till the morning."

He looked at her without answering, as a man might who fails to understand. His nose, which loomed immense on his shorn face, looked like a swollen pimple, while his lower lip hung down. Seeing him such a wreck, Mme Hugon, full of kind compassion, said pitying things to him.

"You work too hard. You ought to rest yourself. At our age we ought to leave work to the young people."

"Work! Ah yes, to be sure, work!" he stammered at last. "Always plenty of work."

He began to pull himself together, straightening up his bent figure and passing his hand, as was his wont, over his scant gray hair, of which a few locks strayed behind his ears.

"At what are you working as late as this?" asked Mme du Joncquoy. "I thought you were at the financial minister's reception?"

But the countess intervened with:

"My father had to study the question of a projected law."

"Yes, a projected law," he said; "exactly so, a projected law. I shut myself up for that reason. It refers to work in factories, and I was anxious for a proper observance of the Lord's day of rest. It is really shameful that the government is unwilling to act with vigor in the matter. Churches are growing empty; we are running headlong to ruin."

Vandeuvres had exchanged glances with Fauchery. They both happened to be behind the marquis, and they were scanning him suspiciously. When Vandeuvres found an opportunity to take him aside and to speak to him about the good-looking creature he was in the habit of taking down into the country, the old man affected extreme surprise. Perhaps someone had seen him with the Baroness Decker, at whose house at Viroflay he sometimes spent a day or so. Vandeuvres's sole vengeance was an abrupt question:

"Tell me, where have you been straying to? Your elbow is covered with cobwebs and plaster."

"My elbow," he muttered, slightly disturbed. "Yes indeed, it's true. A speck or two, I must have come in for them on my way down from my office."

Several people were taking their departure. It was close on midnight. Two footmen were noiselessly removing the empty cups and the plates with cakes. In front of the hearth the ladies had re-formed and, at the same time, narrowed their circle and were chatting more carelessly than before in the languid atmosphere peculiar to the close of a party. The very room was going to sleep, and slowly creeping shadows were cast by its walls. It was then Fauchery spoke of departure. Yet he once more forgot his intention at sight of the Countess Sabine. She was resting from her cares as hostess, and as she sat in her wonted seat, silent, her eyes fixed on a log which was turning into embers, her face appeared so white and so impassable that doubt again possessed him. In the glow of the fire the small black hairs on the mole at the corner of her lip became white. It was Nana's very mole, down to the color of the hair. He could not refrain from whispering something about it in Vandeuvres's ear. Gad, it was true; the other had never noticed it before. And both men continued this comparison of Nana and the countess. They discovered a vague resemblance about the chin and the mouth, but the eyes were not at all alike. Then, too, Nana had a good-natured expression, while with the countess it was hard to decide—she might have been a cat, sleeping with claws withdrawn and paws stirred by a scarce-perceptible nervous quiver.

"All the same, one could have her," declared Fauchery.

Vandeuvres stripped her at a glance.

"Yes, one could, all the same," he said. "But I think nothing of the thighs, you know. Will you bet she has no thighs?"

He stopped, for Fauchery touched him briskly on the arm and showed him Estelle, sitting close to them on her footstool. They had raised their voices without noticing her, and she must have overheard them. Nevertheless, she continued sitting there stiff and motionless, not a hair having lifted on her thin neck, which was that of a girl who has shot up all too quickly. Thereupon they retired three or four paces, and Vandeuvres vowed that the countess was a very honest woman. Just then voices were raised in front of the hearth. Mme du Joncquoy was saying:

"I was willing to grant you that Monsieur de Bismarck was perhaps a witty man. Only, if you go as far as to talk of genius——"

The ladies had come round again to their earliest topic of conversation.

"What the deuce! Still Monsieur de Bismarck!" muttered Fauchery. "This time I make my escape for good and all."

"Wait a bit," said Vandeuvres, "we must have a definite no from the count."

The Count Muffat was talking to his father-in-law and a certain serious-looking gentleman. Vandeuvres drew him away and renewed the invitation, backing it up with the information that he was to be at the supper himself. A man might go anywhere; no one could think of suspecting evil where at most there could only be curiosity. The count listened to these arguments with downcast eyes and expressionless face. Vandeuvres felt him to be hesitating when the Marquis de Chouard approached with a look of interrogation. And when the latter was informed of the question in hand and Fauchery had invited him in his turn, he looked at his son-in-law furtively. There ensued an embarrassed silence, but both men encouraged one another and would doubtless have ended by accepting had not Count Muffat perceived M. Venot's gaze fixed upon him. The little old man was no longer smiling; his face was cadaverous, his eyes bright and keen as steel.

"No," replied the count directly, in so decisive a tone that further insistence became impossible.

Then the marquis refused with even greater severity of expression. He talked morality. The aristocratic classes ought to set a good example. Fauchery smiled and shook hands with Vandeuvres. He did not wait for him and took his departure immediately, for he was due at his newspaper office.

"At Nana's at midnight, eh?"

La Faloise retired too. Steiner had made his bow to the countess. Other men followed them, and the same phrase went round—"At midnight, at Nana's" —as they went to get their overcoats in the anteroom. Georges, who could not leave without his mother, had stationed himself at the door, where he gave the exact address. "Third floor, door on your left." Yet before going out Fauchery gave a final glance. Vandeuvres had again resumed his position among the ladies and was laughing with Léonide de Chezelles. Count Muffat and the Marquis de Chouard were joining in the conversation, while the good Mme Hugon was falling asleep open-eyed. Lost among the petticoats, M. Venot was his own small self again and smiled as of old. Twelve struck slowly in the great solemn room.

"What—what do you mean?" Mme du Joncquoy resumed. "You imagine that Monsieur de Bismarck will make war on us and beat us! Oh, that's unbearable!"

Indeed, they were laughing round Mme Chantereau, who had just repeated an assertion she had heard made in Alsace, where her husband owned a foundry.

"We have the emperor, fortunately," said Count Muffat in his grave, official way.

It was the last phrase Fauchery was able to catch. He closed the door after casting one more glance in the direction of the Countess Sabine. She was talking sedately with the chief clerk and seemed to be interested in that stout individual's conversation. Assuredly he must have been deceiving himself. There was no "little rift" there at all. It was a pity.

"You're not coming down then?" La Faloise shouted up to him from the entrance hall.

And out on the pavement, as they separated, they once more repeated: "Tomorrow, at Nana's."

CHAPTER IV

SINCE MORNING Zoé had delivered up the flat to a managing man who had come from Brebant's with a staff of helpers and waiters. Brebant was to supply everything, from the supper, the plates and dishes, the glass, the linen, the flowers, down to the seats and footstools. Nana could not have mustered a dozen napkins out of all her cupboards, and not having had time to get a proper outfit after her new start in life and scorning to go to the restaurant, she had decided to make the restaurant come to her. It struck her as being more the thing. She wanted to celebrate her great success as an actress with a supper which should set people talking. As her dining room was too small, the manager had arranged the table in the drawing room, a table with twenty-five covers, placed somewhat close together.

"Is everything ready?" asked Nana when she returned at midnight.

"Oh! I don't know," replied Zoé roughly, looking beside herself with worry. "The Lord be thanked, I don't bother about anything. They're making a fearful mess in the kitchen and all over the flat! I've had to fight my battles too. The other two came again. My eye! I did just chuck 'em out!"

She referred, of course, to her employer's old admirers, the tradesman and the Walachian, to whom Nana, sure of her future and longing to shed her skin, as she phrased it, had decided to give the go-by.

"There are a couple of leeches for you!" she muttered.

"If they come back threaten to go to the police."

Then she called Daguenet and Georges, who had remained behind in the anteroom, where they were hanging up their overcoats. They had both met at the stage door in the Passage des Panoramas, and she had brought them home with her in a cab. As there was nobody there yet, she shouted to them to come into the dressing room while Zoé was touching up her toilet. Hurriedly and without changing her dress she had her hair done up and stuck white roses in her chignon and at her bosom. The little room was littered with the drawing-room furniture, which the workmen had been compelled to roll in there, and it was full of a motley assemblage of round tables, sofas and arm-chairs, with their legs in air for the most part. Nana was quite ready when her dress caught on a castor and tore upward. At this she swore furiously; such things only happened to her! Ragingly she took off her dress, a very simple affair of white foulard, of so thin and supple a texture that it clung about her

like a long shift. But she put it on again directly, for she could not find
another to her taste, and with tears in her eyes declared that she was dressed
like a ragpicker. Daguenet and Georges had to patch up the rent with pins,
while Zoé once more arranged her hair. All three hurried round her, especially the boy, who knelt on the floor with his hands among her skirts. And
at last she calmed down again when Daguenet assured her it could not be later
than a quarter past twelve, seeing that by dint of scamping her words and
skipping her lines she had effectually shortened the third act of the *Blonde
Venus*.

"The play's still far too good for that crowd of idiots," she said. "Did you
see? There were thousands there tonight. Zoé, my girl, you will wait in here.
Don't go to bed, I shall want you. By gum, it is time they came. Here's
company!"

She ran off while Georges stayed where he was with the skirts of his coat
brushing the floor. He blushed, seeing Daguenet looking at him. Notwithstanding which, they had conceived a tender regard the one for the other.
They rearranged the bows of their cravats in front of the big dressing glass
and gave each other a mutual dose of the clothesbrush, for they were all white
from their close contact with Nana.

"One would think it was sugar," murmured Georges, giggling like a greedy
little child.

A footman hired for the evening was ushering the guests into the small
drawing room, a narrow slip of a place in which only four armchairs had been
left in order the better to pack in the company. From the large drawing room
beyond came a sound as of the moving of plates and silver, while a clear and
brilliant ray of light shone from under the door. At her entrance Nana found
Clarisse Besnus, whom La Faloise had brought, already installed in one of the
armchairs.

"Dear me, you're the first of 'em!" said Nana, who, now that she was successful, treated her familiarly.

"Oh, it's his doing," replied Clarisse. "He's always afraid of not getting anywhere in time. If I'd taken him at his word I shouldn't have waited to take
off my paint and my wig."

The young man, who now saw Nana for the first time, bowed, paid her a
compliment and spoke of his cousin, hiding his agitation behind an exaggeration of politeness. But Nana, neither listening to him nor recognizing his face,
shook hands with him and then went briskly toward Rose Mignon, with whom
she at once assumed a most distinguished manner.

"Ah, how nice of you, my dear madame! I was so anxious to have you here!"

"It's I who am charmed, I assure you," said Rose with equal amiability.

"Pray, sit down. Do you require anything?"

"Thank you, no! Ah yes, I've left my fan in my pelisse, Steiner; just look
in the right-hand pocket."

Steiner and Mignon had come in behind Rose. The banker turned back and
reappeared with the fan while Mignon embraced Nana fraternally and forced
Rose to do so also. Did they not all belong to the same family in the theatrical

world? Then he winked as though to encourage Steiner, but the latter was disconcerted by Rose's clear gaze and contented himself by kissing Nana's hand.

Just then the Count de Vandeuvres made his appearance with Blanche de Sivry. There was an interchange of profound bows, and Nana with the utmost ceremony conducted Blanche to an armchair. Meanwhile Vandeuvres told them laughingly that Fauchery was engaged in a dispute at the foot of the stairs because the porter had refused to allow Lucy Stewart's carriage to come in at the gate. They could hear Lucy telling the porter he was a dirty blackguard in the anteroom. But when the footman had opened the door she came forward with her laughing grace of manner, announced her name herself, took both Nana's hands in hers and told her that she had liked her from the very first and considered her talent splendid. Nana, puffed up by her novel role of hostess, thanked her and was veritably confused. Nevertheless, from the moment of Fauchery's arrival she appeared preoccupied, and directly she could get near him she asked him in a low voice:

"Will he come?"

"No, he did not want to," was the journalist's abrupt reply, for he was taken by surprise, though he had got ready some sort of tale to explain Count Muffat's refusal.

Seeing the young woman's sudden pallor, he became conscious of his folly and tried to retract his words.

"He was unable to; he is taking the countess to the ball at the Ministry of the Interior tonight."

"All right," murmured Nana, who suspected him of ill will, "you'll pay me out for that, my pippin."

She turned on her heel, and so did he; they were angry. Just then Mignon was pushing Steiner up against Nana, and when Fauchery had left her he said to her in a low voice and with the good-natured cynicism of a comrade in arms who wishes his friends to be happy:

"He's dying of it, you know, only he's afraid of my wife. Won't you protect him?"

Nana did not appear to understand. She smiled and looked at Rose, the husband and the banker and finally said to the latter:

"Monsieur Steiner, you will sit next to me."

With that there came from the anteroom a sound of laughter and whispering and a burst of merry, chattering voices, which sounded as if a runaway convent were on the premises. And Labordette appeared, towing five women in his rear, his boarding school, as Lucy Stewart cruelly phrased it. There was Gaga, majestic in a blue velvet dress which was too tight for her, and Caroline Héquet, clad as usual in ribbed black silk, trimmed with Chantilly lace. Léa de Horn came next, terribly dressed up, as her wont was, and after her the big Tatan Néné, a good-humored fair girl with the bosom of a wet nurse, at which people laughed, and finally little Maria Blond, a young damsel of fifteen, as thin and vicious as a street child, yet on the high road to success, owing to her recent first appearance at the Folies. Labordette had brought the whole collection in a single fly, and they were still laughing at the way they had been squeezed with Maria Blond on her knees. But on entering the room they pursed up their lips, and all grew very conventional as they shook hands and exchanged salutations. Gaga even affected the infantile and lisped through excess of genteel deportment. Tatan Néné alone transgressed. They had been telling her as they came along that six absolutely naked Negroes would serve up Nana's supper, and she now grew anxious about them and asked to see them. Labordette called her a goose and besought her to be silent.

"And Bordenave?" asked Fauchery.

"Oh, you may imagine how miserable I am," cried Nana; "he won't be able to join us."

"Yes," said Rose Mignon, "his foot caught in a trap door, and he's got a fearful sprain. If only you could hear him swearing, with his leg tied up and laid out on a chair!"

Thereupon everybody mourned over Bordenave's absence. No one ever gave a good supper without Bordenave. Ah well, they would try and do without him, and they were already talking about other matters when a burly voice was heard:

"What, eh, what? Is that the way they're going to write my obituary notice?"

There was a shout, and all heads were turned round, for it was indeed Bordenave. Huge and fiery-faced, he was standing with his stiff leg in the doorway, leaning for support on Simonne Cabiroche's shoulder. Simonne was for the time being his mistress. This little creature had had a certain amount of education and could play the piano and talk English. She was a blonde on a tiny, pretty scale and so delicately formed that she seemed to bend under Bordenave's rude weight. Yet she was smilingly submissive withal. He postured there for some moments, for he felt that together they formed a tableau.

"One can't help liking ye, eh?" he continued. "Zounds, I was afraid I should get bored, and I said to myself, 'Here goes.'"

But he interrupted himself with an oath.

"Oh, damn!"

Simonne had taken a step too quickly forward, and his foot had just felt his full weight. He gave her a rough push, but she, still smiling away and ducking her pretty head as some animal might that is afraid of a beating, held him up with all the strength a little plump blonde can command. Amid all these exclamations there was a rush to his assistance. Nana and Rose Mignon rolled up an armchair, into which Bordenave let himself sink, while the other women slid a second one under his leg. And with that all the actresses present kissed him as a matter of course. He kept grumbling and gasping.

"Oh, damn! Oh, damn! Ah well, the stomach's unhurt, you'll see."

Other guests had arrived by this time, and motion became impossible in the room. The noise of clinking plates and silver had ceased, and now a dispute was heard going on in the big drawing room, where the voice of the manager grumbled angrily. Nana was growing impatient, for she expected no more invited guests and wondered why they did not bring in supper. She had just sent Georges to find out what was going on when, to her great surprise, she noticed the arrival of more guests, both male and female. She did not know them in the least. Whereupon with some embarrassment she questioned Bordenave, Mignon and Labordette about them. They did not know them any more than she did, but when she turned to the Count de Vandeuvres he seemed suddenly to recollect himself. They were the young men he had pressed into her service at Count Muffat's. Nana thanked him. That was capital, capital! Only they would all be terribly crowded, and she begged Labordette to go and have seven more covers set. Scarcely had he left the room than the footman ushered in three newcomers. Nay, this time the thing was becoming ridiculous; one certainly could never take them all in. Nana was beginning to grow angry and in her haughtiest manner announced that such conduct was scarcely in good taste. But seeing two more arrive, she began laughing; it was really too funny. So much the worse. People would have to fit in anyhow! The company were all on their feet save Gaga and Rose and Bordenave, who alone took up two armchairs. There was a buzz of voices, people talking in low tones and stifling slight yawns the while.

"Now what d'you say, my lass," asked Bordenave, "to our sitting down at table as if nothing had happened? We are all here, don't you think?"

"Oh yes, we're all here, I promise you!" she answered laughingly.

She looked round her but grew suddenly serious, as though she were surprised at not finding someone. Doubtless there was a guest missing whom she did not mention. It was a case of waiting. But a minute or two later the company noticed in their midst a tall gentleman with a fine face and a beautiful white beard. The most astonishing thing about it was that nobody had seen him come in; indeed, he must have slipped into the little drawing room through the bedroom door, which had remained ajar. Silence reigned, broken only by a sound of whispering. The Count de Vandeuvres certainly knew who the gentleman was, for they both exchanged a discreet handgrip, but to the questions which the women asked him he replied by a smile only. Thereupon Caroline Héquet wagered in a low voice that it was an English lord who was on the eve of returning to London to be married. She knew him quite well—she had had him. And this account of the matter went the round of the ladies present, Maria Blond alone asserting that, for her part, she recognized a German ambassador. She could prove it, because he often passed the night with one of her friends. Among the men his measure was taken in a few rapid phrases. A real swell, to judge by his looks! Perhaps he would pay for the supper! Most likely. It looked like it. Bah! Provided only the supper was a good one! In the end the company remained undecided. Nay, they were already beginning to forget the old white-bearded gentleman when the manager opened the door of the large drawing room.

"Supper is on the table, madame."

Nana had already accepted Steiner's proffered arm without noticing a movement on the part of the old gentleman, who started to walk behind her in solitary state. Thus the march past could not be organized, and men and women entered anyhow, joking with homely good humor over this absence of ceremony. A long table stretched from one end to the other of the great room, which had been entirely cleared of furniture, and this same table was not long enough, for the plates thereon were touching one another. Four candelabra, with ten candles apiece, lit up the supper, and of these one was gorgeous in silver plate with sheaves of flowers to right and left of it. Everything was luxurious after the restaurant fashion; the china was ornamented with a gold line and lacked the customary monogram; the silver had become worn and tarnished through dint of continual washings; the glass was of the kind that you can complete an odd set of in any cheap emporium.

The scene suggested a premature housewarming in an establishment newly smiled on by fortune and as yet lacking the necessary conveniences. There was no central luster, and the candelabra, whose tall tapers had scarcely burned up properly, cast a pale yellow light among the dishes and stands on which fruit, cakes and preserves alternated symmetrically.

"You sit where you like, you know," said Nana. "It's more amusing that way."

She remained standing midway down the side of the table. The old gentleman whom nobody knew had placed himself on her right, while she kept Steiner on her left hand. Some guests were already sitting down when the sound of oaths came from the little drawing room. It was Bordenave. The company had forgotten him, and he was having all the trouble in the world to raise himself out of his two armchairs, for he was howling amain and calling for that cat of a Simonne, who had slipped off with the rest. The women ran in to him, full of pity for his woes, and Bordenave appeared, supported, nay, almost carried, by Caroline, Clarisse, Tatan Néné and Maria Blond. And there was much to-do over his installation at the table.

"In the middle, facing Nana!" was the cry. "Bordenave in the middle! He'll be our president!"

Thereupon the ladies seated him in the middle. But he needed a second chair for his leg, and two girls lifted it up and stretched it carefully out. It wouldn't matter; he would eat sideways.

"God blast it all!" he grumbled. "We're squashed all the same! Ah, my kittens, Papa recommends himself to your tender care!"

He had Rose Mignon on his right and Lucy Stewart on his left hand, and they promised to take good care of him. Everybody was now getting settled. Count de Vandeuvres placed himself between Lucy and Clarisse; Fauchery between Rose Mignon and Caroline Héquet. On the other side of the table Hector de la Faloise had rushed to get next Gaga, and that despite the calls of Clarisse opposite, while Mignon, who never deserted Steiner, was only separated from him by Blanche and had Tatan Néné on his left. Then came Labordette and, finally, at the two ends of the table were irregular crowding groups of young men and of women, such as Simonne, Léa de Horn and Maria Blond. It was in this region that Daguenet and Georges forgathered more warmly than ever while smilingly gazing at Nana.

Nevertheless, two people remained standing, and there was much joking about it. The men offered seats on their knees. Clarisse, who could not move her elbows, told Vandeuvres that she counted on him to feed her. And then that Bordenave did just take up space with his chairs! There was a final effort, and at last everybody was seated, but, as Mignon loudly remarked, they were confoundedly like herrings in a barrel.

"Thick asparagus soup *à la comtesse,* clear soup *à la Deslignac,"* murmured the waiters, carrying about platefuls in rear of the guests.

Bordenave was loudly recommending the thick soup when a shout arose, followed by protests and indignant exclamations. The door had just opened, and three late arrivals, a woman and two men, had just come in. Oh dear, no! There was no space for them! Nana, however, without leaving her chair, began screwing up her eyes in the effort to find out whether she knew them. The woman was Louise Violaine, but she had never seen the men before.

"This gentleman, my dear," said Vandeuvres, "is a friend of mine, a naval officer, Monsieur de Foucarmont by name. I invited him."

Foucarmont bowed and seemed very much at ease, for he added:

"And I took leave to bring one of my friends with me."

"Oh, it's quite right, quite right!" said Nana. "Sit down, pray. Let's see, you —Clarisse—push up a little. You're a good deal spread out down there. That's it—where there's a will——"

They crowded more tightly than ever, and Foucarmont and Louise were given a little stretch of table, but the friend had to sit at some distance from his plate and ate his supper through dint of making a long arm between his neighbors' shoulders. The waiters took away the soup plates and circulated rissoles of young rabbit with truffles and "niokys" and powdered cheese. Bordenave agitated the whole table with the announcement that at one moment he had had the idea of bringing with him Prulliére, Fontan and old Bosc. At this Nana looked sedate and remarked dryly that she would have given them a pretty reception. Had she wanted colleagues, she would certainly have undertaken to ask them herself. No, no, she wouldn't have third-rate play actors. Old Bosc was always drunk; Prulliére was fond of spitting too much, and as to Fontan, he made himself unbearable in society with his loud voice and his stupid doings. Then, you know, third-rate play actors were always out of place when they found themselves in the society of gentlemen such as those around her.

"Yes, yes, it's true," Mignon declared.

All round the table the gentlemen in question looked unimpeachable in the extreme, what with their evening dress and their pale features, the natural distinction of which was still further refined by fatigue. The old gentleman was as deliberate in his movements and wore as subtle a smile as though he were presiding over a diplomatic congress, and Vandeuvres, with his exquisite politeness toward the ladies next to him, seemed to be at one of the Countess Muffat's receptions. That very morning Nana had been remarking to her aunt that in the matter of men one could not have done better—they were all either wellborn or wealthy, in fact, quite the thing. And as to the ladies, they were behaving admirably. Some of them, such as Blanche, Léa and Louise, had come in low dresses, but Gaga's only was perhaps a little too low, the more so

because at her age she would have done well not to show her neck at all.
Now that the company were finally settled the laughter and the light jests
began to fail. Georges was under the impression that he had assisted at merrier
dinner parties among the good folks of Orleans. There was scarcely any conversation. The men, not being mutually acquainted, stared at one another,
while the women sat quite quiet, and it was this which especially surprised
Georges. He thought them all smugs—he had been under the impression that
everybody would begin kissing at once.

The third course, consisting of a Rhine carp *à la Chambord* and a saddle
of venison *à l'anglaise*, was being served when Blanche remarked aloud:

"Lucy, my dear, I met your Ollivier on Sunday. How he's grown!"

"Dear me, yes! He's eighteen," replied Lucy. "It doesn't make me feel any
younger. He went back to his school yesterday."

Her son Ollivier, whom she was wont to speak of with pride, was a pupil
at the Ecole de Marine. Then ensued a conversation about the young people,
during which all the ladies waxed very tender. Nana described her own great
happiness. Her baby, the little Louis, she said, was now at the house of her
aunt, who brought him round to her every morning at eleven o'clock, when
she would take him into her bed, where he played with her griffon dog Lulu.
It was enough to make one die of laughing to see them both burying themselves under the clothes at the bottom of the bed. The company had no idea
how cunning Louiset had already become.

"Oh, yesterday I did just pass a day!" said Rose Mignon in her turn. "Just
imagine, I went to fetch Charles and Henry at their boarding school, and I
had positively to take them to the theater at night. They jumped; they clapped
their little hands: 'We shall see Mamma act! We shall see Mamma act!' Oh,
it was a to-do!"

Mignon smiled complaisantly, his eyes moist with paternal tenderness.

"And at the play itself," he continued, "they were so funny! They behaved
as seriously as grown men, devoured Rose with their eyes and asked me why
Mamma had her legs bare like that."

The whole table began laughing, and Mignon looked radiant, for his pride
as a father was flattered. He adored his children and had but one object in life,
which was to increase their fortunes by administering the money gained by
Rose at the theater and elsewhere with the businesslike severity of a faithful
steward. When as first fiddle in the music hall where she used to sing he had
married her, they had been passionately fond of one another. Now they were
good friends. There was an understanding between them: she labored hard to
the full extent of her talent and of her beauty; he had given up his violin in
order the better to watch over her successes as an actress and as a woman.
One could not have found a more homely and united household anywhere!

"What age is your eldest?" asked Vandeuvres.

"Henry's nine," replied Mignon, "but such a big chap for his years!"

Then he chaffed Steiner, who was not fond of children, and with quiet
audacity informed him that were he a father, he would make a less stupid
hash of his fortune. While talking he watched the banker over Blanche's

shoulders to see if it was coming off with Nana. But for some minutes Rose and Fauchery, who were talking very near him, had been getting on his nerves. Was Rose going to waste time over such a folly as that? In that sort of case, by Jove, he blocked the way. And diamond on finger and with his fine hands in great evidence, he finished discussing a fillet of venison.

Elsewhere the conversation about children continued. La Faloise, rendered very restless by the immediate proximity of Gaga, asked news of her daughter, whom he had had the pleasure of noticing in her company at the Variétés. Lili was quite well, but she was still such a tomboy! He was astonished to learn that Lili was entering on her nineteenth year. Gaga became even more imposing in his eyes, and when he endeavored to find out why she had not brought Lili with her:

"Oh no, no, never!" she said stiffly. "Not three months ago she positively insisted on leaving her boarding school. I was thinking of marrying her off at once, but she loves me so that I had to take her home—oh, so much against my will!"

Her blue eyelids with their blackened lashes blinked and wavered while she spoke of the business of settling her young lady. If at her time of life she hadn't laid by a sou but was still always working to minister to men's pleasures, especially those very young men, whose grandmother she might well be, it was truly because she considered a good match of far greater importance than mere savings. And with that she leaned over La Faloise, who reddened under the huge, naked, plastered shoulder with which she well-nigh crushed him.

"You know," she murmured, "if she fails it won't be my fault. But they're so strange when they're young!"

There was a considerable bustle round the table, and the waiters became very active. After the third course the entrees had made their appearance; they consisted of pullets *à la maréchale*, fillets of sole with shallot sauce and *escalopes* of Strasbourg *pâté*. The manager, who till then had been having Meursault served, now offered Chambertin and Léoville. Amid the slight hubbub which the change of plates involved Georges, who was growing momentarily more astonished, asked Daguenet if all the ladies present were similarly provided with children, and the other, who was amused by this question, gave him some further details. Lucy Stewart was the daughter of a man of English origin who greased the wheels of the trains at the Gare du Nord; she was thirty-nine years old and had the face of a horse but was adorable withal and, though consumptive, never died. In fact, she was the smartest woman there and represented three princes and a duke. Caroline Héquet, born at Bordeaux, daughter of a little clerk long since dead of shame, was lucky enough to be possessed of a mother with a head on her shoulders, who, after having cursed her, had made it up again at the end of a year of reflection, being minded, at any rate, to save a fortune for her daughter. The latter was twenty-five years old and very passionless and was held to be one of the finest women it is possible to enjoy. Her price never varied. The mother, a model of orderliness, kept the accounts and noted down receipts and expenditures with severe precision. She managed the whole household from some small lodging two stories above her daughter's, where, moreover, she had established a workroom for dressmaking and plain sewing. As to Blanche de Sivry, whose real name was Jacqueline Bandu, she hailed from a village near Amiens. Magnificent in person, stupid and untruthful in character, she gave herself out as the granddaughter of a general and never owned to her thirty-two summers. The Russians had a great taste for her, owing to her *embonpoint*. Then Daguenet added a rapid word or two about the rest. There was Clarisse Besnus, whom a lady had brought up from Saint-Aubin-sur-Mer in the capacity of maid while the lady's husband had started her in quite another line. There was Simonne Cabiroche, the daughter of a furniture dealer in the Faubourg Saint-Antoine, who had been educated in a large boarding school with a view to becoming a governess. Finally there were Maria Blond and Louise Violaine and Léa de Horn, who had all shot up to woman's estate on the pavements of Paris, not to mention Tatan Néné, who had herded cows in Champagne till she was twenty.

Georges listened and looked at these ladies, feeling dizzy and excited by the coarse recital thus crudely whispered in his ear, while behind his chair the waiters kept repeating in respectful tones:

"Pullets *à la maréchale;* fillets of sole with ravigote sauce."

"My dear fellow," said Daguenet, giving him the benefit of his experience, "don't take any fish; it'll do you no good at this time of night. And be content with Léoville: it's less treacherous."

A heavy warmth floated upward from the candelabras, from the dishes which were being handed round, from the whole table where thirty-eight human beings were suffocating. And the waiters forgot themselves and ran when crossing the carpet, so that it was spotted with grease. Nevertheless, the supper grew scarce any merrier. The ladies trifled with their meat, left half of it uneaten. Tatan Néné alone partook gluttonously of every dish. At that advance hour of the night hunger was of the nervous order only, a mere whimsical craving born of an exasperated stomach.

At Nana's side the old gentleman refused every dish offered him; he had only taken a spoonful of soup, and he now sat in front of his empty plate, gazing silently about. There was some subdued yawning, and occasionally eyelids closed and faces became haggard and white. It was unutterably slow, as it always was, according to Vandeuvres's dictum. This sort of supper should be served anyhow if it was to be funny, he opined. Otherwise when elegantly and conventionally done you might as well feed in good society, where you were not more bored than here. Had it not been for Bordenave, who was still bawling away, everybody would have fallen asleep. That rum old buffer Bordenave, with his leg duly stretched on its chair, was letting his neighbors, Lucy and Rose, wait on him as though he were a sultan. They were entirely taken up with him, and they helped him and pampered him and watched over his glass and his plate, and yet that did not prevent his complaining.

"Who's going to cut up my meat for me? I can't; the table's a league away."

Every few seconds Simonne rose and took up a position behind his back in order to cut his meat and his bread. All the women took a great interest in the things he ate. The waiters were recalled, and he was stuffed to suffocation.

Simonne having wiped his mouth for him while Rose and Lucy were changing his plate, her act struck him as very pretty and, deigning at length to show contentment:

"There, there, my daughter," he said, "that's as it should be. Women are made for that!"

There was a slight reawakening, and conversation became general as they finished discussing some orange sherbet. The hot roast was a fillet with truffles, and the cold roast a galantine of guinea fowl in jelly. Nana, annoyed by the want of go displayed by her guests, had begun talking with the greatest distinctness.

"You know the Prince of Scots has already had a stage box reserved so as to see the *Blonde Venus* when he comes to visit the exhibition."

"I very much hope that all the princes will come and see it," declared Bordenave with his mouth full.

"They are expecting the shah of Persia next Sunday," said Lucy Stewart. Whereupon Rose Mignon spoke of the shah's diamonds. He wore a tunic entirely covered with gems; it was a marvel, a flaming star; it represented millions. And the ladies, with pale faces and eyes glittering with covetousness, craned forward and ran over the names of the other kings, the other emperors, who were shortly expected. All of them were dreaming of some royal caprice, some night to be paid for by a fortune.

"Now tell me, dear boy," Caroline Héquet asked Vandeuvres, leaning forward as she did so, "how old's the emperor of Russia?"

"Oh, he's 'present time,'" replied the count, laughing. "Nothing to be done in that quarter, I warn you."

Nana made pretense of being hurt. The witticism appeared somewhat too stinging, and there was a murmur of protest. But Blanche gave a description of the king of Italy, whom she had once seen at Milan. He was scarcely good looking, and yet that did not prevent him enjoying all the women. She was put out somewhat when Fauchery assured her that Victor Emmanuel could not come to the exhibition. Louise Violaine and Léa favored the emperor of Austria, and all of a sudden little Maria Blond was heard saying:

"What an old stick the king of Prussia is! I was at Baden last year, and one was always meeting him about with Count Bismarck."

"Dear me, Bismarck!" Simonne interrupted. "I knew him once, I did. A charming man."

"That's what I was saying yesterday," cried Vandeuvres, "but nobody would believe me."

And just as at Countess Sabine's, there ensued a long discussion about Bismarck. Vandeuvres repeated the same phrases, and for a moment or two one was again in the Muffats' drawing room, the only difference being that the ladies were changed. Then, just as last night, they passed on to a discussion on music, after which, Foucarmont having let slip some mention of the assumption of the veil of which Paris was still talking, Nana grew quite interested and insisted on details about Mlle de Fougeray. Oh, the poor child, fancy her burying herself alive like that! Ah well, when it was a question of vocation!

All round the table the women expressed themselves much touched, and Georges, wearied at hearing these things a second time discussed, was beginning to ask Daguenet about Nana's ways in private life, when the conversation veered fatefully back to Count Bismarck. Tatan Néné bent toward Labordette to ask him privily who this Bismarck might be, for she did not know him. Whereupon Labordette, in cold blood, told her some portentous anecdotes. This Bismarck, he said, was in the habit of eating raw meat and when he met a woman near his den would carry her off thither on his back; at forty years of age he had already had as many as thirty-two children that way.

"Thirty-two children at forty!" cried Tatan Néné, stupefied and yet convinced. "He must be jolly well worn out for his age."

There was a burst of merriment, and it dawned on her that she was being made game of.

"You sillies! How am I to know if you're joking?"

Gaga, meanwhile, had stopped at the exhibition. Like all these ladies, she was delightedly preparing for the fray. A good season, provincials and foreigners rushing into Paris! In the long run, perhaps, after the close of the exhibition she would, if her business had flourished, be able to retire to a little house at Jouvisy, which she had long had her eye on.

"What's to be done?" she said to La Faloise. "One never gets what one wants! Oh, if only one were still really loved!"

Gaga behaved meltingly because she had felt the young man's knee gently placed against her own. He was blushing hotly and lisping as elegantly as ever. She weighed him at a glance. Not a very heavy little gentleman, to be sure, but then she wasn't hard to please. La Faloise obtained her address.

"Just look there," murmured Vandeuvres to Clarisse. "I think Gaga's doing you out of your Hector."

"A good riddance, so far as I'm concerned," replied the actress. "That fellow's an idiot. I've already chucked him downstairs three times. You know, I'm disgusted when dirty little boys run after old women."

She broke off and with a little gesture indicated Blanche, who from the commencement of dinner had remained in a most uncomfortable attitude, sitting up very markedly, with the intention of displaying her shoulders to the old distinguished-looking gentleman three seats beyond her.

"You're being left too," she resumed.

Vandeuvres smiled his thin smile and made a little movement to signify he did not care. Assuredly 'twas not he who would ever have prevented poor, dear Blanche scoring a success. He was more interested by the spectacle which Steiner was presenting to the table at large. The banker was noted for his sudden flames. That terrible German Jew who brewed money, whose hands forged millions, was wont to turn imbecile whenever he became enamored of a woman. He wanted them all too! Not one could make her appearance on the stage but he bought her, however expensive she might be. Vast sums were quoted. Twice had his furious appetite for courtesans ruined him. The courtesans, as Vandeuvres used to say, avenged public morality by emptying his moneybags. A big operation in the saltworks of the Landes had rendered him powerful on 'change, and so for six weeks past the Mignons had been getting a pretty slice out of those same saltworks. But people were beginning to lay wagers that the Mignons would not finish their slice, for Nana was showing her white teeth. Once again Steiner was in the toils, and so deeply this time that as he sat by Nana's side he seemed stunned; he ate without appetite; his lip hung down; his face was mottled. She had only to name a figure. Nevertheless, she did not hurry but continued playing with him, breathing her merry laughter into his hairy ear and enjoying the little convulsive movements which kept traversing his heavy face. There would always be time enough to patch all that up if that ninny of a Count Muffat were really to treat her as Joseph did Potiphar's wife.

"Léoville or Chambertin?" murmured a waiter, who came craning forward between Nana and Steiner just as the latter was addressing her in a low voice.

"Eh, what?" he stammered, losing his head. "Whatever you like—I don't care."

Vandeuvres gently nudged Lucy Stewart, who had a very spiteful tongue and a very fierce invention when once she was set going. That evening Mignon was driving her to exasperation.

"He would gladly be bottleholder, you know," she remarked to the count. "He's in hopes of repeating what he did with little Jonquier. You remember? Jonquier was Rose's man, but he was sweet on big Laure. Now Mignon procured Laure for Jonquier and then came back arm in arm with him to Rose, as if he were a husband who had been allowed a little peccadillo. But this time the thing's going to fail. Nana doesn't give up the men who are lent her."

"What ails Mignon that he should be looking at his wife in that severe way?" asked Vandeuvres.

He leaned forward and saw Rose growing exceedingly amorous toward Fauchery. This was the explanation of his neighbor's wrath. He resumed laughingly:

"The devil, are you jealous?"

"Jealous!" said Lucy in a fury. "Good gracious, if Rose is wanting Léon I give him up willingly—for what he's worth! That's to say, for a bouquet a week and the rest to match! Look here, my dear boy, these theatrical trollops are all made the same way. Why, Rose cried with rage when she read Léon's article on Nana; I know she did. So now, you understand, she must have an article, too, and she's gaining it. As for me, I'm going to chuck Léon downstairs—you'll see!"

She paused to say "Léoville" to the waiter standing behind her with his two bottles and then resumed in lowered tones:

"I don't want to shout; it isn't my style. But she's a cocky slut all the same. If I were in her husband's place I should lead her a lovely dance. Oh, she won't be very happy over it. She doesn't know my Fauchery: a dirty gent he is, too, palling up with women like that so as to get on in the world. Oh, a nice lot they are!"

Vandeuvres did his best to calm her down, but Bordenave, deserted by Rose and by Lucy, grew angry and cried out that they were letting Papa perish of hunger and thirst. This produced a fortunate diversion. Yet the supper was flagging; no one was eating now, though platefuls of *cèpes à l'italienne* and pineapple fritters *à la Pompadour* were being mangled. The champagne, however, which had been drunk ever since the soup course, was beginning little by little to warm the guests into a state of nervous exaltation. They ended by paying less attention to decorum than before. The women began leaning on their elbows amid the disordered table arrangements, while the men, in order to breathe more easily, pushed their chairs back, and soon the black coats appeared buried between the light-colored bodices, and bare shoulders, half turned toward the table, began to gleam as soft as silk. It was too hot, and the glare of the candles above the table grew ever yellower and duller. Now and again, when a women bent forward, the back of her neck glowed golden under a rain of curls, and the glitter of a diamond clasp lit up a lofty chignon. There was a touch of fire in the passing jests, in the laughing eyes, in the sudden gleam of white teeth, in the reflection of the candelabra on the surface of a glass of champagne. The company joked at the tops of their voices, gesticulated, asked questions which no one answered and called to one another across the whole length of the room. But the loudest din was made by the waiters; they fancied themselves at home in the corridors of their parent restaurant; they jostled one another and served the ices and the dessert to an accompaniment of guttural exclamations.

"My children," shouted Bordenave, "you know we're playing tomorrow. Be careful! Not too much champagne!"

"As far as I'm concerned," said Foucarmont, "I've drunk every imaginable kind of wine in all the four quarters of the globe. Extraordinary liquors some of 'em, containing alcohol enough to kill a corpse! Well, and what d'you think? Why, it never hurt me a bit. I can't make myself drunk. I've tried and I can't."

He was very pale, very calm and collected, and he lolled back in his chair, drinking without cessation.

"Never mind that," murmured Louise Violaine. "Leave off; you've had enough. It would be a funny business if I had to look after you the rest of the night."

Such was her state of exaltation that Lucy Stewart's cheeks were assuming a red, consumptive flush, while Rose Mignon with moist eyelids was growing excessively melting. Tatan Néné, greatly astonished at the thought that she had overeaten herself, was laughing vaguely over her own stupidity. The others, such as Blanche, Caroline, Simonne and Maria, were all talking at once and telling each other about their private affairs—about a dispute with a coachman, a projected picnic and innumerable complex stories of lovers stolen or restored. Meanwhile a young man near Georges, having evinced a desire to kiss Léa de Horn, received a sharp rap, accompanied by a "Look here, you, let me go!" which was spoken in a tone of fine indignation; and Georges, who was now very tipsy and greatly excited by the sight of Nana, hesitated about carrying out a project which he had been gravely maturing. He had been planning, indeed, to get under the table on all fours and to go and crouch at Nana's feet like a little dog. Nobody would have seen him, and he would have stayed there in the quietest way. But when at Léa's urgent request Daguenet had told the young man to sit still, Georges all at once felt grievously chagrined, as though the reproof had just been leveled at him. Oh, it was all silly and slow, and there was nothing worth living for! Daguenet, nevertheless, began chaffing and obliged him to swallow a big glassful of water, asking him at the same time what he would do if he were to find himself alone with a woman, seeing that three glasses of champagne were able to bowl him over.

"Why, in Havana," resumed Foucarmont, "they make a spirit with a certain wild berry; you think you're swallowing fire! Well now, one evening I drank more than a liter of it, and it didn't hurt me one bit. Better than that, another time when we were on the coast of Coromandel some savages gave us I don't know what sort of a mixture of pepper and vitriol, and that didn't hurt me one bit. I can't make myself drunk."

For some moments past La Faloise's face opposite had excited his displeasure. He began sneering and giving vent to disagreeable witticisms. La Faloise, whose brain was in a whirl, was behaving very restlessly and squeezing up against Gaga. But at length he became the victim of anxiety; somebody had just taken his handkerchief, and with drunken obstinacy he demanded it back again, asked his neighbors about it, stooped down in order to look under the chairs and the guests' feet. And when Gaga did her best to quiet him:

"It's a nuisance," he murmured, "my initials and my coronet are worked in the corner. They may compromise me."

"I say, Monsieur Falamoise, Lamafoise, Mafaloise!" shouted Foucarmont, who thought it exceedingly witty thus to disfigure the young man's name *ad infinitum*.

But La Faloise grew wroth and talked with a stutter about his ancestry. He threatened to send a water bottle at Foucarmont's head, and Count de Vandeuvres had to interfere in order to assure him that Foucarmont was a great joker. Indeed, everybody was laughing. This did for the already flurried young man, who was very glad to resume his seat and to begin eating with childlike submissiveness when in a loud voice his cousin ordered him to feed. Gaga had taken him back to her ample side; only from time to time he cast sly and anxious glances at the guests, for he ceased not to search for his handkerchief.

Then Foucarmont, being now in his witty vein, attacked Labordette right at the other end of the table. Louise Violaine strove to make him hold his tongue, for, she said, "when he goes nagging at other people like that it always ends in mischief for me." He had discovered a witticism which consisted in addressing Labordette as "Madame," and it must have amused him greatly, for he kept on repeating it while Labordette tranquilly shrugged his shoulders and as constantly replied:

"Pray hold your tongue, my dear fellow; it's stupid."

But as Foucarmont failed to desist and even became insulting without his neighbors knowing why, he left off answering him and appealed to Count Vandeuvres.

"Make your friend hold his tongue, monsieur. I don't wish to become angry."

Foucarmont had twice fought duels, and he was in consequence most politely treated and admitted into every circle. But there was now a general uprising against him. The table grew merry at his sallies, for they thought him very witty, but that was no reason why the evening should be spoiled. Vandeuvres, whose subtle countenance was darkening visibly, insisted on his restoring Labordette his sex. The other men—Mignon, Steiner and Bordenave—who were by this time much exalted, also intervened with shouts which drowned his voice. Only the old gentleman sitting forgotten next to Nana retained his stately demeanor and, still smiling in his tired, silent way, watched with lackluster eyes the untoward finish of the dessert.

"What do you say to our taking coffee in here, duckie?" said Bordenave. "We're very comfortable."

Nana did not give an immediate reply. Since the beginning of supper she had seemed no longer in her own house. All this company had overwhelmed and bewildered her with their shouts to the waiters, the loudness of their voices and the way in which they put themselves at their ease, just as though they were in a restaurant. Forgetting her role of hostess, she busied herself exclusively with bulky Steiner, who was verging on apoplexy beside her. She was listening to his proposals and continually refusing them with shakes of the head and that temptress's laughter which is peculiar to a voluptuous blonde. The champagne she had been drinking had flushed her a rosy-red; her lips were moist; her eyes sparkled, and the banker's offers rose with every kittenish movement of her shoulders, with every little voluptuous lift and fall of her throat, which occurred when she turned her head. Close by her ear he kept espying a sweet little satiny corner which drove him crazy. Occasionally Nana was interrupted, and then, remembering her guests, she would try and be as pleased as possible in order to show that she knew how to receive. Toward the end of the supper she was very tipsy. It made her miserable to think of it, but champagne had a way of intoxicating her almost directly! Then an exasperating notion struck her. In behaving thus improperly at her table, these ladies were showing themselves anxious to do her an ugly turn. Oh yes, she could see it all distinctly. Lucy had given Foucarmont a wink in order to egg him on against Labordette, while Rose, Caroline and the others were doing all they could to stir up the men. Now there was such a din you couldn't hear your neighbor speak, and so the story would get about that you might allow yourself every kind of liberty when you supped at Nana's. Very well then! They should see! She might be tipsy, if you like, but she was still the smartest and most ladylike woman there.

"Do tell them to serve the coffee here, duckie," resumed Bordenave. "I prefer it here because of my leg."

But Nana had sprung savagely to her feet after whispering into the astonished ears of Steiner and the old gentleman:

"It's quite right; it'll teach me to go and invite a dirty lot like that."

Then she pointed to the door of the dining room and added at the top of her voice:

"If you want coffee it's there, you know."

The company left the table and crowded toward the dining room without noticing Nana's indignant outburst. And soon no one was left in the drawing room save Bordenave, who advanced cautiously, supporting himself against the wall and cursing away at the confounded women who chucked Papa the moment they were chock-full. The waiters behind him were already busy removing the plates and dishes in obedience to the loudly voiced orders of the manager. They rushed to and fro, jostled one another, caused the whole table to vanish, as a pantomime property might at the sound of the chief scene-shifter's whistle. The ladies and gentlemen were to return to the drawing room after drinking their coffee.

"By gum, it's less hot here," said Gaga with a slight shiver as she entered the dining room.

The window here had remained open. Two lamps illuminated the table, where coffee and liqueurs were set out. There were no chairs, and the guests drank their coffee standing, while the hubbub the waiters were making in the next room grew louder and louder. Nana had disappeared, but nobody fretted about her absence. They did without her excellently well, and everybody helped himself and rummaged in the drawers of the sideboard in search of teaspoons, which were lacking. Several groups were formed; people separated during supper rejoined each other, and there was an interchange of glances, of meaning laughter and of phrases which summed up recent situations.

"Ought not Monsieur Fauchery to come and lunch with us one of these days, Auguste?" said Rose Mignon.

Mignon, who was toying with his watch chain, eyed the journalist for a second or two with his severe glance. Rose was out of her senses. As became a good manager, he would put a stop to such spendthrift courses. In return for a notice, well and good, but afterward, decidedly not. Nevertheless, as he was fully aware of his wife's wrongheadedness and as he made it a rule to wink paternally at a folly now and again, when such was necessary, he answered amiably enough:

"Certainly, I shall be most happy. Pray come tomorrow, Monsieur Fauchery."

Lucy Stewart heard this invitation given while she was talking with Steiner and Blanche and, raising her voice, she remarked to the banker:

"It's a mania they've all of them got. One of them even went so far as to steal my dog. Now, dear boy, am I to blame if you chuck her?"

Rose turned round. She was very pale and gazed fixedly at Steiner as she sipped her coffee. And then all the concentrated anger she felt at his abandonment of her flamed out in her eyes. She saw more clearly than Mignon; it was stupid in him to have wished to begin the Jonquier ruse a second time—those dodgers never succeeded twice running. Well, so much the worse for him! She would have Fauchery! She had been getting enamored of him since the beginning of supper, and if Mignon was not pleased it would teach him greater wisdom!

"You are not going to fight?" said Vandeuvres, coming over to Lucy Stewart.

"No, don't be afraid of that! Only she must mind and keep quiet, or I let the cat out of the bag!"

Then signing imperiously to Fauchery:

"I've got your slippers at home, my little man. I'll get them taken to your porter's lodge for you tomorrow."

He wanted to joke about it, but she swept off, looking like a queen. Clarisse, who had propped herself against a wall in order to drink a quiet glass of kirsch, was seen to shrug her shoulders. A pleasant business for a man! Wasn't it true that the moment two women were together in the presence of their lovers their first idea was to do one another out of them? It was a law of nature! As to herself, why, in heaven's name, if she had wanted to she would have torn out Gaga's eyes on Hector's account! But la, she despised him! Then as La Faloise passed by, she contented herself by remarking to him:

"Listen, my friend, you like 'em well advanced, you do! You don't want 'em ripe; you want 'em mildewed!"

La Faloise seemed much annoyed and not a little anxious. Seeing Clarisse making game of him, he grew suspicious of her.

"No humbug, I say," he muttered. "You've taken my handkerchief. Well then, give it back!"

"He's dreeing us with that handkerchief of his!" she cried. "Why, you ass, why should I have taken it from you?"

"Why should you?" he said suspiciously. "Why, that you may send it to my people and compromise me."

In the meantime Foucarmont was diligently attacking the liqueurs. He continued to gaze sneeringly at Labordette, who was drinking his coffee in the midst of the ladies. And occasionally he gave vent to fragmentary assertions, as thus: "He's the son of a horse dealer; some say the illegitimate child of a countess. Never a penny of income, yet always got twenty-five louis in his pocket! Footboy to the ladies of the town! A big lubber, who never goes with any of 'em! Never, never, never!" he repeated, growing furious. "No, by Jove! I must box his ears."

He drained a glass of chartreuse. The chartreuse had not the slightest effect upon him; it didn't affect him "even to that extent," and he clicked his thumbnail against the edge of his teeth. But suddenly, just as he was advancing upon Labordette, he grew ashy white and fell down in a heap in front of the sideboard. He was dead drunk. Louise Violaine was beside herself. She had been quite right to prophesy that matters would end badly, and now she would have her work cut out for the remainder of the night. Gaga reassured her. She examined the officer with the eye of a woman of experience and declared that there was nothing much the matter and that the gentleman would sleep like that for at least a dozen or fifteen hours without any serious consequences. Foucarmont was carried off.

"Well, where's Nana gone to?" asked Vandeuvres.

Yes, she had certainly flown away somewhere on leaving the table. The company suddenly recollected her, and everybody asked for her. Steiner, who for some seconds had been uneasy on her account, asked Vandeuvres about the old gentleman, for he, too, had disappeared. But the count reassured him—he had just brought the old gentleman back. He was a stranger, whose name it was useless to mention. Suffice it to say that he was a very rich man who was quite pleased to pay for suppers! Then as Nana was once more being forgotten, Vandeuvres saw Daguenet looking out of an open door and beckoning to him. And in the bedroom he found the mistress of the house sitting up, white-lipped and rigid, while Daguenet and Georges stood gazing at her with an alarmed expression.

"What *is* the matter with you?" he asked in some surprise.

She neither answered nor turned her head, and he repeated his question.

"Why, this is what's the matter with me," she cried out at length; "I won't let them make bloody sport of me!"

Thereupon she gave vent to any expression that occurred to her. Yes, oh yes, *she* wasn't a ninny—*she* could see clearly enough. They had been making devilish light of her during supper and saying all sorts of frightful things to show that they thought nothing of her! A pack of sluts who weren't fit to black her boots! Catch her bothering herself again just to be badgered for it after! She really didn't know what kept her from chuckling all that dirty lot out of the house! And with this, rage choked her and her voice broke down in sobs.

"Come, come, my lass, you're drunk," said Vandeuvres, growing familiar. "You must be reasonable."

No, she would give her refusal now; she would stay where she was.

"I am drunk—it's quite likely! But I want people to respect me!"

For a quarter of an hour past Daguenet and Georges had been vainly beseeching her to return to the drawing room. She was obstinate, however; her guests might do what they liked; she despised them too much to come back among them.

No, she never would, never. They might tear her in pieces before she would leave her room!

"I ought to have had my suspicions," she resumed.

"It's that cat of a Rose who's got the plot up! I'm certain Rose 'll have stopped that respectable woman coming whom I was expecting tonight."

She referred to Mme Robert. Vandeuvres gave her his word of honor that Mme Robert had given a spontaneous refusal. He listened and he argued with much gravity, for he was well accustomed to similar scenes and knew how women in such a state ought to be treated. But the moment he tried to take hold of her hands in order to lift her up from her chair and draw her away with him she struggled free of his clasp, and her wrath redoubled. Now, just look at that! They would never get her to believe that Fauchery had not put the Count Muffat off coming! A regular snake was that Fauchery, an envious sort, a fellow capable of growing mad against a woman and of destroying her whole happiness. For she knew this—the count had become madly devoted to her! She could have had him!

"Him, my dear, never!" cried Vandeuvres, forgetting himself and laughing aloud.

"Why not?" she asked, looking serious and slightly sobered.

"Because he's thoroughly in the hands of the priests, and if he were only to touch you with the tips of his fingers he would go and confess it the day after. Now listen to a bit of good advice. Don't let the other man escape you!"

She was silent and thoughtful for a moment or two. Then she got up and went and bathed her eyes. Yet when they wanted to take her into the dining room she still shouted "No!" furiously. Vandeuvres left the bedroom, smiling and without further pressing her, and the moment he was gone she had an access of melting tenderness, threw herself into Daguenet's arms and cried out:

"Ah, my sweetie, there's only you in the world. I love you! *Yes*, I love you from the bottom of my heart! Oh, it would be too nice if we could always live together. My God! How unfortunate women are!"

Then her eye fell upon Georges, who, seeing them kiss, was growing very red, and she kissed him too. Sweetie could not be jealous of a baby! She wanted Paul and Georges always to agree, because it would be so nice for them all three to stay like that, knowing all the time that they loved one another very much. But an extraordinary noise disturbed them: someone was snoring in the room. Whereupon after some searching they perceived Bordenave, who, since taking his coffee, must have comfortably installed himself there. He was sleeping on two chairs, his head propped on the edge of the bed and his leg stretched out in front. Nana thought him so funny with his open mouth and his nose moving with each successive snore that she was shaken with a mad fit of laughter. She left the room, followed by Daguenet and Georges, crossed the dining room, entered the drawing room, her merriment increasing at every step.

"Oh, my dear, you've no idea!" she cried, almost throwing herself into Rose's arms. "Come and see it."

All the women had to follow her. She took their hands coaxingly and drew them along with her willy-nilly, accompanying her action with so frank an outburst of mirth that they all of them began laughing on trust. The band vanished and returned after standing breathlessly for a second or two round Bordenave's lordly, outstretched form. And then there was a burst of laughter, and when one of them told the rest to be quiet Bordenave's distant snorings became audible.

It was close on four o'clock. In the dining room a card table had just been set out, at which Vandeuvres, Steiner, Mignon and Labordette had taken their seats. Behind them Lucy and Caroline stood making bets, while Blanche, nodding with sleep and dissatisfied about her night, kept asking Vandeuvres at intervals of five minutes if they weren't going soon. In the drawing room there was an attempt at dancing. Daguenet was at the piano or "chest of drawers," as Nana called it. She did not want a "thumper," for Mimi would play as many waltzes and polkas as the company desired. But the dance was languishing, and the ladies were chatting drowsily together in the corners of sofas. Suddenly, however, there was an outburst of noise. A band of eleven young men had arrived and were laughing loudly in the anteroom and crowding to the drawing room. They had just come from the ball at the Ministry of the Interior and were in evening dress and wore various unknown orders. Nana was annoyed at this riotous entry, called to the waiters who still remained in the kitchen and ordered them to throw these individuals out of doors. She vowed that she had never seen any of them before. Fauchery, Labordette, Daguenet and the rest of the men had all come forward in order to enforce respectful behavior toward their hostess. Big words flew about; arms were outstretched, and for some seconds a general exchange of fisticuffs was imminent. Notwithstanding this, however, a little sickly looking light-haired man kept insistently repeating:

"Come, come, Nana, you saw us the other evening at Peters' in the great red saloon! Pray remember, you invited us."

The other evening at Peters'? She did not remember it all. To begin with, what evening?

And when the little light-haired man had mentioned the day, which was Wednesday, she distinctly remembered having supped at Peters' on the Wednesday, but she had given no invitation to anyone; she was almost sure of that.

"However, suppose you *have* invited them, my good girl," murmured Labordette, who was beginning to have his doubts. "Perhaps you were a little elevated."

Then Nana fell a-laughing. It was quite possible; she really didn't know. So then, since these gentlemen were on the spot, they had her leave to come in. Everything was quietly arranged; several of the newcomers found friends in the drawing room, and the scene ended in handshakings. The little sickly looking light-haired man bore one of the greatest names in France. Furthermore, the eleven announced that others were to follow them, and, in fact, the door opened every few moments, and men in white gloves and official garb presented themselves. They were still coming from the ball at the Ministry. Fauchery jestingly inquired whether the minister was not coming, too, but Nana answered in a huff that the minister went to the houses of people she didn't care a pin for. What she did not say was that she was possessed with a hope of seeing Count Muffat enter her room among all that stream of people. He might quite have reconsidered his decision, and so while talking to Rose she kept a sharp eye on the door.

Five o'clock struck. The dancing had ceased, and the cardplayers alone persisted in their game. Labordette had vacated his seat, and the women had returned into the drawing room. The air there was heavy with the somnolence which accompanies a long vigil, and the lamps cast a wavering light while their burned-out wicks glowed red within their globes. The ladies had reached that vaguely melancholy hour when they felt it necessary to tell each other their histories. Blanche de Sivry spoke of her grandfather, the general, while Clarisse invented a romantic story about a duke seducing her at her uncle's house, whither he used to come for the boar hunting. Both women, looking different ways, kept shrugging their shoulders and asking themselves how the deuce the other could tell such whoppers! As to Lucy Stewart, she quietly confessed to her origin and of her own accord spoke of her childhood and of the days when her father, the wheel greaser at the Northern Railway Terminus, used to treat her to an apple puff on Sundays.

"Oh, I must tell you about it!" cried the little Maria Blond abruptly. "Opposite to me there lives a gentleman, a Russian, an awfully rich man! Well, just fancy, yesterday I received a basket of fruit—oh, it just was a basket! Enormous peaches, grapes as big as that, simply wonderful for the time of year! And in the middle of them six thousand-franc notes! It was the Russian's doing. Of course I sent the whole thing back again, but I must say my heart ached a little —when I thought of the fruit!"

The ladies looked at one another and pursed up their lips. At her age little Maria Blond had a pretty cheek! Besides, to think that such things should happen to trollops like her! Infinite was their contempt for her among themselves. It was Lucy of whom they were particularly jealous, for they were beside themselves at the thought of her three princes. Since Lucy had begun taking a daily morning ride in the Bois they all had become Amazons, as though a mania possessed them.

Day was about to dawn, and Nana turned her eyes away from the door, for she was relinquishing all hope. The company were bored to distraction. Rose Mignon had refused to sing the "Slipper" and sat huddled up on a sofa, chatting in a low voice with Fauchery and waiting for Mignon, who had by now won some fifty louis from Vandeuvres. A fat gentleman with a decoration and a serious cast of countenance had certainly given a recitation in Alsatian accents of "Abraham's Sacrifice," a piece in which the Almighty says, "By My blasted Name" when He swears, and Isaac always answers with a "Yes, Papa!" Nobody, however, understood what it was all about, and the piece had been voted stupid. People were at their wits' end how to make merry and to finish the night with fitting hilarity. For a moment or two Labordette conceived the idea of denouncing different women in a whisper to La Faloise, who still went prowling round each individual lady, looking to see if she were hiding his handkerchief in her bosom. Soon, as there were still some bottles of champagne on the sideboard, the young men again fell to drinking. They shouted to one another; they stirred each other up, but a dreary species of intoxication, which was stupid enough to drive one to despair, began to overcome the company beyond hope of recovery. Then the little fair-haired fellow, the man who bore one of the greatest names in France and had reached his wit's end and was desperate at the thought that he could not hit upon something really funny, conceived a brilliant notion: he snatched up his bottle of champagne and poured its contents into the piano. His allies were convulsed with laughter.

"La now! Why's he putting champagne into the piano?" asked Tatan Néné in great astonishment as she caught sight of him.

"What, my lass, you don't know why he's doing that?" replied Labordette solemnly. "There's nothing so good as champagne for pianos. It gives 'em tone."

"Ah," murmured Tatan Néné with conviction.

And when the rest began laughing at her she grew angry. How should she know? They were always confusing her.

Decidedly the evening was becoming a big failure. The night threatened to end in the unloveliest way. In a corner by themselves Maria Blond and Léa de Horn had begun squabbling at close quarters, the former accusing the latter

of consorting with people of insufficient wealth. They were getting vastly
abusive over it, their chief stumbling block being the good looks of the men in
question. Lucy, who was plain, got them to hold their tongues. Good looks
were nothing, according to her; good figures were what was wanted. Farther
off, on a sofa, an attaché had slipped his arm round Simonne's waist and was
trying to kiss her neck, but Simonne, sullen and thoroughly out of sorts, pushed
him away at every fresh attempt with cries of "You're pestering me!" and
sound slaps of the fan across his face. For the matter of that, not one of the
ladies allowed herself to be touched. Did people take them for light women?
Gaga, in the meantime, had once more caught La Faloise and had almost
hoisted him upon her knees while Clarisse was disappearing from view between two gentlemen, shaking with nervous laughter as women will when they
are tickled. Round about the piano they were still busy with their little game,
for they were suffering from a fit of stupid imbecility, which caused each man
to jostle his fellow in his frantic desire to empty his bottle into the instru-
ment. It was a simple process and a charming one.

"Now then, old boy, drink a glass! Devil take it, he's a thirsty piano! Hi!
'Tenshun! Here's another bottle! You mustn't lose a drop!"

Nana's back was turned, and she did not see them. Emphatically she was now
falling back on the bulky Steiner, who was seated next to her. So much the
worse! It was all on account of that Muffat, who had refused what was offered
him. Sitting there in her white foulard dress, which was as light and full of
folds as a shift, sitting there with drooped eyelids and cheeks pale with the
touch of intoxication from which she was suffering, she offered herself to him
with that quiet expression which is peculiar to a good-natured courtesan. The
roses in her hair and at her throat had lost their leaves, and their stalks alone
remained. Presently Steiner withdrew his hand quickly from the folds of her
skirt, where he had come in contact with the pins that Georges had stuck there.
Some drops of blood appeared on his fingers, and one fell on Nana's dress and
stained it.

"Now the bargain's struck," said Nana gravely.

The day was breaking apace. An uncertain glimmer of light, fraught with a
poignant melancholy, came stealing through the windows. And with that the
guests began to take their departure. It was a most sour and uncomfortable retreat. Caroline Héquet, annoyed at the loss of her night, announced that it was
high time to be off unless you were anxious to assist at some pretty scenes. Rose
pouted as if her womanly character had been compromised. It was always
so with these girls; they didn't know how to behave and were guilty of disgusting conduct when they made their first appearance in society! And Mignon
having cleaned Vandeuvres out completely, the family took their departure.
They did not trouble about Steiner but renewed their invitation for tomorrow
to Fauchery. Lucy thereupon refused the journalist's escort home and sent him
back shrilly to his "strolling actress." At this Rose turned round immediately
and hissed out a "Dirty sow" by way of answer. But Mignon, who in feminine
quarrels was always paternal, for his experience was a long one and rendered
him superior to them, had already pushed her out of the house, telling her at

the same time to have done. Lucy came downstairs in solitary state behind
them. After which Gaga had to carry off La Faloise, ill, sobbing like a child,
calling after Clarisse, who had long since gone off with her two gentlemen.
Simonne, too, had vanished. Indeed, none remained save Tatan, Léa and Maria,
whom Labordette complaisantly took under his charge.

"Oh, but I don't the least bit want to go to bed!" said Nana. "One ought to
find something to do."

She looked at the sky through the windowpanes. It was a livid sky, and sooty
clouds were scudding across it. It was six o'clock in the morning. Over the
way, on the opposite side of the Boulevard Haussmann, the glistening roofs of
the still-slumbering houses were sharply outlined against the twilight sky while
along the deserted roadway a gang of street sweepers passed with a clatter of
wooden shoes. As she viewed Paris thus grimly awakening, she was overcome
by tender, girlish feelings, by a yearning for the country, for idyllic scenes,
for things soft and white.

"Now guess what you're to do," she said, coming back to Steiner. "You're
going to take me to the Bois de Boulogne, and we'll drink milk there."

She clapped her hands in childish glee. Without waiting for the banker's
reply—he naturally consented, though he was really rather bored and inclined
to think of other things—she ran off to throw a pelisse over her shoulders. In
the drawing room there was now no one with Steiner save the band of young
men. These had by this time dropped the very dregs of their glasses into the
piano and were talking of going, when one of their number ran in triumphantly. He held in his hands a last remaining bottle, which he had brought
back with him from the pantry.

"Wait a minute, wait a minute!" he shouted. "Here's a bottle of chartreuse;
that 'll pick him up! And now, my young friends, let's hook it. We're blooming idiots."

In the dressing room Nana was compelled to wake up Zoé, who had dozed
off on a chair. The gas was still alight, and Zoé shivered as she helped her
mistress on with her hat and pelisse.

"Well, it's over; I've done what you wanted me to," said Nana, speaking
familiarly to the maid in a sudden burst of expansive confidence and much relieved at the thought that she had at last made her election. "You were quite
right; the banker's as good as another."

The maid was cross, for she was still heavy with sleep. She grumbled something to the effect that Madame ought to have come to a decision the first evening. Then following her into the bedroom, she asked what she was going to
do with "those two," meaning Bordenave, who was snoring away as usual, and
Georges, who had slipped in slyly, buried his head in a pillow and, finally falling asleep there, was now breathing as lightly and regularly as a cherub. Nana
in reply told her that she was to let them sleep on. But seeing Daguenet come
into the room, she again grew tender. He had been watching her from the
kitchen and was looking very wretched.

"Come, my sweetie, be reasonable," she said, taking him in her arms and
kissing him with all sorts of little wheedling caresses. "Nothing's changed; you

know that it's sweetie whom I always adore! Eh, dear? I had to do it. Why, I swear to you we shall have even nicer times now. Come tomorrow, and we'll arrange about hours. Now be quick, kiss and hug me as you love me. Oh, tighter, tighter than that!"

And she escaped and rejoined Steiner, feeling happy and once more possessed with the idea of drinking milk. In the empty room the Count de Vandeuvres was left alone with the "decorated" man who had recited "Abraham's Sacrifice." Both seemed glued to the card table; they had lost count of their whereabouts and never once noticed the broad light of day without, while Blanche had made bold to put her feet up on a sofa in order to try and get a little sleep.

"Oh, Blanche is with them!" cried Nana. "We are going to drink milk, dear. Do come; you'll find Vandeuvres here when we return."

Blanche got up lazily. This time the banker's fiery face grew white with annoyance at the idea of having to take that big wench with him too. She was certain to bore him. But the two women had already got him by the arms and were reiterating:

"We want them to milk the cow before our eyes, you know."

CHAPTER V

AT THE VARIÉTIÉS they were giving the thirty-fourth performance of the *Blonde Venus*. The first act had just finished, and in the greenroom Simonne, dressed as the little laundress, was standing in front of a console table, surmounted by a looking glass and situated between the two corner doors which opened obliquely on the end of the dressing-room passage. No one was with her, and she was scrutinizing her face and rubbing her finger up and down below her eyes with a view to putting the finishing touches to her make-up. The gas jets on either side of the mirror flooded her with warm, crude light.

"Has he arrived?" asked Prullière, entering the room in his Alpine admiral's costume, which was set off by a big sword, enormous top boots and a vast tuft of plumes.

"Who d'you mean?" said Simonne, taking no notice of him and laughing into the mirror in order to see how her lips looked.

"The prince."

"I don't know; I've just come down. Oh, he's certainly due here tonight; he comes every time!"

Prullière had drawn near the hearth opposite the console table, where a coke fire was blazing and two more gas jets were flaring brightly. He lifted his eyes and looked at the clock and the barometer on his right hand and on his left. They had gilded sphinxes by way of adornment in the style of the First Empire. Then he stretched himself out in a huge armchair with ears, the green velvet of which had been so worn by four generations of comedians that it looked yellow in places, and there he stayed, with moveless limbs and vacant eyes, in that weary and resigned attitude peculiar to actors who are used to long waits before their turn for going on the stage.

Old Bosc, too, had just made his appearance. He came in dragging one foot behind the other and coughing. He was wrapped in an old box coat, part of which had slipped from his shoulder in such a way as to uncover the gold-laced cloak of King Dagobert. He put his crown on the piano and for a moment or two stood moodily stamping his feet. His hands were trembling slightly with the first beginnings of alcoholism, but he looked a sterling old fellow for all that, and a long white beard lent that fiery tippler's face of his a truly venerable appearance. Then in the silence of the room, while the shower of hail was whipping the panes of the great window that looked out on the courtyard, he shook himself disgustedly.

"What filthy weather!" he growled.

Simonne and Prullière did not move. Four or five pictures—a landscape, a portrait of the actor Vernet—hung yellowing in the hot glare of the gas, and a bust of Potier, one of the bygone glories of the Variétés, stood gazing vacant-eyed from its pedestal. But just then there was a burst of voices outside. It was Fontan, dressed for the second act. He was a young dandy, and his habiliments, even to his gloves, were entirely yellow.

"Now say you don't know!" he shouted, gesticulating. "Today's my patron saint's day!"

"What?" asked Simonne, coming up smilingly, as though attracted by the huge nose and the vast, comic mouth of the man. "D'you answer to the name of Achille?"

"Exactly so! And I'm going to get 'em to tell Madame Bron to send up champagne after the second act."

For some seconds a bell had been ringing in the distance. The long-drawn sound grew fainter, then louder, and when the bell ceased a shout ran up the stair and down it till it was lost along the passages. "All on the stage for the second act! All on the stage for the second act!" The sound drew near, and a little pale-faced man passed by the greenroom doors, outside each of which he yelled at the top of his shrill voice, "On the stage for the second act!"

"The deuce, it's champagne!" said Prullière without appearing to hear the din. "You're prospering!"

"If I were you I should have it in from the café," old Bosc slowly announced. He was sitting on a bench covered with green velvet, with his head against the wall.

But Simonne said that it was one's duty to consider Mme Bron's small perquisites. She clapped her hands excitedly and devoured Fontan with her gaze while his long goatlike visage kept up a continuous twitching of eyes and nose and mouth.

"Oh, that Fontan!" she murmured. "There's no one like him, no one like him!"

The two greenroom doors stood wide open to the corridor leading to the wings. And along the yellow wall, which was brightly lit up by a gas lamp out of view, passed a string of rapidly moving shadows—men in costume, women with shawls over their scant attire, in a word, the whole of the characters in the second act, who would shortly make their appearance as masqueraders in the ball at the Boule Noire. And at the end of the corridor became audible a shuffling of feet as these people clattered down the five wooden steps which led to the stage. As the big Clarisse went running by Simonne called to her, but she said she would be back directly. And, indeed, she reappeared almost at once, shivering in the thin tunic and scarf which she wore as Iris.

"God bless me!" she said. "It isn't warm, and I've left my furs in my dressing room!"

Then as she stood toasting her legs in their warm rose-colored tights in front of the fireplace she resumed:

"The prince has arrived."

"Oh!" cried the rest with the utmost curiosity.

"Yes, that's why I ran down: I wanted to see. He's in the first stage box to the right, the same he was in on Thursday. It's the third time he's been this week, eh? That's Nana; well, she's in luck's way! I was willing to wager he wouldn't come again."

Simonne opened her lips to speak, but her remarks were drowned by a fresh shout which arose close to the greenroom. In the passage the callboy was yelling at the top of his shrill voice, "They've knocked!"

"Three times!" said Simonne when she was again able to speak. "It's getting exciting. You know, he won't go to her place; he takes her to his. And it seems that he has to pay for it too!"

"Egad! It's a case of when one 'has to go out,' " muttered Prullière wickedly, and he got up to have a last look at the mirror as became a handsome fellow whom the boxes adored.

"They've knocked! They've knocked!" the callboy kept repeating in tones that died gradually away in the distance as he passed through the various stories and corridors.

Fontan thereupon, knowing how it had all gone off on the first occasion the prince and Nana met, told the two women the whole story while they in their turn crowded against him and laughed at the tops of their voices whenever he stooped to whisper certain details in their ears. Old Bosc had never budged an inch—he was totally indifferent. That sort of thing no longer interested him now. He was stroking a great tortoise-shell cat which was lying curled up on the bench. He did so quite beautifully and ended by taking her in his arms with the tender good nature becoming a worn-out monarch. The cat arched its back and then, after a prolonged sniff at the big white beard, the gluey odor of which doubtless disgusted her, she turned and, curling herself up, went to sleep again on the bench beside him. Bosc remained grave and absorbed.

"That's all right, but if I were you I should drink the champagne at the restaurant—it's better there," he said, suddenly addressing Fontan when he had finished his recital.

"The curtain's up!" cried the callboy in cracked and long-drawn accents. "The curtain's up! The curtain's up!"

The shout sounded for some moments, during which there had been a noise of rapid footsteps. Through the suddenly opened door of the passage came a burst of music and a far-off murmur of voices, and then the door shut to again, and you could hear its dull thud as it wedged itself into position once more.

A heavy, peaceful atmosphere again pervaded the greenroom, as though the place were situated a hundred leagues from the house where crowds were applauding. Simonne and Clarisse were still on the topic of Nana. There was a girl who never hurried herself! Why, yesterday she had again come on too late! But there was a silence, for a tall damsel had just craned her head in at the door and, seeing that she had made a mistake, had departed to the other end of the passage. It was Satin. Wearing a hat and a small veil for the nonce she was affecting the manner of a lady about to pay a call.

"A pretty trollop!" muttered Prullière, who had been coming across her for a year past at the Café des Variétés. And at this Simonne told them how Nana had recognized in Satin an old schoolmate, had taken a vast fancy to her and was now plaguing Bordenave to let her make a first appearance on the stage.

"How d'ye do?" said Fontan, shaking hands with Mignon and Fauchery, who now came into the room.

Old Bosc himself gave them the tips of his fingers while the two women kissed Mignon.

"A good house this evening?" queried Fauchery.

"Oh, a splendid one!" replied Prullière. "You should see 'em gaping."

"I say, my little dears," remarked Mignon, "it must be your turn!"

Oh, all in good time! They were only at the fourth scene as yet, but Bosc got up in obedience to instinct, as became a rattling old actor who felt that his cue was coming. At that very moment the callboy was opening the door.

"Monsieur Bosc!" he called. "Mademoiselle Simonne!"

Simonne flung a fur-lined pelisse briskly over her shoulders and went out. Bosc, without hurrying at all, went and got his crown, which he settled on his brow with a rap. Then dragging himself unsteadily along in his greatcoat, he took his departure, grumbling and looking as annoyed as a man who has been rudely disturbed.

"You were very amiable in your last notice," continued Fontan, addressing Fauchery. "Only why do you say that comedians are vain?"

"Yes, my little man, why d'you say that?" shouted Mignon, bringing down his huge hands on the journalist's slender shoulders with such force as almost to double him up.

Prullière and Clarisse refrained from laughing aloud. For some time past the whole company had been deriving amusement from a comedy which was going on in the wings. Mignon, rendered frantic by his wife's caprice and annoyed at the thought that this man Fauchery brought nothing but a certain doubtful notoriety to his household, had conceived the idea of revenging himself on the journalist by overwhelming him with tokens of friendship. Every evening, therefore, when he met him behind scenes he would shower friendly slaps on his back and shoulders, as though fairly carried away by an outburst of tenderness, and Fauchery, who was a frail, small man in comparison with such a giant, was fain to take the raps with a strained smile in order not to quarrel with Rose's husband.

"Aha, my buck, you've insulted Fontan," resumed Mignon, who was doing his best to force the joke. "Stand on guard! One—two—got him right in the middle of his chest!"

He lunged and struck the young man with such force that the latter grew very pale and could not speak for some seconds. With a wink Clarisse showed the others where Rose Mignon was standing on the threshold of the greenroom. Rose had witnessed the scene, and she marched straight up to the journalist, as though she had failed to notice her husband and, standing on tiptoe, bare-armed and in baby costume, she held her face up to him with a caressing, infantine pout.

"Good evening, baby," said Fauchery, kissing her familiarly.

Thus he indemnified himself. Mignon, however, did not seem to have observed this kiss, for everybody kissed his wife at the theater. But he laughed and gave the journalist a keen little look. The latter would assuredly have to pay for Rose's bravado.

In the passage the tightly shutting door opened and closed again, and a tempest of applause was blown as far as the greenroom. Simonne came in after her scene.

"Oh, Father Bosc *has* just scored!" she cried. "The prince was writhing with laughter and applauded with the rest as though he had been paid to. I say, do you know the big man sitting beside the prince in the stage box? A handsome man, with a very sedate expression and splendid whiskers!"

"It's Count Muffat," replied Fauchery. "I know that the prince, when he was at the empress's the day before yesterday, invited him to dinner for tonight. He'll have corrupted him afterward!"

"So that's Count Muffat! We know his father-in-law, eh, Auguste?" said Rose, addressing her remark to Mignon. "You know the Marquis de Chouard, at whose place I went to sing? Well, he's in the house too. I noticed him at the back of a box. There's an old boy for you!"

Prullière, who had just put on his huge plume of feathers, turned round and called her.

"Hi, Rose! Let's go now!"

She ran after him, leaving her sentence unfinished. At that moment Mme Bron, the portress of the theater, passed by the door with an immense bouquet in her arms. Simonne asked cheerfully if it was for her, but the porter woman did not vouchsafe an answer and only pointed her chin toward Nana's dressing room at the end of the passage. Oh, that Nana! They were loading her with flowers! Then when Mme Bron returned she handed a letter to Clarisse, who allowed a smothered oath to escape her. That beggar La Faloise again! There was a fellow who wouldn't let her alone! And when she learned the gentleman in question was waiting for her at the porter's lodge she shrieked:

"Tell him I'm coming down after this act. I'm going to catch him one on the face."

Fontan had rushed forward, shouting:

"Madame Bron, just listen. Please listen, Madame Bron. I want you to send up six bottles of champagne between the acts."

But the callboy had again made his appearance. He was out of breath, and in a singsong voice he called out:

"All to go on the stage! It's your turn, Monsieur Fontan. Make haste, make haste!"

"Yes, yes, I'm going, Father Barillot," replied Fontan in a flurry.

And he ran after Mme Bron and continued:

"You understand, eh? Six bottles of champagne in the greenroom between the acts. It's my patron saint's day, and I'm standing the racket."

Simonne and Clarisse had gone off with a great rustling of skirts. Everybody was swallowed up in the distance, and when the passage door had banged with its usual hollow sound a fresh hail shower was heard beating against the windows in the now-silent greenroom. Barillot, a small, pale-faced ancient, who for thirty years had been a servant in the theater, had advanced familiarly toward Mignon and had presented his open snuffbox to him. This proffer of a pinch and its acceptance allowed him a minute's rest in his interminable career up and down stairs and along the dressing-room passage. He certainly had still to look up Mme Nana, as he called her, but she was one of those who followed her own sweet will and didn't care a pin for penalties. Why, if she chose to be too late she was too late! But he stopped short and murmured in great surprise:

"Well, I never! She's ready; here she is! She must know that the prince is here."

Indeed, Nana appeared in the corridor. She was dressed as a fish hag: her arms and face were plastered with white paint, and she had a couple of red dabs under her eyes. Without entering the greenroom she contented herself by nodding to Mignon and Fauchery.

"How do? You're all right?"

Only Mignon shook her outstretched hand, and she hied royally on her way, followed by her dresser, who almost trod on her heels while stooping to adjust the folds of her skirt. In the rear of the dresser came Satin, closing the procession and trying to look quite the lady, though she was already bored to death.

"And Steiner?" asked Mignon sharply.

"Monsieur Steiner has gone away to the Loiret," said Barillot, preparing to return to the neighborhood of the stage. "I expect he's gone to buy a country place in those parts."

"Ah yes, I know, Nana's country place."

Mignon had grown suddenly serious. Oh, that Steiner! He had promised Rose a fine house in the old days! Well, well, it wouldn't do to grow angry with anybody. Here was a position that would have to be won again. From fireplace to console table Mignon paced, sunk in thought yet still unconquered by circumstances. There was no one in the greenroom now save Fauchery and himself. The journalist was tired and had flung himself back into the recesses of the big armchair. There he stayed with half-closed eyes and as quiet as quiet could be, while the other glanced down at him as he passed. When they were alone Mignon scorned to slap him at every turn. What good would it have

done, since nobody would have enjoyed the spectacle? He was far too dis
interested to be personally entertained by the farcical scenes in which h
figured as a bantering husband. Glad of this short-lived respite, Faucher
stretched his feet out languidly toward the fire and let his upturned eye
wander from the barometer to the clock. In the course of his march Mignor
planted himself in front of Potier's bust, looked at it without seeming to se
it and then turned back to the window, outside which yawned the darklin
gulf of the courtyard. The rain had ceased, and there was now a deep silenc
in the room, which the fierce heat of the coke fire and the flare of the gas jet
rendered still more oppressive. Not a sound came from the wings: the staircas
and the passages were deadly still.

That choking sensation of quiet, which behind the scenes immediately pre
cedes the end of an act, had begun to pervade the empty greenroom. Indeed
the place seemed to be drowsing off through very breathlessness amid that fain
murmur which the stage gives forth when the whole troupe are raising th
deafening uproar of some grand finale.

"Oh, the cows!" Bordenave suddenly shouted in his hoarse voice.

He had only just come up, and he was already howling complaints abou
two chorus girls who had nearly fallen flat on the stage because they were play
ing the fool together. When his eye lit on Mignon and Fauchery he calle
them; he wanted to show them something. The prince had just notified a de
sire to compliment Nana in her dressing room during the next interval. But a
he was leading them into the wings the stage manager passed.

"Just you find those hags Fernande and Maria!" cried Bordenave savagely

Then calming down and endeavoring to assume the dignified expression
worn by "heavy fathers," he wiped his face with his pocket handkerchief and
added:

"I am now going to receive His Highness."

The curtain fell amid a long-drawn salvo of applause. Then across the
twilight stage, which was no longer lit up by the footlights, there followed a
disorderly retreat. Actors and supers and chorus made haste to get back to
their dressing rooms while the sceneshifters rapidly changed the scenery.
Simonne and Clarisse, however, had remained "at the top," talking together
in whispers. On the stage, in an interval between their lines, they had just
settled a little matter. Clarisse, after viewing the thing in every light, found she
preferred not to see La Faloise, who could never decide to leave her for Gaga,
and so Simonne was simply to go and explain that a woman ought not to be
palled up to in that fashion! At last she agreed to undertake the mission.

Then Simonne, in her theatrical laundress's attire but with furs over her
shoulders, ran down the greasy steps of the narrow, winding stairs which led
between damp walls to the porter's lodge. This lodge, situated between the
actors' staircase and that of the management, was shut in to right and left by
large glass partitions and resembled a huge transparent lantern in which two
gas jets were flaring.

There was a set of pigeonholes in the place in which were piled letters and
newspapers, while on the table various bouquets lay awaiting their recipients

in close proximity to neglected heaps of dirty plates and to an old pair of stays, the eyelets of which the portress was busy mending. And in the middle of this untidy, ill-kept storeroom sat four fashionable, white-gloved society men. They occupied as many ancient straw-bottomed chairs and, with an expression at once patient and submissive, kept sharply turning their heads in Mme Bron's direction every time she came down from the theater overhead, for on such occasions she was the bearer of replies. Indeed, she had but now handed a note to a young man who had hurried out to open it beneath the gaslight in the vestibule, where he had grown slightly pale on reading the classic phrase— how often had others read it in that very place!—"Impossible tonight, my dearie! I'm booked!" La Faloise sat on one of these chairs at the back of the room, between the table and the stove. He seemed bent on passing the evening there, and yet he was not quite happy. Indeed, he kept tucking up his long legs in his endeavors to escape from a whole litter of black kittens who were gamboling wildly round them while the mother cat sat bolt upright, staring at him with yellow eyes.

"Ah, it's you, Mademoiselle Simonne! What can I do for you?" asked the portress.

Simonne begged her to send La Faloise out to her. But Mme Bron was unable to comply with her wishes all at once. Under the stairs in a sort of deep cupboard she kept a little bar, whither the supers were wont to descend for drinks between the acts, and seeing that just at that moment there were five or six tall lubbers there who, still dressed as Boule Noire masqueraders, were dying of thirst and in a great hurry, she lost her head a bit. A gas jet was flaring in the cupboard, within which it was possible to descry a tin-covered table and some shelves garnished with half-emptied bottles. Whenever the door of this coalhole was opened a violent whiff of alcohol mingled with the scent of stale cooking in the lodge, as well as with the penetrating scent of the flowers upon the table.

"Well now," continued the portress when she had served the supers, "is it the little dark chap out there you want?"

"No, no; don't be silly!" said Simonne. "It's the lanky one by the side of the stove. Your cat's sniffing at his trouser legs!"

And with that she carried La Faloise off into the lobby, while the other gentlemen once more resigned themselves to their fate and to semisuffocation and the masqueraders drank on the stairs and indulged in rough horseplay and guttural drunken jests.

On the stage above Bordenave was wild with the sceneshifters, who seemed never to have done changing scenes. They appeared to be acting of set purpose —the prince would certainly have some set piece or other tumbling on his head.

"Up with it! Up with it!" shouted the foreman.

At length the canvas at the back of the stage was raised into position, and the stage was clear. Mignon, who had kept his eye on Fauchery, seized this opportunity in order to start his pummeling matches again. He hugged him in his long arms and cried:

"Oh, take care! That mast just missed crushing you!"

And he carried him off and shook him before setting him down again. In view of the sceneshifters' exaggerated mirth, Faucery grew white. His lips trembled, and he was ready to flare up in anger while Mignon, shamming good nature, was clapping him on the shoulder with such affectionate violence as nearly to pulverize him.

"I value your health, I do!" he kept repeating. "Egad! I should be in a pretty pickle if anything serious happened to you!"

But just then a whisper ran through their midst: "The prince! The prince!" And everybody turned and looked at the little door which opened out of the main body of the house. At first nothing was visible save Bordenave's round back and beefy neck, which bobbed down and arched up in a series of obsequious obeisances. Then the prince made his appearance. Largely and strongly built, light of beard and rosy of hue, he was not lacking in the kind of distinction peculiar to a sturdy man of pleasure, the square contours of whose limbs are clearly defined by the irreproachable cut of a frock coat. Behind him walked Count Muffat and the Marquis de Chouard, but this particular corner of the theater being dark, the group were lost to view amid huge moving shadows.

In order fittingly to address the son of a queen, who would someday occupy a throne, Bordenave had assumed the tone of a man exhibiting a bear in the street. In a voice tremulous with false emotion he kept repeating:

"If His Highness will have the goodness to follow me—would His Highness deign to come this way? His Highness will take care!"

The prince did not hurry in the least. On the contrary, he was greatly interested and kept pausing in order to look at the sceneshifters' maneuvers. A batten had just been lowered, and the group of gaslights high up among its iron crossbars illuminated the stage with a wide beam of light. Muffat, who had never yet been behind scenes at a theater, was even more astonished than the rest. An uneasy feeling of mingled fear and vague repugnance took possession of him. He looked up into the heights above him, where more battens, the gas jets on which were burning low, gleamed like galaxies of little bluish stars amid a chaos of iron rods, connecting lines of all sizes, hanging stages and canvases spread out in space, like huge cloths hung out to dry.

"Lower away!" shouted the foreman unexpectedly.

And the prince himself had to warn the count, for a canvas was descending. They were setting the scenery for the third act, which was the grotto on Mount Etna. Men were busy planting masts in the sockets, while others went and took frames which were leaning against the walls of the stage and proceeded to lash them with strong cords to the poles already in position. At the back of the stage, with a view to producing the bright rays thrown by Vulcan's glowing forge, a stand had been fixed by a limelight man, who was now lighting various burners under red glasses. The scene was one of confusion, verging to all appearances on absolute chaos, but every little move had been prearranged. Nay, amid all the scurry the whistle blower even took a few turns, stepping short as he did so, in order to rest his legs.

"His Highness overwhelms me," said Bordenave, still bowing low. "The theater is not large, but we do what we can. Now if His Highness deigns to follow me——"

Count Muffat was already making for the dressing-room passage. The really sharp downward slope of the stage had surprised him disagreeably, and he owed no small part of his present anxiety to a feeling that its boards were moving under his feet. Through the open sockets gas was descried burning in the "dock." Human voices and blasts of air, as from a vault, came up thence, and, looking down into the depths of gloom, one became aware of a whole subterranean existence. But just as the count was going up the stage a small incident occurred to stop him. Two little women, dressed for the third act, were chatting by the peephole in the curtain. One of them, straining forward and widening the hole with her fingers in order the better to observe things, was scanning the house beyond.

"I see him," said she sharply. "Oh, what a mug!"

Horrified, Bordenave had much ado not to give her a kick. But the prince smiled and looked pleased and excited by the remark. He gazed warmly at the little woman who did not care a button for His Highness, and she, on her part, laughed unblushingly. Bordenave, however, persuaded the prince to follow him. Muffat was beginning to perspire; he had taken his hat off. What inconvenienced him most was the stuffy, dense, overheated air of the place with its strong, haunting smell, a smell peculiar to this part of a theater, and, as such, compact of the reek of gas, of the glue used in the manufacture of the scenery, of dirty dark nooks and corners and of questionably clean chorus girls. In the passage the air was still more suffocating, and one seemed to breathe a poisoned atmosphere, which was occasionally relieved by the acid scents of toilet waters and the perfumes of various soaps emanating from the dressing rooms. The count lifted his eyes as he passed and glanced up the staircase, for he was well-nigh startled by the keen flood of light and warmth which flowed down upon his back and shoulders. High up above him there was a clicking of ewers and basins, a sound of laughter and of people calling to one another, a banging of doors, which in their continual opening and shutting allowed an odor of womankind to escape—a musky scent of oils and essences mingling with the natural pungency exhaled from human tresses. He did not stop. Nay, he hastened his walk: he almost ran, his skin tingling with the breath of that fiery approach to a world he knew nothing of.

"A theater's a curious sight, eh?" said the Marquis de Chouard with the enchanted expression of a man who once more finds himself amid familiar surroundings.

But Bordenave had at length reached Nana's dressing room at the end of the passage. He quietly turned the door handle; then, cringing again:

"If His Highness will have the goodness to enter——"

They heard the cry of a startled woman and caught sight of Nana as, stripped to the waist, she slipped behind a curtain while her dresser, who had been in the act of drying her, stood, towel in air, before them.

"Oh, it *is* silly to come in that way!" cried Nana from her hiding place. "Don't come in; you see you mustn't come in!"

Bordenave did not seem to relish this sudden flight.

"Do stay where you were, my dear. Why, it doesn't matter," he said. "It's His Highness. Come, come, don't be childish."

And when she still refused to make her appearance—for she was startled as yet, though she had begun to laugh—he added in peevish, paternal tones:

"Good heavens, these gentlemen know perfectly well what a woman looks like. They won't eat you."

"I'm not so sure of that," said the prince wittily.

With that the whole company began laughing in an exaggerated manner in order to pay him proper court.

"An exquisitely witty speech—an altogether Parisian speech," as Bordenave remarked.

Nana vouchsafed no further reply, but the curtain began moving. Doubtless she was making up her mind. Then Count Muffat, with glowing cheeks, began to take stock of the dressing room. It was a square room with a very low ceiling, and it was entirely hung with a light-colored Havana stuff. A curtain of the same material depended from a copper rod and formed a sort of recess at the end of the room, while two large windows opened on the courtyard of the theater and were faced, at a distance of three yards at most, by a leprous-looking wall against which the panes cast squares of yellow light amid the surrounding darkness. A large dressing glass faced a white marble toilet table, which was garnished with a disorderly array of flasks and glass boxes containing oils, essences and powders. The count went up to the dressing glass and discovered that he was looking very flushed and had small drops of perspiration on his forehead. He dropped his eyes and came and took up a position in front of the toilet table, where the basin, full of soapy water, the small, scattered, ivory toilet utensils and the damp sponges, appeared for some moments to absorb his attention. The feeling of dizziness which he had experienced when he first visited Nana in the Boulevard Haussmann once more overcame him. He felt the thick carpet soften under foot, and the gasjets burning by the dressing table and by the glass seemed to shoot whistling flames about his temples. For one moment, being afraid of fainting away under the influence of those feminine odors which he now re-encountered, intensified by the heat under the low-pitched ceiling, he sat down on the edge of a softly padded divan between the two windows. But he got up again almost directly and, returning to the dressing table, seemed to gaze with vacant eyes into space, for he was thinking of a bouquet of tuberoses which had once faded in his bedroom and had nearly killed him in their death. When tuberoses are turning brown they have a human smell.

"Make haste!" Bordenave whispered, putting his head in behind the curtain.

The prince, however, was listening complaisantly to the Marquis de Chouard, who had taken up a hare's-foot on the dressing table and had begun explaining the way grease paint is put on. In a corner of the room Satin, with her pure, virginal face, was scanning the gentlemen keenly, while the dresser, Mme Jules by name, was getting ready Venus' tights and tunic. Mme Jules was a woman of no age. She had the parchment skin and changeless features peculiar to old maids whom no one ever knew in their younger years. She had indeed shriveled up in the burning atmosphere of the dressing rooms and amid the most famous thighs and bosoms in all Paris. She wore everlastingly a faded black dress, and on her flat and sexless chest a perfect forest of pins clustered above the spot where her heart should have been.

"I beg your pardon, gentlemen," said Nana, drawing aside the curtain, "but you took me by surprise."

They all turned round. She had not clothed herself at all, had, in fact, only buttoned on a little pair of linen stays which half revealed her bosom. When the gentlemen had put her to flight she had scarcely begun undressing and was rapidly taking off her fishwife's costume. Through the opening in her drawers behind a corner of her shift was even now visible. There she stood, bare-armed, bare-shouldered, bare-breasted, in all the adorable glory of her youth and plump, fair beauty, but she still held the curtain with one hand, as though ready to draw it to again upon the slightest provocation.

"Yes, you took me by surprise! I never shall dare——" she stammered in pretty, mock confusion, while rosy blushes crossed her neck and shoulders and smiles of embarrassment played about her lips.

"Oh, don't apologize," cried Bordenave, "since these gentlemen approve of your good looks!"

But she still tried the hesitating, innocent, girlish game, and, shivering as though someone were tickling her, she continued:

"His Highness does me too great an honor. I beg His Highness will excuse my receiving him thus——"

"It is I who am importunate," said the prince, "but, madame, I could not resist the desire of complimenting you."

Thereupon, in order to reach her dressing table, she walked very quietly and just as she was through the midst of the gentlemen, who made way for her to pass.

She had strongly marked hips, which filled her drawers out roundly, while with swelling bosom she still continued bowing and smiling her delicate little smile. Suddenly she seemed to recognize Count Muffat, and she extended her hand to him as an old friend. Then she scolded him for not having come to her supper party. His Highness deigned to chaff Muffat about this, and the latter stammered and thrilled again at the thought that for one second he had held in his own feverish clasp a little fresh and perfumed hand. The count had dined excellently at the prince's, who, indeed, was a heroic eater and drinker. Both of them were even a little intoxicated, but they behaved very creditably. To hide the commotion within him Muffat could only remark about the heat.

"Good heavens, how hot it is here!" he said. "How do you manage to live in such a temperature, madame?"

And conversation was about to ensue on this topic when noisy voices were heard at the dressing-room door. Bordenave drew back the slide over a grated peephole of the kind used in convents. Fontan was outside with Prullière and Bosc, and all three had bottles under their arms and their hands full of glasses.

He began knocking and shouting out that it was his patron saint's day and that he was standing champagne round. Nana consulted the prince with a glance. Eh! Oh dear, yes! His Highness did not want to be in anyone's way; he would be only too happy! But without waiting for permission Fontan came in, repeating in baby accents:

"Me not a cad, me pay for champagne!"

Then all of a sudden he became aware of the prince's presence of which he had been totally ignorant. He stopped short and, assuming an air of farcical solemnity, announced:

"King Dagobert is in the corridor and is desirous of drinking the health of His Royal Highness."

The prince having made answer with a smile, Fontan's sally was voted charming. But the dressing room was too small to accommodate everybody, and it became necessary to crowd up anyhow, Satin and Mme Jules standing back against the curtain at the end and the men clustering closely round the half-naked Nana. The three actors still had on the costumes they had been wearing in the second act, and while Prullière took off his Alpine admiral's cocked hat, the huge plume of which would have knocked the ceiling, Bosc, in his purple cloak and tinware crown, steadied himself on his tipsy old legs and greeted the prince as became a monarch receiving the son of a powerful neighbor. The glasses were filled, and the company began clinking them together.

"I drink to Your Highness!" said ancient Bosc royally.

"To the army!" added Prullière.

"To Venus!" cried Fontan.

The prince complaisantly poised his glass, waited quietly, bowed thrice and murmured:

"Madame! Admiral! Your Majesty!"

Then he drank it off. Count Muffat and the Marquis de Chouard had followed his example. There was no more jesting now—the company were at court. Actual life was prolonged in the life of the theater, and a sort of solemn farce was enacted under the hot flare of the gas. Nana, quite forgetting that she was in her drawers and that a corner of her shift stuck out behind, became the great lady, the queen of love, in act to open her most private palace chambers to state dignitaries. In every sentence she used the words "Royal Highness" and, bowing with the utmost conviction, treated the masqueraders, Bosc and Prullière, as if the one were a sovereign and the other his attendant minister. And no one dreamed of smiling at this strange contrast, this real prince, this heir to a throne, drinking a petty actor's champagne and taking his ease amid a carnival of gods, a masquerade of royalty, in the society of dressers and courtesans, shabby players and showmen of venal beauty. Bordenave was simply ravished by the dramatic aspects of the scene and began dreaming of the receipts which would have accrued had His Highness only consented thus to appear in the second act of the *Blonde Venus*.

"I say, shall we have our little women down?" he cried, becoming familiar.

Nana would not hear of it. But notwithstanding this, she was giving way herself. Fontan attracted her with his comic make-up. She brushed against

him and, eying him as a woman in the family way might do when she fancies
some unpleasant kind of food, she suddenly became extremely familiar:

"Now then, fill up again, ye great brute!"

Fontan charged the glasses afresh, and the company drank, repeating the
same toasts.

"To His Highness!"

"To the army!"

"To Venus!"

But with that Nana made a sign and obtained silence. She raised her glass
and cried:

"No, no! To Fontan! It's Fontan's day; to Fontan! To Fontan!"

Then they clinked glasses a third time and drank Fontan with all the honors.
The prince, who had noticed the young woman devouring the actor with her
eyes, saluted him with a "Monsieur Fontan, I drink to your success!" This
he said with his customary courtesy.

But meanwhile the tail of his highness's frock coat was sweeping the marble
of the dressing table. The place, indeed, was like an alcove or narrow bath-
room, full as it was of the steam of hot water and sponges and of the strong
scent of essences which mingled with the tartish, intoxicating fumes of the
champagne. The prince and Count Muffat, between whom Nana was wedged,
had to lift up their hands so as not to brush against her hips or her breast with
every little movement. And there stood Mme Jules, waiting, cool and rigid as
ever, while Satin, marveling in the depths of her vicious soul to see a prince
and two gentlemen in black coats going after a naked woman in the society of
dressed-up actors, secretly concluded that fashionable people were not so very
particular after all.

But Father Barillot's tinkling bell approached along the passage. At the door
of the dressing room he stood amazed when he caught sight of the three actors
still clad in the costumes which they had worn in the second act.

"Gentlemen, gentlemen," he stammered, "do please make haste. They've
just rung the bell in the public foyer."

"Bah, the public will have to wait!" said Bordenave placidly.

However, as the bottles were now empty, the comedians went upstairs to
dress after yet another interchange of civilities. Bosc, having dipped his beard
in the champagne, had taken it off, and under his venerable disguise the drunkard had suddenly reappeared. His was the haggard, empurpled face of the old
actor who has taken to drink. At the foot of the stairs he was heard remarking
to Fontan in his boozy voice:

"I pulverized him, eh?"

He was alluding to the prince.

In Nana's dressing room none now remained save His Highness, the count
and the marquis. Bordenave had withdrawn with Barillot, whom he advised not
to knock without first letting Madame know.

"You will excuse me, gentlemen?" asked Nana, again setting to work to
make up her arms and face, of which she was now particularly careful, owing
to her nude appearance in the third act.

The prince seated himself by the Marquis de Chouard on the divan, and Count Muffat alone remained standing. In that suffocating heat the two glasses of champagne they had drunk had increased their intoxication. Satin, when she saw the gentlemen thus closeting themselves with her friend, had deemed it discreet to vanish behind the curtain, where she sat waiting on a trunk, much annoyed at being compelled to remain motionless, while Mme Jules came and went quietly without word or look.

"You sang your numbers marvelously," said the prince.

And with that they began a conversation, but their sentences were short and their pauses frequent. Nana, indeed, was not always able to reply. After rubbing cold cream over her arms and face with the palm of her hand she laid on the grease paint with the corner of a towel. For one second only she ceased looking in the glass and smilingly stole a glance at the prince.

"His Highness is spoiling me," she murmured without putting down the grease paint.

Her task was a complicated one, and the Marquis de Chouard followed it with an expression of devout enjoyment. He spoke in his turn.

"Could not the band accompany you more softly?" he said. "It drowns your voice, and that's an unpardonable crime."

This time Nana did not turn round. She had taken up the hare's-foot and was lightly manipulating it. All her attention was concentrated on this action, and she bent forward over her toilet table so very far that the white round contour of her drawers and the little patch of chemise stood out with the unwonted tension. But she was anxious to prove that she appreciated the old man's compliment and therefore made a little swinging movement with her hips.

Silence reigned. Mme Jules had noticed a tear in the right leg of her drawers. She took a pin from over her heart and for a second or so knelt on the ground, busily at work about Nana's leg, while the young woman, without seeming to notice her presence, applied the rice powder, taking extreme pains, as she did so, to avoid putting any on the upper part of her cheeks. But when the prince remarked that if she were to come and sing in London all England would want to applaud her, she laughed amiably and turned round for a moment with her left cheek looking very white amid a perfect cloud of powder. Then she became suddenly serious, for she had come to the operation of rouging. And with her face once more close to the mirror, she dipped her finger in a jar and began applying the rouge below her eyes and gently spreading it back toward her temples. The gentlemen maintained a respectful silence.

Count Muffat, indeed, had not yet opened his lips. He was thinking perforce of his own youth. The bedroom of his childish days had been quite cold, and later, when he had reached the age of sixteen and would give his mother a good-night kiss every evening, he used to carry the icy feeling of the embrace into the world of dreams. One day in passing a half-open door he had caught sight of a maidservant washing herself, and that was the solitary recollection which had in any way troubled his peace of mind from the days of puberty till the time of marriage. Afterward he had found his wife strictly obedient to her conjugal duties but had himself felt a species of religious dislike to them.

He had grown to man's estate and was now aging, in ignorance of the flesh, in the humble observance of rigid devotional practices and in obedience to a rule of life full of precepts and moral laws. And now suddenly he was dropped down in this actress's dressing room in the presence of this undraped courtesan.

He, who had never seen the Countess Muffat putting on her garters, was witnessing, amid that wild disarray of jars and basins and that strong, sweet perfume, the intimate details of a woman's toilet. His whole being was in turmoil; he was terrified by the stealthy, all-pervading influence which for some time past Nana's presence had been exercising over him, and he recalled to mind the pious accounts of diabolic possession which had amused his early years. He was a believer in the devil, and, in a confused kind of way, Nana was he, with her laughter and her bosom and her hips, which seemed swollen with many vices. But he promised himself that he would be strong—nay, he would know how to defend himself.

"Well then, it's agreed," said the prince, lounging quite comfortably on the divan. "You will come to London next year, and we shall receive you so cordially that you will never return to France again. Ah, my dear Count, you don't value your pretty women enough. We shall take them all from you!"

"That won't make much odds to him," murmured the Marquis de Chouard wickedly, for he occasionally said a risky thing among friends. "The count is virtue itself."

Hearing his virtue mentioned, Nana looked at him so comically that Muffat felt a keen twinge of annoyance. But directly afterward he was surprised and angry with himself. Why, in the presence of this courtesan, should the idea of being virtuous embarrass him? He could have struck her. But in attempting to take up a brush Nana had just let it drop on the ground, and as she stooped to pick it up he rushed forward. Their breath mingled for one moment, and the loosened tresses of Venus flowed over his hands. But remorse mingled with his enjoyment, a kind of enjoyment, moreover, peculiar to good Catholics, whom the fear of hell torments in the midst of their sin.

At this moment Father Barillot's voice was heard outside the door.

"May I give the knocks, madame? The house is growing impatient."

"All in good time," answered Nana quietly.

She had dipped her paint brush in a pot of kohl, and with the point of her nose close to the glass and her left eye closed she passed it delicately along between her eyelashes. Muffat stood behind her, looking on. He saw her reflection in the mirror, with her rounded shoulders and her bosom half hidden by a rosy shadow. And despite all his endeavors he could not turn away his gaze from that face so merry with dimples and so worn with desire, which the closed eye rendered more seductive. When she shut her right eye and passed the brush along it he understood that he belonged to her.

"They are stamping their feet, madame," the callboy once more cried. "They'll end by smashing the seats. May I give the knocks?"

"Oh, bother!" said Nana impatiently. "Knock away; I don't care! If I'm not ready, well, they'll have to wait for me!"

She grew calm again and, turning to the gentlemen, added with a smile: "It's true: we've only got a minute left for our talk."

Her face and arms were now finished, and with her fingers she put two large dabs of carmine on her lips. Count Muffat felt more excited than ever. He was ravished by the perverse transformation wrought by powders and paints and filled by a lawless yearning for those young painted charms, for the too-red mouth and the too-white face and the exaggerated eyes, ringed round with black and burning and dying for very love. Meanwhile Nana went behind the curtain for a second or two in order to take off her drawers and slip on Venus' tights. After which, with tranquil immodesty, she came out and undid her little linen stays and held out her arms to Mme Jules, who drew the short-sleeved tunic over them.

"Make haste; they're growing angry!" she muttered.

The prince with half-closed eyes marked the swelling lines of her bosom with an air of connoisseurship, while the Marquis de Chouard wagged his head involuntarily. Muffat gazed at the carpet in order not to see any more. At length Venus, with only her gauze veil over her shoulders, was ready to go on the stage. Mme Jules, with vacant, unconcerned eyes and an expression suggestive of a little elderly wooden doll, still kept circling round her. With brisk movements she took pins out of the inexhaustible pincushion over her heart and pinned up Venus' tunic, but as she ran over all those plump nude charms with her shriveled hands, nothing was suggested to her. She was as one whom her sex does not concern.

"There!" said the young woman, taking a final look at herself in the mirror.

Bordenave was back again. He was anxious and said the third act had begun.

"Very well! I'm coming," replied Nana. "Here's a pretty fuss! Why, it's usually I that waits for the others."

The gentlemen left the dressing room, but they did not say good-by, for the prince had expressed a desire to assist behind the scenes at the performance of the third act. Left alone, Nana seemed greatly surprised and looked round her in all directions.

"Where can she be?" she queried.

She was searching for Satin. When she had found her again, waiting on her trunk behind the curtain, Satin quietly replied:

"Certainly I didn't want to be in your way with all those men there!"

And she added further that she was going now. But Nana held her back. What a silly girl she was! Now that Bordenave had agreed to take her on! Why, the bargain was to be struck after the play was over! Satin hesitated. There were too many bothers; she was out of her element! Nevertheless, she stayed.

As the prince was coming down the little wooden staircase a strange sound of smothered oaths and stamping, scuffling feet became audible on the other side of the theater. The actors waiting for their cues were being scared by quite a serious episode. For some seconds past Mignon had been renewing his jokes and smothering Fauchery with caresses. He had at last invented a little game of a novel kind and had begun flicking the other's nose in order, as he phrased it, to keep the flies off him. This kind of game naturally diverted the actors to any extent.

But success had suddenly thrown Mignon off his balance. He had launched forth into extravagant courses and had given the journalist a box on the ear, an actual, a vigorous, box on the ear. This time he had gone too far: in the presence of so many spectators it was impossible for Fauchery to pocket such a blow with laughing equanimity. Whereupon the two men had desisted from their farce, had sprung at one another's throats, their faces livid with hate, and were now rolling over and over behind a set of side lights, pounding away at each other as though they weren't breakable.

"Monsieur Bordenave, Monsieur Bordenave!" said the stage manager, coming up in a terrible flutter.

Bordenave made his excuses to the prince and followed him. When he recognized Fauchery and Mignon in the men on the floor he gave vent to an expression of annoyance. They had chosen a nice time, certainly, with His Highness on the other side of the scenery and all that houseful of people who might have overheard the row! To make matters worse, Rose Mignon arrived out of breath at the very moment she was due on the stage. Vulcan, indeed, was giving her the cue, but Rose stood rooted to the ground, marveling at sight of her husband and her lover as they lay wallowing at her feet, strangling one another, kicking, tearing their hair out and whitening their coats with dust. They barred the way. A sceneshifter had even stopped Fauchery's hat just when the devilish thing was going to bound onto the stage in the middle of the struggle. Meanwhile Vulcan, who had been gagging away to amuse the audience, gave Rose her cue a second time. But she stood motionless, still gazing at the two men.

"Oh, don't look at *them!*" Bordenave furiously whispered to her. "Go on the stage; go on, do! It's no business of yours! Why, you're missing your cue!"

And with a push from the manager, Rose stepped over the prostrate bodies and found herself in the flare of the footlights and in the presence of the audience. She had quite failed to understand why they were fighting on the floor behind her. Trembling from head to foot and with a humming in her ears, she came down to the footlights, Diana's sweet, amorous smile on her lips, and attacked the opening lines of her duet with so feeling a voice that the public gave her a veritable ovation.

Behind the scenery she could hear the dull thuds caused by the two men. They had rolled down to the wings, but fortunately the music covered the noise made by their feet as they kicked against them.

"By God!" yelled Bordenave in exasperation when at last he had succeeded in separating them. "Why couldn't you fight at home? You know as well as I do that I don't like this sort of thing. You, Mignon, you'll do me the pleasure of staying over here on the prompt side, and you, Fauchery, if you leave the O.P. side I'll chuck you out of the theater. You understand, eh? Prompt side and O.P. side or I forbid Rose to bring you here at all."

When he returned to the prince's presence the latter asked what was the matter.

"Oh, nothing at all," he murmured quietly.

Nana was standing wrapped in furs, talking to these gentlemen while await-ing her cue. As Count Muffat was coming up in order to peep between two of the wings at the stage, he understood from a sign made him by the stage manager that he was to step softly. Drowsy warmth was streaming down from the flies, and in the wings, which were lit by vivid patches of light, only a few people remained, talking in low voices or making off on tiptoe. The gasman was at his post amid an intricate arrangement of cocks; a fireman, leaning against the side lights, was craning forward, trying to catch a glimpse of things, while on his seat, high up, the curtain man was watching with resigned expression, careless of the play, constantly on the alert for the bell to ring him to his duty among the ropes. And amid the close air and the shuffling of feet and the sound of whispering, the voices of the actors on the stage sounded strange, deadened, surprisingly discordant. Farther off again, above the con-fused noises of the band, a vast breathing sound was audible. It was the breath of the house, which sometimes swelled up till it burst in vague rumors, in laughter, in applause. Though invisible, the presence of the public could be felt, even in the silences.

"There's something open," said Nana sharply, and with that she tightened the folds of her fur cloak. "Do look, Barillot. I bet they've just opened a window. Why, one might catch one's death of cold here!"

Barillot swore that he had closed every window himself but suggested that possibly there were broken panes about. The actors were always complaining of drafts. Through the heavy warmth of that gaslit region blasts of cold air were constantly passing—it was a regular influenza trap, as Fontan phrased it.

"I should like to see *you* in a low-cut dress," continued Nana, growing annoyed.

"Hush!" murmured Bordenave.

On the stage Rose rendered a phrase in her duet so cleverly that the stalls burst into universal applause. Nana was silent at this, and her face grew grave. Meanwhile the count was venturing down a passage when Barillot stopped him and said he would make a discovery there. Indeed, he obtained an oblique back view of the scenery and of the wings which had been strengthened, as it were, by a thick layer of old posters. Then he caught sight of a corner of the stage, of the Etna cave hollowed out in a silver mine and of Vulcan's forge in the background. Battens, lowered from above, lit up a sparkling substance which had been laid on with large dabs of the brush. Side lights with red glasses and blue were so placed as to produce the appearance of a fiery brazier, while on the floor of the stage, in the far background, long lines of gaslight had been laid down in order to throw a wall of dark rocks into sharp relief. Hard by on a gentle, "practicable" incline, amid little points of light resem-bling the illumination lamps scattered about in the grass on the night of a public holiday, old Mme Drouard, who played Juno, was sitting dazed and sleepy, waiting for her cue.

Presently there was a commotion, for Simonne, while listening to a story Clarisse was telling her, cried out:

"My! It's the Tricon!"

It was indeed the Tricon, wearing the same old curls and looking as like a litigious great lady as ever.

When she saw Nana she went straight up to her.

"No," said the latter after some rapid phrases had been exchanged, "not now."

The old lady looked grave. Just then Prullière passed by and shook hands with her, while two little chorus girls stood gazing at her with looks of deep emotion. For a moment she seemed to hesitate. Then she beckoned to Simonne, and the rapid exchange of sentences began again.

"Yes," said Simonne at last. "In half an hour."

But as she was going upstairs again to her dressing room, Mme Bron, who was once more going the rounds with letters, presented one to her. Bordenave lowered his voice and furiously reproached the portress for having allowed the Tricon to come in. That woman! And on such an evening of all others! It made him so angry because His Highness was there! Mme Bron, who had been thirty years in the theater, replied quite sourly. How was she to know? she asked. The Tricon did business with all the ladies—M. le Directeur had met her a score of times without making remarks. And while Bordenave was muttering oaths the Tricon stood quietly by, scrutinizing the prince as became a woman who weighs a man at a glance. A smile lit up her yellow face. Presently she paced slowly off through the crowd of deeply deferential little women.

"Immediately, eh?" she queried, turning round again to Simonne.

Simonne seemed much worried. The letter was from a young man to whom she had engaged herself for that evening. She gave Mme Bron a scribbled note in which were the words, "Impossible tonight, darling—I'm booked." But she was still apprehensive; the young man might possibly wait for her in spite of everything. As she was not playing in the third act, she had a mind to be off at once and accordingly begged Clarisse to go and see if the man were there. Clarisse was only due on the stage toward the end of the act, and so she went downstairs while Simonne ran up for a minute to their common dressing room.

In Mme Bron's drinking bar downstairs a super, who was charged with the part of Pluto, was drinking in solitude amid the folds of a great red robe diapered with golden flames. The little business plied by the good portress must have been progressing finely, for the cellarlike hole under the stairs was wet with emptied heeltaps and water. Clarisse picked up the tunic of Iris, which was dragging over the greasy steps behind her, but she halted prudently at the turn in the stairs and was content simply to crane forward and peer into the lodge. She certainly had been quick to scent things out! Just fancy! That idiot La Faloise was still there, sitting on the same old chair between the table and the stove! He had made pretense of sneaking off in front of Simonne and had returned after her departure. For the matter of that, the lodge was still full of gentlemen who sat there gloved, elegant, submissive and patient as ever. They were all waiting and viewing each other gravely as they waited. On the table there were now only some dirty plates, Mme Bron having recently distributed the last of the bouquets. A single fallen rose was withering on the floor in the neighborhood of the black cat, who had lain down and curled herself up while the kittens ran wild races and danced fierce gallops among the gentlemen's legs. Clarisse was momentarily inclined to turn La Faloise out. The idiot wasn't fond of animals, and that put the finishing touch to him! He was busy drawing in his legs because the cat was there, and he didn't want to touch her.

"He'll nip you; take care!" said Pluto, who was a joker, as he went upstairs, wiping his mouth with the back of his hand.

After that Clarisse gave up the idea of hauling La Faloise over the coals. She had seen Mme Bron giving the letter to Simonne's young man, and he had gone out to read it under the gas light in the lobby. "Impossible tonight, darling —I'm booked." And with that he had peaceably departed, as one who was doubtless used to the formula. He, at any rate, knew how to conduct himself! Not so the others, the fellows who sat there doggedly on Mme Bron's battered straw-bottomed chairs under the great glazed lantern, where the heat was enough to roast you and there was an unpleasant odor. What a lot of men it must have held! Clarisse went upstairs again in disgust, crossed over behind scenes and nimbly mounted three flights of steps which led to the dressing rooms, in order to bring Simonne her reply.

Downstairs the prince had withdrawn from the rest and stood talking to Nana. He never left her; he stood brooding over her through half-shut eyelids. Nana did not look at him but, smiling, nodded yes. Suddenly, however, Count Muffat obeyed an overmastering impulse, and leaving Bordenave, who was explaining to him the working of the rollers and windlasses, he came up in order to interrupt their confabulations. Nana lifted her eyes and smiled at him as she smiled at His Highness. But she kept her ears open notwithstanding, for she was waiting for her cue.

"The third act is the shortest, I believe," the prince began saying, for the count's presence embarrassed him.

She did not answer; her whole expression altered; she was suddenly intent on her business. With a rapid movement of the shoulders she had let her furs slip from her, and Mme Jules, standing behind, had caught them in her arms. And then after passing her two hands to her hair as though to make it fast, she went on the stage in all her nudity.

"Hush, hush!" whispered Bordenave.

The count and the prince had been taken by surprise. There was profound silence, and then a deep sigh and the far-off murmur of a multitude became audible. Every evening when Venus entered in her godlike nakedness the same effect was produced. Then Muffat was seized with a desire to see; he put his eye to the peephole. Above and beyond the glowing arc formed by the foot-lights the dark body of the house seemed full of ruddy vapor, and against this neutral-tinted background, where row upon row of faces struck a pale, un-certain note, Nana stood forth white and vast, so that the boxes from the bal-cony to the flies were blotted from view. He saw her from behind, noted her swelling hips, her outstretched arms, while down on the floor, on the same level as her feet, the prompter's head—an old man's head with a humble, honest face—stood on the edge of the stage, looking as though it had been severed from the body. At certain points in her opening number an undulating movement seemed to run from her neck to her waist and to die out in the trailing border of her tunic. When amid a tempest of applause she had sung her last note she bowed, and the gauze floated forth round about her limbs, and her hair swept over her waist as she bent sharply backward. And seeing her thus, as with bending form and with exaggerated hips she came backing toward the count's peephole, he stood upright again, and his face was very white. The stage had disappeared, and he now saw only the reverse side of the scenery with its display of old posters pasted up in every direction. On the practicable slope, among the lines of gas jets, the whole of Olympus had rejoined the dozing Mme Drouard. They were waiting for the close of the act. Bosc and Fontan sat on the floor with their knees drawn up to their chins, and Prullière stretched himself and yawned before going on. Everybody was worn out; their eyes were red, and they were longing to go home to sleep.

Just then Fauchery, who had been prowling about on the O.P. side ever since Bordenave had forbidden him the other, came and buttonholed the count in order to keep himself in countenance and offered at the same time to show him the dressing rooms. An increasing sense of languor had left Muffat without any power of resistance, and after looking round for the Marquis de Chouard, who had disappeared, he ended by following the journalist. He experienced a mingled feeling of relief and anxiety as he left the wings whence he had been listening to Nana's songs.

Fauchery had already preceded him up the staircase, which was closed on the first and second floors by low-paneled doors. It was one of those stairways which you find in miserable tenements. Count Muffat had seen many such during his rounds as member of the Benevolent Organization. It was bare and dilapidated: there was a wash of yellow paint on its walls; its steps had been worn by the incessant passage of feet, and its iron balustrade had grown smooth under the friction of many hands. On a level with the floor on every stairhead there was a low window which resembled a deep, square venthole, while in lanterns fastened to the walls flaring gas jets crudely illuminated the surrounding squalor and gave out a glowing heat which, as it mounted up the narrow stairwell, grew ever more intense.

When he reached the foot of the stairs the count once more felt the hot breath upon his neck and shoulders. As of old it was laden with the odor of women, wafted amid floods of light and sound from the dressing rooms above, and now with every upward step he took the musky scent of powders and the tart perfume of toilet vinegars heated and bewildered him more and more. On the first floor two corridors ran backward, branching sharply off and presenting a set of doors to view which were painted yellow and numbered with great white numerals in such a way as to suggest a hotel with a bad reputation. The tiles on the floor had been many of them unbedded, and the old house being in a state of subsidence, they stuck up like hummocks. The count dashed recklessly forward, glanced through a half-open door and saw a very dirty room which resembled a barber's shop in a poor part of the town. In was furnished with two chairs, a mirror and a small table containing a drawer which had been blackened by the grease from brushes and combs. A great perspiring fellow with smoking shoulders was changing his linen there, while in a similar room next door a woman was drawing on her gloves preparatory to departure. Her hair was damp and out of curl, as though she had just had a bath. But Fauchery began calling the count, and the latter was rushing up without delay when a furious "damn!" burst from the corridor on the right. Mathilde, a little drab of a miss, had just broken her washhand basin, the soapy water from which was flowing out to the stairhead. A dressing room door banged noisily. Two women in their stays skipped across the passage, and another, with the hem of her shift in her mouth, appeared and immediately vanished from view. Then followed a sound of laughter, a dispute, the snatch of a song which was suddenly broken off short. All along the passage naked gleams, sudden visions of white skin and wan underlinen were observable through chinks in doorways. Two girls were making very merry, showing each other their birthmarks. One of them, a very young girl, almost a child, had drawn her skirts up over her knees in order to sew up a rent in her drawers, and the dressers, catching sight of the two men, drew some curtains half to for decency's sake. The wild stampede which follows the end of a play had already begun, the grand removal of white paint and rouge, the reassumption amid clouds of rice powder of ordinary attire. The strange animal scent came in whiffs of redoubled intensity through the lines of banging doors. On the third story Muffat abandoned himself to the feeling of intoxication which was overpowering him. For the chorus girls' dressing room was there, and you saw a crowd of twenty women and a wild display of soaps and flasks of lavender water. The place resembled the common room in a slum lodging house. As he passed by he heard fierce sounds of washing behind a closed door and a perfect storm raging in a washhand basin. And as he was mounting up to the topmost story of all, curiosity led him to risk one more little peep through an open loophole. The room was empty, and under the flare of the gas a solitary chamber pot stood forgotten among a heap of petticoats trailing on the floor. This room afforded him his ultimate impression. Upstairs on the fourth floor he was well-nigh suffocated. All the scents, all the blasts of heat, had found their goal there. The yellow ceiling looked as if it had been baked, and a lamp burned amid fumes of russet-colored fog. For some seconds he leaned upon the iron balustrade which felt warm and damp and well-nigh human to the touch. And he shut his eyes and drew a long breath and drank in the sexual atmosphere of the place. Hitherto he had been utterly ignorant of it, but now it beat full in his face.

"Do come here," shouted Fauchery, who had vanished some moments ago. "You're being asked for."

At the end of the corridor was the dressing room belonging to Clarisse and Simonne. It was a long, ill-built room under the roof with a garret ceiling and sloping walls. The light penetrated to it from two deep-set openings high up in the wall, but at that hour of the night the dressing room was lit by flaring gas. It was papered with a paper at seven sous a roll with a pattern of roses twining over green trelliswork. Two boards, placed near one another and covered with oilcloth, did duty for dressing tables. They were black with spilled water, and underneath them was a fine medley of dinted zinc jugs, slop pails and coarse yellow earthenware crocks. There was an array of fancy articles in the room— a battered, soiled and well-worn array of chipped basins, of toothless combs, of all those manifold untidy trifles which, in their hurry and carelessness, two women will leave scattered about when they undress and wash together amid purely temporary surroundings, the dirty aspect of which has ceased to concern them.

"Do come here," Fauchery repeated with the good-humored familiarity which men adopt among their fallen sisters. "Clarisse is wanting to kiss you."

Muffat entered the room at last. But what was his surprise when he found the Marquis de Chouard snugly ensconced on a chair between the two dressing tables! The marquis had withdrawn thither some time ago. He was spreading his feet apart because a pail was leaking and letting a whitish flood spread over the floor. He was visibly much at his ease, as became a man who knew all the snug corners, and had grown quite merry in the close dressing room, where people might have been bathing, and amid those quietly immodest feminine surroundings which the uncleanness of the little place rendered at once natural and poignant.

"D'you go with the old boy?" Simonne asked Clarisse in a whisper.

"Rather!" replied the latter aloud.

The dresser, a very ugly and extremely familiar young girl, who was helping Simonne into her coat, positively writhed with laughter. The three pushed each other and babbled little phrases which redoubled their merriment.

"Come, Clarisse, kiss the gentleman," said Fauchery. "You know, he's got the rhino."

And turning to the count:

"You'll see, she's very nice! She's going to kiss you!"

But Clarisse was disgusted by the men. She spoke in violent terms of the dirty lot waiting at the porter's lodge down below. Besides, she was in a hurry to go downstairs again; they were making her miss her last scene. Then as Fauchery blocked up the doorway, she gave Muffat a couple of kisses on the whiskers, remarking as she did so:

"It's not for you, at any rate! It's for that nuisance Fauchery!"

And with that she darted off, and the count remained much embarrassed in his father-in-law's presence. The blood had rushed to his face. In Nana's dressing room, amid all the luxury of hangings and mirrors, he had not experienced the sharp physical sensation which the shameful wretchedness of that sorry garret excited within him, redolent as it was of these two girls' self-abandonment. Meanwhile the marquis had hurried in the rear of Simonne, who was making off at the top of her pace, and he kept whispering in her ear while she shook her head in token of refusal. Fauchery followed them, laughing. And with that the count found himself alone with the dresser, who was washing out the basins. Accordingly he took his departure, too, his legs almost failing under him. Once more he put up flights of half-dressed women and caused doors to bang as he advanced. But amid the disorderly, disbanded troops of girls to be found on each of the four stories, he was only distinctly aware of a cat, a great tortoise-shell cat, which went gliding upstairs through the ovenlike place where the air was poisoned with musk, rubbing its back against the banisters and keeping its tail exceedingly erect.

"Yes, to be sure!" said a woman hoarsely. "I thought they'd keep us back tonight! What a nuisance they are with their calls!"

The end had come; the curtain had just fallen. There was a veritable stampede on the staircase—its walls rang with exclamations, and everyone was in a savage hurry to dress and be off. As Count Muffat came down the last step or two he saw Nana and the prince passing slowly along the passage. The young woman halted and lowered her voice as she said with a smile:

"All right then—by and by!"

The prince returned to the stage, where Bordenave was awaiting him. And left alone with Nana, Muffat gave way to an impulse of anger and desire. He ran up behind her and, as she was on the point of entering her dressing room, imprinted a rough kiss on her neck among little golden hairs curling low down between her shoulders. It was as though he had returned the kiss that had been given him upstairs. Nana was in a fury; she lifted her hand, but when she recognized the count she smiled.

"Oh, you frightened me," she said simply.

And her smile was adorable in its embarrassment and submissiveness, as though she had despaired of this kiss and were happy to have received it. But she could do nothing for him either that evening or the day after. It was a case of waiting. Nay, even if it had been in her power she would still have let herself be desired. Her glance said as much. At length she continued:

"I'm a landowner, you know. Yes, I'm buying a country house near Orleans, in a part of the world to which you sometimes betake yourself. Baby told me you did—little Georges Hugon, I mean. You know him? So come and see me down there."

The count was a shy man, and the thought of his roughness had frightened him; he was ashamed of what he had done and he bowed ceremoniously, promising at the same time to take advantage of her invitation. Then he walked off as one who dreams.

He was rejoining the prince when, passing in front of the foyer, he heard Satin screaming out:

"Oh, the dirty old thing! Just you bloody well leave me alone!"

It was the Marquis de Chouard who was tumbling down over Satin. The girl had decidedly had enough of the fashionable world! Nana had certainly introduced her to Bordenave, but the necessity of standing with sealed lips for fear of allowing some awkward phrase to escape her had been too much for her feelings, and now she was anxious to regain her freedom, the more so as she had run against an old flame of hers in the wings. This was the super, to whom the task of impersonating Pluto had been entrusted, a pastry cook, who had already treated her to a whole week of love and flagellation. She was waiting for him, much irritated at the things the marquis was saying to her, as though she were one of those theatrical ladies! And so at last she assumed a highly respectable expression and jerked out this phrase:

"My husband's coming! You'll see."

Meanwhile the worn-looking artistes were dropping off one after the other in their outdoor coats. Groups of men and women were coming down the little winding staircase, and the outlines of battered hats and worn-out shawls were visible in the shadows. They looked colorless and unlovely, as became poor play actors who have got rid of their paint. On the stage, where the side lights and battens were being extinguished, the prince was listening to an anecdote Bordenave was telling him. He was waiting for Nana, and when at length she made her appearance the stage was dark, and the fireman on duty was finishing his round, lantern in hand. Bordenave, in order to save His Highness going about by the Passage des Panoramas, had made them open the corridor which led from the porter's lodge to the entrance hall of the theater. Along this narrow alley little women were racing pell-mell, for they were delighted to escape from the men who were waiting for them in the other passage. They went jostling and elbowing along, casting apprehensive glances behind them and only breathing freely when they got outside. Fontan, Bosc and Prullière, on the other hand, retired at a leisurely pace, joking at the figure cut by the serious, paying admirers who were striding up and down the Galerie des Variétés at a time when the little dears were escaping along the boulevard with the men of their hearts. But Clarisse was especially sly. She had her suspicions about La Faloise, and, as a matter of fact, he was still in his place in the lodge among the gentlemen obstinately waiting on Mme Bron's chairs. They all stretched forward, and with that she passed brazenly by in the wake of a friend. The gentlemen were blinking in bewilderment over the wild whirl of petticoats eddying at the foot of the narrow stairs. It made them desperate to think they had waited so long, only to see them all flying away like this without being able to recognize a single one. The litter of little black cats were sleeping on the oilcloth, nestled against their mother's belly, and the latter was stretching her paws out in a state of beatitude while the big tortoise-shell cat sat at the other end of the table, her tail stretched out behind her and her yellow eyes solemnly following the flight of the women.

"If His Highness will be good enough to come this way," said Bordenave at the bottom of the stairs, and he pointed to the passage.

Some chorus girls were still crowding along it. The prince began following Nana while Muffat and the marquis walked behind.

It was a long, narrow passage lying between the theater and the house next door, a kind of contracted by-lane which had been covered with a sloping glass roof. Damp oozed from the walls, and the footfall sounded as hollow on the tiled floor as in an underground vault. It was crowded with the kind of rubbish usually found in a garret. There was a workbench on which the porter was wont to plane such parts of the scenery as required it, besides a pile of wooden barriers which at night were placed at the doors of the theater for the purpose of regulating the incoming stream of people. Nana had to pick up her dress as she passed a hydrant which, through having been carelessly turned off, was flooding the tiles underfoot. In the entrance hall the company bowed and said good-by. And when Bordenave was alone he summed up his opinion of the prince in a shrug of eminently philosophic disdain.

"He's a bit of a duffer all the same," he said to Fauchery without entering on further explanations, and with that Rose Mignon carried the journalist off with her husband in order to effect a reconciliation between them at home.

Muffat was left alone on the sidewalk. His Highness had handed Nana quietly into his carriage, and the marquis had slipped off after Satin and her super. In his excitement he was content to follow this vicious pair in vague hopes of some stray favor being granted him. Then with brain on fire Muffat decided to walk home. The struggle within him had wholly ceased. The ideas and beliefs of the last forty years were being drowned in a flood of new life. While he was passing along the boulevards the roll of the last carriages deafened him with the name of Nana; the gaslights set nude limbs dancing before his eyes—the nude limbs, the lithe arms, the white shoulders, of Nana. And he felt that he was hers utterly: he would have abjured everything, sold everything, to possess her for a single hour that very night. Youth, a lustful puberty of early manhood, was stirring within him at last, flaming up suddenly in the chaste heart of the Catholic and amid the dignified traditions of middle age.

CHAPTER VI

COUNT MUFFAT, accompanied by his wife and daughter, had arrived overnight at Les Fondettes, where Mme Hugon, who was staying there with only her son Georges, had invited them to come and spend a week. The house, which had been built at the end of the eighteenth century, stood in the middle of a huge square enclosure. It was perfectly unadorned, but the garden possessed magnificent shady trees and a chain of tanks fed by running spring water. It stood at the side of the road which leads from Orleans to Paris and with its rich verdure and high-embowered trees broke the monotony of that flat countryside, where fields stretched to the horizon's verge.

At eleven o'clock, when the second lunch bell had called the whole household together, Mme Hugon, smiling in her kindly maternal way, gave Sabine two great kisses, one on each cheek, and said as she did so:

"You know it's my custom in the country. Oh, seeing you here makes me feel twenty years younger. Did you sleep well in your old room?"

Then without waiting for her reply she turned to Estelle:

"And this little one, has she had a nap too? Give me a kiss, my child."

They had taken their seats in the vast dining room, the windows of which looked out on the park. But they only occupied one end of the long table, where they sat somewhat crowded together for company's sake. Sabine, in high good spirits, dwelt on various childish memories which had been stirred up within her—memories of months passed at Les Fondettes, of long walks, of a tumble into one of the tanks on a summer evening, of an old romance of chivalry discovered by her on the top of a cupboard and read during the winter before fires made of vine branches. And Georges, who had not seen the countess for some months, thought there was something curious about her. Her face seemed changed, somehow, while, on the other hand, that stick of an Estelle seemed more insignificant and dumb and awkward than ever.

While such simple fare as cutlets and boiled eggs was being discussed by the company, Mme Hugon, as became a good housekeeper, launched out into complaints. The butchers, she said, were becoming impossible. She bought everything at Orleans, and yet they never brought her the pieces she asked for. Yet, alas, if her guests had nothing worth eating it was their own fault: they had come too late in the season.

"There's no sense in it," she said. "I've been expecting you since June, and now we're half through September. You see, it doesn't look pretty."

And with a movement she pointed to the trees on the grass outside, the leaves of which were beginning to turn yellow. The day was covered, and the distance was hidden by a bluish haze which was fraught with a sweet and melancholy peacefulness.

"Oh, I'm expecting company," she continued. "We shall be gayer then! The first to come will be two gentlemen whom Georges has invited—Monsieur Fauchery and Monsieur Daguenet; you know them, do you not? Then we shall have Monsieur de Vandeuvres, who has promised me a visit these five years past. This time, perhaps, he'll make up his mind!"

"Oh, well and good!" said the countess, laughing. "If we only can get Monsieur de Vandeuvres! But he's too much engaged."

"And Philippe?" queried Muffat.

"Philippe has asked for a furlough," replied the old lady, "but without doubt you won't be at Les Fondettes any longer when he arrives."

The coffee was served. Paris was now the subject of conversation, and Steiner's name was mentioned, at which Mme Hugon gave a little cry.

"Let me see," she said; "Monsieur Steiner is that stout man I met at your house one evening. He's a banker, is he not? Now there's a detestable man for you! Why, he's gone and bought an actress an estate about a league from here, over Gumières way, beyond the Choue. The whole countryside's scandalized. Did you know about that, my friend?"

"I knew nothing about it," replied Muffat. "Ah, then, Steiner's bought a country place in the neighborhood!"

Hearing his mother broach the subject, Georges looked into his coffee cup, but in his astonishment at the count's answer he glanced up at him and stared. Why was he lying so glibly? The count, on his side, noticed the young fellow's movement and gave him a suspicious glance. Mme Hugon continued to go into details: the country place was called La Mignotte. In order to get there one had to go up the bank of the Choue as far as Gumières in order to cross the bridge; otherwise one got one's feet wet and ran the risk of a ducking.

"And what is the actress's name?" asked the countess.

"Oh, I wasn't told," murmured the old lady. "Georges, you were there the morning the gardener spoke to us about it."

Georges appeared to rack his brains. Muffat waited, twirling a teaspoon between his fingers. Then the countess addressed her husband:

"Isn't Monsieur Steiner with that singer at the Variétés, that Nana?"

"Nana, that's the name! A horrible woman!" cried Mme Hugon with growing annoyance. "And they are expecting her at La Mignotte. I've heard all about it from the gardener. Didn't the gardener say they were expecting her this evening, Georges?"

The count gave a little start of astonishment, but Georges replied with much vivacity:

"Oh, Mother, the gardener spoke without knowing anything about it. Directly afterward the coachman said just the opposite. Nobody's expected at La Mignotte before the day after tomorrow."

He tried hard to assume a natural expression while he slyly watched the effect of his remarks on the count. The latter was twirling his spoon again as though reassured. The countess, her eyes fixed dreamily on the blue distances of the park, seemed to have lost all interest in the conversation. The shadow of a smile on her lips, she seemed to be following up a secret thought which had been suddenly awakened within her. Estelle, on the other hand, sitting stiffly on her chair, had heard all that had been said about Nana, but her white, virginal face had not betrayed a trace of emotion.

"Dear me, dear me! I've got no right to grow angry," murmured Mme Hugon after a pause, and with a return to her old good humor she added: "Everybody's got a right to live. If we meet this said lady on the road we shall not bow to her—that's all!"

And as they got up from table she once more gently upbraided the Countess Sabine for having been so long in coming to her that year. But the countess defended herself and threw the blame of the delays upon her husband's shoulders. Twice on the eve of departure, when all the trunks were locked, he counterordered their journey on the plea of urgent business. Then he had suddenly decided to start just when the trip seemed shelved. Thereupon the old lady told them how Georges in the same way had twice announced his arrival without arriving and had finally cropped up at Les Fondettes the day before yesterday, when she was no longer expecting him. They had come down into the garden, and the two men, walking beside the ladies, were listening to them in consequential silence.

"Never mind," said Mme Hugon, kissing her son's sunny locks, "Zizi is a very good boy to come and bury himself in the country with his mother. He's a dear Zizi not to forget me!"

In the afternoon she expressed some anxiety, for Georges, directly after leaving the table, had complained of a heavy feeling in his head and now seemed in for an atrocious sick headache. Toward four o'clock he said he would go upstairs to bed: it was the only remedy. After sleeping till tomorrow morning he would be perfectly himself again. His mother was bent on putting him to bed herself, but as she left the room he ran and locked the door, explaining that he was shutting himself in so that no one should come and disturb him. Then caressingly he shouted, "Good night till tomorrow, little Mother!" and promised to take a nap. But he did not go to bed again and with flushed cheeks and bright eyes noiselessly put on his clothes. Then he sat on a chair and waited. When the dinner bell rang he listened for Count Muffat, who was on his way to the dining room, and ten minutes later, when he was certain that no one would see him, he slipped from the window to the ground with the assistance of a rain pipe. His bedroom was situated on the first floor and looked out upon the rear of the house. He threw himself among some bushes and got out of the park and then galloped across the fields with empty stomach and heart beating with excitement. Night was closing in, and a small fine rain was beginning to fall.

It was the very evening that Nana was due at La Mignotte. Ever since in the preceding May Steiner had bought her this country place she had from time to time been so filled with the desire of taking possession that she had wept hot tears about, but on each of these occasions Bordenave had refused to give her even the shortest leave and had deferred her holiday till September on the plea that he did not intend putting an understudy in her place, even for one evening, now that the exhibition was on. Toward the close of August he spoke of October. Nana was furious and declared that she would be at La Mignotte in the middle of September. Nay, in order to dare Bordenave, she even invited a crowd of guests in his very presence. One afternoon in her rooms, as Muffat, whose advances she still adroitly resisted, was beseeching her with tremulous emotion to yield to his entreaties, she at length promised to be kind, but not in Paris, and to him, too, she named the middle of September. Then on the twelfth she was seized by a desire to be off forthwith with Zoé as her sole companion. It might be that Bordenave had got wind of her intentions and was about to discover some means of detaining her. She was delighted at the notion of putting him in a fix, and she sent him a doctor's certificate. When once the idea had entered her head of being the first to get to La Mignotte and of living there two days without anybody knowing anything about it, she rushed Zoé through the operation of packing and finally pushed her into a cab, where in a sudden burst of extreme contrition she kissed her and begged her pardon. It was only when they got to the station refreshment room that she thought of writing Steiner of her movements. She begged him to wait till the day after tomorrow before rejoining her if he wanted to find her quite bright and fresh. And then, suddenly conceiving another project, she wrote a second letter, in which she besought her aunt to bring little Louis to her at once. It would do Baby so much good! And how happy they would be together in the shade of the trees! In the railway carriage between Paris and Orleans she spoke of nothing else; her eyes were full of tears; she had an unexpected attack of maternal tenderness and mingled together flowers, birds and child in her every sentence.

La Mignotte was more than three leagues away from the station, and Nana lost a good hour over the hire of a carriage, a huge, dilapidated calash, which rumbled slowly along to an accompaniment of rattling old iron. She had at once taken possession of the coachman, a little taciturn old man whom she overwhelmed with questions. Had he often passed by La Mignotte? It was behind this hill then? There ought to be lots of trees there, eh? And the house, could one see it at a distance? The little old man answered with a succession of grunts. Down in the calash Nana was almost dancing with impatience, while Zoé, in her annoyance at having left Paris in such a hurry, sat stiffly sulking beside her. The horse suddenly stopped short, and the young woman thought they had reached their destination. She put her head out of the carriage door and asked:

"Are we there, eh?"

By way of answer the driver whipped up his horse, which was in the act of painfully climbing a hill. Nana gazed ecstatically at the vast plain beneath the gray sky where great clouds were banked up.

"Oh, do look, Zoé! There's greenery! Now, is that all wheat? Good lord, how pretty it is!"

"One can quite see that Madame doesn't come from the country," was the servant's prim and tardy rejoinder. "As for me, I knew the country only too well when I was with my dentist. He had a house at Bougival. No, it's cold, too, this evening. It's damp in these parts."

They were driving under the shadow of a wood, and Nana sniffed up the scent of the leaves as a young dog might. All of a sudden at a turn of the road she caught sight of the corner of a house among the trees. Perhaps it was there! And with that she began a conversation with the driver, who continued shaking his head by way of saying no. Then as they drove down the other side of the hill he contented himself by holding out his whip and muttering, " 'Tis down there."

She got up and stretched herself almost bodily out of the carriage door. "Where is it? Where is it?" she cried with pale cheeks, but as yet she saw nothing.

At last she caught sight of a bit of wall. And then followed a succession of little cries and jumps, the ecstatic behavior of a woman overcome by a new and vivid sensation.

"I see it! I see it, Zoé! Look out at the other side. Oh, there's a terrace with brick ornaments on the roof! And there's a hothouse down there! But the place is immense. Oh, how happy I am! Do look, Zoé! Now, do look!"

The carriage had by this time pulled up before the park gates. A side door was opened, and the gardener, a tall, dry fellow, made his appearance, cap in hand. Nana made an effort to regain her dignity, for the driver seemed now to be suppressing a laugh behind his dry, speechless lips. She refrained from setting off at a run and listened to the gardener, who was a very talkative fellow. He begged Madame to excuse the disorder in which she found everything, seeing that he had only received Madame's letter that very morning. But despite all his efforts, she flew off at a tangent and walked so quickly that Zoé could scarcely follow her. At the end of the avenue she paused for a moment in order to take the house in at a glance. It was a great pavilionlike building in the Italian manner, and it was flanked by a smaller construction, which a rich Englishman, after two years' residence in Naples, had caused to be erected and had forthwith become disgusted with.

"I'll take Madame over the house," said the gardener.

But she had outrun him entirely, and she shouted back that he was not to put himself out and that she would go over the house by herself. She preferred doing that, she said. And without removing her hat she dashed into the different rooms, calling to Zoé as she did so, shouting her impressions from one end of each corridor to the other and filling the empty house, which for long months had been uninhabited, with exclamations and bursts of laughter. In the first place, there was the hall. It was a little damp, but that didn't matter; one wasn't going to sleep in it. Then came the drawing room, quite the thing, the drawing room, with its windows opening on the lawn. Only the red upholsteries there were hideous; she would alter all that. As to the dining room—well, it was a lovely dining room, eh? What big blowouts you might give in Paris if you had a dining room as large as that! As she was going upstairs to the first floor it occurred to her that she had not seen the kitchen, and she went down again and indulged in ecstatic exclamations. Zoé ought to admire the beautiful dimensions of the sink and the width of the hearth, where you might have roasted a sheep! When she had gone upstairs again her bedroom especially enchanted her. It had been hung with delicate rose-colored Louis XVI cretonne by an Orleans upholsterer. Dear me, yes! One ought to sleep jolly sound in such a room as that; why, it was a real best bedroom! Then came four or five guest chambers and then some splendid garrets, which would be extremely convenient for trunks and boxes. Zoé looked very gruff and cast a frigid glance into each of the rooms as she lingered in Madame's wake. She saw Nana disappearing up the steep garret ladder and said, "Thanks, I haven't the least wish to break my legs." But the sound of a voice reached her from far away; indeed, it seemed to come whistling down a chimney.

"Zoé, Zoé, where are you? Come up, do! You've no idea! It's like fairyland!"

Zoé went up, grumbling. On the roof she found her mistress leaning against the brickwork balustrade and gazing at the valley which spread out into the silence. The horizon was immeasurably wide, but it was now covered by masses of gray vapor, and a fierce wind was driving fine rain before it. Nana had to hold her hat on with both hands to keep it from being blown away while her petticoats streamed out behind her, flapping like a flag.

"Not if I know it!" said Zoé, drawing her head in at once. "Madame will be blown away. What beastly weather!"

Madame did not hear what she said. With her head over the balustrade she was gazing at the grounds beneath. They consisted of seven or eight acres of land enclosed within a wall. Then the view of the kitchen garden entirely engrossed her attention. She darted back, jostling the lady's maid at the top of the stairs and bursting out:

"It's full of cabbages! Oh, such woppers! And lettuces and sorrel and onions and everything! Come along, make haste!"

The rain was falling more heavily now, and she opened her white silk sunshade and ran down the garden walks.

"Madame will catch cold," cried Zoé, who had stayed quietly behind under the awning over the garden door.

But Madame wanted to see things, and at each new discovery there was a burst of wonderment.

"Zoé, here's spinach! Do come. Oh, look at the artichokes! They are funny. So they grow in the ground, do they? Now, what can that be? I don't know it. Do come, Zoé, perhaps you know."

The lady's maid never budged an inch. Madame must really be raving mad. For now the rain was coming down in torrents, and the little white silk sunshade was already dark with it. Nor did it shelter Madame, whose skirts were wringing wet. But that didn't put her out in the smallest degree, and in the pouring rain she visited the kitchen garden and the orchard, stopping in front of every fruit tree and bending over every bed of vegetables. Then she ran and looked down the well and lifted up a frame to see what was underneath it and was lost in the contemplation of a huge pumpkin. She wanted to go along every single garden walk and to take immediate possession of all the things she had been wont to dream of in the old days, when she was a slipshod workgirl on the Paris pavements. The rain redoubled, but she never heeded it and was only miserable at the thought that the daylight was fading. She could not see clearly now and touched things with her fingers to find out what they were. Suddenly in the twilight she caught sight of a bed of strawberries, and all that was childish in her awoke.

"Strawberries! Strawberries! There are some here; I can feel them. A plate, Zoé! Come and pick strawberries."

And dropping her sunshade, Nana crouched down in the mire under the full force of the downpour. With drenched hands she began gathering the fruit among the leaves. But Zoé in the meantime brought no plate, and when the young woman rose to her feet again she was frightened. She thought she had seen a shadow close to her.

"It's some beast!" she screamed.

But she stood rooted to the path in utter amazement. It was a man, and she recognized him.

"Gracious me, it's Baby! What *are* you doing there, baby?"

" 'Gad, I've come—that's all!" replied Georges.

Her head swam.

"You knew I'd come through the gardener telling you? Oh, that poor child! Why, he's soaking!"

"Oh, I'll explain that to you! The rain caught me on my way here, and then, as I didn't wish to go upstream as far as Gumières, I crossed the Choue and fell into a blessed hole."

Nana forgot the strawberries forthwith. She was trembling and full of pity. That poor dear Zizi in a hole full of water! And she drew him with her in the direction of the house and spoke of making up a roaring fire.

"You know," he murmured, stopping her among the shadows, "I was in hiding because I was afraid of being scolded, like in Paris, when I come and see you and you're not expecting me."

She made no reply but burst out laughing and gave him a kiss on the forehead. Up till today she had always treated him like a naughty urchin, never taking his declarations seriously and amusing herself at his expense as though he were a little man of no consequence whatever. There was much ado to install him in the house. She absolutely insisted on the fire being lit in her bedroom, as being the most comfortable place for his reception. Georges had not surprised Zoé, who was used to all kinds of encounters, but the gardener, who brought the wood upstairs, was greatly nonplused at sight of this dripping gentleman to whom he was certain he had not opened the front door. He was, however, dismissed, as he was no longer wanted.

A lamp lit up the room, and the fire burned with a great bright flame.

"He'll never get dry, and he'll catch cold," said Nana, seeing Georges beginning to shiver.

And there were no men's trousers in her house! She was on the point of calling the gardener back when an idea struck her. Zoé, who was unpacking the trunks in the dressing room, brought her mistress a change of underwear, consisting of a shift and some petticoats with a dressing jacket.

"Oh, that's first rate!" cried the young woman. "Zizi can put 'em all on. You're not angry with me, eh? When your clothes are dry you can put them on again, and then off with you, as fast as fast can be, so as not to have a scolding from your mamma. Make haste! I'm going to change my things, too, in the dressing room."

Ten minutes afterward, when she reappeared in a tea gown, she clasped her hands in a perfect ecstasy.

"Oh, the darling! How sweet he looks dressed like a little woman!"

He had simply slipped on a long nightgown with an insertion front, a pair of worked drawers and the dressing jacket, which was a long cambric garment trimmed with lace. Thus attired and with his delicate young arms showing and his bright damp hair falling almost to his shoulders, he looked just like a girl.

"Why, he's as slim as I am!" said Nana, putting her arm round his waist. "Zoé, just come here and see how it suits him. It's made for him, eh? All except the bodice part, which is too large. He hasn't got as much as I have, poor, dear Zizi!"

"Oh, to be sure, I'm a bit wanting there," murmured Georges with a smile.

All three grew very merry about it. Nana had set to work buttoning the dressing jacket from top to bottom so as to make him quite decent. Then she turned him round as though he were a doll, gave him little thumps, made the skirt stand well out behind. After which she asked him questions. Was he comfortable? Did he feel warm? Zounds, yes, he was comfortable! Nothing fitted more closely and warmly than a woman's shift; had he been able, he would always have worn one. He moved round and about therein, delighted with the fine linen and the soft touch of that unmanly garment, in the folds of which he thought he discovered some of Nana's own warm life.

Meanwhile Zoé had taken the soaked clothes down to the kitchen in order to dry them as quickly as possible in front of a vine-branch fire. Then Georges, as he lounged in an easy chair, ventured to make a confession.

"I say, are you going to feed this evening? I'm dying of hunger. I haven't dined."

Nana was vexed. The great silly thing to go sloping off from Mamma's with an empty stomach, just to chuck himself into a hole full of water! But she was as hungry as a hunter too. They certainly must feed! Only they would have to eat what they could get. Whereupon a round table was rolled up in front of the fire, and the queerest of dinners was improvised thereon. Zoé ran down to the gardener's, he having cooked a mess of cabbage soup in case Madame should not dine at Orleans before her arrival. Madame, indeed, had forgotten to tell him what he was to get ready in the letter she had sent him. Fortunately the cellar was well furnished. Accordingly they had cabbage soup, followed by a piece of bacon. Then Nana rummaged in her handbag and found quite a heap of provisions which she had taken the precaution of stuffing into it. There was a Strasbourg pâté, for instance, and a bag of sweet-meats and some oranges. So they both ate away like ogres and, while they satisfied their healthy young appetites, treated one another with easy good fellowship. Nana kept calling Georges "dear old girl," a form of address which struck her as at once tender and familiar. At dessert, in order not to give Zoé any more trouble, they used the same spoon turn and turn about while demolishing a pot of preserves they had discovered at the top of a cupboard.

"Oh, you dear old girl!" said Nana, pushing back the round table. "I haven't made such a good dinner these ten years past!"

Yet it was growing late, and she wanted to send her boy off for fear he should be suspected of all sorts of things. But he kept declaring that he had plenty of time to spare. For the matter of that, his clothes were not drying well, and Zoé averred that it would take an hour longer at least, and as she was dropping with sleep after the fatigues of the journey, they sent her off to bed. After which they were alone in the silent house.

It was a very charming evening. The fire was dying out amid glowing embers, and in the great blue room, where Zoé had made up the bed before going upstairs, the air felt a little oppressive. Nana, overcome by the heavy warmth, got up to open the window for a few minutes, and as she did so she uttered a little cry.

"Great heavens, how beautiful it is! Look, dear old girl!"

Georges had come up, and as though the window bar had not been sufficiently wide, he put his arm round Nana's waist and rested his head against her shoulder. The weather had undergone a brisk change: the skies were clearing, and a full moon lit up the country with its golden disk of light. A sovereign quiet reigned over the valley. It seemed wider and larger as it opened on the immense distances of the plain, where the trees loomed like little shadowy islands amid a shining and waveless lake. And Nana grew ten-derhearted, felt herself a child again. Most surely she had dreamed of nights like this at an epoch which she could not recall. Since leaving the train every object of sensation—the wide countryside, the green things with their pun-gent scents, the house, the vegetables—had stirred her to such a degree that now it seemed to her as if she had left Paris twenty years ago. Yesterday's existence was far, far away, and she was full of sensations of which she had no previous experience. Georges, meanwhile, was giving her neck little coaxing kisses, and this again added to her sweet unrest. With hesitating hand she pushed him from her, as though he were a child whose affectionate advances were fatiguing, and once more she told him that he ought to take his departure. He did not gainsay her. All in good time—he would go all in good time!

But a bird raised its song and again was silent. It was a robin in an elder tree below the window.

"Wait one moment," whispered Georges; "the lamp's frightening him. I'll put it out."

And when he came back and took her waist again he added:

"We'll relight it in a minute."

Then as she listened to the robin and the boy pressed against her side, Nana remembered. Ah yes, it was in novels that she had got to know all this! In other days she would have given her heart to have a full moon and robins and a lad dying of love for her. Great God, she could have cried, so good and charming did it all seem to her! Beyond a doubt she had been born to live honestly! So she pushed Georges away again, and he grew yet bolder.

"No, let me be. I don't care about it. It would be very wicked at your age. Now listen—I'll always be your mamma."

A sudden feeling of shame overcame her. She was blushing exceedingly, and yet not a soul could see her. The room behind them was full of black night while the country stretched before them in silence and lifeless solitude. Never had she known such a sense of shame before. Little by little she felt her power of resistance ebbing away, and that despite her embarrassed efforts to the contrary. That disguise of his, that woman's shift and that dressing jacket set her laughing again. It was as though a girl friend were teasing her.

"Oh, it's not right; it's not right!" she stammered after a last effort.

And with that, in face of the lovely night, she sank like a young virgin into the arms of this mere child. The house slept.

Next morning at Les Fondettes, when the bell rang for lunch, the dining-room table was no longer too big for the company. Fauchery and Daguenet had been driven up together in one carriage, and after them another had arrived with the Count de Vandeuvres, who had followed by the next train. Georges was the last to come downstairs. He was looking a little pale, and his eyes were sunken, but in answer to questions he said that he was much better, though he was still somewhat shaken by the violence of the attack. Mme Hugon looked into his eyes with an anxious smile and adjusted his hair which had been carelessly combed that morning, but he drew back as though embarrassed by this tender little action. During the meal she chaffed Vandeuvres very pleasantly and declared that she had expected him for five years past.

"Well, here you are at last! How have you managed it?"

Vandeuvres took her remarks with equal pleasantry. He told her that he had lost a fabulous sum of money at the club yesterday and thereupon had come away with the intention of ending up in the country.

"'Pon my word, yes, if only you can find me an heiress in these rustic parts! There must be delightful women hereabouts."

The old lady rendered equal thanks to Daguenet and Fauchery for having been so good as to accept her son's invitation, and then to her great and joyful surprise she saw the Marquis de Chouard enter the room. A third carriage had brought him.

"Dear me, you've made this your trysting place today!" she cried. "You've passed word round! But what's happening? For years I've never succeeded in bringing you all together, and now you all drop in at once. Oh, I certainly don't complain."

Another place was laid. Fauchery found himself next the Countess Sabine, whose liveliness and gaiety surprised him when he remembered her drooping, languid state in the austere Rue Miromesnil drawing room. Daguenet, on the other hand, who was seated on Estelle's left, seemed slightly put out by his propinquity to that tall, silent girl. The angularity of her elbows was disagreeable to him. Muffat and Chouard had exchanged a sly glance while Vandeuvres continued joking about his coming marriage.

"Talking of ladies," Mme Hugon ended by saying, "I have a new neighbor whom you probably know."

And she mentioned Nana. Vandeuvres affected the liveliest astonishment. "Well, that is strange! Nana's property near here!"

Fauchery and Daguenet indulged in a similar demonstration while the Marquis de Chouard discussed the breast of a chicken without appearing to comprehend their meaning. Not one of the men had smiled.

"Certainly," continued the old lady, "and the person in question arrived at La Mignotte yesterday evening, as I was saying she would. I got my information from the gardener this morning."

At these words the gentlemen could not conceal their very real surprise. They all looked up. Eh? What? Nana had come down! But they were only expecting her next day; they were privately under the impression that they would arrive before her! Georges alone sat looking at his glass with drooped eyelids and a tired expression. Ever since the beginning of lunch he had seemed to be sleeping with open eyes and a vague smile on his lips.

"Are you still in pain, my Zizi?" asked his mother, who had been gazing at him throughout the meal.

He started and blushed as he said that he was very well now, but the worn-out insatiate expression of a girl who has danced too much did not fade from his face.

"What's the matter with your neck?" resumed Mme Hugon in an alarmed tone. "It's all red."

He was embarrassed and stammered. He did not know—he had nothing the matter with his neck. Then drawing his shirt collar up:

"Ah yes, some insect stung me there!"

The Marquis de Chouard had cast a sidelong glance at the little red place. Muffat, too, looked at Georges. The company was finishing lunch and planning various excursions. Fauchery was growing increasingly excited with the

Countess Sabine's laughter. As he was passing her a dish of fruit their hands touched, and for one second she looked at him with eyes so full of dark meaning that he once more thought of the secret which had been communicated to him one evening after an uproarious dinner. Then, too, she was no longer the same woman. Something was more pronounced than of old, and her gray foulard gown which fitted loosely over her shoulders added a touch of license to her delicate, high-strung elegance.

When they rose from the table Daguenet remained behind with Fauchery in order to impart to him the following crude witticism about Estelle: "A nice broomstick that to shove into a man's hands!" Nevertheless, he grew serious when the journalist told him the amount she was worth in the way of dowry.

"Four hundred thousand francs."

"And the mother?" queried Fauchery. "She's all right, eh?"

"Oh, *she'll* work the oracle! But it's no go, my dear man!"

"Bah! How are we to know? We must wait and see."

It was impossible to go out that day, for the rain was still falling in heavy showers. Georges had made haste to disappear from the scene and had double-locked his door. These gentlemen avoided mutual explanations, though they were none of them deceived as to the reasons which had brought them together. Vandeuvres, who had had a very bad time at play, had really conceived the notion of lying fallow for a season, and he was counting on Nana's presence in the neighborhood as a safeguard against excessive boredom. Fauchery had taken advantage of the holidays granted him by Rose, who just then was extremely busy. He was thinking of discussing a second notice with Nana, in case country air should render them reciprocally affectionate. Daguenet, who had been just a little sulky with her since Steiner had come upon the scene, was dreaming of resuming the old connection or at least of snatching some delightful opportunities if occasion offered. As to the Marquis de Chouard, he was watching for times and seasons. But among all those men who were busy following in the tracks of Venus—a Venus with the rouge scarce washed from her cheeks—Muffat was at once the most ardent and the most tortured by the novel sensations of desire and fear and anger warring in his anguished members. A formal promise had been made him; Nana was awaiting him. Why then had she taken her departure two days sooner than was expected?

He resolved to betake himself to La Mignotte after dinner that same evening.

At night as the count was leaving the park Georges fled forth after him. He left him to follow the road to Gumières, crossed the Choue, rushed into Nana's presence, breathless, furious and with tears in his eyes. Ah yes, he understood everything! That old fellow now on his way to her was coming to keep an appointment! Nana was dumfounded by this ebullition of jealousy, and, greatly moved by the way things were turning out, she took him in her arms and comforted him to the best of her ability. Oh no, he was quite beside the mark; she was expecting no one. If the gentleman came it would not be her fault. What a great ninny that Zizi was to be taking on so about nothing at all! By her child's soul she swore she loved nobody except her own Georges And with that she kissed him and wiped away his tears.

"Now just listen! You'll see that it's all for your sake," she went on when he had grown somewhat calmer. "Steiner has arrived—he's up above there now. You know, duckie, I can't turn *him* out of doors."

"Yes, I know; I'm not talking of *him*," whispered the boy.

"Very well then, I've stuck him into the room at the end. I said I was out of sorts. He's unpacking his trunk. Since nobody's seen you, be quick and run up and hide in my room and wait for me."

Georges sprang at her and threw his arms round her neck. It was true after all! She loved him a little! So they would put the lamp out as they did yesterday and be in the dark till daytime! Then as the front-door bell sounded he quietly slipped away. Upstairs in the bedroom he at once took off his shoes so as not to make any noise and straightway crouched down behind a curtain and waited soberly.

Nana welcomed Count Muffat, who, though still shaken with passion, was now somewhat embarrassed. She had pledged her word to him and would even have liked to keep it since he struck her as a serious, practicable lover. But truly, who could have foreseen all that happened yesterday? There was the voyage and the house she had never set eyes on before and the arrival of the drenched little lover! How sweet it had all seemed to her, and how delightful it would be to continue in it! So much the worse for the gentleman! For three months past she had been keeping him dangling after her while she affected conventionality in order the further to inflame him. Well, well! He would have to continue dangling, and if he didn't like that he could go! She would sooner have thrown up everything than have played false to Georges.

The count had seated himself with all the ceremonious politeness becoming a country caller. Only his hands were trembling slightly. Lust, which Nana's skillful tactics daily exasperated, had at last wrought terrible havoc in that sanguine, uncontaminated nature. The grave man, the chamberlain who was wont to tread the state apartments at the Tuileries with slow and dignified step, was now nightly driven to plunge his teeth into his bolster, while with sobs of exasperation he pictured to himself a sensual shape which never changed. But this time he was determined to make an end of the torture. Coming along the highroad in the deep quiet of the gloaming, he had meditated a fierce course of action. And the moment he had finished his opening remarks he tried to take hold of Nana with both hands.

"No, no! Take care!" she said simply. She was not vexed; nay, she even smiled.

He caught her again, clenching his teeth as he did so. Then as she struggled to get free he coarsely and crudely reminded her that he had come to stay the night. Though much embarrassed at this, Nana did not cease to smile. She took his hands and spoke very familiarly in order to soften her refusal.

"Come now, darling, do be quiet! Honor bright, I can't: Steiner's upstairs."

But he was beside himself. Never yet had she seen a man in such a state. She grew frightened and put her hand over his mouth in order to stifle his çries. Then in lowered tones she besought him to be quiet and to let her alone. Steiner was coming downstairs. Things were getting stupid, to be sure! When Steiner entered the room he heard Nana remarking:

"I adore the country."

She was lounging comfortably back in her deep easy chair, and she turned round and interrupted herself.

"It's Monsieur le Comte Muffat, darling. He saw a light here while he was strolling past, and he came in to bid us welcome."

The two men clasped hands. Muffat, with his face in shadow, stood silent for a moment or two. Steiner seemed sulky. Then they chatted about Paris: business there was at a standstill; abominable things had been happening on 'change. When a quarter of an hour had elapsed Muffat took his departure, and, as the young woman was seeing him to the door, he tried without success to make an assignation for the following night. Steiner went up to bed almost directly afterward, grumbling, as he did so, at the everlasting little ailments that seemed to afflict the genus courtesan. The two old boys had been packed off at last! When she was able to rejoin him Nana found Georges still hiding exemplarily behind the curtain. The room was dark. He pulled her down onto the floor as she sat near him, and together they began playfully rolling on the ground, stopping now and again and smothering their laughter with kisses whenever they struck their bare feet against some piece of furniture. Far away, on the road to Gumières, Count Muffat walked slowly home and, hat in hand, bathed his burning forehead in the freshness and silence of the night.

During the days that followed Nana found life adorable. In the lad's arms she was once more a girl of fifteen, and under the caressing influence of this renewed childhood love's white flower once more blossomed forth in a nature which had grown hackneyed and disgusted in the service of the other sex. She would experience sudden fits of shame, sudden vivid emotions, which left her trembling. She wanted to laugh and to cry, and she was beset by nervous, maidenly feelings, mingled with warm desires that made her blush again. Never yet had she felt anything comparable to this. The country filled her with tender thoughts. As a little girl she had long wished to dwell in a meadow, tending a goat, because one day on the talus of the fortifications she had seen a goat bleating at the end of its tether. Now this estate, this stretch of land belonging to her, simply swelled her heart to bursting, so utterly had her old ambition been surpassed. Once again she tasted the novel sensations experienced by chits of girls, and at night when she went upstairs, dizzy with her day in the open air and intoxicated by the scent of green leaves, and rejoined her Zizi behind the curtain, she fancied herself a schoolgirl enjoying a holiday escapade. It was an amour, she thought, with a young cousin to whom she was going to be married. And so she trembled at the slightest noise and dread lest parents should hear her, while making the delicious experiments and suffering the voluptuous terrors attendant on a girl's first slip from the path of virtue.

Nana in those days was subject to the fancies a sentimental girl will indulge in. She would gaze at the moon for hours. One night she had a mind to go down into the garden with Georges when all the household was asleep. When there they strolled under the trees, their arms round each other's waists, and finally went and laid down in the grass, where the dew soaked them through and through. On another occasion, after a long silence up in the bedroom, she fell sobbing on the lad's neck, declaring in broken accents that she was afraid of dying. She would often croon a favorite ballad of Mme Lerat's, which was full of flowers and birds. The song would melt her to tears, and she would break off in order to clasp Georges in a passionate embrace and to extract from him vows of undying affection. In short she was extremely silly, as she herself would admit when they both became jolly good fellows again and sat up smoking cigarettes on the edge of the bed, dangling their bare legs over it the while and tapping their heels against its wooden side.

But what utterly melted the young woman's heart was Louiset's arrival. She had an access of maternal affection which was as violent as a mad fit. She would carry off her boy into the sunshine outside to watch him kicking about; she would dress him like a little prince and roll with him in the grass. The moment he arrived she decided that he was to sleep near her, in the room next hers, where Mme Lerat, whom the country greatly affected, used to begin snoring the moment her head touched the pillow. Louiset did not hurt Zizi's position in the least. On the contrary, Nana said that she had now two children, and she treated them with the same wayward tenderness. At night, more than ten times running, she would leave Zizi to go and see if Louiset were breathing properly, but on her return she would re-embrace her Zizi and lavish on him the caresses that had been destined for the child. She played at being Mamma while he wickedly enjoyed being dandled in the arms of the great wench and allowed himself to be rocked to and fro like a baby that is being sent to sleep. It was all so delightful, and Nana was so charmed with her present existence, that she seriously proposed to him never to leave the country. They would send all the other people away, and he, she and the child would live alone. And with that they would make a thousand plans till daybreak and never once hear Mme Lerat as she snored vigorously after the fatigues of a day spent in picking country flowers.

This charming existence lasted nearly a week. Count Muffat used to come every evening and go away again with disordered face and burning hands. One evening he was not even received, as Steiner had been obliged to run up to Paris. He was told that Madame was not well. Nana grew daily more disgusted at the notion of deceiving Georges. He was such an innocent lad, and he had such faith in her! She would have looked on herself as the lowest of the low had she played him false. Besides, it would have sickened her to do so! Zoé, who took her part in this affair in mute disdain, believed that Madame was growing senseless.

On the sixth day a band of visitors suddenly blundered into Nana's idyl. She had, indeed, invited a whole swarm of people under the belief that none of them would come. And so one fine afternoon she was vastly astonished and annoyed to see an omnibus full of people pulling up outside the gate of La Mignotte.

"It's us!" cried Mignon, getting down first from the conveyance and extracting then his sons Henri and Charles.

Labordette thereupon appeared and began handing out an interminable file of ladies—Lucy Stewart, Caroline Héquet, Tatan Néné, Maria Blond. Nana was in hopes that they would end there, when La Faloise sprang from the step in order to receive Gaga and her daughter Amélie in his trembling arms. That brought the number up to eleven people. Their installation proved a laborious undertaking. There were five spare rooms at La Mignotte, one of which was already occupied by Mme Lerat and Louiset. The largest was devoted to the Gaga and La Faloise establishment, and it was decided that Amélie should sleep on a truckle bed in the dressing room at the side. Mignon and his two sons had the third room. Labordette the fourth. There thus remained one room which was transformed into a dormitory with four beds in it for Lucy, Caroline, Tatan and Maria. As to Steiner, he would sleep on the divan in the drawing room. At the end of an hour, when everyone was duly settled, Nana, who had begun by being furious, grew enchanted at the thought of playing hostess on a grand scale. The ladies complimented her on La Mignotte. "It's a stunning property, my dear!" And then, too, they brought her quite a whiff of Parisian air, and talking all together with bursts of laughter and exclamation and emphatic little gestures, they gave her all the petty gossip of the week just past. By the by, and how about Bordenave? What had he said about her prank? Oh, nothing much! After bawling about having her brought back by the police, he had simply put somebody else in her place at night. Little Violaine was the understudy, and she had even obtained a very pretty success as the Blonde Venus. Which piece of news made Nana rather serious.

It was only four o'clock in the afternoon, and there was some talk of taking a stroll around.

"Oh, I haven't told you," said Nana, "I was just off to get up potatoes when you arrived."

Thereupon they all wanted to go and dig potatoes without even changing their dresses first. It was quite a party. The gardener and two helpers were already in the potato field at the end of the grounds. The ladies knelt down and began fumbling in the mold with their beringed fingers, shouting gaily whenever they discovered a potato of exceptional size. It struck them as so amusing! But Tatan Néné was in a state of triumph! So many were the potatoes she had gathered in her youth that she forgot herself entirely and gave the others much good advice, treating them like geese the while. The gentlemen toiled less strenuously. Mignon looked every inch the good citizen and father and made his stay in the country an occasion for completing his boys' education. Indeed, he spoke to them of Parmentier!

Dinner that evening was wildly hilarious. The company ate ravenously. Nana, in a state of great elevation, had a warm disagreement with her butler, an individual who had been in service at the bishop's palace in Orleans. The ladies smoked over their coffee. An earsplitting noise of merrymaking issued from the open windows and died out far away under the serene evening sky while peasants, belated in the lanes, turned and looked at the flaring rooms.

"It's most tiresome that you're going back the day after tomorrow," said Nana. "But never mind, we'll get up an excursion all the same!"

They decided to go on the morrow, Sunday, and visit the ruins of the old Abbey of Chamont, which were some seven kilometers distant. Five carriages would come out from Orleans, take up the company after lunch and bring them back to dinner at La Mignotte at about seven. It would be delightful.

That evening, as his wont was, Count Muffat mounted the hill to ring at the outer gate. But the brightly lit windows and the shouts of laughter astonished him. When, however, he recognized Mignon's voice, he understood it all and went off, raging at this new obstacle, driven to extremities, bent on some violent act. Georges passed through a little door of which he had the key, slipped along the staircase walls and went quietly up into Nana's room. Only he had to wait for her till past midnight. She appeared at last in a high state of intoxication and more maternal even than on the previous nights. Whenever she had drunk anything she became so amorous as to be absurd. Accordingly she now insisted on his accompanying her to the Abbey of Chamont. But he stood out against this; he was afraid of being seen. If he were to be seen driving with her there would be an atrocious scandal. But she burst into tears and evinced the noisy despair of a slighted woman. And he thereupon consoled her and formally promised to be one of the party.

"So you do love me very much," she blurted out. "Say you love me very much. Oh, my darling old bear, if I were to die would you feel it very much? Confess!"

At Les Fondettes the near neighborhood of Nana had utterly disorganized the party. Every morning during lunch good Mme Hugon returned to the subject despite herself, told her guests the news the gardener had brought her and gave evidence of the absorbing curiosity with which notorious courtesans are able to inspire even the worthiest old ladies. Tolerant though she was, she was revolted and maddened by a vague presentiment of coming ill, which frightened her in the evenings as thoroughly as if a wild beast had escaped from a menagerie and were known to be lurking in the countryside.

She began trying to pick a little quarrel with her guests, whom she each and all accused of prowling round La Mignotte. Count Vandeuvres had been seen laughing on the highroad with a golden-haired lady, but he defended himself against the accusation; he denied that it was Nana, the fact being that Lucy had been with him and had told him how she had just turned her third prince out of doors. The Marquis de Chouard used also to go out every day, but his excuse was doctor's orders. Toward Daguenet and Fauchery Mme Hugon behaved unjustly too. The former especially never left Les Fondettes, for he had given up the idea of renewing the old connection and was busy paying the most respectful attentions to Estelle. Fauchery also stayed with the Muffat ladies. On one occasion only he had met Mignon with an armful of flowers, putting his sons through a course of botanical instruction in a by-path. The two men had shaken hands and given each other the news about Rose. She was perfectly well and happy; they had both received a letter from her that morning in which she besought them to profit by the fresh country air for some days longer. Among all her guests the old lady spared only Count Muffat and Georges. The count, who said he had serious business in Orleans, could certainly not be running after the bad woman, and as to Georges, the poor child was at last causing her grave anxiety, seeing that every evening he was seized with atrocious sick headaches which kept him to his bed in broad daylight.

Meanwhile Fauchery had become the Countess Sabine's faithful attendant in the absence during each afternoon of Count Muffat. Whenever they went to the end of the park he carried her campstool and her sunshade. Besides, he amused her with the original witticisms peculiar to a second-rate journalist, and in so doing he prompted her to one of those sudden intimacies which are allowable in the country. She had apparently consented to it from the first, for she had grown quite a girl again in the society of a young man whose noisy humor seemed unlikely to compromize her. But now and again, when for a second or two they found themselves alone behind the shrubs, their eyes would meet; they would pause amid their laughter, grow suddenly serious and view one another darkly, as though they had fathomed and divined their inmost hearts.

On Friday a fresh place had to be laid at lunch time. M. Théophile Venot, whom Mme Hugon remembered to have invited at the Muffats' last winter, had just arrived. He sat stooping humbly forward and behaved with much good nature, as became a man of no account, nor did he seem to notice the anxious deference with which he was treated. When he had succeeded in getting the company to forget his presence he sat nibbling small lumps of sugar during dessert, looking sharply up at Daguenet as the latter handed Estelle strawberries and listening to Fauchery, who was making the countess very merry over one of his anecdotes. Whenever anyone looked at *him* he smiled in his quiet way. When the guests rose from table he took the count's arm and drew him into the park. He was known to have exercised great influence over the latter ever since the death of his mother. Indeed, singular stories were told about the kind of dominion which the ex-lawyer enjoyed in that household. Fauchery, whom his arrival doubtless embarrassed, began explaining to Georges and Daguenet the origin of the man's wealth. It was a big lawsuit with the management of which the Jesuits had entrusted him in days gone by. In his opinion the worthy man was a terrible fellow despite his gentle, plump face and at this time of day had his finger in all the intrigues of the priesthood. The two young men had begun joking at this, for they thought the little old gentleman had an idiotic expression. The idea of an unknown Venot, a gigantic Venot, acting for the whole body of the clergy, struck them in the light of a comical invention. But they were silenced when, still leaning on the old man's arm, Count Muffat reappeared with blanched cheeks and eyes reddened as if by recent weeping.

"I bet they've been chatting about hell," muttered Fauchery in a bantering tone.

The Countess Sabine overheard the remark. She turned her head slowly, and their eyes met in that long gaze with which they were accustomed to sound one another prudently before venturing once for all.

After the breakfast it was the guests' custom to betake themselves to a little flower garden on a terrace overlooking the plain. This Sunday afternoon was exquisitely mild. There had been signs of rain toward ten in the morning, but the sky, without ceasing to be covered, had, as it were, melted into milky fog, which now hung like a cloud of luminous dust in the golden sunlight. Soon Mme Hugon proposed that they should step down through a little doorway below the terrace and take a walk on foot in the direction of Gumières and as far as the Choue. She was fond of walking and, considering her threescore years, was very active. Besides, all her guests declared that there was no need to drive. So in a somewhat straggling order they reached the wooden bridge over the river. Fauchery and Daguenet headed the column with the Muffat ladies and were followed by the count and the marquis, walking on either side of Mme Hugon, while Vandeuvres, looking fashionable and out of his element on the highroad, marched in the rear, smoking a cigar. M. Venot, now slackening, now hastening his pace, passed smilingly from group to group, as though bent on losing no scrap of conversation.

"To think of poor dear Georges at Orleans!" said Mme Hugon. "He was anxious to consult old Doctor Tavernier, who never goes out now, on the subject of his sick headaches. Yes, you were not up, as he went off before seven o'clock. But it 'll be a change for him all the same."

She broke off, exclaiming:

"Why, what's making them stop on the bridge?"

The fact was the ladies and Fauchery and Daguenet were standing stockstill on the crown of the bridge. They seemed to be hesitating as though some obstacle or other rendered them uneasy and yet the way lay clear before them.

"Go on!" cried the count.

They never moved and seemed to be watching the approach of something which the rest had not yet observed. Indeed the road wound considerably and was bordered by a thick screen of poplar trees. Nevertheless, a dull sound began to grow momentarily louder, and soon there was a noise of wheels, mingled with shouts of laughter and the cracking of whips. Then suddenly five carriages came into view, driving one behind the other. They were crowded to bursting, and bright with a galaxy of white, blue and pink costumes.

"What is it?" said Mme Hugon in some surprise.

Then her instinct told her, and she felt indignant at such an untoward invasion of her road.

"Oh, that woman!" she murmured. "Walk on, pray walk on. Don't appear to notice."

But it was too late. The five carriages which were taking Nana and her circle to the ruins of Chamont rolled on to the narrow wooden bridge. Fauchery, Daguenet and the Muffat ladies were forced to step backward, while Mme Hugon and the others had also to stop in Indian file along the roadside. It was a superb ride past! The laughter in the carriages had ceased, and faces were turned with an expression of curiosity. The rival parties took stock of each other amid a silence broken only by the measured trot of the horses. In the first carriage Maria Blond and Tatan Néné were lolling backward like a pair of duchesses, their skirts swelling forth over the wheels, and as they passed they cast disdainful glances at the honest women who were walking afoot. Then came Gaga, filling up a whole seat and half smothering La Faloise beside her so that little but his small anxious face was visible. Next followed Caroline Héquet with Labordette, Lucy Stewart with Mignon and his boys and at the close of all Nana in a victoria with Steiner and on a bracket seat in front of her that poor, darling Zizi, with his knees jammed against her own.

"It's the last of them, isn't it?" the countess placidly asked Fauchery, pretending at the same time not to recognize Nana.

The wheel of the victoria came near grazing her, but she did not step back. The two women had exchanged a deeply significant glance. It was, in fact, one of those momentary scrutinies which are at once complete and definite. As to the men, they behaved unexceptionably. Fauchery and Daguenet looked icy and recognized no one. The marquis, more nervous than they and afraid of some farcical ebullition on the part of the ladies, had plucked a blade of grass and was rolling it between his fingers. Only Vandeuvres, who had stayed somewhat apart from the rest of the company, winked imperceptibly at Lucy, who smiled at him as she passed.

"Be careful!" M. Venot had whispered as he stood behind Count Muffat.

The latter in extreme agitation gazed after this illusive vision of Nana while his wife turned slowly round and scrutinized him. Then he cast his eyes on the ground as though to escape the sound of galloping hoofs which were sweeping away both his senses and his heart. He could have cried aloud in his agony, for, seeing Georges among Nana's skirts, he understood it all now. A mere child! He was brokenhearted at the thought that she should have preferred a mere child to him! Steiner was his equal, but that child!

Mme Hugon, in the meantime, had not at once recognized Georges. Crossing the bridge, he was fain to jump into the river, but Nana's knees restrained him. Then white as a sheet and icy cold, he sat rigidly up in his place and looked at no one. It was just possible no one would notice him.

"Oh, my God!" said the old lady suddenly. "Georges is with her!"

The carriages had passed quite through the uncomfortable crowd of people who recognized and yet gave no sign of recognition. The short critical encounter seemed to have been going on for ages. And now the wheels whirled away the carriageloads of girls more gaily than ever. Toward the fair open country they went, amid the buffetings of the fresh air of heaven. Bright-colored fabrics fluttered in the wind, and the merry laughter burst forth anew as the voyagers began jesting and glancing back at the respectable folks halting with looks of annoyance at the roadside. Turning round, Nana could see the walking party hesitating and then returning the way they had come without crossing the bridge. Mme Hugon was leaning silently on Count Muffat's arm, and so sad was her look that no one dared comfort her.

"I say, did you see Fauchery, dear?" Nana shouted to Lucy, who was leaning out of the carriage in front. "What a brute he was! He shall pay out for that. And Paul, too, a fellow I've been so kind to! Not a sign! They're polite, I'm sure."

And with that she gave Steiner a terrible dressing, he having ventured to suggest that the gentlemen's attitude had been quite as it should be. So then they weren't even worth a bow? The first blackguard that came by might insult them? Thanks! He was the right sort, too, he was! It couldn't be better! One ought always to bow to a woman.

"Who's the tall one?" asked Lucy at random, shouting through the noise of the wheels.

"It's the Countess Muffat," answered Steiner.

"There now! I suspected as much," said Nana. "Now, my dear fellow, it's all very well her being a countess, for she's no better than she should be. Yes, yes, she's no better that she should be. You know, I've got an eye for such things, I have! And now I know your countess as well as if I had been at the making of her! I'll bet you that she's the mistress of that viper Fauchery! I tell you, she's his mistress! Between women you guess that sort of thing at once!"

Steiner shrugged his shoulders. Since the previous day his irritation had been hourly increasing. He had received letters which necessitated his leaving the following morning, added to which he did not much appreciate coming down to the country in order to sleep on the drawing-room divan.

"And this poor baby boy!" Nana continued, melting suddenly at sight of Georges's pale face as he still sat rigid and breathless in front of her.

"D'you think Mamma recognized me?" he stammered at last.

"Oh, most surely she did! Why, she cried out! But it's my fault. He didn't want to come with us; I forced him to. Now listen, Zizi, would you like me to write to your mamma? She looks such a kind, decent sort of lady! I'll tell her that I never saw you before and that it was Steiner who brought you with him for the first time today."

"No, no, don't write," said Georges in great anxiety. "I'll explain it all myself. Besides, if they bother me about it I shan't go home again."

But he continued plunged in thought, racking his brains for excuses against his return home in the evening. The five carriages were rolling through a flat country along an interminable straight road bordered by fine trees. The country was bathed in a silvery-gray atmosphere. The ladies still continued shouting remarks from carriage to carriage behind the backs of the drivers, who chuckled over their extraordinary fares. Occasionally one of them would rise to her feet to look at the landscape and, supporting herself on her neighbor's shoulder, would grow extremely excited till a sudden jolt brought her down to the seat again. Caroline Héquet in the meantime was having a warm discussion with Labordette. Both of them were agreed that Nana would be selling her country house before three months were out, and Caroline was urging Labordette to buy it back for her for as little as it was likely to fetch. In front of them La Faloise, who was very amorous and could not get at Gaga's apoplectic neck, was imprinting kisses on her spine through her dress, the strained fabric of which was nigh splitting, while Amélie, perching stiffly on the bracket seat, was bidding them be quiet, for she was horrified to be sitting idly by, watching her mother being kissed. In the next carriage Mignon, in order to astonish Lucy, was making his sons recite a fable by La Fontaine. Henri was prodigious at this exercise; he could spout you one without pause or hesitation. But Maria Blond, at the head of the procession, was beginning to feel extremely bored. She was tired of hoaxing that blockhead of a Tatan Néné with a story to the effect that the Parisian dairywomen were wont to fabricate eggs with a mixture of paste and saffron. The distance was too great: were they never going to get to their destination? And the question was transmitted from carriage to carriage and finally reached Nana, who, after questioning her driver, got up and shouted:

"We've not got a quarter of an hour more to go. You see that church behind the trees down there?"

Then she continued:

"Do you know, it appears the owner of the Château de Chamont is an old lady of Napoleon's time? Oh, *she* was a merry one! At least, so Joseph told me, and he heard it from the servants at the bishop's palace. There's no one like it nowadays, and for the matter of that, she's become goody-goody."

"What's her name?" asked Lucy.

"Madame d'Anglars."

"Irma d'Anglars—I knew her!" cried Gaga.

Admiring exclamations burst from the line of carriages and were borne down the wind as the horses quickened their trot. Heads were stretched out in Gaga's direction; Maria Blond and Tatan Néné turned round and knelt on the seat while they leaned over the carriage hood, and the air was full of questions and cutting remarks, tempered by a certain obscure admiration. Gaga had known her! The idea filled them all with respect for that far-off past.

"Dear me, I was young then," continued Gaga. "But never mind, I remember it all. I saw her pass. They said she was disgusting in her own house, but, driving in her carriage, she *was* just smart! And the stunning tales about her! Dirty doings and money flung about like one o'clock! I don't wonder at all that she's got a fine place. Why, she used to clean out a man's pockets as soon as look at him. Irma d'Anglars still in the land of the living! Why, my little pets, she must be near ninety."

At this the ladies became suddenly serious. Ninety years old! The deuce, there wasn't one of them, as Lucy loudly declared, who would live to that age. They were all done for. Besides, Nana said she didn't want to make old bones; it wouldn't be amusing. They were drawing near their destination, and the conversation was interrupted by the cracking of whips as the drivers put their horses to their best paces. Yet amid all the noise Lucy continued talking and, suddenly changing the subject, urged Nana to come to town with them all tomorrow. The exhibition was soon to close, and the ladies must really return to Paris, where the season was surpassing their expectations. But Nana was obstinate. She loathed Paris; she wouldn't set foot there yet!

"Eh, darling, we'll stay?" she said, giving Georges's knees a squeeze, as though Steiner were of no account.

The carriages had pulled up abruptly, and in some surprise the company got out on some waste ground at the bottom of a small hill. With his whip one of the drivers had to point them out the ruins of the old Abbey of Chamont where they lay hidden among trees. It was a great sell! The ladies voted them silly. Why, they were only a heap of old stones with briers growing over them and part of a tumble-down tower. It really wasn't worth coming a couple of leagues to see that! Then the driver pointed out to them the countryseat, the park of which stretched away from the abbey, and he advised them to take a little path and follow the walls surrounding it. They would thus make the tour of the place while the carriages would go and await them in the village square. It was a delightful walk, and the company agreed to the proposition.

"Lord love me, Irma knows how to take care of herself!" said Gaga, halting before a gate at the corner of the park wall abutting on the highroad.

All of them stood silently gazing at the enormous bush which stopped up the gateway. Then following the little path, they skirted the park wall, looking up from time to time to admire the trees, whose lofty branches stretched out over them and formed a dense vault of greenery. After three minutes or so they found themselves in front of a second gate. Through this a wide lawn was visible, over which two venerable oaks cast dark masses of shadow. Three minutes farther on yet another gate afforded them an extensive view of a great avenue, a perfect corridor of shadow, at the end of which a bright spot of sunlight gleamed like a star. They stood in silent, wondering admiration, and then little by little exclamations burst from their lips. They had been trying hard to joke about it all with a touch of envy at heart, but this decidedly and immeasurably impressed them. What a genius that Irma was! A sight like this gave you a rattling notion of the woman! The trees stretched away and away, and there were endlessly recurrent patches of ivy along the wall with glimpses of lofty roofs and screens of poplars interspersed with dense masses of elms and aspens. Was there no end to it then? The ladies would have liked to catch sight of the mansion house, for they were weary of circling on and on, weary of seeing nothing but leafy recesses through every opening they came to. They took the rails of the gate in their hands and pressed their faces against the ironwork. And thus excluded and isolated, a feeling of respect began to overcome them as they thought of the castle lost to view in surrounding immensity. Soon, being quite unused to walking, they grew tired. And the wall did not leave off; at every turn of the small deserted path the same range of gray stones stretched ahead of them. Some of them began to despair of ever getting to the end of it and began talking of returning. But the more their long walk fatigued them, the more respectful they became, for at each successive step they were increasingly impressed by the tranquil, lordly dignity of the domain.

"It's getting silly, this is!" said Caroline Héquet, grinding her teeth.

Nana silenced her with a shrug. For some moments past she had been rather pale and extremely serious and had not spoken a single word. Suddenly the path gave a final turn; the wall ended, and as they came out on the village square the mansion house stood before them on the farther side of its grand outer court. All stopped to admire the proud sweep of the wide steps, the twenty frontage windows, the arrangement of the three wings, which were built of brick framed by courses of stone. Henri IV had erewhile inhabited this historic mansion, and his room, with its great bed hung with Genoa velvet, was still preserved there. Breathless with admiration, Nana gave a little childish sigh.

"Great God!" she whispered very quietly to herself.

But the party were deeply moved when Gaga suddenly announced that Irma herself was standing yonder in front of the church. She recognized her perfectly. She was as upright as of old, the hoary campaigner, and that despite her age, and she still had those eyes which flashed when she moved in that proud way of hers! Vespers were just over, and for a second or two Madame stood in the church porch. She was dressed in a dark brown silk and looked very simple and very tall, her venerable face reminding one of some old marquise who had survived the horrors of the Great Revolution. In her right hand a huge Book of Hours shone in the sunlight, and very slowly she crossed the square, followed some fifteen paces off by a footman in livery. The church was emptying, and all the inhabitants of Chamont bowed before her with extreme respect. An old man even kissed her hand, and a woman wanted to fall on her knees. Truly this was a potent queen, full of years and honors. She mounted her flight of steps and vanished from view.

"That's what one attains to when one has methodical habits!" said Mignon with an air of conviction, looking at his sons and improving the occasion.

Then everybody said his say. Labordette thought her extraordinarily well preserved. Maria Blond let slip a foul expression and vexed Lucy, who declared that one ought to honor gray hairs. All the women, to sum up, agreed that she was a perfect marvel. Then the company got into their conveyances again. From Chamont all the way to La Mignotte Nana remained silent. She had twice turned round to look back at the house, and now, lulled by the sound of the wheels, she forgot that Steiner was at her side and that Georges was in front of her. A vision had come up out of the twilight, and the great lady seemed still to be sweeping by with all the majesty of a potent queen, full of years and of honors.

That evening Georges re-entered Les Fondettes in time for dinner. Nana, who had grown increasingly absent-minded and singular in point of manner, had sent him to ask his mamma's forgiveness. It was his plain duty, she remarked severely, growing suddenly solicitous for the decencies of family life. She even made him swear not to return for the night; she was tired, and in showing proper obedience he was doing no more than his duty. Much bored by this moral discourse, Georges appeared in his mother's presence with heavy heart and downcast head.

Fortunately for him his brother Philippe, a great merry devil of a military man, had arrived during the day, a fact which greatly curtailed the scene he was dreading. Mme Hugon was content to look at him with eyes full of tears while Philippe, who had been put in possession of the facts, threatened to go and drag him home by the scruff of the neck if ever he went back into that woman's society. Somewhat comforted, Georges began slyly planning how to make his escape toward two o'clock next day in order to arrange about future meetings with Nana.

Nevertheless, at dinnertime the house party at Les Fondettes seemed not a little embarrassed. Vandeuvres had given notice of departure, for he was anxious to take Lucy back to Paris with him. He was amused at the idea of carrying off this girl whom he had known for ten years yet never desired. The Marquis de Chouard bent over his plate and meditated on Gaga's young lady. He could well remember dandling Lili on his knee. What a way children had of shooting up! This little thing was becoming extremely plump! But Count Muffat especially was silent and absorbed. His cheeks glowed, and he had given Georges one long look. Dinner over, he went upstairs, intending to shut himself in his bedroom, his pretext being a slight feverish attack. M. Venot had rushed after him, and upstairs in the bedroom a scene ensued. The count threw himself upon the bed and strove to stifle a fit of nervous sobbing in the folds of the pillow while M. Venot, in a soft voice, called him brother and advised him to implore heaven for mercy. But he heard nothing: there was a rattle in his throat. Suddenly he sprang off the bed and stammered:

"I am going there. I can't resist any longer."

"Very well," said the old man, "I go with you."

As they left the house two shadows were vanishing into the dark depths of a garden walk, for every evening now Fauchery and the Countess Sabine left Daguenet to help Estelle make tea. Once on the highroad the count walked so rapidly that his companion had to run in order to follow him. Though utterly out of breath, the latter never ceased showering on him the most conclusive arguments against the temptations of the flesh. But the other never opened his mouth as he hurried away into the night. Arrived in front of La Mignotte, he said simply:

"I can't resist any longer. Go!"

"God's will be done then!" muttered M. Venot. "He uses every method to assure His final triumph. Your sin will become His weapon."

At La Mignotte there was much wrangling during the evening meal. Nana had found a letter from Bordenave awaiting her, in which he advised rest, just as though he were anxious to be rid of her. Little Violaine, he said, was being encored twice nightly. But when Mignon continued urging her to come away with them on the morrow Nana grew exasperated and declared that she did not intend taking advice from anybody. In other ways, too, her behavior at table was ridiculously stuck up. Mme Lerat having made some sharp little speech or other, she loudly announced that, God willing, she wasn't going to let anyone—no, not even her own aunt—make improper remarks in her presence. After which she dreed her guests with honorable sentiments. She seemed to be suffering from a fit of stupid right-mindedness, and she treated them all to projects of religious education for Louiset and to a complete scheme of regeneration for herself. When the company began laughing she gave vent to profound opinions, nodding her head like a grocer's wife who knows what she is saying. Nothing but order could lead to fortune! And so far as she was concerned, she had no wish to die like a beggar! She set the ladies' teeth on edge. They burst out in protest. Could anyone have been converting Nana? No, it was impossible! But she sat quite still and with absent looks once more plunged into dreamland, where the vision of an extremely wealthy and greatly courted Nana rose up before her.

The household were going upstairs to bed when Muffat put in an appearance. It was Labordette who caught sight of him in the garden. He understood it all at once and did him a service, for he got Steiner out of the way and, taking his hand, led him along the dark corridor as far as Nana's bedroom. In affairs of this kind Labordette was wont to display the most perfect tact and cleverness. Indeed, he seemed delighted to be making other people happy. Nana showed no surprise; she was only somewhat annoyed by the excessive heat of Muffat's pursuit. Life was a serious affair, was it not? Love was too silly: it led to nothing. Besides, she had her scruples in view of Zizi's tender age. Indeed, she had scarcely behaved quite fairly toward him. Dear me, yes, she was choosing the proper course again in taking up with an old fellow.

"Zoé," she said to the lady's maid, who was enchanted at the thought of leaving the country, "pack the trunks when you get up tomorrow. We are going back to Paris."

And she went to bed with Muffat but experienced no pleasure.

CHAPTER VII

ONE DECEMBER EVENING three months afterward Count Muffat was strolling in the Passage des Panoramas. The evening was very mild, and owing to a passing shower, the passage had just become crowded with people. There was a perfect mob of them, and they thronged slowly and laboriously along between the shops on either side. Under the windows, white with reflected light, the pavement was violently illuminated. A perfect stream of brilliancy emanated from white globes, red lanterns, blue transparencies, lines of gas jets, gigantic watches and fans, outlined in flame and burning in the open. And the motley displays in the shops, the gold ornaments of the jeweler's, the glass ornaments of the confectioner's, the light-colored silks of the modiste's, seemed to shine again in the crude light of the reflectors behind the clear plate-glass windows, while among the bright-colored, disorderly array of shop signs a huge purple glove loomed in the distance like a bleeding hand which had been severed from an arm and fastened to a yellow cuff.

Count Muffat had slowly returned as far as the boulevard. He glanced out at the roadway and then came sauntering back along the shopwindows. The damp and heated atmosphere filled the narrow passage with a slight luminous mist. Along the flagstones, which had been wet by the drip-drop of umbrellas, the footsteps of the crowd rang continually, but there was no sound of voices. Passers-by elbowed him at every turn and cast inquiring looks at his silent face, which the gaslight rendered pale. And to escape these curious manifestations the count posted himself in front of a stationer's, where with profound attention he contemplated an array of paperweights in the form of glass bowls containing floating landscapes and flowers.

He was conscious of nothing: he was thinking of Nana. Why had she lied t

him again? That morning she had written and told him not to trouble about
her in the evening, her excuse being that Louiset was ill and that she was
going to pass the night at her aunt's in order to nurse him. But he had felt
suspicious and had called at her house, where he learned from the porter that
Madame had just gone off to her theater. He was astonished at this, for she
was not playing in the new piece. Why then should she have told him this
falsehood, and what could she be doing at the Variétés that evening? Hustled
by a passer-by, the count unconsciously left the paperweights and found himself in front of a glass case full of toys, where he grew absorbed over an array
of pocketbooks and cigar cases, all of which had the same blue swallow
stamped on one corner. Nana was most certainly not the same woman! In the
early days after his return from the country she used to drive him wild with
delight, as with pussycat caresses she kissed him all round his face and whiskers
and vowed that he was her own dear pet and the only little man she adored.
He was no longer afraid of Georges, whom his mother kept down at Les
Fondettes. There was only fat Steiner to reckon with, and he believed he was
really ousting him, but he did not dare provoke an explanation on his score.
He knew he was once more in an extraordinary financial scrape and on the
verge of being declared bankrupt on 'change, so much so that he was clinging
fiercely to the shareholders in the Landes Salt Pits and striving to sweat a final
subscription out of them. Whenever he met him at Nana's she would explain
reasonably enough that she did not wish to turn him out of doors like a dog
after all he had spent on her. Besides, for the last three months he had been
living in such a whirl of sensual excitement that, beyond the need of possessing her, he had felt no very distinct impressions. His was a tardy awakening
of the fleshly instinct, a childish greed of enjoyment, which left no room for
either vanity or jealousy. Only one definite feeling could affect him now, and
that was Nana's decreasing kindness. She no longer kissed him on the beard!
It made him anxious, and as became a man quite ignorant of womankind, he
began asking himself what possible cause of offense he could have given her.
Besides, he was under the impression that he was satisfying all her desires.
And so he harked back again and again to the letter he had received that morning with its tissue of falsehoods, invented for the extremely simple purpose
of passing an evening at her own theater. The crowd had pushed him forward
again, and he had crossed the passage and was puzzling his brain in front of
the entrance to a restaurant, his eyes fixed on some plucked larks and on a
huge salmon laid out inside the window.

At length he seemed to tear himself away from this spectacle. He shook
himself, looked up and noticed that it was close on nine o'clock. Nana would
soon be coming out, and he would make her tell the truth. And with that he
walked on and recalled to memory the evenings he once passed in that region
in the days when he used to meet her at the door of the theater.

He knew all the shops, and in the gas-laden air he recognized their different
scents, such, for instance, as the strong savor of Russia leather, the perfume
of vanilla emanating from a chocolate dealer's basement, the savor of musk
blown in whiffs from the open doors of the perfumers. But he did not dare

linger under the gaze of the pale shopwomen, who looked placidly at him as though they knew him by sight. For one instant he seemed to be studying the line of little round windows above the shops, as though he had never noticed them before among the medley of signs. Then once again he went up to the boulevard and stood still a minute or two. A fine rain was now falling, and the cold feel of it on his hands calmed him. He thought of his wife who was staying in a country house near Mâcon, where her friend Mme de Chezelles had been ailing a good deal since the autumn. The carriages in the roadway were rolling through a stream of mud. The country, he thought, must be detestable in such vile weather. But suddenly he became anxious and re-entered the hot, close passage down which he strode among the strolling people. A thought struck him: if Nana were suspicious of his presence there she would be off along the Galerie Montmartre.

After that the count kept a sharp lookout at the very door of the theater, though he did not like this passage end, where he was afraid of being recognized. It was at the corner between the Galerie des Variétés and the Galerie Saint-Marc, an equivocal corner full of obscure little shops. Of these last one was a shoemaker's, where customers never seemed to enter. Then there were two or three upholsterers', deep in dust, and a smoky, sleepy reading room and library, the shaded lamps in which cast a green and slumberous light all the evening through. There was never anyone in this corner save well-dressed, patient gentlemen, who prowled about the wreckage peculiar to a stage door, where drunken sceneshifters and ragged chorus girls congregate. In front of the theater a single gas jet in a ground-glass globe lit up the doorway. For a moment or two Muffat thought of questioning Mme Bron; then he grew afraid lest Nana should get wind of his presence and escape by way of the boulevard. So he went on the march again and determined to wait till he was turned out at the closing of the gates, an event which had happened on two previous occasions. The thought of returning home to his solitary bed simply wrung his heart with anguish. Every time that golden-haired girls and men in dirty linen came out and stared at him he returned to his post in front of the reading room, where, looking in between two advertisements posted on a windowpane, he was always greeted by the same sight. It was a little old man, sitting stiff and solitary at the vast table and holding a green newspaper in his green hands under the green light of one of the lamps. But shortly before ten o'clock another gentleman, a tall, good-looking, fair man with well-fitting gloves, was also walking up and down in front of the stage door. Thereupon at each successive turn the pair treated each other to a suspicious sidelong glance. The count walked to the corner of the two galleries, which was adorned with a high mirror, and when he saw himself therein, looking grave and elegant, he was both ashamed and nervous.

Ten o'clock struck, and suddenly it occurred to Muffat that it would be very easy to find out whether Nana were in her dressing room or not. He went up the three steps, crossed the little yellow-painted lobby and slipped into the court by a door which simply shut with a latch. At that hour of the night the narrow, damp well of a court, with its pestiferous water closets, its fountain, its back view of the kitchen stove and the collection of plants with which the portress used to litter the place, was drenched in dark mist; but the two walls, rising pierced with windows on either hand, were flaming with light, since the property room and the firemen's office were situated on the ground floor, with the managerial bureau on the left, and on the right and upstairs the dressing rooms of the company. The mouths of furnaces seemed to be opening on the outer darkness from top to bottom of this well. The count had at once marked the light in the windows of the dressing room on the first floor, and as a man who is comforted and happy, he forgot where he was and stood gazing upward amid the foul mud and faint decaying smell peculiar to the premises of this antiquated Parisian building. Big drops were dripping from a broken waterspout, and a ray of gaslight slipped from Mme Bron's window and cast a yellow glare over a patch of moss-clad pavement, over the base of a wall which had been rotted by water from a sink, over a whole cornerful of nameless filth amid which old pails and broken crocks lay in fine confusion round a spindling tree growing mildewed in its pot. A window fastening creaked, and the count fled.

Nana was certainly going to come down. He returned to his post in front of the reading room; among its slumbering shadows, which seemed only broken by the glimmer of a night light, the little old man still sat motionless, his side face sharply outlined against his newspaper. Then Muffat walked again and this time took a more prolonged turn and, crossing the large gallery, followed the Galerie des Variétés as far as that of Feydeau. The last mentioned was cold and deserted and buried in melancholy shadow. He returned from it, passed by the theater, turned the corner of the Galerie Saint-Marc and ventured as far as the Galerie Montmartre, where a sugar-chopping machine in front of a grocer's interested him awhile. But when he was taking his third turn he was seized with such dread lest Nana should escape behind his back that he lost all self-respect. Thereupon he stationed himself beside the fair gentleman in front of the very theater. Both exchanged a glance of fraternal humility with which was mingled a touch of distrust, for it was possible they might yet turn out to be rivals. Some sceneshifters who came out smoking their pipes between the acts brushed rudely against them, but neither one nor the other ventured to complain. Three big wenches with untidy hair and dirty gowns appeared on the doorstep. They were munching apples and spitting out the cores, but the two men bowed their heads and patiently braved their impudent looks and rough speeches, though they were hustled and, as it were, soiled by these trollops, who amused themselves by pushing each other down upon them.

At that very moment Nana descended the three steps. She grew very pale when she noticed Muffat.

"Oh, it's you!" she stammered.

The sniggering extra ladies were quite frightened when they recognized her, and they formed in line and stood up, looking as stiff and serious as servants whom their mistress has caught behaving badly. The tall fair gentleman had moved away; he was at once reassured and sad at heart.

"Well, give me your arm," Nana continued impatiently.

They walked quietly off. The count had been getting ready to question her and now found nothing to say.

It was she who in rapid tones told a story to the effect that she had been at her aunt's as late as eight o'clock, when, seeing Louiset very much better, she had conceived the idea of going down to the theater for a few minutes.

"On some important business?" he queried.

"Yes, a new piece," she replied after some slight hesitation. "They wanted my advice."

He knew that she was not speaking the truth, but the warm touch of her arm as it leaned firmly on his own, left him powerless. He felt neither anger nor rancor after his long, long wait; his one thought was to keep her where she was now that he had got hold of her. Tomorrow, and not before, he would try and find out what she had come to her dressing room after. But Nana still appeared to hesitate; she was manifestly a prey to the sort of secret anguish that besets people when they are trying to regain lost ground and to initiate a plan of action. Accordingly, as they turned the corner of the Galerie des Variétés, she stopped in front of the show in a fan seller's window.

"I say, that's pretty," she whispered; "I mean that mother-of-pearl mount with the feathers."

Then, indifferently:

"So you're seeing me home?"

"Of course," he said, with some surprise, "since your child's better."

She was sorry she had told him that story. Perhaps Louiset was passing through another crisis! She talked of returning to the Batignolles. But when he offered to accompany her she did not insist on going. For a second or two she was possessed with the kind of white-hot fury which a woman experiences when she feels herself entrapped and must, nevertheless, behave prettily. But in the end she grew resigned and determined to gain time. If only she could get rid of the count toward midnight everything would happen as she wished.

"Yes, it's true; you're a bachelor tonight," she murmured. "Your wife doesn't return till tomorrow, eh?"

"Yes," replied Muffat. It embarrassed him somewhat to hear her talking familiarly about the countess.

But she pressed him further, asking at what time the train was due and wanting to know whether he were going to the station to meet her. She had begun to walk more slowly than ever, as though the shops interested her very much.

"Now do look!" she said, pausing anew before a jeweler's window, "what a funny bracelet!"

She adored the Passage des Panoramas. The tinsel of the *article de Paris*, the false jewelry, the gilded zinc, the cardboard made to look like leather, had been the passion of her early youth. It remained, and when she passed the shop-windows she could not tear herself away from them. It was the same with her today as when she was a ragged, slouching child who fell into reveries in front of the chocolate maker's sweet-stuff shows or stood listening to a musical box in a neighboring shop or fell into supreme ecstasies over cheap, vulgarly designed knickknacks, such as nutshell workboxes, ragpickers' baskets for holding toothpicks, Vendôme columns and Luxor obelisks on which thermometers were mounted. But that evening she was too much agitated and looked at things without seeing them. When all was said and done, it bored her to think she was not free. An obscure revolt raged within her, and amid it all she felt a wild desire to do something foolish. It was a great thing gained, forsooth, to be mistress of men of position! She had been devouring the prince's substance and Steiner's, too, with her childish caprices, and yet she had no notion where her money went. Even at this time of day her flat in the Boulevard Haussmann was not entirely furnished. The drawing room alone was finished, and with its red satin upholsteries and excess of ornamentation and furniture it struck a decidedly false note. Her creditors, moreover, would now take to tormenting her more than ever before whenever she had no money on hand, a fact which caused her constant surprise, seeing that she was wont to quote herself as a model of economy. For a month past that thief Steiner had been scarcely able to pay up his thousand francs on the occasions when she threatened to kick him out of doors in case he failed to bring them. As to Muffat, he was an idiot: he had no notion as to what it was usual to give, and she could not, therefore, grow angry with him on the score of miserliness. Oh, how gladly she would have turned all these folks off had she not repeated to herself a score of times daily a whole string of economical maxims!

One ought to be sensible, Zoé kept saying every morning, and Nana herself was constantly haunted by the queenly vision seen at Chamont. It had now become an almost religious memory with her, and through dint of being ceaselessly recalled it grew even more grandiose. And for these reasons, though trembling with repressed indignation, she now hung submissively on the count's arm as they went from window to window among the fast-diminishing crowd. The pavement was drying outside, and a cool wind blew along the gallery, swept the close hot air up beneath the glass that imprisoned it and shook the colored lanterns and the lines of gas jets and the giant fan which was flaring away like a set piece in an illumination. At the door of the restaurant a waiter was putting out the gas, while the motionless attendants in the empty, glaring shops looked as though they had dropped off to sleep with their eyes open.

"Oh, what a duck!" continued Nana, retracing her steps as far as the last of the shops in order to go into ecstasies over a porcelain greyhound standing with raised forepaw in front of a nest hidden among roses.

At length they quitted the passage, but she refused the offer of a cab. It was very pleasant out she said; besides, they were in no hurry, and it would be charming to return home on foot. When they were in front of the Café Anglais she had a sudden longing to eat oysters. Indeed, she said that owing to Louiset's illness she had tasted nothing since morning. Muffat dared not oppose her. Yet as he did not in those days wish to be seen about with her he asked for a private supper room and hurried to it along the corridors. She followed him with the air of a woman familiar with the house, and they were on the point of entering a private room, the door of which a waiter held open, when from a neighboring saloon, whence issued a perfect tempest of shouts and laughter, a man rapidly emerged. It was Daguenet.

"By Jove, it's Nana!" he cried.

The count had briskly disappeared into the private room, leaving the door ajar behind him. But Daguenet winked behind his round shoulders and added in chaffing tones:

"The deuce, but you're doing nicely! You catch 'em in the Tuileries nowadays!"

Nana smiled and laid a finger on her lips to beg him to be silent. She could see he was very much exalted, and yet she was glad to have met him, for she still felt tenderly toward him, and that despite the nasty way he had cut her when in the company of fashionable ladies.

"What are you doing now?" she asked amicably.

"Becoming respectable. Yes indeed, I'm thinking of getting married."

She shrugged her shoulders with a pitying air. But he jokingly continued to the effect that to be only just gaining enough on 'change to buy ladies bouquets could scarcely be called an income, provided you wanted to look respectable too! His three hundred thousand francs had only lasted him eighteen months! He wanted to be practical, and he was going to marry a girl with a huge dowry and end off as a *préfet*, like his father before him! Nana still smiled incredulously. She nodded in the direction of the saloon: "Who are you with in there?"

"Oh, a whole gang," he said, forgetting all about his projects under the influence of returning intoxication. "Just think! Léa is telling us about her trip in Egypt. Oh, it's screaming! There's a bathing story——"

And he told the story while Nana lingered complaisantly. They had ended by leaning up against the wall in the corridor, facing one another. Gas jets were flaring under the low ceiling, and a vague smell of cookery hung about the folds of the hangings. Now and again, in order to hear each other's voices when the din in the saloon became louder than ever, they had to lean well forward. Every few seconds, however, a waiter with an armful of dishes found his passage barred and disturbed them. But they did not cease their talk for that; on the contrary, they stood close up to the walls and, amid the uproar of the supper party and the jostlings of the waiters, chatted as quietly as if they were by their own firesides.

"Just look at that," whispered the young man, pointing to the door of the private room through which Muffat had vanished.

Both looked. The door was quivering slightly; a breath of air seemed to be disturbing it, and at last, very, very slowly and without the least sound, it was shut to. They exchanged a silent chuckle. The count must be looking charmingly happy all alone in there!

"By the by," she asked, "have you read Fauchery's article about me?"

"Yes, 'The Golden Fly,'" replied Daguenet; "I didn't mention it to you as I was afraid of paining you."

"Paining me—why? His article's a very long one."

She was flattered to think that the *Figaro* should concern itself about her person. But failing the explanations of her hairdresser Francis, who had brought her the paper, she would not have understood that it was she who was in question. Daguenet scrutinized her slyly, sneering in his chaffing way. Well, well, since she was pleased, everybody else ought to be.

"By your leave!" shouted a waiter, holding a dish of iced cheese in both hands as he separated them.

Nana had stepped toward the little saloon where Muffat was waiting.

"Well, good-by!" continued Daguenet. "Go and find your cuckold again." But she halted afresh.

"Why d'you call him cuckold?"

"Because he is a cuckold, by Jove!"

She came and leaned against the wall again; she was profoundly interested.

"Ah!" she said simply.

"What, d'you mean to say you didn't know that? Why, my dear girl, his wife's Fauchery's mistress. It probably began in the country. Some time ago, when I was coming here, Fauchery left me, and I suspect he's got an assignation with her at his place tonight. They've made up a story about a journey, I fancy."

Overcome with surprise, Nana remained voiceless.

"I suspected it," she said at last, slapping her leg. "I guessed it by merely looking at her on the highroad that day. To think of its being possible for an honest woman to deceive her husband, and with that blackguard Fauchery too! He'll teach her some pretty things!"

"Oh, it isn't her trial trip," muttered Daguenet wickedly. "Perhaps she knows as much about it as he does."

At this Nana gave vent to an indignant exclamation.

"Indeed she does! What a nice world! It's too foul!"

"By your leave!" shouted a waiter, laden with bottles, as he separated them.

Daguenet drew her forward again and held her hand for a second or two. He adopted his crystalline tone of voice, the voice with notes as sweet as those of a harmonica, which had gained him his success among the ladies of Nana's type.

"Good-by, darling! You know I love you always."

She disengaged her hand from his, and while a thunder of shouts and bravos, which made the door in the saloon tremble again, almost drowned her words she smilingly remarked:

"It's over between us, stupid! But that doesn't matter. Do come up one of these days, and we'll have a chat."

Then she became serious again and in the outraged tones of a respectable woman:

"So he's a cuckold, is he?" she cried. "Well, that *is* a nuisance, dear boy. They've always sickened me, cuckolds have."

When at length she went into the private room she noticed that Muffat was sitting resignedly on a narrow divan with pale face and twitching hands. He did not reproach her at all, and she, greatly moved, was divided between feelings of pity and of contempt. The poor man! To think of his being so unworthily cheated by a vile wife! She had a good mind to throw her arms round his neck and comfort him. But it was only fair all the same! He was a fool with women, and this would teach him a lesson! Nevertheless, pity overcame her. She did not get rid of him as she had determined to do after the oysters had been discussed. They scarcely stayed a quarter of an hour in the Café Anglais, and together they went into the house in the Boulevard Haussmann. It was then eleven. Before midnight she would have easily have discovered some means of getting rid of him kindly.

In the anteroom, however, she took the precaution of giving Zoé an order.

"You'll look out for him, and you'll tell him not to make a noise if the other man's still with me."

"But where shall I put him, madame?"

"Keep him in the kitchen. It's more safe."

In the room inside Muffat was already taking off his overcoat. A big fire was burning on the hearth. It was the same room as of old, with its rosewood furniture and its hangings and chair coverings of figured damask with the large blue flowers on a gray background. On two occasions Nana had thought of having it redone, the first in black velvet, the second in white satin with bows, but directly Steiner consented she demanded the money that these changes would cost simply with a view to pillaging him. She had, indeed, only indulged in a tiger skin rug for the hearth and a cut-glass hanging lamp.

"I'm not sleepy; I'm not going to bed," she said the moment they were shut in together.

The count obeyed her submissively, as became a man no longer afraid of being seen. His one care now was to avoid vexing her.

"As you will," he murmured.

Nevertheless, he took his boots off, too, before seating himself in front of the fire. One of Nana's pleasures consisted in undressing herself in front of the mirror on her wardrobe door, which reflected her whole height. She would let everything slip off her in turn and then would stand perfectly naked and gaze and gaze in complete oblivion of all around her. Passion for her own body, ecstasy over her satin skin and the supple contours of her shape, would keep her serious, attentive and absorbed in the love of herself. The hairdresser frequently found her standing thus and would enter without her once turning to look at him. Muffat used to grow angry then, but he only succeeded in astonishing her. What was coming over the man? She was doing it to please herself, not other people.

That particular evening she wanted to have a better view of herself, and she lit the six candles attached to the frame of the mirror. But while letting her shift slip down she paused. She had been preoccupied for some moments past, and a question was on her lips.

"You haven't read the *Figaro* article, have you? The paper's on the table."

Daguenet's laugh had recurred to her recollections, and she was harassed by a doubt. If that Fauchery had slandered her she would be revenged.

"They say that it's about me," she continued, affecting indifference. "What's your notion, eh, darling?"

And letting go her shift and waiting till Muffat should have done reading, she stood naked. Muffat was reading slowly Fauchery's article entitled "The Golden Fly," describing the life of a harlot descended from four or five generations of drunkards and tainted in her blood by a cumulative inheritance of misery and drink, which in her case has taken the form of a nervous exaggeration of the sexual instinct. She has shot up to womanhood in the slums and on the pavements of Paris, and tall, handsome and as superbly grown as a dunghill plant, she avenges the beggars and outcasts of whom she is the ultimate product. With her the rottenness that is allowed to ferment among the populace is carried upward and rots the aristocracy. She becomes a blind power of nature, a leaven of destruction, and unwittingly she corrupts and disorganizes all Paris, churning it between her snow-white thighs as milk is monthly churned by housewives. And it was at the end of this article that the comparison with a fly occurred, a fly of sunny hue which has flown up out of the dung, a fly which sucks in death on the carrion tolerated by the road-side and then buzzing, dancing and glittering like a precious stone enters the windows of palaces and poisons the men within by merely settling on them in her flight.

Muffat lifted his head; his eyes stared fixedly; he gazed at the fire.

"Well?" asked Nana.

But he did not answer. It seemed as though he wanted to read the article again. A cold, shivering feeling was creeping from his scalp to his shoulders. This article had been written anyhow. The phrases were wildly extravagant; the unexpected epigrams and quaint collocations of words went beyond all bounds. Yet notwithstanding this, he was struck by what he had read, for it had rudely awakened within him much that for months past he had not cared to think about.

He looked up. Nana had grown absorbed in her ecstatic self-contemplation. She was bending her neck and was looking attentively in the mirror at a little brown mark above her right haunch. She was touching it with the tip of her finger and by dint of bending backward was making it stand out more clearly than ever. Situated where it was, it doubtless struck her as both quaint and pretty. After that she studied other parts of her body with an amused expression and much of the vicious curiosity of a child. The sight of herself always astonished her, and she would look as surprised and ecstatic as a young girl who has discovered her puberty. Slowly, slowly, she spread out her arms in order to give full value to her figure, which suggested the torso of a plump Venus. She bent herself this way and that and examined herself before and behind, stooping to look at the side view of her bosom and at the sweeping contours of her thighs. And she ended with a strange amusement which consisted of swinging to right and left, her knees apart and her body swaying from the waist with the perpetual jogging, twitching movements peculiar to an oriental dancer in the *danse du ventre*.

Muffat sat looking at her. She frightened him. The newspaper had dropped from his hand. For a moment he saw her as she was, and he despised himself. Yes, it was just that; she had corrupted his life; he already felt himself tainted to his very marrow by impurities hitherto undreamed of. Everything was now destined to rot within him, and in the twinkling of an eye he understood what this evil entailed. He saw the ruin brought about by this kind of "leaven" —himself poisoned, his family destroyed, a bit of the social fabric cracking and crumbling. And unable to take his eyes from the sight, he sat looking fixedly at her, striving to inspire himself with loathing for her nakedness.

Nana no longer moved. With an arm behind her neck, one hand clasped in the other, and her elbows far apart, she was throwing back her head so that he could see a foreshortened reflection of her half-closed eyes, her parted lips, her face clothed with amorous laughter. Her masses of yellow hair were unknotted behind, and they covered her back with the fell of a lioness.

Bending back thus, she displayed her solid Amazonian waist and firm bosom, where strong muscles moved under the satin texture of the skin. A delicate line, to which the shoulder and the thigh added their slight undulations, ran from one of her elbows to her foot, and Muffat's eyes followed this tender profile and marked how the outlines of the fair flesh vanished in golden gleams and how its rounded contours shone like silk in the candlelight. He thought of his old dread of Woman, of the Beast of the Scriptures, at once lewd and wild. Nana was all covered with fine hair; a russet made her body velvety, while the Beast was apparent in the almost equine development of her flanks, in the fleshy exuberances and deep hollows of her body, which lent her sex the mystery and suggestiveness lurking in their shadows. She was, indeed, that Golden Creature, blind as brute force, whose very odor ruined the world. Muffat gazed and gazed as a man possessed, till at last, when he had shut his eyes in order to escape it, the Brute reappeared in the darkness of the brain, larger, more terrible, more suggestive in its attitude. Now, he understood, it would remain before his eyes, in his very flesh, forever.

But Nana was gathering herself together. A little thrill of tenderness seemed to have traversed her members. Her eyes were moist; she tried, as it were, to make herself small, as though she could feel herself better thus. Then she threw her head and bosom back and, melting, as it were, in one great bodily caress, she rubbed her cheeks coaxingly, first against one shoulder, then against the other. Her lustful mouth breathed desire over her limbs. She put out her lips, kissed herself long in the neighborhood of her armpit and laughed at the other Nana who also was kissing herself in the mirror.

Then Muffat gave a long sigh. This solitary pleasure exasperated him. Suddenly all his resolutions were swept away as though by a mighty wind. In a fit of brutal passion he caught Nana to his breast and threw her down on the carpet.

"Leave me alone!" she cried. "You're hurting me!"

He was conscious of his undoing; he recognized in her stupidity, vileness and falsehood, and he longed to possess her, poisoned though she was.

"Oh, you're a fool!" she said savagely when he let her get up.

Nevertheless, she grew calm. He would go now. She slipped on a nightgown trimmed with lace and came and sat down on the floor in front of the fire. It was her favorite position. When she again questioned him about Faucherý's article Muffat replied vaguely, for he wanted to avoid a scene.

Besides, she declared that she had found a weak spot in Fauchery. And with that she relapsed into a long silence and reflected on how to dismiss the count. She would have liked to do it in an agreeable way, for she was still a good-natured wench, and it bored her to cause others pain, especially in the present instance where the man was a cuckold. The mere thought of his being that had ended by rousing her sympathies!

"So you expect your wife tomorrow morning?" she said at last.

Muffat had stretched himself in an armchair. He looked drowsy, and his limbs were tired. He gave a sign of assent. Nana sat gazing seriously at him with a dull tumult in her brain. Propped on one leg, among her slightly rumpled laces she was holding one of her bare feet between her hands and was turning it mechanically about and about.

"Have you been married long?" she asked.

"Nineteen years," replied the count.

"Ah! And is your wife amiable? Do you get on comfortably together?"

He was silent. Then with some embarrassment:

"You know I've begged you never to talk of those matters."

"Dear me, why's that?" she cried, beginning to grow vexed directly. "I'm sure I won't eat your wife if I *do* talk about her. Dear boy, why, every woman's worth——"

But she stopped for fear of saying too much. She contented herself by assuming a superior expression, since she considered herself extremely kind. The poor fellow, he needed delicate handling! Besides, she had been struck by a laughable notion, and she smiled as she looked him carefully over.

"I say," she continued, "I haven't told you the story about you that Fauchery's circulating. There's a viper, if you like! I don't bear him any ill will, because his article may be all right, but he's a regular viper all the same."

And laughing more gaily than ever, she let go her foot and, crawling along the floor, came and propped herself against the count's knees.

"Now just fancy, he swears you were still like a babe when you married your wife. You were still like that, eh? Is it true, eh?"

Her eyes pressed for an answer, and she raised her hands to his shoulders and began shaking him in order to extract the desired confession.

"Without doubt," he at last made answer gravely.

Thereupon she again sank down at his feet. She was shaking with uproarious laughter, and she stuttered and dealt him little slaps.

"No, it's too funny! There's no one like you; you're a marvel. But, my poor pet, you must just have been stupid! When a man doesn't know—oh, it is so comical! Good heavens, I should have liked to have seen you! And it came off well, did it? Now tell me something about it! Oh, do, do tell me!"

She overwhelmed him with questions, forgetting nothing and requiring the veriest details. And she laughed such sudden merry peals which doubled her up with mirth, and her chemise slipped and got turned down to such an extent, and her skin looked so golden in the light of the big fire, that little by little the count described to her his bridal night. He no longer felt at all awkward. He himself began to be amused at last as he spoke. Only he kept choosing his

ohrases, for he still had a certain sense of modesty. The young woman, now
horoughly interested, asked him about the countess. According to his account,
he had a marvelous figure but was a regular iceberg for all that.

"Oh, get along with you!" he muttered indolently. "You have no cause
o be jealous."

Nana had ceased laughing, and she now resumed her former position and,
with her back to the fire, brought her knees up under her chin with her
clasped hands. Then in a serious tone she declared:

"It doesn't pay, dear boy, to look like a ninny with one's wife the first
night."

"Why?" queried the astonished count.

"Because," she replied slowly, assuming a doctorial expression.

And with that she looked as if she were delivering a lecture and shook her
head at him. In the end, however, she condescended to explain herself more
lucidly.

"Well, look here! I know how it all happens. Yes, dearie, women don't like
a man to be foolish. They don't say anything because there's such a thing as
modesty, you know, but you may be sure they think about it for a jolly long
time to come. And sooner or later, when a man's been an ignoramus, they go
and make other arrangements. That's it, my pet."

He did not seem to understand. Whereupon she grew more definite still.
She became maternal and taught him his lesson out of sheer goodness of heart,
as a friend might do. Since she had discovered him to be a cuckold the information had weighed on her spirits; she was madly anxious to discuss his
position with him.

"Good heavens! I'm talking of things that don't concern me. I've said what
I have because everybody ought to be happy. We're having a chat, eh? Well
then, you're to answer me as straight as you can."

But she stopped to change her position, for she was burning herself.

"It's jolly hot, eh? My back's roasted. Wait a second. I'll cook my tummy
a bit. That's what's good for the aches!"

And when she had turned round with her breast to the fire and her feet
tucked under her:

"Let me see," she said; "you don't sleep with your wife any longer?"

"No, I swear to you I don't," said Muffat, dreading a scene.

"And you believe she's really a stick?"

He bowed his head in the affirmative.

"And that's why you love me? Answer me! I shan't be angry."

He repeated the same movement.

"Very well then," she concluded. "I suspected as much! Oh, the poor pet.
Do you know my aunt Lerat? When she comes get her to tell you the story
about the fruiterer who lives opposite her. Just fancy that man—— Damn it,
how hot this fire is! I must turn round. I'm going to roast my left side now."

And as she presented her side to the blaze a droll idea struck her, and like
a good-tempered thing, she made fun of herself for she was delighted to see
that she was looking so plump and pink in the light of the coal fire.

"I look like a goose, eh? Yes, that's it! I'm a goose on the spit, and I'm turning, turning and cooking in my own juice, eh?"

And she was once more indulging in a merry fit of laughter when a sound of voices and slamming doors became audible. Muffat was surprised, and he questioned her with a look. She grew serious, and an anxious expression came over her face. It must be Zoé's cat, a cursed beast that broke everything. It was half-past twelve o'clock. How long was she going to bother herself in her cuckold's behalf? Now that the other man had come she ought to get him out of the way, and that quickly.

"What were you saying?" asked the count complaisantly, for he was charmed to see her so kind to him.

But in her desire to be rid of him she suddenly changed her mood, became brutal and did not take care what she was saying.

"Oh yes! The fruiterer and his wife. Well, my dear fellow, they never once touched one another! Not the least bit! She was very keen on it, you understand, but he, the ninny, didn't know it. He was so green that he thought her a stick, and so he went elsewhere and took up with streetwalkers, who treated him to all sorts of nastiness, while she, on her part, made up for it beautifully with fellows who were a lot slyer than her greenhorn of a husband. And things always turn out that way through people not understanding one another. I know it, I do!"

Muffat was growing pale. At last he was beginning to understand her allusions, and he wanted to make her keep silence. But she was in full swing.

"No, hold your tongue, will you? If you weren't brutes you would be as nice with your wives as you are with us, and if your wives weren't geese they would take as much pains to keep you as we do to get you. That's the way to behave. Yes, my duck, you can put that in your pipe and smoke it."

"Do not talk of honest women," he said in a hard voice. "You do not know them."

At that Nana rose to her knees.

"I don't know them! Why, they aren't even clean, your honest women aren't! They aren't even clean! I defy you to find me one who would dare show herself as I am doing. Oh, you make me laugh with your honest women! Don't drive me to it; don't oblige me to tell you things I may regret afterward."

The count, by way of answer, mumbled something insulting. Nana became quite pale in her turn. For some seconds she looked at him without speaking. Then in her decisive way:

"What would you do if your wife were deceiving you?"

He made a threatening gesture.

"Well, and if I were to?"

"Oh, you," he muttered with a shrug of his shoulders.

Nana was certainly not spiteful. Since the beginning of the conversation she had been strongly tempted to throw his cuckold's reputation in his teeth, but she had resisted. She would have liked to confess him quietly on the subject, but he had begun to exasperate her at last. The matter ought to stop now.

"Well, then, my dearie," she continued, "I don't know what you're getting t with me. For two hours past you've been worrying my life out. Now do ust go and find your wife, for she's at it with Fauchery. Yes, it's quite correct; hey're in the Rue Taitbout, at the corner of the Rue de Provençe. You see, 'm giving you the address."

Then triumphantly, as she saw Muffat stagger to his feet like an ox under he hammer:

"If honest women must meddle in our affairs and take our sweethearts from is—— Oh, you bet they're a nice lot, those honest women!"

But she was unable to proceed. With a terrible push he had cast her full ength on the floor and, lifting his heel, he seemed on the point of crushing in ler head in order to silence her. For the twinkling of an eye she felt sickening dread. Blinded with rage, he had begun beating about the room like a maniac. Then his choking silence and the struggle with which he was shaken melted ler to tears. She felt a mortal regret and, rolling herself up in front of the ire so as to roast her right side, she undertook the task of comforting him.

"I take my oath, darling, I thought you knew it all. Otherwise I shouldn't ave spoken; you may be sure. But perhaps it isn't true. I don't say anything or certain. I've been told it, and people are talking about it, but what does hat prove? Oh, get along! You're very silly to grow riled about it. If I were man I shouldn't care a rush for the women! All the women are alike, you ee, high or low; they're all rowdy and the rest of it."

In a fit of self-abnegation she was severe on womankind, for she wished hus to lessen the cruelty of her blow. But he did not listen to her or hear vhat she said. With fumbling movements he had put on his boots and his overcoat. For a moment longer he raved round, and then in a final outburst, inding himself near the door, he rushed from the room. Nana was very nuch annoyed.

"Well, well! A prosperous trip to you!" she continued aloud, though she vas now alone. "He's polite, too, that fellow is, when he's spoken to! And I lad to defend myself at that! Well, I was the first to get back my temper and made plenty of excuses, I'm thinking! Besides, he had been getting on my lerves!"

Nevertheless, she was not happy and sat scratching her legs with both hands. Then she took high ground:

"Tut, tut, it isn't my fault if he is a cuckold!"

And toasted on every side and as hot as a roast bird, she went and buried lerself under the bedclothes after ringing for Zoé to usher in the other man, vho was waiting in the kitchen.

Once outside, Muffat began walking at a furious pace. A fresh shower had ust fallen, and he kept slipping on the greasy pavement. When he looked nechanically up into the sky he saw ragged, soot-colored clouds scudding in front of the moon. At this hour of the night passers-by were becoming few and far between in the Boulevard Haussmann. He skirted the enclosures round the opera house in his search for darkness, and as he went along he kept mumbling inconsequent phrases. That girl had been lying. She had invented her story out of sheer stupidity and cruelty. He ought to have crushed

her head when he had it under his heel. After all was said and done, the busi
ness was too shameful. Never would he see her; never would he touch her
again, or if he did he would be miserably weak. And with that he breathed
hard, as though he were free once more. Oh, that naked, cruel monster, roast
ing away like any goose and slavering over everything that he had respected
for forty years back. The moon had come out, and the empty street was bathed
in white light. He felt afraid, and he burst into a great fit of sobbing, for he
had grown suddenly hopeless and maddened as though he had sunk into a
fathomless void.

"My God!" he stuttered out. "It's finished! There's nothing left now!"

Along the boulevards belated people were hurrying. He tried hard to be
calm, and as the story told him by that courtesan kept recurring to his burning
consciousness, he wanted to reason the matter out. The countess was coming
up from Mme de Chezelles's country house tomorrow morning. Yet nothing
in fact, could have prevented her from returning to Paris the night before
and passing it with that man. He now began recalling to mind certain details
of their stay at Les Fondettes. One evening, for instance, he had surprised
Sabine in the shade of some trees, when she was so much agitated as to be
unable to answer his questions. The man had been present; why should she
not be with him now? The more he thought about it the more possible the
whole story became, and he ended by thinking it natural and even inevitable.
While he was in his shirt sleeves in the house of a harlot his wife was undressing in her lover's room. Nothing could be simpler or more logical!
Reasoning in this way, he forced himself to keep cool. He felt as if there
were a great downward movement in the direction of fleshly madness, a movement which, as it grew, was overcoming the whole world round about him.
Warm images pursued him in imagination. A naked Nana suddenly evoked a
naked Sabine. At this vision, which seemed to bring them together in shame-
less relationship and under the influence of the same lusts, he literally stumbled,
and in the road a cab nearly ran over him. Some women who had come out
of a café jostled him amid loud laughter. Then a fit of weeping once more
overcame him, despite all his efforts to the contrary, and, not wishing to shed
tears in the presence of others, he plunged into a dark and empty street. It
was the Rue Rossini, and along its silent length he wept like a child.

"It's over with us," he said in hollow tones. "There's nothing left us now,
nothing left us now!"

He wept so violently that he had to lean up against a door as he buried his
face in his wet hands. A noise of footsteps drove him away. He felt a shame
and a fear which made him fly before people's faces with the restless step of
a bird of darkness. When passers-by met him on the pavement he did his
best to look and walk in a leisurely way, for he fancied they were reading his
secret in the very swing of his shoulders. He had followed the Rue de la
Grange Batelière as far as the Rue du Faubourg Montmartre, where the brilliant lamplight surprised him, and he retraced his steps. For nearly an hour
he traversed the district thus, choosing always the darkest corners. Doubtless
there was some goal whither his steps were patiently, instinctively, leading

im through a labyrinth of endless turnings. At length he lifted his eyes up
t a street corner. He had reached his destination, the point where the Rue
Taitbout and the Rue de la Provençe met. He had taken an hour amid his
painful mental sufferings to arrive at a place he could have reached in five
minutes. One morning a month ago he remembered going up to Fauchery's
rooms to thank him for a notice of a ball at the Tuileries, in which the
journalist had mentioned him. The flat was between the ground floor and the
first story and had a row of small square windows which were half hidden
by the colossal signboard belonging to a shop. The last window on the left
was bisected by a brilliant band of lamplight coming from between the half-
closed curtains. And he remained absorbed and expectant, with his gaze fixed
on this shining streak.

The moon had disappeared in an inky sky, whence an icy drizzle was falling.
Two o'clock struck at the Trinité. The Rue de Provençe and the Rue Taitbout lay in shadow, bestarred at intervals by bright splashes of light from the
gas lamps, which in the distance were merged in yellow mist. Muffat did not
move from where he was standing. That was the room. He remembered it
now: it had hangings of red "andrinople," and a Louis XIII bed stood at one
end of it. The lamp must be standing on the chimney piece to the right. Without doubt they had gone to bed, for no shadows passed across the window,
and the bright streak gleamed as motionless as the light of a night lamp. With
his eyes still uplifted he began forming a plan; he would ring the bell, go
upstairs despite the porter's remonstrances, break the doors in with a push of
his shoulder and fall upon them in the very bed without giving them time to
unlace their arms. For one moment the thought that he had no weapon upon
him gave him pause, but directly afterward he decided to throttle them. He
returned to the consideration of his project, and he perfected it while waiting
for some sign, some indication, which should bring certainty with it.

Had a woman's shadow only shown itself at that moment he would have
rung. But the thought that perhaps he was deceiving himself froze him. How
could he be certain? Doubts began to return. His wife could not be with that
man. It was monstrous and impossible. Nevertheless, he stayed where he was
and was gradually overcome by a species of torpor which merged into sheer
feebleness while he waited long, and the fixity of his gaze induced hallucina-
tions.

A shower was falling. Two policemen were approaching, and he was forced
to leave the doorway where he had taken shelter. When these were lost to
view in the Rue de Provençe he returned to his post, wet and shivering. The
luminous streak still traversed the window, and this time he was going away
for good when a shadow crossed it. It moved so quickly that he thought he
had deceived himself. But first one and then another black thing followed
quickly after it, and there was a regular commotion in the room. Riveted
anew to the pavement, he experienced an intolerable burning sensation in his
inside as he waited to find out the meaning of it all. Outlines of arms and legs
flitted after one another, and an enormous hand traveled about with the silhouette of a water jug. He distinguished nothing clearly, but he thought he

recognized a woman's headdress. And he disputed the point with himself; it might well have been Sabine's hair, only the neck did not seem sufficientl slim. At that hour of the night he had lost the power of recognition and o action. In this terrible agony of uncertainty his inside caused him such acut suffering that he pressed against the door in order to calm himself, shivering like a man in rags, as he did so. Then seeing that despite everything he could not turn his eyes away from the window, his anger changed into a fit o moralizing. He fancied himself a deputy; he was haranguing an assembly loudly denouncing debauchery, prophesying national ruin. And he recon structed Fauchery's article on the poisoned fly, and he came before the house and declared that morals such as these, which could only be paralleled in the days of the later Roman Empire, rendered society an impossibility; that did him good. But the shadows had meanwhile disappeared. Doubtless they had gone to bed again, and, still watching, he continued waiting where he was

Three o'clock struck, then four, but he could not take his departure. When showers fell he buried himself in a corner of the doorway, his legs splashed with wet. Nobody passed by now, and occasionally his eyes would close, a though scorched by the streak of light, which he kept watching obstinately fixedly, with idiotic persistence. On two subsequent occasions the shadow flitted about, repeating the same gestures and agitating the silhouette of the same gigantic jug, and twice quiet was re-established, and the night lamp again glowed discreetly out. These shadows only increased his uncertainty. Then too, a sudden idea soothed his brain while it postponed the decisive moment. After all, he had only to wait for the woman when she left the house. He could quite easily recognize Sabine. Nothing could be simpler, and there would be no scandal, and he would be sure of things one way or the other. It was only necessary to stay where he was. Among all the confused feelings which had been agitating him he now merely felt a dull need of certain knowl- edge. But sheer weariness and vacancy began lulling him to sleep under his doorway, and by way of distraction he tried to reckon up how long he would have to wait. Sabine was to be at the station toward nine o'clock; that meant about four hours and a half more. He was very patient; he would even have been content not to move again, and he found a certain charm in fancying that his night vigil would last through eternity.

Suddenly the streak of light was gone. This extremely simple event was to him an unforeseen catastrophe, at once troublesome and disagreeable. Evi- dently they had just put the lamp out and were going to sleep. It was reason- able enough at that hour, but he was irritated thereat, for now the darkened window ceased to interest him. He watched it for a quarter of an hour longer and then grew tired and, leaving the doorway, took a turn upon the pave- ment. Until five o'clock he walked to and fro, looking upward from time to time. The window seemed a dead thing, and now and then he asked himself if he had not dreamed that shadows had been dancing up there behind the panes. An intolerable sense of fatigue weighed him down, a dull, heavy feeling, under the influence of which he forgot what he was waiting for at that particular street corner. He kept stumbling on the pavement and starting into wakeful-

ess with the icy shudder of a man who does not know where he is. Nothing
eemed to justify the painful anxiety he was inflicting on himself. Since those
eople were asleep—well then, let them sleep! What good could it do mixing
a their affairs? It was very dark; no one would ever know anything about this
ight's doings. And with that every sentiment within him, down to curiosity
self, took flight before the longing to have done with it all and to find relief
omewhere. The cold was increasing, and the street was becoming insuffer-
ble. Twice he walked away and slowly returned, dragging one foot behind
he other, only to walk farther away next time. It was all over; nothing was
eft him now, and so he went down the whole length of the boulevard and did
ot return.

His was a melancholy progress through the streets. He walked slowly, never
hanging his pace and simply keeping along the walls of the houses.

His boot heels re-echoed, and he saw nothing but his shadow moving at his
ide. As he neared each successive gaslight it grew taller and immediately
fterward diminished. But this lulled him and occupied him mechanically. He
ever knew afterward where he had been; it seemed as if he had dragged
imself round and round in a circle for hours. One reminiscence only was
ery distinctly retained by him. Without his being able to explain how it
ame about he found himself with his face pressed close against the gate at
he end of the Passage des Panoramas and his two hands grasping the bars.
He did not shake them but, his whole heart swelling with emotion, he simply
ried to look into the passage. But he could make nothing out clearly, for
hadows flooded the whole length of the deserted gallery, and the wind, blow-
ng hard down the Rue Saint-Marc, puffed in his face with the damp breath
of a cellar. For a time he tried doggedly to see into the place, and then,
wakening from his dream, he was filled with astonishment and asked himself
what he could possibly be seeking for at that hour and in that position, for
he had pressed against the railings so fiercely that they had left their mark
n his face. Then he went on tramp once more. He was hopeless, and his heart
vas full of infinite sorrow, for he felt, amid all those shadows, that he was
evermore betrayed and alone.

Day broke at last. It was the murky dawn that follows winter nights and
ooks so melancholy from muddy Paris pavements. Muffat had returned into
he wide streets, which were then in course of construction on either side of
he new opera house. Soaked by the rain and cut up by cart wheels, the
chalky soil had become a lake of liquid mire. But he never looked to see where
he was stepping and walked on and on, slipping and regaining his footing as he
vent. The awakening of Paris, with its gangs of sweepers and early workmen
rooping to their destinations, added to his troubles as day brightened. People
tared at him in surprise as he went by with scared look and soaked hat and
nuddy clothes. For a long while he sought refuge against palings and among
caffoldings, his desolate brain haunted by the single remaining thought that
he was very miserable.

Then he thought of God. The sudden idea of divine help, of superhuman
consolation, surprised him, as though it were something unforeseen and ex-

traordinary. The image of M. Venot was evoked thereby, and he saw his little plump face and ruined teeth. Assuredly M. Venot, whom for months he had been avoiding and thereby rendering miserable, would be delighted were he to go and knock at his door and fall weeping into his arms. In the old days God had been always so merciful toward him. At the least sorrow, the slightest obstacle on the path of life, he had been wont to enter a church, where, kneeling down, he would humble his littleness in the presence of Omnipotence. And he had been used to go forth thence, fortified by prayer, fully prepared to give up the good things of this world, possessed by the single yearning for eternal salvation. But at present he only practiced by fits and starts, when the terror of hell came upon him. All kinds of weak inclinations had overcome him, and the thought of Nana disturbed his devotions. And now the thought of God astonished him. Why had he not thought of God before, in the hour of that terrible agony when his feeble humanity was breaking up in ruin?

Meanwhile with slow and painful steps he sought for a church. But he had lost his bearings; the early hour had changed the face of the streets. Soon, however, as he turned the corner of the Rue de la Chaussée-d'Antin, he noticed a tower looming vaguely in the fog at the end of the Trinité Church. The white statues overlooking the bare garden seemed like so many chilly Venuses among the yellow foliage of a park. Under the porch he stood and panted a little, for the ascent of the wide steps had tired him. Then he went in. The church was very cold, for its heating apparatus had been fireless since the previous evening, and its lofty, vaulted aisles were full of a fine damp vapor which had come filtering through the windows. The aisles were deep in shadow; not a soul was in the church, and the only sound audible amid the unlovely darkness was that made by the old shoes of some verger or other who was dragging himself about in sulky semiwakefulness. Muffat, however, after knocking forlornly against an untidy collection of chairs, sank on his knees with bursting heart and propped himself against the rails in front of a little chapel close by a font. He clasped his hands and began searching within himself for suitable prayers, while his whole being yearned toward a transport. But only his lips kept stammering empty words; his heart and brain were far away, and with them he returned to the outer world and began his long, unresting march through the streets, as though lashed forward by implacable necessity. And he kept repeating, "O my God, come to my assistance! O my God, abandon not Thy creature, who delivers himself up to Thy justice! O my God, I adore Thee: Thou wilt not leave me to perish under the buffetings of mine enemies!" Nothing answered: the shadows and the cold weighed upon him, and the noise of the old shoes continued in the distance and prevented him praying. Nothing, indeed, save that tiresome noise was audible in the deserted church, where the matutinal sweeping was unknown before the early masses had somewhat warmed the air of the place. After that he rose to his feet with the help of a chair, his knees cracking under him as he did so. God was not yet there. And why should he weep in M. Venot's arms? The man could do nothing.

And then mechanically he returned to Nana's house. Outside he slipped,

nd he felt the tears welling to his eyes again, but he was not angry with his
ot—he was only feeble and ill. Yes, he was too tired; the rain had wet him
oo much; he was nipped with cold, but the idea of going back to his great
ark house in the Rue Miromesnil froze his heart. The house door at Nana's
as not open as yet, and he had to wait till the porter made his appearance.
Ie smiled as he went upstairs, for he already felt penetrated by the soft
varmth of that cozy retreat, where he would be able to stretch his limbs and
o to sleep.

When Zoé opened the door to him she gave a start of most uneasy astonish-
nent. Madame had been taken ill with an atrocious sick headache, and she
adn't closed her eyes all night. Still, she could quite go and see whether
Iadame had gone to sleep for good. And with that she slipped into the bed-
oom while he sank back into one of the armchairs in the drawing room. But
lmost at that very moment Nana appeared. She had jumped out of bed and
ad scarce had time to slip on a petticoat. Her feet were bare, her hair in
vild disorder, her nightgown all crumpled.

"What! You here again?" she cried with a red flush on her cheeks.

Up she rushed, stung by sudden indignation, in order herself to thrust him
ut of doors. But when she saw him in such sorry plight—nay, so utterly done
or—she felt infinite pity.

"Well, you are a pretty sight, my dear fellow!" she continued more gently.
But what's the matter? You've spotted them, eh? And it's given you the
ump?"

He did not answer; he looked like a broken-down animal. Nevertheless, she
ame to the conclusion that he still lacked proofs, and to hearten him up
he said:

"You see now? I was on the wrong tack. Your wife's an honest woman, on
ny word of honor! And now, my little friend, you must go home to bed. You
vant it badly."

He did not stir.

"Now then, be off! I can't keep you here. But perhaps you won't presume
o stay at such a time as this?"

"Yes, let's go to bed," he stammered.

She repressed a violent gesture, for her patience was deserting her. Was the
nan going crazy?

"Come, be off!" she repeated.

"No."

But she flared up in exasperation, in utter rebellion.

"It's sickening! Don't you understand I'm jolly tired of your company?
Go and find your wife, who's making a cuckold of you. Yes, she's making
 cuckold of you. I say so—yes, I do now. There, you've got the sack! Will
ou leave me or will you not?"

Muffat's eyes filled with tears. He clasped his hands together.

"Oh, let's go to bed!"

At this Nana suddenly lost all control over herself and was choked by nerv-
us sobs. She was being taken advantage of when all was said and done! What

had these stories to do with her? She certainly had used all manner of delicat
methods in order to teach him his lesson gently. And now he was for makin
her pay the damages! No, thank you! She was kindhearted, but not to tha
extent.

"The devil, but I've had enough of this!" she swore, bringing her fist dow
on the furniture. "Yes, yes, I wanted to be faithful—it was all I could do t
be that! Yet if I spoke the word I could be rich tomorrow, my dear fellow!"

He looked up in surprise. Never once had he thought of the monetar
question. If she only expressed a desire he would realize it at once; his who
fortune was at her service.

"No, it's too late now," she replied furiously. "I like men who give withou
being asked. No, if you were to offer me a million for a single interview
should say no! It's over between us; I've got other fish to fry there! So be o
or I shan't answer for the consequences. I shall do something dreadful!"

She advanced threateningly toward him, and while she was raving, as be
came a good courtesan who, though driven to desperation, was yet firml
convinced of her rights and her superiority over tiresome, honest folks, th
door opened suddenly and Steiner presented himself. That proved the finishin
touch. She shrieked aloud:

"Well, I never. Here's the other one!"

Bewildered by her piercing outcry, Steiner stopped short. Muffat's unex
pected presence annoyed him, for he feared an explanation and had been doin
his best to avoid it these three months past. With blinking eyes he stood firs
on one leg, then on the other, looking embarrassed the while and avoiding
the count's gaze. He was out of breath, and as became a man who had rushe
across Paris with good news, only to find himself involved in unforeseer
trouble, his face was flushed and distorted.

"Que veux-tu, toi?" asked Nana roughly, using the second person singula
in open mockery of the count.

"What—what do I——" he stammered. "I've got it for you—you know what.
"Eh?"

He hesitated. The day before yesterday she had given him to understan
that if he could not find her a thousand francs to pay a bill with she woul
not receive him any more. For two days he had been loafing about the tow
in quest of the money and had at last made the sum up that very morning

"The thousand francs!" he ended by declaring as he drew an envelope fron
his pocket.

Nana had not remembered.

"The thousand francs!" she cried. "D'you think I'm begging alms? Now
look here, that's what I value your thousand francs at!"

And snatching the envelope, she threw it full in his face. As became a pru
dent Hebrew, he picked it up slowly and painfully and then looked at the
young woman with a dull expression of face. Muffat and he exchanged a
despairing glance, while she put her arms akimbo in order to shout more loudly
than before.

"Come now, will you soon have done insulting me? I'm glad you've come,

o, dear boy, because now you see the clearance'll be quite complete. Now
en, gee up! Out you go!"

Then as they did not hurry in the least, for they were paralyzed:

"D'you mean to say I'm acting like a fool, eh? It's likely enough! But you've
red me too much! And, hang it all, I've had enough of swelldom! If I die
what I'm doing—well, it's my fancy!"

They sought to calm her; they begged her to listen to reason.

"Now then, once, twice, thrice! Won't you go? Very well! Look there!
ve got company."

And with a brisk movement she flung wide the bedroom door. Whereupon
the middle of the tumbled bed the two men caught sight of Fontan. He
d not expected to be shown off in this situation; nevertheless, he took things
ry easily, for he was used to sudden surprises on the stage. Indeed, after the
st shock he even hit upon a grimace calculated to tide him honorably over
s difficulty; he "turned rabbit," as he phrased it, and stuck out his lips and
rinkled up his nose, so as completely to transform the lower half of his face.
is base, satyrlike head seemed to exude incontinence. It was this man Fontan
en whom Nana had been to fetch at the Variétiés every day for a week
ast, for she was smitten with that fierce sort of passion which the grimacing
gliness of a low comedian is wont to inspire in the genus courtesan.

"There!" she said, pointing him out with tragic gesture.

Muffat, who hitherto had pocketed everything, rebelled at this affront.

"Bitch!" he stammered.

But Nana, who was once more in the bedroom, came back in order to have
ae last word.

"How am I a bitch? What about your wife?"

And she was off and, slamming the door with a bang, she noisily pushed to
ae bolt. Left alone, the two men gazed at one another in silence. Zoé had just
ome into the room, but she did not drive them out. Nay, she spoke to them
a the most sensible manner. As became a woman with a head on her shoul-
ers, she decided that Madame's conduct was rather too much of a good thing.
ut she defended her, nonetheless: this union with the play actor couldn't
st; the madness must be allowed to pass off! The two men retired without
ttering a sound. On the pavement outside they shook hands silently, as though
vayed by a mutual sense of fraternity. Then they turned their backs on one
nother and went crawling off in opposite directions.

When at last Muffat entered his town house in the Rue Miromesnil his wife
as just arriving. The two met on the great staircase, whose walls exhaled an
y chill. They lifted up their eyes and beheld one another. The count still
ore his muddy clothes, and his pale, bewildered face betrayed the prodigal
eturning from his debauch. The countess looked as though she were utterly
agged out by a night in the train. She was dropping with sleep, but her hair
ad been brushed anyhow, and her eyes were deeply sunken.

CHAPTER VIII

WE ARE in a little set of lodgings on the fourth floor in the Rue Véron at Montmartre. Nana and Fontan have invited a few friends to cut their Twelfth Night cake with them. They are giving their housewarming, though they have been only three days settled.

They had no fixed intention of keeping house together, but the whole thing had come about suddenly in the first glow of the honeymoon. After her grand blowup, when she had turned the count and the banker so vigorously out of doors, Nana felt the world crumbling about her feet. She estimated the situation at a glance; the creditors would swoop down on her anteroom would mix themselves up with her love affairs and threaten to sell her little all unless she continued to act sensibly. Then, too, there would be no end of disputes and carking anxieties if she attempted to save her furniture from their clutches. And so she preferred giving up everything. Besides, the flat in the Boulevard Haussmann was plaguing her to death. It was so stupid with its great gilded rooms! In her access of tenderness for Fontan she began dreaming of a pretty little bright chamber. Indeed, she returned to the old ideal of the florist days, when her highest ambition was to have a rosewood cupboard with a plate-glass door and a bed hung with blue "reps." In the course of two days she sold what she could smuggle out of the house in the way of knickknacks and jewelry and then disappeared, taking with her ten thousand francs and never even warning the porter's wife. It was a plunge into the dark, a merry spree; never a trace was left behind. In this way she would prevent the men from coming dangling after her. Fontain was very nice. He did not say no to anything but just let her do as she liked. Nay, he even displayed an admirable spirit of comradeship. He had, on his part, nearly seven thousand francs, and despite the fact that people accused him of stinginess he consented to add them to the young woman's ten thousand. The sum struck them as a solid foundation on which to begin housekeeping. And so they started away, drawing from their common hoard, in order to hire and furnish the two rooms in the Rue Véron, and sharing everything together like old friends. In the early days it was really delicious.

On Twelfth Night Mme Lerat and Louiset were the first to arrive. As Fontan had not yet come home, the old lady ventured to give expression to her fears, for she trembled to see her niece renouncing the chance of wealth

"Oh, Aunt, I love him so dearly!" cried Nana, pressing her hands to her heart with the prettiest of gestures.

This phrase produced an extraordinary effect on Mme Lerat, and tears came into her eyes.

"That's true," she said with an air of conviction. "Love before all things!"

And with that she went into raptures over the prettiness of the rooms. Nana took her to see the bedroom, the parlor and the very kitchen. Gracious goodness, it wasn't a vast place, but then, they had painted it afresh and put up new wallpapers. Besides, the sun shone merrily into it during the daytime.

Thereupon Mme Lerat detained the young woman in the bedroom, while Louiset installed himself behind the charwoman in the kitchen in order to watch a chicken being roasted. If, said Mme Lerat, she permitted herself to say what was in her mind, it was because Zoé had just been at her house. Zoé had stayed courageously in the breach because she was devoted to her mistress. Madame would pay her later on; she was in no anxiety about that! And amid the breakup of the Boulevard Haussmann establishment it was she who showed the creditors a bold front; it was she who conducted a digni-fied retreat, saving what she could from the wreck and telling everyone that her mistress was traveling. She never once gave them her address. Nay, through fear of being followed, she even deprived herself of the pleasure of calling on Madame. Nevertheless, that same morning she had run round to Mme Lerat's because matters were taking a new turn. The evening before creditors in the persons of the upholsterer, the charcoal merchant and the laundress had put in an appearance and had offered to give Madame an ex-tension of time. Nay, they had even proposed to advance Madame a very considerable amount if only Madame would return to her flat and conduct herself like a sensible person. The aunt repeated Zoé's words. Without doubt there was a gentleman behind it all.

"I'll never consent!" declared Nana in great disgust. "Ah, they're a pretty lot those tradesmen! Do they think I'm to be sold so that they can get their bills paid? Why, look here, I'd rather die of hunger than deceive Fontan."

"That's what I said," averred Mme Lerat. "'My niece,' I said, 'is too noble-hearted!'"

Nana, however, was much vexed to learn that La Mignotte was being sold and that Labordette was buying it for Caroline Héquet at an absurdly low price. It made her angry with that clique. Oh, they were a regular cheap lot, in spite of their airs and graces! Yes, by Jove, she was worth more than the whole lot of them!

"They can have their little joke out," she concluded, "but money will never give them true happiness! Besides, you know, Aunt, I don't even know now whether all that set are alive or not. I'm much too happy."

At that very moment Mme Maloir entered, wearing one of those hats of which she alone understood the shape. It was delightful meeting again. Mme Maloir explained that magnificence frightened her and that *now*, from time to time, she would come back for her game of bezique. A second visit was paid to the different rooms in the lodgings, and in the kitchen Nana talked of economy in the presence of the charwoman, who was basting the fowl, and said that a servant would have cost too much and that she was herself desirous of looking after things. Louiset was gazing beatifically at the roasting process.

But presently there was a loud outburst of voices. Fontan had come in with Bosc and Prullière, and the company could now sit down to table. The soup had been already served when Nana for the third time showed off the lodgings.

"Ah, dear children, how comfortable you are here!" Bosc kept repeating, simply for the sake of pleasing the chums who were standing the dinner.

At bottom the subject of the "nook," as he called it, nowise touched him.

In the bedroom he harped still more vigorously on the amiable note. Ordinarily he was wont to treat women like cattle, and the idea of a man bothering himself about one of the dirty brutes excited within him the only angry feelings of which, in his comprehensive, drunken disdain of the universe, he was still capable.

"Ah, ah, the villains," he continued with a wink, "they've done this on the sly. Well, you were certainly right. It will be charming, and, by heaven, we'll come and see you!"

But when Louiset arrived on the scene astride upon a broomstick, Prullière chuckled spitefully and remarked:

"Well, I never! You've got a baby already?"

This struck everybody as very droll, and Mme Lerat and Mme Maloir shook with laughter. Nana, far from being vexed, laughed tenderly and said that unfortunately this was not the case. She would very much have liked it, both for the little one's sake and for her own, but perhaps one would arrive all the same. Fontan, in his role of honest citizen, took Louiset in his arms and began playing with him and lisping.

"Never mind! It loves its daddy! Call me 'Papa,' you little blackguard!"

"Papa, Papa!" stammered the child.

The company overwhelmed him with caresses, but Bosc was bored and talked of sitting down to table. That was the only serious business in life. Nana asked her guests' permission to put Louiset's chair next her own. The dinner was very merry, but Bosc suffered from the near neighborhood of the child, from whom he had to defend his plate. Mme Lerat bored him too. She was in a melting mood and kept whispering to him all sorts of mysterious things about gentlemen of the first fashion who were still running after Nana. Twice he had to push away her knee, for she was positively invading him in her gushing, tearful mood. Prullière behaved with great incivility toward Mme Maloir and did not once help her to anything. He was entirely taken up with Nana and looked annoyed at seeing her with Fontan. Besides, the turtle doves were kissing so excessively as to be becoming positive bores. Contrary to all known rules, they had elected to sit side by side.

"Devil take it! Why don't you eat? You've got plenty of time ahead of you!" Bosc kept repeating with his mouth full. "Wait till we are gone!"

But Nana could not restrain herself. She was in a perfect ecstasy of love. Her face was as full of blushes as an innocent young girl's, and her looks and her laughter seemed to overflow with tenderness. Gazing on Fontan, she overwhelmed him with pet names—"my doggie, my old bear, my kitten"—and whenever he passed her the water or the salt she bent forward and kissed him at random on lips, eyes, nose or ear. Then if she met with reproof she would return to the attack with the cleverest maneuvers and with infinite submissiveness and the supple cunning of a beaten cat would catch hold of his hand when no one was looking, in order to kiss it again. It seemed she must be touching something belonging to him. As to Fontan, he gave himself airs and let himself be adored with the utmost condescension. His great nose sniffed with entirely sensual content; his goat face, with its quaint, monstrous ugliness, positively glowed in the sunlight of devoted adoration lavished upon him by that superb woman who was so fair and so plump of limb. Occasionally he gave a kiss in return, as became a man who is having all the enjoyment and is yet willing to behave prettily.

"Well, you're growing maddening!" cried Prullière. "Get away from her, you fellow there!"

And he dismissed Fontan and changed covers, in order to take his place at Nana's side. The company shouted and applauded at this and gave vent to some stiffish epigrammatic witticisms. Fontan counterfeited despair and assumed the quaint expression of Vulcan crying for Venus. Straightway Prullière became very gallant, but Nana, whose foot he was groping for under the table, caught him a slap to make him keep quiet. No, no, she was certainly not going to become his mistress. A month ago she had begun to take a fancy to him because of his good looks, but now she detested him. If he pinched her again under pretense of picking up her napkin, she would throw her glass in his face!

Nevertheless, the evening passed off well. The company had naturally begun talking about the Variétés. Wasn't that cad of a Bordenave going to go off the hooks after all? His nasty diseases kept reappearing and causing him such suffering that you couldn't come within six yards of him nowadays. The day before during rehearsal he had been incessantly yelling at Simonne. There was a fellow whom the theatrical people wouldn't shed many tears over. Nana announced that if he were to ask her to take another part she would jolly well send him to the rightabout. Moreover, she began talking of leaving the stage; the theater was not to compare with her home. Fontan, who was not in the present piece or in that which was then being rehearsed, also talked big about the joy of being entirely at liberty and of passing his evenings with his feet on the fender in the society of his little pet. And at this the rest exclaimed delightedly, treating their entertainers as lucky people and pretending to envy their felicity.

The Twelfth-Night cake had been cut and handed round. The bean had fallen to the lot of Mme Lerat, who popped it into Bosc's glass. Whereupon there were shouts of "The king drinks! The king drinks!" Nana took advantage of this outburst of merriment and went and put her arms round Fontan's neck again, kissing him and whispering in his ear. But Prullière, laughing angrily, as became a pretty man, declared that they were not playing the game. Louiset, meanwhile, slept soundly on two chairs. It was nearing one o'clock when the company separated, shouting au revoir as they went downstairs.

For three weeks the existence of the pair of lovers was really charming. Nana fancied she was returning to those early days when her first silk dress had caused her infinite delight. She went out little and affected a life of solitude and simplicity. One morning early, when she had gone down to buy fish *in propria persona* in La Rouchefoucauld Market, she was vastly surprised to meet her old hair dresser Francis face to face. His getup was as scrupulously careful as ever: he wore the finest linen, and his frock coat was beyond reproach; in fact, Nana felt ashamed that he should see her in the street with a dressing jacket and disordered hair and down-at-heel shoes. But he had the tact, if possible, to intensify his politeness toward her. He did not permit himself a single inquiry and affected to believe that Madame was at present on her travels. Ah, but Madame had rendered many persons unhappy when she decided to travel! All the world had suffered loss. The young woman, however, ended by asking him questions, for a sudden fit of curiosity had made her forget her previous embarrassment. Seeing that the crowd was jostling them, she pushed him into a doorway and, still holding her little basket in one hand, stood chatting in front of him. What were people saying about her high jinks? Good heavens! The ladies to whom he went said this and that and all sorts of things. In fact, she had made a great noise and was enjoying a real boom: And Steiner? M. Steiner was in a very bad way, would make an ugly finish if he couldn't hit on some new commercial operation. And Daguenet? Oh, *he* was getting on swimmingly. M. Daguenet was settling down. Nana, under the exciting influence of various recollections, was just opening her mouth with a view to a further examination when she felt it would be awkward to utter Muffat's name. Thereupon Francis smiled and spoke instead of her. As to Monsieur le Comte, it was all a great pity, so sad had been his sufferings since Madame's departure.

He had been like a soul in pain—you might have met him wherever Madame was likely to be found. At last M. Mignon had come across him and had taken him home to his own place. This piece of news caused Nana to laugh a good deal. But her laughter was not of the easiest kind.

"Ah, he's with Rose now," she said. "Well then, you must know, Francis, I've done with him! Oh, the canting thing! It's learned some pretty habits— can't even go fasting for a week now! And to think that he used to swear he wouldn't have any woman after me!"

She was raging inwardly.

"My leavings, if you please!" she continued. "A pretty Johnnie for Rose to go and treat herself to! Oh, I understand it all now: she wanted to have her revenge because I got that brute of a Steiner away from her. Ain't it sly to get a man to come to her when I've chucked him out of doors?"

"M. Mignon doesn't tell that tale," said the hairdresser. "According to his account, it was Monsieur le Comte who chucked you out. Yes, and in a pretty disgusting way too—with a kick on the bottom!"

Nana became suddenly very pale.

"Eh, what?" she cried. "With a kick on my bottom? He's going too far, he is! Look here, my little friend, it was I who threw him downstairs, the cuckold, for he is a cuckold, I must inform you. His countess is making him one with every man she meets—yes, even with that good-for-nothing of a Fauchery. And that Mignon, who goes loafing about the pavement in behalf of his harridan of a wife, whom nobody wants because she's so lean! What a foul lot! What a foul lot!"

She was choking, and she paused for breath.

"Oh, that's what they say, is it? Very well, my little Francis, I'll go and look 'em up, I will. Shall you and I go to them at once? Yes, I'll go, and we'll see

whether they will have the cheek to go telling about kicks on the bottom.
Kicks! I never took one from anybody! And nobody's ever going to strike me
—d'ye see?—for I'd smash the man who laid a finger on me!"
Nevertheless, the storm subsided at last. After all, they might jolly well
say what they liked! She looked upon them as so much filth underfoot! It
would have soiled her to bother about people like that. She had a conscience
of her own, she had! And Francis, seeing her thus giving herself away, what
with her housewife's costume and all, became familiar and, at parting, made so
bold as to give her some good advice. It was wrong of her to be sacrificing
everything for the sake of an infatuation; such infatuations ruined existence.
She listened to him with bowed head while he spoke to her with a pained
expression, as became a connoisseur who could not bear to see so fine a girl
making such a hash of things.

"Well, that's my affair," she said at last. "Thanks all the same, dear boy."
She shook his hand, which despite his perfect dress was always a little greasy,
and then went off to buy her fish. During the day that story about the kick on
the bottom occupied her thoughts. She even spoke about it to Fontan and
again posed as a sturdy woman who was not going to stand the slightest flick
from anybody. Fontan, as became a philosophic spirit, declared that all men
of fashion were beasts whom it was one's duty to despise. And from that moment forth Nana was full of very real disdain.

That same evening they went to the Bouffes-Parisiens Théâtre to see a
little woman of Fontan's acquaintance make her debut in a part of some ten
lines. It was close on one o'clock when they once more trudged up the heights
of Montmartre. They had purchased a cake, a "mocha," in the Rue de la
Chaussée-d'Antin, and they ate it in bed, seeing that the night was not warm
and it was not worth while lighting a fire. Sitting up side by side, with the
bedclothes pulled up in front and the pillows piled up behind, they supped
and talked about the little woman. Nana thought her plain and lacking in style.
Fontan, lying on his stomach, passed up the pieces of cake which had been put
between the candle and the matches on the edge of the night table. But they
ended by quarreling.

"Oh, just to think of it!" cried Nana. "She's got eyes like gimlet holes, and
her hair's the color of tow."

"Hold your tongue, do!" said Fontan. "She has a superb head of hair and
such fire in her looks! It's lovely the way you women always tear each other
to pieces!"

He looked annoyed.

"Come now, we've had enough of it!" he said at last in savage tones. "You
know I don't like being bored. Let's go to sleep, or things 'll take a nasty turn."

And he blew out the candle, but Nana was furious and went on talking. She
was not going to be spoken to in that voice; she was accustomed to being
treated with respect! As he did not vouchsafe any further answer, she was
silenced, but she could not go to sleep and lay tossing to and fro.

"Great God, have you done moving about?" cried he suddenly, giving a
brisk jump upward.

"It isn't my fault if there are crumbs in the bed," she said curtly.

In fact, there were crumbs in the bed. She felt them down to her middle; she was everywhere devoured by them. One single crumb was scorching her and making her scratch herself till she bled. Besides, when one eats a cake isn't it usual to shake out the bedclothes afterward? Fontan, white with rage, had relit the candle, and they both got up and, barefooted and in their night-dresses, they turned down the clothes and swept up the crumbs on the sheet with their hands. Fontan went to bed again, shivering, and told her to go to the devil when she advised him to wipe the soles of his feet carefully. And in the end she came back to her old position, but scarce had she stretched herself out than she danced again. There were fresh crumbs in the bed!

"By Jove, it was sure to happen!" she cried. "You've brought them back again under your feet. I can't go on like this! No, I tell you, I can't go on like this!"

And with that she was on the point of stepping over him in order to jump out of bed again, when Fontan in his longing for sleep grew desperate and dealt her a ringing box on the ear. The blow was so smart that Nana suddenly found herself lying down again with her head on the pillow.

She lay half stunned.

"Oh!" she ejaculated simply, sighing a child's big sigh.

For a second or two he threatened her with a second slap, asking her at the same time if she meant to move again. Then he put out the light, settled him-self squarely on his back and in a trice was snoring. But she buried her face in the pillow and began sobbing quietly to herself. It was cowardly of him to take advantage of his superior strength! She had experienced very real terror all the same, so terrible had that quaint mask of Fontan's become. And her anger began dwindling down as though the blow had calmed her. She began to feel respect toward him and accordingly squeezed herself against the wall in order to leave him as much room as possible. She even ended by going to sleep, her cheek tingling, her eyes full of tears and feeling so deliciously depressed and wearied and submissive that she no longer noticed the crumbs. When she woke up in the morning she was holding Fontain in her naked arms and pressing him tightly against her breast. He would never begin it again, eh? Never again? She loved him too dearly. Why, it was even nice to be beaten if he struck the blow!

After that night a new life began. For a mere trifle—a yes, a no—Fontan would deal her a blow. She grew accustomed to it and pocketed everything. Sometimes she shed tears and threatened him, but he would pin her up against the wall and talk of strangling her, which had the effect of rendering her extremely obedient. As often as not, she sank down on a chair and sobbed for five minutes on end. But afterward she would forget all about it, grow very merry, fill the little lodgings with the sound of song and laughter and the rapid rustle of skirts. The worst of it was that Fontan was now in the habit of disappearing for the whole day and never returning home before mid-night, for he was going to cafés and meeting his old friends again. Nana bore with everything. She was tremulous and caressing, her only fear being that she might never see him again if she reproached him. But on certain days, when she had neither Mme Maloir nor her aunt and Louiset with her, she grew mortally dull. Thus one Sunday, when she was bargaining for some pigeons at La Rochefoucauld Market, she was delighted to meet Satin, who, in her turn, was busy purchasing a bunch of radishes. Since the evening when the prince had drunk Fontan's champagne they had lost sight of one another.

"What? It's you! D'you live in our parts?" said Satin, astounded at seeing her in the street at that hour of the morning and in slippers too. "Oh, my poor, dear girl, you're really ruined then!"

Nana knitted her brows as a sign that she was to hold her tongue, for they were surrounded by other women who wore dressing gowns and were without linen, while their disheveled tresses were white with fluff. In the morning, when the man picked up overnight had been newly dismissed, all the courtesans of the quarter were wont to come marketing here, their eyes heavy with sleep, their feet in old down-at-heel shoes and themselves full of the weariness and ill humor entailed by a night of boredom. From the four converging streets they came down into the market, looking still rather young in some cases and very pale and charming in their utter unconstraint; in others, hideous and old, with bloated faces and peeling skin. The latter did not the least mind being seen thus outside working hours, and not one of them deigned to smile when the passers-by on the sidewalk turned round to look at them. Indeed, they were all very full of business and wore a disdainful expression, as became good housewives for whom men had ceased to exist. Just as Satin, for instance, was paying for her bunch of radishes a young man, who might have been a shop-boy going late to his work, threw her a passing greeting:

"Good morning, duckie."

She straightened herself up at once and with the dignified manner becoming an offended queen remarked:

"What's up with that swine there?"

Then she fancied she recognized him. Three days ago toward midnight, as she was coming back alone from the boulevards, she had talked to him at the corner of the Rue Labruyère for nearly half an hour, with a view to persuading him to come home with her. But this recollection only angered her the more.

"Fancy they're brutes enough to shout things to you in broad daylight!" she continued. "When one's out on business one ought to be respectfully treated, eh?"

Nana had ended by buying her pigeons, although she certainly had her doubts of their freshness. After which Satin wanted to show her where she lived in the Rue Rochefoucauld close by. And the moment they were alone Nana told her of her passion for Fontan. Arrived in front of the house, the girl stopped with her bundle of radishes under her arm and listened eagerly to a final detail which the other imparted to her. Nana fibbed away and vowed that it was she who had turned Count Muffat out of doors with a perfect hail of kicks on the posterior.

"Oh, how smart!" Satin repeated. "How very smart! Kicks, eh? And he never said a word, did he? What a blooming coward! I wish I'd been there to see his ugly mug! My dear girl, you were quite right. A pin for the coin! When I'm on with a mash I starve for it! You'll come and see me, eh? You promise? It's the left-hand door. Knock three knocks, for there's a whole heap of damned squints about."

After that whenever Nana grew too weary of life she went down and saw Satin. She was always sure of finding her, for the girl never went out before six in the evening. Satin occupied a couple of rooms which a chemist had furnished for her in order to save her from the clutches of the police, but in little more than a twelvemonth she had broken the furniture, knocked in the chairs, dirtied the curtains, and that in a manner so furiously filthy and untidy that the lodgings seemed as though inhabited by a pack of mad cats. On the mornings when she grew disgusted with herself and thought about cleaning up a bit, chair rails and strips of curtain would come off in her hands during her struggle with superincumbent dirt. On such days the place was fouler than ever, and it was impossible to enter it, owing to the things which had fallen down across the doorway. At length she ended by leaving her house severely alone. When the lamp was lit the cupboard with plate-glass doors, the clock and what remained of the curtains still served to impose on the men. Besides, for six months past her landlord had been threatening to evict her. Well then, for whom should she be keeping the furniture nice? For him more than anyone else, perhaps! And so whenever she got up in a merry mood she would shout "Gee up!" and give the sides of the cupboard and the chest of drawers such a tremendous kick that they cracked again.

Nana nearly always found her in bed. Even on the days when Satin went out to do her marketing she felt so tired on her return upstairs that she flung herself down on the bed and went to sleep again. During the day she dragged herself about and dozed off on chairs. Indeed, she did not emerge from this languid condition till the evening drew on and the gas was lit outside. Nana felt very comfortable at Satin's, sitting doing nothing on the untidy bed, while basins stood about on the floor at her feet and petticoats which had been bemired last night hung over the backs of armchairs and stained them with mud. They had long gossips together and were endlessly confidential, while Satin lay on her stomach in her nightgown, waving her legs above her head and smoking cigarettes as she listened. Sometimes on such afternoons as they had troubles to retail they treated themselves to absinthe in order, as they termed it, "to forget." Satin did not go downstairs or put on a petticoat but simply went and leaned over the banisters and shouted her order to the portress's little girl, a chit of ten, who when she brought up the absinthe in a glass would look furtively at the lady's bare legs. Every conversation led up to one subject—the beastliness of the men. Nana was overpowering on the subject of Fontan. She could not say a dozen words without lapsing into endless repetitions of his sayings and his doings. But Satin, like a good-natured girl, would listen unwearyingly to everlasting accounts of how Nana had watched for him at the window, how they had fallen out over a burnt dish of hash and how they had made it up in bed after hours of silent sulking. In her desire to be always talking about these things Nana had got to tell of every slap that he dealt her. Last week he had given her a swollen eye; nay, the night before he had given her such a box on the ear as to throw her across the night table, and all because he could not find his slippers. And the other woman did not evince any astonishment but blew out cigarette smoke and only paused a moment to remark that, for her part, she always ducked under, which sent the gentleman pretty nearly sprawling. Both of them settled down with a will to these anecdotes about blows; they grew supremely happy and excited over these same idiotic doings about which they told one another a hundred times or more, while they gave themselves up to the soft and pleasing sense of weariness which was sure to follow the drubbings they talked of. It was the delight of rediscussing Fontan's blows and of explaining his works and his ways, down to the very manner in which he took off his boots, which brought Nana back daily to Satin's place. The latter, moreover, used to end by growing sympathetic in her turn and would cite even more violent cases, as, for instance, that of a pastry cook who had left her for dead on the floor. Yet she loved him, in spite of it all! Then came the days on which Nana cried and declared that things could not go on as they were doing. Satin would escort her back to her own door and would linger an hour out in the street to see that he did not murder her. And the next day the two women would rejoice over the reconciliation the whole afternoon through. Yet though they did not say so, they preferred the days when threshings were, so to speak, in the air, for then their comfortable indignation was all the stronger.

They became inseparable. Yet Satin never went to Nana's, Fontan having announced that he would have no trollops in his house. They used to go out together, and thus it was that Satin one day took her friend to see another woman. This woman turned out to be that very Mme Robert who had interested Nana and inspired her with a certain respect ever since she had refused to come to her supper. Mme Robert lived in the Rue Mosnier, a silent, new street in the Quartier de l'Europe, where there were no shops, and the handsome houses with their small, limited flats were peopled by ladies. It was five o'clock, and along the silent pavements in the quiet, aristocratic shelter of the tall white houses were drawn up the broughams of stock-exchange people and merchants, while men walked hastily about, looking up at the windows, where women in dressing jackets seemed to be awaiting them. At first Nana refused to go up, remarking with some constraint that she had not the pleasure of the lady's acquaintance. But Satin would take no refusal. She was only desirous of paying a civil call, for Mme Robert, whom she had met in a restaurant the day before, had made herself extremely agreeable and had got her to promise to come and see her. And at last Nana consented. At the top of the stairs a little drowsy maid informed them that Madame had not come home yet, but she ushered them into the drawing room notwithstanding and left them there.

"The deuce, it's a smart show!" whispered Satin. It was a stiff, middle-class room, hung with dark-colored fabrics, and suggested the conventional taste of a Parisian shopkeeper who has retired on his fortune. Nana was struck and did her best to make merry about it. But Satin showed annoyance and spoke up for Mme Robert's strict adherence to the proprieties. She was always to be met in the society of elderly, grave-looking men, on whose arms she leaned. At present she had a retired chocolate seller in tow, a serious soul. Whenever he came to see her he was so charmed by the solid, handsome way in which the house was arranged that he had himself announced and addressed its mistress as "dear child."

"Look, here she is!" continued Satin, pointing to a photograph which stood in front of the clock. Nana scrutinized the portrait for a second or so. It represented a very dark brunette with a longish face and lips pursed up in a discreet smile. "A thoroughly fashionable lady," one might have said of the likeness, "but one who is rather more reserved than the rest."

"It's strange," murmured Nana at length, "but I've certainly seen that face somewhere. Where, I don't remember. But it can't have been in a pretty place —oh no, I'm sure it wasn't in a pretty place."

And turning toward her friend, she added, "So she's made you promise to come and see her? What does she want with you?"

"What does she want with me? 'Gad! To talk, I expect—to be with me a bit. It's her politeness."

Nana looked steadily at Satin. "Tut, tut," she said softly. After all, it didn't matter to her! Yet seeing that the lady was keeping them waiting, she declared that she would not stay longer, and accordingly they both took their departure.

The next day Fontan informed Nana that he was not coming home to dinner, and she went down early to find Satin with a view to treating her at a restaurant. The choice of the restaurant involved infinite debate. Satin proposed various brewery bars, which Nana thought detestable, and at last persuaded her to dine at Laure's. This was a table d'hôte in the Rue des Martyrs, where the dinner cost three francs.

Tired of waiting for the dinner hour and not knowing what to do out in the street, the pair went up to Laure's twenty minutes too early. The three dining rooms there were still empty, and they sat down at a table in the very saloon where Laure Piédefer was enthroned on a high bench behind a bar. This Laure was a lady of some fifty summers, whose swelling contours were tightly laced by belts and corsets. Women kept entering in quick procession, and each, in passing, craned upward so as to overtop the saucers raised on the counter and kissed Laure on the mouth with tender familiarity, while the monstrous creature tried, with tears in her eyes, to divide her attentions among them in such a way as to make no one jealous. On the other hand, the servant who waited on the ladies was a tall, lean woman. She seemed wasted with disease, and her eyes were ringed with dark lines and glowed with somber fire. Very rapidly the three saloons filled up. There were some hundred customers, and they had seated themselves wherever they could find vacant places. The majority were nearing the age of forty: their flesh was puffy and so bloated by vice as almost to hide the outlines of their flaccid mouths. But amid all these gross bosoms and figures some slim, pretty girls were observable.

These still wore a modest expression despite their impudent gestures, for they were only beginners in their art, who had started life in the ballrooms of the slums and had been brought to Laure's by some customer or other. Here the tribe of bloated women, excited by the sweet scent of their youth, jostled one another and, while treating them to dainties, formed a perfect court round them, much as old amorous bachelors might have done. As to the men, they were not numerous. There were ten or fifteen of them at the outside, and if we except four tall fellows who had come to see the sight and were cracking jokes and taking things easy, they behaved humbly enough amid this whelming flood of petticoats.

"I say, their stew's very good, ain't it?" said Satin.

Nana nodded with much satisfaction. It was the old substantial dinner you get in a country hotel and consisted of *vol-au-vent à la financière*, fowl boiled in rice, beans with a sauce and vanilla creams, iced and flavored with burnt sugar. The ladies made an especial onslaught on the boiled fowl and rice: their stays seemed about to burst; they wiped their lips with slow, luxurious movements. At first Nana had been afraid of meeting old friends who might have asked her silly questions, but she grew calm at last, for she recognized no one she knew among that extremely motley throng, where faded dresses and lamentable hats contrasted strangely with handsome costumes, the wearers of which fraternized in vice with their shabbier neighbors. She was momentarily interested, however, at the sight of a young man with short curly hair and insolent face who kept a whole tableful of vastly fat women breathlessly attentive to his slightest caprice. But when the young man began to laugh his bosom swelled.

"Good lack, it's a woman!"

She let a little cry escape as she spoke, and Satin, who was stuffing herself with boiled fowl, lifted up her head and whispered:

"Oh yes! I know her. A smart lot, eh? They do just fight for her."

Nana pouted disgustingly. She could not understand the thing as yet. Nevertheless, she remarked in her sensible tone that there was no disputing about tastes or colors, for you never could tell what you yourself might one day have a liking for. So she ate her cream with an air of philosophy, though she was perfectly well aware that Satin with her great blue virginal eyes was throwing the neighboring tables into a state of great excitement. There was one woman in particular, a powerful, fair-haired person who sat close to her and made herself extremely agreeable. She seemed all aglow with affection and pushed toward the girl so eagerly that Nana was on the point of interfering.

But at that very moment a woman who was entering the room gave her a shock of surprise. Indeed, she had recognized Mme Robert. The latter, looking, as was her wont, like a pretty brown mouse, nodded familiarly to the tall, lean serving maid and came and leaned upon Laure's counter. Then both women exchanged a long kiss. Nana thought such an attention on the part of a woman so distinguished looking very amusing, the more so because Mme Robert had quite altered her usual modest expression. On the contrary, her eye roved about the saloon as she kept up a whispered conversation. Laure had resumed her seat and once more settled herself down with all the majesty of an old image of Vice, whose face has been worn and polished by the kisses of the faithful. Above the range of loaded plates she sat enthroned in all the opulence which a hotelkeeper enjoys after forty years of activity, and as she sat there she swayed her bloated following of large women, in comparison with the biggest of whom she seemed monstrous.

But Mme Robert had caught sight of Satin, and leaving Laure, she ran up and behaved charmingly, telling her how much she regretted not having been at home the day before. When Satin, however, who was ravished at this treatment, insisted on finding room for her at the table, she vowed she had already dined. She had simply come up to look about her. As she stood talking behind her new friend's chair she leaned lightly on her shoulders and in a smiling, coaxing manner remarked:

"Now when shall I see you? If you were free——"

Nana unluckily failed to hear more. The conversation vexed her, and she was dying to tell this honest lady a few home truths. But the sight of a troop of new arrivals paralyzed her. It was composed of smart, fashionably dressed women who were wearing their diamonds. Under the influence of perverse impulse they had made up a party to come to Laure's—whom, by the by, they all treated with great familiarity—to eat the three-franc dinner while flashing their jewels of great price in the jealous and astonished eyes of poor, bedraggled prostitutes. The moment they entered, talking and laughing in their shrill, clear tones and seeming to bring sunshine with them from the outside world, Nana turned her head rapidly away. Much to her annoyance she had recognized Lucy Stewart and Maria Blond among them, and for nearly five minutes, during which the ladies chatted with Laure before passing into the saloon beyond, she kept her head down and seemed deeply occupied in rolling bread pills on the cloth in front of her. But when at length she was able to look round, what was her astonishment to observe the chair next to hers vacant! Satin had vanished.

"Gracious, where can she be?" she loudly ejaculated.

The sturdy, fair woman who had been overwhelming Satin with civil attentions laughed ill-temperedly, and when Nana, whom the laugh irritated, looked threatening she remarked in a soft, drawling way:

"It's certainly not me that's done you this turn; it's the other one!"

Thereupon Nana understood that they would most likely make game of her and so said nothing more. She even kept her seat for some moments, as she did not wish to show how angry she felt. She could hear Lucy Stewart laughing at the end of the next saloon, where she was treating a whole table of little women who had come from the public balls at Montmartre and La Chapelle. It was very hot; the servant was carrying away piles of dirty plates with a strong scent of boiled fowl and rice, while the four gentlemen had ended by regaling quite half a dozen couples with capital wine in the hope of making them tipsy and hearing some pretty stiffish things. What at present most exasperated Nana was the thought of paying for Satin's dinner. There was a wench for you, who allowed herself to be amused and then made off with never a thank-you in company with the first petticoat that came by! Without doubt it was only a matter of three francs, but she felt it was hard lines all the same—her way of doing it was too disgusting. Nevertheless, she paid up, throwing the six francs at Laure, whom at the moment she despised more than the mud in the street. In the Rue des Martyrs Nana felt her bitterness increasing. She was certainly not going to run after Satin! It was a nice filthy business for one to be poking one's nose into! But her evening was spoiled, and she walked slowly up again toward Montmartre, raging against Mme Robert in particular. Gracious goodness, that woman had a fine cheek to go playing the lady—yes, the lady in the dustbin! She now felt sure she had met her at the Papillon, a wretched public-house ball in the Rue des Poissonniers, where men conquered her scruples for thirty sous. And to think a thing like that got hold of important functionaries with her modest looks! And to think she refused suppers to which one did her the honor of inviting her because, forsooth, she was playing the virtuous game! Oh yes, she'd get virtued! It was always those conceited prudes who went the most fearful lengths in low corners nobody knew anything about.

Revolving these matters, Nana at length reached her home in the Rue Véron and was taken aback on observing a light in the window. Fontan had come home in a sulk, for he, too, had been deserted by the friend who had been dining with him. He listened coldly to her explanations while she trembled lest he should strike her. It scared her to find him at home, seeing that she had not expected him before one in the morning, and she told him a fib and confessed that she had certainly spent six francs, but in Mme Maloir's society. He was not ruffled, however, and he handed her a letter which, though addressed to her, he had quietly opened. It was a letter from Georges, who was still a prisoner at Les Fondettes and comforted himself weekly with the composition of glowing pages. Nana loved to be written to, especially when the letters were full of grand, loverlike expressions with a sprinkling of vows. She used to read them to everybody. Fontan was familiar with the style employed by Georges and appreciated it. But that evening she was so afraid of a scene that she affected complete indifference, skimming through the letter with a sulky expression and flinging it aside as soon as read. Fontan had begun beating a tattoo on a windowpane; the thought of going to bed so early bored him, and yet he did not know how to employ his evening. He turned briskly round:

"Suppose we answer that young vagabond at once," he said.

It was the custom for him to write the letters in reply. He was wont to vie with the other in point of style. Then, too, he used to be delighted when Nana, grown enthusiastic after the letter had been read over aloud, would kiss him with the announcement that nobody but he could "say things like that." Thus their latent affections would be stirred, and they would end with mutual adoration.

"As you will," she replied. "I'll make tea, and we'll go to bed after."

Thereupon Fontan installed himself at the table on which pen, ink and paper were at the same time grandly displayed. He curved his arm; he drew a long face.

"My heart's own," he began aloud.

And for more than an hour he applied himself to his task, polishing here, weighing a phrase there, while he sat with his head between his hands and laughed inwardly whenever he hit upon a peculiarly tender expression. Nana had already consumed two cups of tea in silence, when at last he read out the letter in the level voice and with the two or three emphatic gestures peculiar to such performances on the stage. It was five pages long, and he spoke therein of "the delicious hours passed at La Mignotte, those hours of which the memory lingered like subtle perfume." He vowed "eternal fidelity to that springtide of love" and ended by declaring that his sole wish was to "recommence that happy time if, indeed, happiness can recommence."

"I say that out of politeness, y'know," he explained. "The moment it becomes laughable—eh, what! I think she's felt it, she has!"

He glowed with triumph. But Nana was unskillful; she still suspected an outbreak and now was mistaken enough not to fling her arms round his neck in a burst of admiration. She thought the letter a respectable performance, nothing more. Thereupon he was much annoyed. If his letter did not please her she might write another! And so instead of bursting out in loverlike speeches and exchanging kisses, as their wont was, they sat coldly facing one another at the table. Nevertheless, she poured him out a cup of tea.

"Here's a filthy mess," he cried after dipping his lips in the mixture. "You've put salt in it, you have!"

Nana was unlucky enough to shrug her shoulders, and at that he grew furious.

"Aha! Things are taking a wrong turn tonight!"

And with that the quarrel began. It was only ten by the clock, and this was a way of killing time. So he lashed himself into a rage and threw in Nana's teeth a whole string of insults and all kinds of accusations which followed one another so closely that she had no time to defend herself. She was dirty; she was stupid; she had knocked about in all sorts of low places! After that he waxed frantic over the money question. Did he spend six francs when he dined out? No, somebody was treating him to a dinner; otherwise he would have eaten his ordinary meal at home. And to think of spending them on that old procuress of a Maloir, a jade he would chuck out of the house tomorrow! Yes, by jingo, they would get into a nice mess if he and she were to go throwing six francs out of the window every day!

"Now to begin with, I want your accounts," he shouted. "Let's see; hand over the money! Now where do we stand?"

All his sordid avaricious instincts came to the surface. Nana was cowed and scared, and she made haste to fetch their remaining cash out of the desk and to bring it him. Up to that time the key had lain on this common treasury, from which they had drawn as freely as they wished.

"How's this?" he said when he had counted up the money. "There are scarcely seven thousand francs remaining out of seventeen thousand, and we've only been together three months. The thing's impossible."

He rushed forward, gave the desk a savage shake and brought the drawer forward in order to ransack it in the light of the lamp. But it actually contained only six thousand eight hundred and odd francs. Thereupon the tempest burst forth.

"Ten thousand francs in three months!" he yelled. "By God! What have you done with it all? Eh? Answer! It all goes to your jade of an aunt, eh? Or you're keeping men; that's plain! Will you answer?"

"Oh well, if you must get in a rage!" said Nana. "Why, the calculation's easily made! You haven't allowed for the furniture; besides, I've had to buy linen. Money goes quickly when one's settling in a new place."

But while requiring explanations he refused to listen to them.

"Yes, it goes a deal too quickly!" he rejoined more calmly. "And look here, little girl, I've had enough of this mutual housekeeping. You know those seven thousand francs are mine. Yes, and as I've got 'em, I shall keep 'em! Hang it, the moment you become wasteful I get anxious not to be ruined. To each man his own."

And he pocketed the money in a lordly way while Nana gazed at him, dumfounded. He continued speaking complaisantly:

"You must understand I'm not such a fool as to keep aunts and likewise children who don't belong to me. You were pleased to spend your own money —well, that's your affair! But my money—no, that's sacred! When in the future you cook a leg of mutton I'll pay for half of it. We'll settle up tonight—there!"

Straightway Nana rebelled. She could not help shouting:

"Come, I say, it's you who've run through my ten thousand francs. It's a dirty trick, I tell you!"

But he did not stop to discuss matters further, for he dealt her a random box on the ear across the table, remarking as he did so:

"Let's have that again!"

She let him have it again despite his blow. Whereupon he fell upon her and kicked and cuffed her heartily. Soon he had reduced her to such a state that she ended, as her wont was, by undressing and going to bed in a flood of tears.

He was out of breath and was going to bed, in his turn, when he noticed the letter he had written to Georges lying on the table. Whereupon he folded it up carefully and, turning toward the bed, remarked in threatening accents:

"It's very well written, and I'm going to post it myself because I don't like women's fancies. Now don't go moaning any more; it puts my teeth on edge."

Nana, who was crying and gasping, thereupon held her breath. When he was in bed she choked with emotion and threw herself upon his breast with a wild burst of sobs. Their scuffles always ended thus, for she trembled at the thought of losing him and, like a coward, wanted always to feel that he belonged entirely to her, despite everything. Twice he pushed her magnificently away, but the warm embrace of this woman who was begging for mercy with great, tearful eyes, as some faithful brute might do, finally aroused desire. And he became royally condescending without, however, lowering his dignity before any of her advances. In fact, he let himself be caressed and taken by force, as became a man whose forgiveness is worth the trouble of winning. Then he was seized with anxiety, fearing that Nana was playing a part with a view to regaining possession of the treasury key. The light had been extinguished when he felt it necessary to reaffirm his will and pleasure.

"You must know, my girl, that this is really very serious and that I keep the money."

Nana, who was falling asleep with her arms round his neck, uttered a sublime sentiment.

"Yes, you need fear nothing! I'll work for both of us!"

But from that evening onward their life in common became more and more difficult. From one week's end to the other the noise of slaps filled the air and resembled the ticking of a clock by which they regulated their existence. Through dint of being much beaten Nana became as pliable as fine linen; her skin grew delicate and pink and white and so soft to the touch and clear to the view that she may be said to have grown more good looking than ever. Prullière, moreover, began running after her like a madman, coming in when Fontan was away and pushing her into corners in order to snatch an embrace. But she used to struggle out of his grasp, full of indignation and blushing with shame. It disgusted her to think of him wanting to deceive a friend. Prullière would thereupon begin sneering with a wrathful expression. Why, she was growing jolly stupid nowadays! How could she take up with such an ape? For, indeed, Fontan was a regular ape with that great swingeing nose of his. Oh, he had an ugly mug! Besides, the man knocked her about too!

"It's possible I like him as he is," she one day made answer in the quiet voice peculiar to a woman who confesses to an abominable taste.

Bosc contented himself by dining with them as often as possible. He shrugged his shoulders behind Prullière's back—a pretty fellow, to be sure, but a frivolous! Bosc had on more than one occasion assisted at domestic scenes, and at dessert, when Fontan slapped Nana, he went on chewing solemnly, for the thing struck him as being quite in the course of nature. In order to give some return for his dinner he used always to go into ecstasies over their happiness. He declared himself a philosopher who had given up everything, glory included. At times Prullière and Fontan lolled back in their chairs, losing count of time in front of the empty table, while with theatrical gestures and intonation they discussed their former successes till two in the morning. But he would sit by, lost in thought, finishing the brandy bottle in silence and only occasionally emitting a little contemptuous sniff. Where was Talma's tradition? Nowhere. Very well, let them leave him jolly well alone! It was too stupid to go on as they were doing!

One evening he found Nana in tears. She took off her dressing jacket in order to show him her back and her arms, which were black and blue. He looked at her skin without being tempted to abuse the opportunity, as that ass of a Prullière would have been. Then, sententiously:

"My dear girl, where there are women there are sure to be ructions. It was Napoleon who said that, I think. Wash yourself with salt water. Salt water's the very thing for those little knocks. Tut, tut, you'll get others as bad, but don't complain so long as no bones are broken. I'm inviting myself to dinner, you know; I've spotted a leg of mutton."

But Mme Lerat had less philosophy. Every time Nana showed her a fresh bruise on the white skin she screamed aloud. They were killing her niece; things couldn't go on as they were doing. As a matter of fact, Fontan had turned Mme Lerat out of doors and had declared that he would not have her at his house in the future, and ever since that day, when he returned home and she happened to be there, she had to make off through the kitchen, which was a horrible humiliation to her. Accordingly she never ceased inveighing against that brutal individual. She especially blamed his ill breeding, pursing up her lips, as she did so, like a highly respectable lady whom nobody could possibly remonstrate with on the subject of good manners.

"Oh, you notice it at once," she used to tell Nana; "he hasn't the barest notion of the very smallest proprieties. His mother must have been common! Don't deny it—the thing's obvious! I don't speak on my own account, though a person of my years has a right to respectful treatment, but *you*—how do *you* manage to put up with his bad manners? For though I don't want to flatter myself, I've always taught you how to behave, and among our own people you always enjoyed the best possible advice. We were all very well bred in our family, weren't we now?"

Nana used never to protest but would listen with bowed head.

"Then, too," continued the aunt, "you've only known perfect gentlemen hitherto. We were talking of that very topic with Zoé at my place yesterday evening. She can't understand it any more than I can. 'How is it,' she said, 'that Madame, who used to have that perfect gentleman, Monsieur le Comte, at her beck and call'—for between you and me, it seems you drove him silly— 'how is it that Madame lets herself be made into mincemeat by that clown of a fellow?' I remarked at the time that you might put up with the beatings but that I would never have allowed him to be lacking in proper respect. In fact, there isn't a word to be said for him. I wouldn't have his portrait in my room even! And you ruin yourself for such a bird as that; yes, you ruin yourself, my darling; you toil and you moil, when there are so many others and such rich men, too, some of them even connected with the government! Ah well, it's not I who ought to be telling you this, of course! But all the same, when next he tries any of his dirty tricks on I should cut him short with a 'Monsieur, what d'you take me for?' You know how to say it in that grand way of yours! It would downright cripple him."

Thereupon Nana burst into sobs and stammered out:

"Oh, Aunt, I love him!"

The fact of the matter was that Mme Lerat was beginning to feel anxious at the painful way her niece doled out the sparse, occasional francs destined to pay for little Louis's board and lodging. Doubtless she was willing to make sacrifices and to keep the child by her whatever might happen while waiting for more prosperous times, but the thought that Fontan was preventing her and the brat and its mother from swimming in a sea of gold made her so savage that she was ready to deny the very existence of true love. Accordingly she ended up with the following severe remarks:

"Now listen, some fine day when he's taken the skin off your back, you'll come and knock at my door, and I'll open it to you."

Soon money began to engross Nana's whole attention. Fontan had caused the seven thousand francs to vanish away. Without doubt they were quite safe; indeed, she would never have dared ask him questions about them, for she was wont to be blushingly diffident with that bird, as Mme Lerat called him. She trembled lest he should think her capable of quarreling with him about halfpence. He had certainly promised to subscribe toward their common household expenses, and in the early days he had given out three francs every morning. But he was as exacting as a boarder; he wanted everything for his three francs—butter, meat, early fruit and early vegetables—and if she ventured to make an observation, if she hinted that you could not have everything in the market for three francs, he flew into a temper and treated her as a useless, wasteful woman, a confounded donkey whom the tradespeople were robbing. Moreover, he was always ready to threaten that he would take lodgings somewhere else. At the end of a month on certain mornings he had forgotten to deposit the three francs on the chest of drawers, and she had ventured to ask for them in a timid, roundabout way. Whereupon there had been such bitter disputes and he had seized every pretext to render her life so miserable that she had found it best no longer to count upon him. Whenever, however, he had omitted to leave behind the three one-franc pieces and found a dinner awaiting him all the same, he grew as merry as a sandboy, kissed Nana gallantly and waltzed with the chairs. And she was so charmed by this conduct that she at length got to hope that nothing would be found on the chest of drawers, despite the difficulty she experienced in making both ends meet. One day she even returned him his three francs, telling him a tale to the effect that she still had yesterday's money. As he had given her nothing then, he hesitated for some moments, as though he dreaded a lecture. But she gazed at him with her loving eyes and hugged him in such utter self-surrender that he pocketed the money again with that little convulsive twitch of the fingers peculiar to a miser when he regains possession of that which has been well-nigh lost. From that day forth he never troubled himself about money again or inquired whence it came. But when there were potatoes on the table he looked intoxicated with delight and would laugh and smack his lips before her turkeys and legs of mutton, though of course this did not prevent his dealing Nana sundry sharp smacks, as though to keep his hand in amid all his happiness.

Nana had indeed found means to provide for all needs, and the place on certain days overflowed with good things. Twice a week, regularly, Bosc had indigestion. One evening as Mme Lerat was withdrawing from the scene in high dudgeon because she had noticed a copious dinner she was not destined to eat in process of preparation, she could not prevent herself asking brutally who paid for it all. Nana was taken by surprise; she grew foolish and began crying.

"Ah, that's a pretty business," said the aunt, who had divined her meaning. Nana had resigned herself to it for the sake of enjoying peace in her own home. Then, too, the Tricon was to blame. She had come across her in the Rue de Laval one fine day when Fontan had gone out raging about a dish of cod. She had accordingly consented to the proposals made her by the Tricon, who happened just then to be in difficulty. As Fontan never came in before six o'clock, she made arrangements for her afternoons and used to bring back forty francs, sixty francs, sometimes more. She might have made it a matter of ten and fifteen louis had she been able to maintain her former position, but as matters stood she was very glad thus to earn enough to keep the pot boiling. At night she used to forget all her sorrows when Bosc sat there bursting with dinner and Fontan leaned on his elbows and with an expression of lofty superiority becoming a man who is loved for his own sake allowed her to kiss him on the eyelids.

In due course Nana's very adoration of her darling, her dear old duck, which was all the more passionately blind, seeing that now she paid for everything, plunged her back into the muddiest depths of her calling. She roamed the streets and loitered on the pavement in quest of a five-franc piece, just as when she was a slipshod baggage years ago. One Sunday at La Rochefoucauld Market she had made her peace with Satin after having flown at her with furious reproaches about Mme Robert. But Satin had been content to answer that when one didn't like a thing there was no reason why one should want to disgust others with it. And Nana, who was by way of being wide-minded, had accepted the philosophic view that you never can tell where your tastes will lead you and had forgiven her. Her curiosity was even excited, and she began questioning her about obscure vices and was astounded to be adding to her information at her time of life and with her knowledge. She burst out laughing and gave vent to various expressions of surprise. It struck her as so queer, and yet she was a little shocked by it, for she was really quite the philistine outside the pale of her own habits. So she went back to Laure's and fed there when Fontan was dining out. She derived much amusement from the stories and the amours and the jealousies which inflamed the female customers without hindering their appetites in the slightest degree. Nevertheless, she still was not quite in it, as she herself phrased it. The vast Laure, meltingly maternal as ever, used often to invite her to pass a day or two at her Asnièries Villa, a country house containing seven spare bedrooms. But she used to refuse; she was afraid. Satin, however, swore she was mistaken about it, that gentlemen from Paris swung you in swings and played tonneau with you, and so she promised to come at some future time when it would be possible for her to leave town.

At that time Nana was much tormented by circumstances and not at all festively inclined. She needed money, and when the Tricon did not want her, which too often happened, she had no notion where to bestow her charms. Then began a series of wild descents upon the Parisian pavement, plunges into the baser sort of vice, whose votaries prowl in muddy bystreets under the restless flicker of gas lamps. Nana went back to the public-house balls in the suburbs, where she had kicked up her heels in the early ill-shod days. She revisited the dark corners on the outer boulevards, where when she was fifteen years old men used to hug her while her father was looking for her in order to give her a hiding. Both the women would speed along, visiting all the ball-rooms and restaurants in a quarter and climbing innumerable staircases which were wet with spittle and spilled beer, or they would stroll quietly about, going up streets and planting themselves in front of carriage gates. Satin, who had served her apprenticeship in the Quartier Latin, used to take Nana to Bullier's and the public houses in the Boulevard Saint-Michel. But the vacations were drawing on, and the Quarter looked too starved. Eventually they always returned to the principal boulevards, for it was there they ran the best chance of getting what they wanted. From the heights of Montmartre to the observatory plateau they scoured the whole town in the way we have been describing. They were out on rainy evenings, when their boots got worn down, and on hot evenings, when their linen clung to their skins. There were long periods of waiting and endless periods of walking; there were jostlings and disputes and the nameless, brutal caresses of the stray passer-by who was taken by them to some miserable furnished room and came swearing down the greasy stairs afterward.

The summer was drawing to a close, a stormy summer of burning nights. The pair used to start out together after dinner, toward nine o'clock. On the pavements of the Rue Notre Dame de la Lorette two long files of women scudded along with tucked-up skirts and bent heads, keeping close to the shops but never once glancing at the displays in the shopwindows as they hurried busily down toward the boulevards. This was the hungry exodus from the Quartier Breda which took place nightly when the street lamps had just been lit. Nana and Satin used to skirt the church and then march off along the Rue le Peletier. When they were some hundred yards from the Café Riche and had fairly reached their scene of operations they would shake out the skirts of their dresses, which up till that moment they had been holding carefully up, and begin sweeping the pavements, regardless of dust. With much swaying of the hips they strolled delicately along, slackening their pace when they crossed the bright light thrown from one of the great cafés. With shoulders thrown back, shrill and noisy laughter and many backward glances at the men who turned to look at them, they marched about and were completely in their element. In the shadow of night their artificially whitened faces, their rouged lips and their darkened eyelids became as charming and suggestive as if the inmates of a make-believe trumpery oriental bazaar had been sent forth into the open street. Till eleven at night they sauntered gaily along among the rudely jostling crowds, contenting themselves with an occasional "dirty ass!" hurled after the clumsy people whose boot heels had torn a flounce or two from their dresses. Little familiar salutations would pass between them and the café waiters, and at times they would stop and chat in front of a small table and accept of drinks, which they consumed with much deliberation, as became people not sorry to sit down for a bit while waiting for the theaters to empty. But as night advanced, if they had not made one or two trips in the direction of the Rue la Rochefoucauld, they became abject strumpets, and their hunt for men grew more ferocious than ever. Beneath the trees in the darkening and fast-emptying boulevards fierce bargainings took place, accompanied by oaths and blows. Respectable family parties—fathers, mothers and daughters—who were used to such scenes, would pass quietly by the while without quickening their pace. Afterward, when they had walked from the opera to the *gymnase* some half-score times and in the deepening night men were rapidly dropping off homeward for good and all, Nana and Satin kept to the sidewalk in the Rue du Faubourg Montmartre. There up till two o'clock in the morning restaurants, bars and ham-and-beef shops were brightly lit up, while a noisy mob of women hung obstinately round the doors of the cafés. This suburb was the only corner of night Paris which was still alight and still alive, the only market still open to nocturnal bargains. These last were openly struck between group and group and from one end of the street to the other, just as in the wide and open corridor of a disorderly house. On such evenings as the pair came home without having had any success they used to wrangle together. The Rue Notre Dame de la Lorette stretched dark and deserted in front of them. Here and there the crawling shadow of a woman was discernible, for the Quarter was going home and going home late, and poor creatures, exasperated at a night of fruitless loitering, were unwilling to give up the chase and would still stand, disputing in hoarse voices with any strayed reveler they could catch at the corner of the Rue Breda or the Rue Fontaine.

Nevertheless, some windfalls came in their way now and then in the shape of louis picked up in the society of elegant gentlemen, who slipped their decorations into their pockets as they went upstairs with them. Satin had an especially keen scent for these. On rainy evenings, when the dripping city exhaled an unpleasant odor suggestive of a great untidy bed, she knew that the soft weather and the fetid reek of the town's holes and corners were sure to send the men mad. And so she watched the best dressed among them, for she knew by their pale eyes what their state was. On such nights it was as though a fit of fleshly madness were passing over Paris. The girl was rather nervous certainly, for the most modish gentlemen were always the most obscene. All the varnish would crack off a man, and the brute beast would show itself, exacting, monstrous in lust, a past master in corruption. But besides being nervous, that trollop of a Satin was lacking in respect. She would blurt out awful things in front of dignified gentlemen in carriages and assure them that their coachmen were better bred than they because they behaved respectfully toward the women and did not half kill them with their diabolical tricks and suggestions. The way in which smart people sprawled head over heels into all the cesspools of vice still caused Nana some surprise, for she had a few prejudices remaining, though Satin was rapidly destroying them.

"Well then," she used to say when talking seriously about the matter, "there's no such thing as virtue left, is there?"

From one end of the social ladder to the other everybody was on the loose! Good gracious! Some nice things ought to be going on in Paris between nine o'clock in the evening and three in the morning! And with that she began making very merry and declaring that if one could only have looked into every room one would have seen some funny sights—the little people going it head over ears and a good lot of swells, too, playing the swine rather harder than the rest. Oh, she was finishing her education!

One evening when she came to call for Satin she recognized the Marquis de Chouard. He was coming downstairs with quaking legs; his face was ashen white, and he leaned heavily on the banisters. She pretended to be blowing her nose. Upstairs she found Satin amid indescribable filth. No household work had been done for a week; her bed was disgusting, and ewers and basins were standing about in all directions. Nana expressed surprise at her knowing the marquis. Oh yes, she knew him! He had jolly well bored her confectioner and her when they were together. At present he used to come back now and then, but he nearly bothered her life out, going sniffing into all the dirty corners—yes, even into her slippers!

"Yes, dear girl, my slippers! Oh, he's the dirtiest old beast, always wanting one to do things!"

The sincerity of these low debauches rendered Nana especially uneasy. Seeing the courtesans around her slowly dying of it every day, she recalled to mind the comedy of pleasure she had taken part in when she was in the heyday of success. Moreover, Satin inspired her with an awful fear of the police. She was full of anecdotes about them. Formerly she had been the mistress of a plain-clothes man, had consented to this in order to be left in peace, and on two occasions he had prevented her from being put "on the lists." But at present she was in a great fright, for if she were to be nabbed again there was a clear case against her. You had only to listen to her! For the sake of perquisites the police used to take up as many women as possible. They laid hold of everybody and quieted you with a slap if you shouted, for they were sure of being defended in their actions and rewarded, even when they had taken a virtuous girl among the rest. In the summer they would swoop upon the boulevard in parties of twelve or fifteen, surround a whole long reach of sidewalk and fish up as many as thirty women in an evening. Satin, however, knew the likely places, and the moment she saw a plain-clothes man heaving in sight she took to her heels, while the long lines of women on the pavements scattered in consternation and fled through the surrounding crowd. The dread of the law and of the magistracy was such that certain women would stand as though paralyzed in the doorways of the cafés while the raid was sweeping the avenue without. But Satin was even more afraid of being denounced, for her pastry cook had proved blackguard enough to threaten to sell her when she had left him. Yes, that was a fake by which men lived on their mistresses! Then, too, there were the dirty women who delivered you up out of sheer treachery if you were prettier than they! Nana listened to these recitals and felt her terrors growing upon her. She had always trembled before the law, that unknown power, that form of revenge practiced by men able and willing to crush her in the certain absence of all defenders. Saint-Lazare she pictured as a grave, a dark hole, in which they buried live women after they had cut off their hair. She admitted that it was only necessary to leave Fontan and seek powerful protectors. But as matters stood it was in vain that Satin talked to

ier of certain lists of women's names, which it was the duty of the plain-
clothes men to consult, and of certain photographs accompanying the lists, the
originals of which were on no account to be touched. The reassurance did
not make her tremble the less, and she still saw herself hustled and dragged
along and finally subjected to the official medical inspection. The thought of
he official armchair filled her with shame and anguish, for had she not bade
it defiance a score of times?

Now it so happened that one evening toward the close of September, as she
was walking with Satin in the Boulevard Poissonnière, the latter suddenly
began tearing along at a terrible pace. And when Nana asked her what she
meant thereby:

"It's the plain-clothes men!" whispered Satin. "Off with you! Off with you!"

A wild stampede took place amid the surging crowd. Skirts streamed out
behind and were torn. There were blows and shrieks. A woman fell down. The
crowd of bystanders stood hilariously watching this rough police raid while
he plain-clothes men rapidly narrowed their circle. Meanwhile Nana had lost
Satin. Her legs were failing her, and she would have been taken up for a certainty had not a man caught her by the arm and led her away in front of the
angry police. It was Prullière, and he had just recognized her. Without saying a word he turned down the Rue Rougemont with her. It was just then
quite deserted, and she was able to regain breath there, but at first her faint-
ness and exhaustion were such that he had to support her. She did not even
thank him.

"Look here," he said, "you must recover a bit. Come up to my rooms."

He lodged in the Rue Bergère close by. But she straightened herself up at
once.

"No, I don't want to."

Thereupon he waxed coarse and rejoined:

"Why don't you want to, eh? Why, everybody visits my rooms."

"Because I don't."

In her opinion that explained everything. She was too fond of Fontan to
betray him with one of his friends. The other people ceased to count the moment there was no pleasure in the business, and necessity compelled her to it.
In view of her idiotic obstinacy Prullière, as became a pretty fellow whose
vanity had been wounded, did a cowardly thing.

"Very well, do as you like!" he cried. "Only I don't side with you, my dear.
You must get out of the scrape by yourself."

And with that he left her. Terrors got hold of her again, and scurrying past
shops and turning white whenever a man drew nigh, she fetched an immense
compass before reaching Montmartre.

On the morrow, while still suffering from the shock of last night's terrors,
Nana went to her aunt's and at the foot of a small empty street in the Batignolles found herself face to face with Labordette. At first they both appeared
embarrassed, for with his usual complaisance he was busy on a secret errand.
Nevertheless, he was the first to regain his self-possession and to announce
himself fortunate in meeting her. Yes, certainly, everybody was still wonder-

ing at Nana's total eclipse. People were asking for her, and old friends were pining. And with that he grew quite paternal and ended by sermonizing.

"Frankly speaking, between you and me, my dear, the thing's getting stupid One can understand a mash, but to go to that extent, to be trampled on like that and to get nothing but knocks! Are you playing up for the 'Virtue Prizes' then?"

She listened to him with an embarrassed expression. But when he told her about Rose, who was triumphantly enjoying her conquest of Count Muffat, a flame came into her eyes.

"Oh, if I wanted to——" she muttered.

As became an obliging friend, he at once offered to act as intercessor. But she refused his help, and he thereupon attacked her in an opposite quarter.

He informed her that Bordenave was busy mounting a play of Fauchery's containing a splendid part for her.

"What, a play with a part!" she cried in amazement. "But he's in it and he's told me nothing about it!"

She did not mention Fontan by name. However, she grew calm again directly and declared that she would never go on the stage again. Labordette doubtless remained unconvinced, for he continued with smiling insistence.

"You know, you need fear nothing with me. I get your Muffat ready for you, and you go on the stage again, and I bring him to you like a little dog!"

"No!" she cried decisively.

And she left him. Her heroic conduct made her tenderly pitiful toward herself. No blackguard of a man would ever have sacrificed himself like that without trumpeting the fact abroad. Nevertheless, she was struck by one thing: Labordette had given her exactly the same advice as Francis had given her. That evening when Fontan came home she questioned him about Fauchery's piece. The former had been back at the Variétés for two months past. Why then had he not told her about the part?

"What part?" he said in his ill-humored tone. "The grand lady's part, maybe? The deuce, you believe you've got talent then! Why, such a part would utterly do for you, my girl! You're meant for comic business—there's no denying it!"

She was dreadfully wounded. All that evening he kept chaffing her, calling her Mlle Mars. But the harder he hit the more bravely she suffered, for she derived a certain bitter satisfaction from this heroic devotion of hers, which rendered her very great and very loving in her own eyes. Ever since she had gone with other men in order to supply his wants her love for him had increased, and the fatigues and disgusts encountered outside only added to the flame. He was fast becoming a sort of pet vice for which she paid, a necessity of existence it was impossible to do without, seeing that blows only stimulated her desires. He, on his part, seeing what a good tame thing she had become, ended by abusing his privileges. She was getting on his nerves, and he began to conceive so fierce a loathing for her that he forgot to keep count of his real interests. When Bosc made his customary remarks to him he cried out in exasperation, for which there was no apparent cause, that he had had

nough of her and of her good dinners and that he would shortly chuck her
ut of doors if only for the sake of making another woman a present of his
even thousand francs. Indeed, that was how their liaison ended.

One evening Nana came in toward eleven o'clock and found the door bolted.
She tapped once—there was no answer; twice—still no answer. Meanwhile she
saw light under the door, and Fontan inside did not trouble to move. She
tapped again unwearyingly; she called him and began to get annoyed. At
length Fontan's voice became audible; he spoke slowly and rather unctuously
and uttered but this one word:

"*Merde!*"

She beat on the door with her fists.

"*Merde!*"

She banged hard enough to smash in the woodwork.

"*Merde!*"

And for upward of a quarter of an hour the same foul expression buffeted
her, answering like a jeering echo to every blow wherewith she shook the
door. At length, seeing that she was not growing tired, he opened sharply,
planted himself on the threshold, folded his arms and said in the same cold,
brutal voice:

"By God, have you done yet? What d'you want? Are you going to let us
sleep in peace, eh? You can quite see I've got company tonight."

He was certainly not alone, for Nana perceived the little woman from the
Bouffes with the untidy tow hair and the gimlet-hole eyes, standing enjoying
herself in her shift among the furniture she had paid for. But Fontan stepped
out on the landing. He looked terrible, and he spread out and crooked his
great fingers as if they were pincers.

"Hook it or I'll strangle you!"

Thereupon Nana burst into a nervous fit of sobbing. She was frightened and
she made off. This time it was she that was being kicked out of doors. And in
her fury the thought of Muffat suddenly occurred to her. Ah, to be sure,
Fontan, of all men, ought never to have done her such a turn!

When she was out in the street her first thought was to go and sleep with
Satin, provided the girl had no one with her. She met her in front of her house,
for she, too, had been turned out of doors by her landlord. He had just had
a padlock affixed to her door—quite illegally, of course, seeing that she had
her own furniture. She swore and talked of having him up before the commissary of police. In the meantime, as midnight was striking, they had to begin
thinking of finding a bed. And Satin, deeming it unwise to let the plain-clothes
men into her secrets, ended by taking Nana to a woman who kept a little
hotel in the Rue de Laval. Here they were assigned a narrow room on the first
floor, the window of which opened on the courtyard. Satin remarked:

"I should gladly have gone to Mme Robert's. There's always a corner there
for me. But with you it's out of the question. She's getting absurdly jealous;
she beat me the other night."

When they had shut themselves in, Nana, who had not yet relieved her
feelings, burst into tears and again and again recounted Fontan's dirty be-

havior. Satin listened complaisantly, comforted her, grew even more angr
than she in denunciation of the male sex.

"Oh, the pigs, the pigs! Look here, we'll have nothing more to do wit
them!"

Then she helped Nana to undress with all the small, busy attentions, be
coming a humble little friend. She kept saying coaxingly:

"Let's go to bed as fast as we can, pet. We shall be better off there! Ol
how silly you are to get crusty about things! I tell you, they're dirty brute:
Don't think any more about 'em. I—I love you very much. Don't cry, an
oblige your own little darling girl."

And once in bed, she forthwith took Nana in her arms and soothed an
comforted her. She refused to hear Fontan's name mentioned again, and eacl
time it recurred to her friend's lips she stopped it with a kiss. Her lips poute
in pretty indignation; her hair lay loose about her, and her face glowed witl
tenderness and childlike beauty. Little by little her soft embrace compelle
Nana to dry her tears. She was touched and replied to Satin's caresses. Whei
two o'clock struck the candle was still burning, and a sound of soft, smothere
laughter and lovers' talk was audible in the room.

But suddenly a loud noise came up from the lower floors of the hotel, an
Satin, with next to nothing on, got up and listened intently.

"The police!" she said, growing very pale.

"Oh, blast our bad luck! We're bloody well done for!"

Often had she told stories about the raids on hotels made by the plain
clothes men. But that particular night neither of them had suspected any
thing when they took shelter in the Rue de Laval. At the sound of the wor
"police" Nana lost her head. She jumped out of bed and ran across the roon
with the scared look of a madwoman about to jump out of the window
Luckily, however, the little courtyard was roofed with glass, which was cov
ered with an iron-wire grating at the level of the girls' bedroom. At sight of
this she ceased to hesitate; she stepped over the window prop, and with hei
chemise flying and her legs bared to the night air she vanished in the gloom

"Stop! Stop!" said Satin in a great fright. "You'll kill yourself."

Then as they began hammering at the door, she shut the window like a
good-natured girl and threw her friend's clothes down into a cupboard. She
was already resigned to her fate and comforted herself with the thought that
after all, if she were to be put on the official list she would no longer be so
"beastly frightened" as of yore. So she pretended to be heavy with sleep. She
yawned; she palavered and ended by opening the door to a tall, burly fellow
with an unkempt beard, who said to her:

"Show your hands! You've got no needle pricks on them: you don't work.
Now then, dress!"

"But I'm not a dressmaker; I'm a burnisher," Satin brazenly declared.

Nevertheless, she dressed with much docility, knowing that argument was
out of the question. Cries were ringing through the hotel; a girl was clinging
to doorposts and refusing to budge an inch. Another girl, in bed with a lover,
who was answering for her legality, was acting the honest woman who had

een grossly insulted and spoke of bringing an action against the prefect of
olice. For close on an hour there was a noise of heavy shoes on the stairs, of
ists hammering on doors, of shrill disputes terminating in sobs, of petticoats
ustling along the walls, of all the sounds, in fact, attendant on the sudden
wakening and scared departure of a flock of women as they were roughly
acked off by three plain-clothes men, headed by a little oily-mannered, fair-
aired commissary of police. After they had gone the hotel relapsed into deep
ilence.

Nobody had betrayed her; Nana was saved. Shivering and half dead with
ear, she came groping back into the room. Her bare feet were cut and
leeding, for they had been torn by the grating. For a long while she re-
nained sitting on the edge of the bed, listening and listening. Toward morn-
ng, however, she went to sleep again, and at eight o'clock, when she woke
p, she escaped from the hotel and ran to her aunt's. When Mme Lerat, who
appened just then to be drinking her morning coffee with Zoé, beheld her
edraggled plight and haggard face, she took note of the hour and at once
nderstood the state of the case.

"It's come to it, eh?" she cried. "I certainly told you that he would take the
kin off your back one of these days. Well, well, come in; you'll always find
kind welcome here."

Zoé had risen from her chair and was muttering with respectful familiarity:
"Madame is restored to us at last. I was waiting for Madame."

But Mme Lerat insisted on Nana's going and kissing Louiset at once, because, she said, the child took delight in his mother's nice ways. Louiset, a
ickly child with poor blood, was still asleep, and when Nana bent over his
white, scrofulous face, the memory of all she had undergone during the last
ew months brought a choking lump into her throat.

"Oh, my poor little one, my poor little one!" she gasped, bursting into a
final fit of sobbing.

CHAPTER IX

THE *Petite Duchesse* was being rehearsed at the Variétés. The first act had
just been carefully gone through, and the second was about to begin. Seated
in old armchairs in front of the stage, Fauchery and Bordenave were discussing various points while the prompter, Father Cossard, a little humpbacked man perched on a straw-bottomed chair, was turning over the pages
of the manuscript, a pencil between his lips.

"Well, what are they waiting for?" cried Bordenave on a sudden, tapping
the floor savagely with his heavy cane. "Barillot, why don't they begin?"

"It's Monsieur Bosc that has disappeared," replied Barillot, who was acting
as second stage manager.

Then there arose a tempest, and everybody shouted for Bosc while Bordenave swore.

"Always the same thing, by God! It's all very well ringing for 'em: they're always where they've no business to be. And then they grumble when they'r kept till after four o'clock."

But Bosc just then came in with supreme tranquillity.

"Eh? What? What do they want me for? Oh, it's my turn! You ough to have said so. All right! Simonne gives the cue: 'Here are the guests,' and I come in. Which way must I come in?"

"Through the door, of course," cried Fauchery in great exasperation.

"Yes, but where is the door?"

At this Bordenave fell upon Barillot and once more set to work swearing and hammering the boards with his cane.

"By God! I said a chair was to be put there to stand for the door, and every day we have to get it done again. Barillot! Where's Barillot? Another of 'em! Why, they're all going!"

Nevertheless, Barillot came and planted the chair down in person, mutely weathering the storm as he did so. And the rehearsal began again. Simonne, in her hat and furs, began moving about like a maidservant busy arranging furniture. She paused to say:

"I'm not warm, you know, so I keep my hands in my muff."

Then changing her voice, she greeted Bosc with a little cry:

"La, it's Monsieur le Comte. You're the first to come, Monsieur le Comte, and Madame will be delighted."

Bosc had muddy trousers and a huge yellow overcoat, round the collar of which a tremendous comforter was wound. On his head he wore an old hat, and he kept his hands in his pockets. He did not act but dragged himself along, remarking in a hollow voice:

"Don't disturb your mistress, Isabelle; I want to take her by surprise."

The rehearsal took its course. Bordenave knitted his brows. He had slipped down low in his armchair and was listening with an air of fatigue. Fauchery was nervous and kept shifting about in his seat. Every few minutes he itched with the desire to interrupt, but he restrained himself. He heard a whispering in the dark and empty house behind him.

"Is she there?" he asked, leaning over toward Bordenave.

The latter nodded affirmatively. Before accepting the part of Géraldine, which he was offering her, Nana had been anxious to see the piece, for she hesitated to play a courtesan's part a second time. She, in fact, aspired to an honest woman's part. Accordingly she was hiding in the shadows of a corner box in company with Labordette, who was managing matters for her with Bordenave. Fauchery glanced in her direction and then once more set himself to follow the rehearsal.

Only the front of the stage was lit up. A flaring gas burner on a support, which was fed by a pipe from the footlights, burned in front of a reflector and cast its full brightness over the immediate foreground. It looked like a big yellow eye glaring through the surrounding semiobscurity, where it flamed in a doubtful, melancholy way. Cossard was holding up his manuscript against the slender stem of this arrangement. He wanted to see more clearly, and in the flood of light his hump was sharply outlined. As to Bordenave and Fau-

:hery, they were already drowned in shadow. It was only in the heart of this
:normous structure, on a few square yards of stage, that a faint glow suggested
he light cast by some lantern nailed up in a railway station. It made the
actors look like eccentric phantoms and set their shadows dancing after them.
The remainder of the stage was full of mist and suggested a house in process
)f being pulled down, a church nave in utter ruin. It was littered with ladders,
with set pieces and with scenery, of which the faded painting suggested
neaped-up rubbish. Hanging high in air, the scenes had the appearance of
great ragged clouts suspended from the rafters of some vast old-clothes shop,
while above these again a ray of bright sunlight fell from a window and
:love the shadow round the flies with a bar of gold.

Meanwhile actors were chatting at the back of the stage while awaiting their
:ues. Little by little they had raised their voices.

"Confound it, will you be silent?" howled Bordenave, raging up and down
in his chair. "I can't hear a word. Go outside if you want to talk; we are at
work. Barillot, if there's any more talking I clap on fines all round!"

They were silent for a second or two. They were sitting in a little group on
a bench and some rustic chairs in the corner of a scenic garden, which was
standing ready to be put in position as it would be used in the opening act the
same evening. In the middle of this group Fontan and Prullière were listening
to Rose Mignon, to whom the manager of the Folies-Dramatique Théâtre
had been making magnificent offers. But a voice was heard shouting:

"The duchess! Saint-Firmin! The duchess and Saint-Firmin are wanted!"

Only when the call was repeated did Prullière remember that he was Saint-
Firmin! Rose, who was playing the Duchess Hélène, was already waiting to
go on with him while old Bosc slowly returned to his seat, dragging one
foot after the other over the sonorous and deserted boards. Clarisse offered
him a place on the bench beside her.

"What's he bawling like that for?" she said in allusion to Bordenave.
"Things will be getting rosy soon! A piece can't be put on nowadays without
its getting on his nerves."

Bosc shrugged his shoulders; he was above such storms. Fontan whispered:
"He's afraid of a fiasco. The piece strikes me as idiotic."

Then he turned to Clarisse and again referred to what Rose had been telling them:

"D'you believe in the offers of the Folies people, eh? Three hundred francs
an evening for a hundred nights! Why not a country house into the bargain?
If his wife were to be given three hundred francs Mignon would chuck my
friend Bordenave and do it jolly sharp too!"

Clarisse was a believer in the three hundred francs. That man Fontan was
always picking holes in his friends' successes! Just then Simonne interrupted
her. She was shivering with cold. Indeed, they were all buttoned up to the
ears and had comforters on, and they looked up at the ray of sunlight which
shone brightly above them but did not penetrate the cold gloom of the theater.
In the streets outside there was a frost under a November sky.

"And there's no fire in the greenroom!" said Simonne. "It's disgusting; h
is just becoming a skinflint! I want to be off; I don't want to get seedy."

"Silence, I say!" Bordenave once more thundered.

Then for a minute or so a confused murmur alone was audible as the actor
went on repeating their parts. There was scarcely any appropriate action, and
they spoke in even tones so as not to tire themselves. Nevertheless, when they
did emphasize a particular shade of meaning they cast a glance at the house
which lay before them like a yawning gulf. It was suffused with vague, ambien
shadow, which resembled the fine dust floating pent in some high, window
less loft. The deserted house, whose sole illumination was the twilight radiance
of the stage, seemed to slumber in melancholy and mysterious effacement
Near the ceiling dense night smothered the frescoes, while from the severa
tiers of stage boxes on either hand huge widths of gray canvas stretched down
to protect the neighboring hangings. In fact, there was no end to these coverings; bands of canvas had been thrown over the velvet-covered ledges in front
of the various galleries which they shrouded thickly. Their pale hue stained
the surrounding shadows, and of the general decorations of the house only the
dark recesses of the boxes were distinguishable. These served to outline the
framework of the several stories, where the seats were so many stains of red
velvet turned black. The chandelier had been let down as far as it would go,
and it so filled the region of the stalls with its pendants as to suggest a flitting
and to set one thinking that the public had started on a journey from which
they would never return.

Just about then Rose, as the little duchess who has been misled into the
society of a courtesan, came to the footlights, lifted up her hands and pouted
adorably at the dark and empty theater, which was as sad as a house of
mourning.

"Good heavens, what queer people!" she said, emphasizing the phrase and
confident that it would have its effect.

Far back in the corner box in which she was hiding Nana sat enveloped in
a great shawl. She was listening to the play and devouring Rose with her eyes.
Turning toward Labordette, she asked him in a low tone:

"You are sure he'll come?"

"Quite sure. Without doubt he'll come with Mignon, so as to have an
excuse for coming. As soon as he makes his appearance you'll go up into Mathilde's dressing room, and I'll bring him to you there."

They were talking of Count Muffat. Labordette had arranged this interview
with him on neutral ground. He had had a serious talk with Bordenave, whose
affairs had been gravely damaged by two successive failures. Accordingly Bordenave had hastened to lend him his theater and to offer Nana a part, for he
was anxious to win the count's favor and hoped to be able to borrow from him.

"And this part of Géraldine, what d'you thing of it?" continued Labordette.

But Nana sat motionless and vouchsafed no reply. After the first act, in
which the author showed how the Duc de Beaurivage played his wife false
with the blonde Géraldine, a comic-opera celebrity, the second act witnessed
the Duchess Hélène's arrival at the house of the actress on the occasion of a

asked ball being given by the latter. The duchess has come to find out by
hat magical process ladies of that sort conquer and retain their husbands' af-
ctions. A cousin, the handsome Oscar de Saint-Firmin, introduces her and
»pes to be able to debauch her. And her first lesson causes her great surprise,
r she hears Géraldine swearing like a hodman at the duke, who suffers with
ost ecstatic submissiveness. The episode causes her to cry out, "Dear me,
that's the way one ought to talk to the men!" Géraldine had scarce any
her scene in the act save this one. As to the duchess, she is very soon pun-
ied for her curiosity, for an old buck, the Baron de Tardiveau, takes her for
courtesan and becomes very gallant, while on her other side Beaurivage
s on a lounging chair and makes his peace with Géraldine by dint of kisses
id caresses. As this last lady's part had not yet been assigned to anyone,
ither Cossard had got up to read it, and he was now figuring away in Bosc's
ms and emphasizing it despite himself. At this point, while the rehearsal was
agging monotonously on, Fauchery suddenly jumped from his chair. He
id restrained himself up to that moment, but now his nerves got the better
him.

"That's not it!" he cried.

The actors paused awkwardly enough while Fontan sneered and asked in his
ost contemptuous voice:

"Eh? What's not it? Who's not doing it right?"

"Nobody is! You're quite wrong, quite wrong!" continued Fauchery, and,
esticulating wildly, he came striding over the stage and began himself to act
ie scene.

"Now look here, you Fontan, do please comprehend the way Tardiveau
ets packed off. You must lean forward like this in order to catch hold of
ie duchess. And then you, Rose, must change your position like that but not
>o soon—only when you hear the kiss."

He broke off and in the heat of explanation shouted to Cossard:

"Géraldine, give the kiss! Loudly, so that it may be heard!"

Father Cossard turned toward Bosc and smacked his lips vigorously.

"Good! That's the kiss," said Fauchery triumphantly. "Once more; let's
ave it once more. Now you see, Rose, I've had time to move, and then I give
little cry—so: 'Oh, she's given him a kiss.' But before I do that, Tardiveau
iust go up the stage. D'you hear, Fontan? You go up. Come, let's try it again,
l together."

The actors continued the scene again, but Fontan played his part with such
1 ill grace that they made no sort of progress. Twice Fauchery had to repeat
is explanation, each time acting it out with more warmth than before. The
ctors listened to him with melancholy faces, gazed momentarily at one an-
ther, as though he had asked them to walk on their heads, and then
wkwardly essayed the passage, only to pull up short directly afterward,
>oking as stiff as puppets whose strings have just been snapped.

"No, it beats me; I can't understand it," said Fontan at length, speaking in
ie insolent manner peculiar to him.

Bordenave had never once opened his lips. He had slipped quite down in his

armchair, so that only the top of his hat was now visible in the doubtf
flicker of the gaslight on the stand. His cane had fallen from his grasp and l
slantwise across his waistcoat. Indeed, he seemed to be asleep. But sudden
he sat bolt upright.

"It's idiotic, my boy," he announced quietly to Fauchery.

"What d'you mean, idiotic?" cried the author, growing very pale. "It's yo
that are the idiot, my dear boy!"

Bordenave began to get angry at once. He repeated the word "idiotic" an
seeking a more forcible expression, hit upon "imbecile" and "damned foolish
The public would hiss, and the act would never be finished! And when Fau
chery, without, indeed, being very deeply wounded by these big phrase
which always recurred when a new piece was being put on, grew savage an
called the other a brute, Bordenave went beyond all bounds, brandished h
cane in the air, snorted like a bull and shouted:

"Good God! Why the hell can't you shut up? We've lost a quarter of a
hour over this folly. Yes, folly! There's no sense in it. And it's so simple, afte
all's said and done! You, Fontan, mustn't move. You, Rose, must make you
little movement, just that, no more; d'ye see? And then you come down. Now
then, let's get it done this journey. Give the kiss, Cossard."

Then ensued confusion. The scene went no better than before. Bordenave
in his turn, showed them how to act it about as gracefully as an elephant migh
have done, while Fauchery sneered and shrugged pityingly. After that Fonta
put his word in, and even Bosc made so bold as to give advice. Rose, thor
oughly tired out, had ended by sitting down on the chair which indicated th
door. No one knew where they had got to, and by way of finish to it a
Simonne made a premature entry, under the impression that her cue had bee
given her, and arrived amid the confusion. This so enraged Bordenave that h
whirled his stick round in a terrific manner and caught her a sounding thwacl
to the rearward. At rehearsal he used frequently to drub his former mistress
Simonne ran away, and this furious outcry followed her:

"Take that, and, by God, if I'm annoyed again I shut the whole shop up a
once!"

Fauchery pushed his hat down over his forehead and pretended to be going
to leave the theater. But he stopped at the top of the stage and came down
again when he saw Bordenave perspiringly resuming his seat. Then he, too
took up his old position in the other armchair. For some seconds they sa
motionless side by side while oppressive silence reigned in the shadowy house
The actors waited for nearly two minutes. They were all heavy with ex
haustion and felt as though they had performed an overwhelming task.

"Well, let's go on," said Bordenave at last. He spoke in his usual voice and
was perfectly calm.

"Yes, let's go on," Fauchery repeated. "We'll arrange the scene tomorrow."

And with that they dragged on again and rehearsed their parts with as much
listlessness and as fine an indifference as ever. During the dispute between
manager and author Fontan and the rest had been taking things very com
fortably on the rustic bench and seats at the back of the stage, where they had

been chuckling, grumbling and saying fiercely cutting things. But when Simonne came back, still smarting from her blow and choking with sobs, they grew melodramatic and declared that had they been in her place they would have strangled the swine. She began wiping her eyes and nodding approval. It was all over between them, she said. She was leaving him, especially as Steiner had offered to give her a grand start in life only the day before. Clarisse was much astonished at this, for the banker was quite ruined, but Prullière began laughing and reminded them of the neat manner in which that confounded Israelite had puffed himself alongside of Rose in order to get his Landes saltworks afloat on 'change. Just at that time he was airing a new project, namely, a tunnel under the Bosporus. Simonne listened with the greatest interest to this fresh piece of information.

As to Clarisse, she had been raging for a week past. Just fancy, that beast La Faloise, whom she had succeeded in chucking into Gaga's venerable embrace, was coming into the fortune of a very rich uncle! It was just her luck; she had always been destined to make things cozy for other people. Then, too, that pig Bordenave had once more given her a mere scrap of a part, a paltry fifty lines, just as if she could not have played Géraldine! She was yearning for that role and hoping that Nana would refuse it.

"Well, and what about me?" said Prullière with much bitterness. "I haven't got more than two hundred lines. I wanted to give the part up. It's too bad to make me play that fellow Saint-Firmin; why, it's a regular failure! And then what a style it's written in, my dears! It 'll fall dead flat, you may be sure."

But just then Simonne, who had been chatting with Father Barillot, came back breathless and announced:

"By the by, talking of Nana, she's in the house."

"Where, where?" asked Clarisse briskly, getting up to look for her.

The news spread at once, and everyone craned forward. The rehearsal was, as it were, momentarily interrupted. But Bordenave emerged from his quiescent condition, shouting:

"What's up, eh? Finish the act, I say. And be quiet out there; it's unbearable!"

Nana was still following the piece from the corner box. Twice Labordette showed an inclination to chat, but she grew impatient and nudged him to make him keep silent. The second act was drawing to a close, when two shadows loomed at the back of the theater. They were creeping softly down, avoiding all noise, and Nana recognized Mignon and Count Muffat. They came forward and silently shook hands with Bordenave.

"Ah, there they are," she murmured with a sigh of relief.

Rose Mignon delivered the last sentences of the act. Thereupon Bordenave said that it was necessary to go through the second again before beginning the third. With that he left off attending to the rehearsal and greeted the count with looks of exaggerated politeness, while Fauchery pretended to be entirely engrossed with his actors, who now grouped themselves round him. Mignon stood whistling carelessly, with his hands behind his back and his eyes fixed complacently on his wife, who seemed rather nervous.

"Well, shall we go upstairs?" Labordette asked Nana. "I'll install you in the dressing room and come down again and fetch him."

Nana forthwith left the corner box. She had to grope her way along the passage outside the stalls, but Bordenave guessed where she was as she passed along in the dark and caught her up at the end of the corridor passing behind the scenes, a narrow tunnel where the gas burned day and night. Here, in order to bluff her into a bargain, he plunged into a discussion of the courtesan's part.

"What a part it is, eh? What a wicked little part! It's made for you. Come and rehearse tomorrow."

Nana was frigid. She wanted to know what the third act was like.

"Oh, it's superb, the third act is! The duchess plays the courtesan in her own house and this disgusts Beaurivage and makes him amend his way. Then there's an awfully funny *quid pro quo*, when Tardiveau arrives and is under the impression that he's at an opera dancer's house."

"And what does Géraldine do in it all?" interrupted Nana.

"Géraldine?" repeated Bordenave in some embarrassment. "She has a scene, not a very long one, but a great success. It's made for you, I assure you! Will you sign?"

She looked steadily at him and at length made answer:

"We'll see about that all in good time."

And she rejoined Labordette, who was waiting for her on the stairs. Everybody in the theater had recognized her, and there was now much whispering, especially between Prullière, who was scandalized at her return, and Clarisse, who was very desirous of the part. As to Fontan, he looked coldly on, pretending unconcern, for he did not think it becoming to round on a woman he had loved. Deep down in his heart, though, his old love had turned to hate, and he nursed the fiercest rancor against her in return for the constant devotion, the personal beauty, the life in common, of which his perverse and monstrous tastes had made him tire.

In the meantime, when Labordette reappeared and went up to the count, Rose Mignon, whose suspicions Nana's presence had excited, understood it all forthwith. Muffat was bothering her to death, but she was beside herself at the thought of being left like this. She broke the silence which she usually maintained on such subjects in her husband's society and said bluntly:

"You see what's going on? My word, if she tries the Steiner trick on again I'll tear her eyes out!"

Tranquilly and haughtily Mignon shrugged his shoulders, as became a man from whom nothing could be hidden.

"Do be quiet," he muttered. "Do me the favor of being quiet, won't you?"

He knew what to rely on now. He had drained his Muffat dry, and he knew that at a sign from Nana he was ready to lie down and be a carpet under her feet. There is no fighting against passions such as that. Accordingly, as he knew what men were, he thought of nothing but how to turn the situation to the best possible account.

It would be necessary to wait on the course of events. And he waited on them.

"Rose, it's your turn!" shouted Bordenave. "The second act's being begun again."

"Off with you then," continued Mignon, "and let me arrange matters."

Then he began bantering, despite all his troubles, and was pleased to congratulate Fauchery on his piece. A very strong piece! Only why was his great lady so chaste? It wasn't natural! With that he sneered and asked who had sat for the portrait of the Duke of Beaurivage, Géraldine's worn-out roué. Fauchery smiled; he was far from annoyed. But Bordenave glanced in Muffat's direction and looked vexed, and Mignon was struck at this and became serious again.

"Let's begin, for God's sake!" yelled the manager. "Now then, Barillot! Eh? What? Isn't Bosc there? Is he bloody well making game of me now?"

Bosc, however, made his appearance quietly enough, and the rehearsal began again just as Labordette was taking the count away with him. The latter was tremulous at the thought of seeing Nana once more. After the rupture had taken place between them there had been a great void in his life. He was idle and fancied himself about to suffer through the sudden change his habits had undergone, and accordingly he had let them take him to see Rose. Besides, his brain had been in such a whirl that he had striven to forget everything and had strenuously kept from seeking out Nana while avoiding an explanation with the countess. He thought, indeed, that he owed his dignity such a measure of forgetfulness. But mysterious forces were at work within, and Nana began slowly to reconquer him. First came thoughts of her, then fleshly cravings and finally a new set of exclusive, tender, well-nigh paternal feelings.

The abominable events attendant on their last interview were gradually effacing themselves. He no longer saw Fontan; he no longer heard the stinging taunt about his wife's adultery with which Nana cast him out of doors. These things were as words whose memory vanished. Yet deep down in his heart there was a poignant smart which wrung him with such increasing pain that it nigh choked him. Childish ideas would occur to him; he imagined that she would never have betrayed him if he had really loved her, and he blamed himself for this. His anguish was becoming unbearable; he was really very wretched. His was the pain of an old wound rather than the blind, present desire which puts up with everything for the sake of immediate possession. He felt a jealous passion for the woman and was haunted by longings for her and her alone, her hair, her mouth, her body. When he remembered the sound of her voice a shiver ran through him; he longed for her as a miser might have done, with refinements of desire beggaring description. He was, in fact, so dolorously possessed by his passion that when Labordette had begun to broach the subject of an assignation he had thrown himself into his arms in obedience to irresistible impulse. Directly afterward he had, of course, been ashamed of an act of self-abandonment which could not but seem very ridiculous in a man of his position; but Labordette was one who knew when to see and when not to see things, and he gave a further proof of his tact when he left the count at the foot of the stairs and without effort let slip only these simple words:

"The right-hand passage on the second floor. The door's not shut."

Muffat was alone in that silent corner of the house. As he passed before the players' waiting room, he had peeped through the open doors and noticed the utter dilapidation of the vast chamber, which looked shamefully stained and worn in broad daylight. But what surprised him most as he emerged from the darkness and confusion of the stage was the pure, clear light and deep quiet at present pervading the lofty staircase, which one evening when he had seen it before had been bathed in gas fumes and loud with the footsteps of women scampering over the different floors. He felt that the dressing rooms were empty, the corridors deserted; not a soul was there; not a sound broke the stillness, while through the square windows on the level of the stairs the pale November sunlight filtered and cast yellow patches of light, full of dancing dust, amid the dead, peaceful air which seemed to descend from the regions above.

He was glad of this calm and the silence, and he went slowly up, trying to regain breath as he went, for his heart was thumping, and he was afraid lest he might behave childishly and give way to sighs and tears. Accordingly on the first-floor landing he leaned up against a wall—for he was sure of not being observed—and pressed his handkerchief to his mouth and gazed at the warped steps, the iron balustrade bright with the friction of many hands, the scraped paint on the walls—all the squalor, in fact, which that house of tolerance so crudely displayed at the pale afternoon hour when courtesans are asleep. When he reached the second floor he had to step over a big yellow cat which was lying curled up on a step. With half-closed eyes this cat was keeping solitary watch over the house, where the close and now frozen odors which the women nightly left behind them had rendered him somnolent.

In the right-hand corridor the door of the dressing room had, indeed, not been closed entirely. Nana was waiting. That little Mathilde, a drab of a young girl, kept her dressing room in a filthy state. Chipped jugs stood about anyhow; the dressing table was greasy, and there was a chair covered with red stains, which looked as if someone had bled over the straw. The paper pasted on walls and ceiling was splashed from top to bottom with spots of soapy water and this smelled so disagreeably of lavender scent turned sour that Nana opened the window and for some moments stayed leaning on the sill, breathing the fresh air and craning forward to catch sight of Mme Bron underneath. She could hear her broom wildly at work on the mildewed pantiles of the narrow court which was buried in shadow. A canary, whose cage hung on a shutter, was trilling away piercingly. The sound of carriages in the boulevard and neighboring streets was no longer audible, and the quiet and the wide expanse of sleeping sunlight suggested the country. Looking farther afield, her eye fell on the small buildings and glass roofs of the galleries in the passage and, beyond these, on the tall houses in the Rue Vivienne, the backs of which rose silent and apparently deserted over against her. There was a succession of terrace roofs close by, and on one of these a photographer had

perched a big cagelike construction of blue glass. It was all very gay, and
Nana was becoming absorbed in contemplation, when it struck her someone
had knocked at the door.

She turned round and shouted:

"Come in!"

At sight of the count she shut the window, for it was not warm, and there
was no need for the eavesdropping Mme Bron to listen. The pair gazed at one
another gravely. Then as the count still kept standing stiffly in front of her,
looking ready to choke with emotion, she burst out laughing and said:

"Well! So you're here again, you silly big beast!"

The tumult going on within him was so great that he seemed a man frozen
to ice. He addressed Nana as "madame" and esteemed himself happy to see
her again. Thereupon she became more familiar than ever in order to bounce
matters through.

"Don't do it in the dignified way! You wanted to see me, didn't you? But
you didn't intend us to stand looking at one another like a couple of china-
ware dogs. We've both been in the wrong—— Oh, I certainly forgive you!"

And herewith they agreed not to talk of that affair again, Muffat nodding
his assent as Nana spoke. He was calmer now but as yet could find nothing to
say, though a thousand things rose tumultuously to his lips. Surprised at his
apparent coldness, she began acting a part with much vigor.

"Come," she continued with a faint smile, "you're a sensible man! Now
that we've made our peace let's shake hands and be good friends in future."

"What? Good friends?" he murmured in sudden anxiety.

"Yes; it's idiotic, perhaps, but I should like you to think well of me. We've
had our little explanation out, and if we meet again we shan't, at any rate
look like a pair of boobies."

He tried to interrupt her with a movement of the hand.

"Let me finish! There's not a man, you understand, able to accuse me of
doing him a blackguardly turn; well, and it struck me as horrid to begin in
your case. We all have our sense of honor, dear boy."

"But that's not my meaning!" he shouted violently. "Sit down—listen to me!"

And as though he were afraid of seeing her take her departure, he pushed
her down on the solitary chair in the room. Then he paced about in growing
agitation. The little dressing room was airless and full of sunlight, and no
sound from the outside world disturbed its pleasant, peaceful, dampish atmosphere. In the pauses of conversation the shrillings of the canary were alone
audible and suggested the distant piping of a flute.

"Listen," he said, planting himself in front of her, "I've come to possess myself of you again. Yes, I want to begin again. You know that well; then why
do you talk to me as you do? Answer me; tell me you consent."

Her head was bent, and she was scratching the blood-red straw of the seat
underneath her. Seeing him so anxious, she did not hurry to answer. But at
last she lifted up her face. It had assumed a grave expression, and into the
beautiful eyes she had succeeded in infusing a look of sadness.

"Oh, it's impossible, little man. Never, never, will I live with you again."

"Why?" he stuttered, and his face seemed contracted in unspeakable suffering.

"Why? Hang it all, because—— It's impossible; that's about it. I don't want to."

He looked ardently at her for some seconds longer. Then his legs curved under him and he fell on the floor. In a bored voice she added this simple advice:

"Ah, don't be a baby!"

But he was one already. Dropping at her feet, he had put his arms round her waist and was hugging her closely, pressing his face hard against her knees. When he felt her thus—when he once more divined the presence of her velvety limbs beneath the thin fabric of her dress—he was suddenly convulsed and trembled, as it were, with fever, while madly, savagely, he pressed his face against her knees as though he had been anxious to force through her flesh. The old chair creaked, and beneath the low ceiling, where the air was pungent with stale perfumes, smothered sobs of desire were audible.

"Well, and after?" Nana began saying, letting him do as he would. "All this doesn't help you a bit, seeing that the thing's impossible. Good God, what a child you are!"

His energy subsided, but he still stayed on the floor, nor did he relax his hold of her as he said in a broken voice:

"Do at least listen to what I came to offer you. I've already seen a town house close to the Parc Monceau—I would gladly realize your smallest wish. In order to have you all to myself, I would give my whole fortune. Yes, that would be my only condition, that I should have you all to myself! Do you understand? And if you were to consent to be mine only, oh, then I should want you to be the loveliest, the richest, woman on earth. I should give you carriages and diamonds and dresses!"

At each successive offer Nana shook her head proudly. Then seeing that he still continued them, that he even spoke of settling money on her—for he was at loss what to lay at her feet—she apparently lost patience.

"Come, come, have you done bargaining with me? I'm a good sort, and I don't mind giving in to you for a minute or two, as your feelings are making you so ill, but I've had enough of it now, haven't I? So let me get up. You're tiring me."

She extricated herself from his clasp, and once on her feet:

"No, no, no!" she said. "I don't want to!"

With that he gathered himself up painfully and feebly dropped into a chair, in which he leaned back with his face in his hands. Nana began pacing up and down in her turn. For a second or two she looked at the stained wallpaper, the greasy toilet table, the whole dirty little room as it basked in the pale sunlight. Then she paused in front of the count and spoke with quiet directness.

"It's strange how rich men fancy they can have everything for their money. Well, and if I don't want to consent—what then? I don't care a pin for your presents! You might give me Paris, and yet I should say no! Always no! Look here, it's scarcely clean in this room, yet I should think it very nice if I wanted to live in it with you. But one's fit to kick the bucket in your palaces if one isn't in love. Ah, as to money, my poor pet, I can lay my hands on that if I want to, but I tell you, I trample on it; I spit on it!"

And with that she assumed a disgusted expression. Then she became sentimental and added in a melancholy tone:

"I know of something worth more than money. Oh, if only someone were to give me what I long for!"

He slowly lifted his head, and there was a gleam of hope in his eyes.

"Oh, you can't give it me," she continued; "it doesn't depend on you, and that's the reason I'm talking to you about it. Yes, we're having a chat, so I may as well mention to you that I should like to play the part of the respectable woman in that show of theirs."

"What respectable woman?" he muttered in astonishment.

"Why, their Duchess Hélène! If they think I'm going to play Géraldine, a part with nothing in it, a scene and nothing besides—if they think that! Besides, that isn't the reason. The fact is I've had enough of courtesans. Why, there's no end to 'em! They'll be fancying I've got 'em on the brain; to be sure they will! Besides, when all's said and done, it's annoying, for I can quite see they seem to think me uneducated. Well, my boy, they're jolly well in the dark about it, I can tell you! When I want to be a perfect lady, why then I am a swell, and no mistake! Just look at this."

And she withdrew as far as the window and then came swelling back with the mincing gait and circumspect air of a portly hen that fears to dirty her claws. As to Muffat, he followed her movements with eyes still wet with tears. He was stupefied by this sudden transition from anguish to comedy. She walked about for a moment or two in order the more thoroughly to show off her paces, and as she walked she smiled subtlely, closed her eyes demurely and managed her skirts with great dexterity. Then she posted herself in front of him again.

"I guess I've hit it, eh?"

"Oh, thoroughly," he stammered with a broken voice and a troubled expression.

"I tell you I've got hold of the honest woman! I've tried at my own place. Nobody's got my little knack of looking like a duchess who don't care a damn for the men. Did you notice it when I passed in front of you? Why, the thing's in my blood! Besides, I want to play the part of an honest woman. I dream about it day and night—I'm miserable about it. I must have the part, d'you hear?"

And with that she grew serious, speaking in a hard voice and looking deeply moved, for she was really tortured by her stupid, tiresome wish. Muffat, still smarting from her late refusals, sat on without appearing to grasp her meaning. There was a silence during which the very flies abstained from buzzing through the quiet, empty place.

"Now, look here," she resumed bluntly, "you're to get them to give me the part."

He was dumfounded, and with a despairing gesture:

"Oh, it's impossible! You yourself were saying just now that it didn't depend on me."

She interrupted him with a shrug of the shoulders.

"You'll just go down, and you'll tell Bordenave you want the part. Now don't be such a silly! Bordenave wants money—well, you'll lend him some, since you can afford to make ducks and drakes of it."

And as he still struggled to refuse her, she grew angry.

"Very well, I understand; you're afraid of making Rose angry. I didn't mention the woman when you were crying down on the floor—I should have had too much to say about it all. Yes, to be sure, when one has sworn to love a woman forever one doesn't usually take up with the first creature that comes by directly after. Oh, that's where the shoe pinches, I remember! Well, dear boy, there's nothing very savory in the Mignon's leavings! Oughtn't you to have broken it off with that dirty lot before coming and squirming on my knees?"

He protested vaguely and at last was able to get out a phrase.

"Oh, I don't care a jot for Rose; I'll give her up at once."

Nana seemed satisfied on this point. She continued:

"Well then, what's bothering you? Bordenave's master here. You'll tell me there's Fauchery after Bordenave——"

She had sunk her voice, for she was coming to the delicate part of the matter. Muffat sat silent, his eyes fixed on the ground. He had remained voluntarily ignorant of Fauchery's assiduous attentions to the countess, and time had lulled his suspicions and set him hoping that he had been deceiving himself during that fearful night passed in a doorway of the Rue Taitbout. But he still felt a dull, angry repugnance to the man.

"Well, what then? Fauchery isn't the devil!" Nana repeated, feeling her way cautiously and trying to find out how matters stood between husband and lover. "One can get over his soft side. I promise you, he's a good sort at bottom! So it's a bargain, eh? You'll tell him that it's for my sake?"

The idea of taking such a step disgusted the count.

"No, no! Never!" he cried.

She paused, and this sentence was on the verge of utterance:

"Fauchery can refuse you nothing."

But she felt that by way of argument it was rather too much of a good thing. So she only smiled a queer smile which spoke as plainly as words. Muffat had raised his eyes to her and now once more lowered them, looking pale and full of embarrassment.

"Ah, you're not good natured," she muttered at last.

"I cannot," he said with a voice and a look of the utmost anguish. "I'll do whatever you like, but not that, dear love! Oh, I beg you not to insist on that!"

Thereupon she wasted no more time in discussion but took his head between her small hands, pushed it back a little, bent down and glued her mouth to his in a long, long kiss. He shivered violently; he trembled beneath her touch; his eyes were closed, and he was beside himself. She lifted him to his feet.

"Go," said she simply.

He walked off, making toward the door. But as he passed out she took him in her arms again, became meek and coaxing, lifted her face to his and rubbed her cheek against his waistcoat, much as a cat might have done.

"Where's the fine house?" she whispered in laughing embarrassment, like a little girl who returns to the pleasant things she has previously refused.

"In the Avenue de Villiers."

"And there are carriages there?"

"Yes."

"Lace? Diamonds?"

"Yes."

"Oh, how good you are, my old pet! You know it was all jealousy just now! And this time I solemnly promise you it won't be like the first, for now you understand what's due to a woman. You give all, don't you? Well then, I don't want anybody but you! Why, look here, there's some more for you! There and there *and* there!"

When she had pushed him from the room after firing his blood with a rain of kisses on hands and on face, she panted awhile. Good heavens, what an unpleasant smell there was in that slut Mathilde's dressing room! It was warm, if you will, with the tranquil warmth peculiar to rooms in the south when the winter sun shines into them, but really, it smelled far too strong of stale lavender water, not to mention other less cleanly things! She opened the window and, again leaning on the window sill, began watching the glass roof of the passage below in order to kill time.

Muffat went staggering downstairs. His head was swimming. What should he say? How should he broach the matter which, moreover, did not concern him? He heard sounds of quarreling as he reached the stage. The second act was being finished, and Prullière was beside himself with wrath, owing to an attempt on Fauchery's part to cut short one of his speeches.

"Cut it all out then," he was shouting. "I should prefer that! Just fancy, I haven't two hundred lines, and they're still cutting me down. No, by Jove, I've had enough of it; I give the part up."

He took a little crumpled manuscript book out of his pocket and fingered its leaves feverishly, as though he were just about to throw it on Cossard's lap. His pale face was convulsed by outraged vanity; his lips were drawn and thin, his eyes flamed; he was quite unable to conceal the struggle that was going on inside him. To think that he, Prullière, the idol of the public, should play a part of only two hundred lines!

"Why not make me bring in letters on a tray?" he continued bitterly.

"Come, come, Prullière, behave decently," said Bordenave, who was anxious to treat him tenderly because of his influence over the boxes. "Don't begin making a fuss. We'll find some points. Eh, Fauchery, you'll add some points? In the third act it would even be possible to lengthen a scene out."

"Well then, I want the last speech of all," the comedian declared. "I certainly deserve to have it."

Fauchery's silence seemed to give consent, and Prullière, still greatly agitated and discontented despite everything, put his part back into his pocket. Bosc and Fontan had appeared profoundly indifferent during the course of this explanation. Let each man fight for his own hand, they reflected; the present dispute had nothing to do with them; they had no interest therein! All the actors clustered round Fauchery and began questioning him and fishing for praise, while Mignon listened to the last of Prullière's complaints without, however, losing sight of Count Muffat, whose return he had been on the watch for.

Entering in the half-light, the count had paused at the back of the stage, for he hesitated to interrupt the quarrel. But Bordenave caught sight of him and ran forward.

"Aren't they a pretty lot?" he muttered. "You can have no idea what I've got to undergo with that lot, Monsieur le Comte. Each man's vainer than his neighbor, and they're wretched players all the same, a scabby lot, always mixed up in some dirty business or other! Oh, they'd be delighted if I were to come to smash. But I beg pardon—I'm getting beside myself."

He ceased speaking, and silence reigned while Muffat sought how to broach his announcement gently. But he failed and, in order to get out of his difficulty the more quickly, ended by an abrupt announcement:

"Nana wants the duchess's part."

Bordenave gave a start and shouted:

"Come now, it's sheer madness!"

Then looking at the count and finding him so pale and so shaken, he was calm at once.

"Devil take it!" he said simply.

And with that there ensued a fresh silence. At bottom he didn't care a pin about it. That great thing Nana playing the duchess might possibly prove amusing! Besides, now that this had happened he had Muffat well in his grasp. Accordingly he was not long in coming to a decision, and so he turned round and called out:

"Fauchery!"

The count had been on the point of stopping him. But Fauchery did not hear him, for he had been pinned against the curtain by Fontan and was being compelled to listen patiently to the comedian's reading of the part of Tardiveau. Fontan imagined Tardiveau to be a native of Marseilles with a dialect, and he imitated the dialect. He was repeating whole speeches. Was that right? Was this the thing? Apparently he was only submitting ideas to Fauchery of which he was himself uncertain, but as the author seemed cold and raised various objections, he grew angry at once.

Oh, very well, the moment the spirit of the part escaped him it would be better for all concerned that he shouldn't act it at all!

"Fauchery!" shouted Bordenave once more.

Thereupon the young man ran off, delighted to escape from the actor, who was wounded not a little by his prompt retreat.

"Don't let's stay here," continued Bordenave. "Come this way, gentlemen."

In order to escape from curious listeners he led them into the property room behind the scenes, while Mignon watched their disappearance in some surprise. They went down a few steps and entered a square room, whose two windows opened upon the courtyard. A faint light stole through the dirty panes and hung wanly under the low ceiling. In pigeonholes and shelves, which filled the whole place up, lay a collection of the most varied kind of bric-a-brac. Indeed, it suggested an old-clothes shop in the Rue de Lappe in process of selling off, so indescribable was the hotchpotch of plates, gilt pasteboard cups, old red umbrellas, Italian jars, clocks in all styles, platters and inkpots, firearms and squirts, which lay chipped and broken and in unrecognizable heaps under a layer of dust an inch deep. An unendurable odor of old iron, rags and damp cardboard emanated from the various piles, where the debris of forgotten dramas had been collecting for half a century.

"Come in," Bordenave repeated. "We shall be alone, at any rate."

The count was extremely embarrassed, and he contrived to let the manager risk his proposal for him. Fauchery was astonished.

"Eh? What?" he asked.

"Just this," said Bordenave finally. "An idea has occurred to us. Now whatever you do, don't jump! It's most serious. What do you think of Nana for the duchess's part?"

The author was bewildered; then he burst out with:

"Ah no, no! You're joking, aren't you? People would laugh far too much."

"Well, and it's a point gained already if they do laugh! Just reflect, my dear boy. The idea pleases Monsieur le Comte very much."

In order to keep himself in countenance Muffat had just picked out of the dust on a neighboring shelf an object which he did not seem to recognize. It was an eggcup, and its stem had been mended with plaster. He kept hold of it unconsciously and came forward, muttering:

"Yes, yes, it would be capital."

Fauchery turned toward him with a brisk, impatient gesture. The count had nothing to do with his piece, and he said decisively:

"Never! Let Nana play the courtesan as much as she likes, but a lady—— No, by Jove!"

"You are mistaken, I assure you," rejoined the count, growing bolder. "This very minute she has been playing the part of a pure woman for my benefit."

"Where?" queried Fauchery with growing surprise.

"Upstairs in a dressing room. Yes, she has, indeed, and with such distinction! She's got a way of glancing at you as she goes by you—something like this, you know!"

And eggcup in hand, he endeavored to imitate Nana, quite forgetting his dignity in his frantic desire to convince the others. Fauchery gazed at him in a state of stupefaction. He understood it all now, and his anger had ceased. The count felt that he was looking at him mockingly and pityingly, and he paused with a slight blush on his face.

"Egad, it's quite possible!" muttered the author complaisantly. "Perhaps she would do very well, only the part's been assigned. We can't take it away from Rose."

"Oh, if that's all the trouble," said Bordenave, "I'll undertake to arrange matters."

But presently, seeing them both against him and guessing that Bordenave had some secret interest at stake, the young man thought to avoid aquiescence by redoubling the violence of his refusal. The consultation was on the verge of being broken up.

"Oh, dear! No, no! Even if the part were unassigned I should never give it her! There, is that plain? Do let me alone; I have no wish to ruin my play!"

He lapsed into silent embarrassment. Bordenave, deeming himself *de trop*, went away, but the count remained with bowed head. He raised it with an effort and said in a breaking voice:

"Supposing, my dear fellow, I were to ask this of you as a favor?"

"I cannot, I cannot," Fauchery kept repeating as he writhed to get free. Muffat's voice became harder.

"I pray and beseech you for it! I want it!"

And with that he fixed his eyes on him. The young man read menaces in that darkling gaze and suddenly gave way with a splutter of confused phrases:

"Do what you like—I don't care a pin about it. Yes, yes, you're abusing your power, but you'll see, you'll see!"

At this the embarrassment of both increased. Fauchery was leaning up against a set of shelves and was tapping nervously on the ground with his foot. Muffat seemed busy examining the eggcup, which he was still turning round and about.

"It's an eggcup," Bordenave obligingly came and remarked.

"Yes, to be sure! It's an eggcup," the count repeated.

"Excuse me, you're covered with dust," continued the manager, putting the thing back on a shelf. "If one had to dust every day there'd be no end to it, you understand. But it's hardly clean here—a filthy mess, eh? Yet you may believe me or not when I tell you there's money in it. Now look, just look at all that!"

He walked Muffat round in front of the pigeonholes and shelves and in the greenish light which filtered through the courtyard, told him the names of different properties, for he was anxious to interest him in his marine-stores inventory, as he jocosely termed it.

Presently, when they had returned into Fauchery's neighborhood, he said carelessly enough:

"Listen, since we're all of one mind, we'll finish the matter at once. Here's Mignon, just when he's wanted."

For some little time past Mignon had been prowling in the adjoining passage, and the very moment Bordenave began talking of a modification of their agreement he burst into wrathful protest. It was infamous—they wanted to spoil his wife's career—he'd go to law about it! Bordenave, meanwhile, was extremely calm and full of reasons. He did not think the part worthy of Rose, and he preferred to reserve her for an operetta, which was to be put on after the *Petite Duchesse*. But when her husband still continued shouting he suddenly offered to cancel their arrangement in view of the offers which the

Folies-Dramatiques had been making the singer. At this Mignon was momentarily put out, so without denying the truth of these offers he loudly professed a vast disdain for money. His wife, he said, had been engaged to play the Duchess Hélène, and she would play the part even if he, Mignon, were to be ruined over it. His dignity, his honor, were at stake! Starting from this basis, the discussion grew interminable. The manager, however, always returned to the following argument: since the Folies had offered Rose three hundred francs a night during a hundred performances, and since she only made a hundred and fifty with him, she would be the gainer by fifteen thousand francs the moment he let her depart. The husband, on his part, did not desert the artist's position. What would people say if they saw his wife deprived of her part? Why, that she was not equal to it; that it had been deemed necessary to find a substitute for her! And this would do great harm to Rose's reputation as an artist; nay, it would diminish it. Oh no, no! Glory before gain! Then without a word of warning he pointed out a possible arrangement: Rose, according to the terms of her agreement, was pledged to pay a forfeit of ten thousand francs in case she gave up the part. Very well then, let them give her ten thousand francs, and she would go to the Folies-Dramatiques. Bordenave was utterly dumfounded while Mignon, who had never once taken his eyes off the count, tranquilly awaited results.

"Then everything can be settled," murmured Muffat in tones of relief; "we can come to an understanding."

"The deuce, no! That would be too stupid!" cried Bordenave, mastered by his commercial instincts. "Ten thousand francs to let Rose go! Why, people would make game of me!"

But the count, with a multiplicity of nods, bade him accept. He hesitated, and at last with much grumbling and infinite regret over the ten thousand francs which, by the by, were not destined to come out of his own pocket he bluntly continued:

"After all, I consent. At any rate, I shall have you off my hands."

For a quarter of an hour past Fontan had been listening in the courtyard. Such had been his curiosity that he had come down and posted himself there, but the moment he understood the state of the case he went upstairs again and enjoyed the treat of telling Rose. Dear me! They were just haggling in her behalf! He dinned his words into her ears; she ran off to the property room. They were silent as she entered. She looked at the four men. Muffat hung his head; Fauchery answered her questioning glance with a despairing shrug of the shoulders; as to Mignon, he was busy discussing the terms of the agreement with Bordenave.

"What's up?" she demanded curtly.

"Nothing," said her husband. "Bordenave here is giving ten thousand francs in order to get you to give up your part."

She grew tremulous with anger and very pale, and she clenched her little fists. For some moments she stared at him, her whole nature in revolt. Ordinarily in matters of business she was wont to trust everything obediently to her husband, leaving him to sign agreements with managers and lovers. Now she could but cry:

"Oh, come, you're too base for anything!"

The words fell like a lash. Then she sped away, and Mignon, in utter astonishment, ran after her. What next? Was she going mad? He began explaining to her in low tones that ten thousand francs from one party and fifteen thousand from the other came to twenty-five thousand. A splendid deal! Muffat was getting rid of her in every sense of the word; it was a pretty trick to have plucked him of this last feather! But Rose in her anger vouchsafed no answer. Whereupon Mignon in disdain left her to her feminine spite and, turning to Bordenave, who was once more on the stage with Fauchery and Muffat, said:

"We'll sign tomorrow morning. Have the money in readiness."

At this moment Nana, to whom Labordette had brought the news, came down to the stage in triumph. She was quite the honest woman now and wore a most distinguished expression in order to overwhelm her friends and prove to the idiots that when she chose she could give them all points in the matter of smartness. But she nearly got into trouble, for at the sight of her Rose darted forward, choking with rage and stuttering:

"Yes, you, I'll pay you out! Things can't go on like this; d'you understand?"

Nana forgot herself in face of this brisk attack and was going to put her arms akimbo and give her what for. But she controlled herself and, looking like a marquise who is afraid of treading on an orange peel, fluted in still more silvery tones.

"Eh, what?" said she. "You're mad, my dear!"

And with that she continued in her graceful affectation while Rose took her departure, followed by Mignon, who now refused to recognize her. Clarisse was enraptured, having just obtained the part of Géraldine from Bordenave. Fauchery, on the other hand, was gloomy; he shifted from one foot to the other; he could not decide whether to leave the theater or no. His piece was bedeviled, and he was seeking how best to save it. But Nana came up, took him by both hands and, drawing him toward her, asked whether he thought her so very atrocious after all. She wasn't going to eat his play—not she! Then she made him laugh and gave him to understand that he would be foolish to be angry with her, in view of his relationship to the Muffats. If, she said, her memory failed her she would take her lines from the prompter. The house, too, would be packed in such a way as to ensure applause. Besides, he was mistaken about her, and he would soon see how she would rattle through her part. By and by it was arranged that the author should make a few changes in the role of the duchess so as to extend that of Prullière. The last-named personage was enraptured. Indeed, amid all the joy which Nana now quite naturally diffused, Fontan alone remained unmoved. In the middle of the yellow lamplight, against which the sharp outline of his goatlike profile shone out with great distinctness, he stood showing off his figure and affecting the pose of one who has been cruelly abandoned. Nana went quietly up and shook hands with him.

"How are you getting on?"

"Oh, pretty fairly. And how are you?"

"Very well, thank you."

That was all. They seemed to have only parted at the doors of the theater the day before. Meanwhile the players were waiting about, but Bordenave said that the third act would not be rehearsed. And so it chanced that old Bosc went grumbling away at the proper time, whereas usually the company were needlessly detained and lost whole afternoons in consequence. Everyone went off. Down on the pavement they were blinded by the broad daylight and stood blinking their eyes in a dazed sort of way, as became people who had passed three hours squabbling with tight-strung nerves in the depths of a cellar. The count, with racked limbs and vacant brain, got into a conveyance with Nana, while Labordette took Fauchery off and comforted him.

A month later the first night of the *Petite Duchesse* proved supremely disastrous to Nana. She was atrociously bad and displayed such pretentions toward high comedy that the public grew mirthful. They did not hiss—they were too amused. From a stage box Rose Mignon kept greeting her rival's successive entrances with a shrill laugh, which set the whole house off. It was the beginning of her revenge. Accordingly, when at night Nana, greatly chagrined, found herself alone with Muffat, she said furiously:

"What a conspiracy, eh? It's all owing to jealousy. Oh, if they only knew how I despise 'em! What do I want them for nowadays? Look here! I'll bet a hundred louis that I'll bring all those who made fun today and make 'em lick the ground at my feet! Yes, I'll fine-lady your Paris for you, I will!"

CHAPTER X

THEREUPON Nana became a smart woman, mistress of all that is foolish and filthy in man, marquise in the ranks of her calling. It was a sudden but decisive start, a plunge into the garish day of gallant notoriety and mad expenditure and that daredevil wastefulness peculiar to beauty. She at once became queen among the most expensive of her kind. Her photographs were displayed in shopwindows, and she was mentioned in the papers. When she drove in her carriage along the boulevards the people would turn and tell one another who that was with all the unction of a nation saluting its sovereign, while the object of their adoration lolled easily back in her diaphanous dresses and smiled gaily under the rain of little golden curls which ran riot above the blue of her made-up eyes and the red of her painted lips. And the wonder of wonders was that the great creature, who was so awkward on the stage, so very absurd the moment she sought to act the chaste woman, was able without effort to assume the role of an enchantress in the outer world. Her movements were lithe as a serpent's, and the studied and yet seemingly involuntary carelessness with which she dressed was really exquisite in its elegance. There was a nervous distinction in all she did which suggested a wellborn Persian cat; she was an aristocrat in vice and proudly and rebelliously trampled upon a prostrate Paris like a sovereign whom none dare disobey. She set the fashion, and great ladies imitated her.

Nana's fine house was situated at the corner of the Rue Cardinet, in the Avenue de Villiers. The avenue was part of the luxurious quarter at that time springing up in the vague district which had once been the Plaine Monceau. The house had been built by a young painter, who was intoxicated by a first success, and had been perforce resold almost as soon as it was habitable. It was in the palatial Renaissance manner and had fantastic interior arrangements which consisted of modern conveniences framed in a setting of somewhat artificial originality. Count Muffat had bought the house ready furnished and full of hosts of beautiful objects—lovely Eastern hangings, old credences, huge chairs of the Louis XIII epoch. And thus Nana had come into artistic surroundings of the choicest kind and of the most extravagantly various dates. But since the studio, which occupied the central portion of the house, could not be of any use to her, she had upset existing arrangements, establishing a small drawing room on the first floor, next to her bedroom and dressing room, and leaving a conservatory, a large drawing room and a dining room to look after themselves underneath. She astonished the architect with her ideas, for, as became a Parisian workgirl who understands the elegancies of life by instinct, she had suddenly developed a very pretty taste for every species of luxurious refinement. Indeed, she did not spoil her house overmuch; nay, she even added to the richness of the furniture, save here and there, where certain traces of tender foolishness and vulgar magnificence betrayed the ex-flower seller who had been wont to dream in front of shopwindows in the arcades.

A carpet was spread on the steps beneath the great awning over the front door in the court, and the moment you entered the hall you were greeted by a perfume as of violets and a soft, warm atmosphere which thick hangings helped to produce. A window, whose yellow- and rose-colored panes suggested the warm pallor of human flesh, gave light to the wide staircase, at the foot of which a Negro in carved wood held out a silver tray full of visiting cards and four white marble women, with bosoms displayed, raised lamps in their uplifted hands. Bronzes and Chinese vases full of flowers, divans covered with old Persian rugs, armchairs upholstered in old tapestry, furnished the entrance hall, adorned the stairheads and gave the first-floor landing the appearance of an anteroom. Here men's overcoats and hats were always in evidence, and there were thick hangings which deadened every sound. It seemed a place apart: on entering it you might have fancied yourself in a chapel, whose very air was thrilling with devotion, whose very silence and seclusion were fraught with mystery.

Nana only opened the large and somewhat too-sumptuous Louis XVI drawing room on those gala nights when she received society from the Tuileries or strangers of distinction. Ordinarily she only came downstairs at mealtimes, and she would feel rather lost on such days as she lunched by herself in the lofty dining room with its Gobelin tapestry and its monumental sideboard, adorned with old porcelain and marvelous pieces of ancient plate. She used to go upstairs again as quickly as possible, for her home was on the first floor, in the three rooms, the bed, dressing and small drawing room above described. Twice already she had done the bedchamber up anew: on the first occasion in mauve satin, on the second in blue silk under lace. But she had not been satisfied with this; it had struck her as "nohowish," and she was still unsuccessfully seeking for new colors and designs. On the elaborately upholstered bed, which was as low as a sofa, there were twenty thousand francs' worth of *point de Venise* lace. The furniture was lacquered blue and white under designs in silver filigree, and everywhere lay such numbers of white bearskins that they hid the carpet. This was a luxurious caprice on Nana's part, she having never been able to break herself of the habit of sitting on the floor to take her stockings off. Next door to the bedroom the little saloon was full of an amusing medley of exquisitely artistic objects. Against the hangings of pale rose-colored silk—a faded Turkish rose color, embroidered with gold thread—a whole world of them stood sharply outlined. They were from every land and in every possible style. There were Italian cabinets, Spanish and Portuguese coffers, models of Chinese pagodas, a Japanese screen of precious workmanship, besides china, bronzes, embroidered silks, hangings of the finest needlework. Armchairs wide as beds and sofas deep as alcoves suggested voluptuous idleness and the somnolent life of the seraglio. The prevailing tone of the room was old gold blended with green and red, and nothing it contained too forcibly indicated the presence of the courtesan save the luxuriousness of the seats. Only two "biscuit" statuettes, a woman in her shift, hunting for fleas, and another with nothing at all on, walking on her hands and waving her feet in the air, sufficed to sully the room with a note of stupid originality.

Through a door, which was nearly always ajar, the dressing room was visible. It was all in marble and glass with a white bath, silver jugs and basins and crystal and ivory appointments. A drawn curtain filled the place with a clear twilight which seemed to slumber in the warm scent of violets, that suggestive perfume peculiar to Nana wherewith the whole house, from the roof to the very courtyard, was penetrated.

The furnishing of the house was a most important undertaking. Nana certainly had Zoé with her, that girl so devoted to her fortunes. For months she had been tranquilly awaiting this abrupt, new departure, as became a woman who was certain of her powers of prescience, and now she was triumphant; she was mistress of the house and was putting by a round sum while serving Madame as honestly as possible. But a solitary lady's maid was no longer sufficient. A butler, a coachman, a porter and a cook were wanted. Besides, it was necessary to fill the stables. It was then that Labordette made himself most useful. He undertook to perform all sorts of errands which bored the count; he made a comfortable job of the purchase of horses; he visited the coachbuilders; he guided the young woman in her choice of things. She was to be met with at the shops, leaning on his arm. Labordette even got in the servants—Charles, a great, tall coachman, who had been in service with the Duc de Corbreuse; Julien, a little, smiling, much-becurled butler, and a married couple, of whom the wife Victorine became cook while the husband François was taken on as porter and footman. The last mentioned in powder and breeches wore Nana's livery, which was a sky-blue one adorned with silver lace, and he received visitors in the hall. The whole thing was princely in the correctness of its style.

At the end of two months the house was set going. The cost had been more than three hundred thousand francs. There were eight horses in the stables, and five carriages in the coach houses, and of these five one was a landau with silver embellishments, which for the moment occupied the attention of all Paris. And amid this great wealth Nana began settling down and making her nest. After the third representation of the *Petite Duchesse* she had quitted the theater, leaving Bordenave to struggle on against a bankruptcy which, despite the count's money, was imminent. Nevertheless, she was still bitter about her failure. It added to that other bitterness, the lesson Fontan had given her, a shameful lesson for which she held all men responsible. Accordingly she now declared herself very firm and quite proof against sudden infatuations, but thoughts of vengeance took no hold of her volatile brain. What did maintain a hold on it in the hours when she was not indignant was an ever-wakeful lust of expenditure, added to a natural contempt for the man who paid and to a perpetual passion for consumption and waste, which took pride in the ruin of her lovers.

At starting Nana put the count on a proper footing and clearly mapped out the conditions of their relationship. The count gave twelve thousand francs monthly, presents excepted, and demanded nothing in return save absolute fidelity. She swore fidelity but insisted also on being treated with the utmost consideration, on enjoying complete liberty as mistress of the house and on having her every wish respected. For instance, she was to receive her friends every day, and he was to come only at stated times. In a word, he was to repose a blind confidence in her in everything. And when he was seized with jealous anxiety and hesitated to grant what she wanted, she stood on her dignity and threatened to give him back all he had given or even swore by little Louiset to perform what she promised. This was to suffice him. There was no love where mutual esteem was wanting. At the end of the first month Muffat respected her.

But she desired and obtained still more. Soon she began to influence him, as became a good-natured courtesan. When he came to her in a moody condition she cheered him up, confessed him and then gave him good advice. Little by little she interested herself in the annoyances of his home life, in his wife, in his daughter, in his love affairs and financial difficulties; she was very sensible, very fair and right-minded. On one occasion only did she let anger get the better of her, and that was when he confided to her that doubtless Daguenet was going to ask for his daughter Estelle in marriage. When the count began making himself notorious Daguenet had thought it a wise move to break off with Nana. He had treated her like a base hussy and had sworn to snatch his future father-in-law out of the creature's clutches. In return Nana abused her old Mimi in a charming fashion. He was a renegade who had devoured his fortune in the company of vile women; he had no moral sense. True, he did not let them pay him money, but he profited by that of others and only repaid them at rare intervals with a bouquet or a dinner. And when the count seemed inclined to find excuses for these failings she bluntly informed him that Daguenet had enjoyed her favors, and she added disgusting particulars. Muffat had grown ashen-pale. There was no question of the young man now. This would teach him to be lacking in gratitude!

Meanwhile the house had not been entirely furnished, when one evening after she had lavished the most energetic promises of fidelity on Muffat Nana kept the Count Xavier de Vandeuvres for the night. For the last fortnight he had been paying her assiduous court, visiting her and sending presents of flowers, and now she gave way not so much out of sudden infatuation as to prove that she was a free woman. The idea of gain followed later when, the day after, Vandeuvres helped her to pay a bill which she did not wish to mention to the other man. From Vandeuvres she would certainly derive from eight to ten thousand francs a month, and this would prove very useful as pocket money. In those days he was finishing the last of his fortune in an access of burning, feverish folly. His horses and Lucy had devoured three of his farms, and at one gulp Nana was going to swallow his last château, near Amiens. He seemed in a hurry to sweep everything away, down to the ruins of the old tower built by a Vandeuvres under Philip Augustus. He was mad for ruin and thought it a great thing to leave the last golden bezants of his coat of arms in the grasp of this courtesan, whom the world of Paris desired. He, too, accepted Nana's conditions, leaving her entire freedom of action and claiming her caresses only on certain days. He was not even naïvely impassioned enough to require her to make vows. Muffat suspected nothing. As to Vandeuvres, he knew things would take place for a certainty, but he never made the least allusion to them and pretended total ignorance, while his lips wore the subtle smile of the skeptical man of pleasure who does not seek the impossible, provided he can have his day and that Paris is aware of it.

From that time forth Nana's house was really properly appointed. The staff of servants was complete in the stable, in the kitchen and in my lady's chamber. Zoé organized everything and passed successfully through the most unforeseen difficulties. The household moved as easily as the scenery in a theater and was regulated like a grand administrative concern. Indeed, it worked with such precision that during the early months there were no jars and no derangements. Madame, however, pained Zoé extremely with her imprudent acts, her sudden fits of unwisdom, her mad bravado. Still the lady's maid grew gradually lenient, for she had noticed that she made increased profits in seasons of wanton waste when Madame had committed a folly which must be made up for. It was then that the presents began raining on her, and she fished up many a louis out of the troubled waters.

One morning when Muffat had not yet left the bedroom Zoé ushered a gentleman into the dressing room, where Nana was changing her underwear. He was trembling violently.

"Good gracious! It's Zizi!" said the young woman in great astonishment. It was, indeed, Georges. But when he saw her in her shift, with her golden hair over her bare shoulders, he threw his arms round her neck and round her waist and kissed her in all directions. She began struggling to get free, for she was frightened, and in smothered tones she stammered:

"Do leave off! He's there! Oh, it's silly of you! And you, Zoé, are you out of your senses? Take him away and keep him downstairs; I'll try and come down."

Zoé had to push him in front of her. When Nana was able to rejoin them in the drawing room downstairs she scolded them both, and Zoé pursed up her lips and took her departure with a vexed expression, remarking that she had only been anxious to give Madame a pleasure. Georges was so glad to see Nana again and gazed at her with such delight that his fine eyes began filling with tears. The miserable days were over now; his mother believed him to have grown reasonable and had allowed him to leave Les Fondettes. Accordingly, the moment he had reached the terminus, he had got a conveyance in order the more quickly to come and kiss his sweet darling. He spoke of living at her side in future, as he used to do down in the country when he waited for her, barefooted, in the bedroom at La Mignotte. And as he told her about himself, he let his fingers creep forward, for he longed to touch her after that cruel year of separation. Then he got possession of her hands, felt about the wide sleeves of her dressing jacket, traveled up as far as her shoulders.

"You still love your baby?" he asked in his child voice.

"Oh, I certainly love him!" answered Nana, briskly getting out of his clutches. "But you come popping in without warning. You know, my little man, I'm not my own mistress; you must be good!"

Georges, when he got out of his cab, had been so dizzy with the feeling that his long desire was at last about to be satisfied that he had not even noticed what sort of house he was entering. But now he became conscious of a change in the things around him. He examined the sumptuous dining room with its lofty decorated ceiling, its Gobelin hangings, its buffet blazing with plate.

"Yes, yes!" he remarked sadly.

And with that she made him understand that he was never to come in the mornings but between four and six in the afternoon, if he cared to. That was her reception time. Then as he looked at her with suppliant, questioning eyes and craved no boon at all, she, in her turn, kissed him on the forehead in the most amiable way.

"Be very good," she whispered. "I'll do all I can."

But the truth was that this remark now meant nothing. She thought Georges very nice and would have liked him as a companion, but as nothing else. Nevertheless, when he arrived daily at four o'clock he seemed so wretched that she was often fain to be as compliant as of old and would hide him in cupboards and constantly allow him to pick up the crumbs from Beauty's table. He hardly ever left the house now and became as much one of its inmates as the little dog Bijou. Together they nestled among Mistress's skirts and enjoyed a little of her at a time, even when she was with another man, while doles of sugar and stray caresses not seldom fell to their share in her hours of loneliness and boredom.

Doubtless Mme Hugon found out that the lad had again returned to that wicked woman's arms, for she hurried up to Paris and came and sought aid from her other son, the Lieutenant Philippe, who was then in garrison at Vincennes. Georges, who was hiding from his elder brother, was seized with despairing apprehension, for he feared the latter might adopt violent tactics, and as his tenderness for Nana was so nervously expansive that he could not keep anything from her, he soon began talking of nothing but his big brother, a great, strong fellow, who was capable of all kinds of things.

"You know," he explained, "Mamma won't come to you while she can send my brother. Oh, she'll certainly send Philippe to fetch me."

The first time he said this Nana was deeply wounded. She said frigidly:

"Gracious me, I should like to see him come! For all that he's a lieutenant in the army, François will chuck him out in double-quick time!"

Soon, as the lad kept returning to the subject of his brother, she ended by taking a certain interest in Philippe, and in a week's time she knew him from head to foot—knew him as very tall and very strong and merry and somewhat rough. She learned intimate details, too, and found out that he had hair on his arms and a birthmark on his shoulder. So thoroughly did she learn her lesson that one day, when she was full of the image of the man who was to be turned out of doors by her orders, she cried out:

"I say, Zizi, your brother's not coming. He's a base deserter!"

The next day, when Georges and Nana were alone together, François came upstairs to ask whether Madame would receive Lieutenant Philippe Hugon. Georges grew extremely white and murmured:

"I suspected it; Mamma was talking about it this morning."

And he besought the young woman to send down word that she could not see visitors. But she was already on her feet and seemed all aflame as she said:

"Why should I not see him? He would think me afraid. Dear me, we'll have a good laugh! Just leave the gentleman in the drawing room for a quarter of an hour, François; afterward bring him up to me."

She did not sit down again but began pacing feverishly to and fro between the fireplace and a Venetian mirror hanging above an Italian chest. And each time she reached the latter she glanced at the glass and tried the effect of a smile, while Georges sat nervously on a sofa, trembling at the thought of the coming scene. As she walked up and down she kept jerking out such little phrases as:

"It will calm the fellow down if he has to wait a quarter of an hour. Besides, if he thinks he's calling on a tottie the drawing room will stun him! Yes, yes, have a good look at everything, my fine fellow! It isn't imitation, and it'll teach you to respect the lady who owns it. Respect's what men need to feel! The quarter of an hour's gone by, eh? No? Only ten minutes? Oh, we've got plenty of time."

She did not stay where she was, however. At the end of the quarter of an hour she sent Georges away after making him solemnly promise not to listen at the door, as such conduct would scarcely look proper in case the servants saw him. As he went into her bedroom Zizi ventured in a choking sort of way to remark:

"It's my brother, you know——"

"Don't you fear," she said with much dignity; "if he's polite I'll be polite."

François ushered in Philippe Hugon, who wore morning dress. Georges began crossing on tiptoe on the other side of the room, for he was anxious to obey the young woman. But the sound of voices retained him, and he hesitated in such anguish of mind that his knees gave way under him. He began imagining that a dread catastrophe would befall, that blows would be struck, that something abominable would happen, which would make Nana everlastingly odious to him. And so he could not withstand the temptation to come back and put his ear against the door. He heard very ill, for the thick portieres deadened every sound, but he managed to catch certain words spoken by Philippe, stern phrases in which such terms as "mere child," "family," "honor," were distinctly audible. He was so anxious about his darling's possible answers that his heart beat violently and filled his head with a confused, buzzing noise. She was sure to give vent to a "Dirty blackguard!" or to a "Leave me bloody well alone! I'm in my own house!" But nothing happened—not a breath came from her direction. Nana seemed dead in there! Soon even his brother's voice grew gentler, and he could not make it out at all, when a strange murmuring sound finally stupefied him. Nana was sobbing! For a moment or two he was the prey of contending feelings and knew not whether to run away or to fall upon Philippe. But just then Zoé came into the room, and he withdrew from the door, ashamed at being thus surprised.

She began quietly to put some linen away in a cupboard while he stood mute and motionless, pressing his forehead against a windowpane. He was tortured by uncertainty. After a short silence the woman asked:

"It's your brother that's with Madame?"

"Yes," replied the lad in a choking voice.

There was a fresh silence.

"And it makes you anxious, doesn't it, Monsieur Georges?"

"Yes," he rejoined in the same painful, suffering tone.

Zoé was in no hurry. She folded up some lace and said slowly:

"You're wrong; Madame will manage it all."

And then the conversation ended; they said not another word. Still she did not leave the room. A long quarter of an hour passed, and she turned round again without seeming to notice the look of exasperation overspreading the lad's face, which was already white with the effects of uncertainty and constraint. He was casting sidelong glances in the direction of the drawing room.

Maybe Nana was still crying. The other must have grown savage and have dealt her blows. Thus when Zoé finally took her departure he ran to the door and once more pressed his ear against it. He was thunderstruck; his head swam, for he heard a brisk outburst of gaiety, tender, whispering voices and the smothered giggles of a woman who is being tickled. Besides, almost directly afterward, Nana conducted Philippe to the head of the stairs, and there was an exchange of cordial and familiar phrases.

When Georges again ventured into the drawing room the young woman was standing before the mirror, looking at herself.

"Well?" he asked in utter bewilderment.

"Well, what?" she said without turning round. Then negligently:

"What did you mean? He's very nice, is your brother!"

"So it's all right, is it?"

"Oh, certainly it's all right! Goodness me, what's come over you? One would have thought we were going to fight!"

Georges still failed to understand.

"I thought I heard—that is, you didn't cry?" he stammered out.

"Me cry!" she exclaimed, looking fixedly at him. "Why, you're dreaming! What makes you think I cried?"

Thereupon the lad was treated to a distressing scene for having disobeyed and played Paul Pry behind the door. She sulked, and he returned with coaxing submissiveness to the old subject, for he wished to know all about it.

"And my brother then?"

"Your brother saw where he was at once. You know, I might have been a tottie, in which case his interference would have been accounted for by your age and the family honor! Oh yes, I understand those kinds of feelings! But a single glance was enough for him, and he behaved like a well-bred man at once. So don't be anxious any longer. It's all over—he's gone to quiet your mamma!"

And she went on laughingly:

"For that matter, you'll see your brother here. I've invited him, and he's going to return."

"Oh, he's going to return," said the lad, growing white. He added nothing, and they ceased talking of Philippe. She began dressing to go out, and he watched her with his great, sad eyes. Doubtless he was very glad that matters had got settled, for he would have preferred death to a rupture of their connection, but deep down in his heart there was a silent anguish, a profound sense of pain, which he had no experience of and dared not talk about. How Philippe quieted their mother's fears he never knew, but three days later she returned to Les Fondettes, apparently satisfied. On the evening of her return, at Nana's house, he trembled when François announced the lieutenant, but the latter jested gaily and treated him like a young rascal, whose escapade he had favored as something not likely to have any consequences. The lad's heart was sore within him; he scarcely dared move and blushed girlishly at the least word that was spoken to him. He had not lived much in Philippe's society; he was ten years his junior, and he feared him as he would a father, from whom stories about women are concealed. Accordingly he experienced an uneasy sense of shame when he saw him so free in Nana's company and heard him laugh uproariously, as became a man who was plunging into a life of pleasure with the gusto born of magnificent health. Nevertheless, when his brother shortly began to present himself every day, Georges ended by getting some-what used to it all. Nana was radiant.

This, her latest installation, had been involving all the riotous waste at-tendant on the life of gallantry, and now her housewarming was being de-fiantly celebrated in a grand mansion positively overflowing with males and with furniture.

One afternoon when the Hugons were there Count Muffat arrived out of hours. But when Zoé told him that Madame was with friends he refused to come in and took his departure discreetly, as became a gallant gentleman. When he made his appearance again in the evening Nana received him with the frigid indignation of a grossly affronted woman.

"Sir," she said, "I have given you no cause why you should insult me. You must understand this: when I am at home to visitors, I beg you to make your appearance just like other people."

The count simply gaped in astonishment. "But, my dear——" he endeavored to explain.

"Perhaps it was because I had visitors! Yes, there were men here, but what d'you suppose I was doing with those men? You only advertise a woman's affairs when you act the discreet lover, and I don't want to be advertised; I don't!"

He obtained his pardon with difficulty, but at bottom he was enchanted. It was with scenes such as these that she kept him in unquestioning and docile submission. She had long since succeeded in imposing Georges on him as a young vagabond who, she declared, amused her. She made him dine with Philippe, and the count behaved with great amiability. When they rose from table he took the young man on one side and asked news of his mother. From that time forth the young Hugons, Vandeuvres and Muffat were openly about the house and shook hands as guests and intimates might have done. It was a more convenient arrangement than the previous one. Muffat alone still abstained discreetly from too-frequent visits, thus adhering to the ceremonious policy of an ordinary strange caller. At night when Nana was sitting on her bearskins drawing off her stockings, he would talk amicably about the other three gentlemen and lay especial stress on Philippe, who was loyalty itself.

"It's very true; they're nice," Nana would say as she lingered on the floor to change her shift. "Only, you know, they see what I am. One word about it and I should chuck 'em all out of doors for you!"

Nevertheless, despite her luxurious life and her group of courtiers, Nana was nearly bored to death. She had men for every minute of the night, and money overflowed even among the brushes and combs in the drawers of her dressing table. But all this had ceased to satisfy her; she felt that there was a void somewhere or other, an empty place provocative of yawns. Her life dragged on, devoid of occupation, and successive days only brought back the same monotonous hours. Tomorrow had ceased to be; she lived like a bird: sure of her food and ready to perch and roost on any branch which she came to. This certainty of food and drink left her lolling effortless for whole days, lulled her to sleep in conventual idleness and submission as though she were

he prisoner of her trade. Never going out except to drive, she was losing her
valking powers. She reverted to low childish tastes, would kiss Bijou from
norning to night and kill time with stupid pleasures while waiting for the
nan whose caresses she tolerated with an appearance of complaisant lassitude.
\mid this species of self-abandonment she now took no thought about any-
hing save her personal beauty; her sole care was to look after herself, to wash
nd to perfume her limbs, as became one who was proud of being able to un-
lress at any moment and in face of anybody without having to blush for her
mperfections.

At ten in the morning Nana would get up. Bijou, the Scotch griffon dog,
used to lick her face and wake her, and then would ensue a game of play last-
ng some five minutes, during which the dog would race about over her arms
nd legs and cause Count Muffat much distress. Bijou was the first little male
te had ever been jealous of. It was not at all proper, he thought, that an
nimal should go poking its nose under the bedclothes like that! After this
Nana would proceed to her dressing room, where she took a bath. Toward
leven o'clock François would come and do up her hair before beginning the
laborate manipulations of the afternoon.

At breakfast, as she hated feeding alone, she nearly always had Mme Maloir
t table with her. This lady would arrive from unknown regions in the morn-
ng, wearing her extravagantly quaint hats, and would return at night to that
nysterious existence of hers, about which no one ever troubled. But the hardest
o bear were the two or three hours between lunch and the toilet. On ordi-
tary occasions she proposed a game of bezique to her old friend; on others
he would read the *Figaro*, in which the theatrical echoes and the fashionable
tews interested her. Sometimes she even opened a book, for she fancied her-
elf in literary matters. Her toilet kept her till close on five o'clock, and then
nly she would wake from her daylong drowse and drive out or receive a
vhole mob of men at her own house. She would often dine abroad and always
·o to bed very late, only to rise again on the morrow with the same languor
s before and to begin another day, differing in nothing from its predecessor.

The great distraction was to go to the Batignolles and see her little Louis
t her aunt's. For a fortnight at a time she forgot all about him, and then
vould follow an access of maternal love, and she would hurry off on foot with
ll the modesty and tenderness becoming a good mother. On such occasions
he would be the bearer of snuff for her aunt and of oranges and biscuits for
he child, the kind of presents one takes to a hospital. Or again she would
lrive up in her landau on her return from the Bois, decked in costumes, the
esplendence of which greatly excited the dwellers in the solitary street. Since
ter niece's magnificent elevation Mme Lerat had been puffed up with vanity.
;he rarely presented herself in the Avenue de Villiers, for she was pleased to re-
nark that it wasn't her place to do so, but she enjoyed triumphs in her own
treet. She was delighted when the young woman arrived in dresses that had
·ost four or five thousand francs and would be occupied during the whole of
he next day in showing off her presents and in citing prices which quite stupe-
ied the neighbors. As often as not, Nana kept Sunday free for the sake of

"her family," and on such occasions, if Muffat invited her, she would refuse with the smile of a good little shopwoman. It was impossible, she would answer; she was dining at her aunt's; she was going to see Baby. Moreover, that poor little man Louiset was always ill. He was almost three years old, growing quite a great boy! But he had had an eczema on the back of his neck, and now concretions were forming in his ears, which pointed, it was feared, to decay of the bones of the skull. When she saw how pale he looked, with his spoiled blood and his flabby flesh all out in yellow patches, she would become serious, but her principal feeling would be one of astonishment. What could be the matter with the little love that he should grow so weakly? She, his mother, was so strong and well!

On the days when her child did not engross attention Nana would again sink back into the noisy monotony of her existence, with its drives in the Bois, first nights at the theater, dinners and suppers at the Maison-d'Or or the Café Anglais, not to mention all the places of public resort, all the spectacles to which crowds rushed—Mabille, the reviews, the races. But whatever happened she still felt that stupid, idle void, which caused her, as it were, to suffer internal cramps. Despite the incessant infatuations that possessed her heart, she would stretch out her arms with a gesture of immense weariness the moment she was left alone. Solitude rendered her low spirited at once, for it brought her face to face with the emptiness and boredom within her. Extremely gay by nature and profession, she became dismal in solitude and would sum up her life in the following ejaculation, which recurred incessantly between her yawns:

"Oh, how the men bother me!"

One afternoon as she was returning home from a concert, Nana, on the sidewalk in the Rue Montmartre, noticed a woman trotting along in down-at-the-heel boots, dirty petticoats and a hat utterly ruined by the rain. She recognized her suddenly.

"Stop, Charles!" she shouted to the coachman and began calling: "Satin, Satin!"

Passers-by turned their heads; the whole street stared. Satin had drawn near and was still further soiling herself against the carriage wheels.

"Do get in, my dear girl," said Nana tranquilly, disdaining the onlookers.

And with that she picked her up and carried her off, though she was in disgusting contrast to her light blue landau and her dress of pearl-gray silk trimmed with Chantilly, while the street smiled at the coachman's loftily dignified demeanor.

From that day forth Nana had a passion to occupy her thoughts. Satin became her vicious foible. Washed and dressed and duly installed in the house in the Avenue de Villiers, during three days the girl talked of Saint-Lazare and the annoyances the sisters had caused her and how those dirty police people had put her down on the official list. Nana grew indignant and comforted her and vowed she would get her name taken off, even though she herself should have to go and find out the minister of the interior. Meanwhile there was no sort of hurry: nobody would come and search for her at Nana's

that was certain. And thereupon the two women began to pass tender after-
oons together, making numberless endearing little speeches and mingling
heir kisses with laughter. The same little sport, which the arrival of the plain-
lothes men had interrupted in the Rue de Laval, was beginning again in a
ocular sort of spirit. One fine evening, however, it became serious, and Nana,
vho had been so disgusted at Laure's, now understood what it meant. She was
pset and enraged by it, the more so because Satin disappeared on the morn-
ıg of the fourth day. No one had seen her go out. She had, indeed, slipped
way in her new dress, seized by a longing for air, full of sentimental regret
or her old street existence.

That day there was such a terrible storm in the house that all the servants
ıung their heads in sheepish silence. Nana had come near beating François
or not throwing himself across the door through which Satin escaped. She
lid her best, however, to control herself, and talked of Satin as a dirty swine.
Oh, it would teach her to pick filthy things like that out of the gutter!

When Madame shut herself up in her room in the afternoon Zoé heard her
obbing. In the evening she suddenly asked for her carriage and had herself
lriven to Laure's. It had occurred to her that she would find Satin at the table
l'hôte in the Rue des Martyrs. She was not going there for the sake of seeing
ıer again but in order to catch her one in the face! As a matter of fact, Satin
vas dining at a little table with Mme Robert. Seeing Nana, she began to laugh,
•ut the former, though wounded to the quick, did not make a scene. On the
ontrary, she was very sweet and very compliant. She paid for champagne,
nade five or six tablefuls tipsy and then carried off Satin when Mme Robert
vas in the closets. Not till they were in the carriage did she make a mordant
ttack on her, threatening to kill her if she did it again.

After that day the same little business began again continually. On twenty
lifferent occasions Nana, tragically furious, as only a jilted woman can be,
an off in pursuit of this sluttish creature, whose flights were prompted by the
•oredom she suffered amid the comforts of her new home. Nana began to talk
•f boxing Mme Robert's ears; one day she even meditated a duel; there was one
voman too many, she said.

In these latter times, whenever she dined at Laure's, she donned her dia-
nonds and occasionally brought with her Louise Violaine, Maria Blond and
Tatan Néné, all of them ablaze with finery; and while the sordid feast was
>rogressing in the three saloons and the yellow gaslight flared overhead, these
our resplendent ladies would demean themselves with a vengeance, for it was
heir delight to dazzle the little local courtesans and to carry them off when
linner was over. On days such as these Laure, sleek and tight-laced as ever,
vould kiss everyone with an air of expanded maternity. Yet notwithstanding
ıll these circumstances Satin's blue eyes and pure virginal face remained as
:alm as heretofore; torn, beaten and pestered by the two women, she would
imply remark that it was a funny business, and they would have done far
•etter to make it up at once. It did no good to slap her; she couldn't cut her-
;elf in two, however much she wanted to be nice to everybody. It was Nana
who finally carried her off in triumph, so assiduously had she loaded Satin

with kindnesses and presents. In order to be revenged, however, Mme Robe
wrote abominable, anonymous letters to her rival's lovers.

For some time past Count Muffat had appeared suspicious, and one mornin
with considerable show of feeling, he laid before Nana an anonymous lette
where in the very first sentences she read that she was accused of deceivin
the count with Vandeuvres and the young Hugons.

"It's false! It's false!" she loudly exclaimed in accents of extraordinar
candor.

"You swear?" asked Muffat, already willing to be comforted.

"I'll swear by whatever you like—yes, by the head of my child!"

But the letter was long. Soon her connection with Satin was described i
the broadest and most ignoble terms. When she had done reading she smile

"Now I know who it comes from," she remarked simply.

And as Muffat wanted her denial to the charges therein contained, she re
sumed quietly enough:

"That's a matter which doesn't concern you, dear old pet. How can it hur
you?"

She did not deny anything. He used some horrified expressions. Thereupo
she shrugged her shoulders. Where had he been all this time? Why, it wa
done everywhere! And she mentioned her friends and swore that fashionabl
ladies went in for it. In fact, to hear her speak, nothing could be commoner o
more natural. But a lie was a lie, and so a moment ago he had seen how angr
she grew in the matter of Vandeuvres and the young Hugons! Oh, if that ha
been true he would have been justified in throttling her! But what was th
good of lying to him about a matter of no consequence? And with that sh
repeated her previous expression:

"Come now, how can it hurt you?"

Then as the scene still continued, she closed it with a rough speech:

"Besides, dear boy, if the thing doesn't suit you it's very simple: the hous
door's open! There now, you must take me as you find me!"

He hung his head, for the young woman's vows of fidelity made him happ
at bottom. She, however, now knew her power over him and ceased to con
sider his feelings. And from that time forth Satin was openly installed in th
house on the same footing as the gentlemen. Vandeuvres had not neede
anonymous letters in order to understand how matters· stood, and accordingl
he joked and tried to pick jealous quarrels with Satin. Philippe and George
on their parts, treated her like a jolly good fellow, shaking hands with he
and cracking the riskiest jokes imaginable.

Nana had an adventure one evening when this slut of a girl had given her th
go-by and she had gone to dine in the Rue des Martyrs without being able t
catch her. While she was dining by herself Daguenet had appeared on th
scene, for although he had reformed, he still occasionally dropped in unde
the influence of his old vicious inclinations. He hoped of course that no on
would meet him in these black recesses, dedicated to the town's lowest de
pravity. Accordingly even Nana's presence seemed to embarrass him at th
outset. But he was not the man to run away and, coming forward with

mile, he asked if Madame would be so kind as to allow him to dine at her
able. Noticing his jocular tone, Nana assumed her magnificently frigid de-
neanor and icily replied:

"Sit down where you please, sir. We are in a public place."

Thus begun, the conversation proved amusing. But at dessert Nana, bored
nd burning for a triumph, put her elbows on the table and began in the old
amiliar way:

"Well, what about your marriage, my lad? Is it getting on all right?"

"Not much," Daguenet averred.

As a matter of fact, just when he was about to venture on his request at the
Muffats', he had met with such a cold reception from the count that he had
prudently refrained. The business struck him as a failure. Nana fixed her clear
yes on him; she was sitting, leaning her chin on her hand, and there was an
ronical curve about her lips.

"Oh yes! I'm a baggage," she resumed slowly. "Oh yes, the future father-
n-law will have to be dragged from between my claws! Dear me, dear me,
or a fellow with *nous*, you're jolly stupid! What! D'you mean to say you're
oing to tell your tales to a man who adores me and tells me everything? Now
ust listen: you shall marry if I wish it, my little man!"

For a minute or two he had felt the truth of this, and now he began
cheming out a method of submission. Nevertheless, he still talked jokingly, not
vishing the matter to grow serious, and after he had put on his gloves he de-
nanded the hand of Mlle Estelle de Beuville in the strict regulation manner.
Nana ended by laughing, as though she had been tickled. Oh, that Mimi! It was
mpossible to bear him a grudge! Daguenet's great successes with ladies of her
lass were due to the sweetness of his voice, a voice of such musical purity
nd pliancy as to have won him among courtesans the sobriquet of "Velvet-
Mouth." Every woman would give way to him when he lulled her with his
onorous caresses. He knew this power and rocked Nana to sleep with end-
ess words, telling her all kinds of idiotic anecdotes. When they left the table
l'hôte she was blushing rosy-red; she trembled as she hung on his arm; he
ad reconquered her. As it was very fine, she sent her carriage away and
valked with him as far as his own place, where she went upstairs with him
aturally enough. Two hours later, as she was dressing again, she said:

"So you hold to this marriage of yours, Mimi?"

"Egad," he muttered, "it's the best thing I could possibly do after all! You
now I'm stony broke."

She summoned him to button her boots, and after a pause:

"Good heavens! I've no objection. I'll shove you on! She's as dry as a lath,
s that little thing, but since it suits your game—oh, I'm agreeable: I'll run the
hing through for you."

Then with bosom still uncovered, she began laughing:

"Only what will you give me?"

He had caught her in his arms and was kissing her on the shoulders in a per-
ect access of gratitude while she quivered with excitement and struggled
nerrily and threw herself backward in her efforts to be free.

"Oh, I know," she cried, excited by the contest. "Listen to what I want in the way of commission. On your wedding day you shall make me a present of your innocence. Before your wife, d'you understand?"

"That's it! That's it!" he said, laughing even louder than Nana.

The bargain amused them—they thought the whole business very good, indeed.

Now as it happened, there was a dinner at Nana's next day. For the matter of that, it was the customary Thursday dinner, and Muffat, Vandeuvres, the young Hugons and Satin were present. The count arrived early. He stood in need of eighty thousand francs wherewith to free the young woman from two or three debts and to give her a set of sapphires she was dying to possess. As he had already seriously lessened his capital, he was in search of a lender, for he did not dare to sell another property. With the advice of Nana herself he had addressed himself to Labordette, but the latter, deeming it too heavy an undertaking, had mentioned it to the hairdresser Francis, who willingly busied himself in such affairs in order to oblige his lady clients. The count put himself into the hands of these gentlemen but expressed a formal desire not to appear in the matter, and they both undertook to keep in hand the bill for a hundred thousand francs which he was to sign, excusing themselves at the same time for charging a matter of twenty thousand francs interest and loudly denouncing the blackguard usurers to whom, they declared, it had been necessary to have recourse. When Muffat had himself announced, Francis was putting the last touches to Nana's coiffure. Labordette also was sitting familiarly in the dressing room, as became a friend of no consequence. Seeing the count, he discreetly placed a thick bundle of bank notes among the powders and pomades, and the bill was signed on the marble-topped dressing table. Nana was anxious to keep Labordette to dinner, but he declined—he was taking a rich foreigner about Paris. Muffat, however, led him aside and begged him to go to Becker, the jeweler, and bring him back thence the set of sapphires, which he wanted to present the young woman by way of surprise that very evening. Labordette willingly undertook the commission, and half an hour later Julien handed the jewel case mysteriously to the count.

During dinnertime Nana was nervous. The sight of the eighty thousand francs had excited her. To think all that money was to go to tradespeople! It was a disgusting thought. After soup had been served she grew sentimental, and in the splendid dining room, glittering with plate and glass, she talked of the bliss of poverty. The men were in evening dress, Nana in a gown of white embroidered satin, while Satin made a more modest appearance in black silk with a simple gold heart at her throat, which was a present from her kind friend. Julien and François waited behind the guests and were assisted in this by Zoé. All three looked most dignified.

"It's certain I had far greater fun when I hadn't a cent!" Nana repeated.

She had placed Muffat on her right hand and Vandeuvres on her left, but she scarcely looked at them, so taken up was she with Satin, who sat in state between Philippe and Georges on the opposite side of the table.

"Eh, duckie?" she kept saying at every turn. "How we did use to laugh in those days when we went to Mother Josse's school in the Rue Polonceau!"

When the roast was being served the two women plunged into a world of reminiscences. They used to have regular chattering fits of this kind when a sudden desire to stir the muddy depths of their childhood would possess them. These fits always occurred when men were present: it was as though they had given way to a burning desire to treat them to the dunghill on which they had grown to woman's estate. The gentlemen paled visibly and looked embarrassed. The young Hugons did their best to laugh, while Vandeuvres nervously toyed with his beard and Muffat redoubled his gravity.

"You remember Victor?" said Nana. "There was a wicked little fellow for you! Why, he used to take the little girls into cellars!"

"I remember him perfectly," replied Satin. "I recollect the big courtyard at your place very well. There was a portress there with a broom!"

"Mother Boche—she's dead."

"And I can still picture your shop. Your mother was a great fatty. One evening when we were playing your father came in drunk. Oh, so drunk!"

At this point Vandeuvres tried to intercept the ladies' reminiscences and to effect a diversion.

"I say, my dear, I should be very glad to have some more truffles. They're simply perfect. Yesterday I had some at the house of the Duc de Corbreuse, which did not come up to them at all."

"The truffles, Julien!" said Nana roughly.

Then returning to the subject:

"By Jove, yes, Dad hadn't any sense! And then what a smash there was! You should have seen it—down, down, down we went, starving away all the time. I can tell you I've had to bear pretty well everything, and it's a miracle I didn't kick the bucket over it, like Daddy and Mamma."

This time Muffat, who was playing with his knife in a state of infinite exasperation, made so bold as to intervene.

"What you're telling us isn't very cheerful."

"Eh, what? Not cheerful!" she cried with a withering glance. "I believe you; it isn't cheerful! Somebody had to earn a living for us, dear boy. Oh yes, you know, I'm the right sort; I don't mince matters. Mamma was a laundress; Daddy used to get drunk, and he died of it! There! If it doesn't suit you—if you're ashamed of my family——"

They all protested. What was she after now? They had every sort of respect for her family! But she went on:

"If you're ashamed of my family you'll please leave me, because I'm not one of those women who deny their father and mother. You must take me and them together, d'you understand?"

They took her as required; they accepted the dad, the mamma, the past; in fact, whatever she chose. With their eyes fixed on the tablecloth, the four now sat shrinking and insignificant while Nana, in a transport of omnipotence, trampled on them in the old muddy boots worn long since in the Rue de la Goutte-d'Or. She was determined not to lay down the cudgels just yet. It

was all very fine to bring her fortunes, to build her palaces; she would neve
leave off regretting the time when she munched apples! Oh, what bosh tha
stupid thing money was! It was made for the tradespeople! Finally her out
burst ended in a sentimentally expressed desire for a simple, openhearte
existence, to be passed in an atmosphere of universal benevolence.

When she got to this point she noticed Julien waiting idly by.

"Well, what's the matter? Hand the champagne then!" she said. "Why d'yo
stand staring at me like a goose?"

During this scene the servants had never once smiled. They apparentl
heard nothing, and the more their mistress let herself down, the more majes
tic they became. Julien set to work to pour out the champagne and did s
without mishap, but François, who was handing round the fruit, was so unfor
tunate as to tilt the fruit dish too low, and the apples, the pears and the grape
rolled on the table.

"You bloody clumsy lot!" cried Nana.

The footman was mistaken enough to try and explain that the fruit had no
been firmly piled up. Zoé had disarranged it by taking out some oranges.

"Then it's Zoé that's the goose!" said Nana.

"Madame——" murmured the lady's maid in an injured tone.

Straightway Madame rose to her feet, and in a sharp voice and with royally
authoritative gesture:

"We've had enough of this, haven't we? Leave the room, all of you! W
don't want you any longer!"

This summary procedure calmed her down, and she was forthwith all sweet
ness and amiability. The dessert proved charming, and the gentlemen grew
quite merry waiting on themselves. But Satin, having peeled a pear, came an
ate it behind her darling, leaning on her shoulder the while and whispering
sundry little remarks in her ear, at which they both laughed very loudly. B
and by she wanted to share her last piece of pear with Nana and presented i
to her between her teeth. Whereupon there was a great nibbling of lips, and th
pear was finished amid kisses. At this there was a burst of comic protest from
the gentlemen, Philippe shouting to them to take it easy and Vandeuvres ask
ing if one ought to leave the room. Georges, meanwhile, had come and pu
his arm round Satin's waist and had brought her back to her seat.

"How silly of you!" said Nana. "You're making her blush, the poor, darling
duck. Never mind, dear girl, let them chaff. It's our own little private affair."

And turning to Muffat, who was watching them with his serious expres
sion:

"Isn't it, my friend?"

"Yes, certainly," he murmured with a slow nod of approval.

He no longer protested now. And so amid that company of gentlemen with
the great names and the old, upright traditions, the two women sat face t
face, exchanging tender glances, conquering, reigning, in tranquil defiance o
the laws of sex, in open contempt for the male portion of the community. Th
gentlemen burst into applause.

The company went upstairs to take coffee in the little drawing room, wher a couple of lamps cast a soft glow over the rosy hangings and the lacquer and old gold of the knickknacks. At that hour of the evening the light played discreetly over coffers, bronzes and china, lighting up silver or ivory inlaid work, bringing into view the polished contours of a carved stick and gleaming over a panel with glossy silky reflections. The fire, which had been burning since the afternoon, was dying out in glowing embers. It was very warm—the air behind the curtains and hangings was languid with warmth. The room was full of Nana's intimate existence: a pair of gloves, a fallen handkerchief, an open book, lay scattered about, and their owner seemed present in careless attire with that well-known odor of violets and that species of untidiness which became her in her character of good-natured courtesan and had such a charming effect among all those rich surroundings. The very armchairs, which were as wide as beds, and the sofas, which were as deep as alcoves, invited to slumber oblivious of the flight of time and to tender whispers in shadowy corners.

Satin went and lolled back in the depths of a sofa near the fireplace. She had lit a cigarette, but Vandeuvres began amusing himself by pretending to be ferociously jealous. Nay, he even threatened to send her his seconds if she still persisted in keeping Nana from her duty. Philippe and Georges joined him and teased her and badgered her so mercilessly that at last she shouted out:

"Darling! Darling! Do make 'em keep quiet! They're still after me!"

"Now then, let her be," said Nana seriously. "I won't have her tormented; you know that quite well. And you, my pet, why d'you always go mixing yourself up with them when they've got so little sense?"

Satin, blushing all over and putting out her tongue, went into the dressing room, through the widely open door of which you caught a glimpse of pale marbles gleaming in the milky light of a gas flame in a globe of rough glass. After that Nana talked to the four men as charmingly as hostess could. During the day she had read a novel which was at that time making a good deal of noise. It was the history of a courtesan, and Nana was very indignant, declaring the whole thing to be untrue and expressing angry dislike to that kind of monstrous literature which pretends to paint from nature. "Just as though one could describe everything," she said. Just as though a novel ought not to be written so that the reader may while away an hour pleasantly! In the matter of books and of plays Nana had very decided opinions: she wanted tender and noble productions, things that would set her dreaming and would elevate her soul. Then allusion being made in the course of conversation to the troubles agitating Paris, the incendiary articles in the papers, the incipient popular disturbances which followed the calls to arms nightly raised at public meetings, she waxed wroth with the Republicans. What on earth did those dirty people who never washed really want? Were folks not happy? Had not the emperor done everything for the people? A nice filthy lot of people! She knew 'em; she could talk about 'em, and, quite forgetting the respect which at dinner she had just been insisting should be paid to her humble circle in the Rue de la Goutte-d'Or, she began blackguarding her own class with all the terror and disgust peculiar to a woman who had risen successfully above it. That very afternoon she had read in the *Figaro* an account of the proceedings at a public meeting which had verged on the comic. Owing to the slang words that had been used and to the piggish behavior of a drunken man who had got himself chucked, she was laughing at those proceedings still.

"Oh, those drunkards!" she said with a disgusted air. "No, look you here, their republic would be a great misfortune for everybody! Oh, may God preserve us the emperor as long as possible!"

"God will hear your prayer, my dear," Muffat replied gravely. "To be sure, the emperor stands firm."

He liked her to express such excellent views. Both, indeed, understood one another in political matters. Vandeuvres and Philippe Hugon likewise indulged in endless jokes against the "cads," the quarrelsome set who scuttled off the moment they clapped eyes on a bayonet. But Georges that evening remained pale and somber.

"What can be the matter with that baby?" asked Nana, noticing his troubled appearance.

"With me? Nothing—I am listening," he muttered.

But he was really suffering. On rising from table he had heard Philippe joking with the young woman, and now it was Philippe, and not himself, who sat beside her. His heart, he knew not why, swelled to bursting. He could not bear to see them so close together; such vile thoughts oppressed him that shame mingled with his anguish. He who laughed at Satin, who had accepted Steiner and Muffat and all the rest, felt outraged and murderous at the thought that Philippe might someday touch that woman.

"Here, take Bijou," she said to comfort him, and she passed him the little dog which had gone to sleep on her dress.

And with that Georges grew happy again, for with the beast still warm from her lap in his arms, he held, as it were, part of her.

Allusion had been made to a considerable loss which Vandeuvres had last night sustained at the Imperial Club. Muffat, who did not play, expressed great astonishment, but Vandeuvres smilingly alluded to his imminent ruin, about which Paris was already talking. The kind of death you chose did not much matter, he averred; the great thing was to die handsomely. For some time past Nana had noticed that he was nervous and had a sharp downward droop of the mouth and a fitful gleam in the depths of his clear eyes. But he retained his haughty aristocratic manner and the delicate elegance of his impoverished race, and as yet these strange manifestations were only, so to speak, momentary fits of vertigo overcoming a brain already sapped by play and by debauchery. One night as he lay beside her he had frightened her with a dreadful story. He had told her he contemplated shutting himself up in his stable and setting fire to himself and his horses at such time as he should have devoured all his substance. His only hope at that period was a horse, Lusignan by name, which he was training for the Prix de Paris. He was living on this horse, which was the sole stay of his shaken credit, and whenever Nana grew exacting he would put her off till June and to the probability of Lusignan winning.

"Bah! He may very likely lose," she said merrily, "since he's going to clear them all out at the races."

By way of reply he contented himself by smiling a thin, mysterious smile. Then carelessly:

"By the by, I've taken the liberty of giving your name to my outsider, the filly. Nana, Nana—that sounds well. You're not vexed?"

"Vexed, why?" she said in a state of inward ecstasy.

The conversation continued, and same mention was made of an execution shortly to take place. The young woman said she was burning to go to it when Satin appeared at the dressing-room door and called her in tones of entreaty. She got up at once and left the gentlemen lolling lazily about, while they finished their cigars and discussed the grave question as to how far a murderer subject to chronic alcoholism is responsible for his act. In the dressing room Zoé sat helpless on a chair, crying her heart out, while Satin vainly endeavored to console her.

"What's the matter?" said Nana in surprise.

"Oh, darling, do speak to her!" said Satin. "I've been trying to make her listen to reason for the last twenty minutes. She's crying because you called her a goose."

"Yes, madame, it's very hard—very hard," stuttered Zoe, choked by a fresh fit of sobbing.

This sad sight melted the young woman's heart at once. She spoke kindly, and when the other woman still refused to grow calm she sank down in front of her and took her round the waist with truly cordial familiarity:

"But, you silly, I said 'goose' just as I might have said anything else. How shall I explain? I was in a passion—it was wrong of me; now calm down."

"I who love Madame so," stuttered Zoé; "after all I've done for Madame."

Thereupon Nana kissed the lady's maid and, wishing to show her she wasn't vexed, gave her a dress she had worn three times. Their quarrels always ended up in the giving of presents! Zoé plugged her handkerchief into her eyes. She carried the dress off over her arm and added before leaving that they were very sad in the kitchen and that Julien and François had been unable to eat, so entirely had Madame's anger taken away their appetites. Thereupon Madame sent them a louis as a pledge of reconciliation. She suffered too much if people around her were sorrowful.

Nana was returning to the drawing room, happy in the thought that she had patched up a disagreement which was rendering her quietly apprehensive of the morrow, when Satin came and whispered vehemently in her ear. She was full of complaint, threatened to be off if those men still went on teasing her and kept insisting that her darling should turn them all out of doors for that night, at any rate. It would be a lesson to them. And then it would be so nice to be alone, both of them! Nana, with a return of anxiety, declared it to be impossible. Thereupon the other shouted at her like a violent child and tried hard to overrule her.

"I wish it, d'you see? Send 'em away or I'm off!"

And she went back into the drawing room, stretched herself out in the recesses of a divan, which stood in the background near the window, and lay waiting, silent and deathlike, with her great eyes fixed upon Nana.

The gentlemen were deciding against the new criminological theories Granted that lovely invention of irresponsibility in certain pathological cases and criminals ceased to exist and sick people alone remained. The young woman, expressing approval with an occasional nod, was busy considering how best to dismiss the count. The others would soon be going, but he would assuredly prove obstinate. In fact, when Philippe got up to withdraw, George followed him at once—he seemed only anxious not to leave his brother behind Vandeuvres lingered some minutes longer, feeling his way, as it were, and waiting to find out if, by any chance, some important business would oblige Muffat to cede him his place. Soon, however, when he saw the count de liberately taking up his quarters for the night, he desisted from his purpos and said good-by, as became a man of tact. But on his way to the door, he noticed Satin staring fixedly at Nana, as usual. Doubtless he understood what this meant, for he seemed amused and came and shook hands with her.

"We're not angry, eh?" he whispered. "Pray pardon me. You're the nicer attraction of the two, on my honor!"

Satin deigned no reply. Nor did she take her eyes off Nana and the count who were now alone. Muffat, ceasing to be ceremonious, had come to sit be side the young woman. He took her fingers and began kissing them. Where upon Nana, seeking to change the current of his thoughts, asked him if hi daughter Estelle were better. The previous night he had been complaining o the child's melancholy behavior—he could not even spend a day happily a his own house, with his wife always out and his daughter icily silent.

In family matters of this kind Nana was always full of good advice, and when Muffat abandoned all his usual self-control under the influence of menta and physical relaxation and once more launched out into his former plaints she remembered the promise she had made.

"Suppose you were to marry her?" she said. And with that she ventured t talk of Daguenet. At the mere mention of the name the count was filled with disgust. "Never," he said after what she had told him!

She pretended great surprise and then burst out laughing and put her arm round his neck.

"Oh, the jealous man! To think of it! Just argue it out a little. Why, they slandered me to you—I was furious. At present I should be ever so sorry if——

But over Muffat's shoulder she met Satin's gaze. And she left him anxiously and in a grave voice continued:

"This marriage must come off, my friend; I don't want to prevent you daughter's happiness. The young man's most charming; you could not possibly find a better sort."

And she launched into extraordinary praise of Daguenet. The count had again taken her hands; he no longer refused now; he would see about it, he said, they would talk the matter over. By and by, when he spoke of going t bed, she sank her voice and excused herself. It was impossible; she was no well. If he loved her at all he would not insist! Nevertheless, he was obstinate

he refused to go away, and she was beginning to give in when she met Satin's
eyes once more. Then she grew inflexible. No, the thing was out of the question! The count, deeply moved and with a look of suffering, had risen and
was going in quest of his hat. But in the doorway he remembered the set of
sapphires; he could feel the case in his pocket. He had been wanting to hide it
at the bottom of the bed so that when she entered it before him she should feel
it against her legs. Since dinnertime he had been meditating this little surprise
like a schoolboy, and now, in trouble and anguish of heart at being thus dismissed, he gave her the case without further ceremony.

"What is it?" she queried. "Sapphires? Dear me! Oh yes, it's that set. How
sweet you are! But I say, my darling, d'you believe it's the same one? In the
shopwindow it made a much greater show."

That was all the thanks he got, and she let him go away. He noticed Satin
stretched out silent and expectant, and with that he gazed at both women and
without further insistence submitted to his fate and went downstairs. The hall
door had not yet closed when Satin caught Nana round the waist and danced
and sang. Then she ran to the window.

"Oh, just look at the figure he cuts down in the street!" The two women
leaned upon the wrought-iron window rail in the shadow of the curtains. One
o'clock struck. The Avenue de Villiers was deserted, and its double file of
gas lamps stretched away into the darkness of the damp March night through
which great gusts of wind kept sweeping, laden with rain. There were vague
stretches of land on either side of the road which looked like gulfs of shadow,
while scaffoldings round mansions in process of construction loomed upward
under the dark sky. They laughed uncontrollably as they watched Muffat's
rounded back and glistening shadow disappearing along the wet sidewalk into
the glacial, desolate plains of new Paris. But Nana silenced Satin.

"Take care; there are the police!"

Thereupon they smothered their laughter and gazed in secret fear at two
dark figures walking with measured tread on the opposite side of the avenue.
Amid all her luxurious surroundings, amid all the royal splendors of the woman
whom all must obey, Nana still stood in horror of the police and did not like
to hear them mentioned any oftener than death. She felt distinctly unwell
when a policeman looked up at her house. One never knew what such people
might do! They might easily take them for loose women if they heard them
laughing at that hour of the night. Satin, with a little shudder, had squeezed
herself up against Nana. Nevertheless, the pair stayed where they were and
were soon interested in the approach of a lantern, the light of which danced
over the puddles in the road. It was an old ragpicker woman who was busy
raking in the gutters. Satin recognized her.

"Dear me," she exclaimed, "it's Queen Pomaré with her wickerwork shawl!"

And while a gust of wind lashed the fine rain in their faces she told her beloved the story of Queen Pomaré. Oh, she had been a splendid girl once upon
a time: all Paris had talked of her beauty. And such devilish go and such
cheek! Why, she led the men about like dogs, and great people stood blub-
bering on her stairs! Now she was in the habit of getting tipsy, and the women

round about would make her drink absinthe for the sake of a laugh, after which the street boys would throw stones at her and chase her. In fact, it was a regular smashup; the queen had tumbled into the mud! Nana listened, feeling cold all over.

"You shall see," added Satin.

She whistled a man's whistle, and the ragpicker, who was then below the window, lifted her head and showed herself by the yellow flare of her lantern. Framed among rags, a perfect bundle of them, a face looked out from under a tattered kerchief—a blue, seamed face with a toothless, cavernous mouth and fiery bruises where the eyes should be. And Nana, seeing the frightful old woman, the wanton drowned in drink, had a sudden fit of recollection and saw far back amid the shadows of consciousness the vision of Chamont—Irma d'Anglars, the old harlot crowned with years and honors, ascending the steps in front of her château amid abjectly reverential villagers. Then as Satin whistled again, making game of the old hag, who could not see her:

"Do leave off; there are the police!" she murmured in changed tones. "In with us, quick, my pet!"

The measured steps were returning, and they shut the window. Turning round again, shivering, and with the damp of night on her hair, Nana was momentarily astounded at sight of her drawing room. It seemed as though she had forgotten it and were entering an unknown chamber. So warm, so full of perfume, was the air she encountered that she experienced a sense of delighted surprise. The heaped-up wealth of the place, the Old World furniture, the fabrics of silk and gold, the ivory, the bronzes, were slumbering in the rosy light of the lamps, while from the whole of the silent house a rich feeling of great luxury ascended, the luxury of the solemn reception rooms, of the comfortable, ample dining room, of the vast retired staircase, with their soft carpets and seats. Her individuality, with its longing for domination and enjoyment and its desire to possess everything that she might destroy everything, was suddenly increased. Never before had she felt so profoundly the puissance of her sex. She gazed slowly round and remarked with an expression of grave philosophy:

"Ah well, all the same, one's jolly well right to profit by things when one's young!"

But now Satin was rolling on the bearskins in the bedroom and calling her.

"Oh, do come! Do come!"

Nana undressed in the dressing room, and in order to be quicker about it she took her thick fell of blonde hair in both hands and began shaking it above the silver wash hand basin, while a downward hail of long hairpins rang a little chime on the shining metal.

CHAPTER XI

ONE SUNDAY the race for the Grand Prix de Paris was being run in the Bois de Boulogne beneath skies rendered sultry by the first heats of June. The sun that morning had risen amid a mist of dun-colored dust, but toward eleven o'clock, just when the carriages were reaching the Longchamps course, a southerly wind had swept away the clouds; long streamers of gray vapor were disappearing across the sky, and gaps showing an intense blue beyond were spreading from one end of the horizon to the other. In the bright bursts of sunlight which alternated with the clouds the whole scene shone again, from the field which was gradually filling with a crowd of carriages, horsemen and pedestrians, to the still-vacant course, where the judge's box stood, together with the posts and the masts for signaling numbers, and thence on to the five symmetrical stands of brickwork and timber, rising gallery upon gallery in the middle of the weighing enclosure opposite. Beyond these, bathed in the light of noon, lay the vast level plain, bordered with little trees and shut in to the westward by the wooded heights of Saint-Cloud and the Suresnes, which, in their turn, were dominated by the severe outlines of Mont-Valérien.

Nana, as excited as if the Grand Prix were going to make her fortune, wanted to take up a position by the railing next the winning post. She had arrived very early—she was, in fact, one of the first to come—in a landau adorned with silver and drawn, à la Daumont, by four splendid white horses. This landau was a present from Count Muffat. When she had made her appearance at the entrance to the field with two postilions jogging blithely on the near horses and two footmen perching motionless behind the carriage, the people had rushed to look as though a queen were passing. She sported the blue and white colors of the Vandeuvres stable, and her dress was remarkable. It consisted of a little blue silk bodice and tunic, which fitted closely to the body and bulged out enormously behind her waist, thereby bringing her lower limbs into bold relief in such a manner as to be extremely noticeable in that epoch of voluminous skirts. Then there was a white satin dress with white satin sleeves and a sash worn crosswise over the shoulders, the whole ornamented with silver guipure which shone in the sun. In addition to this, in order to be still more like a jockey, she had stuck a blue toque with a white feather jauntily upon her chignon, the fair tresses from which flowed down beyond her shoulders and resembled an enormous russet pigtail.

Twelve struck. The public would have to wait more than three hours for the Grand Prix to be run. When the landau had drawn up beside the barriers Nana settled herself comfortably down as though she were in her own house. A whim had prompted her to bring Bijou and Louiset with her, and the dog crouched among her skirts, shivering with cold despite the heat of the day, while amid a bedizenment of ribbons and laces the child's poor little face looked waxen and dumb and white in the open air. Meanwhile the young woman, without troubling about the people near her, talked at the top of her voice with Georges and Philippe Hugon, who were seated opposite on the front seat among such a mountain of bouquets of white roses and blue myosotis that they were buried up to their shoulders.

"Well then," she was saying, "as he bored me to death, I showed him the door. And now it's two days that he's been sulking."

She was talking of Muffat, but she took care not to confess to the young men the real reason for this first quarrel, which was that one evening he had found a man's hat in her bedroom. She had indeed brought home a passer-by out of sheer ennui—a silly infatuation.

"You have no idea how funny he is," she continued, growing merry over the particulars she was giving. "He's a regular bigot at bottom, so he says his prayers every evening. Yes, he does. He's under the impression I notice nothing because I go to bed first so as not to be in his way, but I watch him out of the corner of my eye. Oh, he jaws away, and then he crosses himself when he turns round to step over me and get to the inside of the bed."

"Jove, it's sly," muttered Philippe. "That's what happens before, but afterward, what then?"

She laughed merrily.

"Yes, just so, before and after! When I'm going to sleep I hear him jawing away again. But the biggest bore of all is that we can't argue about anything now without his growing 'pi.' I've always been religious. Yes, chaff as much as you like; that won't prevent me believing what I do believe! Only he's too much of a nuisance: he blubbers; he talks about remorse. The day before yesterday, for instance, he had a regular fit of it after our usual row, and I wasn't the least bit reassured when all was over."

But she broke off, crying out:

"Just look at the Mignons arriving. Dear me, they've brought the children! Oh, how those little chaps are dressed up!"

The Mignons were in a landau of severe hue; there was something substantially luxurious about their turnout, suggesting rich retired tradespeople. Rose was in a gray silk gown trimmed with red knots and with puffs; she was smiling happily at the joyous behavior of Henri and Charles, who sat on the front seat, looking awkward in their ill-fitting collegians' tunics. But when the landau had drawn up by the rails and she perceived Nana sitting in triumph among her bouquets, with her four horses and her liveries, she pursed up her lips, sat bolt upright and turned her head away. Mignon, on the other hand, looking the picture of freshness and gaiety, waved her a salutation. He made it a matter of principle to keep out of feminine disagreements.

"By the by," Nana resumed, "d'you know a little old man who's very clean and neat and has bad teeth—a Monsieur Venot? He came to see me this morning."

"Monsieur Venot?" said Georges in great astonishment. "It's impossible! Why, the man's a Jesuit!"

"Precisely; I spotted that. Oh, you have no idea what our conversation was like! It was just funny! He spoke to me about the count, about his divided house, and begged me to restore a family its happiness. He was very polite and very smiling for the matter of that. Then I answered to the effect that I wanted nothing better, and I undertook to reconcile the count and his wife. You know it's not humbug. I should be delighted to see them all happy again, the poor things! Besides, it would be a relief to me, for there are days—yes, there are days—when he bores me to death."

The weariness of the last months escaped her in this heartfelt outburst.

Moreover, the count appeared to be in big money difficulties; he was anxious, and it seemed likely that the bill which Labordette had put his name to would not be met.

"Dear me, the countess is down yonder," said Georges, letting his gaze wander over the stands.

"Where, where?" cried Nana. "What eyes that baby's got! Hold my sunshade, Philippe."

But with a quick forward dart Georges had outstripped his brother. It enchanted him to be holding the blue silk sunshade with its silver fringe. Nana was scanning the scene through a huge pair of field glasses.

"Ah yes! I see her," she said at length. "In the right-hand stand, near a pillar, eh? She's in mauve, and her daughter in white by her side. Dear me, there's Daguenet going to bow to them."

Thereupon Philippe talked of Daguenet's approaching marriage with that lath of an Estelle. It was a settled matter—the banns were being published. At first the countess had opposed it, but the count, they said, had insisted. Nana smiled.

"I know, I know," she murmured. "So much the better for Paul. He's a nice boy—he deserves it."

And leaning toward Louiset:

"You're enjoying yourself, eh? What a grave face!"

The child never smiled. With a very old expression he was gazing at all those crowds, as though the sight of them filled him with melancholy reflections. Bijou, chased from the skirts of the young woman who was moving about a great deal, had come to nestle, shivering, against the little fellow.

Meanwhile the field was filling up. Carriages, a compact, interminable file of them, were continually arriving through the Porte de la Cascade. There were big omnibuses such as the Pauline, which had started from the Boulevard des Italiens, freighted with its fifty passengers, and was now going to draw up to the right of the stands. Then there were dogcarts, victorias, landaus, all superbly well turned out, mingled with lamentable cabs which jolted along behind sorry old hacks, and four-in-hands, sending along their four horses, and mail coaches, where the masters sat on the seats above and left the servants to take care of the hampers of champagne inside, and "spiders," the immense wheels of which were a flash of glittering steel, and light tandems, which looked as delicately formed as the works of a clock and slipped along amid a peal of little bells. Every few seconds an equestrian rode by, and a swarm of people on foot rushed in a scared way among the carriages. On the green the far-off rolling sound which issued from the avenues in the Bois died out suddenly in dull rustlings, and now nothing was audible save the hubbub of the ever-increasing crowds and cries and calls and the crackings of whips in the open. When the sun, amid bursts of wind, reappeared at the edge of a cloud, a long ray of golden light ran across the field, lit up the harness and the varnished coach panels and touched the ladies' dresses with fire, while amid the dusty radiance the coachmen, high up on their boxes, flamed beside their great whips.

Labordette was getting out of an open carriage where Gaga, Clarisse and Blanche de Sivry had kept a place for him. As he was hurrying to cross the course and enter the weighing enclosure Nana got Georges to call him. Then when he came up:

"What's the betting on me?" she asked laughingly.

She referred to the filly Nana, the Nana who had let herself be shamefully beaten in the race for the Prix de Diane and had not even been placed in April and May last when she ran for the Prix des Cars and the Grande Poule des Produits, both of which had been gained by Lusignan, the other horse in the Vandeuvres stable. Lusignan had all at once become prime favorite, and since yesterday he had been currently taken at two to one.

"Always fifty to one against," replied Labordette.

"The deuce! I'm not worth much," rejoined Nana, amused by the jest. "I don't back myself then; no, by jingo! I don't put a single louis on myself."

Labordette went off again in a great hurry, but she recalled him. She wanted some advice. Since he kept in touch with the world of trainers and jockeys he had special information about various stables. His prognostications had come true a score of times already, and people called him the "King of Tipsters."

"Let's see, what horses ought I to choose?" said the young woman. "What's the betting on the Englishman?"

"Spirit? Three to one against. Valerio II, the same. As to the others, they're laying twenty-five to one against Cosinus, forty to one against Hazard, thirty to one against Boum, thirty-five to one against Pichenette, ten to one against Frangipane."

"No, I don't bet on the Englishman, I don't. I'm a patriot. Perhaps Valerio II would do, eh? The Duc de Corbreuse was beaming a little while ago. Well, no, after all! Fifty louis on Lusignan; what do you say to that?"

Labordette looked at her with a singular expression. She leaned forward and asked him questions in a low voice, for she was aware that Vandeuvres commissioned him to arrange matters with the bookmakers so as to be able to bet the more easily. Supposing him to have got to know something, he might quite well tell it her. But without entering into explanations Labordette persuaded her to trust to his sagacity. He would put on her fifty louis for her as he might think best, and she would not repent of his arrangement.

"All the horses you like!" she cried gaily, letting him take his departure, "but no Nana; she's a jade!"

There was a burst of uproarious laughter in the carriage. The young men thought her sally very amusing, while Louiset in his ignorance lifted his pale eyes to his mother's face, for her loud exclamations surprised him. However, there was no escape for Labordette as yet. Rose Mignon had made a sign to him and was now giving him her commands while he wrote figures in a notebook. Then Clarisse and Gaga called him back in order to change their bets, for they had heard things said in the crowd, and now they didn't want to have anything more to do with Valerio II and were choosing Lusignan. He wrote down their wishes with an impassible expression and at length managed to escape. He could be seen disappearing between two of the stands on the other side of the course.

Carriages were still arriving. They were by this time drawn up five rows deep, and a dense mass of them spread along the barriers, checkered by the light coats of white horses. Beyond them other carriages stood about in comparative isolation, looking as though they had stuck fast in the grass. Wheels and harness were here, there and everywhere, according as the conveyances to which they belonged were side by side, at an angle, across and across or head to head. Over such spaces of turf as still remained unoccupied cavaliers kept trotting, and black groups of pedestrians moved continually. The scene resembled the field where a fair is being held, and above it all, amid the confused motley of the crowd, the drinking booths raised their gray canvas roofs, which gleamed white in the sunshine. But a veritable tumult, a mob, an eddy of hats, surged round the several bookmakers, who stood in open carriages, gesticulating like itinerant dentists while their odds were pasted up on tall boards beside them.

"All the same, it's stupid not to know on what horse one's betting," Nana was remarking. "I really must risk some louis in person."

She had stood up to select a bookmaker with a decent expression of face but forgot what she wanted on perceiving a perfect crowd of her acquaintance. Besides the Mignons, besides Gaga, Clarisse and Blanche, there were present, to the right and left, behind and in the middle of the mass of carriages now hemming in her landau, the following ladies: Tatan Néné and Maria Blond in a victoria, Caroline Héquet with her mother and two gentlemen in an open carriage, Louise Violaine quite alone, driving a little basket chaise, decked with orange and green ribbons, the colors of the Méchain stables, and finally, Léa de Horn on the lofty seat of a mail coach, where a band of young men were making a great din. Farther off, in a *huit ressorts* of aristocratic appearance, Lucy Stewart, in a very simple black silk dress, sat, looking distinguished beside a tall young man in the uniform of a naval cadet. But what most astounded Nana was the arrival of Simonne in a tandem which Steiner was driving, while a footman sat motionless, with folded arms, behind them. She looked dazzling in white satin striped with yellow and was covered with diamonds from waist to hat. The banker, on his part, was handling a tremendous whip and sending along his two horses, which were harnessed tandemwise, the leader being a little warm-colored chestnut with a mouselike trot, the shaft horse a big brown bay, a stepper, with a fine action.

"Deuce take it!" said Nana. "So that thief Steiner has cleared the Bourse again, has he? I say, isn't Simonne a swell! It's too much of a good thing; he'll get into the clutches of the law!"

Nevertheless, she exchanged greetings at a distance. Indeed, she kept waving her hand and smiling, turning round and forgetting no one in her desire to be seen by everybody. At the same time she continued chatting.

"It's her son Lucy's got in tow! He's charming in his uniform. That's why she's looking so grand, of course! You know she's afraid of him and that she passes herself off as an actress. Poor young man, I pity him all the same! He seems quite unsuspicious."

"Bah," muttered Philippe, laughing, "she'll be able to find him an heiress in the country when she likes."

Nana was silent, for she had just noticed the Tricon amid the thick of the carriages. Having arrived in a cab, whence she could not see anything, the Tricon had quietly mounted the coach box. And there, straightening up her tall figure, with her noble face enshrined in its long curls, she dominated the crowd as though enthroned amid her feminine subjects. All the latter smiled discreetly at her while she, in her superiority, pretended not to know them. She wasn't there for business purposes: she was watching the races for the love of the thing, as became a frantic gambler with a passion for horseflesh.

"Dear me, there's that idiot La Faloise!" said Georges suddenly.

It was a surprise to them all. Nana did not recognize her La Faloise, for since he had come into his inheritance he had grown extraordinarily up to date. He wore a low collar and was clad in a cloth of delicate hue which fitted close to his meager shoulders. His hair was in little bandeaux, and he affected a weary kind of swagger, a soft tone of voice and slang words and phrases which he did not take the trouble to finish.

"But he's quite the thing!" declared Nana in perfect enchantment.

Gaga and Clarisse had called La Faloise and were throwing themselves at him in their efforts to regain his allegiance, but he left them immediately, rolling off in a chaffing, disdainful manner. Nana dazzled him. He rushed up to her and stood on the carriage step, and when she twitted him about Gaga he murmured:

"Oh dear, no! We've seen the last of the old lot! Mustn't play her off on me any more. And then, you know, it's you now, Juliet mine!"

He had put his hand to his heart. Nana laughed a good deal at this exceedingly sudden out-of-door declaration. She continued:

"I say, that's not what I'm after. You're making me forget that I want to lay wagers. Georges, you see that bookmaker down there, a great red-faced man with curly hair? He's got a dirty blackguard expression which I like. You're to go and choose—— Oh, I say, what can one choose?"

"I'm not a patriotic soul—oh dear, no!" La Faloise blurted out. "I'm all for the Englishman. It will be ripping if the Englishman gains! The French may go to Jericho!"

Nana was scandalized. Presently the merits of the several horses began to be discussed, and La Faloise, wishing to be thought very much in the swim, spoke of them all as sorry jades. Frangipane, Baron Verdier's horse, was by The Truth out of Lenore. A big bay horse he was, who would certainly have stood a chance if they hadn't let him get foundered during training. As to Valerio II from the Corbreuse stable, he wasn't ready yet; he'd had the colic in April. Oh yes, they were keeping that dark, but he was sure of it, on his honor! In the end he advised Nana to choose Hazard, the most defective of the lot, a horse nobody would have anything to do with. Hazard, by jingo—

such superb lines and such an action! That horse was going to astonish the people.

"No," said Nana, "I'm going to put ten louis on Lusignan and five on Boum." La Faloise burst forth at once:

"But, my dear girl, Boum's all rot! Don't choose him! Gasc himself is chucking up backing his own horse. And your Lusignan—never! Why, it's all humbug! By Lamb and Princess—just think! By Lamb and Princess—no, by Jove! All too short in the legs!"

He was choking. Philippe pointed out that, notwithstanding this, Lusignan had won the Prix des Cars and the Grande Poule des Produits. But the other ran on again. What did that prove? Nothing at all. On the contrary, one ought to distrust him. And besides, Gresham rode Lusignan; well then, let them jolly well dry up! Gresham had bad luck; he would never get to the post.

And from one end of the field to the other the discussion raging in Nana's landau seemed to spread and increase. Voices were raised in a scream; the passion for gambling filled the air, set faces glowing and arms waving excitedly, while the bookmakers, perched on their conveyances, shouted odds and jotted down amounts right furiously. Yet these were only the small fry of the betting world; the big bets were made in the weighing enclosure. Here, then, raged the keen contest of people with light purses who risked their five-franc pieces and displayed infinite covetousness for the sake of a possible gain of a few louis. In a word, the battle would be between Spirit and Lusignan. Englishmen, plainly recognizable as such, were strolling about among the various groups. They were quite at home; their faces were fiery with excitement; they were already triumphant. Bramah, a horse belonging to Lord Reading, had gained the Grand Prix the previous year, and this had been a defeat over which hearts were still bleeding. This year it would be terrible if France were beaten anew. Accordingly all the ladies were wild with national pride. The Vandeuvres stable became the rampart of their honor, and Lusignan was pushed and defended and applauded exceedingly. Gaga, Blanche, Caroline and the rest betted on Lusignan. Lucy Stewart abstained from this on account of her son, but it was bruited abroad that Rose Mignon had commissioned Labordette to risk two hundred louis for her. The Tricon, as she sat alone next her driver, waited till the last moment. Very cool, indeed, amid all these disputes, very far above the ever-increasing uproar in which horses' names kept recurring and lively Parisian phrases mingled with guttural English exclamations, she sat listening and taking notes majestically.

"And Nana?" said Georges. "Does no one want her?"

Indeed, nobody was asking for the filly; she was not even being mentioned. The outsider of the Vandeuvres's stud was swamped by Lusignan's popularity. But La Faloise flung his arms up, crying:

"I've an inspiration. I'll bet a louis on Nana."

"Bravo! I bet a couple," said Georges.

"And I three," added Philippe.

And they mounted up and up, bidding against one another good-humoredly and naming prices as though they had been haggling over Nana at an auction.

La Faloise said he would cover her with gold. Besides, everybody was to be made to back her; they would go and pick up backers. But as the three young men were darting off to propagandize, Nana shouted after them:

"You know I don't want to have anything to do with her; I don't for the world! Georges, ten louis on Lusignan and five on Valerio II."

Meanwhile they had started fairly off, and she watched them gaily as they slipped between wheels, ducked under horses' heads and scoured the whole field. The moment they recognized anyone in a carriage they rushed up and urged Nana's claims. And there were great bursts of laughter among the crowd when sometimes they turned back, triumphantly signaling amounts with their fingers, while the young woman stood and waved her sunshade. Nevertheless, they made poor enough work of it. Some men let themselves be persuaded; Steiner, for instance, ventured three louis, for the sight of Nana stirred him. But the women refused point-blank. "Thanks," they said; "to lose for a certainty!" Besides, they were in no hurry to work for the benefit of a dirty wench who was overwhelming them all with her four white horses, her postilions and her outrageous assumption of side. Gaga and Clarisse looked exceedingly prim and asked La Faloise whether he was jolly well making fun of them. When Georges boldly presented himself before the Mignons' carriage Rose turned her head away in the most marked manner and did not answer him. One must be a pretty foul sort to let one's name be given to a horse! Mignon, on the contrary, followed the young man's movements with a look of amusement and declared that the women always brought luck.

"Well?" queried Nana when the young men returned after a prolonged visit to the bookmakers.

"The odds are forty to one against you," said La Faloise.

"What's that? Forty to one!" she cried, astounded. "They were fifty to one against me. What's happened?"

Labordette had just then reappeared. The course was being cleared, and the pealing of a bell announced the first race. Amid the expectant murmur of the bystanders she questioned him about this sudden rise in her value. But he replied evasively; doubtless a demand for her had arisen. She had to content herself with this explanation. Moreover, Labordette announced with a pre-occupied expression that Vandeuvres was coming if he could get away.

The race was ending unnoticed; people were all waiting for the Grand Prix to be run—when a storm burst over the Hippodrome. For some minutes past the sun had disappeared, and a wan twilight had darkened over the multitude. Then the wind rose, and there ensued a sudden deluge. Huge drops, perfect sheets of water, fell. There was a momentary confusion, and people shouted and joked and swore, while those on foot scampered madly off to find refuge under the canvas of the drinking booths. In the carriages the women did their best to shelter themselves, grasping their sunshades with both hands, while the bewildered footmen ran to the hoods. But the shower was already nearly over, and the sun began shining brilliantly through escaping clouds of fine rain. A blue cleft opened in the stormy mass, which was blown off over the Bois, and the skies seemed to smile again and to set the women laughing in a reassured manner, while amid the snorting of horses and the disarray and agitation of the drenched multitude that was shaking itself dry a broad flush of golden light lit up the field, still dripping and glittering with crystal drops.

"Oh, that poor, dear Louiset!" said Nana. "Are you very drenched, my darling?"

The little thing silently allowed his hands to be wiped. The young woman had taken out her handkerchief. Then she dabbed it over Bijou, who was trembling more violently than ever. It would not matter in the least; there were a few drops on the white satin of her dress, but she didn't care a pin for them. The bouquets, refreshed by the rain, glowed like snow, and she smelled one ecstatically, drenching her lips in it as though it were wet with dew.

Meanwhile the burst of rain had suddenly filled the stands. Nana looked at them through her field glasses. At that distance you could only distinguish a compact, confused mass of people, heaped up, as it were, on the ascending ranges of steps, a dark background relieved by light dots which were human faces. The sunlight filtered in through openings near the roof at each end of the stand and detached and illumined portions of the seated multitude, where the ladies' dresses seemed to lose their distinguishing colors. But Nana was especially amused by the ladies whom the shower had driven from the rows of chairs ranged on the sand at the base of the stands. As courtesans were absolutely forbidden to enter the enclosure, she began making exceedingly bitter remarks about all the fashionable women therein assembled. She thought them fearfully dressed up, and such guys!

There was a rumor that the empress was entering the little central stand, a pavilion built like a chalet, with a wide balcony furnished with red armchairs.

"Why, there he is!" said Georges. "I didn't think he was on duty this week."

The stiff and solemn form of the Count Muffat had appeared behind the empress. Thereupon the young men jested and were sorry that Satin wasn't there to go and dig him in the ribs. But Nana's field glass focused the head of the Prince of Scots in the imperial stand.

"Gracious, it's Charles!" she cried.

She thought him stouter than formerly. In eighteen months he had broadened, and with that she entered into particulars. Oh yes, he was a big, solidly built fellow!

All round her in the ladies' carriages they were whispering that the count had given her up. It was quite a long story. Since he had been making himself noticeable, the Tuileries had grown scandalized at the chamberlain's conduct. Whereupon, in order to retain his position, he had recently broken it off with Nana. La Faloise bluntly reported this account of matters to the young woman and, addressing her as his Juliet, again offered himself. But she laughed merrily and remarked:

"It's idiotic! You won't know him; I've only to say, 'Come here,' for him to chuck up everything."

For some seconds past she had been examining the Countess Sabine and Estelle. Daguenet was still at their side. Fauchery had just arrived and was disturbing the people round him in his desire to make his bow to them. He, too, stayed smilingly beside them. After that Nana pointed with disdainful action at the stands and continued:

"Then, you know, those people don't fetch me any longer now! I know 'em too well. You should see 'em behind scenes. No more honor! It's all up with honor! Filth belowstairs, filth abovestairs, filth everywhere. That's why I won't be bothered about 'em!"

And with a comprehensive gesture she took in everybody, from the grooms leading the horses on to the course to the sovereign lady busy chatting with with Charles, a prince and a dirty fellow to boot.

"Bravo, Nana! Awfully smart, Nana!" cried La Faloise enthusiastically.

The tolling of a bell was lost in the wind; the races continued. The Prix d'Ispahan had just been run for and Berlingot, a horse belonging to the Méchain stable, had won. Nana recalled Labordette in order to obtain news of the hundred louis, but he burst out laughing and refused to let her know the horses he had chosen for her, so as not to disturb the luck, as he phrased it. Her money was well placed; she would see that all in good time. And when she confessed her bets to him and told him how she had put ten louis on Lusignan and five on Valerio II, he shrugged his shoulders, as who should say that women did stupid things whatever happened. His action surprised her; she was quite at sea.

Just then the field grew more animated than before. Open-air lunches were arranged in the interval before the Grand Prix. There was much eating and more drinking in all directions, on the grass, on the high seats of the four-in-hands and mail coaches, in the victorias, the broughams, the landaus. There was a universal spread of cold viands and a fine disorderly display of champagne baskets which footmen kept handing down out of the coach boots. Corks came out with feeble pops, which the wind drowned. There was an interchange of jests, and the sound of breaking glasses imparted a note of discord to the high-strung gaiety of the scene. Gaga and Clarisse, together with Blanche, were making a serious repast, for they were eating sandwiches on the carriage rug with which they had been covering their knees. Louise Violaine had got down from her basket carriage and had joined Caroline Héquet. On the turf at their feet some gentlemen had instituted a drinking bar, whither Tatan, Maria, Simonne and the rest came to refresh themselves, while high in air and close at hand bottles were being emptied on Léa de Horn's mail coach, and, with infinite bravado and gesticulation, a whole band were making themselves tipsy in the sunshine, above the heads of the crowd. Soon, however, there was an especially large crowd by Nana's landau. She had risen to her feet and had set herself to pour out glasses of champagne for the men who came to pay her their respects. François, one of the footmen, was passing up the bottles while La Faloise, trying hard to imitate a coster's accents, kept pattering away:

" 'Ere y're, given away, given away! There's some for everybody!"

"Do be still, dear boy," Nana ended by saying. "We look like a set of tumblers."

She thought him very droll and was greatly entertained. At one moment she conceived the idea of sending Georges with a glass of champagne to Rose Mignon, who was affecting temperance. Henri and Charles were bored to distraction; they would have been glad of some champagne, the poor little fellows. But Georges drank the glassful, for he feared an argument. Then Nana remembered Louiset, who was sitting forgotten behind her. Maybe he was thirsty, and she forced him to take a drop or two of wine, which made him cough dreadfully.

" 'Ere y'are, 'ere y'are, gemmen!" La Faloise reiterated. "It don't cost two sous; it don't cost one. We give it away."

But Nana broke in with an exclamation:

"Gracious, there's Bordenave down there! Call him. Oh, run, please, please do!"

It was indeed Bordenave. He was strolling about with his hands behind his back, wearing a hat that looked rusty in the sunlight and a greasy frock coat that was glossy at the seams. It was Bordenave shattered by bankruptcy, yet furious despite all reverses, a Bordenave who flaunted his misery among all the fine folks with the hardihood becoming a man ever ready to take Dame Fortune by storm.

"The deuce, how smart we are!" he said when Nana extended her hand to him like the good-natured wench she was.

Presently, after emptying a glass of champagne, he gave vent to the following profoundly regretful phrase:

"Ah, if only I were a woman! But, by God, that's nothing! Would you like to go on the stage again? I've a notion: I'll hire the Gaîté, and we'll gobble up Paris between us. You certainly owe it me, eh?"

And he lingered, grumbling, beside her, though glad to see her again; for, he said, that confounded Nana was balm to his feelings. Yes, it was balm to them merely to exist in her presence! She was his daughter; she was blood of his blood!

The circle increased, for now La Faloise was filling glasses, and Georges and Philippe were picking up friends. A stealthy impulse was gradually bringing in the whole field. Nana would fling everyone a laughing smile or an amusing phrase. The groups of tipplers were drawing near, and all the champagne scattered over the place was moving in her direction. Soon there was only one noisy crowd, and that was round her landau, where she queened it among outstretched glasses, her yellow hair floating on the breeze and her snowy face bathed in the sunshine. Then by way of a finishing touch and to make the other women, who were mad at her triumph, simply perish of envy, she lifted a brimming glass on high and assumed her old pose as Venus Victrix.

But somebody touched her shoulder, and she was surprised, on turning round, to see Mignon on the seat. She vanished from view an instant and sat herself down beside him, for he had come to communicate a matter of importance. Mignon had everywhere declared that it was ridiculous of his wife to bear Nana a grudge; he thought her attitude stupid and useless.

"Look here, my dear," he whispered. "Be careful: don't madden Rose too much. You understand, I think it best to warn you. Yes, she's got a weapon in store, and as she's never forgiven you the *Petite Duchesse* business——"

"A weapon," said Nana; "what's that blooming well got to do with me?"

"Just listen: it's a letter she must have found in Fauchery's pocket, a letter written to that screw Fauchery by the Countess Muffat. And, by Jove, it's clear the whole story's in it. Well then, Rose wants to send the letter to the count so as to be revenged on him and on you."

"What the deuce has that got to do with me?" Nana repeated. "It's a funny business. So the whole story about Fauchery's in it! Very well, so much the better; the woman has been exasperating me! We shall have a good laugh!"

"No, I don't wish it," Mignon briskly rejoined. "There 'll be a pretty scandal! Besides, we've got nothing to gain."

He paused, fearing lest he should say too much, while she loudly averred that she was most certainly not going to get a chaste woman into trouble.

But when he still insisted on his refusal she looked steadily at him. Doubtless he was afraid of seeing Fauchery again introduced into his family in case he broke with the countess. While avenging her own wrongs, Rose was anxious for that to happen, since she still felt a kindness toward the journalist. And Nana waxed meditative and thought of M. Venot's call, and a plan began to take shape in her brain, while Mignon was doing his best to talk her over.

"Let's suppose that Rose sends the letter, eh? There's food for scandal: you're mixed up in the business, and people say you're the cause of it all. Then to begin with, the count separates from his wife."

"Why should he?" she said. "On the contrary——"

She broke off, in her turn. There was no need for her to think aloud. So in order to be rid of Mignon she looked as though she entered into his view of the case, and when he advised her to give Rose some proof of her submission —to pay her a short visit on the racecourse, for instance, where everybody would see her—she replied that she would see about it, that she would think the matter over.

A commotion caused her to stand up again. On the course the horses were coming in amid a sudden blast of wind. The prize given by the city of Paris had just been run for, and Cornemuse had gained it. Now the Grand Prix was about to be run, and the fever of the crowd increased, and they were tortured by anxiety and stamped and swayed as though they wanted to make the minutes fly faster. At this ultimate moment the betting world was surprised and startled by the continued shortening of the odds against Nana, the outsider of the Vandeuvres stables. Gentlemen kept returning every few moments with a new quotation: the betting was thirty to one against Nana; it was twenty-five to one against Nana, then twenty to one, then fifteen to one. No one could understand it. A filly beaten on all the racecourses! A filly which that same morning no single sportsman would take at fifty to one against! What did this sudden madness betoken? Some laughed at it and spoke of the pretty doing awaiting the duffers who were being taken in by the joke. Others looked serious and uneasy and sniffed out something ugly under it all. Perhaps there was a "deal" in the offing. Allusion was made to well-known stories about the robberies which are winked at on racecourses, but on this occasion the great name of Vandeuvres put a stop to all such accusations, and the skeptics in the end prevailed when they prophesied that Nana would come in last of all.

"Who's riding Nana?" queried La Faloise.

Just then the real Nana reappeared, whereat the gentlemen lent his question an indecent meaning and burst into an uproarious fit of laughter. Nana bowed.

"Price is up," she replied.

And with that the discussion began again. Price was an English celebrity. Why had Vandeuvres got this jockey to come over, seeing that Gresham ordinarily rode Nana? Besides, they were astonished to see him confiding Lusignan to this man Gresham, who, according to La Faloise, never got a place. But all these remarks were swallowed up in jokes, contradictions and an extraordinarily noisy confusion of opinions. In order to kill time the company once more set themselves to drain bottles of champagne. Presently a whisper ran round, and the different groups opened outward. It was Vandeuvres. Nana affected vexation.

"Dear me, you're a nice fellow to come at this time of day! Why, I'm burning to see the enclosure."

"Well, come along then," he said; "there's still time. You'll take a stroll round with me. I just happen to have a permit for a lady about me."

And he led her off on his arm while she enjoyed the jealous glances with which Lucy, Caroline and the others followed her. The young Hugons and La Faloise remained in the landau behind her retreating figure and continued to do the honors of her champagne. She shouted to them that she would return immediately.

But Vandeuvres caught sight of Labordette and called him, and there was an interchange of brief sentences.

"You've scraped everything up?"

"Yes."

"To what amount?"

"Fifteen hundred louis—pretty well all over the place."

As Nana was visibly listening, and that with much curiosity, they held their tongues. Vandeuvres was very nervous, and he had those same clear eyes, shot with little flames, which so frightened her the night he spoke of burning himself and his horses together. As they crossed over the course she spoke low and familiarly.

"I say, do explain this to me. Why are the odds on your filly changing?"

He trembled, and this sentence escaped him:

"Ah, they're talking, are they? What a set those betting men are! When I've got the favorite they all throw themselves upon him, and there's no chance for me. After that, when an outsider's asked for, they give tongue and yell as though they were being skinned."

"You ought to tell me what's going to happen—I've made my bets," she rejoined. "Has Nana a chance?"

A sudden, unreasonable burst of anger overpowered him.

"Won't you deuced well let me be, eh? Every horse has a chance. The odds are shortening because, by Jove, people have taken the horse. Who, I don't know. I should prefer leaving you if you must needs badger me with your idiotic questions."

Such a tone was not germane either to his temperament or his habits, and Nana was rather surprised than wounded. Besides, he was ashamed of himself directly afterward, and when she begged him in a dry voice to behave politely he apologized. For some time past he had suffered from such sudden changes of temper. No one in the Paris of pleasure or of society was ignorant of the fact that he was playing his last trump card today. If his horses did not win, if, moreover, they lost him the considerable sums wagered upon them, it would mean utter disaster and collapse for him, and the bulwark of his credit and the lofty appearance which, though undermined, he still kept up, would come ruining noisily down. Moreover, no one was ignorant of the fact that Nana was the devouring siren who had finished him off, who had been the last to attack his crumbling fortunes and to sweep up what remained of them. Stories were told of wild whims and fancies, of gold scattered to the four winds, of a visit to Baden-Baden, where she had not left him enough to pay the hotel bill, of a handful of diamonds cast on the fire during an evening of drunkenness in order to see whether they would burn like coal. Little by little her great limbs and her coarse, plebeian way of laughing had gained complete mastery over this elegant, degenerate son of an ancient race. At that time he was risking his all, for he had been so utterly overpowered by his taste for ordure and stupidity as to have even lost the vigor of his skepticism. A week before Nana had made him promise her a château on the Norman coast between Havre and Trouville, and now he was staking the very foundations of his honor on the fulfillment of his word. Only she was getting on his nerves, and he could have beaten her, so stupid did he feel her to be.

The man at the gate, not daring to stop the woman hanging on the count's arm, had allowed them to enter the enclosure. Nana, greatly puffed up at the thought that at last she was setting foot on the forbidden ground, put on her best behavior and walked slowly by the ladies seated at the foot of the stands. On ten rows of chairs the toilets were densely massed, and in the blithe open air their bright colors mingled harmoniously. Chairs were scattered about, and as people met one another friendly circles were formed, just as though the company had been sitting under the trees in a public garden. Children had been allowed to go free and were running from group to group, while overhead the stands rose tier above crowded tier and the light-colored dresses therein faded into the delicate shadows of the timberwork. Nana stared at all these ladies. She stared steadily and markedly at the Countess Sabine. After which, as she was passing in front of the imperial stand, the sight of Muffat, looming in all his official stiffness by the side of the empress, made her very merry.

"Oh, how silly he looks!" she said at the top of her voice to Vandeuvres.

She was anxious to pay everything a visit. This small parklike region, with its green lawns and groups of trees, rather charmed her than otherwise. A

vendor of ices had set up a large buffet near the entrance gates, and beneath a
rustic thatched roof a dense throng of people were shouting and gesticulating.
This was the ring. Close by were some empty stalls, and Nana was disappointed at discovering only a gendarme's horse there. Then there was the pad-
dock, a small course some hundred meters in circumference, where a stable
help was walking about Valerio II in his horsecloths. And, oh, what a lot of
men on the graveled sidewalks, all of them with their tickets forming an
orange-colored patch in their bottonholes! And what a continual parade of
people in the open galleries of the grandstands! The scene interested her for
a moment or two, but truly, it was not worth while getting the spleen because
they didn't admit you inside here.

Daguenet and Fauchery passed by and bowed to her. She made them a sign,
and they had to come up. Thereupon she made hay of the weighing-in enclosure. But she broke off abruptly:

"Dear me, there's the Marquis de Chouard! How old he's growing! That
old man's killing himself! Is he still as mad about it as ever?"

Thereupon Daguenet described the old man's last brilliant stroke. The story
dated from the day before yesterday, and no one knew it as yet. After dangling about for months he had bought her daughter Amélie from Gaga for
thirty thousand francs, they said.

"Good gracious! That's a nice business!" cried Nana in disgust. "Go in
for the regular thing, please! But now that I come to think of it, that must be
Lili down there on the grass with a lady in a brougham. I recognized the
face. The old boy will have brought her out."

Vandeuvres was not listening; he was impatient and longed to get rid of her.
But Fauchery having remarked at parting that if she had not seen the bookmakers she had seen nothing, the count was obliged to take her to them in
spite of his obvious repugnance. And she was perfectly happy at once; that
truly was a curious sight, she said!

Amid lawns bordered by young horse-chestnut trees there was a round open
enclosure, where, forming a vast circle under the shadow of the tender green
leaves, a dense line of bookmakers was waiting for betting men, as though
they had been hucksters at a fair. In order to overtop and command the surrounding crowd they had taken up positions on wooden benches, and they
were advertising their prices on the trees beside them. They had an ever-
vigilant glance, and they booked wagers in answer to a single sign, a mere
wink, so rapidly that certain curious onlookers watched them openmouthed,
without being able to understand it all. Confusion reigned; prices were shouted,
and any unexpected change in a quotation was received with something like
tumult. Occasionally scouts entered the place at a run and redoubled the uproar as they stopped at the entrance to the rotunda and, at the tops of their
voices, announced departures and arrivals. In this place, where the gambling
fever was pulsing in the sunshine, such announcements were sure to raise a
prolonged muttering sound.

"They *are* funny!" murmured Nana, greatly entertained.

"Their features look as if they had been put on the wrong way. Just you see that big fellow there; I shouldn't care to meet him all alone in the middle of a wood."

But Vandeuvres pointed her out a bookmaker, once a shopman in a fancy repository, who had made three million francs in two years. He was slight of build, delicate and fair, and people all round him treated him with great respect. They smiled when they addressed him, while others took up positions close by in order to catch a glimpse of him.

They were at length leaving the ring when Vandeuvres nodded slightly to another bookmaker, who thereupon ventured to call him. It was one of his former coachmen, an enormous fellow with the shoulders of an ox and a high color. Now that he was trying his fortunes at race meetings on the strength of some mysteriously obtained capital, the count was doing his utmost to push him, confiding to him his secret bets and treating him on all occasions as a servant to whom one shows one's true character. Yet despite this protection, the man had in rapid succession lost very heavy sums, and today he, too, was playing his last card. There was blood in his eyes; he looked fit to drop with apoplexy.

"Well, Maréchal," queried the count in the lowest of voices, "to what amount have you laid odds?"

"To five thousand louis, Monsieur le Comte," replied the bookmaker, likewise lowering his voice. "A pretty job, eh? I'll confess to you that I've increased the odds; I've made it three to one."

Vandeuvres looked very much put out.

"No, no, I don't want you to do that. Put it at two to one again directly. I shan't tell you any more, Maréchal."

"Oh, how can it hurt, Monsieur le Comte, at this time o' day?" rejoined the other with the humble smile befitting an accomplice. "I had to attract the people so as to lay your two thousand louis."

At this Vandeuvres silenced him. But as he was going off Maréchal remembered something and was sorry he had not questioned him about the shortening of the odds on the filly. It would be a nice business for him if the filly stood a chance, seeing that he had just laid fifty to one about her in two hundreds.

Nana, though she did not understand a word of what the count was whispering, dared not, however, ask for new explanations. He seemed more nervous than before and abruptly handed her over to Labordette, whom they came upon in front of the weighing-in room.

"You'll take her back," he said. "I've got something on hand. Au revoir!"

And he entered the room, which was narrow and low-pitched and half filled with a great pair of scales. It was like a waiting room in a suburban station, and Nana was again hugely disillusioned, for she had been picturing to herself something on a very vast scale, a monumental machine, in fact, for weighing horses. Dear me, they only weighed the jockeys! Then it wasn't worth while making such a fuss with their weighing! In the scale a jockey with an idiotic expression was waiting, harness on knee, till a stout man in a frock coat should have done verifying his weight. At the door a stable help was holding a horse,

Cosinus, round which a silent and deeply interested throng was clustering.

The course was about to be cleared. Labordette hurried Nana but retraced his steps in order to show her a little man talking with Vandeuvres at some distance from the rest.

"Dear me, there's Price!" he said.

"Ah yes, the man who's mounting me," she murmured laughingly.

And she declared him to be exquisitely ugly. All jockeys struck her as looking idiotic, doubtless, she said, because they were prevented from growing bigger. This particular jockey was a man of forty, and with his long, thin, deeply furrowed, hard, dead countenance, he looked like an old shriveled-up child. His body was knotty and so reduced in size that his blue jacket with its white sleeves looked as if it had been thrown over a lay figure.

"No," she resumed as she walked away, "he would never make me very happy, you know."

A mob of people were still crowding the course, the turf of which had been wet and trampled on till it had grown black. In front of the two telegraphs, which hung very high up on their cast-iron pillars, the crowd were jostling together with upturned faces, uproariously greeting the numbers of the different horses as an electric wire in connection with the weighing room made them appear. Gentlemen were pointing at programs: Pichenette had been scratched by his owner, and this caused some noise. However, Nana did not do more than cross over the course on Labordette's arm. The bell hanging on the flagstaff was ringing persistently to warn people to leave the course.

"Ah, my little dears," she said as she got up into her landau again, "their enclosure's all humbug!"

She was welcomed with acclamation; people around her clapped their hands. "Bravo, Nana! Nana's ours again!"

What idiots they were, to be sure! Did they think she was the sort to cut old friends? She had come back just at the auspicious moment. Now then, 'tenshun! The race was beginning! And the champagne was accordingly forgotten, and everyone left off drinking.

But Nana was astonished to find Gaga in her carriage, sitting with Bijou and Louiset on her knees. Gaga had indeed decided on this course of action in order to be near La Faloise, but she told Nana that she had been anxious to kiss Baby. She adored children.

"By the by, what about Lili?" asked Nana. "That's certainly she over there in that old fellow's brougham. They've just told me something very nice!"

Gaga had adopted a lachrymose expression.

"My dear, it's made me ill," she said dolorously. "Yesterday I had to keep my bed, I cried so, and today I didn't think I should be able to come. You know what my opinions were, don't you? I didn't desire that kind of thing at all. I had her educated in a convent with a view to a good marriage. And then to think of the strict advice she had and the constant watching! Well, my dear, it was she who wished it. We had such a scene—tears—disagreeable speeches! It even got to such a point that I caught her a box on the ear. She was too much bored by existence, she said; she wanted to get out of it. By and by, when she began to say, ' 'Tisn't you, after all, who've got the right to prevent me,' I said to her: 'you're a miserable wretch; you're bringing dishonor upon us. Begone!' And it was done. I consented to arrange about it. But my last hope's blooming well blasted, and, oh, I used to dream about such nice things!"

The noise of a quarrel caused them to rise. It was Georges in the act of defending Vandeuvres against certain vague rumors which were circulating among the various groups.

"Why should you say that he's laying off his own horse?" the young man was exclaiming. "Yesterday in the Salon des Courses he took the odds on Lusignan for a thousand louis."

"Yes, I was there," said Philippe in affirmation of this. "And he didn't put a single louis on Nana. If the betting's ten to one against Nana he's got nothing to win there. It's absurd to imagine people are so calculating. Where would his interest come in?"

Labordette was listening with a quiet expression. Shrugging his shoulders, he said:

"Oh, leave them alone; they must have their say. The count has again laid at least as much as five hundred louis on Lusignan, and if he's wanted Nana to run to a hundred louis it's because an owner ought always to look as if he believes in his horses."

"Oh, bosh! What the deuce does that matter to us?" shouted La Faloise with a wave of his arms. "Spirit's going to win! Down with France—bravo, England!"

A long shiver ran through the crowd, while a fresh peal from the bell announced the arrival of the horses upon the racecourse. At this Nana got up and stood on one of the seats of her carriage so as to obtain a better view, and in so doing she trampled the bouquets of roses and myosotis underfoot. With a sweeping glance she took in the wide, vast horizon. At this last feverish moment the course was empty and closed by gray barriers, between the posts of which stood a line of policemen. The strip of grass which lay muddy in front of her grew brighter as it stretched away and turned into a tender green carpet in the distance. In the middle landscape, as she lowered her eyes, she saw the field swarming with vast numbers of people, some on tiptoe, others perched on carriages, and all heaving and jostling in sudden passionate excitement.

Horses were neighing; tent canvases flapped, while equestrians urged their hacks forward amid a crowd of pedestrians rushing to get places along the barriers. When Nana turned in the direction of the stands on the other side the faces seemed diminished, and the dense masses of heads were only a confused and motley array, filling gangways, steps and terraces and looming in deep, dark, serried lines against the sky. And beyond these again she overlooked the plain surrounding the course. Behind the ivy-clad mill to the right, meadows, dotted over with great patches of umbrageous wood, stretched away into the distance, while opposite to her, as far as the Seine flowing at the foot of a hill, the avenues of the park intersected one another, filled at that moment with long, motionless files of waiting carriages; and in the direction of Boulogne, on the left, the landscape widened anew and opened out toward the blue distances of Meudon through an avenue of paulownias, whose rosy, leafless tops were one stain of brilliant lake color. People were still arriving, and a long procession of human ants kept coming along the narrow ribbon of road which crossed the distance, while very far away, on the Paris side, the nonpaying public, herding like sheep among the wood, loomed in a moving line of little dark spots under the trees on the skirts of the Bois.

Suddenly a cheering influence warmed the hundred thousand souls who covered this part of the plain like insects swarming madly under the vast expanse of heaven. The sun, which had been hidden for about a quarter of an hour, made his appearance again and shone out amid a perfect sea of light. And everything flamed afresh: the women's sunshades turned into countless golden targets above the heads of the crowd. The sun was applauded, saluted with bursts of laughter. And people stretched their arms out as though to brush apart the clouds.

Meanwhile a solitary police officer advanced down the middle of the deserted racecourse, while higher up, on the left, a man appeared with a red flag in his hand.

"It's the starter, the Baron de Mauriac," said Labordette in reply to a question from Nana. All round the young woman exclamations were bursting from the men who were pressing to her very carriage step. They kept up a disconnected conversation, jerking out phrases under the immediate influence of passing impressions. Indeed, Philippe and Georges, Bordenave and La Faloise, could not be quiet.

"Don't shove! Let me see! Ah, the judge is getting into his box. D'you say it's Monsieur de Souvigny? You must have good eyesight—eh?—to be able to tell what half a head is out of a fakement like that! Do hold your tongue—the banner's going up. Here they are—'tenshun! Cosinus is the first!"

A red and yellow banner was flapping in mid-air at the top of a mast. The horses came on the course one by one; they were led by stableboys, and the jockeys were sitting idle-handed in the saddles, the sunlight making them look like bright dabs of color. After Cosinus appeared Hazard and Boum. Presently a murmur of approval greeted Spirit, a magnificent big brown bay, the harsh citron color and black of whose jockey were cheerlessly Britannic. Valerio II scored a success as he came in; he was small and very lively, and his colors were soft green bordered with pink. The two Vandeuvres horses were slow to make their appearance, but at last, in Frangipane's rear, the blue and white showed themselves. But Lusignan, a very dark bay of irreproachable shape, was almost forgotten amid the astonishment caused by Nana. People had not seen her looking like this before, for now the sudden sunlight was dyeing the chestnut filly the brilliant color of a girl's red-gold hair. She was shining in the light like a new gold coin; her chest was deep; her head and neck tapered lightly from the delicate, high-strung line of her long back.

"Gracious, she's got my hair!" cried Nana in an ecstasy. "You bet you know I'm proud of it!"

The men clambered up on the landau, and Bordenave narrowly escaped putting his foot on Louiset, whom his mother had forgotten. He took him up with an outburst of paternal grumbling and hoisted him on his shoulder, muttering at the same time:

"The poor little brat, he must be in it too! Wait a bit, I'll show you Mamma. Eh? Look at Mummy out there."

And as Bijou was scratching his legs, he took charge of him, too, while Nana, rejoicing in the brute that bore her name, glanced round at the other women to see how they took it. They were all raging madly. Just then on the summit of her cab the Tricon, who had not moved till that moment, began waving her hand and giving her bookmaker her orders above the heads of the crowd. Her instinct had at last prompted her; she was backing Nana.

La Faloise meanwhile was making an insufferable noise. He was getting wiid over Frangipane.

"I've an inspiration," he kept shouting. "Just look at Frangipane. What an action, eh? I back Frangipane at eight to one. Who'll take me?"

"Do keep quiet now," said Labordette at last. "You'll be sorry for it if you do."

"Frangipane's a screw," Philippe declared. "He's been utterly blown upon already. You'll see the canter."

The horses had gone up to the right, and they now started for the preliminary canter, passing in loose order before the stands. Thereupon there was a passionate fresh burst of talk, and people all spoke at once.

"Lusignan's too long in the back, but he's very fit. Not a cent, I tell you, on Valerio II; he's nervous—gallops with his head up—it's a bad sign. Jove! Burne's riding Spirit. I tell you, he's got no shoulders. A well-made shoulder —that's the whole secret. No, decidedly, Spirit's too quiet. Now listen, Nana, I saw her after the Grande Poule des Produits, and she was dripping and draggled, and her sides were trembling like one o'clock. I lay twenty louis she isn't placed! Oh, shut up! He's boring us with his Frangipane. There's no time to make a bet now; there, they're off!"

Almost in tears, La Faloise was struggling to find a bookmaker. He had to be reasoned with. Everyone craned forward, but the first go-off was bad, the starter, who looked in the distance like a slim dash of blackness, not having lowered his flag. The horses came back to their places after galloping a moment or two. There were two more false starts. At length the starter got the horses together and sent them away with such address as to elicit shouts of applause.

"Splendid! No, it was mere chance! Never mind—it's done it!"

The outcries were smothered by the anxiety which tortured every breast. The betting stopped now, and the game was being played on the vast course itself. Silence reigned at the outset, as though everyone were holding his breath. White faces and trembling forms were stretched forward in all directions. At first Hazard and Cosinus made the running at the head of the rest; Valerio II followed close by, and the field came on in a confused mass behind. When they passed in front of the stands, thundering over the ground in their course like a sudden stormwind, the mass was already some fourteen lengths in extent. Frangipane was last, and Nana was slightly behind Lusignan and Spirit.

"Egad!" muttered Labordette, "how the Englishman is pulling it off out there!"

The whole carriageload again burst out with phrases and exclamations. Everyone rose on tiptoe and followed the bright splashes of color which were the jockeys as they rushed through the sunlight.

At the rise Valerio II took the lead, while Cosinus and Hazard lost ground, and Lusignan and Spirit were running neck and neck with Nana still behind them.

"By jingo, the Englishman's gained! It's palpable!" said Bordenave. "Lusignan's in difficulties, and Valerio II can't stay."

"Well, it will be a pretty biz if the Englishman wins!" cried Philippe in an access of patriotic grief.

A feeling of anguish was beginning to choke all that crowded multitude. Another defeat! And with that a strange ardent prayer, which was almost religious, went up for Lusignan, while people heaped abuse on Spirit and his dismal mute of a jockey. Among the crowd scattered over the grass the wind of excitement put up whole groups of people and set their boot soles flashing in air as they ran. Horsemen crossed the green at a furious gallop. And Nana, who was slowly revolving on her own axis, saw beneath her a surging waste of beasts and men, a sea of heads swayed and stirred all round the course by the whirlwind of the race, which clove the horizon with the bright lightning flash of the jockeys. She had been following their movement from behind while the cruppers sped away and the legs seemed to grow longer as they raced and then diminished till they looked slender as strands of hair. Now the horses were running at the end of the course, and she caught a side view of them looking minute and delicate of outline against the green distances of the Bois. Then suddenly they vanished behind a great clump of trees growing in the middle of the Hippodrome.

"Don't talk about it!" cried Georges, who was still full of hope. "It isn't over yet. The Englishman's touched."

But La Faloise was again seized with contempt for his country and grew positively outrageous in his applause of Spirit. Bravo! That was right! France needed it! Spirit first and Frangipane second—that would be a nasty one for his native land! He exasperated Labordette, who threatened seriously to throw him off the carriage.

"Let's see how many minutes they'll be about it," said Bordenave peaceably, for though holding up Louiset, he had taken out his watch.

One after the other the horses reappeared from behind the clump of trees. There was stupefaction; a long murmur arose among the crowd. Valerio II was still leading, but Spirit was gaining on him, and behind him Lusignan had slackened while another horse was taking his place. People could not make this out all at once; they were confused about the colors. Then there was a burst of exclamations.

"But it's Nana! Nana? Get along! I tell you Lusignan hasn't budged. Dear me, yes, it's Nana. You can certainly recognize her by her golden color. D'you see her now? She's blazing away. Bravo, Nana! What a ripper she is! Bah, it doesn't matter a bit: she's making the running for Lusignan!"

For some seconds this was everybody's opinion. But little by little the filly kept gaining and gaining, spurting hard all the while. Thereupon a vast wave of feeling passed over the crowd, and the tail of horses in the rear ceased to interest. A supreme struggle was beginning between Spirit, Nana, Lusignan and Valerio II. They were pointed out; people estimated what ground they had gained or lost in disconnected, gasping phrases. And Nana, who had mounted up on the coach box, as though some power had lifted her thither, stood white and trembling and so deeply moved as not to be able to speak. At her side Labordette smiled as of old.

"The Englishman's in trouble, eh?" said Philippe joyously. "He's going badly."

"In any case, it's all up with Lusignan," shouted La Faloise. "Valerio II is coming forward. Look, there they are all four together."

The same phrase was in every mouth.

"What a rush, my dears! By God, what a rush!"

The squad of horses was now passing in front of them like a flash of lightning. Their approach was perceptible—the breath of it was as a distant muttering which increased at every second. The whole crowd had thrown themselves impetuously against the barriers, and a deep clamor issued from innumerable chests before the advance of the horses and drew nearer and nearer like the sound of a foaming tide. It was the last fierce outburst of colossal partisanship; a hundred thousand spectators were possessed by a single passion, burning with the same gambler's lust, as they gazed after the beasts, whose galloping feet were sweeping millions with them. The crowd pushed and crushed—fists were clenched; people gaped, openmouthed; every man was fighting for himself; every man with voice and gesture was madly speeding the horse of his choice. And the cry of all this multitude, a wild beast's cry despite the garb of civilization, grew ever more distinct:

"Here they come! Here they come! Here they come!"

But Nana was still gaining ground, and now Valerio II was distanced, and she was heading the race, with Spirit two or three necks behind. The rolling thunder of voices had increased. They were coming in; a storm of oaths greeted them from the landau.

"Gee up, Lusignan, you great coward! The Englishman's stunning! Do it again, old boy; do it again! Oh, that Valerio! It's sickening! Oh, the carcass! My ten louis damned well lost! Nana's the only one! Bravo, Nana! Bravo!"

And without being aware of it Nana, upon her seat, had begun jerking her hips and waist as though she were racing herself. She kept striking her side —she fancied it was a help to the filly. With each stroke she sighed with fatigue and said in low, anguished tones:

"Go it, go it!"

Then a splendid sight was witnessed. Price, rising in his stirrups and brandishing his whip, flogged Nana with an arm of iron. The old shriveled-up child with his long, hard, dead face seemed to breath flame. And in a fit of furious audacity and triumphant will he put his heart into the filly, held her up, lifted her forward, drenched in foam, with eyes of blood. The whole rush of horses passed with a roar of thunder: it took away people's breaths; it swept the air with it while the judge sat frigidly waiting, his eye adjusted to its task. Then there was an immense re-echoing burst of acclamation. With a supreme effort Price had just flung Nana past the post, thus beating Spirit by a head.

There was an uproar as of a rising tide. "Nana! Nana! Nana!" The cry rolled up and swelled with the violence of a tempest, till little by little it filled the distance, the depths of the Bois as far as Mont Valérien, the meadows of Longchamps and the Plaine de Boulogne. In all parts of the field the wildest enthusiasm declared itself. "Vive Nana! Vive la France! Down with England!" The women waved their sunshades; men leaped and spun round, vociferating as they did so, while others with shouts of nervous laughter threw their hats in the air. And from the other side of the course the enclosure made answer; the people on the stands were stirred, though nothing was distinctly visible save a tremulous motion of the air, as though an invisible flame were burning in a brazier above the living mass of gesticulating arms and little wildly moving faces, where the eyes and gaping mouths looked like black dots. The noise did not cease but swelled up and recommenced in the recesses of faraway avenues and among the people encamped under the trees, till it spread on and on and attained its climax in the imperial stand, where the empress herself had applauded. "Nana! Nana! Nana!" The cry rose heavenward in the glorious sunlight, whose golden rain beat fiercely on the dizzy heads of the multitude.

Then Nana, looming large on the seat of her landau, fancied that it was she whom they were applauding. For a moment or two she had stood devoid of motion, stupefied by her triumph, gazing at the course as it was invaded by so dense a flood of people that the turf became invisible beneath the sea of black hats. By and by, when this crowd had become somewhat less disorderly and a lane had been formed as far as the exit and Nana was again applauded as she went off with Price hanging lifelessly and vacantly over her neck, she smacked her thigh energetically, lost all self-possession, triumphed in crude phrases:

"Oh, by God, it's me; it's me. Oh, by God, what luck!"

And, scarce knowing how to give expression to her overwhelming joy, she hugged and kissed Louiset, whom she now discovered high in the air on Bordenave's shoulder.

"Three minutes and fourteen seconds," said the latter as he put his watch back in his pocket.

Nana kept hearing her name; the whole plain was echoing it back to her. Her people were applauding her while she towered above them in the sunlight, in the splendor of her starry hair and white-and-sky-blue dress. Labordette, as he made off, had just announced to her a gain of two thousand louis, for he had put her fifty on Nana at forty to one. But the money stirred her less than this unforeseen victory, the fame of which made her queen of Paris. All the other ladies were losers. With a raging movement Rose Mignon had snapped her sunshade, and Caroline Héquet and Clarisse and Simonne—nay, Lucy Stewart herself, despite the presence of her son—were swearing low in their exasperation at that great wench's luck, while the Tricon, who had made the sign of the cross at both start and finish, straightened up her tall form above them, went into an ecstasy over her intuition and damned Nana admiringly as became an experienced matron.

Meanwhile round the landau the crush of men increased. The band of Nana's immediate followers had made a fierce uproar, and now Georges, choking with emotion, continued shouting all by himself in breaking tones. As the champagne had given out, Philippe, taking the footmen with him, had run to the wine bars. Nana's court was growing and growing, and her present triumph caused many loiterers to join her. Indeed, that movement which had made her carriage a center of attraction to the whole field was now ending in an apotheosis, and Queen Venus was enthroned amid suddenly maddened subjects. Bordenave, behind her, was muttering oaths, for he yearned to her as a father. Steiner himself had been reconquered—he had deserted Simonne and had hoisted himself upon one of Nana's carriage steps. When the champagne had arrived, when she lifted her brimming glass, such applause burst forth, and "Nana! Nana! Nana!" was so loudly repeated that the crowd looked round in astonishment for the filly, nor could any tell whether it was the horse or the woman that filled all hearts.

While this was going on Mignon came hastening up in defiance of Rose's terrible frown. That confounded girl simply maddened him, and he wanted to kiss her. Then after imprinting a paternal salute on both her cheeks:

"What bothers me," he said, "is that now Rose is certainly going to send the letter. She's raging, too, fearfully."

"So much the better! It'll do my business for me!" Nana let slip.

But noting his utter astonishment, she hastily continued:

"No, no, what am I saying? Indeed, I don't rightly know what I'm saying now! I'm drunk."

And drunk, indeed, drunk with joy, drunk with sunshine, she still raised her glass on high and applauded herself.

"To Nana! To Nana!" she cried amid a redoubled uproar of laughter and bravoes, which little by little overspread the whole Hippodrome.

The races were ending, and the Prix Vaublanc was run for. Carriages began driving off one by one. Meanwhile, amid much disputing, the name of Vandeuvres was again mentioned. It was quite evident now: for two years past Vandeuvres had been preparing his final stroke and had accordingly told Gresham to hold Nana in, while he had only brought Lusignan forward in order to make play for the filly. The losers were vexed; the winners shrugged their shoulders. After all, wasn't the thing permissible? An owner was free to run his stud in his own way. Many others had done as he had! In fact, the majority thought Vandeuvres had displayed great skill in raking in all he could get about Nana through the agency of friends, a course of action which explained the sudden shortening of the odds. People spoke of his having laid two thousand louis on the horse, which, supposing the odds to be thirty to one against, gave him twelve hundred thousand francs, an amount so vast as to inspire respect and to excuse everything.

But other rumors of a very serious nature were being whispered about: they issued in the first instance from the enclosure, and the men who returned thence were full of exact particulars. Voices were raised; an atrocious scandal began to be openly canvassed. That poor fellow Vandeuvres was done for; he had spoiled his splendid hit with a piece of flat stupidity, an idiotic robbery, for he had commissioned Maréchal, a shady bookmaker, to lay two thousand louis on his account against Lusignan, in order thereby to get back his thousand and odd openly wagered louis. It was a miserable business, and it proved to be the last rift necessary to the utter breakup of his fortune. The bookmaker being thus warned that the favorite would not win, had realized some sixty thousand francs over the horse. Only Labordette, for lack of exact and detailed instructions, had just then gone to him to put two hundred louis on Nana, which the bookmaker, in his ignorance of the stroke actually intended, was still quoting at fifty to one against. Cleared of one hundred thousand francs over the filly and a loser to the tune of forty thousand, Maréchal, who felt the world crumbling under his feet, had suddenly divined the situation when he saw the count and Labordette talking together in front of the enclosure just after the race was over. Furious, as became an ex-coachman of the count's, and brutally frank as only a cheated man can be, he had just made a frightful scene in public, had told the whole story in atrocious terms and had thrown everyone into angry excitement. It was further stated that the stewards were about to meet.

Nana, whom Philippe and Georges were whisperingly putting in possession of the facts, gave vent to a series of reflections and yet ceased not to laugh and drink. After all, it was quite likely; she remembered such things, and then that Maréchal had a dirty, hangdog look. Nevertheless, she was still rather doubtful when Labordette appeared. He was very white.

"Well?" she asked in a low voice.

"Bloody well smashed up!" he replied simply.

And he shrugged his shoulders. That Vandeuvres was a mere child! She made a bored little gesture.

That evening at the Bal Mabille Nana obtained a colossal success. When toward ten o'clock she made her appearance, the uproar was already formidable. That classic night of madness had brought together all that was young and pleasure loving, and now this smart world was wallowing in the coarseness and imbecility of the servants' hall. There was a fierce crush under the festoons of gas lamps, and men in evening coats and women in outrageous low-necked old toilets, which they did not mind soiling, were howling and surging to and fro under the maddening influence of a vast drunken fit. At a distance of thirty paces the brass instruments of the orchestra were inaudible. Nobody was dancing. Stupid witticisms, repeated no one knew why, were going the round of the various groups. People were straining after wit without succeeding in being funny. Seven women, imprisoned in the cloakroom, were crying to be set free. A shallot had been found, put up to auction and knocked down at two louis. Just then Nana arrived, still wearing her blue-and-white racecourse costume, and amid a thunder of applause the shallot was presented to her. People caught hold of her in her own despite, and three gentlemen bore her triumphantly into the garden, across ruined glassplots and ravaged masses of greenery. As the bandstand presented an obstacle to her advance, it was taken by storm, and chairs and music stands were smashed. A paternal police organized the disorder.

It was only on Tuesday that Nana recovered from the excitements of victory. That morning she was chatting with Mme Lerat, the old lady having come in to bring her news of Louiset, whom the open air had upset. A long story, which was occupying the attention of all Paris, interested her beyond measure. Vandeuvres, after being warned off all racecourses and posted at the Cercle Imperial on the very evening after the disaster, had set fire to his stable on the morrow and had burned himself and his horses to death.

"He certainly told me he was going to," the young woman kept saying. "That man was a regular maniac! Oh, how they did frighten me when they told me about it yesterday evening! You see, he might easily have murdered me some fine night. And besides, oughtn't he to have given me a hint about his horse? I should at any rate have made my fortune! He said to Labordette that if I knew about the matter I would immediately inform my hairdresser and a whole lot of other men. How polite, eh? Oh dear, no, I certainly can't grieve much for him."

After some reflection she had grown very angry. Just then Labordette came in; he had seen about her bets and was now the bearer of some forty thousand francs. This only added to her bad temper, for she ought to have gained a million. Labordette, who during the whole of this episode had been pretending entire innocence, abandoned Vandeuvres in decisive terms. Those old families, he opined, were worn out and apt to make a stupid ending.

"Oh dear no!" said Nana. "It isn't stupid to burn oneself in one's stable as he did. For my part, I think he made a dashing finish; but, oh, you know, I'm not defending that story about him and Maréchal. It's too silly. Just to think that Blanche has had the cheek to want to lay the blame of it on me! I said to her: 'Did I tell him to steal?' Don't you think one can ask a man for money without urging him to commit crime? If he had said to me, 'I've got nothing left,' I should have said to him, 'All right, let's part.' And the matter wouldn't have gone further."

"Just so," said the aunt gravely. "When men are obstinate about a thing, so much the worse for them!"

"But as to the merry little finish up, oh, that was awfully smart!" continued Nana. "It appears to have been terrible enough to give you the shudders! He sent everybody away and boxed himself up in the place with a lot of petro-leum. And it blazed! You should have seen it! Just think, a great big affair, almost all made of wood and stuffed with hay and straw! The flames simply towered up, and the finest part of the business was that the horses didn't want to be roasted. They could be heard plunging, throwing themselves against the doors, crying aloud just like human beings. Yes, people haven't got rid of the horror of it yet."

Labordette let a low, incredulous whistle escape him. For his part, he did not believe in the death of Vandeuvres. Somebody had sworn he had seen him escaping through a window. He had set fire to his stable in a fit of aberration, but when it had begun to grow too warm it must have sobered him. A man so besotted about the women and so utterly worn out could not possibly die so pluckily.

Nana listened in her disillusionment and could only remark:

"Oh, the poor wretch, it was so beautiful!"

CHAPTER XII

Toward one in the morning, in the great bed of the Venice point draperies, Nana and the count lay still awake. He had returned to her that evening after a three days' sulking fit. The room, which was dimly illumined by a lamp, seemed to slumber amid a warm, damp odor of love, while the furniture, with its white lacquer and silver incrustations, loomed vague and wan through the gloom. A curtain had been drawn to, so that the bed lay flooded with shadow. A sigh became audible; then a kiss broke the silence, and Nana, slipping off the coverlet, sat for a moment or two, barelegged, on the edge of the bed. The count let his head fall back on the pillow and remained in darkness.

"Dearest, you believe in the good God, don't you?" she queried after some moments' reflection. Her face was serious; she had been overcome by pious terrors on quitting her lover's arms.

Since morning, indeed, she had been complaining of feeling uncomfortable, and all her stupid notions, as she phrased it, notions about death and hell, were secretly torturing her. From time to time she had nights such as these, during which childish fears and atrocious fancies would thrill her with waking nightmares. She continued:

"I say, d'you think I shall go to heaven?"

And with that she shivered, while the count, in his surprise at her putting such singular questions at such a moment, felt his old religious remorse returning upon him. Then with her chemise slipping from her shoulders and her hair unpinned, she again threw herself upon his breast, sobbing and clinging to him as she did so.

"I'm afraid of dying! I'm afraid of dying!" He had all the trouble in the world to disengage himself. Indeed, he was himself afraid of giving in to the sudden madness of this woman clinging to his body in her dread of the Invisible. Such dread is contagious, and he reasoned with her. Her conduct was perfect—she had only to conduct herself well in order one day to merit pardon. But she shook her head. Doubtless she was doing no one any harm; nay, she was even in the constant habit of wearing a medal of the Virgin, which she showed to him as it hung by a red thread between her breasts.

Only it had been foreordained that all unmarried women who held conversation with men would go to hell. Scraps of her catechism recurred to her remembrance. Ah, if one only knew for certain, but, alas, one was sure of nothing; nobody ever brought back any information, and then, truly, it would be stupid to bother oneself about things if the priests were talking foolishness all the time. Nevertheless, she religiously kissed her medal, which was still warm from contact with her skin, as though by way of charm against death, the idea of which filled her with icy horror. Muffat was obliged to accompany her into the dressing room, for she shook at the idea of being alone there for one moment, even though she had left the door open. When he had lain down again she still roamed about the room, visiting its several corners and starting and shivering at the slightest noise. A mirror stopped her, and as of old she lapsed into obvious contemplation of her nakedness. But the sight of her breast, her waist and her thighs only doubled her terror, and she ended by feeling with both hands very slowly over the bones of her face.

"You're ugly when you're dead," she said in deliberate tones.

And she pressed her cheeks, enlarging her eyes and pushing down her jaw, in order to see how she would look. Thus disfigured, she turned toward the count.

"Do look! My head 'll be quite small, it will!"

At this he grew vexed.

"You're mad; come to bed!"

He fancied he saw her in a grave, emaciated by a century of sleep, and he joined his hands and stammered a prayer. It was some time ago that the religious sense had reconquered him, and now his daily access of faith had again assumed the apoplectic intensity which was wont to leave him well-nigh stunned. The joints of his fingers used to crack, and he would repeat without cease these words only: "My God, my God, my God!" It was the cry of his impotence, the cry of that sin against which, though his damnation was certain, he felt powerless to strive. When Nana returned she found him hidden beneath the bedclothes; he was haggard; he had dug his nails into his bosom, and his eyes stared upward as though in search of heaven. And with that she started to weep again. Then they both embraced, and their teeth chattered they knew not why, as the same imbecile obsession overmastered them. They had already passed a similar night, but on this occasion the thing was utterly idiotic, as Nana declared when she ceased to be frightened. She suspected something, and this caused her to question the count in a prudent sort of way. It might be that Rose Mignon had sent the famous letter! But that was not the case; it was sheer fright, nothing more, for he was still ignorant whether he was a cuckold or no.

Two days later, after a fresh disappearance, Muffat presented himself in the morning, a time of day at which he never came. He was livid; his eyes were red and his whole man still shaken by a great internal struggle. But Zoé, being scared herself, did not notice his troubled state. She had run to meet him and now began crying:

"Oh, monsieur, do come in! Madame nearly died yesterday evening!"

And when he asked for particulars:

"Something it's impossible to believe has happened—a miscarriage, monsieur."

Nana had been in the family way for the past three months. For long she had simply thought herself out of sorts, and Dr Boutarel had himself been in doubt. But when afterward he made her a decisive announcement, she felt so bored thereby that she did all she possibly could to disguise her condition. Her nervous terrors, her dark humors, sprang to some extent from this unfortunate state of things, the secret of which she kept very shamefacedly, as became a courtesan mother who is obliged to conceal her plight. The thing struck her as a ridiculous accident, which made her appear small in her own eyes and would, had it been known, have led people to chaff her.

"A poor joke, eh?" she said. "Bad luck, too, certainly."

She was necessarily very sharp set when she thought her last hour had come. There was no end to her surprise, too; her sexual economy seemed to her to have got out of order; it produced children then even when one did not want them and when one employed it for quite other purposes! Nature drove her to exasperation; this appearance of serious motherhood in a career of pleasure, this gift of life amid all the deaths she was spreading around, exasperated her. Why could one not dispose of oneself as fancy dictated, without all this fuss? And whence had this brat come? She could not even suggest a father. Ah, dear heaven, the man who made him would have a splendid notion had he kept him in his own hands, for nobody asked for him; he was in everybody's way, and he would certainly not have much happiness in life!

Meanwhile Zoé described the catastrophe.

"Madame was seized with colic toward four o'clock. When she didn't come back out of the dressing room I went in and found her lying stretched on the floor in a faint. Yes, monsieur, on the floor in a pool of blood, as though she had been murdered. Then I understood, you see. I was furious; Madame might quite well have confided her trouble to me. As it happened, Monsieur Georges was there, and he helped me to lift her up, and directly a miscarriage was mentioned he felt ill in his turn! Oh, it's true I've had the hump since yesterday!"

In fact, the house seemed utterly upset. All the servants were galloping upstairs, downstairs and through the rooms. Georges had passed the night on an armchair in the drawing room. It was he who had announced the news to Madame's friends at that hour of the evening when Madame was in the habit of receiving. He had still been very pale, and he had told his story very feelingly, and as though stupefied. Steiner, La Faloise, Philippe and others, besides, had presented themselves, and at the end of the lad's first phrase they burst into exclamations. The thing was impossible! It must be a farce! After which they grew serious and gazed with an embarrassed expression at her bedroom door. They shook their heads; it was no laughing matter.

Till midnight a dozen gentlemen had stood talking in low voices in front of the fireplace. All were friends; all were deeply exercised by the same idea of paternity. They seemed to be mutually excusing themselves, and they looked as confused as if they had done something clumsy. Eventually, however, they put a bold face on the matter. It had nothing to do with them: the fault was hers! What a stunner that Nana was, eh? One would never have believed her capable of such a fake! And with that they departed one by one, walking on tiptoe, as though in a chamber of death where you cannot laugh.

"Come up all the same, monsieur," said Zoé to Muffat. "Madame is much better and will see you. We are expecting the doctor, who promised to come back this morning."

The lady's maid had persuaded Georges to go back home to sleep, and upstairs in the drawing room only Satin remained. She lay stretched on a divan, smoking a cigarette and scanning the ceiling. Amid the household scare which had followed the accident she had been white with rage, had shrugged her shoulders violently and had made ferocious remarks. Accordingly, when Zoé was passing in front of her and telling Monsieur that poor, dear Madame had suffered a great deal:

"That's right; it'll teach him!" said Satin curtly.

They turned round in surprise, but she had not moved a muscle; her eyes were still turned toward the ceiling, and her cigarette was still wedged tightly between her lips.

"Dear me, you're charming, you are!" said Zoé.

But Satin sat up, looked savagely at the count and once more hurled her remark at him.

"That's right; it'll teach him!"

And she lay down again and blew forth a thin jet of smoke, as though she had no interest in present events and were resolved not to meddle in any of them. No, it was all too silly!

Zoé, however, introduced Muffat into the bedroom, where a scent of ether lingered amid warm, heavy silence, scarce broken by the dull roll of occasional carriages in the Avenue de Villiers. Nana, looking very white on her pillow, was lying awake with wide-open, meditative eyes. She smiled when she saw the count but did not move.

"Ah, dear pet!" she slowly murmured. "I really thought I should never see you again."

Then as he leaned forward to kiss her on the hair, she grew tender toward him and spoke frankly about the child, as though he were its father.

"I never dared tell you; I felt so happy about it! Oh, I used to dream about it; I should have liked to be worthy of you! And now there's nothing left. Ah well, perhaps that's best. I don't want to bring a stumbling block into your life."

Astounded by this story of paternity, he began stammering vague phrases. He had taken a chair and had sat down by the bed, leaning one arm on the coverlet. Then the young woman noticed his wild expression, the blood reddening his eyes, the fever that set his lips aquiver.

"What's the matter then?" she asked. "You're ill too."

"No," he answered with extreme difficulty.

She gazed at him with a profound expression. Then she signed to Zoé to retire, for the latter was lingering round arranging the medicine bottles. And when they were alone she drew him down to her and again asked:

"What's the matter with you, darling? The tears are ready to burst from your eyes—I can see that quite well. Well now, speak out; you've come to tell me something."

"No, no, I swear I haven't," he blurted out. But he was choking with suffering, and this sickroom, into which he had suddenly entered unawares, so worked on his feelings that he burst out sobbing and buried his face in the bedclothes to smother the violence of his grief. Nana understood. Rose Mignon had most assuredly decided to send the letter. She let him weep for some moments, and he was shaken by convulsions so fierce that the bed trembled under her. At length in accents of motherly compassion she queried:

"You've had bothers at your home?"

He nodded affirmatively. She paused anew, and then very low:

"Then you know all?"

He nodded assent. And a heavy silence fell over the chamber of suffering. The night before, on his return from a party given by the empress, he had received the letter Sabine had written her lover. After an atrocious night passed in the meditation of vengeance he had gone out in the morning in order to resist a longing which prompted him to kill his wife. Outside, under a sudden, sweet influence of a fine June morning, he had lost the thread of his thoughts and had come to Nana's, as he always came at terrible moments in his life. There only he gave way to his misery, for he felt a cowardly joy at the thought that she would console him.

"Now look here, be calm!" the young woman continued, becoming at the same time extremely kind. "I've known it a long time, but it was certainly not I that would have opened your eyes. You remember you had your doubts last year, but then things arranged themselves, owing to my prudence. In fact, you wanted proofs. The deuce, you've got one today, and I know it's hard lines. Nevertheless, you must look at the matter quietly: you're not dishonored because it's happened."

He had left off weeping. A sense of shame restrained him from saying what he wanted to, although he had long ago slipped into the most intimate confessions about his household. She had to encourage him. Dear me, she was a woman; she could understand everything. When in a dull voice he exclaimed:

"You're ill. What's the good of tiring you? It was stupid of me to have come. I'm going—"

"No," she answered briskly enough. "Stay! Perhaps I shall be able to give you some good advice. Only don't make me talk too much; the medical man's forbidden it."

He had ended by rising, and he was now walking up and down the room. Then she questioned him:

"Now what are you going to do?

"I'm going to box the man's ears—by heavens, yes!"

She pursed up her lips disapprovingly.

"That's not very wise. And about your wife?"

"I shall go to law; I've proofs."

"Not at all wise, my dear boy. It's stupid even. You know I shall never let you do that!"

And in her feeble voice she showed him decisively how useless and scandalous a duel and a trial would be. He would be a nine days' newspaper sensation; his whole existence would be at stake, his peace of mind, his high situation at court, the honor of his name, and all for what? That he might have the laughers against him.

"What will it matter?" he cried. "I shall have had my revenge."

"My pet," she said, "in a business of that kind one never has one's revenge if one doesn't take it directly."

He paused and stammered. He was certainly no poltroon, but he felt that she was right. An uneasy feeling was growing momentarily stronger within him, a poor, shameful feeling which softened his anger now that it was at its hottest. Moreover, in her frank desire to tell him everything, she dealt him a fresh blow.

"And d'you want to know what's annoying you, dearest? Why, that you are deceiving your wife yourself. You don't sleep away from home for nothing, eh? Your wife must have her suspicions. Well then, how can you blame her? She'll tell you that you've set her the example, and that 'll shut you up. There, now, that's why you're stamping about here instead of being at home murdering both of 'em."

Muffat had again sunk down on the chair; he was overwhelmed by these home thrusts. She broke off and took breath, and then in a low voice:

"Oh, I'm a wreck! Do help me sit up a bit. I keep slipping down, and my head's too low."

When he had helped her she sighed and felt more comfortable. And with that she harked back to the subject. What a pretty sight a divorce suit would be! Couldn't he imagine the advocate of the countess amusing Paris with his remarks about Nana? Everything would have come out—her fiasco at the Variétés, her house, her manner of life. Oh dear, no! She had no wish for all that amount of advertising. Some dirty women might, perhaps, have driven him to it for the sake of getting a thundering big advertisement, but she—she desired his happiness before all else. She had drawn him down toward her and, after passing her arm around his neck, was nursing his head close to hers on the edge of the pillow. And with that she whispered softly:

"Listen, my pet, you shall make it up with your wife."

But he rebelled at this. It could never be! His heart was nigh breaking at the thought; it was too shameful. Nevertheless, she kept tenderly insisting.

"You shall make it up with your wife. Come, come, you don't want to hear all the world saying that I've tempted you away from your home? I should have too vile a reputation! What would people think of me? Only swear that you'll always love me, because the moment you go with another woman——"

Tears choked her utterance, and he intervened with kisses and said:
"You're beside yourself; it's impossible!"

"Yes, yes," she rejoined, "you must. But I'll be reasonable. After all, she's your wife, and it isn't as if you were to play me false with the firstcomer."

And she continued in this strain, giving him the most excellent advice. She even spoke of God, and the count thought he was listening to M. Venot, when that old gentleman endeavored to sermonize him out of the grasp of sin. Nana, however, did not speak of breaking it off entirely: she preached indulgent good nature and suggested that, as became a dear, nice old fellow, he should divide his attentions between his wife and his mistress, so that they would all enjoy a quiet life, devoid of any kind of annoyance, something, in fact, in the nature of a happy slumber amid the inevitable miseries of existence. Their life would be nowise changed: he would still be the little man of her heart. Only he would come to her a bit less often and would give the countess the nights not passed with her. She had got to the end of her strength and left off, speaking under her breath:

"After that I shall feel I've done a good action, and you'll love me all the more."

Silence reigned. She had closed her eyes and lay wan upon her pillow. The count was patiently listening to her, not wishing her to tire herself. A whole minute went by before she reopened her eyes and murmured:

"Besides, how about the money? Where would you get the money from if you must grow angry and go to law? Labordette came for the bill yesterday. As for me, I'm out of everything; I have nothing to put on now."

Then she shut her eyes again and looked like one dead. A shadow of deep anguish had passed over Muffat's brow. Under the present stroke he had since yesterday forgotten the money troubles from which he knew not how to escape. Despite formal promises to the contrary, the bill for a hundred thousand francs had been put in circulation after being once renewed, and Labordette, pretending to be very miserable about it, threw all the blame on Francis, declaring that he would never again mix himself up in such a matter with an uneducated man. It was necessary to pay, for the count would never have allowed his signature to be protested. Then in addition to Nana's novel demands, his home expenses were extraordinarily confused. On their return from Les Fondettes the countess had suddenly manifested a taste for luxury, a longing for worldly pleasures, which was devouring their fortune. Her ruinous caprices began to be talked about. Their whole household management was altered, and five hundred thousand francs were squandered in utterly transforming the old house in the Rue Miromesnil. Then there were extravagantly magnificent gowns and large sums disappeared, squandered or perhaps given away, without her ever dreaming of accounting for them. Twice Muffat ventured to mention this, for he was anxious to know how the money went, but on these occasions she had smiled and gazed at him with so singular an expression that he dared not interrogate her further for fear of a too-unmistakable answer. If he were taking Daguenet as son-in-law as a gift from Nana it was chiefly with the hope of being able to reduce Estelle's dower to two hundred thousand francs and of then being free to make any arrangements he chose about the remainder with a young man who was still rejoicing in this unexpected match.

Nevertheless, for the last week, under the immediate necessity of finding Labordette's hundred thousand francs, Muffat had been able to hit on but one expedient, from which he recoiled. This was that he should sell the Bordes, a magnificent property valued at half a million, which an uncle had recently left the countess. However, her signature was necessary, and she herself, according to the terms of the deed, could not alienate the property without the count's authorization. The day before he had indeed resolved to talk to his wife about this signature. And now everything was ruined; at such a moment he would never accept of such a compromise. This reflection added bitterness to the frightful disgrace of the adultery. He fully understood what Nana was asking for, since in that ever-growing self-abandonment which prompted him to put her in possession of all his secrets, he had complained to her of his position and had confided to her the tiresome difficulty he was in with regard to the signature of the countess.

Nana, however, did not seem to insist. She did not open her eyes again, and, seeing her so pale, he grew frightened and made her inhale a little ether. She gave a sigh and without mentioning Daguenet asked him some questions.

"When is the marriage?"

"We sign the contract on Tuesday, in five days' time," he replied.

Then still keeping her eyelids closed, as though she were speaking from the darkness and silence of her brain:

"Well then, pet, see to what you've got to do. As far as I'm concerned, I want everybody to be happy and comfortable."

He took her hand and soothed her. Yes, he would see about it; the important thing now was for her to rest. And the revolt within him ceased, for this warm and slumberous sickroom, with its all-pervading scent of ether, had ended by lulling him into a mere longing for happiness and peace. All his manhood, erewhile maddened by wrong, had departed out of him in the neighborhood of that warm bed and that suffering woman, whom he was nursing under the influence of her feverish heat and of remembered delights. He leaned over her and pressed her in a close embrace, while despite her unmoved features her lips wore a delicate, victorious smile. But Dr Boutarel made his appearance.

"Well, and how's this dear child?" he said familiarly to Muffat, whom he treated as her husband. "The deuce, but we've made her talk!"

The doctor was a good-looking man and still young. He had a superb practice among the gay world, and being very merry by nature and ready to laugh and joke in the friendliest way with the demimonde ladies with whom, however, he never went farther, he charged very high fees and got them paid with the greatest punctuality. Moreover, he would put himself out to visit them on the most trivial occasions, and Nana, who was always trembling at the fear of death, would send and fetch him two or three times a week and would anxiously confide to him little infantile ills which he would cure to an accompaniment of amusing gossip and harebrained anecdotes. The ladies all adored him. But this time the little ill was serious.

Muffat withdrew, deeply moved. Seeing his poor Nana so very weak, his sole feeling was now one of tenderness. As he was leaving the room she motioned him back and gave him her forehead to kiss. In a low voice and with a playfully threatening look she said:

"You know what I've allowed you to do. Go back to your wife, or it's all over and I shall grow angry!"

The Countess Sabine had been anxious that her daughter's wedding contract should be signed on a Tuesday in order that the renovated house, where the paint was still scarcely dry, might be reopened with a grand entertainment. Five hundred invitations had been issued to people in all kinds of sets. On the morning of the great day the upholsterers were still nailing up hangings, and toward nine at night, just when the lusters were going to be lit, the architect, accompanied by the eager and interested countess, was given his final orders.

It was one of those spring festivities which have a delicate charm of their own. Owing to the warmth of the June nights, it had become possible to open the two doors of the great drawing room and to extend the dancing floor to the sanded paths of the garden. When the first guests arrived and were welcomed at the door by the count and the countess they were positively dazzled. One had only to recall to mind the drawing room of the past, through which flitted the icy, ghostly presence of the Countess Muffat, that antique room full of an atmosphere of religious austerity with its massive First Empire mahogany furniture, its yellow velvet hangings, its moldy ceiling through which the damp had soaked. Now from the very threshold of the entrance hall mosaics set off with gold were glittering under the lights of lofty candelabras, while the marble staircase unfurled, as it were, a delicately chiseled balustrade. Then, too, the drawing room looked splendid; it was hung with Genoa velvet, and a huge decorative design by Boucher covered the ceiling, a design for which the architect had paid a hundred thousand francs at the sale of the Château de Dampierre. The lusters and the crystal ornaments lit up a luxurious display of mirrors and precious furniture. It seemed as though Sabine's long chair, that solitary red silk chair, whose soft contours were so marked in the old days, had grown and spread till it filled the whole great house with voluptuous idleness and a sense of tense enjoyment not less fierce and hot than a fire which has been long in burning up.

People were already dancing. The band, which had been located in the garden, in front of one of the open windows, was playing a waltz, the supple rhythm of which came softly into the house through the intervening night air. And the garden seemed to spread away and away, bathed in transparent shadow and lit by Venetian lamps, while in a purple tent pitched on the edge of a lawn a table for refreshments had been established. The waltz, which was none other than the quaint, vulgar one in the *Blonde Venus*, with its laughing, blackguard lilt, penetrated the old hotel with sonorous waves of sound and sent a feverish thrill along its walls. It was as though some fleshly wind had come up out of the common street and were sweeping the relics of a vanished epoch out of the proud old dwelling, bearing away the Muffats' past, the age of honor and religious faith which had long slumbered beneath the lofty ceilings.

Meanwhile near the hearth, in their accustomed places, the old friends of the count's mother were taking refuge. They felt out of their element—they were dazzled and they formed a little group amid the slowly invading mob. Mme du Joncquoy, unable to recognize the various rooms, had come in through the dining saloon. Mme Chantereau was gazing with a stupefied expression at the garden, which struck her as immense. Presently there was a sound of low voices, and the corner gave vent to all sorts of bitter reflections.

"I declare," murmured Mme Chantereau, "just fancy if the countess were to return to life. Why, can you not imagine her coming in among all these crowds of people! And then there's all this gilding and this uproar! It's scandalous!"

"Sabine's out of her senses," replied Mme du Joncquoy. "Did you see her at the door? Look, you can catch sight of her here; she's wearing all her diamonds."

For a moment or two they stood up in order to take a distant view of the count and countess. Sabine was in a white dress trimmed with marvelous English point lace. She was triumphant in beauty; she looked young and gay, and there was a touch of intoxication in her continual smile. Beside her stood Muffat, looking aged and a little pale, but he, too, was smiling in his calm and worthy fashion.

"And just to think that he was once master," continued Mme Chantereau, "and that not a single rout seat would have come in without his permission! Ah well, she's changed all that; it's her house now. D'you remember when she did not want to do her drawing room up again? She's done up the entire house."

But the ladies grew silent, for Mme de Chezelles was entering the room, followed by a band of young men. She was going into ecstasies and marking her approval with a succession of little exclamations.

"Oh, it's delicious, exquisite! What taste!" And she shouted back to her followers:

"Didn't I say so? There's nothing equal to these old places when one takes them in hand. They become dazzling! It's quite in the grand seventeenth-century style. Well, *now* she can receive."

The two old ladies had again sat down and with lowered tones began talking about the marriage, which was causing astonishment to a good many people. Estelle had just passed by them. She was in a pink silk gown and was as pale, flat, silent and virginal as ever. She had accepted Daguenet very quietly and now evinced neither joy nor sadness, for she was still as cold and white as on those winter evenings when she used to put logs on the fire.

This whole fete given in her honor, these lights and flowers and tunes, left her quite unmoved.

"An adventurer," Mme du Joncquoy was saying. "For my part, I've never seen him."

"Take care, here he is," whispered Mme Chantereau.

Daguenet, who had caught sight of Mme Hugon and her sons, had eagerly offered her his arm. He laughed and was effusively affectionate toward her, as though she had had a hand in his sudden good fortune.

"Thank you," she said, sitting down near the fireplace. "You see, it's my old corner."

"You know him?" queried Mme du Joncquoy, when Daguenet had gone.

"Certainly I do—a charming young man. Georges is very fond of him. Oh, they're a most respected family."

And the good lady defended him against the mute hostility which was apparent to her. His father, held in high esteem by Louis Philippe, had been a *préfet* up to the time of his death. The son had been a little dissipated, perhaps; they said he was ruined, but in any case, one of his uncles, who was a great landowner, was bound to leave him his fortune. The ladies, however, shook their heads, while Mme Hugon, herself somewhat embarrassed, kept harking back to the extreme respectability of his family. She was very much fatigued and complained of her feet. For some months she had been occupying her house in the Rue Richelieu, having, as she said, a whole lot of things on hand. A look of sorrow overshadowed her smiling, motherly face.

"Never mind," Mme Chantereau concluded. "Estelle could have aimed at something much better."

There was a flourish. A quadrille was about to begin, and the crowd flowed back to the sides of the drawing room in order to leave the floor clear. Bright dresses flitted by and mingled together amid the dark evening coats, while the intense light set jewels flashing and white plumes quivering and lilacs and roses gleaming and flowering amid the sea of many heads. It was already very warm, and a penetrating perfume was exhaled from light tulles and crumpled silks and satins, from which bare shoulders glimmered white, while the orchestra played its lively airs. Through open doors ranges of seated ladies were visible in the background of adjoining rooms; they flashed a discreet smile; their eyes glowed, and they made pretty mouths as the breath of their fans caressed their faces. And guests still kept arriving, and a footman announced their names while gentlemen advanced slowly amid the surrounding groups, striving to find places for ladies, who hung with difficulty on their arms, and stretching forward in quest of some far-off vacant armchair. The house kept filling, and crinolined skirts got jammed together with a little rustling sound. There were corners where an amalgam of laces, bunches and puffs would completely bar the way, while all the other ladies stood waiting, politely resigned and imperturbably graceful, as became people who were made to take part in these dazzling crushes. Meanwhile across the garden couples, who had been glad to escape from the close air of the great drawing room, were wandering away under the roseate gleam of the Venetian lamps, and shadowy dresses kept flitting along the edge of the lawn, as though in rhythmic time to the music of the quadrille, which sounded sweet and distant behind the trees.

Steiner had just met with Foucarmont and La Faloise, who were drinking a glass of champagne in front of the buffet.

"It's beastly smart," said La Faloise as he took a survey of the purple tent, which was supported by gilded lances. "You might fancy yourself at the Gingerbread Fair. That's it—the Gingerbread Fair!"

In these days he continually affected a bantering tone, posing as the young man who has abused every mortal thing and now finds nothing worth taking seriously.

"How surprised poor Vandeuvres would be if he were to come back," murmured Foucarmont. "You remember how he simply nearly died of boredom in front of the fire in there. Egad, it was no laughing matter."

"Vandeuvres—oh, let him be. He's a gone coon!" La Faloise disdainfully rejoined. "He jolly well choused himself, he did, if he thought he could make us sit up with his roast-meat story! Not a soul mentions it now. Blotted out, done for, buried—that's what's the matter with Vandeuvres! Here's to the next man!"

Then as Steiner shook hands with him:

"You know Nana's just arrived. Oh, my boys, it was a state entry. It was too brilliant for anything! First of all she kissed the countess. Then when the children came up she gave them her blessing and said to Daguenet, 'Listen, Paul, if you go running after the girls you'll have to answer for it to me.' What, d'you mean to say you didn't see that? Oh, it *was* smart. A success, if you like!"

The other two listened to him, openmouthed, and at last burst out laughing. He was enchanted and thought himself in his best vein.

"You thought it had really happened, eh? Confound it, since Nana's made the match! Anyway, she's one of the family."

The young Hugons were passing, and Philippe silenced him. And with that they chatted about the marriage from the male point of view. Georges was vexed with La Faloise for telling an anecdote. Certainly Nana had fubbed off on Muffat one of her old flames as son-in-law; only it was not true that she had been to bed with Daguenet as lately as yesterday. Foucarmont made bold to shrug his shoulders. Could anyone ever tell when Nana was in bed with anyone? But Georges grew excited and answered with an "I can tell, sir!" which set them all laughing. In a word, as Steiner put it, it was all a very funny kettle of fish!

The buffet was gradually invaded by the crowd, and, still keeping together, they vacated their positions there. La Faloise stared brazenly at the women as though he believed himself to be Mabille. At the end of a garden walk the little band was surprised to find M. Venot busily conferring with Daguenet, and with that they indulged in some facile pleasantries which made them very merry. He was confessing him, giving him advice about the bridal night! Presently they returned in front of one of the drawing-room doors, within

which a polka was sending the couples whirling to and fro till they seemed
to leave a wake behind them among the crowd of men who remained standing about. In the slight puffs of air which came from outside the tapers flared
up brilliantly, and when a dress floated by in time to the rat-tat of the measure, a little gust of wind cooled the sparkling heat which streamed down
from the lusters.

"Egad, they're not cold in there!" muttered La Faloise.

They blinked after emerging from the mysterious shadows of the garden.
Then they pointed out to one another the Marquis de Chouard where he stood
apart, his tall figure towering over the bare shoulders which surrounded him.
His face was pale and very stern, and beneath its crown of scant white hair
it wore an expression of lofty dignity. Scandalized by Count Muffat's conduct,
he had publicly broken off all intercourse with him and was by way of never
again setting foot in the house. If he had consented to put in an appearance
that evening it was because his granddaughter had begged him to. But he dis-
approved of her marriage and had inveighed indignantly against the way in
which the government classes were being disorganized by the shameful com-
promises engendered by modern debauchery.

"Ah, it's the end of all things," Mme du Joncquoy whispered in Mme
Chantereau's ear as she sat near the fireplace. "That bad woman has be-
witched the unfortunate man. And to think we once knew him such a true believer, such a noblehearted gentleman!"

"It appears he is ruining himself," continued Mme Chantereau. "My husband
has had a bill of his in his hands. At present he's living in that house in the
Avenue de Villiers; all Paris is talking about it. Good heavens! I don't make
excuses for Sabine, but you must admit that he gives her infinite cause of complaint, and, dear me, if she throws money out of the window, too——"

"She does not only throw money," interrupted the other. "In fact, between
them, there's no knowing where they'll stop; they'll end in the mire, my dear."

But just then a soft voice interrupted them. It was M. Venot, and he had
come and seated himself behind them, as though anxious to disappear from
view. Bending forward, he murmured:

"Why despair? God manifests Himself when all seems lost."

He was assisting peacefully at the downfall of the house which he erewhile
governed. Since his stay at Les Fondettes he had been allowing the madness to
increase, for he was very clearly aware of his own powerlessness. He had, indeed, accepted the whole position—the count's wild passion for Nana,
Fauchery's presence, even Estelle's marriage with Daguenet. What did these
things matter? He even became more supple and mysterious, for he nursed a
hope of being able to gain the same mastery over the young as over the dis-
united couple, and he knew that great disorders lead to great conversions.
Providence would have its opportunity.

"Our friend," he continued in a low voice, "is always animated by the best
religious sentiments. He has given me the sweetest proofs of this."

"Well," said Mme du Joncquoy, "he ought first to have made it up with
his wife."

"Doubtless. At this moment I have hopes that the reconciliation will be shortly effected."

Whereupon the two old ladies questioned him.

But he grew very humble again. "Heaven," he said, "must be left to act." His whole desire in bringing the count and the countess together again was to avoid a public scandal, for religion tolerated many faults when the proprieties were respected.

"In fact," resumed Mme du Joncquoy, "you ought to have prevented this union with an adventurer."

The little old gentleman assumed an expression of profound astonishment.

"You deceive yourself. Monsieur Daguenet is a young man of the greatest merit. I am acquainted with his thoughts; he is anxious to live down the errors of his youth. Estelle will bring him back to the path of virtue, be sure of that."

"Oh, Estelle!" Mme Chantereau murmured disdainfully. "I believe the dear young thing to be incapable of willing anything; she is so insignificant!"

This opinion caused M. Venot to smile. However, he went into no explanations about the young bride and, shutting his eyes, as though to avoid seeming to take any further interest in the matter, he once more lost himself in his corner behind the petticoats. Mme Hugon, though weary and absent-minded, had caught some phrases of the conversation, and she now intervened and summed up in her tolerant way by remarking to the Marquis de Chouard, who just then bowed to her:

"These ladies are too severe. Existence is so bitter for every one of us! Ought we not to forgive others much, my friend, if we wish to merit forgiveness ourselves?"

For some seconds the marquis appeared embarrassed, for he was afraid of allusions. But the good lady wore so sad a smile that he recovered almost at once and remarked:

"No, there is no forgiveness for certain faults. It is by reason of this kind of accommodating spirit that a society sinks into the abyss of ruin."

The ball had grown still more animated. A fresh quadrille was imparting a slight swaying motion to the drawing-room floor, as though the old dwelling had been shaken by the impulse of the dance. Now and again amid the wan confusion of heads a woman's face with shining eyes and parted lips stood sharply out as it was whirled away by the dance, the light of the lusters gleaming on the white skin. Mme du Joncquoy declared that the present proceedings were senseless. It was madness to crowd five hundred people into a room which would scarcely contain two hundred. In fact, why not sign the wedding contract on the Place du Carrousel? This was the outcome of the new code of manners, said Mme Chantereau. In old times these solemnities took place in the bosom of the family, but today one must have a mob of people; the whole street must be allowed to enter quite freely, and there must be a great crush, or else the evening seems a chilly affair. People now advertised their luxury and introduced the mere foam on the wave of Parisian society into their houses, and accordingly it was only too natural if illicit proceedings such as they had been discussing afterward polluted the hearth. The ladies complained that they could not recognize more than fifty people. Where did all this crowd spring from? Young girls with low necks were making a great display of their shoulders. A woman had a golden dagger stuck in her chignon, while a bodice thickly embroidered with jet beads clothed her in what looked like a coat of mail. People's eyes kept following another lady smilingly, so singularly marked were her clinging skirts. All the luxuriant splendor of the departing winter was there—the overtolerant world of pleasure, the scratch gathering a hostess can get together after a first introduction, the sort of society, in fact, in which great names and great shames jostle together in the same fierce quest of enjoyment. The heat was increasing, and amid the overcrowded rooms the quadrille unrolled the cadenced symmetry of its figures.

"Very smart—the countess!" La Faloise continued at the garden door. "She's ten years younger than her daughter. By the by, Foucarmont, you must decide on a point. Vandeuvres once bet that she had no thighs."

This affectation of cynicism bored the other gentlemen, and Foucarmont contented himself by saying:

"Ask your cousin, dear boy. Here he is."

"Jove, it's a happy thought!" cried La Faloise. "I bet ten louis she has thighs."

Fauchery did indeed come up. As became a constant inmate of the house, he had gone round by the dining room in order to avoid the crowded doors. Rose had taken him up again at the beginning of the winter, and he was now dividing himself between the singer and the countess, but he was extremely fatigued and did not know how to get rid of one of them. Sabine flattered his vanity, but Rose amused him more than she. Besides, the passion Rose felt was a real one: her tenderness for him was marked by a conjugal fidelity which drove Mignon to despair.

"Listen, we want some information," said La Faloise as he squeezed his cousin's arm. "You see that lady in white silk?"

Ever since his inheritance had given him a kind of insolent dash of manner he had affected to chaff Fauchery, for he had an old grudge to satisfy and wanted to be revenged for much bygone raillery, dating from the days when he was just fresh from his native province.

"Yes, that lady with the lace."

The journalist stood on tiptoe, for as yet he did not understand.

"The countess?" he said at last.

"Exactly, my good friend. I've bet ten louis—now, has she thighs?"

And he fell a-laughing, for he was delighted to have succeeded in snubbing a fellow who had once come heavily down on him for asking whether the countess slept with anyone. But Fauchery, without showing the very slightest astonishment, looked fixedly at him.

"Get along, you idiot!" he said finally as he shrugged his shoulders.

Then he shook hands with the other gentlemen, while La Faloise, in his discomfiture, felt rather uncertain whether he had said something funny. The men chatted. Since the races the banker and Foucarmont had formed part of the set in the Avenue de Villiers. Nana was going on much better, and every eve-ning the count came and asked how she did. Meanwhile Fauchery, though he listened, seemed preoccupied, for during a quarrel that morning Rose had roundly confessed to the sending of the letter. Oh yes, he might present him-self at his great lady's house; he would be well received! After long hesitation he had come despite everything—out of sheer courage. But La Faloise's im-becile pleasantry had upset him in spite of his apparent tranquillity.

"What's the matter?" asked Philippe. "You seem in trouble."

"I do? Not at all. I've been working: that's why I came so late."

Then coldly, in one of those heroic moods which, although unnoticed, are wont to solve the vulgar tragedies of existence:

"All the same, I haven't made my bow to our hosts. One must be civil."

He even ventured on a joke, for he turned to La Faloise and said:

"Eh, you idiot?"

And with that he pushed his way through the crowd. The valet's full voice was no longer shouting out names, but close to the door the count and countess were still talking, for they were detained by ladies coming in. At length he joined them, while the gentlemen who were still on the garden steps stood on tiptoe so as to watch the scene. Nana, they thought, must have been chattering.

"The count hasn't noticed him," muttered Georges. "Look out! He's turn-ing round; there, it's done!"

The band had again taken up the waltz in the *Blonde Venus*. Fauchery had begun by bowing to the countess, who was still smiling in ecstatic serenity. After which he had stood motionless a moment, waiting very calmly behind the count's back. That evening the count's deportment was one of lofty gravity: he held his head high, as became the official and the great dignitary. And when at last he lowered his gaze in the direction of the journalist he seemed still further to emphasize the majesty of his attitude. For some seconds the two men looked at one another. It was Fauchery who first stretched out his hand. Muffat gave him his. Their hands remained clasped, and the Countess Sabine with downcast eyes stood smiling before them, while the waltz con-tinually beat out its mocking, vagabond rhythm.

"But the thing's going on wheels!" said Steiner.

"Are their hands glued together?" asked Foucarmont, surprised at this pro-longed clasp. A memory he could not forget brought a faint glow to Fau-chery's pale cheeks, and in his mind's eye he saw the property room bathed in greenish twilight and filled with dusty bric-a-brac. And Muffat was there, eggcup in hand, making a clever use of his suspicions. At this moment Muffat was no longer suspicious, and the last vestige of his dignity was crumbling in ruin. Fauchery's fears were assuaged, and when he saw the frank gaiety of the countess he was seized with a desire to laugh. The thing struck him as comic.

"Aha, here she is at last!" cried La Faloise, who did not abandon a jest when he thought it a good one. "D'you see Nana coming in over there?"

"Hold your tongue, do, you idiot!" muttered Philippe.

"But I tell you, it is Nana! They're playing her waltz for her, by Jove! She's making her entry. And she takes part in the reconciliation, the devil she does!

What? You don't see her? She's squeezing all three of 'em to her heart—my cousin Fauchery, my lady cousin and her husband, and she's calling 'em her dear kitties. Oh, those family scenes give me a turn!"

Estelle had come up, and Fauchery complimented her while she stood stiffly up in her rose-colored dress, gazing at him with the astonished look of a silent child and constantly glancing aside at her father and mother. Daguenet, too, exchanged a hearty shake of the hand with the journalist. Together they made up a smiling group, while M. Venot came gliding in behind them. He gloated over them with a beatified expression and seemed to envelop them in his pious sweetness, for he rejoiced in these last instances of self-abandonment which were preparing the means of grace.

But the waltz still beat out its swinging, laughing, voluptuous measure; it was like a shrill continuation of the life of pleasure which was beating against the old house like a rising tide. The band blew louder trills from their little flutes; their violins sent forth more swooning notes. Beneath the Genoa velvet hangings, the gilding and the paintings, the lusters exhaled a living heat and a great glow of sunlight, while the crowd of guests, multiplied in the surrounding mirrors, seemed to grow and increase as the murmur of many voices rose ever louder. The couples who whirled round the drawing room, arm about waist, amid the smiles of the seated ladies, still further accentuated the quaking of the floors. In the garden a dull, fiery glow fell from the Venetian lanterns and threw a distant reflection of flame over the dark shadows moving in search of a breath of air about the walks at its farther end. And this trembling of walls and this red glow of light seemed to betoken a great ultimate conflagration in which the fabric of an ancient honor was cracking and burning on every side. The shy early beginnings of gaiety, of which Fauchery one April evening had heard the vocal expression in the sound of breaking glass, had little by little grown bolder, wilder, till they had burst forth in this festival. Now the rift was growing; it was crannying the house and announcing approaching downfall. Among drunkards in the slums it is black misery, an empty cupboard, which put an end to ruined families; it is the madness of drink which empties the wretched beds. Here the waltz tune was sounding the knell of an old race amid the suddenly ignited ruins of accumulated wealth, while Nana, although unseen, stretched her lithe limbs above the dancers' heads and sent corruption through their caste, drenching the hot air with the ferment of her exhalations and the vagabond lilt of the music.

On the evening after the celebration of the church marriage Count Muffat made his appearance in his wife's bedroom, where he had not entered for the last two years. At first, in her great surprise, the countess drew back from him. But she was still smiling the intoxicated smile which she now always wore. He began stammering in extreme embarrassment; whereupon she gave him a short moral lecture. However, neither of them risked a decisive explanation. It was religion, they pretended, which required this process of mutual forgiveness, and they agreed by a tacit understanding to retain their freedom. Before going to bed, seeing that the countess still appeared to hesitate, they had a business conversation, and the count was the first to speak of selling the Bordes. She consented at once. They both stood in great want of money, and they would share and share alike. This completed the reconciliation, and Muffat, remorseful though he was, felt veritably relieved.

That very day, as Nana was dozing toward two in the afternoon, Zoé made so bold as to knock at her bedroom door. The curtains were drawn to, and a hot breath of wind kept blowing through a window into the fresh twilight stillness within. During these last days the young woman had been getting up and about again, but she was still somewhat weak. She opened her eyes and asked:

"Who is it?"

Zoé was about to reply, but Daguenet pushed by her and announced himself in person. Nana forthwith propped herself up on her pillow and, dismissing the lady's maid:

"What! Is that you?" she cried. "On the day of your marriage? What can be the matter?"

Taken aback by the darkness, he stood still in the middle of the room. However, he grew used to it and came forward at last. He was in evening dress and wore a white cravat and gloves.

"Yes, to be sure, it's me!" he said. "You don't remember?"

No, she remembered nothing, and in his chaffing way he had to offer himself frankly to her.

"Come now, here's your commission. I've brought you the handsel of my innocence!"

And with that, as he was now by the bedside, she caught him in her bare arms and shook with merry laughter and almost cried, she thought it so pretty of him.

"Oh, that Mimi, how funny he is! He's thought of it after all! And to think I didn't remember it any longer! So you've slipped off; you're just out of church. Yes, certainly, you've got a scent of incense about you. But kiss me, kiss me! Oh, harder than that, Mimi dear! Bah! Perhaps it's for the last time."

In the dim room, where a vague odor of ether still lingered, their tender laughter died away suddenly. The heavy, warm breeze swelled the window curtains, and children's voices were audible in the avenue without. Then the lateness of the hour tore them asunder and set them joking again. Daguenet took his departure with his wife directly after the breakfast.

CHAPTER XIII

Toward the end of September Count Muffat, who was to dine at Nana's that evening, came at nightfall to inform her of a summons to the Tuileries. The lamps in the house had not been lit yet, and the servants were laughing uproariously in the kitchen regions as he softly mounted the stairs, where the tall windows gleamed in warm shadow. The door of the drawing room upstairs opened noiselessly. A faint pink glow was dying out on the ceiling of the room, and the red hangings, the deep divans, the lacquered furniture, with their medley of embroidered fabrics and bronzes and china, were already sleeping under a slowly creeping flood of shadows, which drowned nooks and corners and blotted out the gleam of ivory and the glint of gold. And there in the darkness, on the white surface of a wide, outspread petticoat, which alone remained clearly visible, he saw Nana lying stretched in the arms of Georges. Denial in any shape or form was impossible. He gave a choking cry and stood gaping at them.

Nana had bounded up, and now she pushed him into the bedroom in order to give the lad time to escape.

"Come in," she murmured with reeling senses, "I'll explain."

She was exasperated at being thus surprised. Never before had she given way like this in her own house, in her own drawing room, when the doors were open. It was a long story: Georges and she had had a disagreement; he had been mad with jealousy of Philippe, and he had sobbed so bitterly on her bosom that she had yielded to him, not knowing how else to calm him and really very full of pity for him at heart. And on this solitary occasion, when she had been stupid enough to forget herself thus with a little rascal who could not even now bring her bouquets of violets, so short did his mother keep him—on this solitary occasion the count turned up and came straight down on them. 'Gad, she had very bad luck! That was what one got if one was a good-natured wench!

Meanwhile in the bedroom, into which she had pushed Muffat, the darkness was complete. Whereupon after some groping she rang furiously and asked for a lamp. It was Julien's fault too! If there had been a lamp in the drawing room the whole affair would not have happened. It was the stupid nightfall which had got the better of her heart.

"I beseech you to be reasonable, my pet," she said when Zoé had brought in the lights.

The count, with his hands on his knees, was sitting gazing at the floor. He was stupefied by what he had just seen. He did not cry out in anger. He only trembled, as though overtaken by some horror which was freezing him. This dumb misery touched the young woman, and she tried to comfort him.

"Well, yes, I've done wrong. It's very bad what I did. You see I'm sorry for my fault. It makes me grieve very much because it annoys you. Come now, be nice, too, and forgive me."

She had crouched down at his feet and was striving to catch his eye with a look of tender submission. She was fain to know whether he was very vexed with her. Presently, as he gave a long sigh and seemed to recover himself, she grew more coaxing and with grave kindness of manner added a final reason:

"You see, dearie, you must try and understand how it is: I can't refuse it to my poor friends."

The count consented to give way and only insisted that Georges should be dismissed once for all. But all his illusions had vanished, and he no longer believed in her sworn fidelity. Next day Nana would deceive him anew, and he only remained her miserable possessor in obedience to a cowardly necessity and to terror at the thought of living without her.

This was the epoch in her existence when Nana flared upon Paris with re-doubled splendor. She loomed larger than heretofore on the horizon of vice and swayed the town with her impudently flaunted splendor and that contempt of money which made her openly squander fortunes. Her house had become a sort of glowing smithy, where her continual desires were the flames and the slightest breath from her lips changed gold into fine ashes, which the wind hourly swept away. Never had eye beheld such a rage of expenditure. The great house seemed to have been built over a gulf in which men—their worldly possessions, their fortunes, their very names—were swallowed up without leaving even a handful of dust behind them. This courtesan, who had the tastes of a parrot and gobbled up radishes and burnt almonds and pecked at the meat upon her plate, had monthly table bills amounting to five thousand francs. The wildest waste went on in the kitchen: the place, metaphorically speaking, was one great river which stove in cask upon cask of wine and swept great bills with it, swollen by three or four successive manipulators. Victorine and François reigned supreme in the kitchen, whither they invited friends. In addition to these there was quite a little tribe of cousins, who were cockered up in their homes with cold meats and strong soup. Julien made the tradespeople give him commissions, and the glaziers never put up a pane of glass at a cost of a franc and a half but he had a franc put down to himself. Charles devoured the horses' oats and doubled the amount of their provender, reselling at the back door what came in at the carriage gate, while amid the general pillage, the sack of the town after the storm, Zoé, by dint of cleverness, succeeded in saving appearances and covering the thefts of all in order the better to slur over and make good her own. But the household waste was worse than the household dishonesty. Yesterday's food was thrown into the gutter, and the collection of provisions in the house was such that the servants grew disgusted with it. The glass was all sticky with sugar, and the gas burners flared and flared till the rooms seemed ready to explode. Then, too, there were instances of negligence and mischief and sheer accident—of everything, in fact, which can hasten the ruin of a house devoured by so many mouths. Upstairs in Madame's quarters destruction raged more fiercely still. Dresses, which cost ten thousand francs and had been twice worn, were sold by Zoé; jewels vanished as though they had crumbled deep down in their drawers; stupid purchases were made; every novelty of the day was brought and left to lie forgotten in some corner the morning after or swept up by ragpickers in the street. She could not see any very expensive object without wanting to possess it, and so she constantly surrounded herself with the wrecks of bouquets and costly knickknacks and was the happier the more her passing fancy cost. Nothing remained intact in her hands; she broke everything, and this object withered, and that grew dirty in the clasp of her lithe white fingers. A perfect heap of nameless debris, of twisted shreds and muddy rags, followed her and marked her passage. Then amid this utter squandering of pocket money cropped up a question about the big bills and their settlement. Twenty thousand francs were due to the modiste, thirty thousand to the linen draper, twelve thousand to the bootmaker. Her stable devoured fifty thousand for her, and in six months she ran up a bill of a hundred and twenty thousand francs at her ladies' tailor. Though she had not enlarged her scheme of expenditure, which Labordette reckoned at four hundred thousand francs on an average, she ran up that same year to a million. She was herself stupefied by the amount and was unable to tell whither such a sum could have gone. Heaps upon heaps of men, barrowfuls of gold, failed to stop up the hole, which, amid this ruinous luxury, continually gaped under the floor of her house.

Meanwhile Nana had cherished her latest caprice. Once more exercised by the notion that her room needed redoing, she fancied she had hit on something at last. The room should be done in velvet of the color of tea roses, with silver buttons and golden cords, tassels and fringes, and the hangings should be caught up to the ceiling after the manner of a tent. This arrangement ought to be both rich and tender, she thought, and would form a splendid background to her blonde vermeil-tinted skin. However, the bedroom was only designed to serve as a setting to the bed, which was to be a dazzling affair, a prodigy. Nana meditated a bed such as had never before existed; it was to be a throne, an altar, whither Paris was to come in order to adore her sovereign nudity. It was to be all in gold and silver beaten work—it should suggest a great piece of jewelry with its golden roses climbing on a trelliswork of silver. On the headboard a band of Loves should peep forth laughing from amid the flowers, as though they were watching the voluptuous dalliance within the shadow of the bed curtains. Nana had applied to Labordette who had brought two goldsmiths to see her. They were already busy with the designs. The bed would cost fifty thousand francs, and Muffat was to give it her as a New Year's present.

What most astonished the young woman was that she was endlessly short of money amid a river of gold, the tide of which almost enveloped her. On certain days she was at her wit's end for want of ridiculously small sums—sums of only a few louis. She was driven to borrow from Zoé, or she scraped up cash as well as she could on her own account. But before resignedly adopting extreme measures she tried her friends and in a joking sort of way got the men to give her all they had about them, even down to their coppers. For the last three months she had been emptying Philippe's pockets especially, and now on days of passionate enjoyment he never came away but he left his purse behind him. Soon she grew bolder and asked him for loans of two hundred francs, three hundred francs—never more than that—wherewith to pay the interest of bills or to stave off outrageous debts. And Philippe, who in July had been appointed paymaster to his regiment, would bring the money the day after, apologizing at the same time for not being rich, seeing that good Mamma Hugon now treated her sons with singular financial severity. At the close of three months these little oft-renewed loans mounted up to a sum of ten thousand francs. The captain still laughed his hearty-sounding laugh, but he was growing visibly thinner, and sometimes he seemed absent-minded, and a shade of suffering would pass over his face. But one look from Nana's eyes would transfigure him in a sort of sensual ecstasy. She had a very coaxing way with him and would intoxicate him with furtive kisses and yield herself to him in sudden fits of self-abandonment, which tied him to her apron strings the moment he was able to escape from his military duties.

One evening, Nana having announced that her name, too, was Thérèse and that her fete day was the fifteenth of October, the gentlemen all sent her presents. Captain Philippe brought his himself; it was an old comfit dish in Dresden china, and it had a gold mount. He found her alone in her dressing room. She had just emerged from the bath, had nothing on save a great red-and-white flannel bathing wrap and was very busy examining her presents, which were ranged on a table. She had already broken a rock-crystal flask in her attempts to unstopper it.

"Oh, you're too nice!" she said. "What is it? Let's have a peep! What a baby you are to spend your pennies in little fakements like that!"

She scolded him, seeing that he was not rich, but at heart she was delighted to see him spending his whole substance for her. Indeed, this was the only proof of love which had power to touch her. Meanwhile she was fiddling away at the comfit dish, opening it and shutting it in her desire to see how it was made.

"Take care," he murmured, "it's brittle."

But she shrugged her shoulders. Did he think her as clumsy as a street porter? And all of a sudden the hinge came off between her fingers and the lid fell and was broken. She was stupefied and remained gazing at the fragments as she cried:

"Oh, it's smashed!"

Then she burst out laughing. The fragments lying on the floor tickled her fancy. Her merriment was of the nervous kind, the stupid, spiteful laughter of a child who delights in destruction. Philippe had a little fit of disgust, for the wretched girl did not know what anguish this curio had cost him. Seeing him thoroughly upset, she tried to contain herself.

"Gracious me, it isn't my fault! It was cracked; those old things barely hold together. Besides, it was the cover! Didn't you see the bound it gave?"

And she once more burst into uproarious mirth.

But though he made an effort to the contrary, tears appeared in the young man's eyes, and with that she flung her arms tenderly round his neck.

"How silly you are! You know I love you all the same. If one never broke anything the tradesmen would never sell anything. All that sort of thing's made to be broken. Now look at this fan; it's only held together with glue!"

She had snatched up a fan and was dragging at the blades so that the silk was torn in two. This seemed to excite her, and in order to show that she scorned the other presents, the moment she had ruined his she treated herself to a general massacre, rapping each successive object and proving clearly that not one was solid in that she had broken them all. There was a lurid glow in her vacant eyes, and her lips, slightly drawn back, displayed her white teeth. Soon, when everything was in fragments, she laughed cheerily again and with flushed cheeks beat on the table with the flat of her hands, lisping like a naughty little girl:

"All over! Got no more! Got no more!"

Then Philippe was overcome by the same mad excitement, and, pushing her down, he merrily kissed her bosom. She abandoned herself to him and clung to his shoulders with such gleeful energy that she could not remember having enjoyed herself so much for an age past. Without letting go of him she said caressingly:

"I say, dearie, you ought certainly to bring me ten louis tomorrow. It's a bore, but there's the baker's bill worrying me awfully."

He had grown pale. Then imprinting a final kiss on her forehead, he said simply:

"I'll try."

Silence reigned. She was dressing, and he stood pressing his forehead against the windowpanes. A minute passed, and he returned to her and deliberately continued:

"Nana, you ought to marry me."

This notion straightway so tickled the young woman that she was unable to finish tying on her petticoats.

"My poor pet, you're ill! D'you offer me your hand because I ask you for ten louis? No, never! I'm too fond of you. Good gracious, what a silly question!"

And as Zoé entered in order to put her boots on, they ceased talking of the matter. The lady's maid at once espied the presents lying broken in pieces on the table. She asked if she should put these things away, and, Madame having bidden her get rid of them, she carried the whole collection off in the folds of her dress. In the kitchen a sorting-out process began, and Madame's debris were shared among the servants.

That day Georges had slipped into the house despite Nana's orders to the contrary. François had certainly seen him pass, but the servants had now got to laugh among themselves at their good lady's embarrassing situations. He had just slipped as far as the little drawing room when his brother's voice stopped him, and, as one powerless to tear himself from the door, he overheard everything that went on within, the kisses, the offer of marriage. A feeling of horror froze him, and he went away in a state bordering on imbecility, feeling as though there were a great void in his brain. It was only in his own room above his mother's flat in the Rue Richelieu that his heart broke in a storm of furious sobs. This time there could be no doubt about the state of things; a horrible picture of Nana in Philippe's arms kept rising before his mind's eye. It struck him in the light of an incest. When he fancied himself calm again the remembrance of it all would return, and in fresh access of raging jealousy he would throw himself on the bed, biting the coverlet, shouting infamous accusations which maddened him the more. Thus the day passed. In order to stay shut up in his room he spoke of having a sick headache. But the night proved more terrible still; a murder fever shook him amid continual nightmares. Had his brother lived in the house, he would have gone and killed him with the stab of a knife. When day returned he tried to reason things out. It was he who ought to die, and he determined to throw himself out of the window when an omnibus was passing. Nevertheless, he went out toward ten o'clock and traversed Paris, wandered up and down on the bridges and at the last moment felt an unconquerable desire to see Nana once more. With one word, perhaps, she would save him. And three o'clock was striking when he entered the house in the Avenue de Villiers.

Toward noon a frightful piece of news had simply crushed Mme Hugon Philippe had been in prison since the evening of the previous day, accused of having stolen twelve thousand francs from the chest of his regiment. For the last three months he had been withdrawing small sums therefrom in the hope of being able to repay them, while he had covered the deficit with false money Thanks to the negligence of the administrative committee, this fraud had been constantly successful. The old lady, humbled utterly by her child's crime, had at once cried out in anger against Nana. She knew Philippe's connection with her, and her melancholy had been the result of this miserable state of things which kept her in Paris in constant dread of some final catastrophe. But she had never looked forward to such shame as this, and now she blamed herself for refusing him money, as though such refusal had made her accessory to his act. She sank down on an armchair; her legs were seized with paralysis, and she felt herself to be useless, incapable of action and destined to stay where she was till she died. But the sudden thought of Georges comforted her. Georges was still left her; he would be able to act, perhaps to save them. Thereupon, without seeking aid of anyone else—for she wished to keep these matters shrouded in the bosom of her family—she dragged herself up to the next story, her mind possessed by the idea that she still had someone to love about her. But upstairs she found an empty room. The porter told her that M. Georges had gone out at an early hour. The room was haunted by the ghost of yet another calamity; the bed with its gnawed bedclothes bore witness to someone's anguish, and a chair which lay amid a heap of clothes on the ground looked like something dead. Georges must be at that woman's house, and so with dry eyes and feet that had regained their strength Mme Hugon went downstairs. She wanted her sons; she was starting to reclaim them.

Since morning Nana had been much worried. First of all it was the baker, who at nine o'clock had turned up, bill in hand. It was a wretched story. He had supplied her with bread to the amount of a hundred and thirty-three francs, and despite her royal housekeeping she could not pay it. In his irritation at being put off he had presented himself a score of times since the day he had refused further credit, and the servants were now espousing his cause. François kept saying that Madame would never pay him unless he made a fine scene; Charles talked of going upstairs, too, in order to get an old unpaid straw bill settled, while Victorine advised them to wait till some gentleman was with her, when they would get the money out of her by suddenly asking for it in the middle of conversation. The kitchen was in a savage mood: the tradesmen were all kept posted in the course events were taking, and there were gossiping consultations, lasting three or four hours on a stretch, during which Madame was stripped, plucked and talked over with the wrathful eagerness peculiar to an idle, overprosperous servants' hall. Julien, the house steward, alone pretended to defend his mistress. She was quite the thing, whatever they

night say! And when the others accused him of sleeping with her he laughed
~~atuously~~, thereby driving the cook to distraction, for she would have liked
~~o~~ be a man in order to "spit on such women's backsides," so utterly would
~~h~~ey have disgusted her. François, without informing Madame of it, had
~~w~~ickedly posted the baker in the hall, and when she came downstairs at lunch
~~t~~ime she found herself face to face with him. Taking the bill, she told him
~~t~~o return toward three o'clock, whereupon, with many foul expressions, he
~~d~~eparted, vowing that he would have things properly settled and get his
~~m~~oney by hook or by crook.

Nana made a very bad lunch, for the scene had annoyed her. Next time the
man would have to be definitely got rid of. A dozen times she had put his
money aside for him, but it had as constantly melted away, sometimes in the
purchase of flowers, at others in the shape of a subscription got up for the
benefit of an old gendarme. Besides, she was counting on Philippe and was
astonished not to see him make his appearance with his two hundred francs.
It was regular bad luck, seeing that the day before yesterday she had again
given Satin an outfit, a perfect trousseau this time, some twelve hundred francs'
worth of dresses and linen, and now she had not a louis remaining.

Toward two o'clock, when Nana was beginning to be anxious, Labordette
presented himself. He brought with him the designs for the bed, and this
caused a diversion, a joyful interlude which made the young woman forget
all her troubles. She clapped her hands and danced about. After which, her
heart bursting with curiosity, she leaned over a table in the drawing room and
examined the designs, which Labordette proceeded to explain to her.

"You see," he said, "this is the body of the bed. In the middle here there's
a bunch of roses in full bloom, and then comes a garland of buds and flowers.
The leaves are to be in yellow and the roses in red-gold. And here's the grand
design for the bed's head; Cupids dancing in a ring on a silver trelliswork."

But Nana interrupted him, for she was beside herself with ecstasy.

"Oh, how funny that little one is, that one in the corner, with his behind in
the air! Isn't he now? And what a sly laugh! They've all got such dirty,
wicked eyes! You know, dear boy, I shall never dare play any silly tricks
before *them!*"

Her pride was flattered beyond measure. The goldsmiths had declared that
no queen anywhere slept in such a bed. However, a difficulty presented itself.
Labordette showed her two designs for the footboard, one of which repro-
duced the pattern on the sides, while the other, a subject by itself, represented Night wrapped in her veil and discovered by a faun in all her splendid
nudity. He added that if she chose this last subject the goldsmiths intended
making Night in her own likeness. This idea, the taste of which was rather
risky, made her grow white with pleasure, and she pictured herself as a silver
statuette, symbolic of the warm, voluptuous delights of darkness.

"Of course you will only sit for the head and shoulders," said Labordette.
She looked quietly at him.

"Why? The moment a work of art's in question I don't mind the sculptor
that takes my likeness a blooming bit!"

Of course it must be understood that she was choosing the subject. But at this he interposed.

"Wait a moment; it's six thousand francs extra."

"It's all the same to me, by Jove!" she cried, bursting into a laugh. "Hasn't my little rough got the rhino?"

Nowadays among her intimates she always spoke thus of Count Muffat, and the gentlemen had ceased to inquire after him otherwise.

"Did you see your little rough last night?" they used to say.

"Dear me, I expected to find the little rough here!"

It was a simple familiarity enough, which, nevertheless, she did not as yet venture on in his presence.

Labordette began rolling up the designs as he gave the final explanations. The goldsmiths, he said, were undertaking to deliver the bed in two months' time, toward the twenty-fifth of December, and next week a sculptor would come to make a model for the Night. As she accompanied him to the door Nana remembered the baker and briskly inquired:

"By the by, you wouldn't be having ten louis about you?"

Labordette made it a solemn rule, which stood him in good stead, never to lend women money. He used always to make the same reply.

"No, my girl, I'm short. But would you like me to go to your little rough?"

She refused; it was useless. Two days before she had succeeded in getting five thousand francs out of the count. However, she soon regretted her discreet conduct, for the moment Labordette had gone the baker reappeared, though it was barely half-past two, and with many loud oaths roughly settled himself on a bench in the hall. The young woman listened to him from the first floor. She was pale, and it caused her especial pain to hear the servants' secret rejoicings swelling up louder and louder till they even reached her ears. Down in the kitchen they were dying of laughter. The coachman was staring across from the other side of the court; François was crossing the hall without any apparent reason. Then he hurried off to report progress, after sneering knowingly at the baker. They didn't care a damn for Madame; the walls were echoing to their laughter, and she felt that she was deserted on all hands and despised by the servants' hall, the inmates of which were watching her every movement and liberally bespattering her with the filthiest of chaff. Thereupon she abandoned the intention of borrowing the hundred and thirty-three francs from Zoé; she already owed the maid money, and she was too proud to risk a refusal now. Such a burst of feeling stirred her that she went back into her room, loudly remarking:

"Come, come, my girl, don't count on anyone but yourself. Your body's your own property, and it's better to make use of it than to let yourself be insulted."

And without even summoning Zoé she dressed herself with feverish haste in order to run round to the Tricon's. In hours of great embarrassment this was her last resource. Much sought after and constantly solicited by the old lady, she would refuse or resign herself according to her needs, and on these increasingly frequent occasions when both ends would not meet in her royally conducted establishment, she was sure to find twenty-five louis awaiting her at the other's house. She used to betake herself to the Tricon's with the ease born of use, just as the poor go to the pawnshop.

But as she left her own chamber Nana came suddenly upon Georges standing in the middle of the drawing room. Not noticing his waxen pallor and the somber fire in his wide eyes, she gave a sigh of relief.

"Ah, you've come from your brother."

"No," said the lad, growing yet paler.

At this she gave a despairing shrug. What did he want? Why was he barring her way? She was in a hurry—yes, she was. Then returning to where he stood:

"You've no money, have you?"

"No."

"That's true. How silly of me! Never a stiver; not even their omnibus fares. Mamma doesn't wish it! Oh, what a set of men!"

And she escaped. But he held her back; he wanted to speak to her. She was fairly under way and again declared she had no time, but he stopped her with a word.

"Listen, I know you're going to marry my brother."

Gracious! The thing was too funny! And she let herself down into a chair in order to laugh at her ease.

"Yes," continued the lad, "and I don't wish it. It's I you're going to marry. That's why I've come."

"Eh, what? You too?" she cried. "Why, it's a family disease, is it? No, never! What a fancy, to be sure! Have I ever asked you to do anything so nasty? Neither one nor t'other of you! No, never!"

The lad's face brightened. Perhaps he had been deceiving himself! He continued:

"Then swear to me that you don't go to bed with my brother."

"Oh, you're beginning to bore me now!" said Nana, who had risen with renewed impatience. "It's amusing for a little while, but when I tell you I'm in a hurry—— I go to bed with your brother if it pleases me. Are you keeping me—are you paymaster here that you insist on my making a report? Yes, I go to bed with your brother."

He had caught hold of her arm and squeezed it hard enough to break it as he stuttered:

"Don't say that! Don't say that!"

With a slight blow she disengaged herself from his grasp.

"He's maltreating me now! Here's a young ruffian for you! My chicken, you'll leave this jolly sharp. I used to keep you about out of niceness. Yes, I did! You may stare! Did you think I was going to be your mamma till I died? I've got better things to do than to bring up brats."

He listened to her stark with anguish, yet in utter submission. Her every word cut him to the heart so sharply that he felt he should die. She did not so much as notice his suffering and continued delightedly to revenge herself on him for the annoyance of the morning.

"It's like your brother; he's another pretty Johnny, he is! He promised me two hundred francs. Oh, dear me; yes, I can wait for 'em. It isn't his money I care for! I've not got enough to pay for hair oil. Yes, he's leaving me in a jolly fix! Look here, d'you want to know how matters stand? Here goes then: it's all owing to your brother that I'm going out to earn twenty-five louis with another man."

At these words his head spun, and he barred her egress. He cried; he besought her not to go, clasping his hands together and blurting out:

"Oh no! Oh no!"

"I want to, I do," she said. "Have you the money?"

No, he had not got the money. He would have given his life to have the money! Never before had he felt so miserable, so useless, so very childish. All his wretched being was shaken with weeping and gave proof of such heavy suffering that at last she noticed it and grew kind. She pushed him away softly.

"Come, my pet, let me pass; I must. Be reasonable. You're a baby boy, and it was very nice for a week, but nowadays I must look after my own affairs. Just think it over a bit. Now your brother's a man; what I'm saying doesn't apply to him. Oh, please do me a favor; it's no good telling him all this. He needn't know where I'm going. I always let out too much when I'm in a rage."

She began laughing. Then taking him in her arms and kissing him on the forehead:

"Good-by, baby," she said; "it's over, quite over between us; d'you understand? And now I'm off!"

And she left him, and he stood in the middle of the drawing room. Her last words rang like the knell of a tocsin in his ears: "It's over, quite over!" And he thought the ground was opening beneath his feet. There was a void in his brain from which the man awaiting Nana had disappeared. Philippe alone remained there in the young woman's bare embrace forever and ever. She did not deny it: she loved him, since she wanted to spare him the pain of her infidelity. It was over, quite over. He breathed heavily and gazed round the room, suffocating beneath a crushing weight. Memories kept recurring to him one after the other—memories of merry nights at La Mignotte, of amorous hours during which he had fancied himself her child, of pleasures stolen in this very room. And now these things would never, never recur! He was too small; he had not grown up quickly enough; Philippe was supplanting him because he was a bearded man. So then this was the end; he could not go on living. His vicious passion had become transformed into an infinite tenderness, a sensual adoration, in which his whole being was merged. Then, too, how was he to forget it all if his brother remained—his brother, blood of his blood, a second self, whose enjoyment drove him mad with jealousy? It was the end of all things; he wanted to die.

All the doors remained open, as the servants noisily scattered over the house after seeing Madame make her exit on foot. Downstairs on the bench in the hall the baker was laughing with Charles and François. Zoé came running across the drawing room and seemed surprised at sight of Georges. She asked

him if he were waiting for Madame. Yes, he was waiting for her; he had forgotten to give her an answer to a question. And when he was alone he set to
work and searched. Finding nothing else to suit his purpose, he took up in the
dressing room a pair of very sharply pointed scissors with which Nana had a
mania for ceaselessly trimming herself, either by polishing her skin or cutting
off little hairs. Then for a whole hour he waited patiently, his hand in his
pocket and his fingers tightly clasped round the scissors.

"Here's Madame," said Zoé, returning. She must have espied her through
the bedroom window.

There was a sound of people racing through the house, and laughter died
away and doors were shut. Georges heard Nana paying the baker and speaking in the curtest way. Then she came upstairs.

"What, you're here still!" she said as she noticed him. "Aha! We're going
to grow angry, my good man!"

He followed her as she walked toward her bedroom.

"Nana, will you marry me?"

She shrugged her shoulders. It was too stupid; she refused to answer any
more and conceived the idea of slamming the door in his face.

"Nana, will you marry me?"

She slammed the door. He opened it with one hand while he brought the
other and the scissors out of his pocket. And with one great stab he simply
buried them in his breast.

Nana, meanwhile, had felt conscious that something dreadful would happen,
and she had turned round. When she saw him stab himself she was seized with
indignation.

"Oh, what a fool he is! What a fool! And with my scissors! Will you leave
off, you naughty little rogue? Oh, my God! Oh, my God!"

She was scared. Sinking on his knees, the boy had just given himself a second
stab, which sent him down at full length on the carpet. He blocked the threshold of the bedroom. With that Nana lost her head utterly and screamed with
all her might, for she dared not step over his body, which shut her in and
prevented her from running to seek assistance.

"Zoé! Zoé! Come at once. Make him leave off. It's getting stupid—a child
like that! He's killing himself now! And in my place too! Did you ever see
the like of it?"

He was frightening her. He was all white, and his eyes were shut. There
was scarcely any bleeding—only a little blood, a tiny stain which was oozing
down into his waistcoat. She was making up her mind to step over the body
when an apparition sent her starting back. An old lady was advancing through
the drawing-room door, which remained wide open opposite. And in her
terror she recognized Mme Hugon but could not explain her presence. Still
wearing her gloves and hat, Nana kept edging backward, and her terror grew
so great that she sought to defend herself, and in a shaky voice:

"Madame," she cried, "it isn't I; I swear to you it isn't. He wanted to marry
me, and I said no, and he's killed himself!"

Slowly Mme Hugon drew near—she was in black, and her face showed pale under her white hair. In the carriage, as she drove thither, the thought of Georges had vanished and that of Philippe's misdoing had again taken complete possession of her. It might be that this woman could afford explanations to the judges which would touch them, and so she conceived the project of begging her to bear witness in her son's favor. Downstairs the doors of the house stood open, but as she mounted to the first floor her sick feet failed her, and she was hesitating as to which way to go when suddenly horror-stricken cries directed her. Then upstairs she found a man lying on the floor with bloodstained shirt. It was Georges—it was her other child.

Nana, in idiotic tones, kept saying:

"He wanted to marry me, and I said no, and he's killed himself."

Uttering no cry, Mme Hugon stooped down. Yes, it was the other one; it was Georges. The one was brought to dishonor, the other murdered! It caused her no surprise, for her whole life was ruined. Kneeling on the carpet, utterly forgetting where she was, noticing no one else, she gazed fixedly at her boy's face and listened with her hand on his heart. Then she gave a feeble sigh— she had felt the heart beating. And with that she lifted her head and scrutinized the room and the woman and seemed to remember. A fire glowed forth in her vacant eyes, and she looked so great and terrible in her silence that Nana trembled as she continued to defend herself above the body that divided them.

"I swear it, madame! If his brother were here he could explain it to you."

"His brother has robbed—he is in prison," said the mother in a hard voice.

Nana felt a choking sensation. Why, what was the reason of it all? The other had turned thief now! They were mad in that family! She ceased struggling in self-defense; she seemed no longer mistress in her own house and allowed Mme Hugon to give what orders she liked. The servants had at last hurried up, and the old lady insisted on their carrying the fainting Georges down to her carriage. She preferred killing him rather than letting him remain in that house. With an air of stupefaction Nana watched the retreating servants as they supported poor, dear Zizi by his legs and shoulders. The mother walked behind them in a state of collapse; she supported herself against the furniture; she felt as if all she held dear had vanished in the void. On the landing a sob escaped her; she turned and twice ejaculated:

"Oh, but you've done us infinite harm! You've done us infinite harm!"

That was all. In her stupefaction Nana had sat down; she still wore her gloves and her hat. The house once more lapsed into heavy silence; the carriage had driven away, and she sat motionless, not knowing what to do next, her head swimming after all she had gone through. A quarter of an hour later Count Muffat found her thus, but at sight of him she relieved her feelings in an overflowing current of talk. She told him all about the sad incident, repeated the same details twenty times over, picked up the bloodstained scissors in order to imitate Zizi's gesture when he stabbed himself. And above all she nursed the idea of proving her own innocence.

"Look you here, dearie, is it my fault? If you were the judge would you condemn me? I certainly didn't tell Philippe to meddle with the till any more than I urged that wretched boy to kill himself. I've been most unfortunate throughout it all. They come and do stupid things in my place; they make me miserable; they treat me like a hussy."

And she burst into tears. A fit of nervous expansiveness rendered her soft and doleful, and her immense distress melted her utterly.

"And you, too, look as if you weren't satisfied. Now do just ask Zoé if I'm at all mixed up in it. Zoé, do speak: explain to Monsieur——"

The lady's maid, having brought a towel and a basin of water out of the dressing room, had for some moments past been rubbing the carpet in order to remove the bloodstains before they dried.

"Oh, monsieur, " she declared, "Madame is utterly miserable!"

Muffat was still stupefied; the tragedy had frozen him, and his imagination was full of the mother weeping for her sons. He knew her greatness of heart and pictured her in her widow's weeds, withering solitarily away at Les Fondettes. But Nana grew ever more despondent, for now the memory of Zizi lying stretched on the floor, with a red hole in his shirt, almost drove her senseless.

"He used to be such a darling, so sweet and caressing. Oh, you know, my pet—I'm sorry if it vexes you—I loved that baby! I can't help saying so; the words must out. Besides, now it ought not to hurt you at all. He's gone. You've got what you wanted; you're quite certain never to surprise us again."

And this last reflection tortured her with such regret that he ended by turning comforter. Well, well, he said, she ought to be brave; she was quite right; it wasn't her fault! But she checked her lamentations of her own accord in order to say:

"Listen, you must run round and bring me news of him. At once! I wish it!"

He took his hat and went to get news of Georges. When he returned after some three quarters of an hour he saw Nana leaning anxiously out of a window, and he shouted up to her from the pavement that the lad was not dead and that they even hoped to bring him through. At this she immediately exchanged grief for excess of joy and began to sing and dance and vote existence delightful. Zoé, meanwhile, was still dissatisfied with her washing. She kept looking at the stain, and every time she passed it she repeated:

"You know it's not gone yet, madame."

As a matter of fact, the pale red stain kept reappearing on one of the white roses in the carpet pattern. It was as though, on the very threshold of the room, a splash of blood were barring the doorway.

"Bah!" said the joyous Nana. "That 'll be rubbed out under people's feet."

After the following day Count Muffat had likewise forgotten the incident. For a moment or two, when in the cab which drove him to the Rue Richelieu, he had busily sworn never to return to that woman's house. Heaven was warning him; the misfortunes of Philippe and Georges were, he opined, prophetic of his proper ruin. But neither the sight of Mme Hugon in tears nor that of the boy burning with fever had been strong enough to make him keep his vow, and the short-lived horror of the situation had only left behind it a sense of secret delight at the thought that he was now well quit of a rival, the charm of whose youth had always exasperated him. His passion had by this time grown exclusive; it was, indeed, the passion of a man who has had no youth. He loved Nana as one who yearned to be her sole possessor, to listen to her, to touch her, to be breathed on by her. His was now a supersensual tenderness, verging on pure sentiment; it was an anxious affection and as such was jealous of the past and apt at times to dream of a day of redemption and pardon received, when both should kneel before God the Father. Every day religion kept regaining its influence over him. He again became a practicing Christian; he confessed himself and communicated, while a ceaseless struggle raged within him, and remorse redoubled the joys of sin and of repentance. Afterward, when his director gave him leave to spend his passion, he had made a habit of this daily perdition and would redeem the same by ecstasies of faith, which were full of pious humility. Very naïvely he offered heaven, by way of expiatory anguish, the abominable torment from which he was suffering. This torment grew and increased, and he would climb his Calvary with the deep and solemn feelings of a believer, though steeped in a harlot's fierce sensuality. That which made his agony most poignant was this woman's continued faithlessness. He could not share her with others, nor did he understand her imbecile caprices. Undying, unchanging love was what he wished for. However, she had sworn, and he paid her as having done so. But he felt that she was untruthful, incapable of common fidelity, apt to yield to friends, to stray passers-by, like a good-natured animal, born to live minus a shift.

One morning when he saw Foucarmont emerging from her bedroom at an unusual hour, he made a scene about it. But in her weariness of his jealousy she grew angry directly. On several occasions ere that she had behaved rather prettily. Thus the evening when he surprised her with Georges she was the first to regain her temper and to confess herself in the wrong. She had loaded him with caresses and dosed him with soft speeches in order to make him swallow the business. But he had ended by boring her to death with his obstinate refusals to understand the feminine nature, and now she was brutal.

"Very well, yes! I've slept with Foucarmont. What then? That's flattened you out a bit, my little rough, hasn't it?"

It was the first time she had thrown "my little rough" in his teeth. The frank directness of her avowal took his breath away, and when he began clenching his fists she marched up to him and looked him full in the face.

"We've had enough of this, eh? If it doesn't suit you you'll do me the pleasure of leaving the house. I don't want you to go yelling in my place. Just you get it into your noodle that I mean to be quite free. When a man pleases me I go to bed with him. Yes, I do—that's my way! And you must make up your mind directly. Yes or no! If it's no, out you may walk!"

She had gone and opened the door, but he did not leave. That was her way now of binding him more closely to her. For no reason whatever, at the slightest approach to a quarrel she would tell him he might stop or go as he liked, and she would accompany her permission with a flood of odious reflections. She said she could always find better than he; she had only too many from whom to choose; men in any quantity could be picked up in the street, and men a good deal smarter, too, whose blood boiled in their veins. At this he would hang his head and wait for those gentler moods when she wanted money. She would then become affectionate, and he would forget it all, one night of tender dalliance making up for the tortures of a whole week. His reconciliation with his wife had rendered his home unbearable. Fauchery, having again fallen under Rose's dominion, the countess was running madly after other loves. She was entering on the forties, that restless, feverish time in the life of women, and ever hysterically nervous, she now filled her mansion with the maddening whirl of her fashionable life. Estelle, since her marriage, had seen nothing of her father; the undeveloped, insignificant girl had suddenly become a woman of iron will, so imperious withal that Daguenet trembled in her presence. In these days he accompanied her to mass: he was converted, and he raged against his father-in-law for ruining them with a courtesan. M. Venot alone still remained kindly inclined toward the count, for he was biding his time. He had even succeeded in getting into Nana's immediate circle. In fact, he frequented both houses, where you encountered his continual smile behind doors. So Muffat, wretched at home, driven out by ennui and shame, still preferred to live in the Avenue de Villiers, even though he was abused there.

Soon there was but one question between Nana and the count, and that was "money." One day after having formally promised her ten thousand francs he had dared keep his appointment empty handed. For two days past she had been surfeiting him with love, and such a breach of faith, such a waste of caresses, made her ragingly abusive. She was white with fury.

"So you've not got the money, eh? Then go back where you came from, my little rough, and look sharp about it! There's a bloody fool for you! He wanted to kiss me again! Mark my words—no money, no nothing!"

He explained matters; he would be sure to have the money the day after tomorrow. But she interrupted him violently:

"And my bills! They'll sell me up while Monsieur's playing the fool. Now then, look at yourself. D'ye think I love you for your figure? A man with a mug like yours has to pay the women who are kind enough to put up with him. By God, if you don't bring me that ten thousand francs tonight you shan't even have the tip of my little finger to suck. I mean it! I shall send you back to your wife!"

At night he brought the ten thousand francs. Nana put up her lips, and he took a long kiss which consoled him for the whole day of anguish. What annoyed the young woman was to have him continually tied to her apron strings. She complained to M. Venot, begging him to take her little rough off to the countess. Was their reconciliation good for nothing then? She was sorry she had mixed herself up in it, since despite everything he was always at her heels. On the days when, out of anger, she forgot her own interest, she swore to play him such a dirty trick that he would never again be able to set foot in her place. But when she slapped her leg and yelled at him she might quite as well have spat in his face too: he would still have stayed and even thanked her. Then the rows about money matters kept continually recurring. She demanded money savagely; she rowed him over wretched little amounts; she was odiously stingy with every minute of her time; she kept fiercely informing him that she slept with him for his money, not for any other reasons, and that she did not enjoy it a bit, that, in fact, she loved another and was awfully unfortunate in needing an idiot of his sort! They did not even want him at court now, and there was some talk of requiring him to send in his resignation. The empress had said, "He is too disgusting." It was true enough. So Nana repeated the phrase by way of closure to all their quarrels.

"Look here! You disgust me!"

Nowadays she no longer minded her ps and qs; she had regained the most perfect freedom.

Every day she did her round of the lake, beginning acquaintanceships which ended elsewhere. Here was the happy hunting ground par excellence, where courtesans of the first water spread their nets in open daylight and flaunted themselves amid the tolerating smiles and brilliant luxury of Paris. Duchesses pointed her out to one another with a passing look—rich shopkeepers' wives copied the fashion of her hats. Sometimes her landau, in its haste to get by, stopped a file of puissant turnouts, wherein sat plutocrats able to buy up all Europe or Cabinet ministers with plump fingers tight-pressed to the throat of France. She belonged to this Bois society, occupied a prominent place in it, was known in every capital and asked about by every foreigner. The splendors of this crowd were enhanced by the madness of her profligacy as though it were the very crown, the darling passion, of the nation. Then there were unions of a night, continual passages of desire, which she lost count of the morning after, and these sent her touring through the grand restaurants and on fine days, as often as not, to "Madrid." The staffs of all the embassies visited her, and she, Lucy Stewart, Caroline Héquet and Maria Blond would dine in the society of gentlemen who murdered the French language and paid to be amused, engaging them by the evening with orders to be funny and yet proving so blasé and so worn out that they never even touched them. This the ladies called "going on a spree," and they would return home happy at having been despised and would finish the night in the arms of the lovers of their choice.

When she did not actually throw the men at his head Count Muffat pretended not to know about all this. However, he suffered not a little from the lesser indignities of their daily life. The mansion in the Avenue de Villiers was becoming a hell, a house full of mad people, in which every hour of the day wild disorders led to hateful complications. Nana even fought with her servants. One moment she would be very nice with Charles, the coachman. When she stopped at a restaurant she would send him out beer by the waiter and would talk with him from the inside of her carriage when he slanged the cabbies at a block in the traffic, for then he struck her as funny and cheered her up. Then the next moment she called him a fool for no earthly reason. She was always squabbling over the straw, the bran or the oats; in spite of her love for animals she thought her horses ate too much. Accordingly one day when she was settling up she accused the man of robbing her. At this Charles got in a rage and called her a whore right out; his horses, he said, were distinctly better than she was, for they did not sleep with everybody. She answered him in the same strain, and the count had to separate them and give the coachman the sack. This was the beginning of a rebellion among the servants. When her diamonds had been stolen Victorine and François left. Julien himself disappeared, and the tale ran that the master had given him a big bribe and had begged him to go, because he slept with the mistress. Every week there were new faces in the servants' hall. Never was there such a mess; the house was like a passage down which the scum of the registry offices galloped, destroying everything in their path. Zoé alone kept her place; she always looked clean, and her only anxiety was how to organize this riot until she had got enough together to set up on her own account in fulfillment of a plan she had been hatching for some time past.

These, again, were only the anxieties he could own to. The count put up with the stupidity of Mme Maloir, playing bezique with her in spite of her musty smell. He put up with Mme Lerat and her encumbrances, with Louiset and the mournful complaints peculiar to a child who is being eaten up with the rottenness inherited from some unknown father. But he spent hours worse than these. One evening he had heard Nana angrily telling her maid that a man pretending to be rich had just swindled her—a handsome man calling himself an American and owning gold mines in his own country, a beast who had gone off while she was asleep without giving her a copper and had even taken a packet of cigarette papers with him. The count had turned very pale and had gone downstairs again on tiptoe so as not to hear more. But later he had to hear all. Nana, having been smitten with a baritone in a music hall and having been thrown over by him, wanted to commit suicide during a fit of sentimental melancholia. She swallowed a glass of water in which she had soaked a box of matches. This made her terribly sick but did not kill her. The count had to nurse her and to listen to the whole story of her passion, her tearful protests and her oaths never to take to any man again. In her contempt for those swine, as she called them, she could not, however, keep her heart free, for she always had some sweetheart round her, and her exhausted body inclined to incomprehensible fancies and perverse tastes. As Zoé designedly relaxed her efforts the service of the house had got to such a pitch that Muffat did not dare to push open a door, to pull a curtain or to unclose a cupboard. The bells did not ring; men lounged about everywhere and at every moment knocked up against one another. He had now to cough before entering a room, having almost caught the girl hanging round Francis' neck one evening that he had just gone out of the dressing room for two minutes to tell the coachman to put the horses to, while her hairdresser was finishing her hair. She gave herself up suddenly behind his back; she took her pleasure in every corner, quickly, with the first man she met. Whether she was in her chemise or in full dress did not matter. She would come back to the count red all over, happy at having cheated him. As for him, he was plagued to death; it was an abominable infliction!

In his jealous anguish the unhappy man was comparatively at peace when he left Nana and Satin alone together. He would have willingly urged her on to this vice, to keep the men off her. But all was spoiled in this direction too. Nana deceived Satin as she deceived the count, going mad over some monstrous fancy or other and picking up girls at the street corners. Coming back in her carriage, she would suddenly be taken with a little slut that she saw on the pavement; her senses would be captivated, her imagination excited. She would take the little slut in with her, pay her and send her away again. Then, disguised as a man, she would go to infamous houses and look on at scenes of debauch to while away hours of boredom. And Satin, angry at being thrown over every moment, would turn the house topsy-turvy with the most awful scenes. She had at last acquired a complete ascendancy over Nana, who now respected her. Muffat even thought of an alliance between them. When he dared not say anything he let Satin loose. Twice she had compelled her darling to take up with him again, while he showed himself obliging and effaced himself in her favor at the least sign. But this good understanding lasted no time, for Satin, too, was a little cracked. On certain days she would very nearly go mad and would smash everything, wearing herself out in tempest of love and anger, but pretty all the time. Zoé must have excited her, for the maid took her into corners as if she wanted to tell her about her great design of which she as yet spoke to no one.

At times, however, Count Muffat was still singularly revolted. He who had tolerated Satin for months, who had at last shut his eyes to the unknown herd of men that scampered so quickly through Nana's bedroom, became terribly enraged at being deceived by one of his own set or even by an acquaintance. When she confessed her relations with Foucarmont he suffered so acutely, he thought the treachery of the young man so base, that he wished to insult him and fight a duel. As he did not know where to find seconds for such an affair, he went to Labordette. The latter, astonished, could not help laughing.

"A duel about Nana? But, my dear sir, all Paris would be laughing at you. Men do not fight for Nana; it would be ridiculous."

The count grew very pale and made a violent gesture.

"Then I shall slap his face in the open street."

For an hour Labordette had to argue with him. A blow would make the affair odious; that evening everyone would know the real reason of the meeting; it would be in all the papers. And Labordette always finished with the same expression:

"It is impossible; it would be ridiculous."

Each time Muffat heard these words they seemed sharp and keen as a stab. He could not even fight for the woman he loved; people would have burst out laughing. Never before had he felt more bitterly the misery of his love, the contrast between his heavy heart and the absurdity of this life of pleasure in which it was now lost. This was his last rebellion; he allowed Labordette to convince him, and he was present afterward at the procession of his friends, who lived there as if at home.

Nana in a few months finished them up greedily, one after the other. The growing needs entailed by her luxurious way of life only added fuel to her desires, and she finished a man up at one mouthful. First she had Foucarmont, who did not last a fortnight. He was thinking of leaving the navy, having saved about thirty thousand francs in his ten years of service, which he wished to invest in the United States. His instincts, which were prudential, even miserly, were conquered; he gave her everything, even his signature to notes of hand, which pledged his future. When Nana had done with him he was penniless. But then she proved very kind; she advised him to return to his ship. What was the good of getting angry? Since he had no money their relations were no longer possible. He ought to understand that and to be reasonable. A ruined man fell from her hands like a ripe fruit, to rot on the ground by himself.

Then Nana took up with Steiner without disgust but without love. She called him a dirty Jew; she seemed to be paying back an old grudge, of which she had no distinct recollection. He was fat; he was stupid, and she got him down and took two bites at a time in order the quicker to do for this Prussian. As for him, he had thrown Simonne over. His Bosphorous scheme was getting shaky, and Nana hastened the downfall by wild expenses. For a month he struggled on, doing miracles of finance. He filled Europe with posters, advertisements and prospectuses of a colossal scheme and obtained money from the most distant climes. All these savings, the pounds of speculators and the pence of the poor, were swallowed up in the Avenue de Villiers. Again he was partner in an ironworks in Alsace, where in a small provincial town workmen, blackened with coal dust and soaked with sweat, day and night strained their sinews and heard their bones crack to satisfy Nana's pleasures. Like a huge fire she devoured all the fruits of stock-exchange swindling and the profits of labor. This time she did for Steiner; she brought him to the ground, sucked him dry to the core, left him so cleaned out that he was unable to invent a new roguery.When his bank failed he stammered and trembled at the idea of prosecution. His bankruptcy had just been published, and the simple mention of money flurried him and threw him into a childish embarrassment. And this was he who had played with millions. One evening at Nana's he began to cry and asked her for a loan of a hundred francs wherewith to pay his maidservant. And Nana, much affected and amused at the end of this terrible old man who had squeezed Paris for twenty years, brought it to him and said:

"I say, I'm giving it you because it seems so funny! But listen to me, my boy, you are too old for me to keep. You must find something else to do."

Then Nana started on La Faloise at once. He had for some time been longing for the honor of being ruined by her in order to put the finishing stroke on his smartness. He needed a woman to launch him properly; it was the one thing still lacking. In two months all Paris would be talking of him, and he would see his name in the papers. Six weeks were enough. His inheritance was in landed estate, houses, fields, woods and farms. He had to sell all, one after the other, as quickly as he could. At every mouthful Nana swallowed an acre. The foliage trembling in the sunshine, the wide fields of ripe grain, the vineyards so golden in September, the tall grass in which the cows stood knee-deep, all passed through her hands as if engulfed by an abyss. Even fishing rights, a stone quarry and three mills disappeared. Nana passed over them like an invading army or one of those swarms of locusts whose flight scours a whole province. The ground was burned up where her little foot had rested. Farm by farm, field by field, she ate up the man's patrimony very prettily and quite inattentively, just as she would have eaten a box of sweetmeats flung into her lap between mealtimes. There was no harm in it all; they were only sweets! But at last one evening there only remained a single little wood. She swallowed it up disdainfully, as it was hardly worth the trouble opening one's mouth for. La Faloise laughed idiotically and sucked the top of his stick. His debts were crushing him; he was not worth a hundred francs a year, and he saw that he would be compelled to go back into the country and live with his maniacal uncle. But that did not matter; he had achieved smartness; the *Figaro* had printed his name twice. And with his meager neck sticking up between the turndown points of his collar and his figure squeezed into all too short a coat, he would swagger about, uttering his parrotlike exclamations and affecting a solemn listlessness suggestive of an emotionless marionette. He so annoyed Nana that she ended by beating him.

Meanwhile Fauchery had returned, his cousin having brought him. Poor Fauchery had now set up housekeeping. After having thrown over the countess he had fallen into Rose's hands, and she treated him as a lawful wife would have done. Mignon was simply Madame's major-domo. Installed as master of the house, the journalist lied to Rose and took all sorts of precautions when he deceived her. He was as scrupulous as a good husband, for he really wanted to settle down at last. Nana's triumph consisted in possessing and in ruining a newspaper that he had started with a friend's capital. She did not proclaim her triumph; on the contrary, she delighted in treating him as a man who had to be circumspect, and when she spoke of Rose it was as "poor Rose." The newspaper kept her in flowers for two months. She took all the provincial subscriptions; in fact, she took everything, from the column of news and gossip down to the dramatic notes. Then the editorial staff having been turned topsy-turvy and the management completely disorganized, she satisfied a fanciful caprice and had a winter garden constructed in a corner of her house: that carried off all the type. But then it was no joke after all! When in his delight at the whole business Mignon came to see if he could not saddle Fauchery on her altogether, she asked him if he took her for a fool. A penniless fellow living by his articles and his plays—not if she knew it! That sort of foolishness might be all very well for a clever woman like her poor, dear Rose! She grew distrustful: she feared some treachery on Mignon's part, for he was quite capable of preaching to his wife, and so she gave Fauchery his *congé* as he now only paid her in fame.

But she always recollected him kindly. They had both enjoyed themselves so much at the expense of that fool of a La Faloise! They would never have thought of seeing each other again if the delight of fooling such a perfect idiot had not egged them on! It seemed an awfully good joke to kiss each other under his very nose. They cut a regular dash with his coin; they would send him off full speed to the other end of Paris in order to be alone and then, when he came back, they would crack jokes and make allusions he could not understand. One day, urged by the journalist, she bet that she would smack his face, and that she did the very same evening and went on to harder blows, for she thought it a good joke and was glad of the opportunity of showing how cowardly men were. She called him her "slapjack" and would tell him to come and have his smack! The smacks made her hands red, for as yet she was not up to the trick. La Faloise laughed in his idiotic, languid way, though his eyes were full of tears. He was delighted at such familiarity; he thought it simply stunning.

One night when he had received sundry cuffs and was greatly excited:

"Now, d'you know," he said, "you ought to marry me. We should be as jolly as grigs together, eh?"

This was no empty suggestion. Seized with a desire to astonish Paris, he had been slyly projecting this marriage. "Nana's husband! Wouldn't that sound smart, eh?" Rather a stunning apotheosis that! But Nana gave him a fine snubbing.

"Me marry you! Lovely! If such an idea had been tormenting me I should have found a husband a long time ago! And he'd have been a man worth twenty of you, my pippin! I've had a heap of proposals. Why, look here, just reckon 'em up with me: Philippe, Georges, Foucarmont, Steiner—that makes four, without counting the others you don't know. It's a chorus they all sing. I can't be nice, but they forthwith begin yelling, 'Will you marry me? Will you marry me?'"

She lashed herself up and then burst out in fine indignation:

"Oh dear, no! I don't want to! D'you think I'm built that way? Just look at me a bit! Why, I shouldn't be Nana any longer if I fastened a man on behind! And, besides, it's too foul!"

And she spat and hiccuped with disgust, as though she had seen all the dirt in the world spread out beneath her.

One evening La Faloise vanished, and a week later it became known that he was in the country with an uncle whose mania was botany. He was pasting his specimens for him and stood a chance of marrying a very plain, pious cousin. Nana shed no tears for him. She simply said to the count:

"Eh, little rough, another rival less! You're chortling today. But he was becoming serious! He wanted to marry me."

He waxed pale, and she flung her arms round his neck and hung there, laughing, while she emphasized every little cruel speech with a caress.

"You can't marry Nana! Isn't that what's fetching you, eh? When they're all bothering me with their marriages you're raging in your corner. It isn't possible; you must wait till your wife kicks the bucket. Oh, if she were only to do that, how you'd come rushing round! How you'd fling yourself on the ground and make your offer with all the grand accompaniments—sighs and tears and vows! Wouldn't it be nice, darling, eh?"

Her voice had become soft, and she was chaffing him in a ferociously wheedling manner. He was deeply moved and began blushing as he paid her back her kisses. Then she cried:

"By God, to think I should have guessed! He's thought about it; he's waiting for his wife to go off the hooks! Well, well, that's the finishing touch! Why, he's even a bigger rascal than the others!"

Muffat had resigned himself to "the others." Nowadays he was trusting to the last relics of his personal dignity in order to remain "Monsieur" among the servants and intimates of the house, the man, in fact, who because he gave most was the official lover. And his passion grew fiercer. He kept his position because he paid for it, buying even smiles at a high price. He was even robbed and he never got his money's worth, but a disease seemed to be gnawing his vitals from which he could not prevent himself suffering. Whenever he entered Nana's bedroom he was simply content to open the windows for a second or two in order to get rid of the odors the others left behind them, the essential smells of fair-haired men and dark, the smoke of cigars, of which the pungency choked him. This bedroom was becoming a veritable thoroughfare, so continually were boots wiped on its threshold. Yet never a man among them was stopped by the bloodstain barring the door. Zoé was still preoccupied by this stain; it was a simple mania with her, for she was a clean girl, and it horrified her to see it always there. Despite everything her eyes would wander in its direction, and she now never entered Madame's room without remarking:

"It's strange that don't go. All the same, plenty of folk come in this way."

Nana kept receiving the best news from Georges, who was by that time already convalescent in his mother's keeping at Les Fondettes, and she used always to make the same reply.

"Oh, hang it, time's all that's wanted. It's apt to grow paler as feet cross it."

As a matter of fact, each of the gentlemen, whether Foucarmont, Steiner, La Faloise or Fauchery, had borne away some of it on their bootsoles. And Muffat, whom the bloodstain preoccupied as much as it did Zoé, kept studying it in his own despite, as though in its gradual rosy disappearance he would read the number of men that passed. He secretly dreaded it and always stepped over it out of a vivid fear of crushing some live thing, some naked limb lying on the floor.

But in the bedroom within he would grow dizzy and intoxicated and would forget everything—the mob of men which constantly crossed it, the sign of mourning which barred its door. Outside, in the open air of the street, he would weep occasionally out of sheer shame and disgust and would vow never to enter the room again. And the moment the portiere had closed behind him he was under the old influence once more and felt his whole being melting in the damp warm air of the place, felt his flesh penetrated by a perfume, felt himself overborne by a voluptuous yearning for self-annihilation. Pious and habituated to ecstatic experiences in sumptuous chapels, he there re-encountered precisely the same mystical sensations as when he knelt under some painted window and gave way to the intoxication of organ music and incense. Woman swayed him as jealously and despotically as the God of wrath, terrifying him, granting him moments of delight, which were like spasms in their keenness, in return for hours filled with frightful, tormenting visions of hell and eternal tortures. In Nana's presence, as in church, the same stammering accents were his, the same prayers and the same fits of despair—nay, the same paroxysms of humility peculiar to an accursed creature who is crushed down in the mire from whence he has sprung. His fleshly desires, his spiritual needs, were confounded together and seemed to spring from the obscure depths of his being and to bear but one blossom on the tree of his existence. He abandoned himself to the power of love and of faith, those twin levers which move the world. And despite all the struggles of his reason this bedroom of Nana's always filled him with madness, and he would sink shuddering under the almighty dominion of sex, just as he would swoon before the vast unknown of heaven.

Then when she felt how humble he was Nana grew tyrannously triumphant. The rage for debasing things was inborn in her. It did not suffice her to destroy them; she must soil them too. Her delicate hands left abominable traces and themselves decomposed whatever they had broken. And he in his imbecile condition lent himself to this sort of sport, for he was possessed by vaguely remembered stories of saints who were devoured by vermin and in turn devoured their own excrements. When once she had him fast in her room and the doors were shut, she treated herself to a man's infamy. At first they joked together, and she would deal him light blows and impose quaint tasks on him, making him lisp like a child and repeat tags of sentences.

"Say as I do: 'tonfound it! Ickle man damn vell don't tare about it!"

He would prove so docile as to reproduce her very accent.

" 'Tonfound it! Ickle man damn vell don't tare about it!"

Or again she would play bear, walking on all fours on her rugs when she had only her chemise on and turning round with a growl as though she wanted to eat him. She would even nibble his calves for the fun of the thing. Then, getting up again:

"It's your turn now; try it a bit. I bet you don't play bear like me."

It was still charming enough. As bear she amused him with her white skin and her fell of ruddy hair. He used to laugh and go down on all fours, too, and growl and bite her calves, while she ran from him with an affectation of terror.

"Are we beasts, eh?" she would end by saying. "You've no notion how ugly you are, my pet! Just think if they were to see you like that at the Tuileries!"

But ere long these little games were spoiled. It was not cruelty in her case, for she was still a good-natured girl; it was as though a passing wind of madness were blowing ever more strongly in the shut-up bedroom. A storm of lust disordered their brains, plunged them into the delirious imaginations of the flesh. The old pious terrors of their sleepless nights were now transforming themselves into a thirst for bestiality, a furious longing to walk on all fours, to growl and to bite. One day when he was playing bear she pushed him so roughly that he fell against a piece of furniture, and when she saw the lump on his forehead she burst into involuntary laughter. After that her experiments on La Faloise having whetted her appetite, she treated him like an animal, threshing him and chasing him to an accompaniment of kicks.

"Gee up! Gee up! You're a horse. Hoi! Gee up! Won't you hurry up, you dirty screw?"

At other times he was a dog. She would throw her scented handkerchief to the far end of the room, and he had to run and pick it up with his teeth, dragging himself along on hands and knees.

"Fetch it, Caesar! Look here, I'll give you what for if you don't look sharp! Well done, Caesar! Good dog! Nice old fellow! Now behave pretty!"

And he loved his abasement and delighted in being a brute beast. He longed to sink still further and would cry:

"Hit harder. On, on! I'm wild! Hit away!"

She was seized with a whim and insisted on his coming to her one night clad in his magnificent chamberlain's costume. Then how she did laugh and make fun of him when she had him there in all his glory, with the sword and the cocked hat and the white breeches and the full-bottomed coat of red cloth laced with gold and the symbolic key hanging on its left-hand skirt. This key made her especially merry and urged her to a wildly fanciful and extremely filthy discussion of it. Laughing without cease and carried away by her irreverence for pomp and by the joy of debasing him in the official dignity of his costume, she shook him, pinched him, shouted, "Oh, get along with ye, Chamberlain!" and ended by an accompaniment of swinging kicks behind. Oh, those kicks! How heartily she rained them on the Tuileries and the majesty of the imperial court, throning on high above an abject and trembling people. That's what she thought of society! That was her revenge! It was an affair of unconscious hereditary spite; it had come to her in her blood. Then when once the chamberlain was undressed and his coat lay spread on the ground she shrieked, "Jump!" And he jumped. She shrieked, "Spit!" And he spat. With a shriek she bade him walk on the gold, on the eagles, on the decorations, and he walked on them. Hi tiddly hi ti! Nothing was left; everything was going to pieces. She smashed a chamberlain just as she smashed a flask or a comfit box, and she made filth of him, reduced him to a heap of mud at a street corner.

Meanwhile the goldsmiths had failed to keep their promise, and the bed was not delivered till one day about the middle of January. Muffat was just then in Normandy, whither he had gone to sell a last stray shred of property, but Nana demanded four thousand francs forthwith. He was not due in Paris till the day after tomorrow, but when his business was once finished he hastened his return and without even paying a flying visit in the Rue Miromesnil came direct to the Avenue de Villiers. Ten o'clock was striking. As he had a key of a little door opening on the Rue Cardinet, he went up unhindered. In the drawing room upstairs Zoé, who was polishing the bronzes, stood dumfounded at sight of him, and not knowing how to stop him, she began with much circumlocution, informing him that M. Venot, looking utterly beside himself, had been searching for him since yesterday and that he had already come twice to beg her to send Monsieur to his house if Monsieur arrived at Madame's before going home. Muffat listened to her without in the least understanding the meaning of her recital; then he noticed her agitation and was seized by a sudden fit of jealousy of which he no longer believed himself capable. He threw himself against the bedroom door, for he heard the sound of laughter within. The door gave; its two flaps flew asunder, while Zoé withdrew, shrugging her shoulders. So much the worse for Madame! As Madame was bidding good-by to her wits, she might arrange matters for herself.

And on the threshold Muffat uttered a cry at the sight that was presented to his view.

"My God! My God!"

The renovated bedroom was resplendent in all its royal luxury. Silver buttons gleamed like bright stars on the tea-rose velvet of the hangings. These last were of that pink flesh tint which the skies assume on fine evenings, when Venus lights her fires on the horizon against the clear background of fading daylight. The golden cords and tassels hanging in corners and the gold lacework surrounding the panels were like little flames of ruddy strands of loosened hair, and they half covered the wide nakedness of the room while they emphasized its pale, voluptuous tone. Then over against him there was the gold and silver bed, which shone in all the fresh splendor of its chiseled workmanship, a throne this of sufficient extent for Nana to display the outstretched glory of her naked limbs, an altar of Byzantine sumptuousness, worthy of the almighty puissance of Nana's sex, which at this very hour lay nudely displayed there in the religious immodesty befitting an idol of all men's worship. And close by, beneath the snowy reflections of her bosom and amid the triumph of the goddess, lay wallowing a shameful, decrepit thing, a comic and lamentable ruin, the Marquis de Chouard in his nightshirt.

The count had clasped his hands together and, shaken by a paroxysmal shuddering, he kept crying:

"My God! My God!"

It was for the Marquis de Chouard, then, that the golden roses flourished on the side panels, those bunches of golden roses blooming among the golden leaves; it was for him that the Cupids leaned forth with amorous, roguish laughter from their tumbling ring on the silver trelliswork. And it was for him that the faun at his feet discovered the nymph sleeping, tired with dalliance, the figure of Night copied down to the exaggerated thighs—which caused her to be recognizable of all—from Nana's renowned nudity. Cast there like the rag of something human which has been spoiled and dissolved by sixty years of debauchery, he suggested the charnelhouse amid the glory of the woman's dazzling contours. Seeing the door open, he had risen up, smitten with sudden terror as became an infirm old man. This last night of passion had rendered him imbecile; he was entering on his second childhood; and, his speech failing him, he remained in an attitude of flight, half-paralyzed, stammering, shivering, his nightshirt half up his skeleton shape, and one leg outside the clothes, a livid leg, covered with gray hair. Despite her vexation Nana could not keep from laughing.

"Do lie down! Stuff yourself into the bed," she said, pulling him back and burying him under the coverlet, as though he were some filthy thing she could not show anyone.

Then she sprang up to shut the door again. She was decidedly never lucky with her little rough. He was always coming when least wanted. And why had he gone to fetch money in Normandy? The old man had brought her the four thousand francs, and she had let him have his will of her. She pushed back the two flaps of the door and shouted:

"So much the worse for you! It's your fault. Is that the way to come into a room? I've had enough of this sort of thing. Ta ta!"

Muffat remained standing before the closed door, thunderstruck by what he had just seen. His shuddering fit increased. It mounted from his feet to his heart and brain. Then like a tree shaken by a mighty wind, he swayed to and fro and dropped on his knees, all his muscles giving way under him. And with hands despairingly outstretched he stammered:

"This is more than I can bear, my God! More than I can bear!"

He had accepted every situation but he could do so no longer. He had come to the end of his strength and was plunged in the dark void where man and his reason are together overthrown. In an extravagant access of faith he raised his hands ever higher and higher, searching for heaven, calling on God.

"Oh no, I do not desire it! Oh, come to me, my God! Succor me; nay, let me die sooner! Oh no, not that man, my God! It is over; take me, carry me away, that I may not see, that I may not feel any longer! Oh, I belong to you, my God! Our Father which art in heaven——"

And burning with faith, he continued his supplication, and an ardent prayer escaped from his lips. But someone touched him on the shoulder. He lifted his eyes; it was M. Venot. He was surprised to find him praying before that closed door. Then as though God Himself had responded to his appeal, the count flung his arms round the little old gentleman's neck. At last he could weep, and he burst out sobbing and repeated:

"My brother, my brother."

All his suffering humanity found comfort in that cry. He drenched M. Venot's face with tears; he kissed him, uttering fragmentary ejaculations.

"Oh, my brother, how I am suffering! You only are left me, my brother. Take me away forever—oh, for mercy's sake, take me away!"

Then M. Venot pressed him to his bosom and called him "brother" also. But he had a fresh blow in store for him. Since yesterday he had been searching for him in order to inform him that the Countess Sabine, in a supreme fit of moral aberration, had but now taken flight with the manager of one of the departments in a large, fancy emporium. It was a fearful scandal, and all Paris was already talking about it. Seeing him under the influence of such religious exaltation, Venot felt the opportunity to be favorable and at once told him of the meanly tragic shipwreck of his house. The count was not touched thereby. His wife had gone? That meant nothing to him; they would see what would happen later on. And again he was seized with anguish, and gazing with a look of terror at the door, the walls, the ceiling, he continued pouring forth his single supplication:

"Take me away! I cannot bear it any longer! Take me away!"

M. Venot took him away as though he had been a child. From that day forth Muffat belonged to him entirely; he again became strictly attentive to the duties of religion; his life was utterly blasted. He had resigned his position as chamberlain out of respect for the outraged modesty of the Tuileries, and soon Estelle, his daughter, brought an action against him for the recovery of a sum of sixty thousand francs, a legacy left her by an aunt to which she ought to have succeeded at the time of her marriage. Ruined and living narrowly on the remains of his great fortune, he let himself be gradually devoured by the countess, who ate up the husks Nana had rejected. Sabine was indeed ruined by the example of promiscuity set her by her husband's intercourse with the wanton. She was prone to every excess and proved the ultimate ruin and destruction of his very hearth. After sundry adventures she had returned home, and he had taken her back in a spirit of Christian resignation and forgiveness. She haunted him as his living disgrace, but he grew more and more indifferent and at last ceased suffering from these distresses. Heaven took him out of his wife's hands in order to restore him to the arms of God, and so the voluptuous pleasures he had enjoyed with Nana were prolonged in religious ecstasies, accompanied by the old stammering utterances, the old prayers and despairs, the old fits of humility which befit an accursed creature who is crushed beneath the mire whence he sprang. In the recesses of churches, his knees chilled by the pavement, he would once more experience the delights of the past, and his muscles would twitch, and his brain would whirl deliciously, and the satisfaction of the obscure necessities of his existence would be the same as of old.

On the evening of the final rupture Mignon presented himself at the house in the Avenue de Villiers. He was growing accustomed to Fauchery and was beginning at last to find the presence of his wife's husband infinitely advantageous to him. He would leave all the little household cares to the journalist and would trust him in the active superintendence of all their affairs. Nay, he devoted the money gained by his dramatic successes to the daily expenditure of the family, and as, on his part, Fauchery behaved sensibly, avoiding ridiculous jealousy and proving not less pliant than Mignon himself whenever Rose found her opportunity, the mutual understanding between the two men constantly improved. In fact, they were happy in a partnership which was so fertile in all kinds of amenities, and they settled down side by side and adopted a family arrangement which no longer proved a stumbling block. The whole thing was conducted according to rule; it suited admirably, and each man vied with the other in his efforts for the common happiness. That very evening Mignon had come by Fauchery's advice to see if he could not steal Nana's lady's maid from her, the journalist having formed a high opinion of the woman's extraordinary intelligence. Rose was in despair; for a month past she had been falling into the hands of inexperienced girls who were causing her continual embarrassment. When Zoé received him at the door he forthwith pushed her into the dining room. But at his opening sentence she smiled. The thing was impossible, she said, for she was leaving Madame and establishing herself on her own account. And she added with an expression of discreet vanity that she was daily receiving offers, that the ladies were fighting for her and that Mme Blanche would give a pile of gold to have her back.

Zoé was taking the Tricon's establishment. It was an old project and had been long brooded over. It was her ambition to make her fortune thereby, and she was investing all her savings in it. She was full of great ideas and meditated increasing the business and hiring a house and combining all the delights within its walls. It was with this in view that she had tried to entice Satin, a little pig at that moment dying in hospital, so terribly had she done for herself.

Mignon still insisted with his offer and spoke of the risks run in the commercial life, but Zoé, without entering into explanations about the exact nature of her establishment, smiled a pinched smile, as though she had just put a sweetmeat in her mouth, and was content to remark:

"Oh, luxuries always pay. You see, I've been with others quite long enough, and now I want others to be with me."

And a fierce look set her lip curling. At last she would be "Madame," and for the sake of earning a few louis all those women whose slops she had emptied during the last fifteen years would prostrate themselves before her.

Mignon wished to be announced, and Zoé left him for a moment after remarking that Madame had passed a miserable day. He had only been at the house once before, and he did not know it at all. The dining room with its Gobelin tapestry, its sideboard and its plate filled him with astonishment. He opened the doors familiarly and visited the drawing room and the winter garden, returning thence into the hall. This overwhelming luxury, this gilded furniture, these silks and velvets, gradually filled him with such a feeling of admiration that it set his heart beating. When Zoé came down to fetch him she offered to show him the other rooms, the dressing room, that is to say, and the bedroom. In the latter Mignon's feelings overcame him; he was carried away by them; they filled him with tender enthusiasm.

That damned Nana was simply stupefying him, and yet he thought he knew a thing or two. Amid the downfall of the house and the servants' wild, wasteful race to destruction, massed-up riches still filled every gaping hole and overtopped every ruined wall. And Mignon, as he viewed this lordly monument of wealth, began recalling to mind the various great works he had seen. Near Marseilles they had shown him an aqueduct, the stone arches of which bestrode an abyss, a Cyclopean work which cost millions of money and ten years of intense labor. At Cherbourg he had seen the new harbor with its enormous works, where hundreds of men sweated in the sun while cranes filled the sea with huge squares of rock and built up a wall where a workman now and again remained crushed into bloody pulp. But all that now struck him as insignificant. Nana excited him far more. Viewing the fruit of her labors, he once more experienced the feelings of respect that had overcome him one festal evening in a sugar refiner's château. This château had been erected for the refiner, and its palatial proportions and royal splendor had been paid for by a single material—sugar. It was with something quite different, with a little laughable folly, a little delicate nudity—it was with this shameful trifle, which is so powerful as to move the universe, that she alone, without workmen, without the inventions of engineers, had shaken Paris to its foundations and had built up a fortune on the bodies of dead men.

"Oh, by God, what an implement!"

Mignon let the words escape him in his ecstasy, for he felt a return of personal gratitude.

Nana had gradually lapsed into a most mournful condition. To begin with, the meeting of the marquis and the count had given her a severe fit of feverish nervousness, which verged at times on laughter. Then the thought of this old man going away half dead in a cab and of her poor rough, whom she would never set eyes on again now that she had driven him so wild, brought on what looked like the beginnings of melancholia. After that she grew vexed to hear about Satin's illness. The girl had disappeared about a fortnight ago and was now ready to die at Lariboisière, to such a damnable state had Mme Robert reduced her. When she ordered the horses to be put to in order that she might have a last sight of this vile little wretch Zoé had just quietly given her a week's notice. The announcement drove her to desperation at once! It seemed to her she was losing a member of her own family. Great heavens! What was to become of her when left alone? And she besought Zoé to stay, and the latter, much flattered by Madame's despair, ended by kissing her to show that she was not going away in anger. No, she had positively to go: the heart could have no voice in matters of business.

But that day was one of annoyances. Nana was thoroughly disgusted and gave up the idea of going out. She was dragging herself wearily about the little drawing room when Labordette came up to tell her of a splendid chance of buying magnificent lace and in the course of his remarks casually let slip the information that Georges was dead. The announcement froze her.

"Zizi dead!" she cried.

And involuntarily her eyes sought the pink stain on the carpet, but it had vanished at last; passing footsteps had worn it away. Meanwhile Labordette entered into particulars. It was not exactly known how he died. Some spoke of a wound reopening, others of suicide. The lad had plunged, they said, into a tank at Les Fondettes. Nana kept repeating:

"Dead! Dead!"

She had been choking with grief since morning, and now she burst out sobbing and thus sought relief. Hers was an infinite sorrow: it overwhelmed her with its depth and immensity. Labordette wanted to comfort her as touching Georges, but she silenced him with a gesture and blurted out:

"It isn't only he; it's everything, everything. I'm very wretched. Oh yes, I know! They'll again be saying I'm a hussy. To think of the mother mourning down there and of the poor man who was groaning in front of my door this morning and of all the other people that are now ruined after running through all they had with me! That's it; punish Nana; punish the beastly thing! Oh, I've got a broad back! I can hear them as if I were actually there! 'That dirty wench who lies with everybody and cleans out some and drives others to death and causes a whole heap of people pain!' "

She was obliged to pause, for tears choked her utterance, and in her anguish she flung herself athwart a divan and buried her face in a cushion. The miseries she felt to be around her, miseries of which she was the cause, overwhelmed her with a warm, continuous stream of self-pitying tears, and her voice failed as she uttered a little girl's broken plaint:

"Oh, I'm wretched! Oh, I'm wretched! I can't go on like this: it's choking me. It's too hard to be misunderstood and to see them all siding against you because they're stronger. However, when you've got nothing to reproach yourself with and your conscious is clear, why, then I say, 'I won't have it! I won't have it!' "

In her anger she began rebeling against circumstances, and getting up, she dried her eyes, and walked about in much agitation.

"I won't have it! They can say what they like, but it's not my fault! Am I a bad lot, eh? I give away all I've got; I wouldn't crush a fly! It's they who are bad! Yes, it's they! *I* never wanted to be horrid to them. And they came dangling after me, and today they're kicking the bucket and begging and going to ruin on purpose."

Then she paused in front of Labordette and tapped his shoulders.

"Look here," she said, "you were there all along; now speak the truth: did I urge them on? Weren't there always a dozen of 'em squabbling who could invent the dirtiest trick? They used to disgust me, they did! I did all I knew not to copy them: I was afraid to. Look here, I'll give you a single instance: they all wanted to marry me! A pretty notion, eh? Yes, dear boy, I could have been countess or baroness a dozen times over and more, if I'd consented. Well now, I refused because I was reasonable. Oh yes, I saved 'em some crimes and other foul acts! They'd have stolen, murdered, killed father and mother. I had only to say one word, and I didn't say it. You see what I've got for it today. There's Daguenet, for instance; I married that chap off! I made a position for the beggarly fellow after keeping him gratis for weeks! And I met him yesterday, and he looks the other way! Oh, get along, you swine! I'm less dirty than you!"

She had begun pacing about again, and now she brought her fist violently down on a round table.

"By God, it isn't fair! Society's all wrong. They come down on the women when it's the men who want you to do things. Yes, I can tell you this now: when I used to go with them—see? I didn't enjoy it; no, I didn't enjoy it one bit. It bored me, on my honor. Well then, I ask you whether I've got anything to do with it! Yes, they bored me to death! If it hadn't been for them and what they made of me, dear boy, I should be in a convent saying my prayers to the good God, for I've always had my share of religion. Dash it, after all, if they have dropped their money and their lives over it, what do I care? It's their fault. I've had nothing to do with it!"

"Certainly not," said Labordette with conviction.

Zoé ushered in Mignon, and Nana received him smilingly. She had cried a good deal, but it was all over now. Still glowing with enthusiasm, he complimented her on her installation, but she let him see that she had had enough of her mansion and that now she had other projects and would sell everything up one of these days. Then as he excused himself for calling on the ground that he had come about a benefit performance in aid of old Bosc, who was tied to his armchair by paralysis, she expressed extreme pity and took two boxes. Meanwhile Zoé announced that the carriage was waiting for Madame, and she asked for her hat and as she tied the strings told them about poor, dear Satin's mishap, adding:

"I'm going to the hospital. Nobody ever loved me as she did. Oh, they're quite right when they accuse the men of heartlessness! Who knows? Perhaps I shan't see her alive. Never mind, I shall ask to see her: I want to give her a kiss."

Labordette and Mignon smiled, and as Nana was no longer melancholy she smiled too. Those two fellows didn't count; they could enter into her feelings. And they both stood and admired her in silent abstraction while she finished buttoning her gloves. She alone kept her feet amid the heaped-up riches of her mansion, while a whole generation of men lay stricken down before her. Like those antique monsters whose redoubtable domains were covered with skeletons, she rested her feet on human skulls. She was ringed round with catastrophes. There was the furious immolation of Vandeuvres; the melancholy state of Foucarmont, who was lost in the China seas; the smashup of Steiner, who now had to live like an honest man; the satisfied idiocy of La Faloise, and the tragic shipwreck of the Muffats. Finally there was the white corpse of Georges, over which Philippe was now watching, for he had come out of prison but yesterday. She had finished her labor of ruin and death. The fly that had flown up from the ordure of the slums, bringing with it the leaven of social rottenness, had poisoned all these men by merely alighting on them. It was well done—it was just. She had avenged the beggars and the wastrels from whose caste she issued. And while, metaphorically speaking, her sex rose in a halo of glory and beamed over prostrate victims like a mounting sun shining brightly over a field of carnage, the actual woman remained as unconscious as a splendid animal, and in her ignorance of her mission was the good-natured courtesan to the last. She was still big; she was still plump; her health was excellent, her spirits capital. But this went for nothing now, for her house struck her as ridiculous. It was too small; it was full of furniture which got in her way. It was a wretched business, and the long and the short of the matter was she would have to make a fresh start. In fact, she was meditating something much better, and so she went off to kiss Satin for the last time. She was in all her finery and looked clean and solid and as brand new as if she had never seen service before.

CHAPTER XIV

NANA suddenly disappeared. It was a fresh plunge, an escapade, a flight into barbarous regions. Before her departure she had treated herself to a new sensation: she had held a sale and had made a clean sweep of everything—house, furniture, jewelry, nay, even dresses and linen. Prices were cited—the five days' sale produced more than six hundred thousand francs. For the last time Paris had seen her in a fairy piece. It was called *Mélusine*, and it played at the Théâtre de la Gaîté, which the penniless Bordenave had taken out of sheer audacity. Here she again found herself in company with Prullière and Fontan. Her part was simply spectacular, but it was the great attraction of the piece, consisting, as it did, of three *poses plastiques*, each of which represented the same dumb and puissant fairy. Then one fine morning amid his grand success, when Bordenave, who was mad after advertisement, kept firing the Parisian imagination with colossal posters, it became known that she must have started for Cairo the previous day. She had simply had a few words with her manager. Something had been said which did not please her; the whole thing was the caprice of a woman who is too rich to let herself be annoyed. Besides, she had indulged an old infatuation, for she had long meditated visiting the Turks.

Months passed—she began to be forgotten. When her name was mentioned among the ladies and gentlemen, the strangest stories were told, and everybody gave the most contradictory and at the same time prodigious information. She had made a conquest of the viceroy; she was reigning, in the recesses of a palace, over two hundred slaves whose heads she now and then cut off for the sake of a little amusement. No, not at all! She had ruined herself with a great big nigger! A filthy passion this, which had left her wallowing without a chemise to her back in the crapulous debauchery of Cairo. A fortnight later much astonishment was produced when someone swore to having met her in Russia. A legend began to be formed: she was the mistress of a prince, and her diamonds were mentioned. All the women were soon acquainted with them from the current descriptions, but nobody could cite the precise source of all this information. There were finger rings, earrings, bracelets, a *revière* of phenomenal width, a queenly diadem surmounted by a central brilliant the size of one's thumb. In the retirement of those faraway countries she began to gleam forth as mysteriously as a gem-laden idol. People now mentioned her without laughing, for they were full of meditative respect for this fortune acquired among the barbarians.

One evening in July toward eight o'clock, Lucy, while getting out of her carriage in the Rue du Faubourg Saint-Honoré, noticed Caroline Héquet, who had come out on foot to order something at a neighboring tradesman's. Lucy called her and at once burst out with:

"Have you dined? Are you disengaged? Oh, then come with me, my dear. Nana's back."

The other got in at once, and Lucy continued:

"And you know, my dear, she may be dead while we're gossiping."

"Dead! What an idea!" cried Caroline in stupefaction. "And where is she? And what's it of?"

"At the Grand Hôtel, of smallpox. Oh, it's a long story!"

Lucy had bidden her coachman drive fast, and while the horses trotted rapidly along the Rue Royale and the boulevards, she told what had happened to Nana in jerky, breathless sentences.

"You can't imagine it. Nana plumps down out of Russia. I don't know why
—some dispute with her prince. She leaves her traps at the station; she lands
at her aunt's—you remember the old thing. Well, and then she finds her baby
dying of smallpox. The baby dies next day, and she has a row with the aunt
about some money she ought to have sent, of which the other one has never
seen a sou. Seems the child died of that: in fact, it was neglected and badly
cared for. Very well; Nana slopes, goes to a hotel, then meets Mignon just
as she was thinking of her traps. She has all sorts of queer feelings, shivers,
wants to be sick, and Mignon takes her back to her place and promises to look
after her affairs. Isn't it odd, eh? Doesn't it all happen pat? But this is the best
part of the story: Rose finds out about Nana's illness and gets indignant at the
idea of her being alone in furnished apartments. So she rushes off, crying, to
look after her. You remember how they used to detest one another—like
regular furies! Well then, my dear, Rose has had Nana transported to the
Grand Hôtel, so that she should, at any rate, die in a smart place, and now
she's already passed three nights there and is free to die of it after. It's Labordette who told me all about it. Accordingly I wanted to see for myself——"
"Yes, yes," interrupted Caroline in great excitement. "We'll go up to her."
They had arrived at their destination. On the boulevard the coachman had
had to rein in his horses amid a block of carriages and people on foot. During
the day the Corps Législatif had voted for war, and now a crowd was streaming
down all the streets, flowing along all the pavements, invading the middle of
the roadway. Beyond the Madeleine the sun had set behind a blood-red cloud,
which cast a reflection as of a great fire and set the lofty windows flaming.
Twilight was falling, and the hour was oppressively melancholy, for now the
avenues were darkening away into the distance but were not as yet dotted
over by the bright sparks of the gas lamps. And among the marching crowds
distant voices swelled and grew ever louder, and eyes gleamed from pale faces,
while a great spreading wind of anguish and stupor set every head whirling.
"Here's Mignon," said Lucy. "He'll give us news."
Mignon was standing under the vast porch of the Grand Hôtel. He looked
nervous and was gazing at the crowd. After Lucy's first few questions he grew
impatient and cried out:
"How should I know? These last two days I haven't been able to tear Rose
away from up there. It's getting stupid, when all's said, for her to be risking
her life like that! She'll be charming if she gets over it, with holes in her face!
It 'll suit us to a tee!"
The idea that Rose might lose her beauty was exasperating him. He was
giving up Nana in the most downright fashion, and he could not in the least
understand these stupid feminine devotions. But Fauchery was crossing the
boulevard, and he, too, came up anxiously and asked for news. The two men
egged each other on. They addressed one another familiarly in these days.
"Always the same business, my sonny," declared Mignon. "You ought to go
upstairs; you would force her to follow you."
"Come now, you're kind, you are!" said the journalist. "Why don't you go
upstairs yourself?"

Then as Lucy began asking for Nana's number, they besought her to make Rose come down; otherwise they would end by getting angry.

Nevertheless, Lucy and Caroline did not go up at once. They had caught sight of Fontan strolling about with his hands in his pockets and greatly amused by the quaint expressions of the mob. When he became aware that Nana was lying ill upstairs he affected sentiment and remarked:

"The poor girl! I'll go and shake her by the hand. What's the matter with her, eh?"

"Smallpox," replied Mignon.

The actor had already taken a step or two in the direction of the court, but he came back and simply murmured with a shiver:

"Oh, damn it!"

The smallpox was no joke. Fontan had been near having it when he was five years old, while Mignon gave them an account of one of his nieces who had died of it. As to Fauchery, he could speak of it from personal experience, for he still bore marks of it in the shape of three little lumps at the base of his nose, which he showed them. And when Mignon again egged him on to the ascent, on the pretext that you never had it twice, he violently combated this theory and with infinite abuse of the doctors instanced various cases. But Lucy and Caroline interrupted them, for the growing multitude filled them with astonishment.

"Just look! Just look what a lot of people!" The night was deepening, and in the distance the gas lamps were being lit one by one. Meanwhile interested spectators became visible at windows, while under the trees the human flood grew every minute more dense, till it ran in one enormous stream from the Madeleine to the Bastille. Carriages rolled slowly along. A roaring sound went up from this compact and as yet inarticulate mass. Each member of it had come out, impelled by the desire to form a crowd, and was now trampling along, steeping himself in the pervading fever. But a great movement caused the mob to flow asunder. Among the jostling, scattering groups a band of men in workmen's caps and white blouses had come in sight, uttering a rhythmical cry which suggested the beat of hammers upon an anvil.

"To Ber-lin! To Ber-lin! To Ber-lin!" And the crowd stared in gloomy distrust yet felt themselves already possessed and inspired by heroic imaginings, as though a military band were passing.

"Oh yes, go and get your throats cut!" muttered Mignon, overcome by an access of philosophy.

But Fontan thought it very fine, indeed, and spoke of enlisting. When the enemy was on the frontier all citizens ought to rise up in defense of the fatherland! And with that he assumed an attitude suggestive of Bonaparte at Austerlitz.

"Look here, are you coming up with us?" Lucy asked him.

"Oh dear, no! To catch something horrid?" he said.

On a bench in front of the Grand Hôtel a man sat hiding his face in a handkerchief. On arriving Fauchery had indicated him to Mignon with a wink of the eye. Well, he was still there; yes, he was always there. And the jour-

nalist detained the two women also in order to point him out to them. When
the man lifted his head they recognized him; an exclamation escaped them. It
was the Count Muffat, and he was giving an upward glance at one of the
windows.

"You know, he's been waiting there since this morning," Mignon informed
them. "I saw him at six o'clock, and he hasn't moved since. Directly Labordette spoke about it he came there with his handkerchief up to his face.
Every half-hour he comes dragging himself to where we're standing to ask if
the person upstairs is doing better, and then he goes back and sits down. Hang
it, that room isn't healthy! It's all very well being fond of people, but one
doesn't want to kick the bucket."

The count sat with uplifted eyes and did not seem conscious of what was
going on around him. Doubtless he was ignorant of the declaration of war,
and he neither felt nor saw the crowd.

"Look, here he comes!" said Fauchery. "Now you'll see."

The count had, in fact, quitted his bench and was entering the lofty porch.
But the porter, who was getting to know his face at last, did not give him time
to put his question. He said sharply:

"She's dead, monsieur, this very minute."

Nana dead! It was a blow to them all. Without a word Muffat had gone
back to the bench, his face still buried in his handkerchief. The others burst
into exclamations, but they were cut short, for a fresh band passed by, howling, "*A Berlin! A Berlin! A Berlin!*" Nana dead! Hang it, and such a fine girl
too! Mignon sighed and looked relieved, for at last Rose would come down. A
chill fell on the company. Fontan, meditating a tragic role, had assumed a look
of woe and was drawing down the corners of his mouth and rolling his eyes
askance, while Fauchery chewed his cigar nervously, for despite his cheap
journalistic chaff he was really touched. Nevertheless, the two women continued to give vent to their feelings of surprise. The last time Lucy had seen
her was at the Gaîté; Blanche, too, had seen her in *Mélusine*. Oh, how stunning it was, my dear, when she appeared in the depths of the crystal grot! The
gentlemen remembered the occasion perfectly. Fontan had played the Prince
Cocorico. And their memories once stirred up, they launched into interminable particulars. How ripping she looked with that rich coloring of hers in
the crystal grot! Didn't she, now? She didn't say a word: the authors had
even deprived her of a line or two, because it was superfluous. No, never a
word! It was grander that way, and she drove her public wild by simply
showing herself. You wouldn't find another body like hers! Such shoulders
as she had, and such legs and such a figure! Strange that she should be dead!
You know, above her tights she had nothing on but a golden girdle which
hardly concealed her behind and in front. All round her the grotto, which
was entirely of glass, shone like day. Cascades of diamonds were flowing down;
strings of brilliant pearls glistened among the stalactites in the vault overhead,
and amid the transparent atmosphere and flowing fountain water, which was
crossed by a wide ray of electric light, she gleamed like the sun with that
flamelike skin and hair of hers. Paris would always picture her thus—would see

her shining high up among crystal glass like the good God Himself. No, it was too stupid to let herself die under such conditions! She must be looking pretty by this time in that room up there!

"And what a lot of pleasures bloody well wasted!" said Mignon in melancholy tones, as became a man who did not like to see good and useful things lost.

He sounded Lucy and Caroline in order to find out if they were going up after all. Of course they were going up; their curiosity had increased. Just then Blanche arrived, out of breath and much exasperated at the way the crowds were blocking the pavement, and when she heard the news there was a fresh outburst of exclamations, and with a great rustling of skirts the ladies moved toward the staircase. Mignon followed them, crying out:

"Tell Rose that I'm waiting for her. She'll come at once, eh?"

"They do not exactly know whether the contagion is to be feared at the beginning or near the end," Fontan was explaining to Fauchery. "A medical I know was assuring me that the hours immediately following death are particularly dangerous. There are miasmatic exhalations then. Ah, but I do regret this sudden ending; I should have been so glad to shake hands with her for the last time."

"What good would it do you now?" said the journalist.

"Yes, what good?" the two others repeated.

The crowd was still on the increase. In the bright light thrown from shop-windows and beneath the wavering glare of the gas two living streams were distinguishable as they flowed along the pavement, innumerable hats apparently drifting on their surface. At that hour the popular fever was gaining ground rapidly, and people were flinging themselves in the wake of the bands of men in blouses. A constant forward movement seemed to sweep the roadway, and the cry kept recurring; obstinately, abruptly, there rang from thousands of throats:

"*A Berlin! A Berlin! A Berlin!*"

The room on the fourth floor upstairs cost twelve francs a day, since Rose had wanted something decent and yet not luxurious, for sumptuousness is not necessary when one is suffering. Hung with Louis XIII cretonne, which was adorned with a pattern of large flowers, the room was furnished with the mahogany commonly found in hotels. On the floor there was a red carpet variegated with black foliage. Heavy silence reigned save for an occasional whispering sound caused by voices in the corridor.

"I assure you we're lost. The waiter told us to turn to the right. What a barrack of a house!"

"Wait a bit; we must have a look. Room number 401; room number 401!"

"Oh, it's this way: 405, 403. We ought to be there. Ah, at last, 401! This way! Hush now, hush!"

The voices were silent. Then there was a slight coughing and a moment or of mental preparation. Then the door opened slowly, and Lucy entered, followed by Caroline and Blanche. But they stopped directly; there were already five women in the room; Gaga was lying back in the solitary armchair, which was a red velvet Voltaire. In front of the fireplace Simonne and Clarisse were now standing talking to Léa de Horn, who was seated, while by the bed, to the left of the door, Rose Mignon, perched on the edge of a chest, sat gazing fixedly at the body where it lay hidden in the shadow of the curtains. All the others had their hats and gloves on and looked as if they were paying a call: she alone sat there with bare hands and untidy hair and cheeks rendered pale by three nights of watching. She felt stupid in the face of this sudden death, and her eyes were swollen with weeping. A shaded lamp standing on the corner of the chest of drawers threw a bright flood of light over Gaga.

"What a sad misfortune, is it not?" whispered Lucy as she shook hands with Rose. "We wanted to bid her good-by."

And she turned round and tried to catch sight of her, but the lamp was too far off, and she did not dare bring it nearer. On the bed lay stretched a gray mass, but only the ruddy chignon was distinguishable and a pale blotch which might be the face. Lucy added:

"I never saw her since that time at the Gaîté, when she was at the end of the grotto."

At this Rose awoke from her stupor and smiled as she said:

"Ah, she's changed; she's changed."

Then she once more lapsed into contemplation and neither moved nor spoke. Perhaps they would be able to look at her presently! And with that the three women joined the others in front of the fireplace. Simonne and Clarisse were discussing the dead woman's diamonds in low tones. Well, did they really exist—those diamonds? Nobody had seen them; it must be a bit of humbug. But Léa de Horn knew someone who knew all about them. Oh, they were monster stones! Besides, they weren't all; she had brought back lots of other precious property from Russia—embroidered stuffs, for instance, valuable knickknacks, a gold dinner service, nay, even furniture. "Yes, my dear, fifty-two boxes, enormous cases some of them, three truckloads of them!" They were all lying at the station. "Wasn't it hard lines, eh?—to die without even having time to unpack one's traps?" Then she had a lot of tin, besides—something like a million! Lucy asked who was going to inherit it all. Oh, distant relations—the aunt, without doubt! It would be a pretty surprise for that old body. She knew nothing about it yet, for the sick woman had obstinately refused to let them warn her, for she still owed her a grudge over her little boy's death. Thereupon they were all moved to pity about the little boy, and they remembered seeing him at the races. Oh, it was a wretchedly sickly baby; it looked so old and so sad. In fact, it was one of those poor brats who never asked to be born!

"He's happier under the ground," said Blanche.

"Bah, and so's she!" added Caroline. "Life isn't so funny!"

In that gloomy room melancholy ideas began to take possession of their imaginations. They felt frightened. It was silly to stand talking so long, but a longing to see her kept them rooted to the spot. It was very hot—the lamp glass threw a round, moonlike patch of light upon the ceiling, but the rest of the room was drowned in steamy darkness. Under the bed a deep plate full of phenol exhaled an insipid smell. And every few moments tiny gusts of wind swelled the window curtains. The window opened on the boulevard, whence rose a dull roaring sound.

"Did she suffer much?" asked Lucy, who was absorbed in contemplation of the clock, the design of which represented the three Graces as nude young women, smiling like opera dancers.

Gaga seemed to wake up.

"My word, yes! I was present when she died. I promise you it was not at all pleasant to see. Why, she was taken with a shuddering fit——"

But she was unable to proceed with her explanation, for a cry arose outside: "*A Berlin! A Berlin! A Berlin!*"

And Lucy, who felt suffocated, flung wide the window and leaned upon the sill. It was pleasant there; the air came fresh from the starry sky. Opposite her the windows were all aglow with light, and the gas sent dancing reflections over the gilt lettering of the shop signs.

Beneath these, again, a most amusing scene presented itself. The streams of people were discernible rolling torrentwise along the sidewalks and in the roadway, where there was a confused procession of carriages. Everywhere there were vast moving shadows in which lanterns and lampposts gleamed like sparks. But the band which now came roaring by carried torches, and a red glow streamed down from the direction of the Madeleine, crossed the mob like a trail of fire and spread out over the heads in the distance like a vivid reflection of a burning house. Lucy called Blanche and Caroline, forgetting where she was and shouting:

"Do come! You get a capital view from this window!"

They all three leaned out, greatly interested. The trees got in their way, and occasionally the torches disappeared under the foliage. They tried to catch a glimpse of the men of their own party below, but a protruding balcony hid the door, and they could only make out Count Muffat, who looked like a dark parcel thrown down on the bench where he sat. He was still burying his face in his handkerchief. A carriage had stopped in front, and yet another woman hurried up, in whom Lucy recognized Maria Blond. She was not alone; a stout man got down after her.

"It's that thief of a Steiner," said Caroline. "How is it they haven't sent him back to Cologne yet? I want to see how he looks when he comes in."

They turned round, but when after the lapse of ten minutes Maria Blond appeared, she was alone. She had twice mistaken the staircase. And when Lucy, in some astonishment, questioned her:

"What, he?" she said. "My dear, don't you go fancying that he'll come upstairs! It's a great wonder he's escorted me as far as the door. There are nearly a dozen of them smoking cigars."

As a matter of fact, all the gentlemen were meeting downstairs. They had come strolling thither in order to have a look at the boulevards, and they hailed one another and commented loudly on that poor girl's death. Then they began discussing politics and strategy. Bordenave, Daguenet, Labordette,

Prullière and others, besides, had swollen the group, and now they were all listening to Fontan, who was explaining his plan for taking Berlin within a week.

Meanwhile Maria Blond was touched as she stood by the bedside and murmured, as the others had done before her:

"Poor pet! The last time I saw her was in the grotto at the Gaîté."

"Ah, she's changed; she's changed!" Rose Mignon repeated with a smile of gloomiest dejection.

Two more women arrived. These were Tatan Néné and Louise Violaine. They had been wandering about the Grand Hôtel for twenty minutes past, bandied from waiter to waiter, and had ascended and descended more than thirty flights of stairs amid a perfect stampede of travelers who were hurrying to leave Paris amid the panic caused by the war and the excitement on the boulevards. Accordingly they just dropped down on chairs when they came in, for they were too tired to think about the dead. At that moment a loud noise came from the room next door, where people were pushing trunks about and striking against furniture to an accompaniment of strident, outlandish syllables. It was a young Austrian couple, and Gaga told how during her agony the neighbors had played a game of catch as catch can and how, as only an unused door divided the two rooms, they had heard them laughing and kissing when one or the other was caught.

"Come, it's time we were off," said Clarisse. "We shan't bring her to life again. Are you coming, Simonne?"

They all looked at the bed out of the corners of their eyes, but they did not budge an inch. Nevertheless, they began getting ready and gave their skirts various little pats. Lucy was again leaning out of window. She was alone now, and a sorrowful feeling began little by little to overpower her, as though an intense wave of melancholy had mounted up from the howling mob. Torches still kept passing, shaking out clouds of sparks, and far away in the distance the various bands stretched into the shadows, surging unquietly to and fro like flocks being driven to the slaughterhouse at night. A dizzy feeling emanated from these confused masses as the human flood rolled them along— a dizzy feeling, a sense of terror and all the pity of the massacres to come. The people were going wild; their voices broke; they were drunk with a fever of excitement which sent them rushing toward the unknown "out there" beyond the dark wall of the horizon.

"A Berlin! A Berlin! A Berlin!"

Lucy turned round. She leaned her back against the window, and her face was very pale.

"Good God! What's to become of us?"

The ladies shook their heads. They were serious and very anxious about the turn events were taking.

"For my part," said Caroline Héquet in her decisive way, "I start for London the day after tomorrow. Mamma's already over there getting a house ready for me. I'm certainly not going to let myself be massacred in Paris."

Her mother, as became a prudent woman, had invested all her daughters' money in foreign lands. One never knows how a war may end! But Maria Blond grew vexed at this. She was a patriot and spoke of following the army.

"There's a coward for you! Yes, if they wanted me I should put on man's clothes just to have a good shot at those pigs of Prussians! And if we all die after? What of that? Our wretched skins aren't so valuable!"

Blanche de Sivry was exasperated.

"Please don't speak ill of the Prussians! They are just like other men, and they're not always running after the women, like your Frenchmen. They've just expelled the little Prussian who was with me. He was an awfully rich fellow and so gentle: he couldn't have hurt a soul. It's disgraceful; I'm ruined by it. And, you know, you mustn't say a word or I go and find him out in Germany!"

After that, while the two were at loggerheads, Gaga began murmuring in dolorous tones:

"It's all over with me; my luck's always bad. It's only a week ago that I finished paying for my little house at Juvisy. Ah, God knows what trouble it cost me! I had to go to Lili for help! And now here's the war declared, and the Prussians 'll come and they'll burn everything. How am I to begin again at my time of life, I should like to know?"

"Bah!" said Clarisse. "I don't care a damn about it. I shall always find what I want."

"Certainly you will," added Simonne. "It 'll be a joke. Perhaps, after all, it 'll be good biz."

And her smile hinted what she thought. Tatan Néné and Louise Violaine were of her opinion. The former told them that she had enjoyed the most roaring jolly good times with soldiers. Oh, they were good fellows and would have done any mortal thing for the girls. But as the ladies had raised their voices unduly Rose Mignon, still sitting on the chest by the bed, silenced them with a softly whispered "Hush!" They stood quite still at this and glanced obliquely toward the dead woman, as though this request for silence had emanated from the very shadows of the curtains. In the heavy, peaceful stillness which ensued, a void, deathly stillness which made them conscious of the stiff dead body lying stretched close by them, the cries of the mob burst forth:

"*A Berlin! A Berlin! A Berlin!*"

But soon they forgot. Léa de Horn, who had a political salon where former ministers of Louis Philippe were wont to indulge in delicate epigrams, shrugged her shoulders and continued the conversation in a low tone:

"What a mistake this war is! What a bloodthirsty piece of stupidity!"

At this Lucy forthwith took up the cudgels for the empire. She had been the mistress of a prince of the imperial house, and its defense became a point of family honor with her.

"Do leave them alone, my dear. We couldn't let ourselves be further insulted! Why, this war concerns the honor of France. Oh, you know I don't say that because of the prince. He *was* just mean! Just imagine, at night when he was going to bed he hid his gold in his boots, and when we played at

bezique he used beans, because one day I pounced down on the stakes for fun.
But that doesn't prevent my being fair. The emperor was right."

Léa shook her head with an air of superiority, as became a woman who was
repeating the opinions of important personages. Then raising her voice:
"This is the end of all things. They're out of their minds at the Tuileries.
France ought to have driven them out yesterday. Don't you see?"

They all violently interrupted her. What was up with her? Was she mad
about the emperor? Were people not happy? Was business doing badly?
Paris would never enjoy itself so thoroughly again.

Gaga was beside herself; she woke up and was very indignant.

"Be quiet! It's idiotic! You don't know what you're saying. I—I've seen
Louis Philippe's reign: it was full of beggars and misers, my dear. And then
came '48! Oh, it was a pretty disgusting business was their republic! After
February I was simply dying of starvation—yes, I, Gaga. Oh, if only you'd
been through it all you would go down on your knees before the emperor,
for he's been a father to us; yes, a father to us."

She had to be soothed but continued with pious fervor:

"O my God, do Thy best to give the emperor the victory. Preserve the
empire to us!"

They all repeated this aspiration, and Blanche confessed that she burned
candles for the emperor. Caroline had been smitten by him and for two whole
months had walked where he was likely to pass but had failed to attract his
attention. And with that the others burst forth into furious denunciations of
the Republicans and talked of exterminating them on the frontiers so that
Napoleon III, after having beaten the enemy, might reign peacefully amid
universal enjoyment.

"That dirty Bismarck—there's another cad for you!" Maria Blond remarked.

"To think that I should have known him!" cried Simonne. "If only I could
have foreseen, I'm the one that would have put some poison in his glass."

But Blanche, on whose heart the expulsion of her Prussian still weighed,
ventured to defend Bismarck. Perhaps he wasn't such a bad sort. To every
man his trade!

"You know," she added, "he adores women."

"What the hell has that got to do with us?" said Clarisse. "We don't want
to cuddle him, eh?"

"There's always too many men of that sort!" declared Louise Violaine
gravely. "It's better to do without 'em than to mix oneself up with such
monsters!"

And the discussion continued, and they stripped Bismarck, and, in her
Bonapartist zeal, each of them gave him a sounding kick, while Tatan Néné
kept saying:

"Bismarck! Why, they've simply driven me crazy with the chap! Oh, I
hate him! I didn't know that there Bismarck! One can't know everybody."

"Never mind," said Léa de Horn by way of conclusion, "that Bismarck
will give us a jolly good threshing."

But she could not continue. The ladies were all down on her at once. Eh, what? A threshing? It was Bismarck they were going to escort home with blows from the butt ends of their muskets. What was this bad Frenchwoman going to say next?

"Hush," whispered Rose, for so much noise hurt her.

The cold influence of the corpse once more overcame them, and they all paused together. They were embarrassed; the dead woman was before them again; a dull thread of coming ill possessed them. On the boulevard the cry was passing, hoarse and wild:

"À Berlin! À Berlin! À Berlin!"

Presently, when they were making up their minds to go, a voice was heard calling from the passage:

"Rose! Rose!"

Gaga opened the door in astonishment and disappeared for a moment. When she returned:

"My dear," she said, "it's Fauchery. He's out there at the end of the corridor. He won't come any further, and he's beside himself because you still stay near that body."

Mignon had at last succeeded in urging the journalist upstairs. Lucy, who was still at the window, leaned out and caught sight of the gentlemen out on the pavement. They were looking up, making energetic signals to her. Mignon was shaking his fists in exasperation, and Steiner, Fontan, Bordenave and the rest were stretching out their arms with looks of anxious reproach, while Daguenet simply stood smoking a cigar with his hands behind his back, so as not to compromise himself.

"It's true, dear," said Lucy, leaving the window open; "I promised to make you come down. They're all calling us now."

Rose slowly and painfully left the chest.

"I'm coming down; I'm coming down," she whispered. "It's very certain she no longer needs me. They're going to send in a Sister of Mercy."

And she turned round, searching for her hat and shawl. Mechanically she filled a basin of water on the toilet table and while washing her hands and face continued:

"I don't know! It's been a great blow to me. We used scarcely to be nice to one another. Ah well! You see I'm quite silly over it now. Oh! I've got all sorts of strange ideas—I want to die myself—I feel the end of the world's coming. Yes, I need air."

The corpse was beginning to poison the atmosphere of the room. And after long heedlessness there ensued a panic.

"Let's be off; let's be off, my little pets!" Gaga kept saying. "It isn't wholesome here."

They went briskly out, casting a last glance at the bed as they passed it. But while Lucy, Blanche and Caroline still remained behind, Rose gave a final look round, for she wanted to leave the room in order. She drew a curtain across the window, and then it occurred to her that the lamp was not the proper thing and that a taper should take its place. So she lit one of the copper candelabra on the chimney piece and placed it on the night table beside the corpse. A brilliant light suddenly illumined the dead woman's face. The women were horror-struck. They shuddered and escaped.

"Ah, she's changed; she's changed!" murmured Rose Mignon, who was the last to remain.

She went away; she shut the door. Nana was left alone with upturned face in the light cast by the candle. She was fruit of the charnel house, a heap of matter and blood, a shovelful of corrupted flesh thrown down on the pillow. The pustules had invaded the whole of the face, so that each touched its neighbor. Fading and sunken, they had assumed the grayish hue of mud; and on that formless pulp, where the features had ceased to be traceable, they already resembled some decaying damp from the grave. One eye, the left eye, had completely foundered among bubbling purulence, and the other, which remained half open, looked like a deep, black, ruinous hole. The nose was still suppurating. Quite a reddish crush was peeling from one of the cheeks and invading the mouth, which it distorted into a horrible grin. And over this loathsome and grotesque mask of death the hair, the beautiful hair, still blazed like sunlight and flowed downward in rippling gold. Venus was rotting. It seemed as though the poison she had assimilated in the gutters and on the carrion tolerated by the roadside, the leaven with which she had poisoned a whole people, had but now remounted to her face and turned it to corruption.

The room was empty. A great despairing breath came up from the boulevard and swelled the curtain.

"A Berlin! A Berlin! A Berlin!"

THE MILLER'S DAUGHTER

CHAPTER I

The Betrothal

Père Merlier's mill, one beautiful summer evening, was arranged for a grand fete. In the courtyard were three tables, placed end to end, which awaited the guests. Everyone knew that Françoise, Merlier's daughter, was that night to be betrothed to Dominique, a young man who was accused of idleness but whom the fair sex for three leagues around gazed at with sparkling eyes, such a fine appearance had he.

Père Merlier's mill was pleasing to look upon. It stood exactly in the center of Rocreuse, where the highway made an elbow. The village had but one street, with two rows of huts, a row on each side of the road; but at the elbow meadows spread out, and huge trees which lined the banks of the Morelle covered the extremity of the valley with lordly shade. There was not, in all Lorraine, a corner of nature more adorable. To the right and to the left thick woods, centenarian forests, towered up from gentle slopes, filling the horizon with a sea of verdure, while toward the south the plain stretched away, of marvelous fertility, displaying as far as the eye could reach patches of ground divided by green hedges. But what constituted the special charm of Rocreuse was the coolness of that cut of verdure in the most sultry days of July and August. The Morelle descended from the forests of Gagny and seemed to have gathered the cold from the foliage beneath which it flowed for leagues; it brought with it the murmuring sounds, the icy and concentrated shade of the woods. And it was not the sole source of coolness: all sorts of flowing streams gurgled through the forest; at each step springs bubbled up; one felt, on following the narrow pathways, that there must exist subterranean lakes which pierced through beneath the moss and availed themselves of the smallest crevices at the feet of trees or between the rocks to burst forth in crystalline fountains. The whispering voices of these brooks were so numerous and so loud that they drowned the song of the bullfinches. It was like some enchanted park with cascades falling from every portion.

Below the meadows were damp. Gigantic chestnut trees cast dark shadows. On the borders of the meadows long hedges of poplars exhibited in lines their rustling branches. Two avenues of enormous plane trees stretched across the fields toward the ancient Château de Gagny, then a mass of ruins. In this constantly watered district the grass grew to an extraordinary height. It resembled a garden between two wooded hills, a natural garden, of which the meadows were the lawns, the giant trees marking the colossal flower beds. When the sun's rays at noon poured straight downward the shadows assumed a bluish tint; scorched grass slept in the heat, while an icy shiver passed beneath the foliage.

And there it was that Père Merlier's mill enlivened with its ticktack a corner of wild verdure. The structure, built of plaster and planks, seemed as old as the world. It dipped partially in the Morelle, which rounded at that point into a transparent basin. A sluice had been made, and the water fell from a height of several meters upon the mill wheel, which cracked as it turned, with the asthmatic cough of a faithful servant grown old in the house. When Père Merlier was advised to change it he shook his head, saying that a new wheel would be lazier and would not so well understand the work, and he mended the old one with whatever he could put his hands on: cask staves, rusty iron, zinc and lead. The wheel appeared gayer than ever for it, with its profile grown odd, all plumed with grass and moss. When the water beat upon it with its silvery flood it was covered with pearls; its strange carcass wore a sparkling attire of necklaces of mother-of-pearl.

The part of the mill which dipped in the Morelle had the air of a barbaric arch stranded there. A full half of the structure was built on piles. The water flowed beneath the floor, and deep places were there, renowned throughout the district for the enormous eels and crayfish caught in them. Below the fall the basin was as clear as a mirror, and when the wheel did not cover it with foam schools of huge fish could be seen swimming with the slowness of a squadron. Broken steps led down to the river near a stake to which a boat was moored. A wooden gallery passed above the wheel. Windows opened, pierced irregularly. It was a pell-mell of corners, of little walls, of constructions added too late, of beams and of roofs, which gave the mill the aspect of an old, dismantled citadel. But ivy had grown; all sorts of clinging plants stopped the too-wide chinks and threw a green cloak over the ancient building. The young ladies who passed by sketched Père Merlier's mill in their albums.

On the side facing the highway the structure was more solid. A stone gateway opened upon the wide courtyard, which was bordered to the right and to the left by sheds and stables. Beside a well an immense elm covered half the courtyard with its shadow. In the background the building displayed the four windows of its second story, surmounted by a pigeon house. Père Merlier's sole vanity was to have this front plastered every ten years. It had just received a new coating and dazzled the village when the sun shone on it at noon.

For twenty years Père Merlier had been mayor of Rocreuse. He was esteemed for the fortune he had acquired. His wealth was estimated at something like eighty thousand francs, amassed sou by sou. When he married Madeleine Guillard, who brought him the mill as her dowry, he possessed only his two arms. But Madeleine never repented of her choice, so briskly did he manage the business. Now his wife was dead, and he remained a widower with his daughter Françoise. Certainly he might have rested, allowed the mill wheel to slumber in the moss, but that would have been too dull for him, and in his eyes the building would have seemed dead. He toiled on for pleasure.

Père Merlier was a tall old man with a long, still face, who never laughed but who possessed, notwithstanding, a very gay heart. He had been chosen mayor because of his money and also on account of the imposing air he could assume during a marriage ceremony.

Françoise Merlier was just eighteen. She did not pass for one of the handsome girls of the district, as she was not robust. Up to her fifteenth year she had been even ugly.

The Rocreuse people had not been able to understand why the daughter of Père and Mère Merlier, both of whom had always enjoyed excellent health grew ill and with an air of regret. But at fifteen, though yet delicate, her little face became one of the prettiest in the world. She had black hair, black eyes, and was as rosy as a peach; her lips constantly wore a smile; there were dimples in her cheeks, and her fair forehead seemed crowned with sunlight. Although not considered robust in the district, she was far from thin; the idea was simply that she could not lift a sack of grain, but she would become plump as she grew older—she would eventually be as round and dainty as a quail. Her father's long periods of silence had made her thoughtful very young. If she smiled constantly it was to please others. By nature she was serious.

Of course all the young men of the district paid court to her, more on account of her ècus than her pretty ways. At last she made a choice which scandalized the community.

On the opposite bank of the Morelle lived a tall youth named Dominique Penquer. He did not belong to Rocreuse. Ten years before he had arrived from Belgium as the heir of his uncle, who had left him a small property upon the very border of the forest of Gagny, just opposite the mill, a few gunshots distant. He had come to sell this property, he said, and return home But the district charmed him, it appeared, for he did not quit it. He was seen cultivating his little field, gathering a few vegetables upon which he subsisted. He fished and hunted; many times the forest guards nearly caught him and were on the point of drawing up procès-verbaux against him. This free existence, the resources of which the peasants could not clearly discover, at length gave him a bad reputation. He was vaguely styled a poacher. At any rate, he was lazy, for he was often found asleep on the grass when he should have been at work. The hut he inhabited beneath the last trees on the edge of the forest did not seem at all like the dwelling of an honest young fellow. If he had had dealings with the wolves of the ruins of Gagny the old women would not have been the least bit surprised. Nevertheless, the young girls sometimes risked defending him, for this doubtful man was superb; supple and tall as a poplar, he had a very white skin, with flaxen hair and beard which gleamed like gold in the sun.

One fine morning Françoise declared to Père Merlier that she loved Dominique and would never wed any other man.

It may well be imagined what a blow this was to Père Merlier. He said nothing, according to his custom, but his face grew thoughtful and his internal gaiety no longer sparkled in his eyes. He looked gruff for a week. Françoise also was exceedingly grave. What tormented Père Merlier was to find out how this rogue of a poacher had managed to fascinate his daughter. Dominique had never visited the mill. The miller watched and saw the gallant on the other side of the Morelle, stretched out upon the grass and feigning to be asleep. Françoise could see him from her chamber window. Everything was plain: they had fallen in love by casting sheep's eyes at each other over the mill wheel.

Another week went by. Françoise became more and more grave. Père Merlier still said nothing. Then one evening he himself silently brought in Dominique. Françoise at that moment was setting the table. She did not seem astonished; she contented herself with putting on an additional plate, knife and fork, but the little dimples were again seen in her cheeks, and her smile reappeared. That morning Père Merlier had sought out Dominique in his hut on the border of the wood.

There the two men had talked for three hours with doors and windows closed. What was the purport of their conversation no one ever knew. Certain it was, however, that Père Merlier, on taking his departure, already called Dominique his son-in-law. Without doubt the old man had found the youth he had gone to seek a worthy youth in the lazy fellow who stretched himself out upon the grass to make the girls fall in love with him.

All Rocreuse clamored. The women at the doors had plenty to say on the subject of the folly of Père Merlier, who had thus introduced a reprobate into his house. The miller let people talk on. Perhaps he remembered his own marriage. He was without a sou when he wedded Madeleine and her mill; this, however, had not prevented him from making a good husband. Besides, Dominique cut short the gossip by going so vigorously to work that all the district was amazed. The miller's assistant had just been drawn to serve as a soldier, and Dominique would not suffer another to be engaged. He carried the sacks, drove the cart, fought with the old mill wheel when it refused to turn, and all this with such good will that people came to see him out of curiosity. Père Merlier had his silent laugh. He was excessively proud of having formed a correct estimate of this youth. There is nothing like love to give courage to young folks. Amid all these heavy labors Françoise and Dominique adored each other. They did not indulge in lovers' talks, but there was a smiling gentleness in their glances.

Up to that time Père Merlier had not spoken a single word on the subject of marriage, and they respected this silence, awaiting the old man's will. Finally one day toward the middle of July he caused three tables to be placed in the courtyard, beneath the great elm, and invited his friends of Rocreuse to come in the evening and drink a glass of wine with him.

When the courtyard was full and all had their glasses in their hands, Père Merlier raised his very high and said:

"I have the pleasure to announce to you that Françoise will wed this young fellow here in a month, on Saint Louis's Day."

Then they drank noisily. Everybody smiled. But Père Merlier, again lifting his voice, exclaimed:

"Dominique, embrace your fiancée. It is your right."

They embraced, blushing to the tips of their ears, while all the guests laughed joyously. It was a genuine fete. They emptied a small cask of wine. Then when all were gone but intimate friends the conversation was carried on without noise. The night had fallen, a starry and cloudless night. Dominique and Françoise, seated side by side on a bench, said nothing.

An old peasant spoke of the war the emperor had declared against Prussia. All the village lads had already departed. On the preceding day troops had again passed through the place. There was going to be hard fighting.

"Bah!" said Père Merlier with the selfishness of a happy man. "Dominique is a foreigner; he will not go to the war. And if the Prussians come here he will be on hand to defend his wife!"

The idea that the Prussians might come there seemed a good joke. They were going to receive a sound whipping, and the affair would soon be over.

"I have already seen them; I have already seen them," repeated the old peasant in a hollow voice.

There was silence. Then they drank again. Françoise and Dominique had heard nothing; they had gently taken each other by the hand behind the bench, so that nobody could see them, and it seemed so delightful that they remained where they were, their eyes plunged into the depths of the shadows.

What a warm and superb night it was! The village slumbered on both edges of the white highway in infantile quietude. From time to time was heard the crowing of some chanticleer aroused too soon. From the huge wood near by came long breaths, which passed over the roofs like caresses. The meadows, with their dark shadows, assumed a mysterious and dreamy majesty, while all the springs, all the flowing waters which gurgled in the darkness, seemed to be the cool and rhythmical respiration of the sleeping country. Occasionally the ancient mill wheel, lost in a doze, appeared to dream like those old watchdogs that bark while snoring; it cracked; it talked to itself, rocked by the fall of the Morelle, the surface of which gave forth the musical and continuous sound of an organ pipe. Never had more profound peace descended upon a happier corner of nature.

CHAPTER II

The Attack on the Mill

A MONTH LATER, on the day preceding that of Saint Louis, Rocreuse was in a state of terror. The Prussians had beaten the emperor and were advancing by forced marches toward the village. For a week past people who hurried along the highway had been announcing them thus: "They are at Lormière—they are at Novelles!" And on hearing that they were drawing near so rapidly, Rocreuse every morning expected to see them descend from the wood of Gagny. They did not come, however, and that increased the fright. They would surely fall upon the village during the night and slaughter everybody.

That morning, a little before sunrise, there was an alarm. The inhabitants were awakened by the loud tramp of men on the highway. The women were already on their knees, making the sign of the cross, when some of the people, peering cautiously through the partially opened windows, recognized the red pantaloons. It was a French detachment. The captain immediately asked for the mayor of the district and remained at the mill after having talked with Père Merlier.

The sun rose gaily that morning. It would be hot at noon. Over the wood floated a golden brightness, while in the distance white vapors arose from the meadows. The neat and pretty village awoke amid the fresh air, and the country, with its river and its springs, had the moist sweetness of a bouquet. But that beautiful day caused nobody to smile. The captain was seen to take a turn around the mill, examine the neighboring houses, pass to the other side of the Morelle and from there study the district with a field glass; Père Merlier, who accompanied him, seemed to be giving him explanations. Then the captain posted soldiers behind the walls, behind the trees and in the ditches. The main body of the detachment encamped in the courtyard of the mill. Was there going to be a battle? When Père Merlier returned he was questioned. He nodded his head without speaking. Yes, there was going to be a battle!

Françoise and Dominique were in the courtyard; they looked at him. At last he took his pipe from his mouth and said:

"Ah, my poor young ones, you cannot get married tomorrow!"

Dominique, his lips pressed together, with an angry frown on his forehead, at times raised himself on tiptoe and fixed his eyes upon the wood of Gagny, as if he wished to see the Prussians arrive. Françoise, very pale and serious, came and went, furnishing the soldiers with what they needed. The troops were making soup in a corner of the courtyard; they joked while waiting for it to get ready.

The captain was delighted. He had visited the chambers and the huge hall of the mill which looked out upon the river. Now, seated beside the well, he was conversing with Père Merlier.

"Your mill is a real fortress," he said. "We can hold it without difficulty until evening. The bandits are late. They ought to be here."

The miller was grave. He saw his mill burning like a torch, but he uttered no complaint, thinking such a course useless. He merely said:

"You had better hide the boat behind the wheel; there is a place there just fit for that purpose. Perhaps it will be useful to have the boat."

The captain gave the requisite order. This officer was a handsome man of forty; he was tall and had an amiable countenance. The sight of Françoise and Dominique seemed to please him. He contemplated them as if he had forgotten the coming struggle. He followed Françoise with his eyes, and his look told plainly that he thought her charming. Then turning toward Dominique, he asked suddenly:

"Why are you not in the army, my good fellow?"

"I am a foreigner," answered the young man.

The captain evidently did not attach much weight to this reason. He winked his eye and smiled. Françoise was more agreeable company than a cannon. On seeing him smile, Dominique added:

"I am a foreigner, but I can put a ball in an apple at five hundred meters. There is my hunting gun behind you."

"You may have use for it," responded the captain dryly.

Françoise had approached, somewhat agitated. Without heeding the strangers present Dominique took and grasped in his the two hands she extended to him, as if to put herself under his protection. The captain smiled again but said not a word. He remained seated, his sword across his knees and his eyes plunged into space, lost in a reverie.

It was already ten o'clock. The heat had become very great. A heavy silence prevailed. In the courtyard, in the shadows of the sheds, the soldiers had begun to eat their soup. Not a sound came from the village; all its inhabitants had barricaded the doors and windows of their houses. A dog, alone upon the highway, howled. From the neighboring forests and meadows, swooning in the heat, came a prolonged and distant voice made up of all the scattered breaths. A cuckoo sang. Then the silence grew more intense.

Suddenly in that slumbering air a shot was heard. The captain leaped briskly to his feet; the soldiers left their plates of soup, yet half full. In a few seconds everybody was at the post of duty; from bottom to top the mill was occupied. Meanwhile the captain, who had gone out upon the road, had discovered nothing; to the right and to the left the highway stretched out, empty and white. A second shot was heard, and still nothing visible, not even a shadow. But as he was returning the captain perceived in the direction of Gagny, between two trees, a light puff of smoke whirling away like thistledown. The wood was calm and peaceful.

"The bandits have thrown themselves into the forest," he muttered. "They know we are here."

Then the firing continued, growing more and more vigorous, between the French soldiers posted around the mill and the Prussians hidden behind the trees. The balls whistled above the Morelle without damaging either side. The fusillade was irregular, the shots coming from every bush, and still only the little puffs of smoke, tossed gently by the breeze, were seen. This lasted nearly two hours. The officer hummed a tune with an air of indifference. Françoise and Dominique, who had remained in the courtyard, raised themselves on tiptoe and looked over a low wall. They were particularly interested in a little soldier posted on the shore of the Morelle, behind the remains of an old bateau; he stretched himself out flat on the ground, watched, fired and then glided into a ditch a trifle farther back to reload his gun; and his movements were so droll, so tricky and so supple, that they smiled as they looked at him. He must have perceived the head of a Prussian, for he arose quickly and brought his weapon to his shoulder, but before he could fire he uttered a cry, fell and rolled into the ditch, where for an instant his legs twitched convulsively like the claws of a chicken just killed. The little soldier had received a ball full in the breast. He was the first man slain. Instinctively Françoise seized Dominique's hand and clasped it with a nervous contraction.

"Move away," said the captain. "You are within range of the balls."

At that moment a sharp little thud was heard in the old elm, and a fragment of a branch came whirling down. But the two young folks did not stir; they were nailed to the spot by anxiety to see what was going on. On the edge of the wood a Prussian had suddenly come out from behind a tree as from a theater stage entrance, beating the air with his hands and falling backward. Nothing further moved; the two corpses seemed asleep in the broad sunlight; not a living soul was seen in the scorching country. Even the crack of the fusillade had ceased. The Morelle alone whispered in its clear tones.

Père Merlier looked at the captain with an air of surprise, as if to ask him if the struggle was over.

"They are getting ready for something worse," muttered the officer. "Don't trust appearances. Move away from there."

He had not finished speaking when there was a terrible discharge of musketry. The great elm was riddled, and a host of leaves shot into the air. The Prussians had happily fired too high. Dominique dragged, almost carried, Françoise away, while Père Merlier followed them, shouting:

"Go down into the cellar; the walls are solid!"

But they did not heed him; they entered the huge hall where ten soldiers were waiting in silence, watching through the chinks in the closed window shutters. The captain was alone in the courtyard, crouching behind the little wall, while the furious discharges continued. Without, the soldiers he had posted gave ground only foot by foot. However, they re-entered one by one, crawling, when the enemy had dislodged them from their hiding places. Their orders were to gain time and not show themselves, that the Prussians might remain in ignorance as to what force was before them. Another hour went by. As a sergeant arrived, saying that but two or three more men remained without, the captain glanced at his watch, muttering:

"Half-past two o'clock. We must hold the position four hours longer."

He caused the great gate of the courtyard to be closed, and every preparation was made for an energetic resistance. As the Prussians were on the opposite side of the Morelle, an immediate assault was not to be feared. There was a bridge two kilometers away, but they evidently were not aware of its existence, and it was hardly likely that they would attempt to ford the river. The officer, therefore, simply ordered the highway to be watched. Every effort would be made in the direction of the country.

Again the fusillade had ceased. The mill seemed dead beneath the glowing sun. Not a shutter was open; no sound came from the interior. At length, little by little, the Prussians showed themselves at the edge of the forest of Gagny. They stretched their necks and grew bold. In the mill several soldiers had already raised their guns to their shoulders, but the captain cried:

"No, no; wait. Let them come nearer."

They were exceedingly prudent, gazing at the mill with a suspicious air. The silent and somber old structure with its curtains of ivy filled them with uneasiness. Nevertheless, they advanced. When fifty of them were in the opposite meadow the officer uttered the single word:

"Fire!"

A crash was heard; isolated shots followed. Françoise, all of a tremble, had mechanically put her hands to her ears. Dominique, behind the soldiers, looked on; when the smoke had somewhat lifted he saw three Prussians stretched upon their backs in the center of the meadow. The others had thrown themselves behind the willows and poplars. Then the siege began.

For more than an hour the mill was riddled with balls. They dashed against the old walls like hail. When they struck the stones they were heard to flatten and fall into the water. They buried themselves in the wood with a hollow sound. Occasionally a sharp crack announced that the mill wheel had been hit. The soldiers in the interior were careful of their shots; they fired only when they could take aim. From time to time the captain consulted his watch. As a ball broke a shutter and plowed into the ceiling he said to himself:

"Four o'clock. We shall never be able to hold out!"

Little by little the terrible fusillade weakened the old mill. A shutter fell into the water, pierced like a bit of lace, and it was necessary to replace it with a mattress. Père Merlier constantly exposed himself to ascertain the extent of the damage done to his poor wheel, the cracking of which made his heart ache. All would be over with it this time; never could he repair it. Dominique had implored Françoise to withdraw, but she refused to leave him; she was seated behind a huge oaken clothespress, which protected her. A ball, however, struck the clothespress, the sides of which gave forth a hollow sound. Then Dominique placed himself in front of Françoise. He had not yet fired a shot; he held his gun in his hand but was unable to approach the windows, which were altogether occupied by the soldiers. At each discharge the floor shook.

"Attention! Attention!" suddenly cried the captain.

He had just seen a great dark mass emerge from the wood. Immediately a formidable platoon fire opened. It was like a waterspout passing over the mill. Another shutter was shattered, and through the gaping opening of the window the balls entered. Two soldiers rolled upon the floor. One of them lay like a stone; they pushed the body against the wall because it was in the way. The other twisted in agony, begging his comrades to finish him, but they paid no attention to him. The balls entered in a constant stream; each man took care of himself and strove to find a loophole through which to return the fire. A third soldier was hit; he uttered not a word; he fell on the edge of a table, with eyes fixed and haggard. Opposite these dead men Françoise, stricken with horror, had mechanically pushed away her chair to sit on the floor against the wall; she thought she would take up less room there and not be in so much danger. Meanwhile the soldiers had collected all the mattresses of the household and partially stopped up the windows with them. The hall was filled with wrecks, with broken weapons and demolished furniture.

"Five o'clock," said the captain. "Keep up your courage! They are about to try to cross the river!"

At that moment Françoise uttered a cry. A ball which had ricocheted had grazed her forehead. Several drops of blood appeared. Dominique stared at her; then, approaching the window, he fired his first shot. Once started, he did not stop. He loaded and fired without heeding what was passing around him, but from time to time he glanced at Françoise. He was very deliberate and aimed with care. The Prussians, keeping beside the poplars, attempted the passage of the Morelle, as the captain had predicted, but as soon as a man strove to cross he fell, shot in the head by Dominique. The captain, who had his eyes on the young man, was amazed. He complimented him, saying that he should be glad to have many such skillful marksmen. Dominique did not hear him. A ball cut his shoulder; another wounded his arm, but he continued to fire.

There were two more dead men. The mangled mattresses no longer stopped the windows. The last discharge seemed as if it would have carried away the mill. The position had ceased to be tenable. Nevertheless, the captain said firmly:

"Hold your ground for half an hour more!"

Now he counted the minutes. He had promised his chiefs to hold the enemy in check there until evening, and he would not give an inch before the hour he had fixed on for the retreat. He preserved his amiable air and smiled upon Françoise to reassure her. He had picked up the gun of a dead soldier and himself was firing.

Only four soldiers remained in the hall. The Prussians appeared in a body on the other side of the Morelle, and it was clear that they intended speedily to cross the river. A few minutes more elapsed. The stubborn captain would not order the retreat. Just then a sergeant hastened to him and said:

"They are upon the highway; they will take us in the rear!"

The Prussians must have found the bridge. The captain pulled out his watch and looked at it.

"Five minutes longer," he said. "They cannot get here before that time!"

Then at six o'clock exactly he at last consented to lead his men out through a little door which opened into a lane. From there they threw themselves into a ditch; they gained the forest of Sauval. Before taking his departure the captain bowed very politely to Père Merlier and made his excuses, adding:

"Amuse them! We will return!"

Dominique was now alone in the hall. He was still firing, hearing nothing, understanding nothing. He felt only the need of defending Françoise. He had not the least suspicion in the world that the soldiers had retreated. He aimed and killed his man at every shot. Suddenly there was a loud noise. The Prussians had entered the courtyard from behind. Dominique fired a last shot, and they fell upon him while his gun was yet smoking.

Four men held him. Others vociferated around him in a frightful language. They were ready to slaughter him on the spot. Françoise, with a supplicating look, had cast herself before him. But an officer entered and ordered the prisoner to be delivered up to him. After exchanging a few words in German with the soldiers he turned toward Dominique and said to him roughly in very good French:

"You will be shot in two hours!"

CHAPTER III

THE FLIGHT

IT WAS a settled rule of the German staff that every Frenchman, not belonging to the regular army, taken with arms in his hands should be shot. The militia companies themselves were not recognized as belligerents. By thus making terrible examples of the peasants who defended their homes, the Germans hoped to prevent the levy en masse, which they feared.

The officer, a tall, lean man of fifty, briefly questioned Dominique. Although he spoke remarkably pure French he had a stiffness altogether Prussian.

"Do you belong to this district?" he asked.

"No; I am a Belgian," answered the young man.

"Why then did you take up arms? The fighting did not concern you!"

Dominique made no reply. At that moment the officer saw Françoise who was standing by, very pale, listening; upon her white forehead her slight wound had put a red bar. He looked at the young folks, one after the other, seemed to understand matters and contented himself with adding:

"You do not deny having fired, do you?"

"I fired as often as I could!" responded Dominique tranquilly.

This confession was useless, for he was black with powder, covered with sweat and stained with a few drops of blood which had flowed from the scratch on his shoulder.

"Very well," said the officer. "You will be shot in two hours!"

Françoise did not cry out. She clasped her hands and raised them with a gesture of mute despair. The officer noticed this gesture. Two soldiers had taken Dominique to a neighboring apartment, where they were to keep watch over him. The young girl had fallen upon a chair, totally overcome; she could not weep; she was suffocating. The officer had continued to examine her. At last he spoke to her.

"Is that young man your brother?" he demanded.

She shook her head negatively. The German stood stiffly on his feet without a smile. Then after a short silence he again asked:

"Has he lived long in the district?"

She nodded affirmatively.

"In that case, he ought to be thoroughly acquainted with the neighboring forests."

This time she spoke.

"He is thoroughly acquainted with them, monsieur," she said, looking at him with considerable surprise.

He said nothing further to her but turned upon his heel, demanding that the mayor of the village should be brought to him. But Françoise had arisen with a slight blush on her countenance; thinking that she had seized the aim of the officer's questions, she had recovered hope. She herself ran to find her father.

Père Merlier, as soon as the firing had ceased, had quickly descended to the wooden gallery to examine his wheel. He adored his daughter; he had a solid friendship for Dominique, his future son-in-law, but his wheel also held a large place in his heart. Since the two young ones, as he called them, had come safe and sound out of the fight, he thought of his other tenderness, which had suffered greatly. Bent over the huge wooden carcass, he was studying its wounds with a sad air. Five buckets were shattered to pieces; the central framework was riddled. He thrust his fingers in the bullet holes to measure their depth; he thought how he could repair all these injuries. Françoise found him already stopping up the clefts with rubbish and moss.

"Father," she said, "you are wanted."

And she wept at last as she told him what she had just heard. Père Merlier tossed his head. People were not shot in such a summary fashion. The matter must be looked after. He re-entered the mill with his silent and tranquil air. When the officer demanded of him provisions for his men he replied that the inhabitants of Rocreuse were not accustomed to be treated roughly and that nothing would be obtained from them if violence were employed. He would see to everything but on condition that he was not interfered with. The officer at first seemed irritated by his calm tone; then he gave way before the old man's short and clear words. He even called him back and asked him:

"What is the name of that wood opposite?"

"The forest of Sauval."

"What is its extent?"

The miller looked at him fixedly.

"I do not know," he answered.

And he went away. An hour later the contribution of war in provisions and money, demanded by the officer, was in the courtyard of the mill. Night came on. Françoise watched with anxiety the movements of the soldiers. She hung about the room in which Dominique was imprisoned. Toward seven o'clock she experienced a poignant emotion. She saw the officer enter the prisoner's apartment and for a quarter of an hour heard their voices in loud conversation. For an instant the officer reappeared upon the threshold to give an order in German, which she did not understand, but when twelve men ranged themselves in the courtyard, their guns on their shoulders, she trembled and felt as if about to faint. All then was over: the execution was going to take place. The twelve men stood there ten minutes, Dominique's voice continuing to be raised in a tone of violent refusal. Finally the officer came out, saying, as he roughly shut the door:

"Very well; reflect. I give you until tomorrow morning."

And with a gesture he ordered the twelve men to break ranks. Françoise was stupefied. Père Merlier, who had been smoking his pipe and looking at the platoon simply with an air of curiosity, took her by the arm with paternal gentleness. He led her to her chamber.

"Be calm," he said, "and try to sleep. Tomorrow, when it is light, we will see what can be done."

As he withdrew he prudently locked her in. It was his opinion that women were good for nothing and that they spoiled everything when they took a hand in a serious affair. But Françoise did not retire. She sat for a long while upon the side of her bed, listening to the noises of the house. The German soldiers encamped in the courtyard sang and laughed; they must have been eating and drinking until eleven o'clock, for the racket did not cease an instant. In the mill itself heavy footsteps resounded from time to time, without doubt those of the sentinels who were being relieved. But she was interested most by the sounds she could distinguish in the apartment beneath her chamber. Many times she stretched herself out at full length and put her ear to the floor. That apartment was the one in which Dominique was confined. He must have been walking back and forth from the window to the wall, for she long heard the regular cadence of his steps. Then deep silence ensued; he had doubtless seated himself. Finally every noise ceased and all was as if asleep. When slumber appeared to her to have settled on the house she opened her window as gently as possible and leaned her elbows on the sill.

Without, the night had a warm serenity. The slender crescent of the moon, which was sinking behind the forest of Sauval, lit up the country with the glimmer of a night lamp. The lengthened shadows of the tall trees barred the meadows with black, while the grass in uncovered spots assumed the softness of greenish velvet. But Françoise did not pause to admire the mysterious charms of the night. She examined the country, searching for the sentinels whom the Germans had posted obliquely. She clearly saw their shadows extending like the rounds of a ladder along the Morelle. Only one was before the mill, on the other shore of the river, beside a willow, the branches of which dipped in the water. Françoise saw him plainly. He was a tall man and was standing motionless, his face turned toward the sky with the dreamy air of a shepherd.

When she had carefully inspected the locality she again seated herself on her bed. She remained there an hour, deeply absorbed. Then she listened once more: there was not a sound in the mill. She returned to the window and glanced out, but doubtless one of the horns of the moon, which was still visible behind the trees, made her uneasy, for she resumed her waiting attitude. At last she thought the proper time had come. The night was as black as jet; she could no longer see the sentinel opposite; the country spread out like a pool of ink. She strained her ear for an instant and made her decision. Passing near the window was an iron ladder, the bars fastened to the wall, which mounted from the wheel to the garret and formerly enabled the millers to reach certain machinery; afterward the mechanism had been altered, and for a long while the ladder had been hidden under the thick ivy which covered that side of the mill.

Françoise bravely climbed out of her window and grasped one of the bars of the ladder. She began to descend. Her skirts embarrassed her greatly. Suddenly a stone was detached from the wall and fell into the Morelle with a loud splash. She stopped with an icy shiver of fear. Then she realized that the waterfall with its continuous roar would drown every noise she might make, and she descended more courageously, feeling the ivy with her foot, assuring herself that the rounds were firm. When she was at the height of the chamber which served as Dominique's prison she paused. An unforeseen difficulty nearly caused her to lose all her courage: the window of the chamber was not directly below that of her apartment. She hung off from the ladder, but when she stretched out her arm her hand encountered only the wall. Must she, then, ascend without pushing her plan to completion? Her arms were fatigued; the murmur of the Morelle beneath her commenced to make her dizzy. Then she tore from the wall little fragments of plaster and threw them against Dominique's window. He did not hear; he was doubtless asleep. She crumbled more plaster from the wall, scraping the skin off her fingers. She was utterly exhausted; she felt herself falling backward, when Dominique at last softly opened the window.

"It is I!" she murmured. "Catch me quickly; I'm falling!"

It was the first time that she had addressed him familiarly. Leaning out, he seized her and drew her into the chamber. There she gave vent to a flood of tears, stifling her sobs that she might not be heard. Then by a supreme effort she calmed herself.

"Are you guarded?" she asked in a low voice.

Dominique, still stupefied at seeing her thus, nodded his head affirmatively, pointing to the door. On the other side they heard someone snoring; the sentinel, yielding to sleep, had thrown himself on the floor against the door, arguing that by disposing himself thus the prisoner could not escape.

"You must fly," resumed Françoise excitedly. "I have come to beg you to do so and to bid you farewell."

But he did not seem to hear her. He repeated:

"What? Is it you; is it you? Oh, what fear you caused me! You might have killed yourself!"

He seized her hands; he kissed them.

"How I love you, Françoise!" he murmured. "You are as courageous as good. I had only one dread: that I should die without seeing you again. But you are here, and now they can shoot me. When I have passed a quarter of an hour with you I shall be ready."

Little by little he had drawn her to him, and she leaned her head upon his shoulder. The danger made them dearer to each other. They forgot everything in that warm clasp.

"Ah, Françoise," resumed Dominique in a caressing voice, "this is Saint Louis's Day, the day, so long awaited, of our marriage. Nothing has been able to separate us, since we are both here alone, faithful to the appointment. Is not this our wedding morning?"

"Yes, yes," she repeated, "it is our wedding morning."

They tremblingly exchanged a kiss. But all at once she disengaged herself from Dominique's arms; she remembered the terrible reality.

"You must fly; you must fly," she whispered. "There is not a minute to be lost!"

And as he stretched out his arms in the darkness to clasp her again, she said tenderly:

"Oh, I implore you to listen to me! If you die I shall die also! In an hour it will be light. I want you to go at once."

Then rapidly she explained her plan. The iron ladder descended to the mill wheel; there he could climb down the buckets and get into the boat which was hidden away in a nook. Afterward it would be easy for him to reach the other bank of the river and escape.

"But what of the sentinels?" he asked.

"There is only one, opposite, at the foot of the first willow."

"What if he should see me and attempt to give an alarm?"

Françoise shivered. She placed in his hand a knife she had brought with her. There was a brief silence.

"What is to become of your father and yourself?" resumed Dominique. "No, I cannot fly! When I am gone those soldiers will, perhaps, massacre you both! You do not know them. They offered me my life if I would consent to guide them through the forest of Sauval. When they discover my escape they will be capable of anything!"

The young girl did not stop to argue. She said simply in reply to all the reasons he advanced:

"Out of love for me, fly! If you love me, Dominique, do not remain here another moment!"

Then she promised to climb back to her chamber. No one would know that she had helped him. She finally threw her arms around him to convince him with an embrace, with a burst of extraordinary love. He was vanquished. He asked but one more question:

"Can you swear to me that your father knows what you have done and that he advises me to fly?"

"My father sent me!" answered Françoise boldly.

She told a falsehood. At that moment she had only one immense need: to know that he was safe, to escape from the abominable thought that the sun would be the signal for his death. When he was far away every misfortune might fall upon her; that would seem delightful to her from the moment he was secure. The selfishness of her tenderness desired that he should live before everything.

"Very well," said Dominique; "I will do what you wish."

They said nothing more. Dominique reopened the window. But suddenly a sound froze them. The door was shaken, and they thought that it was about to be opened. Evidently a patrol had heard their voices. Standing locked in each other's arms, they waited in unspeakable anguish. The door was shaken a second time, but it did not open. They uttered low sighs of relief; they comprehended that the soldier who was asleep against the door must have turned over. In fact, silence succeeded; the snoring was resumed.

Dominique exacted that Françoise should ascend to her chamber before he departed. He clasped her in his arms and bade her a mute adieu. Then he aided her to seize the ladder and clung to it in his turn. But he refused to descend a single round until convinced that she was in her apartment. When

Françoise had entered her window she let fall in a voice as light as a breath: "Au revoir, my love!"

She leaned her elbows on the sill and strove to follow Dominique with her eyes. The night was yet very dark. She searched for the sentinel but could not see him; the willow alone made a pale stain in the midst of the gloom. For an instant she heard the sound produced by Dominique's body in passing along the ivy. Then the wheel cracked, and there was a slight agitation in the water which told her that the young man had found the boat. A moment afterward she distinguished the somber silhouette of the bateau on the gray surface of the Morelle. Terrible anguish seized upon her. Each instant she thought she heard the sentinel's cry of alarm; the smallest sounds scattered through the gloom seemed to her the hurried tread of soldiers, the clatter of weapons, the charging of guns. Nevertheless, the seconds elapsed and the country maintained its profound peace. Dominique must have reached the other side of the river. Françoise saw nothing more. The silence was majestic. She heard a shuffling of feet, a hoarse cry and the hollow fall of a body. Afterward the silence grew deeper. Then as if she had felt Death pass by, she stood, chilled through and through, staring into the thick night.

CHAPTER IV

A Terrible Experience

At dawn a clamor of voices shook the mill. Père Merlier opened the door of Françoise's chamber. She went down into the courtyard, pale and very calm. But there she could not repress a shiver as she saw the corpse of a Prussian soldier stretched out on a cloak beside the well.

Around the body troops gesticulated, uttering cries of fury. Many of them shook their fists at the village. Meanwhile the officer had summoned Père Merlier as the mayor of the commune.

"Look!" he said to him in a voice almost choking with anger. "There lies one of our men who was found assassinated upon the bank of the river. We must make a terrible example, and I count on you to aid us in discovering the murderer."

"As you choose," answered the miller with his usual stoicism, "but you will find it no easy task."

The officer stooped and drew aside a part of the cloak which hid the face of the dead man. Then appeared a horrible wound. The sentinel had been struck in the throat, and the weapon had remained in the cut. It was a kitchen knife with a black handle.

"Examine that knife," said the officer to Père Merlier; "perhaps it will help us in our search."

The old man gave a start but recovered control of himself immediately. He replied without moving a muscle of his face:

"Everybody in the district has similar knives. Doubtless your man was weary of fighting and put an end to his own life. It looks like it!"

"Mind what you say!" cried the officer furiously. "I do not know what prevents me from setting fire to the four corners of the village!"

Happily in his rage he did not notice the deep trouble pictured on Françoise's countenance. She had been forced to sit down on a stone bench near the well. Despite herself her eyes were fixed upon the corpse stretched out on the ground almost at her feet. It was that of a tall and handsome man who resembled Dominique, with flaxen hair and blue eyes. This resemblance made her heart ache. She thought that perhaps the dead soldier had left behind him in Germany a sweetheart who would weep her eyes out for him. She recognized her knife in the throat of the murdered man. She had killed him.

The officer was talking of striking Rocreuse with terrible measures, when soldiers came running to him. Dominique's escape had just been discovered. It caused an extreme agitation. The officer went to the apartment in which the prisoner had been confined, looked out of the window which had remained open, understood everything and returned, exasperated.

Père Merlier seemed greatly vexed by Dominique's flight.

"The imbecile!" he muttered. "He has ruined all!"

Françoise heard him and was overcome with anguish. But the miller did not suspect her of complicity in the affair. He tossed his head, saying to her in an undertone:

"We are in a nice scrape!"

"It was that wretch who assassinated the soldier! I am sure of it!" cried the officer. "He has undoubtedly reached the forest. But he must be found for us or the village shall pay for him!"

Turning to the miller, he said:

"See here, you ought to know where he is hidden!"

Père Merlier laughed silently, pointing to the wide stretch of wooden hills.

"Do you expect to find a man in there?" he said.

"Oh, there must be nooks there with which you are acquainted. I will give you ten men. You must guide them."

"As you please. But it will take a week to search all the wood in the vicinity."

The old man's tranquillity enraged the officer. In fact, the latter comprehended the absurdity of this search. At that moment he saw Françoise, pale and trembling, on the bench. The anxious attitude of the young girl struck him. He was silent for an instant, during which he in turn examined the miller and his daughter.

At length he demanded roughly of the old man:

"Is not that fellow your child's lover?"

Père Merlier grew livid and seemed about to hurl himself upon the officer to strangle him. He stiffened himself but made no answer. Françoise buried her face in her hands.

"Yes, that's it!" continued the Prussian. "And you or your daughter helped him to escape! One of you is his accomplice! For the last time, will you give him up to us?"

The miller uttered not a word. He turned away and looked into space with an air of indifference, as if the officer had not addressed him. This brought the latter's rage to a head.

"Very well!" he shouted. "You shall be shot in his place!"

And he again ordered out the platoon of execution. Père Merlier remained as stoical as ever. He hardly even shrugged his shoulders; all this drama appeared to him in bad taste. Without doubt he did not believe that they would shoot a man so lightly. But when the platoon drew up before him he said gravely:

"So it is serious, is it? Go on with your bloody work then! If you must have a victim I will do as well as another!"

But Françoise started up, terrified, stammering:

"In pity, monsieur, do no harm to my father! Kill me in his stead! I aided Dominique to fly! I alone am guilty!"

"Hush, my child!" cried Père Merlier. "Why do you tell an untruth? She passed the night locked in her chamber, monsieur. She tells a falsehood, I assure you!"

"No, I do not tell a falsehood!" resumed the young girl ardently. "I climbed out of my window and went down the iron ladder; I urged Dominique to fly. This is the truth, the whole truth!"

The old man became very pale. He saw clearly in her eyes that she did not lie, and her story terrified him. Ah, these children with their hearts, how they spoil everything! Then he grew angry and exclaimed:

"She is mad; do not heed her. She tells you stupid tales. Come, finish your work!"

She still protested. She knelt, clasping her hands. The officer tranquilly watched this dolorous struggle.

"*Mon Dieu!*" he said at last. "I take your father because I have not the other. Find the fugitive and the old man shall be set at liberty!"

She gazed at him with staring eyes, astonished at the atrocity of the proposition.

"How horrible!" she murmured. "Where do you think I can find Dominique at this hour? He has departed; I know no more about him."

"Come, make your choice—him or your father."

"Oh, *mon Dieu!* How can I choose? If I knew where Dominique was I could not choose! You are cutting my heart. I would rather die at once. Yes, it would be the sooner over. Kill me, I implore you, kill me!"

This scene of despair and tears finally made the officer impatient. He cried out:

"Enough! I will be merciful. I consent to give you two hours. If in that time your lover is not here your father will be shot in his place!"

He caused Père Merlier to be taken to the chamber which had served as Dominique's prison. The old man demanded tobacco and began to smoke. Upon his impassible face not the slightest emotion was visible. But when alone, as he smoked, he shed two big tears which ran slowly down his cheeks. His poor, dear child, how she was suffering!

Françoise remained in the middle of the courtyard. Prussian soldiers passed, laughing. Some of them spoke to her, uttered jokes she could not understand. She stared at the door through which her father had disappeared. With a slow movement she put her hand to her forehead, as if to prevent it from bursting.

The officer turned upon his heel, saying:

"You have two hours. Try to utilize them."

She had two hours. This phrase buzzed in her ears. Then mechanically she quitted the courtyard; she walked straight ahead. Where should she go? —what should she do? She did not even try to make a decision because she well understood the inutility of her efforts. However, she wished to see Dominique. They could have an understanding together; they might, perhaps, find an expedient. And amid the confusion of her thoughts she went down to the shore of the Morelle, which she crossed below the sluice at a spot where there were huge stones. Her feet led her beneath the first willow, in the corner of the meadow. As she stooped she saw a pool of blood which made her turn pale. It was there the murder had been committed. She followed the track of Dominique in the trodden grass; he must have run, for she perceived a line of long footprints stretching across the meadow. Then farther on she lost these traces. But in a neighboring field she thought she found them again. The new trail conducted her to the edge of the forest, where every indication was effaced.

Françoise, nevertheless, plunged beneath the trees. It solaced her to be alone. She sat down for an instant, but at the thought that time was passing she leaped to her feet. How long had it been since she left the mill? Five minutes?—half an hour? She had lost all conception of time. Perhaps Dominique had concealed himself in a copse she knew of, where they had one afternoon eaten filberts together. She hastened to the copse, searched it. Only a blackbird flew away, uttering its soft, sad note. Then she thought he might have taken refuge in a hollow of the rocks, where it had sometimes been his custom to lie in wait for game, but the hollow of the rocks was empty. What good was it to hunt for him? She would never find him, but little by little the desire to discover him took entire possession of her, and she hastened her steps. The idea that he might have climbed a tree suddenly occurred to her. She advanced with uplifted eyes, and that he might be made aware of her presence she called him every fifteen or twenty steps. Cuckoos answered; a breath of wind which passed through the branches made her believe that he was there and was descending. Once she even imagined she saw him; she stopped, almost choked, and wished to fly. What was she to say to him? Had she come to take him back to be shot? Oh no, she would not tell him what had happened. She would cry out to him to escape, not to remain in the neighborhood. Then the thought that her father was waiting for her gave her a sharp pain. She fell upon the turf, weeping, crying aloud:

"*Mon Dieu! Mon Dieu!* Why am I here?"

She was mad to have come. And as if seized with fear, she ran; she sought to leave the forest. Three times she deceived herself; she thought she never again would find the mill, when she entered a meadow just opposite Rocreuse.

As soon as she saw the village she paused. Was she going to return alone?
  She was still hesitating when a voice softly called:
  "Françoise! Françoise!"
  And she saw Dominique, who had raised his head above the edge of a ditch. Just God! She had found him! Did heaven wish his death? She restrained a cry; she let herself glide into the ditch.
  "Are you searching for me?" asked the young man.
  "Yes," she answered, her brain in a whirl, not knowing what she said.
  "What has happened?"
  She lowered her eyes, stammered:
  "Nothing. I was uneasy; I wanted to see you."
  Then, reassured, he explained to her that he had resolved not to go away. He was doubtful about the safety of herself and her father. Those Prussian wretches were fully capable of taking vengeance upon women and old men. But everything was getting on well. He added with a laugh:
  "Our wedding will take place in a week—I am sure of it."
  Then as she remained overwhelmed, he grew grave again and said:
  "But what ails you? You are concealing something from me!"
  "No; I swear it to you. I am out of breath from running."
  He embraced her, saying that it was imprudent for them to be talking, and he wished to climb out of the ditch to return to the forest. She restrained him. She trembled.
  "Listen," she said: "it would, perhaps, be wise for you to remain where you are. No one is searching for you; you have nothing to fear."
  "Françoise, you are concealing something from me," he repeated.
  Again she swore that she was hiding nothing. She had simply wished to know that he was near her. And she stammered forth still further reasons. She seemed so strange to him that he now could not be induced to flee. Besides, he had faith in the return of the French. Troops had been seen in the direction of Sauval.
  "Ah, let them hurry; let them get here as soon as possible," she murmured fervently.
  At that moment eleven o'clock sounded from the belfry of Rocreuse. The strokes were clear and distinct. She arose with a terrified look; two hours had passed since she quitted the mill.
  "Hear me," she said rapidly: "if we have need of you I will wave my handkerchief from my chamber window."
  And she departed on a run, while Dominique, very uneasy, stretched himself out upon the edge of the ditch to watch the mill. As she was about to enter Rocreuse, Françoise met an old beggar, Père Bontemps, who knew everybody in the district. He bowed to her; he had just seen the miller in the midst of the Prussians; then, making the sign of the cross and muttering broken words, he went on his way.
  "The two hours have passed," said the officer when Françoise appeared.
  Père Merlier was there, seated upon the bench beside the well. He was smoking. The young girl again begged, wept, sank on her knees. She wished

to gain time. The hope of seeing the French return had increased in her, and while lamenting she thought she heard in the distance, the measured tramp of an army. Oh, if they would come, if they would deliver them all!

"Listen, monsieur," she said: "an hour, another hour; you can grant us another hour!"

But the officer remained inflexible. He even ordered two men to seize her and take her away, that they might quietly proceed with the execution of the old man. Then a frightful struggle took place in Françoise's heart. She could not allow her father to be thus assassinated. No, no; she would die rather with Dominique. She was running toward her chamber when Dominique himself entered the courtyard.

The officer and the soldiers uttered a shout of triumph. But the young man, calmly, with a somewhat severe look, went up to Françoise, as if she had been the only person present.

"You did wrong," he said. "Why did you not bring me back? It remained for Père Bontemps to tell me everything. But I am here!"

CHAPTER V

THE RETURN OF THE FRENCH

IT WAS THREE O'CLOCK in the afternoon. Great black clouds, the trail of some neighboring storm, had slowly filled the sky. The yellow heavens, the brass-covered uniforms, had changed the valley of Rocreuse, so gay in the sunlight, into a den of cutthroats full of sinister gloom. The Prussian officer had contented himself with causing Dominique to be imprisoned without announcing what fate he reserved for him. Since noon Françoise had been torn by terrible anguish. Despite her father's entreaties she would not quit the courtyard. She was awaiting the French. But the hours sped on; night was approaching, and she suffered the more as all the time gained did not seem to be likely to change the frightful denouement.

About three o'clock the Prussians made their preparations for departure. For an instant past the officer had, as on the previous day, shut himself up with Dominique. Françoise realized that the young man's life was in balance. She clasped her hands; she prayed. Père Merlier, beside her, maintained silence and the rigid attitude of an old peasant who does not struggle against fate.

"Oh, *mon Dieu!* Oh, *mon Dieu!*" murmured Françoise. "They are going to kill him!"

The miller drew her to him and took her on his knees as if she had been a child.

At that moment the officer came out, while behind him two men brought Dominique.

"Never! Never!" cried the latter. "I am ready to die!"

"Think well," resumed the officer. "The service you refuse me another will render us. I am generous: I offer you your life. I want you simply to guide us through the forest to Montredon. There must be pathways leading there."

Dominique was silent.

"So you persist in your infatuation, do you?"

"Kill me and end all this!" replied the young man.

Françoise, her hands clasped, supplicated him from afar. She had forgotten everything; she would have advised him to commit an act of cowardice. But Père Merlier seized her hands that the Prussians might not see her wild gestures.

"He is right," he whispered: "it is better to die!"

The platoon of execution was there. The officer awaited a sign of weakness on Dominique's part. He still expected to conquer him. No one spoke. In the distance violent crashes of thunder were heard. Oppressive heat weighed upon the country. But suddenly, amid the silence, a cry broke forth:

"The French! The French!"

Yes, the French were at hand. Upon the Sauval highway, at the edge of the wood, the line of red pantaloons could be distinguished. In the mill there was an extraordinary agitation. The Prussian soldiers ran hither and thither with guttural exclamations. Not a shot had yet been fired.

"The French! The French!" cried Françoise, clapping her hands.

She was wild with joy. She escaped from her father's grasp; she laughed and tossed her arms in the air. At last they had come and come in time, since Dominique was still alive!

A terrible platoon fire, which burst upon her ears like a clap of thunder, caused her to turn. The officer muttered between his teeth:

"Before everything, let us settle this affair!"

And with his own hand pushing Dominique against the wall of a shed he ordered his men to fire. When Françoise looked Dominique lay upon the ground with blood streaming from his neck and shoulders.

She did not weep; she stood stupefied. Her eyes grew fixed, and she sat down under the shed, a few paces from the body. She stared at it, wringing her hands. The Prussians had seized Père Merlier as a hostage.

It was a stirring combat. The officer had rapidly posted his men, comprehending that he could not beat a retreat without being cut to pieces. Hence he would fight to the last. Now the Prussians defended the mill, and the French attacked it. The fusillade began with unusual violence. For half an hour it did not cease. Then a hollow sound was heard, and a ball broke a main branch of the old elm. The French had cannon. A battery, stationed just above the ditch in which Dominique had hidden himself, swept the wide street of Rocreuse. The struggle could not last long.

Ah, the poor mill! Balls pierced it in every part. Half of the roof was carried away. Two walls were battered down. But it was on the side of the Morelle that the destruction was most lamentable. The ivy, torn from the tottering edifice, hung like rags; the river was encumbered with wrecks of all kinds, and through a breach was visible Françoise's chamber with its bed, the white curtains of which were carefully closed. Shot followed shot; the old wheel received two balls and gave vent to an agonizing groan; the buckets were borne off by the current; the framework was crushed. The soul of the gay mill had left it!

Then the French began the assault. There was a furious fight with swords and bayonets. Beneath the rust-colored sky the valley was choked with the dead. The broad meadows had a wild look with their tall, isolated trees and their hedges of poplars which stained them with shade. To the right and to the left the forests were like the walls of an ancient ampitheater which enclosed the fighting gladiators, while the springs, the fountains and the flowing brooks seemed to sob amid the panic of the country.

Beneath the shed Françoise still sat near Dominique's body; she had not moved. Père Merlier had received a slight wound. The Prussians were exterminated, but the ruined mill was on fire in a dozen places. The French rushed into the courtyard, headed by their captain. It was his first success of the war. His face beamed with triumph. He waved his sword, shouting:

"Victory! Victory!"

On seeing the wounded miller, who was endeavoring to comfort Françoise, and noticing the body of Dominique, his joyous look changed to one of sadness. Then he knelt beside the young man and, tearing open his blouse, put his hand to his heart.

"Thank God!" he cried. "It is yet beating! Send for the surgeon!"

At the captain's words Françoise leaped to her feet.

"There is hope!" she cried. "Oh, tell me there is hope!"

At that moment the surgeon appeared. He made a hasty examination and said:

"The young man is severely hurt, but life is not extinct; he can be saved!"

By the surgeon's orders Dominique was transported to a neighboring cottage, where he was placed in bed. His wounds were dressed; restoratives were administered, and he soon recovered consciousness. When he opened his eyes he saw Françoise sitting beside him and through the open window caught sight of Père Merlier talking with the French captain. He passed his hand over his forehead with a bewildered air and said:

"They did not kill me after all!"

"No," replied Françoise. "The French came, and their surgeon saved you."

Père Merlier turned and said through the window:

"No talking yet, my young ones!"

In due time Dominique was entirely restored, and when peace again blessed the land he wedded his beloved Françoise.

The mill was rebuilt, and Père Merlier had a new wheel upon which to bestow whatever tenderness was not engrossed by his daughter and her husband.

CAPTAIN BURLE

CHAPTER I

The Swindle

IT WAS NINE O'CLOCK. The little town of Vauchamp, dark and silent, had just retired to bed amid a chilly November rain. In the Rue des Recollets, one of the narrowest and most deserted streets of the district of Saint-Jean, a single window was still alight on the third floor of an old house, from whose damaged gutters torrents of water were falling into the street. Mme Burle was sitting up before a meager fire of vine stocks, while her little grandson Charles pored over his lessons by the pale light of a lamp.

The apartment, rented at one hundred and sixty francs per annum, consisted of four large rooms which it was absolutely impossible to keep warm during the winter. Mme Burle slept in the largest chamber, her son Captain and Quartermaster Burle occupying a somewhat smaller one overlooking the street, while little Charles had his iron cot at the farther end of a spacious drawing room with mildewed hangings, which was never used. The few pieces of furniture belonging to the captain and his mother, furniture of the massive style of the First Empire, dented and worn by continuous transit from one garrison town to another, almost disappeared from view beneath the lofty ceilings whence darkness fell. The flooring of red-colored tiles was cold and hard to the feet; before the chairs there were merely a few threadbare little rugs of poverty-stricken aspect, and athwart this desert all the winds of heaven blew through the disjointed doors and windows.

Near the fireplace sat Mme Burle, leaning back in her old yellow velvet armchair and watching the last vine branch smoke, with that stolid, blank stare of the aged who live within themselves. She would sit thus for whole days together, with her tall figure, her long stern face and her thin lips that never smiled. The widow of a colonel who had died just as he was on the point of becoming a general, the mother of a captain whom she had followed even in his campaigns, she had acquired a military stiffness of bearing and formed for herself a code of honor, duty and patriotism which kept her rigid, desiccated, as it were, by the stern application of discipline. She seldom, if ever, complained. When her son had become a widower after five years of married life she had undertaken the education of little Charles as a matter of course, performing her duties with the severity of a sergeant drilling recruits. She watched over the child, never tolerating the slightest waywardness or irregularity, but compelling him to sit up till midnight when his exercises were not finished, and sitting up herself until he had completed them. Under such implacable despotism Charles, whose constitution was delicate, grew up pale and thin, with beautiful eyes, inordinately large and clear, shining in his white, pinched face.

During the long hours of silence Mme Burle dwelt continuously upon one and the same idea: she had been disappointed in her son. This thought sufficed to occupy her mind, and under its influence she would live her whole life over again, from the birth of her son, whom she had pictured rising amid glory to the highest rank, till she came down to mean and narrow garrison life, the dull, monotonous existence of nowadays, that stranding in the post of a quartermaster, from which Burle would never rise and in which he seemed to sink more and more heavily. And yet his first efforts had filled her with pride, and she had hoped to see her dreams realized. Burle had only just left Saint-Cyr when he distinguished himself at the battle of Solferino, where he had captured a whole battery of the enemy's artillery with merely a handful of men. For this feat he had won the cross; the papers had recorded his heroism, and he had become known as one of the bravest soldiers in the army. But gradually the hero had grown stout, embedded in flesh, timorous, lazy and satisfied. In 1870, still a captain, he had been made a prisoner in the first encounter, and he returned from Germany quite furious, swearing that he would never be caught fighting again, for it was too absurd. Being prevented from leaving the army, as he was incapable of embracing any other profession, he applied for and obtained the position of captain quartermaster, "a kennel," as he called it, "in which he would be left to kick the bucket in peace." That day Mme Burle experienced a great internal disruption. She felt that it was all over, and she ever afterward preserved a rigid attitude with tightened lips.

A blast of wind shook the Rue des Recollets and drove the rain angrily against the windowpanes. The old lady lifted her eyes from the smoking vine roots now dying out, to make sure that Charles was not falling asleep over his Latin exercise. This lad, twelve years of age, had become the old lady's supreme hope, the one human being in whom she centered her obstinate yearning for glory. At first she had hated him with all the loathing she had felt for his mother, a weak and pretty young lacemaker whom the captain had been foolish enough to marry when he found out that she would not listen to his passionate addresses on any other condition. Later on, when the mother had died and the father had begun to wallow in vice, Mme Burle dreamed again in presence of that little ailing child whom she found it so hard to rear. She wanted to see him robust, so that he might grow into the hero that Burle had declined to be, and for all her cold ruggedness she watched him anxiously, feeling his limbs and instilling courage into his soul. By degrees, blinded by her passionate desires, she imagined that she had at last found the man of the family. The boy, whose temperament was of a gentle, dreamy character, had a physical horror of soldiering, but as he lived in mortal dread of his grandmother and was extremely shy and submissive, he would echo all she said and resignedly express his intention of entering the army when he grew up.

Mme Burle observed that the exercise was not progressing. In fact, little Charles, overcome by the deafening noise of the storm, was dozing, albeit his pen was between his fingers and his eyes were staring at the paper. The old lady at once struck the edge of the table with her bony hand; whereupon the lad started, opened his dictionary and hurriedly began to turn over the leaves.

Then, still preserving silence, his grandmother drew the vine roots together on the hearth and unsuccessfully attempted to rekindle the fire.

At the time when she had still believed in her son she had sacrificed her small income, which he had squandered in pursuits she dared not investigate. Even now he drained the household; all its resources went to the streets, and it was through him that she lived in penury, with empty rooms and cold kitchen. She never spoke to him of all those things, for with her sense of discipline he remained the master. Only at times she shuddered at the sudden fear that Burle might someday commit some foolish misdeed which would prevent Charles from entering the army.

She was rising up to fetch a fresh piece of wood in the kitchen when a fearful hurricane fell upon the house, making the doors rattle, tearing off a shutter, and whirling the water in the broken gutters like a spout against the window. In the midst of the uproar a ring at the bell startled the old lady. Who could it be at such an hour and in such weather? Burle never returned till after midnight, if he came home at all. However, she went to the door. An officer stood before her, dripping with rain and swearing savagely.

"Hell and thunder!" he growled. "What cursed weather!"

It was Major Laguitte, a brave old soldier who had served under Colonel Burle during Mme Burle's palmy days. He had started in life as a drummer boy and, thanks to his courage rather than his intellect, had attained to the command of a battalion, when a painful infirmity—the contraction of the muscles of one of his thighs, due to a wound—obliged him to accept the post of major. He was slightly lame, but it would have been imprudent to tell him so, as he refused to own it.

"What, you, Major?" said Mme Burle with growing astonishment.

"Yes, thunder," grumbled Laguitte, "and I must be confoundedly fond of you to roam the streets on such a night as this. One would think twice before sending even a parson out."

He shook himself, and little rivulets fell from his huge boots onto the floor. Then he looked round him.

"I particularly want to see Burle. Is the lazy beggar already in bed?"

"No, he is not in yet," said the old woman in her harsh voice.

The major looked furious, and, raising his voice, he shouted: "What, not at home? But in that case they hoaxed me at the café, Mélanie's establishment, you know. I went there, and a maid grinned at me, saying that the captain had gone home to bed. Curse the girl! I suspected as much and felt like pulling her ears!"

After this outburst he became somewhat calmer, stamping about the room in an undecided way, withal seeming greatly disturbed. Mme Burle looked at him attentively.

"Is it the captain personally whom you want to see?" she said at last.

"Yes," he answered.

"Can I not tell him what you have to say?"

"No."

She did not insist but remained standing without taking her eyes off the major, who did not seem able to make up his mind to leave. Finally in a fresh burst of rage he exclaimed with an oath: "It can't be helped. As I am here you may as well know—after all, it is, perhaps, best."

He sat down before the chimney piece, stretching out his muddy boots as if a bright fire had been burning. Mme Burle was about to resume her own seat when she remarked that Charles, overcome by fatigue, had dropped his head between the open pages of his dictionary. The arrival of the major had at first interested him, but, seeing that he remained unnoticed, he had been unable to struggle against his sleepiness. His grandmother turned toward the table to slap his frail little hands, whitening in the lamplight, when Laguitte stopped her.

"No—no!" he said. "Let the poor little man sleep. I haven't got anything funny to say. There's no need for him to hear me."

The old lady sat down in her armchair; deep silence reigned, and they looked at one another.

"Well, yes," said the major at last, punctuating his words with an angry motion of his chin, "he has been and done it; that hound Burle has been and done it!"

Not a muscle of Mme Burle's face moved, but she became livid, and her figure stiffened. Then the major continued: "I had my doubts. I had intended mentioning the subject to you. Burle was spending too much money, and he had an idiotic look which I did not fancy. Thunder and lightning! What a fool a man must be to behave so filthily!"

Then he thumped his knee furiously with his clenched fist and seemed to choke with indignation. The old woman put the straightforward question:

"He has stolen?"

"You can't have an idea of it. You see, I never examined his accounts; I approved and signed them. You know how those things are managed. However, just before the inspection—as the colonel is a crotchety old maniac—I said to Burle: 'I say, old man, look to your accounts; I am answerable, you know,' and then I felt perfectly secure. Well, about a month ago, as he seemed queer and some nasty stories were circulating, I peered a little closer into the books and pottered over the entries. I thought everything looked straight and very well kept——"

At this point he stopped, convulsed by such a fit of rage that he had to relieve himself by a volley of appalling oaths. Finally he resumed: "It isn't the swindle that angers me; it is his disgusting behavior to me. He has gammoned me, Madame Burle. By God! Does he take me for an old fool?"

"So he stole?" the mother again questioned.

"This evening," continued the major more quietly, "I had just finished my dinner when Gagneux came in—you know Gagneux, the butcher at the corner of the Place aux Herbes? Another dirty beast who got the meat contract and makes our men eat all the diseased cow flesh in the neighborhood! Well, I received him like a dog, and then he let it all out—blurted out the whole thing, and a pretty mess it is! It appears that Burle only paid him in driblets and had got himself into a muddle—a confusion of figures which the devil himself couldn't disentangle. In short, Burle owes the butcher two thousand francs, and Gagneux threatens that he'll inform the colonel if he is not paid. To make matters worse, Burle, just to blind me, handed me every week a forged receipt which he had squarely signed with Gagneux's name. To think he did that to me, his old friend! Ah, curse him!"

With increasing profanity the major rose to his feet, shook his fist at the ceiling and then fell back in his chair. Mme Burle again repeated: "He has stolen. It was inevitable."

Then without a word of judgment or condemnation she added simply: "Two thousand francs—we have not got them. There are barely thirty francs in the house."

"I expected as much," said Laguitte. "And do you know where all the money goes? Why, Mélanie gets it—yes, Mélanie, a creature who has turned Burle into a perfect fool. Ah, those women! Those fiendish women! I always said they would do for him! I cannot conceive what he is made of! He is only five years younger than I am, and yet he is as mad as ever. What a woman hunter he is!"

Another long silence followed. Outside the rain was increasing in violence, and throughout the sleepy little town one could hear the crashing of slates and chimney pots as they were dashed by the blast onto the pavements of the streets.

"Come," suddenly said the major, rising, "my stopping here won't mend matters. I have warned you—and now I'm off."

"What is to be done? To whom can we apply?" muttered the old woman drearily.

"Don't give way—we must consider. If I only had the two thousand francs —but you know that I am not rich."

The major stopped short in confusion. This old bachelor, wifeless and child-less, spent his pay in drink and gambled away at écarté whatever money his cognac and absinthe left in his pocket. Despite that, however, he was scrupulously honest from a sense of discipline.

"Never mind," he added as he reached the threshold. "I'll begin by stirring him up. I shall move heaven and earth! What! Burle, Colonel Burle's son, condemned for theft! That cannot be! I would sooner burn down the town. Now, thunder and lightning, don't worry; it is far more annoying for me than for you."

He shook the old lady's hand roughly and vanished into the shadows of the staircase, while she held the lamp aloft to light the way. When she returned and replaced the lamp on the table she stood for a moment motionless in front of Charles, who was still asleep with his face lying on the dictionary. His pale cheeks and long fair hair made him look like a girl, and she gazed at him dreamily, a shade of tenderness passing over her harsh countenance. But it was only a passing emotion; her features regained their look of cold, obstinate determination, and, giving the youngster a sharp rap on his little hand, she said:

"Charles—your lessons."

The boy awoke, dazed and shivering, and again rapidly turned over the leaves. At the same moment Major Laguitte, slamming the house door behind him, received on his head a quantity of water falling from the gutters above, whereupon he began to swear in so loud a voice that he could be heard above the storm. And after that no sound broke upon the pelting downpour save the slight rustle of the boy's pen traveling over the paper. Mme Burle had resumed her seat near the chimney piece, still rigid, with her eyes fixed on the dead embers, preserving, indeed, her habitual attitude and absorbed in her one idea.

CHAPTER II

The Café

The café de paris, kept by Mélanie Cartier, a widow, was situated on the Place du Palais, a large irregular square planted with meager, dusty elm trees. The place was so well known in Vauchamp that it was customary to say, "Are you coming to Mélanie's?" At the farther end of the first room, which was a spacious one, there was another called "the divan," a narrow apartment having sham leather benches placed against the walls, while at each corner there stood a marble-topped table. The widow, deserting her seat in the front room, where she left her little servant Phrosine, spent her evenings in the inner apartment, ministering to a few customers, the usual frequenters of the place, those who were currently styled "the gentlemen of the divan." When a man belonged to that set it was as if he had a label on his back; he was spoken of with smiles of mingled contempt and envy.

Mme Cartier had become a widow when she was five and twenty. Her husband, a wheelwright, who on the death of an uncle had amazed Vauchamp by taking the Café de Paris, had one fine day brought her back with him from Montpellier, where he was wont to repair twice a year to purchase liqueurs. As he was stocking his establishment he selected, together with divers beverages, a woman of the sort he wanted—of an engaging aspect and apt to stimulate the trade of the house. It was never known where he had picked her up, but he married her after trying her in the café during six months or so. Opinions were divided in Vauchamp as to her merits, some folks declaring that she was superb, while others asserted that she looked like a drum-major. She was a tall woman with large features and coarse hair falling low over her forehead. However, everyone agreed that she knew very well how to fool the sterner sex. She had fine eyes and was wont to fix them with a bold stare on the gentlemen of the divan, who colored and became like wax in her hands. She also had the reputation of possessing a wonderfully fine figure, and southerners appreciate a statuesque style of beauty.

Cartier had died in a singular way. Rumor hinted at a conjugal quarrel, a kick, producing some internal tumor. Whatever may have been the truth, Mélanie found herself encumbered with the café, which was far from doing a prosperous business. Her husband had wasted his uncle's inheritance in drinking his own absinthe and wearing out the cloth of his own billiard table. For a while it was believed that the widow would have to sell out, but she liked the life and the establishment just as it was. If she could secure a few customers the bigger room might remain deserted. So she limited herself to re-papering the divan in white and gold and recovering the benches. She began by entertaining a chemist. Then a vermicelli maker, a lawyer and a retired magistrate put in an appearance; and thus it was that the café remained open, although the waiter did not receive twenty orders a day. No objections were raised by the authorities, as appearances were kept up; and, indeed, it was not deemed advisable to interfere, for some respectable folks might have been worried.

Of an evening five or six well-to-do citizens would enter the front room and play at dominoes there. Although Cartier was dead and the Café de Paris had got a queer name, they saw nothing and kept up their old habits. In course of time, the waiter having nothing to do, Mélanie dismissed him and made Phrosine light the solitary gas burner in the corner where the domino players congregated. Occasionally a party of young men, attracted by the gossip that circulated through the town, would come in, wildly excited and laughing loudly and awkwardly. But they were received there with icy dignity. As a rule they did not even see the widow, and even if she happened to be present she treated them with withering disdain, so that they withdrew, stammering and confused. Mélanie was too astute to indulge in any compromising whims. While the front room remained obscure, save in the corner where the few townsfolk rattled their dominoes, she personally waited on the gentlemen of the divan, showing herself amiable without being free, merely venturing in moments of familiarity to lean on the shoulder of one or another of them, the better to watch a skillfully played game of écarté.

One evening the gentlemen of the divan, who had ended by tolerating each other's presence, experienced a disagreeable surprise on finding Captain Burle at home there. He had casually entered the café that same morning to get a glass of vermouth, so it seemed, and he had found Mélanie there. They had conversed, and in the evening when he returned Phrosine immediately showed him to the inner room.

Two days later Burle reigned there supreme; still he had not frightened the chemist, the vermicelli maker, the lawyer or the retired magistrate away. The captain, who was short and dumpy, worshiped tall, plump women. In his regiment he had been nicknamed "Petticoat Burle" on account of his constant philandering. Whenever the officers, and even the privates, met some monstrous-looking creature, some giantess puffed out with fat, whether she were in velvet or in rags, they would invariably exclaim, "There goes one to Petticoat Burle's taste!" Thus Mélanie, with her opulent presence, quite conquered him. He was lost—quite wrecked. In less than a fortnight he had fallen to vacuous imbecility. With much the expression of a whipped hound in the tiny sunken eyes which lighted up his bloated face, he was incessantly watching the widow in mute adoration before her masculine features and stubby hair. For fear that he might be dismissed, he put up with the presence of the other gentlemen of the divan and spent his pay in the place down to the last copper. A sergeant reviewed the situation in one sentence: "Petticoat Burle is done for; he's a buried man!"

It was nearly ten o'clock when Major Laguitte furiously flung the door of the café open. For a moment those inside could see the deluged square transformed into a dark sea of liquid mud, bubbling under the terrible downpour. The major, now soaked to the skin and leaving a stream behind him, strode up to the small counter where Phrosine was reading a novel.

"You little wretch," he yelled, "you have dared to gammon an officer; you deserve——"

And then he lifted his hand as if to deal a blow such as would have felled an ox. The little maid shrank back, terrified, while the amazed domino players looked, openmouthed. However, the major did not linger there—he pushed the divan door open and appeared before Mélanie and Burle just as the widow was playfully making the captain sip his grog in small spoonfuls, as if she were feeding a pet canary. Only the ex-magistrate and the chemist had come that evening, and they had retired early in a melancholy frame of mind. Then Mélanie, being in want of three hundred francs for the morrow, had taken advantage of the opportunity to cajole the captain.

"Come." she said, "open your mouth; ain't it nice, you greedy piggy-wiggy?"

Burle, flushing scarlet, with glazed eyes and sunken figure, was sucking the spoon with an air of intense enjoyment.

"Good heavens!" roared the major from the threshold. "You now play tricks on me, do you? I'm sent to the roundabout and told that you never came here, and yet all the while here you are, addling your silly brains."

Burle shuddered, pushing the grog away, while Mélanie stepped angrily in front of him as if to shield him with her portly figure, but Laguitte looked at her with that quiet, resolute expression well known to women who are familiar with bodily chastisement.

"Leave us," he said curtly.

She hesitated for the space of a second. She almost felt the gust of the expected blow, and then, white with rage, she joined Phrosine in the outer room.

When the two men were alone Major Laguitte walked up to Burle, looked at him and, slightly stooping, yelled into his face these two words: "You pig!"

The captain, quite dazed, endeavored to retort, but he had not time to do so.

"Silence!" resumed the major. "You have bamboozled a friend. You palmed off on me a lot of forged receipts which might have sent both of us to the gallows. Do you call that proper behavior? Is that the sort of trick to play a friend of thirty years' standing?"

Burle, who had fallen back in his chair, was livid; his limbs shook as if with ague. Meanwhile the major, striding up and down and striking the tables wildly with his fists, continued: "So you have become a thief like the veriest scribbling cur of a clerk, and all for the sake of that creature here! If at least you had stolen for your mother's sake it would have been honorable! But, curse it, to play tricks and bring the money into this shanty is what I cannot understand! Tell me—what are you made of at your age to go to the dogs as you are going all for the sake of a creature like a grenadier!"

"*You* gamble——" stammered the captain.

"Yes, I do—curse it!" thundered the major, lashed into still greater fury by this remark. "And I am a pitiful rogue to do so, because it swallows up all my pay and doesn't redound to the honor of the French army. However, I don't steal. Kill yourself, if it pleases you; starve your mother and the boy, but respect the regimental cashbox and don't drag your friends down with you."

He stopped. Burle was sitting there with fixed eyes and a stupid air. Nothing was heard for a moment save the clatter of the major's heels.

"And not a single copper," he continued aggressively. "Can you picture yourself between two gendarmes, eh?"

He then grew a little calmer, caught hold of Burle's wrists and forced him to rise.

"Come!" he said gruffly. "Something must be done at once, for I cannot go to bed with this affair on my mind—I have an idea."

In the front room Mélanie and Phrosine were talking eagerly in low voices. When the widow saw the two men leaving the divan she moved toward Burle and said coaxingly: "What, are you going already, Captain?"

"Yes, he's going," brutally answered Laguitte, "and I don't intend to let him set foot here again."

The little maid felt frightened and pulled her mistress back by the skirt of her dress; in doing so she imprudently murmured the word "drunkard" and thereby brought down the slap which the major's hand had been itching to deal for some time past. Both women having stooped, however, the blow only fell on Phrosine's back hair, flattening her cap and breaking her comb. The domino players were indignant.

"Let's cut it," shouted Laguitte, and he pushed Burle on the pavement. "If I remained I should smash everyone in the place."

To cross the square they had to wade up to their ankles in mud. The rain, driven by the wind, poured off their faces. The captain walked on in silence, while the major kept on reproaching him with his cowardice and its disastrous consequences. Wasn't it sweet weather for tramping the streets? If he hadn't been such an idiot they would both be warmly tucked in bed instead of paddling about in the mud. Then he spoke of Gagneux—a scoundrel whose diseased meat had on three separate occasions made the whole regiment ill. In a week, however, the contract would come to an end, and the fiend himself would not get it renewed.

"It rests with me," the major grumbled. "I can select whomsoever I choose, and I'd rather cut off my right arm than put that poisoner in the way of earning another copper."

Just then he slipped into a gutter and, half choked by a string of oaths, he gasped:

"You understand—I am going to rout up Gagneux. You must stop outside while I go in. I must know what the rascal is up to and if he'll dare to carry out his threat of informing the colonel tomorrow. A butcher—curse him! The idea of compromising oneself with a butcher! Ah, you aren't over-proud, and I shall never forgive you for all this."

They had now reached the Place aux Herbes. Gagneux's house was quite dark, but Laguitte knocked so loudly that he was eventually admitted. Burle remained alone in the dense obscurity and did not even attempt to seek any shelter. He stood at a corner of the market under the pelting rain, his head filled with a loud buzzing noise which prevented him from thinking. He did not feel impatient, for he was unconscious of the flight of time. He stood there looking at the house, which, with its closed door and windows, seemed quite lifeless. When at the end of an hour the major came out again it appeared to the captain as if he had only just gone in.

Laguitte was so grimly mute that Burle did not venture to question him. For a moment they sought each other, groping about in the dark; then they resumed their walk through the somber streets, where the water rolled as in the bed of a torrent. They moved on in silence side by side, the major being so abstracted that he even forgot to swear. However, as they again crossed the Place du Palais, at the sight of the Café de Paris, which was still lit up, he dropped his hand on Burle's shoulder and said, "If you ever re-enter that hole I——"

"No fear!" answered the captain without letting his friend finish his sentence.

Then he stretched out his hand.

"No, no," said Laguitte, "I'll see you home; I'll at least make sure that you'll sleep in your bed tonight."

They went on, and as they ascended the Rue des Recollets they slackened their pace. When the captain's door was reached and Burle had taken out his latchkey he ventured to ask:

"Well?"

"Well," answered the major gruffly, "I am as dirty a rogue as you are. Yes! I have done a scurrilous thing. The fiend take you! Our soldiers will eat carrion for three months longer."

Then he explained that Gagneux, the disgusting Gagneux, had a horribly level head and that he had persuaded him—the major—to strike a bargain. He would refrain from informing the colonel, and he would even make a present of the two thousand francs and replace the forged receipts by genuine ones, on condition that the major bound himself to renew the meat contract. It was a settled thing.

"Ah," continued Laguitte, "calculate what profits the brute must make out of the meat to part with such a sum as two thousand francs."

Burle, choking with emotion, grasped his old friend's hands, stammering confused words of thanks. The vileness of the action committed for his sake brought tears into his eyes.

"I never did such a thing before," growled Laguitte, "but I was driven to it. Curse it, to think that I haven't those two thousand francs in my drawer!

It is enough to make one hate cards. It is my own fault. I am not worth much; only, mark my words, don't begin again, for, curse it—*I* shan't."

The captain embraced him, and when he had entered the house the major stood a moment before the closed door to make certain that he had gone upstairs to bed. Then as midnight was striking and the rain was still belaboring the dark town, he slowly turned homeward. The thought of his men almost broke his heart, and, stopping short, he said aloud in a voice full of compassion:

"Poor devils! what a lot of cow beef they'll have to swallow for those two thousand francs!"

CHAPTER III

Again?

THE REGIMENT was altogether nonplused: Petticoat Burle had quarreled with Mélanie. When a week had elapsed it became a proved and undeniable fact; the captain no longer set foot inside the Café de Paris, where the chemist, it was averred, once more reigned in his stead, to the profound sorrow of the retired magistrate. An even more incredible statement was that Captain Burle led the life of a recluse in the Rue des Recollets. He was becoming a reformed character; he spent his evenings at his own fireside, hearing little Charles repeat his lessons. His mother, who had never breathed a word to him of his manipulations with Gagneux, maintained her old severity of demeanor as she sat opposite to him in her armchair, but her looks seemed to imply that she believed him reclaimed.

A fortnight later Major Laguitte came one evening to invite himself to dinner. He felt some awkwardness at the prospect of meeting Burle again, not on his own account but because he dreaded awakening painful memories. However, as the captain was mending his ways he wished to shake hands and break a crust with him. He thought this would please his old friend.

When Laguitte arrived Burle was in his room, so it was the old lady who received the major. The latter, after announcing that he had come to have a plate of soup with them, added, lowering his voice:

"Well, how goes it?"

"It is all right," answered the old lady.

"Nothing queer?"

"Absolutely nothing. Never away—in bed at nine—and looking quite happy."

"Ah, confound it," replied the major, "I knew very well he only wanted a shaking. He has some heart left, the dog!"

When Burle appeared he almost crushed the major's hands in his grasp, and standing before the fire, waiting for the dinner, they conversed peacefully, honestly, together, extolling the charms of home life. The captain vowed he wouldn't exchange his home for a kingdom and declared that when he had removed his braces, put on his slippers and settled himself in his armchair, no king was fit to hold a candle to him. The major assented and examined him. At all events his virtuous conduct had not made him any thinner; he still looked bloated; his eyes were bleared, and his mouth was heavy. He seemed to be half asleep as he repeated mechanically: "Home life! There's nothing like home life, nothing in the world!"

"No doubt," said the major; "still, one mustn't exaggerate—take a little exercise and come to the café now and then."

"To the café, why?" asked Burle. "Do I lack anything here? No, no, I remain at home."

When Charles had laid his books aside Laguitte was surprised to see a maid come in to lay the cloth.

"So you keep a servant now," he remarked to Mme Burle.

"I had to get one," she answered with a sigh. "My legs are not what they used to be, and the household was going to rack and ruin. Fortunately Cabrol let me have his daughter. You know old Cabrol, who sweeps the market? He did not know what to do with Rose—I am teaching her how to work."

Just then the girl left the room.

"How old is she?" asked the major.

"Barely seventeen. She is stupid and dirty, but I only give her ten francs a month, and she eats nothing but soup."

When Rose returned with an armful of plates Laguitte, though he did not care about women, began to scrutinize her and was amazed at seeing so ugly a creature. She was very short, very dark and slightly deformed, with a face like an ape's: a flat nose, a huge mouth and narrow greenish eyes. Her broad back and long arms gave her an appearance of great strength.

"What a snout!" said Laguitte, laughing, when the maid had again left the room to fetch the cruets.

"Never mind," said Burle carelessly, "she is very obliging and does all one asks her. She suits us well enough as a scullion."

The dinner was very pleasant. It consisted of boiled beef and mutton hash. Charles was encouraged to relate some stories of his school, and Mme Burle repeatedly asked him the same question: "Don't you want to be a soldier?" A faint smile hovered over the child's wan lips as he answered with the frightened obedience of a trained dog, "Oh yes, Grandmother." Captain Burle, with his elbows on the table, was masticating slowly with an absent-minded expression. The big room was getting warmer; the single lamp placed on the table left the corners in vague gloom. There was a certain amount of heavy comfort, the familiar intimacy of penurious people who do not change their plates at every course but become joyously excited at the unexpected appearance of a bowl of whipped egg cream at the close of the meal.

Rose, whose heavy tread shook the floor as she paced round the table, had not yet opened her mouth. At last she stopped behind the captain's chair and asked in a gruff voice: "Cheese, sir?"

Burle started. "What, eh? Oh yes—cheese. Hold the plate tight."

He cut a piece of Gruyère, the girl watching him the while with her narrow eyes. Laguitte laughed; Rose's unparalleled ugliness amused him immensely. He whispered in the captain's ear, "She is ripping! There never was such a nose and such a mouth! You ought to send her to the colonel's someday as a curiosity. It would amuse him to see her."

More and more struck by this phenomenal ugliness, the major felt a paternal desire to examine the girl more closely.

"Come here," he said, "I want some cheese too."

She brought the plate, and Laguitte, sticking the knife in the Gruyère, stared at her, grinning the while because he discovered that she had one nostril broader than the other. Rose gravely allowed herself to be looked at, waiting till the gentleman had done laughing.

She removed the cloth and disappeared. Burle immediately went to sleep in the chimney corner while the major and Mme Burle began to chat. Charles had returned to his exercises. Quietude fell from the loft ceiling; the quietude of a middle-class household gathered in concord around their fireside. At nine o'clock Burle woke up, yawned and announced that he was going off to bed; he apologized but declared that he could not keep his eyes open. Half an hour later, when the major took his leave, Mme Burle vainly called for Rose to light him downstairs; the girl must have gone up to her room; she was, indeed, a regular hen, snoring the round of the clock without waking.

"No need to disturb anybody," said Laguitte on the landing; "my legs are not much better than yours, but if I get hold of the banisters I shan't break any bones. Now, my dear lady, I leave you happy; your troubles are ended at last. I watched Burle closely, and I'll take my oath that he's guileless as a child. Dash it—after all, it was high time for Petticoat Burle to reform; he was going downhill fast."

The major went away fully satisfied with the house and its inmates; the walls were of glass and could harbor no equivocal conduct. What particularly delighted him in his friend's return to virtue was that it absolved him from the obligation of verifying the accounts. Nothing was more distasteful to him than the inspection of a number of ledgers, and as long as Burle kept steady, he—Laguitte—could smoke his pipe in peace and sign the books in all confidence. However, he continued to keep one eye open for a little while longer and found the receipts genuine, the entries correct, the columns admirably balanced. A month later he contented himself with glancing at the receipts and running his eye over the totals. Then one morning, without the slightest suspicion of there being anything wrong, simply because he had lit a second pipe and had nothing to do, he carelessly added up a row of figures and fancied that he detected an error of thirteen francs. The balance seemed perfectly correct, and yet he was not mistaken; the total outlay was thirteen francs more than the various sums for which receipts were furnished. It looked queer, but he said nothing to Burle, just making up his mind to examine the next accounts closely. On the following week he detected a fresh error of nineteen francs, and then, suddenly becoming alarmed, he shut himself up with the books and spent a wretched morning poring over them, perspiring, swearing and feeling as if his very skull were bursting with the figures. At every page he discovered thefts of a few francs—the most miserable petty thefts—ten, eight, eleven francs, latterly, three and four; and, indeed, there was one column showing that Burle had pilfered just one franc and a half. For two months, however, he had been steadily robbing the cashbox, and by comparing dates the major found to his disgust that the famous lesson respecting Gagneux had only kept him straight for one week! This last discovery infuriated Laguitte, who struck the books with his clenched fists, yelling through a shower of oaths:

"This is more abominable still! At least there was some pluck about those forged receipts of Gagneux. But this time he is as contemptible as a cook charging twopence extra for her cabbages. Powers of hell! To pilfer a franc and a half and clap it in his pocket! Hasn't the brute got any pride then? Couldn't he run away with the safe or play the fool with actresses?"

The pitiful meanness of these pilferings revolted the major, and, moreover, he was enraged at having been duped a second time, deceived by the simple, stupid dodge of falsified additions. He rose at last and paced his office for a whole hour, growling aloud.

"This gives me his measure. Even if I were to thresh him to a jelly every morning he would still drop a couple of coins into his pocket every afternoon. But where can he spend it all? He is never seen abroad; he goes to bed at nine, and everything looks so clean and proper over there. Can the brute have vices that nobody knows of?"

He returned to the desk, added up the subtracted money and found a total of five hundred and forty-five francs. Where was this deficiency to come from? The inspection was close at hand, and if the crotchety colonel should take it into his head to examine a single page, the murder would be out and Burle would be done for.

This idea froze the major, who left off cursing, picturing Mme Burle erect and despairing, and at the same time he felt his heart swell with personal grief and shame.

"Well," he muttered, "I must first of all look into the rogue's business; I will act afterward."

As he walked over to Burle's office he caught sight of a skirt vanishing through the doorway. Fancying that he had a clue to the mystery, he slipped up quietly and listened and speedily recognized Mélanie's shrill voice. She was complaining of the gentlemen of the divan. She had signed a promissory note which she was unable to meet; the bailiffs were in the house, and all her goods would be sold. The captain, however, barely replied to her. He alleged that he had no money, whereupon she burst into tears and began to coax him. But her blandishments were apparently ineffectual, for Burle's husky voice could be heard repeating, "Impossible! Impossible!" And finally the widow withdrew in a towering passion. The major, amazed at the turn affairs were taking, waited a few moments longer before entering the office, where Burle had remained alone. He found him very calm, and despite his furious inclination to call him names he also remained calm, determined to begin by finding out the exact truth.

The office certainly did not look like a swindler's den. A cane-seated chair, covered with an honest leather cushion, stood before the captain's desk, and in a corner there was the locked safe. Summer was coming on, and the song of a canary sounded through the open window. The apartment was very neat and tidy, redolent of old papers, and altogether its appearance inspired one with confidence.

"Wasn't it Mélanie who was leaving here as I came along?" asked Laguitte. Burle shrugged his shoulders.

"Yes," he mumbled. "She has been dunning me for two hundred francs, but she can't screw ten out of me—not even tenpence."

"Indeed!" said the major, just to try him. "I heard that you had made up with her."

"I? Certainly not. I have done with the likes of her for good."

Laguitte went away, feeling greatly perplexed. Where had the five hundred and forty-five francs gone? Had the idiot taken to drinking or gambling? He decided to pay Burle a surprise visit that very evening at his own house, and maybe by questioning his mother he might learn something. However, during the afternoon his leg became very painful; latterly he had been feeling in ill-health, and he had to use a stick so as not to limp too outrageously. This stick grieved him sorely, and he declared with angry despair that he was now no better than a pensioner. However, toward the evening, making a strong effort, he pulled himself out of his armchair and, leaning heavily on his stick, dragged himself through the darkness to the Rue des Recollets, which he reached about nine o'clock. The street door was still unlocked, and on going up he stood panting on the third landing, when he heard voices on the upper floor. One of these voices was Burle's, so he fancied, and out of curiosity he ascended another flight of stairs. Then at the end of a passage on the left he saw a ray of light coming from a door which stood ajar. As the creaking of his boots resounded, this door was sharply closed, and he found himself in the dark.

"Some cook going to bed!" he muttered angrily. "I'm a fool."

All the same he groped his way as gently as possible to the door and listened. Two people were talking in the room, and he stood aghast, for it was Burle and that fright Rose! Then he listened, and the conversation he heard left him no doubt of the awful truth. For a moment he lifted his stick as if to beat down the door. Then he shuddered and, staggering back, leaned against the wall. His legs were trembling under him, while in the darkness of the staircase he brandished his stick as if it had been a saber.

What was to be done? After his first moment of passion there had come thoughts of the poor old lady below. And these made him hesitate. It was all over with the captain now; when a man sank as low as that he was hardly worth the few shovelfuls of earth that are thrown over carrion to prevent them from polluting the atmosphere. Whatever might be said of Burle, however much one might try to shame him, he would assuredly begin the next day. Ah, heavens, to think of it! The money! The honor of the army! The name of Burle, that respected name, dragged through the mire! By all that was holy this could and should not be!

Presently the major softened. If he had only possessed five hundred and forty-five francs! But he had not got such an amount. On the previous day he had drunk too much cognac, just like a mere sub, and had lost shockingly at cards. It served him right—he ought to have known better! And if he was so lame he richly deserved it too; by rights, in fact, his leg ought to be much worse.

At last he crept downstairs and rang at the bell of Mme Burle's flat. Five minutes elapsed, and then the old lady appeared.

"I beg your pardon for keeping you waiting," she said; "I thought that dormouse Rose was still about. I must go and shake her."

But the major detained her.

"Where is Burle?" he asked.

"Oh, he has been snoring since nine o'clock. Would you like to knock at his door?"

"No, no, I only wanted to have a chat with you."

In the parlor Charles sat at his usual place, having just finished his exercises. He looked terrified, and his poor little white hands were tremulous. In point of fact, his grandmother, before sending him to bed, was wont to read some martial stories aloud so as to develop the latent family heroism in his bosom. That night she had selected the episode of the Vengeur, the man-of-war freighted with dying heroes and sinking into the sea. The child, while listening, had become almost hysterical, and his head was racked as with some ghastly nightmare.

Mme Burle asked the major to let her finish the perusal. "Long live the republic!" She solemnly closed the volume. Charles was as white as a sheet.

"You see," said the old lady, "the duty of every French soldier is to die for his country."

"Yes, Grandmother."

Then the lad kissed her on the forehead and, shivering with fear, went to bed in his big room, where the faintest creak of the paneling threw him into a cold sweat.

The major had listened with a grave face. Yes, by heavens! Honor was honor, and he would never permit that wretched Burle to disgrace the old woman and the boy! As the lad was so devoted to the military profession, it was necessary that he should be able to enter Saint-Cyr with his head erect.

When Mme Burle took up the lamp to show the major out, she passed the door of the captain's room, and stopped short, surprised to see the key outside, which was a most unusual occurrence.

"Do go in," she said to Laguitte; "it is bad for him to sleep so much."

And before he could interpose she had opened the door and stood transfixed on finding the room empty. Laguitte turned crimson and looked so foolish that she suddenly understood everything, enlightened by the sudden recollection of several little incidents to which she had previously attached no importance.

"You knew it—you knew it!" she stammered. "Why was I not told? Oh, my God, to think of it! Ah, he has been stealing again—I feel it!"

She remained erect, white and rigid. Then she added in a harsh voice:

"Look you—I wish he were dead!"

Laguitte caught hold of both her hands, which for a moment he kept tightly clasped in his own. Then he left her hurriedly, for he felt a lump rising in his throat and tears coming to his eyes. Ah, by all the powers, this time his mind was quite made up.

CHAPTER IV

INSPECTION

THE REGIMENTAL INSPECTION was to take place at the end of the month. The major had ten days before him. On the very next morning, however, he crawled, limping, as far as the Café de Paris, where he ordered some beer. Mélanie grew pale when she saw him enter, and it was with a lively recollection of a certain slap that Phrosine hastened to serve him. The major seemed very calm, however; he called for a second chair to rest his bad leg upon and drank his beer quietly like any other thirsty man. He had sat there for about an hour when he saw two officers crossing the Place du Palais—Morandot, who commanded one of the battalions of the regiment, and Captain Doucet. Thereupon he excitedly waved his cane and shouted: "Come in and have a glass of beer with me!"

The officers dared not refuse, but when the maid had brought the beer Morandot said to the major: "So you patronize this place now?"

"Yes—the beer is good."

Captain Doucet winked and asked archly: "Do you belong to the divan, Major?"

Laguitte chuckled but did not answer. Then the others began to chaff him about Mélanie, and he took their remarks good-naturedly, simply shrugging his shoulders. The widow was undoubtedly a fine woman, however much people might talk. Some of those who disparaged her would, in reality, be only too pleased to win her good graces. Then turning to the little counter and assuming an engaging air, he shouted:

"Three more glasses, madame."

Mélanie was so taken aback that she rose and brought the beer herself. The major detained her at the table and forgot himself so far as to softly pat the hand which she had carelessly placed on the back of a chair. Used as she was to alternate brutality and flattery, she immediately became confident, believing in a sudden whim of gallantry on the part of the "old wreck," as she was wont to style the major when talking with Phrosine. Doucet and Morandot looked at each other in surprise. Was the major actually stepping into Petticoat Burle's shoes? The regiment would be convulsed if that were the case.

Suddenly, however, Laguitte, who kept his eye on the square, gave a start. "Hallo, there's Burle!" he exclaimed.

"Yes, it is his time," explained Phrosine. "The captain passes every afternoon on his way from the office."

In spite of his lameness the major had risen to his feet, pushing aside the chairs as he called out: "Burle! I say—come along and have a glass."

The captain, quite aghast and unable to understand why Laguitte was at the widow's, advanced mechanically. He was so perplexed that he again hesitated at the door.

"Another glass of beer," ordered the major, and then turning to Burle, he added, "What's the matter with you? Come in. Are you afraid of being eaten alive?"

The captain took a seat, and an awkward pause followed. Mélanie, who brought the beer with trembling hands, dreaded some scene which might result in the closing of her establishment. The major's gallantry made her uneasy, and she endeavored to slip away, but he invited her to drink with them, and before she could refuse he had ordered Phrosine to bring a liqueur glass of anisette, doing so with as much coolness as if he had been master of the house. Mélanie was thus compelled to sit down between the captain and Laguitte, who exclaimed aggressively: "I *will* have ladies respected. We are French officers! Let us drink Madame's health!"

Burle, with his eyes fixed on his glass, smiled in an embarrassed way. The two officers, shocked at the proceedings, had already tried to get off. Fortunately the café was deserted, save that the domino players were having their afternoon game. At every fresh oath which came from the major they glanced around, scandalized by such an unusual accession of customers and ready to threaten Mélanie that they would leave her for the Café de la Gare if the soldiery was going to invade her place like flies that buzzed about, attracted by the stickiness of the tables which Phrosine scoured only on Saturdays. She was now reclining behind the counter, already reading a novel again.

"How's this—you are not drinking with Madame?" roughly said the major to Burle. "Be civil at least!"

Then as Doucet and Morandot were again preparing to leave, he stopped them.

"Why can't you wait? We'll go together. It is only this brute who never knows how to behave himself."

The two officers looked surprised at the major's sudden bad temper. Mélanie attempted to restore peace and with a light laugh placed her hands on the arms of both men. However, Laguitte disengaged himself.

"No," he roared, "leave me alone. Why does he refuse to chink glasses with you? I shall not allow you to be insulted—do you hear? I am quite sick of him."

Burle, paling under the insult, turned slightly and said to Morandot, "What does this mean? He calls me in here to insult me. Is he drunk?"

With a wild oath the major rose on his trembling legs and struck the captain's cheek with his open hand. Mélanie dived and thus escaped one half of the smack. An appalling uproar ensued. Phrosine screamed behind the counter as if she herself had received the blow; the domino players also entrenched themselves behind their table in fear lest the soldiers should draw their swords and massacre them. However, Doucet and Morandot pinioned the captain to prevent him from springing at the major's throat and forcibly let him to the door. When they got him outside they succeeded in quieting him a little by repeating that Laguitte was quite in the wrong. They would lay the affair before the colonel, having witnessed it, and the colonel would give his decision. As soon as they had got Burle away they returned to the café where they found Laguitte in reality greatly disturbed, with tears in his eyes but affecting stolid indifference and slowly finishing his beer.

"Listen, Major," began Morandot, "that was very wrong on your part. The captain is your inferior in rank, and you know that he won't be allowed to fight you."

"That remains to be seen," answered the major.

"But how has he offended you? He never uttered a word. Two old comrades too; it is absurd."

The major made a vague gesture. "No matter. He annoyed me."

He could never be made to say anything else. Nothing more as to his motive was ever known. All the same, the scandal was a terrible one. The regiment was inclined to believe that Mélanie, incensed by the captain's defection, had contrived to entrap the major, telling him some abominable stories and prevailing upon him to insult and strike Burle publicly. Who would have thought it of that old fogy Laguitte, who professed to be a woman hater? they said. So he, too, had been caught at last. Despite the general indignation against Mélanie, this adventure made her very conspicuous, and her establishment soon drove a flourishing business.

On the following day the colonel summoned the major and the captain into his presence. He censured them sternly, accusing them of disgracing their uniform by frequenting unseemly haunts. What resolution had they come to, he asked, as he could not authorize them to fight? This same question had occupied the whole regiment for the last twenty-four hours. Apologies were unacceptable on account of the blow, but as Laguitte was almost unable to stand, it was hoped that, should the colonel insist upon it, some reconciliation might be patched up.

"Come," said the colonel, "will you accept me as arbitrator?"

"I beg your pardon, Colonel," interrupted the major; "I have brought you my resignation. Here it is. That settles everything. Please name the day for the duel."

Burle looked at Laguitte in amazement, and the colonel thought it his duty to protest.

"This is a most serious step, Major," he began. "Two years more and you would be entitled to your full pension."

But again did Laguitte cut him short, saying gruffly, "That is my own affair."

"Oh, certainly! Well, I will send in your resignation, and as soon as it is accepted I will fix a day for the duel."

The unexpected turn that events had taken startled the regiment. What possessed that lunatic major to persist in cutting the throat of his old comrade Burle? The officers again discussed Mélanie; they even began to dream of her. There must surely be something wonderful about her since she had completely fascinated two such tough old veterans and brought them to a deadly feud. Morandot, having met Laguitte, did not disguise his concern. If he—the major—was not killed, what would he live upon? He had no fortune, and the pension to which his cross of the Legion of Honor entitled him, with the half of a full regimental pension which he would obtain on resigning, would barely find him in bread. While Morandot was thus speaking Laguitte simply stared before him with his round eyes, persevering in the dumb obstinacy born of his narrow mind; and when his companion tried to question him regarding his hatred for Burle, he simply made the same vague gesture as before and once again repeated:

"He annoyed me; so much the worse."

Every morning at mess and at the canteen the first words were: "Has the acceptance of the major's resignation arrived?" The duel was impatiently expected and ardently discussed. The majority believed that Laguitte would be run through the body in three seconds, for it was madness for a man to fight with a paralyzed leg which did not even allow him to stand upright. A few, however, shook their heads. Laguitte had never been a marvel of intellect, that was true; for the last twenty years, indeed, he had been held up as an example of stupidity, but there had been a time when he was known as the best fencer of the regiment, and although he had begun as a drummer he had won his epaulets as the commander of a battalion by the sanguine bravery of a man who is quite unconscious of danger. On the other hand, Burle fenced indifferently and passed for a poltroon. However, they would soon know what to think.

Meanwhile the excitement became more and more intense as the acceptance of Laguitte's resignation was so long in coming. The major was unmistakably the most anxious and upset of everybody. A week had passed by, and the general inspection would commence two days later. Nothing, however, had come as yet. He shuddered at the thought that he had, perhaps, struck his old friend and sent in his resignation all in vain, without delaying the exposure for a single minute. He had in reality reasoned thus: If he himself were killed he would not have the worry of witnessing the scandal, and if he killed Burle, as he expected to do, the affair would undoubtedly be hushed up. Thus he would save the honor of the army, and the little chap would be able to get in at Saint-Cyr. Ah, why wouldn't those wretched scribblers at the War Office hurry up a bit? The major could not keep still but was forever wandering about before the post office, stopping the estafettes and questioning the colonel's orderly to find out if the acceptance had arrived. He lost his sleep and, careless as to people's remarks, he leaned more and more heavily on his stick, hobbling about with no attempt to steady his gait.

On the day before that fixed for the inspection he was, as usual, on his way to the colonel's quarters when he paused, startled, to see Mme Burle (who was taking Charles to school) a few paces ahead of him. He had not met her since the scene at the Café de Paris, for she had remained in seclusion at home. Unmanned at thus meeting her, he stepped down to leave the whole sidewalk free. Neither he nor the old lady bowed, and the little boy lifted his large inquisitive eyes in mute surprise. Mme Burle, cold and erect, brushed past the major without the least sign of emotion or recognition. When she had passed he looked after her with an expression of stupefied compassion.

"Confound it, I am no longer a man," he growled, dashing away a tear.

When he arrived at the colonel's quarters a captain in attendance greeted him with the words: "It's all right at last. The papers have come."

"Ah!" murmured Laguitte, growing very pale.

And again he beheld the old lady walking on, relentlessly rigid and holding the little boy's hand. What! He had longed so eagerly for those papers for eight days past, and now when the scraps had come he felt his brain on fire and his heart lacerated.

The duel took place on the morrow, in the barrack yard behind a low wall. The air was keen, the sun shining brightly. Laguitte had almost to be carried to the ground; one of his seconds supported him on one side, while on the other he leaned heavily, on his stick. Burle looked half asleep; his face was puffy with unhealthy fat, as if he had spent a night of debauchery. Not a word was spoken. They were all anxious to have it over.

Captain Doucet crossed the swords of the two adversaries and then drew back, saying: "Set to, gentlemen."

Burle was the first to attack; he wanted to test Laguitte's strength and ascertain what he had to expect. For the last ten days the encounter had seemed to him a ghastly nightmare which he could not fathom. At times a hideous suspicion assailed him, but he put it aside with terror, for it meant death, and he refused to believe that a friend could play him such a trick, even to set things right. Besides, Laguitte's leg reasssured him; he would prick the major on the shoulder, and then all would be over.

During well-nigh a couple of minutes the swords clashed, and then the captain lunged, but the major, recovering his old suppleness of wrist, parried in a masterly style, and if he had returned the attack Burle would have been pierced through. The captain now fell back; he was livid, for he felt that he was at the mercy of the man who had just spared him. At last he understood that this was an execution.

Laguitte, squarely poised on his infirm legs and seemingly turned to stone, stood waiting. The two men looked at each other fixedly. In Burle's blurred eyes there arose a supplication—a prayer for pardon. He knew why he was going to die, and like a child he promised not to transgress again. But the major's eyes remained implacable; honor had spoken, and he silenced his emotion and his pity.

"Let it end," he muttered between his teeth.

Then it was he who attacked. Like a flash of lightning his sword flamed, flying from right to left, and then with a resistless thrust it pierced the breast of the captain, who fell like a log without even a groan.

Laguitte had released his hold upon his sword and stood gazing at that poor old rascal Burle, who was stretched upon his back with his fat stomach bulging out.

"Oh, my God! My God!" repeated the major furiously and despairingly, and then he began to swear.

They led him away, and, both his legs failing him, he had to be supported on either side, for he could not even use his stick.

Two months later the ex-major was crawling slowly along in the sunlight down a lonely street of Vauchamp, when he again found himself face to face with Mme Burle and little Charles. They were both in deep mourning. He tried to avoid them, but he now only walked with difficulty, and they advanced straight upon him without hurrying or slackening their steps. Charles still had the same gentle, girlish, frightened face, and Mme Burle retained her stern, rigid demeanor, looking even harsher than ever.

As Laguitte shrank into the corner of a doorway to leave the whole street to them, she abruptly stopped in front of him and stretched out her hand. He hesitated and then took it and pressed it, but he trembled so violently that he made the old lady's arm shake. They exchanged glances in silence.

"Charles," said the boy's grandmother at last, "shake hands with the major."

The boy obeyed without understanding. The major, who was very pale, barely ventured to touch the child's frail fingers; then, feeling that he ought to speak, he stammered out: "You still intend to send him to Saint-Cyr?"

"Of course, when he is old enough," answered Mme Burle.

But during the following week Charles was carried off by typhoid fever. One evening his grandmother had again read him the story of the Vengeur to make him bold, and in the night he had become delirious. The poor little fellow died of fright.

THE DEATH OF OLIVIER BECAILLE

CHAPTER I
My Passing

It was on a Saturday, at six in the morning, that I died after a three days' illness. My wife was searching a trunk for some linen, and when she rose and turned she saw me rigid, with open eyes and silent pulses. She ran to me, fancying that I had fainted, touched my hands and bent over me. Then she suddenly grew alarmed, burst into tears and stammered:

"My God, my God! He is dead!"

I heard everything, but the sounds seemed to come from a great distance. My left eye still detected a faint glimmer, a whitish light in which all objects melted, but my right eye was quite bereft of sight. It was the coma of my whole being, as if a thunderbolt had struck me. My will was annihilated; not a fiber of flesh obeyed my bidding. And yet amid the impotency of my inert limbs my thoughts subsisted, sluggish and lazy, still perfectly clear.

My poor Marguerite was crying; she had dropped on her knees beside the bed, repeating in heart-rending tones:

"He is dead! My God, he is dead!"

Was this strange state of torpor, this immobility of the flesh, really death, although the functions of the intellect were not arrested? Was my soul only lingering for a brief space before it soared away forever? From my childhood upward I had been subject to hysterical attacks, and twice in early youth I had nearly succumbed to nervous fevers. By degrees all those who surrounded me had got accustomed to consider me an invalid and to see me sickly. So much so that I myself had forbidden my wife to call in a doctor when I had taken to my bed on the day of our arrival at the cheap lodginghouse of the Rue Dauphine in Paris. A little rest would soon set me right again; it was only the fatigue of the journey which had caused my intolerable weariness. And yet I was conscious of having felt singularly uneasy. We had left our province somewhat abruptly; we were very poor and had barely enough money to support ourselves till I drew my first month's salary in the office where I had obtained a situation. And now a sudden seizure was carrying me off!

Was it really death? I had pictured to myself a darker night, a deeper silence. As a little child I had already felt afraid to die. Being weak and compassionately petted by everyone, I had concluded that I had not long to live, that I should soon be buried, and the thought of the cold earth filled me with a dread I could not master—a dread which haunted me day and night. As I grew older the same terror pursued me. Sometimes, after long hours spent in reasoning with myself, I thought that I had conquered my fear. I reflected, "After all, what does it matter? One dies and all is over. It is the common fate; nothing could be better or easier."

I then prodded myself on being able to look death boldly in the face, but suddenly a shiver froze my blood, and my dizzy anguish returned, as if a giant hand had swung me over a dark abyss. It was some vision of the earth returning and setting reason at naught. How often at night did I start up in bed, not knowing what cold breath had swept over my slumbers but clasping my despairing hands and moaning, "Must I die?" In those moments an icy horror would stop my pulses while an appalling vision of dissolution rose before me. It was with difficulty that I could get to sleep again. Indeed, sleep alarmed me; it so closely resembled death. If I closed my eyes they might never open again—I might slumber on forever.

I cannot tell if others have endured the same torture; I only know that my own life was made a torment by it. Death ever rose between me and all I loved; I can remember how the thought of it poisoned the happiest moments I spent with Marguerite. During the first months of our married life, when she lay sleeping by my side and I dreamed of a fair future for her and with her, the foreboding of some fatal separation dashed my hopes aside and embittered my delights. Perhaps we should be parted on the morrow—nay, perhaps in an hour's time. Then utter discouragement assailed me; I wondered what the bliss of being united availed me if it were to end in so cruel a disruption.

My morbid imagination reveled in scenes of mourning. I speculated as to who would be the first to depart, Marguerite or I. Either alternative caused me harrowing grief, and tears rose to my eyes at the thought of our shattered lives. At the happiest periods of my existence I often became a prey to grim dejection such as nobody could understand but which was caused by the thought of impending nihility. When I was most successful I was to general wonder most depressed. The fatal question, "What avails it?" rang like a knell in my ears. But the sharpest sting of this torment was that it came with a secret sense of shame, which rendered me unable to confide my thoughts to another. Husband and wife lying side by side in the darkened room may quiver with the same shudder and yet remain mute, for people do not mention death any more than they pronounce certain obscene words. Fear makes it nameless.

I was musing thus while my dear Marguerite knelt sobbing at my feet. It grieved me sorely to be unable to comfort her by telling her that I suffered no pain. If death were merely the annihilation of the flesh it had been foolish of me to harbor so much dread. I experienced a selfish kind of restfulness in which all my cares were forgotten. My memory had become extraordinarily vivid. My whole life passed before me rapidly like a play in which I no longer acted a part; it was a curious and enjoyable sensation—I seemed to hear a far-off voice relating my own history.

I saw in particular a certain spot in the country near Guérande, on the way to Piriac. The road turns sharply, and some scattered pine trees carelessly dot a rocky slope. When I was seven years old I used to pass through those pines with my father as far as a crumbling old house, where Marguerite's parents gave me pancakes. They were salt gatherers and earned a scanty livelihood by working the adjacent salt marshes. Then I remembered the school at Nantes, where I had grown up, leading a monotonous life within its ancient walls and yearning for the broad horizon of Guérande and the salt marshes stretching to the limitless sea widening under the sky.

Next came a blank—my father was dead. I entered the hospital as clerk to the managing board and led a dreary life with one solitary diversion: my Sunday visits to the old house on Piriac road. The saltworks were doing badly; poverty reigned in the land, and Marguerite's parents were nearly penniless. Marguerite, when merely a child, had been fond of me because I trundled her about in a wheelbarrow, but on the morning when I asked her in marriage she shrank from me with a frightened gesture, and I realized that she thought me hideous. Her parents, however, consented at once; they looked upon my offer as a godsend, and the daughter submissively acquiesced. When she became accustomed to the idea of marrying me she did not seem to dislike it so much. On our wedding day at Guérande the rain fell in torrents, and when we got home my bride had to take off her dress, which was soaked through, and sit in her petticoats.

That was all the youth I ever had. We did not remain long in our province. One day I found my wife in tears. She was miserable; life was so dull; she wanted to get away. Six months later I had saved a little money by taking in extra work after office hours, and through the influence of a friend of my father's I obtained a petty appointment in Paris. I started off to settle there with the dear little woman so that she might cry no more. During the night, which we spent in the third-class railway carriage, the seats being very hard, I took her in my arms in order that she might sleep.

That was the past, and now I had just died on the narrow couch of a Paris lodginghouse, and my wife was crouching on the floor, crying bitterly. The white light before my left eye was growing dim, but I remembered the room perfectly. On the left there was a chest of drawers, on the right a mantelpiece surmounted by a damaged clock without a pendulum, the hands of which marked ten minutes past ten. The window overlooked the Rue Dauphine, a long, dark street. All Paris seemed to pass below, and the noise was so great that the window shook.

We knew nobody in the city; we had hurried our departure, but I was not expected at the office till the following Monday. Since I had taken to my bed I had wondered at my imprisonment in this narrow room into which we had tumbled after a railway journey of fifteen hours, followed by a hurried, confusing transit through the noisy streets. My wife had nursed me with smiling tenderness, but I knew that she was anxious. She would walk to the window, glance out and return to the bedside, looking very pale and startled by the sight of the busy thoroughfare, the aspect of the vast city of which she did not know a single stone and which deafened her with its continuous roar. What would happen to her if I never woke up again—alone, friendless and unknowing as she was?

Marguerite had caught hold of one of my hands which lay passive on the coverlet, and, covering it with kisses, she repeated wildly: "Olivier, answer me. Oh, my God, he is dead, dead!"

So death was not complete annihilation. I could hear and think. I had been uselessly alarmed all those years. I had not dropped into utter vacancy as I had anticipated. I could not picture the disappearance of my being, the suppression of all that I had been, without the possibility of renewed existence. I had been wont to shudder whenever in any book or newspaper I came across a date of a hundred years hence. A date at which I should no longer be alive, a future which I should never see, filled me with unspeakable uneasiness. Was I not the whole world, and would not the universe crumble away when I was no more?

To dream of life had been a cherished vision, but this could not possibly be death. I should assuredly awake presently. Yes, in a few moments I would lean over, take Marguerite in my arms and dry her tears. I would rest a little while longer before going to my office, and then a new life would begin, brighter than the last. However, I did not feel impatient; the commotion had been too strong. It was wrong of Marguerite to give way like that when I had not even the strength to turn my head on the pillow and smile at her. The next time that she moaned out, "He is dead! Dead!" I would embrace her and murmer softly so as not to startle her: "No, my darling, I was only asleep. You see, I am alive, and I love you."

CHAPTER II

FUNERAL PREPARATIONS

MARGUERITE'S CRIES had attracted attention, for all at once the door was opened and a voice exclaimed: "What is the matter, neighbor? Is he worse?"

I recognized the voice; it was that of an elderly woman, Mme Gabin, who occupied a room on the same floor. She had been most obliging since our arrival and had evidently become interested in our concerns. On her own side she had lost no time in telling us her history. A stern landlord had sold her furniture during the previous winter to pay himself his rent, and since then she had resided at the lodginghouse in the Rue Dauphine with her daughter Dédé, a child of ten. They both cut and pinked lamp shades, and between them they earned at the utmost only two francs a day.

"Heavens! Is it all over?" cried Mme Gabin, looking at me.

I realized that she was drawing nearer. She examined me, touched me and, turning to Marguerite, murmured compassionately: "Poor girl! Poor girl!"

My wife, wearied out, was sobbing like a child. Mme Gabin lifted her, placed her in a dilapidated armchair near the fireplace and proceeded to comfort her.

"Indeed, you'll do yourself harm if you go on like this, my dear. It's no reason because your husband is gone that you should kill yourself with weeping. Sure enough, when I lost Gabin I was just like you. I remained three days without swallowing a morsel of food. But that didn't help me—on the contrary, it pulled me down. Come, for the Lord's sake, be sensible!"

By degrees Marguerite grew calmer; she was exhausted, and it was only at intervals that she gave way to a fresh flow of tears. Meanwhile the old woman had taken possession of the room with a sort of rough authority.

"Don't worry yourself," she said as she bustled about. "Neighbors must help each other. Luckily Dédé has just gone to take the work home. Ah, I see your trunks are not yet all unpacked, but I suppose there is some linen in the chest of drawers, isn't there?"

I heard her pull a drawer open; she must have taken out a napkin which she spread on the little table at the bedside. She then struck a match, which made me think that she was lighting one of the candles on the mantelpiece and placing it near me as a religious rite. I could follow her movements in the room and divine all her actions.

"Poor gentleman," she muttered. "Luckily I heard you sobbing, poor dear!"

Suddenly the vague light which my left eye had detected vanished. Mme Gabin had just closed my eyelids, but I had not felt her finger on my face. When I understood this I felt chilled.

The door had opened again, and Dédé, the child of ten, now rushed in, calling out in her shrill voice: "Mother, Mother! Ah, I knew you would be here! Look here, there's the money—three francs and four sous. I took back three dozen lamp shades."

"Hush, hush! Hold your tongue," vainly repeated the mother, who, as the little girl chattered on, must have pointed to the bed, for I guessed that the child felt perplexed and was backing toward the door.

"Is the gentleman asleep?" she whispered.

"Yes, yes—go and play," said Mme Gabin.

But the child did not go. She was, no doubt, staring at me with widely opened eyes, startled and vaguely comprehending. Suddenly she seemed convulsed with terror and ran out, upsetting a chair.

"He is dead, Mother; he is dead!" she gasped.

Profound silence followed. Marguerite, lying back in the armchair, had left off crying. Mme Gabin was still rummaging about the room and talking under her breath.

"Children know everything nowadays. Look at that girl. Heaven knows how carefully she's brought up! When I send her on an errand or take the shades back I calculate the time to a minute so that she can't loiter about, but for all that she learns everything. She saw at a glance what had happened here—and yet I never showed her but one corpse, that of her uncle François, and she was then only four years old. Ah well, there are no children left—it can't be helped."

She paused and without any transition passed to another subject.

"I say, dearie, we must think of the formalities—there's the declaration at the municipal offices to be made and the seeing about the funeral. You are not in a fit state to attend to business. What do you say if I look in at Monsieur Simoneau's to find out if he's at home?"

Marguerite did not reply. It seemed to me that I watched her from afar and at times changed into a subtle flame hovering above the room, while a stranger lay heavy and unconscious on my bed. I wished that Marguerite had declined the assistance of Simoneau. I had seen him three or four times during my brief illness, for he occupied a room close to ours and had been civil and neighborly. Mme Gabin had told us that he was merely making a short stay in Paris, having come to collect some old debts due to his father, who had settled in the country and recently died. He was a tall, strong, handsome young man, and I hated him, perhaps on account of his healthy appearance. On the previous evening he had come in to make inquiries, and I had much disliked seeing him at Marguerite's side; she had looked so fair and pretty, and he had gazed so intently into her face when she smilingly thanked him for his kindness.

"Ah, here is Monsieur Simoneau," said Mme Gabin, introducing him.

He gently pushed the door ajar, and as soon as Marguerite saw him enter she burst into a flood of tears. The presence of a friend, of the only person she knew in Paris besides the old woman, recalled her bereavement. I could not see the young man, but in the darkness that encompassed me I conjured up his appearance. I pictured him distinctly, grave and sad at finding poor Marguerite in such distress. How lovely she must have looked with her golden hair unbound, her pale face and her dear little baby hands burning with fever!

"I am at your disposal, madame," he said softly. "Pray allow me to manage everything."

She only answered him with broken words, but as the young man was leaving, accompanied by Mme Gabin, I heard the latter mention money. These things were always expensive, she said, and she feared that the poor little body hadn't a farthing—anyhow, he might ask her. But Simoneau silenced the old woman; he did not want to have the widow worried; he was going to the municipal office and to the undertaker's.

When silence reigned once more I wondered if my nightmare would last much longer. I was certainly alive, for I was conscious of passing incidents, and I began to realize my condition. I must have fallen into one of those cataleptic states that I had read of. As a child I had suffered from syncopes which had lasted several hours, but surely my heart would beat anew, my blood circulate and my muscles relax. Yes, I should wake up and comfort Marguerite, and, reasoning thus, I tried to be patient.

Time passed. Mme Gabin had brought in some breakfast, but Marguerite refused to taste any food. Later on the afternoon waned. Through the open window I heard the rising clamor of the Rue Dauphine. By and by a slight ringing of the brass candlestick on the marble-topped table made me think that a fresh candle had been lighted. At last Simoneau returned.

"Well?" whispered the old woman.

"It is all settled," he answered; "the funeral is ordered for tomorrow at eleven. There is nothing for you to do, and you needn't talk of these things before the poor lady."

Nevertheless, Mme Gabin remarked: "The doctor of the dead hasn't come yet."

Simoneau took a seat beside Marguerite and after a few words of encouragement remained silent. The funeral was to take place at eleven! Those words rang in my brain like a passing bell. And the doctor coming—the doctor of the dead, as Mme Gabin had called him. *He* could not possibly fail to find out that I was only in a state of lethargy; he would do whatever might be necessary to rouse me, so I longed for his arrival with feverish anxiety.

The day was drawing to a close. Mme Gabin, anxious to waste no time, had brought in her lamp shades and summoned Dédé without asking Marguerite's permission. "To tell the truth," she observed, "I do not like to leave children too long alone."

"Come in, I say," she whispered to the little girl; "come in, and don't be frightened. Only don't look toward the bed or you'll catch it."

She thought it decorous to forbid Dédé to look at me, but I was convinced that the child was furtively glancing at the corner where I lay, for every now and then I heard her mother rap her knuckles and repeat angrily: "Get on with your work or you shall leave the room, and the gentleman will come during the night and pull you by the feet."

The mother and daughter had sat down at our table. I could plainly hear the click of their scissors as they clipped the lamp shades, which no doubt required very delicate manipulation, for they did not work rapidly. I counted the shades one by one as they were laid aside, while my anxiety grew more and more intense.

The clicking of the scissors was the only noise in the room, so I concluded that Marguerite had been overcome by fatigue and was dozing. Twice Simoneau rose, and the torturing thought flashed through me that he might be taking advantage of her slumbers to touch her hair with his lips. I hardly knew the man and yet felt sure that he loved my wife. At last little Dédé began to giggle, and her laugh exasperated me.

"Why are you sniggering, you idiot?" asked her mother. "Do you want to be turned out on the landing? Come, out with it; what makes you laugh so?"

The child stammered: she had not laughed; she had only coughed, but I felt certain she had seen Simoneau bending over Marguerite and had felt amused.

The lamp had been lit when a knock was heard at the door.

"It must be the doctor at last," said the old woman.

It was the doctor; he did not apologize for coming so late, for he had no doubt ascended many flights of stairs during the day. The room being but imperfectly lighted by the lamp, he inquired: "Is the body here?"

"Yes, it is," answered Simoneau.

Marguerite had risen, trembling violently. Mme Gabin dismissed Dédé, saying it was useless that a child should be present, and then she tried to lead my wife to the window, to spare her the sight of what was about to take place.

The doctor quickly approached the bed. I guessed that he was bored, tired and impatient. Had he touched my wrist? Had he placed his hand on my heart? I could not tell, but I fancied that he had only carelessly bent over me.

"Shall I bring the lamp so that you may see better?" asked Simoneau obligingly.

"No, it is not necessary," quietly answered the doctor.

Not necessary! That man held my life in his hands, and he did not think it worth while to proceed to a careful examination! I was not dead! I wanted to cry out that I was not dead!

"At what o'clock did he die?" asked the doctor.

"At six this morning," volunteered Simoneau.

A feeling of frenzy and rebellion rose within me, bound as I was in seemingly iron chains. Oh, for the power of uttering one word, of moving a single limb!

"This close weather is unhealthy," resumed the doctor; "nothing is more trying than these early spring days."

And then he moved away. It was like my life departing. Screams, sobs and insults were choking me, struggling in my convulsed throat, in which even my breath was arrested. The wretch! Turned into a mere machine by professional habits, he only came to a deathbed to accomplish a perfunctory formality; he knew nothing; his science was a lie, since he could not at a glance distinguish life from death—and now he was going—going!

"Good night, sir," said Simoneau.

There came a moment's silence; the doctor was probably bowing to Marguerite, who had turned while Mme Gabin was fastening the window. He left the room, and I heard his footsteps descending the stairs.

It was all over; I was condemned. My last hope had vanished with that man. If I did not wake before eleven on the morrow I should be buried alive. The horror of that thought was so great that I lost all consciousness of my surroundings—'twas something like a fainting fit in death. The last sound I heard was the clicking of the scissors handled by Mme Gabin and Dédé. The funeral vigil had begun; nobody spoke.

Marguerite had refused to retire to rest in the neighbor's room. She remained reclining in her armchair, with her beautiful face pale, her eyes closed and her long lashes wet with tears, while before her in the gloom Simoneau sat silently watching her.

CHAPTER III

The Procession

I CANNOT DESCRIBE my agony during the morning of the following day. I remember it as a hideous dream in which my impressions were so ghastly and so confused that I could not formulate them. The persistent yearning for a sudden awakening increased my torture, and as the hour for the funeral drew nearer my anguish became more poignant still.

It was only at daybreak that I had recovered a fuller consciousness of what was going on around me. The creaking of hinges startled me out of my stupor. Mme Gabin had just opened the window. It must have been about seven o'clock, for I heard the cries of hawkers in the street, the shrill voice of a girl offering groundsel and the hoarse voice of a man shouting "Carrots!" The clamorous awakening of Paris pacified me at first. I could not believe that I should be laid under the sod in the midst of so much life; and, besides, a sudden thought helped to calm me. It had just occurred to me that I had witnessed a case similar to my own when I was employed at the hospital of Guérande. A man had been sleeping twenty-eight hours, the doctors hesitating in presence of his apparent lifelessness, when suddenly he had sat up in bed and was almost at once able to rise. I myself had already been asleep for some twenty-five hours; if I awoke at ten I should still be in time.

I endeavored to ascertain who was in the room and what was going on there. Dédé must have been playing on the landing, for once when the door opened I heard her shrill childish laughter outside. Simoneau must have retired, for nothing indicated his presence. Mme Gabin's slipshod tread was still audible over the floor. At last she spoke.

"Come, my dear," she said. "It is wrong of you not to take it while it is hot. It would cheer you up."

She was addressing Marguerite, and a slow trickling sound as of something filtering indicated that she had been making some coffee.

"I don't mind owning," she continued, "that I needed it. At my age sitting up *is* trying. The night seems so dreary when there is a misfortune in the house. *Do* have a cup of coffee, my dear—just a drop."

She persuaded Marguerite to taste it.

"Isn't it nice and hot?" she continued, "and doesn't it set one up? Ah, you'll be wanting all your strength presently for what you've got to go through today. Now if you were sensible you'd step into my room and just wait there."

"No, I want to stay here," said Marguerite resolutely.

Her voice, which I had not heard since the previous evening, touched me strangely. It was changed, broken as by tears. To feel my dear wife near me was a last consolation. I knew that her eyes were fastened on me and that she was weeping with all the anguish of her heart.

The minutes flew by. An inexplicable noise sounded from beyond the door. It seemed as if some people were bringing a bulky piece of furniture upstairs and knocking against the walls as they did so. Suddenly I understood, as I heard Marguerite begin to sob; it was the coffin.

"You are too early," said Mme Gabin crossly. "Put it behind the bed."

What o'clock was it? Nine, perhaps. So the coffin had come. Amid the opaque night around me I could see it plainly, quite new, with roughly planed boards. Heavens! Was this the end then? Was I to be borne off in that box which I realized was lying at my feet?

However, I had one supreme joy. Marguerite, in spite of her weakness, insisted upon discharging all the last offices. Assisted by the old woman, she dressed me with all the tenderness of a wife and a sister. Once more I felt myself in her arms as she clothed me in various garments. She paused at times, overcome by grief; she clasped me convulsively, and her tears rained on my face. Oh, how I longed to return her embrace and cry, "I live!" And yet I was lying there powerless, motionless, inert!

"You are foolish," suddenly said Mme Gabin; "it is all wasted."

"Never mind," answered Marguerite, sobbing. "I want him to wear his very best things."

I understood that she was dressing me in the clothes I had worn on my wedding day. I had kept them carefully for great occasions. When she had finished she fell back exhausted in the armchair.

Simoneau now spoke; he had probably just entered the room.

"They are below," he whispered.

"Well, it ain't any too soon," answered Mme Gabin, also lowering her voice. "Tell them to come up and get it over."

"But I dread the despair of the poor little wife."

The old woman seemed to reflect and presently resumed: "Listen to me, Monsieur Simoneau. You must take her off to my room. I wouldn't have her stop here. It is for her own good. When she is out of the way we'll get it done in a jiffy."

These words pierced my heart, and my anguish was intense when I realized that a struggle was actually taking place. Simoneau had walked up to Marguerite, imploring her to leave the room.

"Do, for pity's sake, come with me!" he pleaded. "Spare yourself useless pain."

"No, no!" she cried. "I will remain till the last minute. Remember that I have only him in the world, and when he is gone I shall be all alone!"

From the bedside Mme Gabin was prompting the young man.

"Don't parley—take hold of her, carry her off in your arms."

Was Simoneau about to lay his hands on Marguerite and bear her away? She screamed. I wildly endeavored to rise, but the springs of my limbs were broken. I remained rigid, unable to lift my eyelids to see what was going on. The struggle continued, and my wife clung to the furniture, repeating, "Oh, don't, don't! Have mercy! Let me go! I will not——"

He must have lifted her in his stalwart arms, for I heard her moaning like a child. He bore her away; her sobs were lost in the distance, and I fancied I saw them both—he, tall and strong, pressing her to his breast; she, fainting, powerless and conquered, following him wherever he listed.

"Drat it all! What a to-do!" muttered Mme Gabin. "Now for the tug of war, as the coast is clear at last."

In my jealous madness I looked upon this incident as a monstrous outrage. I had not been able to see Marguerite for twenty-four hours, but at least I had still heard her voice. Now even this was denied me; she had been torn away; a man had eloped with her even before I was laid under the sod. He was alone with her on the other side of the wall, comforting her—embracing her, perhaps!

But the door opened once more, and heavy footsteps shook the floor.

"Quick, make haste," repeated Mme Gabin. "Get it done before the lady comes back."

She was speaking to some strangers, who merely answered her with uncouth grunts.

"You understand," she went on, "I am not a relation; I'm only a neighbor.

I have no interest in the matter. It is out of pure good nature that I have mixed myself up in their affairs. And I ain't overcheerful, I can tell you. Yes, yes, I sat up the whole blessed night—it was pretty cold, too, about four o'clock. That's a fact. Well, I have always been a fool—I'm too soft-hearted."

The coffin had been dragged into the center of the room. As I had not awakened I was condemned. All clearness departed from my ideas; everything seemed to revolve in a black haze, and I experienced such utter lassitude that it seemed almost a relief to leave off hoping.

"They haven't spared the material," said one of the undertaker's men in a gruff voice. "The box is too long."

"He'll have all the more room," said the other, laughing.

I was not heavy, and they chuckled over it since they had three flights of stairs to descend. As they were seizing me by the shoulders and feet I heard Mme Gabin fly into a violent passion.

"You cursed little brat," she screamed, "what do you mean by poking your nose where you're not wanted? Look here, I'll teach you to spy and pry."

Dédé had slipped her tousled head through the doorway to see how the gentleman was being put into the box. Two ringing slaps resounded, however, by an explosion of sobs. And as soon as the mother returned she began to gossip about her daughter for the benefit of the two men who were settling me in the coffin.

"She is only ten, you know. She is not a bad girl, but she is frightfully inquisitive. I do not beat her often; only I *will* be obeyed."

"Oh," said one of the men, "all kids are alike. Whenever there is a corpse lying about they always want to see it."

I was commodiously stretched out, and I might have thought myself still in bed, had it not been that my left arm felt a trifle cramped from being squeezed against a board. The men had been right. I was pretty comfortable inside on account of my diminutive stature.

"Stop!" suddenly exclaimed Mme Gabin. "I promised his wife to put a pillow under his head."

The men, who were in a hurry, stuffed in the pillow roughly. One of them, who had mislaid his hammer, began to swear. He had left the tool below and went to fetch it, dropping the lid, and when two sharp blows of the hammer drove in the first nail, a shock ran through my being—I had ceased to live. The nails then entered in rapid succession with a rhythmical cadence. It was as if some packers had been closing a case of dried fruit with easy dexterity. After that such sounds as reached me were deadened and strangely prolonged, as if the deal coffin had been changed into a huge musical box. The last words spoken in the room of the Rue Dauphine—at least the last ones that I heard distinctly—were uttered by Mme Gabin.

"Mind the staircase," she said; "the banister of the second flight isn't safe, so be careful."

While I was being carried down I experienced a sensation similar to that of pitching. as when one is on board a ship in a rough sea. However, from that moment my impressions became more and more vague. I remember that the only distinct thought that still possessed me was an imbecile, impulsive curiosity as to the road by which I should be taken to the cemetery. I was not acquainted with a single street of Paris, and I was ignorant of the position of the large burial grounds (though of course I had occasionally heard their names), and yet every effort of my mind was directed toward ascertaining whether we were turning to the right or to the left. Meanwhile the jolting of the hearse over the paving stones, the rumbling of passing vehicles, the steps of the foot passengers, all created a confused clamor, intensified by the acoustical properties of the coffin.

At first I followed our course pretty closely; then came a halt. I was again lifted and carried about, and I concluded that we were in church, but when the funeral procession once more moved onward I lost all consciousness of the road we took. A ringing of bells informed me that we were passing another church, and then the softer and easier progress of the wheels indicated that we were skirting a garden or park. I was like a victim being taken to the gallows, awaiting in stupor a deathblow that never came.

At last they stopped and pulled me out of the hearse. The business proceeded rapidly. The noises had ceased; I knew that I was in a deserted space amid avenues of trees and with the broad sky over my head. No doubt a few persons followed the bier, some of the inhabitants of the lodginghouse, perhaps—Simoneau and others, for instance—for faint whisperings reached my ear. Then I heard a psalm chanted and some Latin words mumbled by a priest, and afterward I suddenly felt myself sinking, while the ropes rubbing against the edges of the coffin elicited lugubrious sounds, as if a bow were being drawn across the strings of a cracked violoncello. It was the end. On the left side of my head I felt a violent shock like that produced by the bursting of a bomb, with another under my feet and a third more violent still on my chest. So forcible, indeed, was this last one that I thought the lid was cleft atwain. I fainted from it.

CHAPTER IV

THE NAIL

IT IS IMPOSSIBLE for me to say how long my swoon lasted. Eternity is not of longer duration than one second spent in nihility. I was no more. It was slowly and confusedly that I regained some degree of consciousness. I was still asleep, but I began to dream; a nightmare started into shape amid the blackness of my horizon, a nightmare compounded of a strange fancy which in other days had haunted my morbid imagination whenever with my propensity for dwelling upon hideous thoughts I had conjured up catastrophes.

Thus I dreamed that my wife was expecting me somewhere—at Guérande, I believe—and that I was going to join her by rail. As we passed through a tunnel a deafening roll thundered over our head, and a sudden subsidence blocked up both issues of the tunnel, leaving our train intact in the center.

We were walled up by blocks of rock in the heart of a mountain. Then a long and fearful agony commenced. No assistance could possibly reach us; even with powerful engines and incessant labor it would take a month to clear the tunnel. We were prisoners there with no outlet, and so our death was only a question of time.

My fancy had often dwelt on that hideous drama and had constantly varied the details and touches. My actors were men, women and children; their number increased to hundreds, and they were ever furnishing me with new incidents. There were some provisions in the train, but these were soon exhausted, and the hungry passengers, if they did not actually devour human flesh, at least fought furiously over the last piece of bread. Sometimes an aged man was driven back with blows and slowly perished; a mother struggled like a she-wolf to keep three or four mouthfuls for her child. In my own compartment a bride and bridegroom were dying, clasped in each other's arms in mute despair.

The line was free along the whole length of the train, and people came and went, prowling round the carriages like beasts of prey in search of carrion. All classes were mingled together. A millionaire, a high functionary, it was said, wept on a workman's shoulder. The lamps had been extinguished from the first, and the engine fire was nearly out. To pass from one carriage to another it was necessary to grope about, and thus, too, one slowly reached the engine, recognizable by its enormous barrel, its cold, motionless flanks, its useless strength, its grim silence, in the overwhelming night. Nothing could be more appalling than this train entombed alive with its passengers perishing one by one.

I gloated over the ghastliness of each detail; howls resounded through the vault; somebody whom one could not see, whose vicinity was not even suspected, would suddenly drop upon another's shoulder. But what affected me most of all was the cold and the want of air. I have never felt so chilled; a mantle of snow seemed to enwrap me; heavy moisture rained upon my skull; I was gasping; the rocky vault seemed to crush my chest; the whole mountain was seemingly weighing upon me.

Suddenly a cry of deliverance sounded. For some time past we fancied that we could hear a dull sound, and we tried to hope that men were at work and that help was coming, but it came not thus. One of the passengers, however, had discovered an air shaft in the tunnel, and, crowding round, we all saw this shaft, above which we could discern a blue patch about the size of a wafer. That blue patch filled us with rapture, for it was the sky. We stretched ourselves and stood on tiptoes to breathe more freely. Then we distinguished some black specks moving about, specks that must surely be workmen about to deliver us. A furious clamor arose. The cry "Saved! Saved!" burst from every mouth, while trembling arms were uplifted toward the tiny azure patch above.

That roar of voices aroused me. Where was I? In the tunnel, of course. I was lying at full length; hard walls were pressing against my ribs. Then I attempted to rise and struck my head roughly. Was it the rock closing in on all sides? The blue speck had vanished—aye, the sky had disappeared—and I was still suffocating, shivering, with chattering teeth.

All at once I remembered. Intense horror raised my hair on end. I felt the hideous truth freeze me from head to foot like ice. I had shaken off the long coma which for many hours had stricken me with corpselike rigidity. Yes, I could move; my hands could feel the boards of my coffin; my lips parted; words came to me, and instinctively I called out Marguerite's name. It was a scream I raised. In that deal box my voice took so hoarse and weird a sound that it terrified me. Oh, my God, was this thing true? I was able to walk, speak, cry out that I was living, and yet my voice could not be heard; I was entombed under the earth.

I made a desperate effort to remain calm and reflect. Was there no means of getting out? Then my dream began afresh in my troubled brain. The fanciful air shaft with the blue bit of sky overhead was mingled with the real grave in which I was lying. I stared at the darkness with widely opened eyes; perhaps I might discover a hole, a slit, a glimmer of light, but only sparks of fire flitted through that night, with rays that broadened and then faded away. I was in a somber abyss again. With returning lucidity I struggled against these fatal visions. Indeed, I should need all my reason if I meant to try to save myself.

The most immediate peril lay in an increasing sense of suffocation. If I had been able to live so long without air it was owing to suspended animation, which had changed all the normal conditions of my existence, but now that my heart beat and my lungs breathed I should die, asphyxiated, if I did not promptly liberate myself. I also suffered from cold and dreaded lest I should succumb to the mortal numbness of those who fall asleep in the snow, never to wake again. Still, while unceasingly realizing the necessity of remaining calm, I felt maddening blasts sweep through my brain, and to quiet my senses I exhorted myself to patience, trying to remember the circumstances of my burial. Probably the ground had been bought for five years, and this would be against my chances of self-deliverance, for I remembered having noticed at Nantes that in the trenches of the common graves one end of the last lowered coffins protruded into the next open cavity, in which case I should only have had to break through one plank. But if I were in a separate hole, filled up above me with earth, the obstacles would prove too great. Had I not been told that the dead were buried six feet deep in Paris? How was I to get through the enormous mass of soil above me? Even if I succeeded in slitting the lid of my bier open the mold would drift in like fine sand and fill my mouth and eyes. That would be death again, a ghastly death, like drowning in mud.

However, I began to feel the planks carefully. The coffin was roomy, and I found that I was able to move my arms with tolerable ease. On both sides the roughly planed boards were stout and resistive. I slipped my arm onto my chest to raise it over my head. There I discovered in the top plank a knot in the wood which yielded slightly at my pressure. Working laboriously, I finally succeeded in driving out this knot, and on passing my finger through the hole I found that the earth was wet and clayey. But that availed me little. I even regretted having removed the knot, vaguely dreading the irruption of the mold. A second experiment occupied me for a while. I tapped all over the coffin to ascertain if perhaps there were any vacuum outside. But the sound was everywhere the same. At last, as I was slightly kicking the foot of the coffin, I fancied that it gave out a clearer echoing noise, but that might merely be produced by the sonority of the wood.

At any rate, I began to press against the boards with my arms and my closed fists. In the same way, too, I used my knees, my back and my feet without eliciting even a creak from the wood. I strained with all my strength, indeed, with so desperate an effort of my whole frame, that my bruised bones seemed breaking. But nothing moved, and I became insane.

Until that moment I had held delirium at bay. I had mastered the intoxicating rage which was mounting to my head like the fumes of alcohol; I had silenced my screams, for I feared that if I again cried out aloud I should be undone. But now I yelled; I shouted; unearthly howls which I could not repress came from my relaxed throat. I called for help in a voice that I did not recognize, growing wilder with each fresh appeal and crying out that I would not die. I also tore at the wood with my nails; I writhed with the contortions of a caged wolf. I do not know how long this fit of madness lasted, but I can still feel the relentless hardness of the box that imprisoned me; I can still hear the storm of shrieks and sobs with which I filled it; a remaining glimmer of reason made me try to stop, but I could not do so.

Great exhaustion followed. I lay waiting for death in a state of somnolent pain. The coffin was like stone, which no effort could break, and the conviction that I was powerless left me unnerved, without courage to make any fresh attempts. Another suffering—hunger—was presently added to cold and want of air. The torture soon became intolerable. With my finger I tried to pull small pinches of earth through the hole of the dislodged knot, and I swallowed them eagerly, only increasing my torment. Tempted by my flesh, I bit my arms and sucked my skin with a fiendish desire to drive my teeth in, but I was afraid of drawing blood.

Then I ardently longed for death. All my life long I had trembled at the thought of dissolution, but I had come to yearn for it, to crave for an everlasting night that could never be dark enough. How childish it had been of me to dread the long, dreamless sleep, the eternity of silence and gloom! Death was kind, for in suppressing life it put an end to suffering. Oh, to sleep like the stones, to be no more!

With groping hands I still continued feeling the wood, and suddenly I pricked my left thumb. That slight pain roused me from my growing numbness. I felt again and found a nail—a nail which the undertaker's men had driven in crookedly and which had not caught in the lower wood. It was long and very sharp; the head was secured to the lid, but it moved. Henceforth I had but one idea—to possess myself of that nail—and I slipped my right hand across my body and began to shake it. I made but little progress, however; it was a difficult job, for my hands soon tired, and I had to use them alternately.

The left one, too, was of little use on account of the nail's awkward position.

While I was obstinately persevering a plan dawned on my mind. That nail meant salvation, and I must have it. But should I get it in time? Hunger was torturing me; my brain was swimming; my limbs were losing their strength; my mind was becoming confused. I had sucked the drops that trickled from my punctured finger, and suddenly I bit my arm and drank my own blood! Thereupon, spurred on by pain, revived by the tepid, acrid liquor that moistened my lips, I tore desperately at the nail and at last I wrenched it off!

I then believed in success. My plan was a simple one; I pushed the point of the nail into the lid, dragging it along as far as I could in a straight line and working it so as to make a slit in the wood. My fingers stiffened, but I doggedly persevered, and when I fancied that I had sufficiently cut into the board I turned on my stomach and, lifting myself on my knees and elbows, thrust the whole strength of my back against the lid. But although it creaked it did not yield; the notched line was not deep enough. I had to resume my old position—which I only managed to do with infinite trouble—and work afresh. At last after another supreme effort the lid was cleft from end to end.

I was not saved as yet, but my heart beat with renewed hope. I had ceased pushing and remained motionless, lest a sudden fall of earth should bury me. I intended to use the lid as a screen and, thus protected, to open a sort of shaft in the clayey soil. Unfortunately I was assailed by unexpected difficulties. Some heavy clods of earth weighed upon the boards and made them unmanageable; I foresaw that I should never reach the surface in that way, for the mass of soil was already bending my spine and crushing my face.

Once more I stopped, affrighted; then suddenly, while I was stretching my legs, trying to find something firm against which I might rest my feet, I felt the end board of the coffin yielding. I at once gave a desperate kick with my heels in the faint hope that there might be a freshly dug grave in that direction.

It was so. My feet abruptly forced their way into space. An open grave was there; I had only a slight partition of earth to displace, and soon I rolled into the cavity. I was saved!

I remained for a time lying on my back in the open grave, with my eyes raised to heaven. It was dark; the stars were shining in a sky of velvety blueness. Now and then the rising breeze wafted a springlike freshness, a perfume of foliage, upon me. I was saved! I could breathe; I felt warm, and I wept and I stammered, with my arms prayerfully extended toward the starry sky. O God, how sweet seemed life!

CHAPTER V

My Resurrection

My first impulse was to find the custodian of the cemetery and ask him to have me conducted home, but various thoughts that came to me restrained me from following that course. My return would create general alarm; why should I hurry now that I was master of the situation? I felt my limbs; I had only an insignificant wound on my left arm, where I had bitten myself, and a slight feverishness lent me unhoped-for strength. I should no doubt be able to walk unaided.

Still I lingered; all sorts of dim visions confused my mind. I had felt beside me in the open grave some sextons' tools which had been left there, and I conceived a sudden desire to repair the damage I had done, to close up the hole through which I had crept, so as to conceal all traces of my resurrection. I do not believe that I had any positive motive in doing so. I only deemed it useless to proclaim my adventure aloud, feeling ashamed to find myself alive when the whole world thought me dead. In half an hour every trace of my escape was obliterated, and then I climbed out of the hole.

The night was splendid, and deep silence reigned in the cemetery; the black trees threw motionless shadows over the white tombs. When I endeavored to ascertain my bearings I noticed that one half of the sky was ruddy, as if lit by a huge conflagration; Paris lay in that direction, and I moved toward it, following a long avenue amid the darkness of the branches.

However, after I had gone some fifty yards I was compelled to stop, feeling faint and weary. I then sat down on a stone bench and for the first time looked at myself. I was fully attired with the exception that I had no hat. I blessed my beloved Marguerite for the pious thought which had prompted her to dress me in my best clothes—those which I had worn at our wedding. That remembrance of my wife brought me to my feet again. I longed to see her without delay.

At the farther end of the avenue I had taken a wall arrested my progress. However, I climbed to the top of a monument, reached the summit of the wall and then dropped over the other side. Although roughly shaken by the fall, I managed to walk for a few minutes along a broad deserted street skirting the cemetery. I had no notion as to where I might be, but with the re-iteration of monomania I kept saying to myself that I was going toward Paris and that I should find the Rue Dauphine somehow or other. Several people passed me but, seized with sudden distrust, I would not stop them and ask my way. I have since realized that I was then in a burning fever and already nearly delirious. Finally, just as I reached a large thoroughfare, I became giddy and fell heavily upon the pavement.

Here there is a blank in my life. For three whole weeks I remained unconscious. When I awoke at last I found myself in a strange room. A man who was nursing me told me quietly that he had picked me up one morning on the Boulevard Montparnasse and had brought me to his house. He was an old doctor who had given up practicing.

When I attempted to thank him he sharply answered that my case had seemed a curious one and that he had wished to study it. Moreover, during the first days of my convalescence he would not allow me to ask a single question, and later on he never put one to me. For eight days longer I remained in bed, feeling very weak and not even trying to remember, for memory was a weariness and a pain. I felt half ashamed and half afraid. As soon as I could leave the house I would go and find out whatever I wanted to know. Possibly in the delirium of fever a name had escaped me; however, the doctor never alluded to anything I may have said. His charity was not only generous; it was discreet.

The summer had come at last, and one warm June morning I was permitted to take a short walk. The sun was shining with that joyous brightness which imparts renewed youth to the streets of old Paris. I went along slowly, questioning the passers-by at every crossing I came to and asking the way to Rue Dauphine. When I reached the street I had some difficulty in recognizing the lodginghouse where we had alighted on our arrival in the capital. A childish terror made me hesitate. If I appeared suddenly before Marguerite the shock might kill her. It might be wiser to begin by revealing myself to our neighbor Mme Gabin; still I shrank from taking a third party into confidence. I seemed unable to arrive at a resolution, and yet in my innermost heart I felt a great void, like that left by some sacrifice long since consummated.

The building looked quite yellow in the sunshine. I had just recognized it by a shabby eating house on the ground floor, where we had ordered our meals, having them sent up to us. Then I raised my eyes to the last window of the third floor on the left-hand side, and as I looked at it a young woman with tumbled hair, wearing a loose dressing gown, appeared and leaned her elbows on the sill. A young man followed and printed a kiss upon her neck. It was not Marguerite. Still I felt no surprise. It seemed to me that I had dreamed all this with other things, too, which I was to learn presently.

For a moment I remained in the street, uncertain whether I had better go upstairs and question the lovers, who were still laughing in the sunshine. However, I decided to enter the little restaurant below. When I started on my walk the old doctor had placed a five-franc piece in my hand. No doubt I was changed beyond recognition, for my beard had grown during the brain fever, and my face was wrinkled and haggard. As I took a seat at a small table I saw Mme Gabin come in carrying a cup; she wished to buy a pennyworth of coffee. Standing in front of the counter, she began to gossip with the landlady of the establishment.

"Well," asked the latter, "so the poor little woman of the third floor has made up her mind at last, eh?"

"How could she help herself?" answered Mme Gabin. "It was the very best thing for her to do. Monsieur Simoneau showed her so much kindness. You see, he had finished his business in Paris to his satisfaction, for he has inherited a pot of money. Well, he offered to take her away with him to his own part of the country and place her with an aunt of his, who wants a housekeeper and companion."

The landlady laughed archly. I buried my face in a newspaper which I picked off the table. My lips were white and my hands shook.

"It will end in a marriage, of course," resumed Mme Gabin. "The little widow mourned for her husband very properly, and the young man was extremely well behaved. Well, they left last night—and, after all, they were free to please themselves."

Just then the side door of the restaurant, communicating with the passage of the house, opened, and Dédé appeared.

"Mother, ain't you coming?" she cried. "I'm waiting, you know; do be quick."

"Presently," said the mother testily. "Don't bother."

The girl stood listening to the two women with the precocious shrewdness of a child born and reared amid the streets of Paris.

"When all is said and done," explained Mme Gabin, "the dear departed did not come up to Monsieur Simoneau. I didn't fancy him overmuch; he was a puny sort of a man, a poor, fretful fellow, and he hadn't a penny to bless himself with. No, candidly, he wasn't the kind of husband for a young and healthy wife, whereas Monsieur Simoneau is rich, you know, and as strong as a Turk."

"Oh yes!" interrupted Dédé. "I saw him once when he was washing—his door was open. His arms are so hairy!"

"Get along with you," screamed the old woman, shoving the girl out of the restaurant. "You are always poking your nose where it has no business to be."

Then she concluded with these words: "Look here, to my mind the other one did quite right to take himself off. It was fine luck for the little woman!"

When I found myself in the street again I walked along slowly with trembling limbs. And yet I was not suffering much; I think I smiled once at my shadow in the sun. It was quite true. I *was* very puny. It had been a queer notion of mine to marry Marguerite. I recalled her weariness at Guérande, her impatience, her dull, monotonous life. The dear creature had been very good to me, but I had never been a real lover; she had mourned for me as a sister for her brother, not otherwise. Why should I again disturb her life? A dead man is not jealous.

When I lifted my eyelids I saw the garden of the Luxembourg before me. I entered it and took a seat in the sun, dreaming with a sense of infinite restfulness. The thought of Marguerite stirred me softly. I pictured her in the provinces, beloved, petted and very happy. She had grown handsomer, and she was the mother of three boys and two girls. It was all right. I had behaved like an honest man in dying, and I would not commit the cruel folly of coming to life again.

Since then I have traveled a good deal. I have been a little everywhere. I am an ordinary man who has toiled and eaten like anybody else. Death no longer frightens me, but it does not seem to care for me now that I have no motive in living, and I sometimes fear that I have been forgotten upon earth.

THE INUNDATION

CHAPTER I

Glorious Days

My name is Louis Roubieu. I am seventy years of age and was born in the village of Saint-Jory, at a few leagues from Toulouse, on the banks of the Garonne. During fourteen years I battled with the soil in order to obtain from it enough bread to feed me. Affluence came at last, and only a month ago I was the richest farmer of the whole countryside.

Our home was blessed. Happiness had its abode under our roof. The sun was our ally, and I do not remember a bad harvest. We were nearly a dozen at the farm, all sharing the same happiness: myself, still hale and hearty, teaching the young ones how to work; my younger brother Pierre, a bachelor and formerly a sergeant in the army; my sister Agathe, a shrewd housewife, extremely stout and gay, who had come to live with us after her husband's death and whose laughter rang out from one end of the village to the other. Next came the whole brood: my son Jacques and Rose, his wife, with their three daughters, Aimée, Véronique and Marie. The first was married to Cyprien Bouisson, a strapping young fellow, to whom she had given two babies, one two years old and the other ten months old; Véronique, on her side, had just become engaged to Gaspard Rabuteau, while Marie, white and very fair, looked more like a town-born lady than a farmer's daughter. This made up ten; I was both a grandfather and a great-grandfather.

When we assembled round the supper table I used to place my sister Agathe on my right, my brother Pierre on my left, and the children completed the circle, seated by order of seniority, down to the mite but ten months old. The whole lot ate heartily, and how gay they all were between each mouthful! I felt both pride and pleasure glowing in my veins when the little ones, stretching out their hands to me, shouted:

"Grandfather, give us some more bread. A big piece, Grandfather, please!"

Those were glorious days. The busy house sang through all its windows; in the evenings Pierre invented new games or told old stories of his regiment; on Sundays Aunt Agathe baked cakes for the girls, and Marie knew some beautiful hymns which she sang with the voice of a young chorister, looking like a saint, too, with her fair hair falling low on her neck and her hands folded in her lap. At the time of Aimée's marriage with Cyprien I had added a story to the house, and I used to say jokingly that when Véronique married Gaspard I should have to add another, and that if I did so at each successive wedding the house would end by reaching the sky. None of us wanted to leave it; we would rather have erected a town in the enclosure behind the farm. When the members of a large family agree it is good to live and die on the spot where one was born.

This last spring the month of May was superb; the crops had not looked so promising for years. That day I went the round of the land with my son Jacques. We started at about three o'clock. Our meadows, still of a tender green, stretched alongside the Garonne; the grass had nearly reached its full height, and in a willow copse planted only last year there were shoots a yard long. We passed on, examining our cornfields and vineyards, the land bought bit by bit as our means increased. The wheat was growing apace; the vines were in full bloom, heralding a rich vintage. Jacques laughed his hearty laugh and, slapping me on the shoulder, said: "Well, Father, we shan't lack bread or wine. You must be in the good graces of God Almighty, as He lets money rain upon your land like this."

Jacques was right. I had no doubt gained the good graces of some saint in heaven, for all the good luck of the district appeared to fall on us. During a storm the hail would stop at the edge of our fields; if our neighbors' vines were ailing a protecting wall seemed to rise around ours, and gradually I had come to deem this just. Harming no one, I believed happiness to be my due.

On our way home we crossed some land belonging to us on the opposite side of the village. A plantation of mulberry trees was coming on splendidly, and the almond trees in a grove were bearing all they could. We chatted gaily and made plans for the future. As soon as we had saved the necessary capital we would purchase certain patches of ground lying between our various lots and thus become the owners of an entire corner of the parish. If the crops turned out as well as they promised our dream could be realized in the autumn.

As we drew near the farm we saw Rose gesticulating and shouting: "Come on, hurry up!"

One of our cows had just calved, and the whole household was astir. Aunt Agathe went rolling about, while the girls watched the little calf, whose advent seemed like an additional benison. Quite recently we had been compelled to enlarge our sheds, which contained nearly a hundred head of cattle without reckoning the horses.

"Another lucky day," I said. "We must have a bottle of good wine tonight."

Just then Rose took us aside to inform us that as Gaspard, Véronique's lover, had come to fix the wedding day, she had kept him to dinner. Gaspard, the eldest son of a farmer of Moranges, was a young man of twenty, known all through our part for his prodigious strength. At a public fete at Toulouse he had wrestled with and defeated Martial, the Lion of the South. Withal he was extremely good-natured and tenderhearted and so shy, indeed, that he blushed whenever Véronique's calm eyes met his own.

I told Rose to call him. He had stayed in the yard, helping the maids to hang out the linen of a three months' washing. When he entered the parlor, where we were all assembled, Jacques turned to me, saying, "It's for you to speak, Father."

"Well, my boy, you have come to settle the day," I said.

"Yes, that's why I came," he answered with a deep color on his cheeks.

"Don't blush, my lad," I resumed. "Shall we say the tenth of July, the day of Sainte Félicité? Today's the twenty-eighth of June, so you won't have long to wait. My poor dead wife's name was Félicité—it will be a good omen. Well, is it a settled thing?"

"Yes, all right; the day of Sainte Félicité will do," replied Gaspard.

Then as he came up to Jacques and me his hand fell on our outstretched palms with a might sufficient to fell an ox. Next he kissed Rose, calling her "mother." This stalwart young fellow with such redoubtable fists was losing sleep and flesh for love of Véronique; he told us that he should have fallen ill if we had not consented to let him have her.

"Now," I resumed, "let us go to our meal. All of you to your places. Thunder and lightning! I am as hungry as a wolf!"

That evening we sat down eleven. We had placed Gaspard and Véronique side by side, and he kept gazing at her, forgetting his supper and so disturbed by the thought that she was his that big tears moistened his eyelashes. Cyprien and Aimée, who had been married three years, smiled as they watched them; Jacques and Rose, with their twenty-five years of wedlock, were graver, still they stealthily exchanged moist glances, born of long-abiding tenderness. As for myself, I felt as if I were growing young again and living anew in those lovers, whose happiness seemed to bring a nook of paradise to our board. How excellent the soup tasted that evening! Aunt Agathe, who was always one for laughing, ventured to make a few jocose remarks, whereupon Pierre insisted upon relating his love passages with a lady of Lyons. Fortunately we had got to the dessert and were all talking at the same time. I had brought two bottles of sweet wine from the cellar, and we drank to Gaspard and Véronique's good luck, as the fashion is with us. Luck is never to quarrel, to have heaps of children and put by bags of money. Later on we had some singing; Gaspard knew some love ballads in our dialect, and by way of conclusion we asked Marie for a hymn. She stood up and began at once, her flutelike and delicate voice falling like a caress on the ear.

I had moved toward the window, and as Gaspard joined me I said, "There is nothing new over your way, is there?"

"No," he answered; "they talk a good deal about the heavy rains of the last few days; some say they might turn out badly."

It had, indeed, recently been raining during sixty consecutive hours, and since the previous day the Garonne had been greatly swollen; still we trusted her, and as long as she did not overflow we could not think of her as a dangerous neighbor. She was so useful; her expanse of water was so broad and gentle, and, moreover, peasants do not readily quit their homes even if the roof be about to fall.

"Nonsense," I said; "nothing will happen; it's the same every year. The river puts up its back as if it were in a rage, then it quiets down in a single night and subsides as gently as a lamb. Take my word, lad, it's only a joke. Just look out of the window and see what splendid weather we are having!"

Then with my hand I pointed to the sky.

It was seven o'clock; the sun was setting. All was blue; the sky showed like an immense expanse of azure, through which the sunset swam like golden dust. From above there slowly descended a delight, reaching to the verge of the distant horizon. I had never seen the village in such tender rest-fulness. A pink glow was fading under the eaves. I could hear a neighbor laughing and children chattering at the bend of the road opposite our house, while from farther off the lowing of herds returning to their sheds reached us, softened by the distance.

Meanwhile the deep roar of the Garonne sounded incessantly, but I was so used to the voice of the river that it seemed to be merely the voice of silence. By degrees the sky whitened and the village seemed falling into a serener sleep. It was the end of a beautiful day, and I fancied that all our happiness, our rich harvests, Véronique's engagement, came to us wafted from above, in the purity of the dying light. A benediction spread over us with the farewell of day.

I had returned to the center of the room where the girls were chatting merrily, and we were listening to them with smiling lips when suddenly, through the great peace of the twilight, an appalling shriek rang out—a shriek of terror and of death:

"The Garonne! The Garonne!"

CHAPTER II

The Garonne!

WE RAN to the yard.

Saint-Jory lies at the very bottom of a dip in the land, lower than the river and some five hundred yards away from it. A screen of poplars dividing some meadows shuts out all view of the water.

We could see nothing, but the shriek still resounded: "The Garonne! The Garonne!"

Then coming from the road in front of us, two men and three women abruptly appeared, one of the latter holding a child in her arms. They were shouting, frenzied with terror, and running as fast as they could over the hard ground. Every now and then they looked back with scared faces, as if they were being pursued by a pack of wolves.

"What has happened?" cried Cyprien. "Can you make out anything, Grandfather?"

"No," I answered; "the leaves are not even stirring."

The low line of the horizon lay still and peaceful, but before I had done speaking a sharp exclamation broke from the others. Behind the fugitives, between the trunks of the poplars, over the tall grass, we caught sight of something resembling a pack of gray, yellowish spotted animals racing onward. They appeared on all sides—waves hurrying upon waves, an invasion of masses of water crested with foam, shaking white saliva, and making the ground quiver with the heavy gallop of their serried ranks.

Then we also echoed the despairing cry, "The Garonne! The Garonne!"

The two men and the three women were still flying along the road, and they could hear the hideous gallop gaining upon them. Presently the waves formed in a single line, rolling and crashing with the thunder of charging battalions. Under their first onset three poplars snapped; their tall foliage tottered and disappeared. Then a shed was swollen up; a wall burst; unharnessed carts were carried away like wisps of straw. But the water seemed specially to pursue the fugitives. At a bend of the road, which is very steep at that particular spot, the flood suddenly fell in immense volume, cutting off their retreat. We saw them still attempting to run, splashing in the water, but silent now and maddened with fear. The waves rose to their knees; at last a huge billow dashed upon the woman who was carrying the child. Then all were submerged.

"Quick, quick!" I cried. "Come in! The house is strong. We have nothing to fear."

However, out of prudence we at once ascended to the first floor, making the girls pass before us; I was determined to be the last. Our house was built on a bank above the road, and the water was now slowly invading the yard with a soft little ripple. We were not much alarmed.

"Never mind," said Jacques reassuringly; "there is no danger. Do you remember, Father, how in '55 the water came into the yard just as it does now? It rose to a foot and then receded."

"It's a pity for the crops, anyhow," muttered Cyprien, half aloud.

"No, no; it won't be much," I said, noting the dilated, questioning eyes of the women. Aimée had laid her children on her bed and sat close to them with Véronique and Marie. Aunt Agathe talked of warming some wine which she had brought with her in order to cheer us. Jacques and Rose looked out of the window, and I stood at the other with my brother, Cyprien and Gaspard.

"Come up, can't you?" I called to the two maids who were paddling about in the yard. "Don't stop there and get your legs wet."

"But the poor beasts," they answered; "they are frightened and will get killed in the sheds."

"Never mind! Come up. We will look after the cattle presently."

If the water continued to rise it would be impossible to save the cattle, but I thought it best not to alarm the servants. I tried to appear quite at ease and, leaning over the window sill, I gave an account of the progress of the flood. After rushing to the assault of the village the river had taken possession of even its narrowest lanes. The race of the charging waves had ceased; there was now a stealthy, invincible invasion. The hollow in which Saint-Jory lies was being transformed into a lake. In our yard the water had risen to a height of three feet already: I watched its ascent, but I affirmed that it remained stationary, and once I even hinted that it was subsiding.

"You will have to sleep here tonight, my boy," I said, turning to Gaspard; "that is, unless the roads get clear in a few hours, which might easily be the case."

He looked at me; his face was very pale, and I saw his eyes turn to Véronique, gleaming the while with intolerable anguish.

It was half-past eight. Out of doors it was still light—a white glimmer.

unspeakably mournful, dropping from the pale sky. Before the maids joined us they had thought of bringing two lamps. I had them lit, hoping that they would brighten the darkening room in which we had taken refuge. Aunt Agathe now pushed a table forward and suggested a game of cards. The excellent woman, whose eyes sought mine anxiously every now and then, was especially desirous of diverting the children: her cheerfulness was grandly brave, and she laughed to conjure away the terror which she felt was creeping over all the others. The game was arranged; Aunt Agathe forced Aimée, Véronique and Marie into their chairs, placed the cards in their resistless fingers and began shuffling, dealing and cutting with such a flow of words that she almost stifled the sound of the rising flood. But our daughters could not fix their minds on the game; they remained pale, with feverish hands, bending their heads to listen. Every now and then one or another of them would turn uneasily and whisper:

"Grandfather, is it still rising?"

It *was* rising with fearful rapidity, but I answered carelessly, "No, no; go on playing—there is no danger."

Never before had I felt my heart wrung by such cruel dread. All the men had grouped themselves in front of the windows to shut out the appalling scene; we tried to look unconcerned when our faces were turned to the room, facing the lamps whose circular light fell on the table as amid the gentle peace of homely vigils. I remembered winter evenings when we had sat thus at the table. It was the same quiet picture, full of the soft warmth of affection. But while perfect peace dwelt within, I could hear behind my back the bellowing of the overflowing river, which was ever rising and rushing onward.

"Louis," whispered my brother Pierre, "the water is only three feet from the window; something must be done."

I pressed his arm to silence him, but it was too late to conceal our peril. The cattle had become frantic in the outhouses: we plainly heard the bleating and lowing of the maddened animals and particularly the wild shrieks of the horses who felt themselves in danger.

"Oh my God! My God!" murmured Aimée, who stood up, convulsed by a long shudder and with her closed fists pressed to her temples.

The women had all risen, and we were powerless to keep them from the windows; they stood there erect and mute, their hair lifted by a wind of terror. The twilight had come; a treacherous gleam hovered above the watery sheet; the pale sky looked like a white pall thrown over the earth; afar off some smoke was trailing; then everything became blurred: it was the close of a day of horror, sinking into a night of death. And not a human sound— only the dull roar of the infinitely widening expanse of water and the lowing and neighing of the frenzied animals!

"Oh God! Oh God!" repeated the women under their breath, as if afraid to speak aloud.

A loud crash silenced them. The infuriated cattle had broken through the stable doors; they passed by in the yellow flood, rolling as they were carried away by the current; the sheep were hurled along in droves like dead leaves whirling in pools; the cows and the horses struggled, trying to feel the ground but losing their footing; our big gray horse refused to die: he reared, stretched out his long neck and panted like the bellows of a forge till the eager waters dashed on his hindquarters, and then we saw him yield himself up and disappear.

Then for the first time we screamed; our cries seemed to come unconsciously, propelled by some alien will. With hands outstretched toward all those dear animals hurried away forever, we moaned and wept, sobbing aloud, giving vent to the tears and lamentations we had restrained. It was indeed our ruin! The crops lost, the cattle drowned, our fortune gone in a few brief hours! Oh, God was not just! We had not offended Him, and yet He had taken back all He had given! I shook my fist at heaven! I recalled our afternoon walk, the meadows, the wheat fields, the vineyards, all so promising! They had all lied! Happiness had lied! The very sun, when he had set so gently and calmly in the deep serenity of evening, had lied.

The flood was still rising, and all at once my brother Pierre, who had been watching it, exclaimed sharply: "Louis, look out! The water has reached the windows. We can't stay here."

These words broke upon our despair. I pulled myself together and, shrugging my shoulders, said, "After all, money is nothing. As long as we are all together and safe there is nothing to regret. We must begin work afresh; that is all."

"Yes, yes—you are right, Father," returned Jacques feverishly, "and we *are* safe—the walls are solid. Let us get upon the roof."

It was our only refuge. The water, after mounting the staircase step by step with a persevering gurgle, was entering at the door. We repaired to the loft, keeping close together, with the vague instinct which makes people in peril anxious to remain side by side. Cyprien alone had vanished. I called to him, and he came out of an adjoining room with a white, scared face. Then as I suddenly became aware of the absence of the two maids and stopped to wait for them, he looked at me strangely and whispered:

"Dead—the outbuilding where their room was has just given way."

The poor creatures must have gone to get their savings out of their boxes. Cyprien, in the same tone, told me that they had managed to throw a ladder across to the building where they slept and had used it as a bridge. I warned him to say nothing, but I felt a great chill at the back of my neck. It was the breath of death entering our house.

We did not even think of turning out the lamps when we went up to the roof in our turn; the cards remained spread out on the table; there was a foot of water in the room.

CHAPTER III

A Crisis

FORTUNATELY the roof was broad and the incline a gentle one. It was reached by a skylight opening on to a little platform, upon which our party took refuge. The women sat down, and presently the men stepped out on the tiles to reconnoiter, going as far as the two tall chimney stacks at either end of the roof. I remained leaning against the aperture of the skylight, looking toward the four points of the horizon.

"Help cannot fail to come soon," I said with forced hopefulness. "The folks of Saintin have some boats, and they will pass this way. See over there, isn't that a lantern on the water?"

I received no answer. Pierre had mechanically lighted his pipe and was smoking so furiously that with every puff he spat out bits of the stem which he had broken between his teeth. Jacques and Cyprien stared into the distance with mournful faces, while Gaspard, with clenched fists, went on pacing the roof as if seeking for some outlet. The women, crouching and shuddering at our feet, covered their eyes to avoid the terrible sight. Presently, however, Rose, raising her head, looked round her.

"Where are the servants?" she asked. "Why don't they come up?"

I pretended not to hear, but she turned to me and fixed her eyes on mine.

"Where are the girls?" she repeated.

I turned away. I could not lie to her, and I felt that the deadly chill which had already touched me was passing over our wives and daughters. They had understood. Marie rose to her full height; a deep sigh parted her lips, and then, sinking down, she burst into a passion of tears. Aimée kept the heads of her two children in her lap, covering them up with her skirts as if to shield them. Véronique, who had her face in her hands, remained motionless. Aunt Agathe, growing paler, was repeatedly making the sign of the cross and muttering Paters and Aves.

All around us the scene was one of supreme grandeur. The night, which had now completely fallen, had the clear limpidity of summer darkness. There was no moon as yet, but the sky was studded with countless stars, and it was of so pure a blue that all the surrounding space was filled with an azure light. The horizon was so clearly defined that it seemed to harbor the twilight, and meanwhile the immense sheet of water, spreading out under the soft skies, became quite white, luminous as with a glow of its own, a phosphorescence which tipped the crest of every wave with tiny flamelets. Land was nowhere visible; the whole plain must have been submerged. One evening on the coast near Marseilles I had seen the sea looking like this and had remained gazing at it, transfixed with admiration.

"The water rises; the water rises," repeated my brother Pierre, still biting the stem of his pipe, which he had allowed to go out.

Indeed, the water was now only a yard from the edge of the roof. It was losing its tranquillity, its lakelike quietude, and currents were forming. When it reached a certain height we were no longer sheltered by the rising ground before the village, and as soon as this was covered, in less than an hour's time, the flood became threatening, lashing the houses with all the wreckage, staved-in barrels, timbers and trusses of hay, which it carried on its bosom. In the distance we heard the deafening shocks of the onsets against the walls. Poplars snapped and fell with a sinister splash, and houses crashed down like cartfuls of stones turned over on the roadside.

Jacques, unnerved by the women's sobs, kept on repeating: "We cannot stop here. Something must be done. Father, I implore you, let us try something."

Hesitating and stammering, I repeated after him: "Yes, yes, let us try something."

And none of us knew what to try. Gaspard proposed that he should take Véronique on his back and swim away with her. Pierre suggested a raft. They were both crazy. At last, however, Cyprien said: "If we could only reach the church."

And, indeed, high above the flood the church still rose up intact with its little square tower. We were separated from it by seven dwellings. Our house, the first of the village, adjoined a taller building, which in its turn leaned against its neighbor. It might be feasible to reach the presbytery by the roofs, and thence it would be easy to get into the church. Many of the villagers had already sought that refuge probably, for the neighboring roofs were deserted, and we heard a murmur of voices which certainly came from the belfry. But at best it was a perilous and uncertain undertaking.

"It is impossible," said Pierre. "Rambeau's house is too lofty; we should need some ladders."

"At any rate, I'll go and see," said Cyprien. "If we cannot get across I'll return; if we can we must all go, the men carrying the women."

I let him start. He was right: situated as we were, everything must be attempted. With the help of an iron clamp fixed to a chimney stack he had just succeeded in climbing onto the next house when his wife Aimée raised her eyes and saw that he was gone.

"Where is he?" she said. "I will not let him leave me. We are one—we must die together."

Then as she caught sight of him on the other roof she darted across the tiles, still carrying her children.

"Wait for me, Cyprien," she panted; "I am coming with you. I will die with you."

She would not be denied. Her husband, leaning over, implored her to remain with us, promising to return and assuring her that he was only acting for our common rescue. But shaking her head and with a wild look in her eyes, she still repeated excitedly: "I am coming with you. I will die with you."

He yielded; first he took the children, and then he helped his wife to climb up to him. We could see them walking slowly on the apex of the roof.

Aimée had again taken her weeping children in her arms, and at every step Cyprien turned and supported her.

"As soon as she is in safety," I shouted, "come back to us."

I saw him wave his hand, but the roar of the water did not allow me to hear his answer. They were soon out of sight; they had descended onto the house beyond, the roof of which was lower. Five minutes later they again appeared on the third roof, which must have been very steep, for we could see that they were crawling up it on their knees. A sudden dread possessed me and, raising my hands to my mouth, I shouted out with all my strength: "Come back, come back!"

All of us, Pierre, Jacques and Gaspard, called to them to return; our voices seemed to stay them for a moment, but they soon moved on. They had reached the corner where the street turned in front of Rambeau's house, a tall building rising nearly nine feet above all the neighboring roofs. For a moment they wavered, and then Cyprien began to climb up a chimney with catlike agility. Aimée, who had evidently consented to wait for him, remained erect amid the tiles. We could plainly distinguish her clasping her babies to her bosom, standing out black against the clear sky and looking much taller than she really was. It was then that the awful catastrophe began.

Rambeau's house, originally intended for some business purposes, was very flimsily built, and, moreover, its frontage received the full shock of the current in the street. I fancied I could see it tremble under the onset of flood, and with bated breath I watched Cyprien's progress along the roof. Suddenly we heard a deep growl. The round moon had risen, freely pacing the sky, her yellow disk lighting up the immense lake with the clear brightness of a lamp. Not a single detail was lost to us. That growl was the noise of Rambeau's house falling in. A scream of terror escaped us as we saw Cyprien sink down. In that tempestuous crash we could only see the splashing of the waves under the remnants of the roof. Then all was calm again; the lake became level once more, with the black carcass of the submerged house bristling above the water with its snapped floors—a confused mass of tangled timbers, looking like the framework of some half-destroyed cathedral. Between those timbers I thought I could see a body moving, a living form wrestling with superhuman efforts.

"He lives!" I cried. "Ah, blessed be God, he lives! There, above that white sheet of water lit up by the moon!"

We shook with hysterical laughter and clapped our hands for joy, as if all danger had passed away.

"He will get up again," said Pierre.

"Yes, yes," explained Gaspard. "See? He is trying to catch hold of the beam on his left."

But our laughter was suddenly hushed. We remained dumb, silenced by anxiety. We had just realized in what an awful position Cyprien had now found himself. In the fall of the house his feet had been caught between two beams, and he was hanging head downward at a few inches above the water and quite unable to free himself. His agony was horrible. On the roof of the other house stood Aimée with her two children, shaken by convulsive shudders. There she remained, a witness of her husband's death struggle, never once taking her eyes off him. From her rigid lips there came a continuous lugubrious sound, like the howl of a dog frenzied by terror.

"We cannot let him die like that," said Jacques in distraction. "We must go to him."

"One might crawl down the beams, perhaps," muttered Pierre, "and disengage him."

They were already moving toward the nearest roof when the house it covered suddenly shook and crumbled in its turn. The way was cut off. Our blood froze in our veins. We seized each other's hands and pressed them nervously, unable to turn our eyes away from the ghastly sight.

Cyprien had at first attempted to stiffen himself, and with extraordinary muscular strength he had finally succeeded in getting farther away from the water and maintaining a sidelong position. But fatigue was mastering him; he tried to resist, to lay hold of the beams, beating the air with his arms in the hope of finding something to which he might cling; then, accepting death, he fell back and again hung down quite motionless. Death was slow to come; his hair barely touched the water, which was patiently rising—he must have felt its coolness on his head. A first wave wet his brow; another closed his eyes—slowly his head vanished from our view.

The women, huddled at our feet, hid their faces with their clasped hands. We fell on our knees with outstretched arms, stammering supplications and crying bitterly. On the other roof Aimée, still erect, with her children close pressed to her bosom, shrieked still louder and louder amid the night.

CHAPTER IV

THE BATTLE

I CANNOT TELL how long the stupor of that crisis lasted. When I recovered my senses the water was higher still; it now reached the tiles, and our roof was only a narrow island, barely emerging from the immense watery expanse. On the right and left the houses had fallen. The sea was widening on all sides.

"We are moving," whispered Rose as she clutched at the tiles.

And, indeed, we all felt a pitching motion, as if the roof had changed into a floating raft; the heavy swell seemed to carry us along. It was only by turning to the motionless church tower that we got rid of this delusion and realized that we were on the same spot amid the angry surf.

It was then that the siege began in earnest. The current so far had followed the street, but the increasing wreckage that barred the way now caused it to flow back. A furious onset commenced. As soon as a plank or beam passed within the current's grasp it was seized, swung round and hurled like a ram against our house; the water never loosened its grasp; the current sucked the wreckage back merely to launch it again at our walls, which it assailed with regular repeated blows. Sometimes ten or twelve large pieces of wood would attack us at once on all sides. The water hissed; foamy splashes wet our feet. We heard the dull moan of the sonorous house filling with water and the creaking of the broken partitions, and whenever a more savage assault made the whole building quiver, we fancied that it was all over—that the walls were opening and giving us up to the river through their yawning breaches.

Gaspard, who had ventured to the very edge of the roof, succeeded in catching a passing beam, which he dragged out of the water with his powerful athletic arms.

"We must defend ourselves," he shouted.

Then Jacques, with the assistance of Pierre, endeavored to stop a long pole. I cursed my old age, which left me useless and as weak as a child. However, the defense was being organized; it was the fight of three men against the flood. Gaspard, armed with his beam, waited for the passing timbers, which the current turned into battering-rams, and kept them off at some little distance from the walls. The shock at times was so great that he fell down. Meantime Pierre and Jacques were maneuvering with their long pole, shoving away the nearer wreckage.

This fierce and senseless battle lasted during nearly an hour. As the time passed the combatants grew wildly excited; they beat the water, insulted it and swore at it. Gaspard hacked at it as if in a bodily struggle, lunged out with his beam as if he were trying to pierce a human breast. And all this time the water remained quietly obstinate, without a wound—invincible. Jacques and Pierre at last sank down on the roof, exhausted, and Gaspard, while making a final effort, saw the current wrest his beam from his grasp and hurl it against us. The struggle had become impossible.

Marie and Véronique, clasped in each other's arms, were repeating the same words in broken tones—words of terror, the echo of which still sounds incessantly in my ears: "I will not die! I will not die!"

Rose embraced them both, trying to reassure and comfort them, but at last she herself, trembling and shivering, lifted her white face and unconsciously cried aloud, "I will not die!"

Aunt Agathe alone remained quite silent. She had ceased praying and crossing herself. In a sort of dumb stupor she now let her eyes wander over the scene, and whenever they chanced to meet mine she still attempted a smile.

The water was lapping the tiles. No help could reach us now. We still heard the sound of voices issuing from the church; two lanterns had gleamed for an instant in the distance, then again the silence deepened amid the desolate immensity of the yellow expanse. In all probability the people of Saintin who owned some boats had been surprised by the flood before us.

Gaspard was still wandering about the roof, and suddenly he called to us, saying: "Look out! Help me—hold me tight!"

He had again snatched hold of a passing timber and was lying in wait for a huge black mass which was slowly swimming toward us. It was the broad, solid plank roof of a shed, wrenched away entire and floating like a raft.

When it came within reach Gaspard arrested it, and, feeling that he was being dragged off, he called to us to help him. We seized him round the waist and clasped him tight. As soon as the wreck entered the current it advanced of its own accord against our roof, coming forward with so much violence that for a moment we feared we should see it fly asunder.

However, Gaspard boldly jumped upon this raft thus sent to us by Providence; he walked all over it to make sure of its strength, while Jacques and Pierre maintained it in position at the edge of our roof. Then he began to laugh and said exultingly, "You see, Grandfather, we are saved. Come, you women, leave off crying! It is as good as a real boat. Look here, my feet are dry. It can carry us all too. It feels like home already."

However, he thought it better to strengthen it and, securing some more beams, he bound them with some ropes which Pierre had happened to bring up with him on the chance of their being wanted. While thus engaged Gaspard once fell overboard, but he soon came up again and answered our cry of alarm with renewed hilarity.

"The Garonne knows me," he laughed; "I have often swum it for a league at a time." Then when he had got on the roof again he shook himself and exclaimed, "Come aboard—there's no time to lose!"

The women had fallen on their knees, and Gaspard had to carry Véronique and Marie to the middle of the raft, where he made them sit down. Rose and Agathe slipped off the tiles unaided and joined the girls. At that moment I again glanced toward the church. Aimée was still on the same roof, only she was now leaning against a chimney stack, holding her children aloft with rigidly uplifted arms. The water had risen to her waist.

"Do not worry, Grandfather," said Gaspard. "I promise you that we'll pick her up as we pass by."

Pierre and Jacques were already on the raft. I jumped after them. It tilted over a little on one side but seemed strong enough to carry us all. Gaspard was the last to leave the roof and gave each of us one of the poles which he had in readiness to be used as oars, he himself keeping a very long one, which he handled with great dexterity. He had taken command, and by his instructions we all pressed against the tiles with our poles, trying to shove off. But our efforts were fruitless; the raft seemed to adhere to the roof; at every fresh attempt we made the current hurled us back against the house. We were incurring great danger, for every fresh shock threatened to shatter the boards on which we stood.

Once more we became conscious of our impotency. We had thought ourselves saved, but we still belonged to the greedy river. I even began to regret that the women had left the roof, for I expected every minute to see them hurled into the furious water and carried away. But when I suggested that we should return to the house they one and all rebelled.

"No, no, let us try again," they pleaded, "or die here."

Gaspard was not laughing now. We multiplied our efforts, weighing on the poles with feverish strength, but all in vain. At last Pierre had an idea. He climbed onto the roof again and with a long rope managed to pull the raft to the left and get it out of the current. Then after he had jumped onto the raft again a few strokes of our poles enabled us to get into the open.

But Gaspard remembered his promise to rescue my poor Aimée, whose plaintive wail had not once ceased. To effect the rescue it was necessary to cross the street where raged that terrible current against which we had fought so desperately. He cast a questioning look at me. I was overcome. Never had I been placed in so cruel an alternative. Eight lives must be endangered, and yet if for their sakes I hesitated just one moment, I lacked the strength to resist the mother's lugubrious call.

"Yes, yes," I said to Gaspard. "We cannot go without her."

He bent his head in silence and began to ply his pole, taking advantage of such walls as were still standing. We slowly skirted the adjoining house, passing over our own cowsheds, but as soon as we turned the bend of the street we shrieked aloud. The current had captured us again and was carrying us off, forcing us back to our roof.

It lasted only a few seconds. We were indeed whirled away so suddenly that the screams we immediately raised expired amid the deafening crash of the raft against the tiles. It was rent asunder; the shivered boards were scattered, and we were hurled into the foaming whirlpool. I do not know what followed. I only remember that as I fell I saw Aunt Agathe lying at full length on the water, buoyed up by her skirts. Then without a struggle she slowly sank, her head thrown backward.

A sharp pain made me open my eyes. Pierre was dragging me by the hair along the tiles. I remained lying there, stupefied, with open eyes. Pierre had left me to dive again, and in the confusion of my mind I thought it strange when I espied Gaspard on the spot just vacated by my brother. The young man had Véronique in his arms. He laid her near me, plunged in again and brought up Marie, who was so white, rigid and motionless that I thought her dead. Then for the third time he threw himself into the water, but now he sought in vain and returned empty handed. Pierre had joined him; they were talking low, and I could not hear what they said. As they were coming, seemingly quite exhausted, up the incline of the roof I moaned out: "And Aunt Agathe and Jacques and Rose?"

They shook their heads; big tears were welling in their eyes. From the brief, husky words they spoke I gathered that Jacques's brains had been dashed out by a passing beam. Rose had clung to her husband's corpse and been dragged away with it. As for Aunt Agathe, she had not reappeared; we presumed that her body, driven forward by the current, had entered the house beneath us through one of the open windows.

Raising myself, I turned toward the chimney stack which Aimée had been clutching hold of a few moments previously. The flood had risen higher still; Aimée was no longer wailing; I only saw her two stiffened arms holding the children above the water. Then all collapsed: the sheet of water closed over her arms and her babes amid the sleepy glimmer of the full moon.

CHAPTER V

DARKNESS

THERE WERE now only five of us on the roof. The water had left us but a narrow dry strip on the crest of the tiles. One of the chimney stacks had been swept away. We had to raise Véronique and Marie, who had fainted, and keep them erect to prevent the surf from wetting their legs. At last they regained consciousness, and our anguish increased as we saw them shivering in their soaked garments and heard them wailing that they would not die. We comforted them as one quiets children, assuring them that they were not going to die, that we would prevent death from taking them. But they no longer believed us; they realized that their life was nearly spent. Each time that the word "die" fell like a knell from their lips their teeth chattered, and mutual dread threw them into each other's arms.

It was the end. A few ruined walls marked here and there the spot where the submerged village had stood. The church, alone intact, raised its belfry on high, and a sound of voices still proceeded from it, telling of people who were safely sheltered. In the distance the vast overflow of the raging waters roared continuously. We no longer heard the crash of crumbling houses, resembling the rough unloading of gravel on a road. The wreck was forsaken as if it were in mid-ocean, a thousand miles from land.

Once we fancied that we detected a splash of oars on our left: it was like a rhythmical, gentle beat growing clearer and nearer. Ah, what a hopeful music it seemed! We craned our necks forward to question space. We held our breath. But we saw nothing. The yellow expanse stretched out, spotted with black, shadowy things, but none of those things, crests of trees, fragments of shattered walls, were stirring. Tufts of herbage, empty barrels, planks, brought us delusive joys. We waved our handkerchiefs till, recognizing our error, we again became the prey of anxiety, wondering whence came the sound that ever fell upon our ears.

"Ah, I see it!" suddenly cried Gaspard. "A large boat—look, over there!"

And with his outstretched arm he pointed to a distant spot. Neither Pierre nor I could distinguish anything, but Gaspard obstinately insisted that it was a boat. The strokes of the oars became more distinct, and finally we all saw it. It was moving slowly, and it seemed to be circling round us without drawing any nearer. I remember that we then became almost mad, waving our arms, raving, shouting, insanely apostrophizing the boat, insulting it and calling it a coward. The craft, still silent and dark, appeared to turn more slowly. Was it really a boat? I cannot tell; I only know that when we realized that it was gone we felt that it had carried our last hope away.

After that we expected every second to be engulfed in the fall of the house. By this time it must be undermined and was probably only held up by some stouter wall, which would drag down the whole building when it gave way. What especially terrified me was to feel the roof sinking under our weight;

the house might possibly have resisted all night, but the tiles were loosened and broken by the attacking beams. We took refuge on the left, where the rafters seemed to be less impaired, but even there they soon seemed to weaken and would infallibly yield if the five of us remained together on so narrow a space.

For the last few moments my brother Pierre had mechanically placed his pipe between his lips again. He was twisting his thick, military-looking mustache and muttering confusedly, with his dark brows knit. The increasing peril which surrounded us on all sides and against which there was no possible fighting made him more and more irritated. He had two or three times spat into the water with angry contempt; then as we were sinking more and more, he made up his mind and walked down the slope of the roof.

"Pierre! Pierre!" I cried, afraid to understand.

He turned and answered quietly, "Good-by, Louis; this lasts too long to suit me, and my going will give you more room."

Then having thrown his pipe into the water, he resolutely flung himself after it, adding: "Good night; I've had enough of it!"

He did not rise again; he was but an indifferent swimmer, and no doubt he surrendered himself to the flood, brokenhearted by our ruin, the loss of those he loved, and feeling unwilling to survive them.

Two o'clock struck at the church tower. The night was almost over, that horrible night, so full of agony and tears. The dry strip under our feet was gradually becoming smaller. There was a soft gurgle of running water, with little caressing wavelets playing and tossing. Then again the current changed; the wreckage was carried to the right of the village, floating lazily along, as if the flood, now seemingly about to reach its greatest height, were resting, weary and satisfied.

All at once Gaspard removed his shoes and coat. During the last moment or two I had watched him wringing his hands and crushing his fingers. In answer to my question he said: "Listen, Grandfather. It kills me to wait here. I cannot stop any longer. Let me act—I can save her!"

He was alluding to Véronique. I attempted to reason with him, saying that he would never be strong enough to swim with the girl as far as the church. But he obstinately insisted, repeating: "I love her—I shall save her!"

I remained silent, simply drawing Marie to my breast. He thought, no doubt, that I was reproaching him with his loverlike selfishness.

"I will come back for Marie," he stammered; "I swear it. I will find a boat somehow and manage to get help. Trust me, Grandfather!"

He stripped, merely retaining his trousers, and then in a low and hurried voice he gave some urgent advice to Véronique, telling her not to struggle but to yield herself to him and, above all, not to get alarmed. The girl stared at him and huskily answered "Yes" to each sentence he spoke.

At last, having made the sign of the cross, although he was not habitually devout, he let himself slide down the roof, holding Véronique by a rope which he had passed under her arms. She gave a loud scream, beat the water with her limbs and fainted away.

"It is best so!" shouted Gaspard. "Now I can answer for her."

With unspeakable anguish I watched their progress. On the white water I easily discerned Gaspard's slightest movements; he supported the girl by means of the rope which he had also twined around himself, and he had thrown her partially across his right shoulder. Her dead weight occasionally made him sink, but he rallied, swimming on with supernatural energy.

I was getting hopeful, for he had already covered one third of the distance, when he struck against some obstacle—some wall hidden below the water's surface. The shock was appalling; they both disappeared. Then I saw Gaspard rise alone; the rope had broken. He plunged twice, and finally he reappeared, again carrying Véronique. He slung her upon his back, but as the supporting rope was gone, she weighed him down more heavily than before. In spite of this he was still advancing. A moment later, as they neared the church, I began to tremble violently; then suddenly I attempted to call out, for I had caught sight of some floating timber coming upon them sideways. My mouth remained wide open; a second concussion parted them; then the waters met again, but they were gone.

From that moment I remained stupefied, retaining merely the animal instinct of self-preservation and shrinking back whenever the water gained on me. Amid this stupor I continued hearing a sound of laughter without understanding whence it came. The day was rising in a great white dawn; the air was pleasant, very fresh and very calm, as it is beside a mere before the sunrise. But laughter still rang out, and on turning round I saw Marie standing near me in her dripping garments. It was she who was laughing!

How sweet and gentle she looked, poor darling, amid the advent of the morning! I saw her stoop, take a little water in the hollow of her palm and bathe her face. Then she twisted her rich golden hair and bound it round her head. She was dressing; she fancied herself back in her little room preparing for church on a Sunday morning while the bells were ringing merrily, and still she laughed her childish laughter, with a happy face and serene, clear eyes.

Her madness was contagious, for I began to laugh with her; terror had demented her, and it was a mercy vouchsafed by heaven, for she seemed conscious only of the enchanting beauty of the springtide dawn.

I watched her quietly, nodding gently and without comprehending. She went on with her toilet till she considered herself ready to start, and then, raising her pure crystalline voice, she began to sing one of her favorite hymns. Presently, however, she stopped, and, as if answering a call which she alone could hear, she cried: "I am coming! I am coming!"

Then resuming her chant, she descended the incline of the roof and stepped into the water, which softly, tenderly, closed over her without shock or struggle. For myself, I continued to smile, looking with a happy, contented face on the spot where she had disappeared.

After that I do not remember. I was quite alone on the roof, the water touching me. A single chimney stack remained standing, and I think I must have clung to it with all my strength, like an animal who refuses to perish. Beyond that I know nothing—nothing—all is black and vacant in my mind.

CHAPTER VI

Heroic Love

WHY AM I HERE? I have been told that the people of Saintin arrived at about six o'clock with their boats and found me in a dead faint, hanging onto the chimney. The water had been so cruel as not to take me away with those I loved while I remained unconscious of my bereavement.

I—the old one—have obstinately lived on. All the others are gone, the children in swaddling clothes, the girls and their lovers, the young and the old married couples. And yet I remain living like a coarse, dry weed rooted to the stones. If I had the courage I would do what Pierre did. Like him, I would say, "Good night; I have had enough of this," and then I would fling myself into the Garonne, following the course that all the others have taken. I have not one child left me; my house is a ruin; my fields lie waste. Oh, for the nights when we all sat at the table, the elders in the center, the young ones in a row, when their merriment warmed my blood! Oh, for the grand days of harvest and vintage, when we all toiled together and came home in the gloaming, exultant in the pride of our wealth! Oh, for the handsome children and the fair vines, the lovely girls and the golden corn, the joy of my old age, the living reward of my whole life! Now that all this is dead and gone, tell me, O God, why wilt Thou have me stay?

I cannot be comforted. I want no help. I shall give my land to those of the village folk who possess children, for they will have the heart to clear it and till it afresh. Those who have no children need but a corner wherein to die.

I have had one wish, a last desire—I wanted to find the corpses of my dear ones and to bury them in our churchyard under a stone which would someday cover me also. I heard that a great many bodies which had been washed away by the river had been recovered at Toulouse, so I started to go and see them.

Was there ever so ghastly a scene? Nearly two thousand houses destroyed, seven hundred victims, all the bridges swept away, a whole district of the city razed, drowned in the mud; poignant tragedies, twenty thousand wretches half naked and dying of starvation, the town poisoned by the stench of unburied corpses and terrified by the fear of typhus. And mourning everywhere, funerals in all the streets, distress such as no alms could allay. But I walked on among the ruins of others, regardless of aught save my own—my own dear dead, the thought of whom weighed me down.

People told me that many bodies had been found and that they had already been buried in long rows in the cemetery. However, the precaution had been taken to photograph the unrecognized ones. It was among the piteous portraits shown me that I came across those of Gaspard and Véronique. The lovers were still clasped in a passionate embrace; they had given and received their nuptial kiss in death. They clung to each other so closely, mouth pressed to mouth and arms entwined, that it would have been impossible to part them without breaking their limbs. So they had been photographed together, and they slept united beneath the sod.

And that is all I have left, that horrible picture of those two fair children, disfigured and swollen by the water, but still bearing on their livid faces the imprint of their heroic love. I gaze upon them and I weep.

NANTAS

CHAPTER I
His Room

THE ROOM in which Nantas had resided since his arrival from Marseilles was on the top floor of a house in the Rue de Lille, next to the mansion of Baron Danvilliers, a member of the Council of State. This house belonged to the baron, who had built it on the site of some old outbuildings. By leaning out of his window Nantas could see a corner of the baron's garden, across which some magnificent trees cast their shade. Beyond, by looking over their leafy crests, a glimpse of Paris was to be had: the open space left by the Seine, with the Tuileries, the Louvre, the quays, a whole sea of roofs and the Père Lachaise Cemetery in the dim distance.

Nantas's room was a small attic with a dormer window amid the tiles. He had furnished it simply with a bed, a table and a chair. He had taken up his abode there because he was attracted by the low rent and had made up his mind to rough it until he found a situation of some kind. The dirty paper, the black ceiling, the general misery and barrenness of this garret did not deter him. Living in sight of the Louvre and the Tuileries, he compared himself with a general sleeping in some miserable inn at the roadside, within view of the wealthy city which he means to carry by assault on the morrow.

Nantas's story was a short one. The son of a Marseilles mason, he had begun his studies at the lycée in that city, stimulated by the ambitious affection of his mother, who had set her heart upon making a gentleman of him. His parents had stinted themselves to give him a good education, but, his mother having died, Nantas had been obliged to accept an unprofitable situation in the office of a merchant, where for twelve years he had led a life of exasperating monotony. He would have taken himself off a score of times if his sense of filial duty had not tied him to Marseilles, for his father, who had fallen from a scaffolding, was quite unable to work. One night, however, when Nantas returned home, he found the old fellow dead, with his pipe lying still warm at his side. Three days later the young man had sold the few sticks about the place and started for Paris with just two hundred francs in his pocket.

Nantas had inherited boundless ambition from his mother. He was a young fellow of ready decision and firm will, and even when quite a boy he had been wont to say that he was a power. He was often laughed at when he so far forgot himself as to repeat his favorite expression confidingly, "I am a power," an expression which sounded comical, indeed, when one looked at him in his thin black coat, all out at the elbows and with the cuffs halfway up his arms. However, he had gradually made power a religion, seeing nothing else in the world and feeling convinced that the strong are necessarily the successful. According to his idea, to be willing and able ought to suffice one. All the rest was of no importance.

One Sunday while he was walking about alone in the scorching suburbs of Marseilles, he felt genius within him; in his innermost being there was, as it were, an instinctive impulse driving him onward, and when he went home to eat a plateful of potatoes with his bedridden father he determined in his own mind that someday or other he would carve his own way in that world in which, at the age of thirty, he was still a nonentity. This was no low greed, no appetite for vulgar pleasures, on his part; it was the clearly defined longing of a will and intellect which, not being in their proper sphere, strove to attain to that sphere by the natural force of logic.

As soon as Nantas felt the paving stones of Paris under his feet he thought that he had merely to put forth his hands to find a situation worthy of him. On the very first day he began his search. He had been given various letters of introduction, which he presented, and, moreover, he called upon several of his own countrymen, thinking that they would help him. But at the end of a month there was still no result. The times were bad, people said; besides which, they merely made promises to break them. His little store of money was swiftly diminishing—indeed, at the most, some twenty francs were left him. It was upon those twenty francs, however, that he was forced to live for another month, eating nothing but bread, scouring Paris from morning till evening and going home to bed without a light, feeling tired to death and still as poor as ever. His courage did not fail him, but mute anger arose within him. Destiny appeared to be illogical and unjust.

One evening Nantas returned home supperless. He had finished his last morsel of bread on the day before. No money and not a friend to lend him even a franc. Rain had been falling all day, one of those raw downfalls which are so cold in Paris. Rivers of mud were running in the streets, and Nantas, drenched to the skin, had gone to Bercy and afterward to Montmartre, where he had been told of employment. But the situation at Bercy was filled, and at Montmartre they had decided that his handwriting was not good enough. Those were his two last hopes. He would have accepted anything, with the certainty that he would soon command success. He only asked for bread at first, something to live upon in Paris, a foundation stone upon which he might build his fortune. He walked slowly from Montmartre to the Rue de Lille with his heart full of bitterness. The rain had ceased falling, and busy throngs crowded the streets. He stopped for a few minutes in front of a money-changer's office. Five francs would perhaps suffice him to become one day the master of them all. On five francs he could indeed live for a week, and in a week a man may achieve great things. While he was dreaming thus a cab ran against him and splashed him with mud. He then walked on more quickly, setting his teeth and experiencing a savage desire to rush with clenched fists upon the crowd which barred his way. It would have been taking a kind of vengeance for the cruelty of fate.

In the Rue Richelieu he was almost run over by an omnibus, but he made his way to the Place du Carrousel, whence he threw a jealous glance at the Tuileries. On the Saints-Pères Bridge a little well-dressed girl obliged him to deviate from the straight path which he was following with the obstinacy of a wild boar tracked by hounds, and this deviation appeared to him a supreme humiliation. The very children impeded his progress! Finally when he had taken refuge in his room, as a wounded animal returns to its lair to die, he threw himself heavily upon his chair, dead-beat, gazing at his trousers which the mud had stiffened and at his worn-out boots which had left wet marks along the floor.

The end had come then. Nantas debated how he should kill himself. His pride held good, and he imagined that his suicide would injure Paris. To be a power, to feel one's own worth and not to find a soul to appreciate you, not one to give you the first crown which you have ever wanted! It seemed monstrous to him, and his whole being revolted at the thought. Then he felt immense regret as his glance fell upon his useless arms. No work had any terror for him. With the tip of his little finger he would have raised the world, and yet there he was, cast into a corner, reduced to impotence and fuming with impatience like a caged lion! But presently he became calmer; death seemed to him grander. When he was a little boy he had been told the story of an inventor who, having constructed a marvelous machine, had one day smashed it to pieces with a hammer because of the indifference of the world. Well, he was like that man; he bore within him a new force, a rare mechanism of intelligence and will, and he was about to destroy his machine by dashing out his brains in the street.

The sun was going down behind the tall trees of the Danvilliers mansion; an autumn sun it was, with golden rays lighting up the yellow leaves. Nantas rose as if attracted by the farewell beams of the heavenly body. He was about to die; he wanted light. For a moment he leaned out of the window. Between the masses of foliage he had often seen a tall, fair young girl walking with a queenly step in the garden. He was not romantic; he had passed that age when young men in garrets dream that wellborn ladies approach them with their love and fortunes. Yet it chanced that at this supreme hour of suicide he suddenly recollected that fair and haughty girl. What could be her name? He knew not. But at the same time he clenched his fists, for his only feeling was one of hatred for the inhabitants of that mansion, glimpses of whose luxury were afforded him by the partially opened windows, and he muttered in a burst of rage:

"I would sell myself; I would sell myself if someone would only give me the first coppers I need for my fortune to come!"

This idea of selling himself occupied his mind for a moment. If there had been such a place as a pawnshop where people advanced money on energy and willingness, he would have gone and pledged himself. He set about imagining cases: a politician might buy him to make a tool of him, a banker to make use of every atom of his intelligence; and he accepted, scorning honor and telling himself that it would suffice if he someday acquired strength and ended by winning the fight. Then he smiled. Did a man ever get a chance to sell himself? Rogues, who watch every opportunity, die of want without finding a purchaser. Now that suicide seemed his only course he was fearful lest he should be overcome by cowardice, and he tried in this way to divert his thoughts. He had sat down again, swearing that he would throw himself out of the window as soon as it was dark.

So great was his fatigue, however, that he fell asleep upon his chair. Suddenly he was awakened by the sound of a voice. It was the doorkeeper of the house, who was showing a lady into his room.

"Sir," the doorkeeper began, "I took the liberty to come up——"

Then seeing no light in the room, she quickly went downstairs and fetched a candle. She seemed to know the person whom she had brought with her and showed herself at once complaisant and respectful.

"There," she said, on leaving the room after placing the candle on the table, "you can talk at your ease; nobody will disturb you."

Nantas, who had awakened with a start, looked with astonishment at the lady who had called upon him. She had now raised her veil and appeared to be about five and forty, short, very stout and with the face of a devotee. He had never seen her before. When he offered her the only chair, casting an inquiring glance at her, she gave her name: "Mademoiselle Chuin—I have come, sir, to talk to you about a very important matter."

Nantas had sat down on the edge of the bed. The name of Mlle Chuin told him nothing, and his only course was to wait until she should think fit to explain herself. But she seemed in no hurry to do so; she had given a glance round the tiny room and appeared to be hesitating as to the way in which she might start the conversation. Finally she spoke in a very gentle voice, emphasizing her remarks with a smile.

"Well, sir, I come as a friend. I have been told your touching story. Do not think that I am a spy; my only wish is to be of use to you. I know how full of trials your life has been till now, with what courage you have struggled to find a situation and the final result of all your painful efforts. Once more, sir, forgive me for intruding upon you. I assure you that sympathy alone——"

Nantas, however, did not interrupt her; his curiosity was aroused, and he surmised that the doorkeeper of the house had furnished the lady with all those particulars. Mlle Chuin, being at liberty to continue, seemed solely desirous of paying compliments and putting things in the most attractive way.

"You have a great future before you, sir," she resumed. "I have taken the liberty to follow your endeavors, and I have been greatly struck by your praiseworthy courage in misfortune. In one word, in my opinion there is a great future before you if someone gives you a helping hand."

She stopped again. She was waiting for a word. The young man, who believed that the lady had come to offer him a situation, replied that he would accept anything. But she, now that the ice was broken, asked him point-blank:

"Would you have any objection to marry?"

"Marry!" cried Nantas. "Goodness, madame, who would have me? Some poor girl that I could not even feed!"

"No, a very pretty girl, very rich, splendidly connected, and who will at once put you in possession of the means to attain to the highest position."

Nantas laughed no longer.

"Then what are the terms?" he asked, instinctively lowering his voice.

"The girl has had a misfortune, and you must assume responsibility," said

Mlle Chuin, and, putting aside her unctuous phraseology in her desire to come straight to the point, she gave some details.

Nantas's first impulse was to turn her out of doors.

"It's an infamous thing to propose," he muttered.

"Infamous!" exclaimed Mlle Chuin, affecting her honied tones again. "I can't admit that ugly word. The truth is, sir, that you will save a family from despair. Her father knows nothing as yet; this misfortune has not long fallen upon her, and it was I myself who conceived the idea of thus marrying her as soon as possible. I know her father; it would kill him if nothing were done. My plan would soften the blow; he would think the wrong half redressed. The unfortunate part of it is that the real culprit is married. Ah, sir, there are men who really have no moral sense."

She might have gone on like this for a long while, for Nantas was not listening to her. He was thinking, why should he refuse? Had he not been proposing to sell himself a little while back? Very well, here was a buyer. Fair exchange is no robbery. He would give his name, and he would be given a situation. It was an ordinary contract. He looked at his muddy trousers and felt that he had eaten nothing since the day before; all the disgust born of two months' struggling and humiliation rose up within him. At last he was about to set his foot on the world which had repulsed him and driven him to the verge of suicide!

"I accept," he said curtly.

Then he asked for clear explanations from Mlle Chuin. What did she want for her services? She protested at first that she wanted nothing. However, she ended by claiming twenty thousand francs out of the dowry which the young man would receive. And as he did not haggle over the terms, she became expansive.

"Listen," she said, "it was I who thought of you, and the young lady did not refuse when I mentioned your name. Oh, you will thank me later on. I might have got a title; I know a man who would have jumped at the chance. But I preferred to choose someone outside of the poor child's sphere. It will appear more romantic. And then I like you. You are good looking and have plenty of sense. You will make your way, and you mustn't forget me. Remember that I am devoted to you."

So far no name had been mentioned, and upon Nantas making an inquiry in this respect the old maid stood up and said, introducing herself afresh:

"Mlle Chuin; I have been living as governess in Baron Danvilliers's family since the baroness's death. I educated Mademoiselle Flavie—the baron's daughter. Mademoiselle Flavie is the young lady in question."

Then she withdrew after formally placing on the table an envelope containing a five-hundred-franc note. It was an advance which she herself made to defray preliminary expenses.

When Nantas found himself alone he went to the window again. The night was very dark; nothing was to be seen but the dark masses of shadow cast by the trees; one window only in the gloomy frontage of the mansion showed a light. So it was that tall, fair girl who walked with such a queenly step and did not deign to notice him. She or some other, what mattered it? The girl was no part of the bargain. Then Nantas raised his eyes still higher, upon Paris roaring in the gloom, upon the quays, the streets, the squares, upon the whole left bank of the river, illuminated by the flickering gaslights, and like a superior being he addressed the city, saying:

"Now you are mine!"

CHAPTER II

The Baron

Baron danvilliers was sitting in the room which served him as a study, a cold, lofty apartment, furnished with old-fashioned leather-covered furniture. For the last two days he had been in a state of stupor, Mlle Chuin having informed him of what had befallen Flavie. In vain had she softened and toned down the facts; the old man had been overcome by the blow, and it was only the thought that the culprit was in a position to offer the sole reparation possible that kept him from death. That morning he was waiting the visit of this man, who was utterly unknown to him but who had robbed him of his daughter. He rang the bell.

"Joseph, a young man will call, whom you will show in here at once. I am not at home to anybody else," he said.

Sitting alone at his fireside, he brooded bitterly. The son of a mason, a starveling without any position! Mlle Chuin had certainly spoken of him as a promising youth, but what a disgrace to a family whose honor had hitherto been stainless! Flavie had accused herself with a kind of passionate eagerness so as to acquit her governess of the slightest blame. Since the painful scene between them she had kept to her room, and, indeed, the baron had refused to see her. Before forgiving her he was determined to look into the matter. All his plans were laid. But his hair had grown whiter, and his head shook with age.

"Monsieur Nantas," announced Joseph.

The baron did not rise. He simply turned his head and looked fixedly at Nantas, who walked forward. The latter had had the good sense not to yield to any desire to dress himself up; he had simply bought a black coat and a pair of trousers, which were decent but very worn and gave him the appearance of a poor but careful student, with nothing of the adventurer about him. He stopped in the middle of the room and waited, standing up, but without humility.

"So it is you, sir," stammered the old man.

But he could not continue, for his emotion choked him, and he feared lest he might commit some act of violence. After a pause he said simply, "You have committed a wicked deed, sir."

Then when Nantas was about to make some excuse he repeated more emphatically, "A wicked deed. I wish to know nothing; I request you to explain nothing to me. In fact, no explanation can lessen your crime. Only robbers break in upon families in this way."

Nantas hung his head again.

"It is making money very easily, setting a trap in which one is certain of catching both child and father."

"Allow me, sir," interrupted the young man, stung by these words.

But the baron made a violent gesture.

"What? Why should I allow anything? It is not for you to speak here. I am telling you what I am in duty bound to tell you and what you are bound to hear, since you come before me as a culprit. Look at this house. Our family has lived here for more than three centuries without reproach. Standing here, are you not conscious of our ancient honor and dignity? Well, sir, you have trifled with all that. It nearly killed me, and today my hands tremble as if I had suddenly grown ten years older. Be silent and listen to me."

Nantas had turned very pale. He had taken a difficult part upon himself. He felt anxious to make the blindness of passionate love serve as his pretext.

"I lost my head," he muttered, trying to make up some tale. "I could not look at Mademoiselle Flavie——"

At his daughter's name the baron rose and cried in a voice like thunder:

"Silence! I have told you that I do not wish to know anything. Whatever happened matters little to me. I have asked her nothing, and I ask you nothing. Keep your confessions to yourselves, I will have nothing to do with them."

Then he sat down again, trembling and exhausted. Nantas bent his head, feeling deeply moved, in spite of the command he had over himself. After a pause the old man continued in the dry tone of a person discussing business matters:

"I beg pardon, sir. I had determined to keep cool but failed. You are not at my disposal; I am at yours, since I am in your power. You are here to carry out a transaction which has become necessary. To business, sir."

And thenceforward he affected to speak like a lawyer, settling as agreeably as possible some shameful case in which he was loath to dabble. He began formally: "Mademoiselle Flavie Danvilliers inherited at the death of her mother a sum of two hundred thousand francs, which she was not to receive until her marriage. That sum has produced interest, but here are the accounts of my guardianship which I will communicate to you."

He opened a book and began to read some figures. Nantas in vain tried to stop him. Emotion seized him in the presence of this old man, who appeared so upright and simple and who seemed to him so great because he was so calm.

"Finally," the baron concluded, "I bestow on you, by an agreement which my notary drew up this morning, another sum of two hundred thousand francs. I know that you have nothing. You can draw those two hundred thousand francs at my banker's on the day after the marriage."

"But I don't ask for your money, sir," said Nantas. "I only want your daughter."

The baron cut him short.

"You have not the right to refuse," he said, "and my daughter could not marry a man with less money than herself. I give you the dowry which I intended for her; that is all. Possibly you reckoned on more, for I have the credit of being richer than I really am."

And as the young man remained mute at this last thrust the baron put an end to the interview by ringing the bell.

"Joseph, tell Mademoiselle Flavie that I want her in my room at once."

He had risen from his chair and now began to walk slowly about the room. Nantas remained motionless. He was deceiving this old man, and he felt small and powerless before him. At last Flavie appeared.

"My child," said the baron, "here is the man. The marriage will take place as soon as possible."

Then he went out of the room, leaving them alone, as if, so far as he was concerned, the marriage were over.

When the door was shut silence reigned. Nantas and Flavie looked at one another. They had never met before. He thought her very handsome with her pale and haughty face and her large gray eyes which never drooped. Perhaps she had been crying during the three days that she had spent in her room; however, the coldness of her cheeks must have frozen her tears. She it was who spoke first.

"Then the matter is settled, sir?" she said.

"Yes, madame," replied Nantas simply.

Her face contracted involuntarily as she cast a long look at him, a look which seemed to be fathoming his baseness.

"Well, so much the better," she continued. "I was afraid I should not find anyone to agree to such a bargain."

Nantas could distinguish in her voice all the scorn which she felt for him, but he raised his head. If he had trembled before the father, knowing that he was deceiving him, he determined to be firm with the daughter, who was his accomplice.

"Excuse me, madame," he said calmly and with the greatest politeness. "I think you misconceive the position in which what you rightly call the bargain has placed us. I apprehend that from today forth we are on a footing of perfect equality."

"Indeed!" interrupted Flavie with a scornful smile.

"Yes, perfect equality. You require a name in order to conceal a fault which I do not presume to condemn, and I give you my name. On my side I require money and a certain social position in order to carry out some great enterprise, and you furnish me with that money and position. We thus become two partners whose capitals balance. It only remains for us to express our mutual thanks for the service which we are rendering to one another."

She smiled no longer; indeed, a look of irritated pride appeared upon her face. After a pause she asked him, "You know my conditions?"

"No, madame," said Nantas, preserving perfect calmness. "Be good enough to name them. I agree to them in advance."

Upon this she spoke as follows, without hesitating or blushing: "Our lives will remain completely distinct and separate. You will give up all rights over me, and I shall owe no duty toward you."

At each sentence Nantas made an affirmative sign. This was precisely what he desired.

"If I thought it part of my duty to be gallant," he said, "I should assert that such conditions would drive me to despair. But we are above empty compliments. I am pleased to see that you have such a correct appreciation of our respective positions. We are not entering upon life by the path of roses. I only ask one thing of you, madame, which is that you will not make use of the liberty I shall accord you in such a way as to necessitate any interference on my part."

"What, sir!" exclaimed Flavie violently, her pride revolting.

Nantas bowed respectfully and entreated her not to be offended. Their position was a delicate one; they must both of them put up with certain allusions, without which a perfect understanding would be impossible. He refrained from insisting further. Mlle Chuin, in a second interview, had given him further particulars and had named to him a certain M. des Fondettes as the person to whom all the trouble was due.

Suddenly Nantas felt a friendly impulse. Like all those who are conscious of their own power, he was fond of being good-natured.

"Listen, madame," he exclaimed. "We don't know one another, but it would be really wrong of us to hate one another at first sight. Perhaps we are made to understand each other. I can see that you despise me, but perhaps that is because you do not know my story."

Then he began to talk feverishly, throwing himself into a state of excitement as he spoke of his life, his ambition and his desperate, fruitless efforts in Paris. Then he displayed his scorn of what he called social conventionalism, in which ordinary men became entangled. What mattered the opinion of the world, he asked, when a man had his foot on it? He must show his superiority. Power was an excuse for all. And in glowing terms he painted the sovereign existence which he would make for himself. He feared no further obstacle; nothing prevailed against power. He would be powerful and, therefore, he would be happy.

"Don't imagine that I am miserably sordid," he continued. "I am not selling myself for your fortune; I only take your money as a means to rise. Oh, if you only knew what is working within me! If you only knew the burning nights which I have spent, always meditating over the same idea, which was only swept away by the reality of the morrow, then you would understand me! You would then, perhaps, be proud to lean on my arm, saying to yourself that you at least had furnished me with the means to become someone!"

She listened to him in silence without a single movement of her features. And he asked himself a question which he had been turning over in his mind for three days past without being able to find answer to it: Had she noticed him at his window that she had so readily accepted Mlle Chuin's scheme when the latter had mentioned him? The singular idea occurred to him that perhaps she might have loved him with a romantic love if he had indignantly refused the bargain which the governess had proposed to him.

He stopped at last, and Flavie maintained an icy silence. Then, as if he had not made his confession, she repeated in a dry voice: "Then it is understood, our lives completely distinct, absolute liberty."

Nantas at once resumed his ceremonious air and in the curt voice of a man discussing an agreement replied: "It is settled, madame."

Ill pleased with himself, he then withdrew. How was it that he had yielded to the foolish desire to overcome that woman? She was very handsome, but it was better that there should be nothing in common between them, for she might hamper him in life.

CHAPTER III

THE QUESTION

TEN YEARS HAD PASSED. One morning Nantas was sitting in the study in which Baron Danvilliers had given him such a formidable reception on the occasion of their first meeting. That study was now his own; the baron, after being reconciled to his daughter and his son-in-law, had given up the house to them, merely reserving for his own use a little building situated at the other end of the garden and overlooking the Rue de Beaume. In ten years' time Nantas had won for himself one of the highest positions attainable in the financial and mercantile worlds. Having a hand in all the great railway enterprises, engaged in all the land speculations which signalized the earlier period of the Second Empire, he had rapidly accumulated an immense fortune. But his ambition did not halt at that; he was determined to play a part in politics, and he had succeeded to get elected as a deputy in a department where he had several farms. Since taking his seat in the Corps Législatif, he had posed as a future finance minister. Thanks to his practical knowledge and his ready tongue, he was day by day acquiring a more important position. He was skillful enough to effect absolute devotion to the empire, but at the same time he professed theories on financial subjects which made a great stir and which he knew gave the emperor a deal to think of.

On that particular morning Nantas was overladen with business. The greatest activity prevailed in the spacious offices which he had arranged on the ground floor of the mansion. There was a crowd of clerks, some sitting motionless at wickets and others constantly going backward and forward to the sound of banging doors. Bags of gold lay open and overflowing on the tables. There was a constant ring of precious metal, a tinkling music of wealth such as might have flooded the streets. In the anterooms a crowd was surging; place hunters, financial agents, politicians, all Paris on its knees before power. Great men frequently waited there patiently for an hour at a stretch. And he, sitting at his table, in correspondence with people far and near, able to grasp the world with his outstretched arms, was carrying his former dream of force into fulfillment, conscious that he was the intelligent motor of a colossal machine which moved kingdoms and empires.

Suddenly he rang for his usher. He seemed anxious.

"Germain," he said, "do you know whether your mistress has come in?"

And when the man replied that he did not know, he told him to summon his wife's maid. But Germain did not move.

"Excuse me, sir," he whispered; "the president of the Corps Législatif insists on seeing you."

Nantas made an impatient gesture and replied: "Well, show him in and do as I told you."

On the previous day a speech which Nantas had made on an important budgetary question had produced such an impression that the matter had been referred to a commission to be amended according to his views. After the sitting of the Chamber a rumor had spread that the finance minister intended to resign, and Nantas was at once spoken of as his probable successor. For his part, he shrugged his shoulders; nothing had been done; he had only had an interview with the emperor with regard to certain special points. However, the president's visit might have vast significance. At this thought Nantas tried to throw off the feeling of worry which was weighing on him and rose to grasp his president's hand.

"Ah, Monsieur le Duc," he said, "I beg your pardon. I did not know you were here. Believe me, I am deeply sensible of the honor which you are paying me."

For a minute they talked cordially; then the president, without saying anything definite, gave him to understand that he had been sent by the emperor to sound him. Would he accept the finance portfolio, and what would be his program? Upon this Nantas, with superb calmness, named his conditions. But beneath the impassibility of his face mute triumph was swelling. At last he had mounted the final rung; he was at the top of the ladder. Another step and he would have all heads save that of the sovereign beneath him. As the president concluded, saying that he was going at once to the emperor to communicate Nantas's program, a small door which communicated with the private part of the house opened, and the maid of the financier's wife appeared.

Nantas, suddenly turning pale, stopped short in the middle of a sentence and hurried to the girl, saying to the duke:

"Pray excuse me."

Then he questioned the servant in whispers. Madame had gone out early? Had she said where she was going? When was she expected home? The maid replied vaguely, like a clever girl who did not wish to compromise herself. Understanding the absurdity of the situation, Nantas concluded by remarking, "Tell your mistress as soon as she comes in that I wish to speak to her."

The president of the Chamber, somewhat surprised, had stepped up to a window and was looking into the courtyard. Nantas returned to him, again apologizing. But he had lost his self-possession; he stammered and astonished the duke by his clumsy remarks.

"There, I've spoiled the whole business," he exclaimed aloud when the other had gone. "I've missed the portfolio."

He sat down, feeling disgusted and angry. Several more visitors were then shown in. An engineer had a report to present to him, showing that enormous profits would arise from the working of a certain mine. A diplomatist interviewed him on the subject of a loan which a foreign power wanted to negotiate in Paris. His tools flocked in, rendering account of twenty different schemes. Finally he received a large number of his colleagues of the Chamber, all of whom went into raptures about his speech of the day before.

Leaning back in his chair, he accepted all this flattery without a smile. The clink of gold was still audible in the neighboring rooms; the house seemed to tremble like a factory, as if all that money were manufactured there. He had only to take up a pen to dispatch telegrams which would have spread joy or consternation through the markets of Europe; he could prevent or precipitate war by supporting or opposing the loan of which he had been told; he even held the fate of the French budget in his hands, and he would soon know whether it would be best for him to support or oppose the empire. This was his triumph; his formidable personality had become the axis upon which a world was turning. And yet he did not enjoy his triumph, as he had thought he would. He experienced a feeling of listlessness; his mind was elsewhere, on the alert at the slightest audible sound. Scarcely had a flame, a flush of satisfied ambition, risen to his cheeks than he felt himself turn pale again, as if a cold hand from behind had been laid upon his neck.

Two hours had passed, and Flavie had not yet appeared. Nantas at last called Germain and gave him orders to summon Baron Danvilliers if the old gentleman was at home. Then he began to pace his study, refusing to see anyone else that day. Little by little his agitation had increased. His wife had evidently been to keep some appointment. She must have renewed her acquaintance with M. des Fondettes. The latter's wife had died six months previously. True, Nantas disclaimed any idea of being jealous; during ten years he had strictly observed the agreement to which he had been a party, but he drew the line, as he said, at being made a dupe of. Never would he allow his wife to compromise his position by making him a laughingstock. His strength forsook him as he became a prey to the feelings of a husband who requires respect. He experienced agony such as he had never endured, not even in his most hazardous speculations at the commencement of his career.

At last Flavie entered the room, still in her outdoor costume; she had merely taken off her gloves and hat. Nantas, whose voice trembled, told her that he would have gone to her if he had known that she had come in. But without sitting down she motioned to him to have done quickly.

"Madame," he began, "an explanation has become necessary between us. Where were you this morning?"

Her husband's quivering voice and the pointedness of his question astonished her profoundly.

"Where it pleased me to go," she replied in a cold tone.

"That is exactly what, in future, I must object to," he resumed, turning very pale. "It is your duty to recollect what I said to you: I will not allow you to make use of the liberty I grant you in a way which may bring disgrace upon my name."

Flavie smiled in sovereign disdain.

"Disgrace your name, sir? But that is a question which regards yourself. It is a thing which no longer remains to be done."

Upon this Nantas, wild with passion, advanced as if to strike her.

"You wretched creature!" he stammered. "You have just left Monsieur des Fondettes. You have a lover; I know it!"

"You are wrong," she replied without recoiling; "I have never seen Monsieur des Fondettes again. But even if I had a lover it would not be for you to reproach me. What difference would it make to you? You forget our compact."

He looked at her for a moment with wild eyes; then, choking with sobs and throwing into one cry all the passion which he had so long stifled, he flung himself at her feet.

"Oh, Flavie, I love you!"

Unbending still, she drew back, for he had touched the hem of her dress. But the wretched man followed her, dragging himself upon his knees with his hands uplifted.

"I love you, Flavie; I love you to madness! How it happened I know not. It began years ago, and it grew and grew, till now it has absorbed my whole being. Oh, I have struggled. I thought this passion unworthy of me. I called our first interview to mind. But now I suffer too much. I must speak——"

For a long time he continued thus. It was the shattering of all his principles. This man, who had put his trust in force, who maintained that violation was the sole lever capable of moving the world, was crushed, feeble as a child, disarmed by a woman. And his dream of fortune realized, his present high position, he would have given all for that woman to have raised him by a kiss upon his brow! She marred his triumph. He no longer heard the gold which sounded in his office; he no longer thought of the endless procession of flatterers who came to bow their knees to him; he forgot that the emperor at that moment, perhaps, was summoning him to power. All those things had no existence for him. He possessed everything, save the only thing he wished for—his wife's love. And if she denied it, then he had nothing left him!

"Listen," he continued; "whatever I have done I have done for you. At first, it is true, you were for nothing in it; I simply worked to gratify my own pride. But soon you became the one object of all my thoughts, of all my efforts. I told myself that I must mount as high as possible in order to become worthy of you. I hoped to make you unbend on the day when I should lay my power at your feet. See what I now am. Have I not won your forgiveness? Do not despise me any longer, I entreat you."

As yet she had not spoken. Now, however, she said calmly: "Get up, sir. Somebody might come in."

He refused and still went on entreating. Perhaps he would have bided his time if he had not been jealous of M. des Fondettes. It was that torture which maddened him. At last he became very humble.

"I see that you still despise me. Very well, wait, do not bestow your love on anybody. I can promise you so much that I shall know how to move you. You must forgive me if I was harsh just now. I am out of my senses. Oh, let me hope that you will love me someday!"

"Never!" she answered energetically.

Then as he still remained upon the floor, seemingly crushed, she would have left the room, but suddenly beside himself with fury, he sprang up and caught her by the wrists. A woman braved him thus when the world was at his feet! He was capable of anything, could overthrow states, rule France as he pleased, and yet he could not obtain his wife's love! He, so strong, so powerful, he whose slightest desires were orders, he had but one longing now, and that longing would never be gratified because a creature who was as weak as a child spurned him! He grasped her arms and repeated in a hoarse whisper: "You must, you must——"

"And I will not," replied Flavie, pale and obstinate.

The struggle was still going on when Baron Danvilliers opened the door. On seeing him, Nantas released Flavie and cried:

"Your daughter has just come from her lover, sir! Tell her that a woman should respect her husband's name, even if she does not love him, even if the thought of her own honor does not stand in the way."

The baron, who was greatly aged, remained standing on the threshold, gazing at this violent scene. It was a melancholy surprise for him. He had believed them to be united, and he looked with approval on their ceremonious intercourse in public, considering that to be a mere matter of form. His son-in-law and he belonged to different generations, but although he disliked the financier's somewhat unscrupulous activity, although he condemned certain undertakings which he regarded as undesirable, he was forced to recognize Nantas's strength of will and his quick intellect. And now he suddenly came upon this drama, which he had never even suspected.

When Nantas accused Flavie of having a lover the baron, who still treated his married daughter with the same severity as he had shown her when a child, advanced with a stately step.

"I swear to you that she has just come from her lover's," repeated Nantas, "and look at her; she defies me."

Flavie turned away her head disdainfully. She was arranging her cuffs, which her husband had crushed in his roughness. Not a blush was to be seen on her face. Her father spoke to her.

"My child," he said, "why do you not defend yourself? Can your husband be speaking the truth? Can you have reserved this last grief for my old age? The offense would fall on me as well, for the fault of one member of a family falls upon the others."

Flavie made a gesture of impatience. Her father had well chosen his time to accuse her! For a moment longer she bore his questions, wishing to spare him the shame of an explanation. But as he, in his turn, lost patience, seeing her mute and obstinate, she finally replied, "Father, let this man play his part. You do not know him. For your own sake do not force me to speak out."

"He is your husband," said the old man, "the father of your child."

Flavie started, stung to the quick. "No, no, he is not the father of my child. I will tell you everything now. This man was never my lover, for it would be at least some excuse for him if he had loved me. This man simply sold himself and agreed to hide another's sin."

The baron turned toward Nantas, who had recoiled, deadly pale.

"Do you hear me, Father?" continued Flavie more violently. "He sold himself, sold himself for money! I have never loved him, and he has never been anything to me. I wished to spare you a great sorrow. I bought him so that he might lie to you. Look at him now. See whether I am not telling you the truth."

Nantas hid his face in his hands.

"And now," resumed the young woman, "he actually wants me to love him. He went down on his knees just now and wept. Some comedy, no doubt! Forgive me for having deceived you, Father, but how can I love such a man? Now that you know all, take me away. Indeed, he treated me with violence just now, and I will not remain here a moment longer."

The baron straightened his bent figure. In silence he stepped forward and gave his arm to his daughter. The two crossed the room without Nantas making a movement to detain them. Then upon reaching the door the old man spoke these two words: "Farewell, sir."

The door closed. Nantas remained alone, crushed, gazing wildly into the void around him. Germain came in and placed a letter on the table; Nantas opened it mechanically and cast his eyes over it. This letter, written by the emperor in person, gave him the appointment of finance minister and was couched in the most flattering terms. He could hardly understand it; the realization of all his ambition did not affect him in the least.

Meanwhile in the neighboring rooms the rattle of money had grown louder; it was the busiest hour of the day, the hour when Nantas's house seemed to shake the world. And he, amid that colossal machinery which was his work, he, at the apogee of his power, with his eyes stupidly fixed on the emperor's letter, gave vent to a childish complaint, the negation of his whole life:

"Ah, how unhappy I am! How unhappy I am!"

Then resting his head upon the table, he wept, and the hot tears that gushed forth from his eyes blotted the letter which appointed him minister of finance.

CHAPTER IV

TOIL

DURING the whole of the eighteen months that Nantas had been a minister he had been trying to drown the past by superhuman toil. On the day after the scene in his study he had had an interview with Baron Danvilliers, and Flavie, acting on her father's advice, had consented to return to her husband's roof. But they spoke no word together, except when they were forced to play a comedy in the eyes of the world. Nantas had determined not to leave his home. In the evening his secretaries came to him from the Ministry, and he got through all his work in his own study.

It was at this period of his life that he performed his greatest deeds. A secret voice suggested lofty and fruitful aspirations to him. Whenever he passed by a murmur of sympathy and admiration was heard. But he remained insensible to eulogy. It may be said that he worked without hope of reward, with the sole idea of performing prodigies, of which the only aim was to compass the impossible. At each step on his upward career he consulted Flavie's face. Was she touched at last? Did she pardon him his former baseness? Had she still any thought save of the development of his intellect? But never did he detect any emotion on that woman's mute countenance, and he said to himself as he redoubled his efforts: "I am not high enough for her yet; I must climb, still climb."

He was determined to compel happiness as he had compelled fortune. All his old belief in his power returned; he would not admit that there was any other lever in this world; it was will which produced humanity. When discouragement seized on him at times he shut himself up so that nobody should witness the weakness of his flesh. His struggles could only be read in his deep-set, dark-circled eyes, in which an ardent fire blazed.

He was devoured by jealousy now. To fail to win Flavie's love was a torture, but the thought that she might care for another drove him mad. By way of asserting her liberty it was quite possible that she might intrigue with M. des Fondettes. Her husband affected not to occupy himself with her, but all the time he endured agony whenever she absented herself, even if it were only for an hour. If he had not feared to make himself look ridiculous he would have followed her in the streets. That course displeasing him, he determined to have someone beside her whose devotion he could purchase.

Mlle Chuin had remained an inmate of the house. The baron was used to her, not to mention that she knew too many things to make it advisable to get rid of her. At one time the old maid had resolved to retire on the twenty thousand francs that Nantas had paid her on the day after his marriage. But she had no doubt calculated that there would be further pickings in such a household. So she awaited her opportunity, having found, moreover, that she needed yet another twenty thousand francs to buy the long-desired notary's house at Roinville, the little market town she came from.

There was no occasion for Nantas to mince matters with this old lady, whose pious mien no longer deceived him. However, on the morning when he called her into his study and openly proposed to her that she should keep him informed as to his wife's slightest actions, she professed to be insulted and asked him what he took her for.

"Come," said he impatiently, "I'm very busy; someone is waiting for me. Let us be brief, please."

But she would listen to nothing which was not couched in proper terms. One of her principles was that things are not ugly in themselves, that they only become ugly or cease to be so according to the way in which they are presented.

"Very well," said Nantas, "a good action is involved in this. I am fearful that my wife is hiding some sorrow from me. For the last few weeks I have observed that she has been very much depressed, and I thought that you could find out the cause of it."

"You can rely on me," said Mlle Chuin with a maternal outburst on hearing these words. "I am devoted to your wife; I will do anything for her sake or yours. From tomorrow we will keep a watch on her."

Nantas promised to reward the old maid for her services. She pretended to be angry at first, but she had the adroitness to make him fix a sum, and it was agreed that he should give her ten thousand francs upon her furnishing him with positive proof of his wife's conduct, whatever it might be. Little by little they had come to call things by their proper names.

From that time forward Nantas was less uneasy. Three months passed, and he was engaged upon a great task—the preparation of the budget. With the emperor's sanction he had introduced some important modifications into the financial system. He knew that he would be fiercely attacked in the Chamber, and he had to prepare a large quantity of documents. Frequently he sat up all night, and this hard work deadened him, as it were, to emotion and made him patient. Whenever he saw Mlle Chuin he questioned her briefly. Did she know anything? Had his wife paid many visits? Had she stopped long at certain houses? Mlle Chuin kept a journal of the slightest incidents, but so far she had not succeeded in making any important discovery. Nantas felt reassured, while the old woman occasionally blinked her eyes, saying that she should perhaps have some news for him soon.

The truth was that Mlle Chuin had indulged in further reflection. Ten thousand francs was not enough; she needed twenty thousand to purchase the notary's house. She at first thought of selling herself to the wife after having sold herself to the husband. But she knew Flavie, and she was fearful of being dismissed at the first word. For a long time past, before she had even been charged with this matter, she had kept watch over Mme Nantas on her own account, remarking to herself that a servant's profits lie in the master's or mistress's vices. However, she had discovered that she had to deal with a virtue which was all the more rigid since it was based upon pride. One effect of Flavie's stumble had been that it had inspired her with positive hatred for the other sex. So Mlle Chuin was in despair, when one day she met M. des Fondettes in the street, and after they had had some conversation together, realizing that he desired to be reconciled to her mistress, she made up her mind: she would serve both him and Nantas—a combination worthy of genius.

Everything favored her. M. des Fondettes had met Flavie in society and had been scorned by her. He was in despair thereat. At the end of a week's time, after a great parade of feeling on his side and of scruples on that of Mlle Chuin, the matter was settled; he was to give her ten thousand francs, and she was to smuggle him into the house one evening so that he might have a private interview with Flavie.

The arrangement having been effected, Mlle Chuin sought Nantas.

"What have you learned?" he asked, turning pale.

She would not say anything definite at first. But Nantas displayed such furious impatience that before long she told him that M. des Fondettes had an appointment with Flavie that evening in her private apartments.

"Very good—thank you," stammered Nantas. And he sent her off with a wave of the hand; he was afraid of giving way before her.

This abrupt dismissal astonished and delighted the old woman, for she had prepared herself for a long cross-examination and had even prearranged her answers so that she might not contradict herself. She made a bow and then retired, putting on a mournful face.

Nantas had risen. As soon as he was alone he said aloud:

"This evening in her private apartments."

Then he carried his hands to his head, as if he feared it would burst. That appointment under his own roof seemed to him monstrous audacity. He clenched his fists, and his rage made him think of murder. And yet he had his task to finish—those budgetary documents to complete. Three times did he sit down at his table, and three times a heaving of his whole body raised him to his feet again, while behind him something seemed to be urging him to go at once to his wife and denounce her. At last, however, he conquered himself and resumed his work, swearing that he would strangle them both that very evening. It was the greatest victory that he had ever won over his feelings.

That same afternoon Nantas went to submit to the emperor the definite plan of the budget. The sovereign having raised certain objections, he discussed them with perfect clearness. But it became necessary that he should modify an important part of his program—a difficult matter, as the debate was to take place on the next day.

"I will pass the night over it," he said.

And on his way home he thought, "I'll kill them at midnight, and I shall have the whole night afterward to finish this task."

At dinner that evening Baron Danvilliers began talking about the budget, which was making some little stir. He did not approve of all his son-in-law's views on financial matters, but he admitted that they were very broad and very remarkable. While Nantas was replying to the baron he fancied, on several occasions, that he noticed his wife's eyes fixed upon him. She frequently looked at him in that way now. Her glance was not softened, however; she simply listened and seemed to be trying to read his thoughts. Nantas fancied that she feared she was betrayed. Accordingly he made an effort to appear careless; he talked a good deal, affected great animation and finally overcame the objections of his great intellect. Flavie was still looking at him, and suddenly a hardly perceptible glimpse of tenderness darted across her face.

Nantas worked in his study until midnight. Little by little he had become absorbed in his task, and soon he lost consciousness of everything save that creation of his brain, that great financial scheme which he had painfully built up piece by piece in the midst of innumerable obstacles. When the clock struck twelve he instinctively raised his head. Deep silence reigned in the house. Suddenly he recollected everything. But it was a trial for him to leave his chair; he laid his pen down regretfully and at last took a few steps, as if in obedience to a will which had forsaken him. Then his face flushed, and a flame blazed forth in his eyes. He started for his wife's rooms.

That evening Flavie had dismissed her maid early, saying that she wished to be alone. She had a suite of rooms for her own use. Until midnight she remained in a little boudoir where, stretched upon a sofa, she took up a book and began to read. But again and again the book fell from her hands, and, closing her eyes at last, she became absorbed in thought. Her face still wore a softened expression, and a faint smile played upon it at intervals. Suddenly she started up. There was a knock outside.

"Who is there?" she asked.

"Open the door," replied Nantas.

She was so surprised that she opened it mechanically. Never before had her husband presented himself in this way. He entered the room half distracted; his rage had mastered him while he ascended the stairs. Mlle Chuin, who was watching for him on the landing, had just told him that M. des Fondettes had been there for some hours. Accordingly he was determined to show his wife no mercy.

"There is a man concealed in your rooms," he said.

Flavie did not reply at first, so greatly did these words surprise her. At last she grasped their meaning.

"You are mad, sir!" she answered.

But without stopping to argue he was already looking about him. Then he made his way to the next room. With one bound, however, she threw herself before the door, crying: "You shall not go in. These are my rooms, and you have no right here."

Quivering with passion and looking taller in her pride, she guarded the door. For a moment they stood thus, motionless, speechless, gazing into one another's eyes. Nantas with his head thrust forward, his arms opened, seemed about to throw himself upon her to force a passage.

"Come away," he said in a hoarse whisper. "I'm stronger than you, and go in I will!"

"You shall not; I will not permit it."

And as Nantas kept on repeating accusations, she, without even deigning to deny them, shrugged her shoulders and replied, "Even if it were true what difference can it make to you? Am I not free?"

He recoiled at these words, which struck him like a blow. It was quite true; she was free. A cold shudder ran through him; he plainly realized that she had the best of the argument and that he was playing the part of a feeble and illogical child. He was not observing their compact; his foolish passion had made it hateful to him. Why had he not remained at work in his study? The blood fled from his cheeks, and an indefinable expression of suffering overspread his face. When Flavie saw his pitiable condition she left the door before which she had been standing, while a tender gleam came into her eyes. "Look," she said simply.

And then she passed into the adjoining room herself, carrying a lamp in her hand, while Nantas remained standing at the door. He had made her a sign as if to say that it was sufficient, that he did not wish to enter. But it was she who insisted now. When she had drawn aside the curtains and perceived M. des Fondettes, who had been concealed behind them, so intense was her amazement and horror that she shrieked.

"It was true," she stammered; "it was true this man was here, but I did not know it. On my life I swear it!"

Then with an effort she calmed herself and even seemed to regret the impulse which had prompted her to defend herself.

"You were right, sir, and I crave your pardon," she said to Nantas, endeavoring to speak in her usual tone of voice.

M. des Fondettes, however, felt somewhat foolish and would have given a good deal if the husband had only flown into a passion. But Nantas remained silent. He had simply turned very pale. When he had carried his eyes from M. de Fondettes to Flavie he bowed to the latter, merely saying: "Excuse me, madame; you are free."

Then he turned and walked away. Something seemed to have broken within him; merely a machinery of muscle and bone still worked. When he reached his study again he walked straight to a drawer where he kept a revolver. Having examined the weapon, he said aloud, as if making a formal engagement with himself: "That suffices; I will kill myself presently."

He turned up his lamp, sat down at his table and quietly resumed his work. Amid the deep silence he completed without an instant's hesitation a sentence that he had previously left unfinished. One by one were fresh sheets of paper covered with writing and set in a heap. Two hours later, when Flavie, who had driven M. des Fondettes from the house, came down with bare feet to listen at the door, she only heard her husband's pen scratching as it traveled over the paper. She bent down and applied her eye to the keyhole. Nantas was still calmly writing; his face was expressive of peace and satisfaction at his work, but a ray of the lamp fell upon the barrel of the revolver at his side.

CHAPTER V
Her Reason

The house adjoining the garden of the mansion was now the property of Nantas, who had bought it from his father-in-law. By a personal caprice he had refrained from letting the wretched garret where he had struggled against want for two months after his arrival in Paris. Since he had acquired an enormous fortune he had on more than one occasion felt impelled to go and shut himself up in that little room for hours at a time. It was there that he had suffered, and it was there that he liked to enjoy his triumph. Again, whenever he met with any obstacle he was wont to go there to reflect and to form great resolutions. Once there he again became what he had formerly been. And now when the hand of death hovered over him, it was in that attic that he determined to meet it.

He did not finish his work until eight o'clock in the morning. Fearing that fatigue might overcome him, he took a cold bath. Then he summoned several of his clerks for the purpose of giving them instructions. When his secretary arrived he had an interview with him, and the secretary received orders to take the plan of the budget to the Tuileries and to furnish certain explanations if the emperor should raise any fresh objections. That settled, Nantas considered that he had done enough. He had left everything in order; he was not going off like a demented bankrupt. After all, he was his own property; he could dispose of himself without being accused of selfishness or cowardice.

Nine o'clock struck. The time had come. But just as he was leaving his study, taking the revolver with him, he had to put up with the final humiliation. Mlle Chuin presented herself to claim the ten thousand francs which he had promised her. He paid her and was forced to put up with her familiarity. She assumed a maternal air and seemed to treat him as a successful pupil. Even if he had had any hesitation left, this shameful complicity would have confirmed him in his intentions. He sought the garret quickly, and in his haste he left the door unlocked.

Nothing was changed there. There were the same rents in the wallpaper; the bed, the table and the chair were still there, with their same old look of poverty. For a moment he inhaled the atmosphere which reminded him of his former struggles. Then he approached the window and caught sight of the same stretch of Paris as formerly: the trees in the garden, the Seine, the quays and a part of the right bank of the river, where the houses rose up in confused masses until they were lost to sight at the point where the Père Lachaise Cemetery appeared in the far distance.

The revolver was lying within his reach on the rickety table. There was no hurry now; he felt certain that nobody would disturb him and that he might kill himself whenever he pleased. He became absorbed in thought, and he reflected that he was at precisely the same point as formerly—led back to the same spot, with the same intention of suicide. One evening before, in that very room, he had determined to dash his brains out. In those days he had been too poor to purchase a pistol; he had only had the stones in the streets at his disposal, but death was awaiting him now as then. Thus in this world death is the only thing which never fails, which is always sure and always ready. Nothing that he knew of was like death; he sought in vain; all else had given way beneath him: death alone remained a certainty. He regretted that he had lived ten years too long. The experience that he had acquired of life in his ascent to fortune and power seemed to him puerile. Why had he put himself to that expenditure of will; what purpose had been served by that waste of force, since will and force were as nothing? One passion had sufficed to destroy him: he had foolishly allowed himself to love Flavie, and now the edifice which he had built up was cracking, collapsing like a mere house of cards swept away by the breath of a child. It was lamentable; it resembled the punishment that overtakes a marauding school-boy, under whom a branch snaps and who perishes on the spot where he has sinned. Life was a mistake; the best men ended it as tamely as the biggest fools.

Nantas had taken the revolver from the table and slowly raised it. At that supreme moment one last regret made him hesitate for a second. What great things would he not have accomplished if Flavie had understood him! Had she but thrown herself on his neck one day, saying, "I love you!" he would have found a lever to move the world. And his last thought was one of disdain for force and strength, since they which were to have given him everything had not been able to give him Flavie.

He raised the revolver. The morning was a glorious one. Through the open window the sun poured in, lending even a look of brightness to that wretched garret. In the distance Paris was awakening to its giant life. Nantas pressed the weapon to his temple.

But the door was suddenly flung open, and Flavie entered. With one movement she dashed the revolver aside, and the bullet lodged itself in the ceiling. They looked at one another. She was so out of breath, so choked with emotion, that she could not articulate. At last, embracing Nantas for the first time, she spoke the words for which he longed, the only words which could have determined him to live.

"I love you!" she cried, sobbing on his breast and tearing the avowal from her pride, her mastered being. "I love you, for you are truly strong."

NAÏS MICOULIN

CHAPTER I

NAÏS

DURING the fruit season a brown-skinned little girl with bushy black hair used to come every month to the house of M. Rostand, a lawyer of Aix, in Provence, bringing with her a huge basket of apricots or peaches, so heavy that she had hardly strength enough to carry it. She would wait in the large entrance hall, whither all the family went to greet her.

"So it's you, Naïs," the lawyer would say. "You've brought us some fruit, eh? Come, you're a good girl. And how is your father?"

"Quite well, sir," replied the little girl, showing her white teeth.

The Mme Rostand would take her into the kitchen and ask her about the olives, the almonds and the vines. But the most important question was whether there had been any rain at L'Estaque, where the Rostands' estate was situated, a place called La Blancarde, which was cultivated by the Micoulins. There were but a few dozen almond and olive trees, but the question of rain was, nonetheless, an important one in this province, where everything perishes from drought.

"There have been a few drops," Naïs would say. "The vines want more."

Then having imparted her news, she ate a piece of bread and some scraps of meat and set out again for L'Estaque in a butcher's cart which came to Aix every fortnight. Frequently she brought some shellfish, a lobster, a fine eel, for Micoulin fished more than he tilled the ground. When she came during the holidays Frédéric, the lawyer's son, used to rush into the kitchen to tell her that the family would soon take up their quarters at La Blancarde and that she must get some nets and lines ready. He was almost like a brother to her, for they had played together as children. Since the age of twelve, however, she had called him "Monsieur Frédéric," out of respect. Every time old Micoulin heard her speak familiarly to the young man he boxed her ears, but in spite of this the two children were sworn allies.

"Don't forget to mend the nets," repeated the schoolboy.

"No fear, Monsieur Frédéric," replied Naïs. "They'll be ready for you."

M. Rostand was very wealthy. He had bought a splendid seignorial mansion in the Rue du Collège at a very low price. The Hôtel de Coiron, built during the latter part of the seventeenth century, had twelve windows in its frontage and contained enough rooms to house a religious order. Amid those vast rooms the family, consisting of five persons, including the two old servants, seemed lost. The lawyer occupied merely the first floor. For ten years he had tried, without success, to let the ground and second floors, and finally he had decided to lock them up, thus abandoning two thirds of the house to the spiders. Echoes like those of a cathedral resounded through the empty, sonorous mansion at the least noise in the entrance hall, an enormous hall with a staircase from which one could easily have obtained sufficient material to build a modern dwelling.

Immediately after his purchase M. Rostand had divided the grand drawing room into two offices by means of a partition. It was a room thirty-six feet long by twenty-four broad, lighted by six windows. Of one of the two parts he had formed his own private room, the other being allotted to his clerks. The first floor contained four other apartments, the smallest of which measured twenty feet by fifteen. Mme Rostand, Frédéric and the two old servants had bedrooms as lofty as churches. The lawyer had been forced, for convenience's sake, to convert an old boudoir into a kitchen, for at an earlier stage, when they had made use of the kitchen on the ground floor, the food, after passing through the chilly atmosphere of the entrance hall and staircase, had come to table quite cold. To make matters worse, the gigantic apartments were furnished in the most sparing manner. In the lawyer's private room an ancient suite of furniture, upholstered in green Utrecht velvet and of the stiff and comfortless-looking Empire style, did its best to fill up the space with its sofa and eight chairs; a little round table, belonging to the same period, looked like a toy in that immensity; on the chimney piece there was nothing beyond a horrible modern marble clock between two vases, while the tiled floor, looking much the worse for age, showed a dirty red. The bedrooms were more empty still. The whole house brought home to one the tranquil disdain which southern families—even the richest of them—display for comfort and luxury in that happy land of the sun, where life is mainly spent out of doors. The Rostands were certainly not conscious of the sad, mortal chilliness which brooded over those huge rooms, mainly through the scantiness and poverty-stricken aspect of the furniture.

Yet the lawyer was a shrewd man. His father had left him one of the best practices in Aix, and he had managed to improve it considerably by displaying an amount of activity rare in that land of indolence. Small, brisk, weasel-faced, his sole thought was of his work. No other matters troubled his brain; he never even looked at a paper during the rare hours of idleness he spent at his club. His wife, on the contrary, had the reputation of being one of the cleverest and most accomplished women in the town. She was a De Villebonne, a fact which invested her with a certain amount of dignity, in spite of her *mésalliance*. But she was strait-laced to such a point, she practiced her religious duties with such bigoted fortitude, that she had, as it were, become shriveled up by the methodical life she led.

As for Frédéric, he grew up between his busy father and rigid mother. During his schoolboy days he was a dunce of the first water, trembling before his mother but having such a distaste for work that he would often sit in the drawing room during the evening, poring for hours over his books without reading a single line, his mind wandering, while his parents imagined from the look of him that he was preparing his lessons. Irritated by his laziness, they put him to board at the college, but he then worked less than ever, being less looked after than at home and delighted to feel that he was no longer under his parents' stern eyes. Accordingly, alarmed by the airs of liberty which he put on, they took him away in order to have him under their ferule again. So narrowly did they look after him that he was forced to work; his mother examined his exercises, made him repeat his lessons and mounted guard over him unremittingly, like a gendarme. Thanks to this supervision, Frédéric failed but twice in passing the examination for his degree.

Aix is celebrated for its law school, and young Rostand was naturally sent to it. In that ancient town the population is largely composed of barristers, notaries and solicitors practicing at the Appeals Court. A youth takes a law degree as a matter of course, following it up or not as he pleases. So Frédéric remained at the college, working as little as possible but trying to make his parents believe that he was working a great deal. Mme Rostand, to her great sorrow, had been forced to give him more liberty. He now went out when he chose in the daytime and was only expected to be at home to meals. He had, however, to be in by nine o'clock in the evening, except on those days when he was allowed to go to the theater. Thus began that country student's life, so full of vice when it is not entirely devoted to work.

A person must know Aix, be acquainted with the quiet grass-grown streets, the state of torpor which enwraps the whole town, in order to understand the purposeless life which the students lead there. Those who work can manage to kill time over their books, but those who refuse to exert themselves steadily have no other places where they can while away their leisure save the cafés and other resorts, where people gamble and drink and call it "seeing life." Thus Frédéric soon became an inveterate gambler; he passed the greater part of his evenings at cards and finished them elsewhere. When he found his evenings too short for him he managed, by stealing a key of the house door, to have all night as well. In this way his years of probation passed pleasantly enough.

Frédéric had sense enough to see that he must play the part of a tractable son. The hypocrisy of a child curbed by fear had little by little grown upon him. His mother now declared herself satisfied; he took her to church, behaved most properly with her, told her with the greatest calmness the most unheard-of lies, which she believed, thanks to his air of candor. And so clever did he become in this respect that he never allowed himself to be outwitted, being always ready with an excuse, always prepared in advance with the most extraordinary stories in support of his statements. He paid his gaming debts with money borrowed from his cousins, and his pecuniary transactions would have filled a book. Once after an unhoped-for stroke of good luck he was able to turn a dream he had of spending a week in Paris into reality by getting himself invited thither by a friend who had a little estate near the Durance.

Frédéric was a fine young fellow, tall, with regular features and a black beard. His vices made him good company, especially with ladies. He was quoted for his good manners. Those who knew his goings on smiled a little, but, as he had the sense to throw a veil over this side of his life, he came in for a certain amount of credit for not making an exhibition of his excesses, as did other students, who were the scandal of the town.

Frédéric was nearly twenty-one and was soon to pass his last examination. His father, who was still young and not inclined as yet to hand his practice over to him, talked of making him enter the magistrature to begin with. He had friends in Paris to whom he could apply to get him an appointment as public prosecutor's assessor. The young man raised no objection, for he never openly opposed his parents, but a certain expressive smile on his face betokened his firm determination to prolong the pleasant existence which suited him so well. He knew that his father was rich, that he was his only son, so why should he trouble himself? In the meantime he smoked his cigar on the Promenade, gambled in the neighboring cafés and paid his attentions to a variety of damsels, though all this did not prevent him from holding himself at his mother's orders and loading her with attentions. At times when he felt out of sorts he stayed at home in the huge, gloomy mansion in the Rue du Collège and enjoyed delicious repose. The emptiness of the rooms, the sense of constraint perceptible on every side, seemed to him to possess a soothing influence. There he collected himself afresh, making his mother believe that he was stopping at home for her sake, until the day when, health and appetite having returned, he devised some fresh escapade. In one word, he was the best fellow in the world, so long as his pleasures were not interfered with.

Every year, however, Naïs came to the Rostands with her fish and fruit, and every year she grew. She was of the same age as Frédéric, or, to be correct, she was just three months older. Mme Rostand would often say to her:

"What a big girl you are growing to be, Naïs!"

And Naïs would smile, showing her white teeth. As a rule, Frédéric was not there, but one day during the last year of his probation he was going out when he found Naïs standing in the hall with her basket. He stopped short in astonishment. He did not recognize the girl, though he had seen her only the year before at La Blancarde. Naïs looking superb with her dark face beneath a swarthy covering of thick black hair, her broad shoulders, her supple waist and her magnificent arms, of which the bare wrists were exposed. In a single year she had grown like a young tree.

"You!" he said in hesitating voice.

"Yes, Monsieur Frédéric," replied Naïs, looking him in the face with her big eyes in which a somber fire smoldered. "I've brought some sea urchins. When are you coming? Shall I get the nets ready?"

He was still looking at her and muttering, as if he had not heard her speak: "How handsome you are, Naïs! What is there in you?"

The compliment made her smile. Then as he took her hands playfully, as he had done in the days gone by, she became serious and said in a hoarse whisper: "No, no; not here. Take care! Here comes your mother."

CHAPTER II

FRÉDÉRIC

A FORTNIGHT LATER the Rostand family started for La Blancarde. The lawyer had to rest during the vacation, and September was a charming month at the seaside. The great heat was past, and the nights were deliciously cool.

La Blancarde was not actually in L'Estaque, a village situated on the extreme outskirts of Marseilles and nestling among the rocks which bound the bay. The house was built on a cliff overlooking the village, and its yellow walls, glistening among the pines, could be seen from any part of the bay. It was one of those heavy square buildings, pierced with irregular windows and called "châteaux" in Provence. In front of the house a broad terrace extended, rising almost perpendicularly above the pebbly beach. Behind there was a vast enclosure of poor land, upon which nothing but a few vines, almond or olive trees would grow. One of the inconveniences, indeed, one of the dangers, of La Blancarde was the fact that the sea was gradually eating away the cliff; infiltrations proceeding from neighboring springs were constantly at work in that softening mountain of clay and rock, and every year enormous masses fell away, being precipitated with a deafening crash into the sea. The property was thus becoming smaller and smaller; the pines had already begun to fall.

The Micoulins had been settled at La Blancarde for forty years. According to the Provençal custom, they cultivated the land and shared the crops with the landlord. These crops were scanty, and they would have died of starvation if, during the summer, they had not turned their attention to the sea. Between tilling and sowing there came an interval of fishing. The family consisted of Micoulin, a stern old man with a black and seamy face, before whom the others trembled; of his wife, a tall woman, whose intellect was dulled by hard toil in the blazing sun; of a son, who at that time was serving on board the Arrogant man-of-war, and of Naïs, whom her father, in spite of her numerous tasks at home, sent to work at a tile manufactory. Rarely did the sound of a laugh or a song enliven the tenants' dwelling, a hovel built against one of the sides of La Blancarde. Micoulin, buried in his reflections, preserved gloomy silence. The two women exhibited toward him that cringing respect which southern wives and daughters always display for the head of the family. It was not often that silence was broken, except if it were by the mother's calls, as she stood with her hands on her hips, her throat ready to burst, shouting out the name of Naïs whenever her daughter disappeared. Naïs heard her a mile away and returned home pale with stifled anger.

The handsome Naïs, as they called her at L'Estaque, was by no means happy. At the age of sixteen Micoulin, on the slightest provocation, would strike her so roughly in the face as to make the blood fly from her nose, and even now, in spite of her twenty years, her bruised shoulders bore the marks of her father's brutality for weeks together. Not that he was cruel; he simply exercised a rigorous rule, insisting on implicit obedience, having in his blood the old Roman feeling of authority over his own family—the authority of life and death. One day Naïs, on being unmercifully threshed, dared to raise her hand to defend herself, and her father came near killing her. After a correction of this kind the girl would throw herself trembling into a dark corner and, with dry eyes, brood over the insult. Black rage would hold her there mute for hours together, gloating over revenge which lay beyond her power. It was her father's blood which rose within her—his blind passion, his furious determination to be the master. When she saw her trembling and submissive mother humble herself before Micoulin she looked at her with scorn. She would often say, "If I'd a husband like that I'd kill him."

And yet Naïs preferred those days when she was beaten, for his violence was a diversion. At other times she led such a dreary, monotonous life that it almost killed her. Her father forbade her to go down to L'Estaque, keeping her constantly at work at home; even when she had nothing to do it was his will that she should stay there beneath his eyes. Accordingly she looked forward impatiently to September, for as soon as the family took up their quarters at La Blancarde Micoulin's surveillance necessarily became less strict, and Naïs, who was wont to run errands for Mme Rostand, was only too glad to make up for all her imprisonment.

One day the idea struck old Micoulin that this big girl might bring him in a franc or two a day. So he emancipated her and sent her to work at a tile manufactory. Although the labor was severe Naïs felt delighted. She left home early, proceeded to the other side of L'Estaque and remained until evening in the hot sun, turning over the tiles set out to dry. Sad work it made with her hands, but she was freed from her father, and she used to joke with the boys. Here it was, in the midst of this rough toil, that she filled out and became a handsome woman. The blazing sun tinted her face and decked her neck with a ring of amber; her black hair grew and enveloped her, as if to protect her with its flying tresses; her body, continually on the move during the progress of her work, acquired the supple vigor of a young warrior's frame. When she stood up on the beaten ground at her full height amid the ruddy tiles she looked like some Amazon, like a statue suddenly imbued with life by the rain of fire falling from the sky. Micoulin glowered at her with his little eyes on seeing her so fair. She laughed too much; it did not seem to him natural that a girl should be so happy. And he swore to himself he would throttle all lovers, should any ever venture to dangle around her!

Lovers! Naïs might have had them by the dozen, but she gave them no encouragement. She tossed her head at all the youths. Her only friend was a hunchback who was employed at the same manufactory as herself—a little fellow called Toine, whom the Foundling Hospital of Aix had sent to L'Estaque and who remained there, adopted, so to say, by the district. This hunchback had a ringing laugh and a comical profile. Naïs found an attraction in his gentleness. She did what she liked with him and often tormented him when she felt inclined to take vengeance on someone for her father's violence toward herself. All this, however, had no further consequences. People used to make sport of Toine, and Micoulin himself said: "She's welcome to Toine. I know her; she's too proud."

That year when Mme Rostand came to La Blancarde she asked Micoulin to lend her Naïs, one of her servants being ill. Work was slack just then at the manufactory, and, moreover, Micoulin, although brutal toward his own family, was politeness with his master's; he would not have refused, even if the request had been against his wishes. But that very day M. Rostand was forced to go to Paris on sudden and important business, and Frédéric was thus left alone with his mother.

As a rule, on his arrival the young man was mad after outdoor exercise, and, intoxicated by the seaside air, he would go with Micoulin to set or draw up the nets or take long walks with Naïs in the gorges which abound in the neighborhood of L'Estaque. Then his ardor cooled down, and he remained for whole days lying under the pines on the edge of the terrace, half asleep and gazing at the sea, of which the monotonous azure finally palled upon him. As a rule, he had had enough of La Blancarde at the end of a fortnight and was wont to invent some excuse in order to slip off to Marseilles.

That year, on the day after their arrival, Micoulin called Frédéric at sunrise. He was going to take up the traps, the long baskets with a narrow opening in which deep-water fish are caught. But the young man turned a deaf ear to him. Fishing appeared to have lost its attraction, for when he got up he threw himself on his back under the pines and fixed his eyes on the sky. His mother was astonished not to see him set off for one of the long walks from which he usually returned as hungry as a wolf.

"You are not going out?" she asked.

"No, Mother," he replied. "I shall stop with you, as Father is not here."

Micoulin, who heard this, muttered in his dialect: "It won't be long before Monsieur Frédéric's off to Marseilles."

But Frédéric did not go to Marseilles. The week passed by and found him still stretched on his back, simply changing his position whenever the sunrays fell on him. For appearance's sake he had taken a book, but it was little he read; the greater part of the time the book remained lying on the dry pine spikes. The young man did not even look at the sea; with his face turned toward the house, he appeared to be interested in the domestic arrangements, in watching the servants go backward and forward, crossing the terrace at every moment, and whenever it was Naïs who happened to pass him a flash shot from his eyes. But Naïs, although she would slacken her pace and move off with the rhythmical sway of her body, never cast a look behind her.

For several days this comedy went on. In his mother's presence Frédéric treated Naïs almost roughly, as if she had been some awkward servant. Then the young girl would cast her eyes down in pleased bashfulness, as if enjoying the harsh words.

One morning at breakfast she broke a salad bowl, and Frédéric flew into a rage.

"How clumsy she is!" he cried. "Wherever is her head?"

And he jumped up furiously, saying that his trousers were spoiled. A drop of oil had stained his knee, and it sufficed to make him raise the house.

"What are you staring at? Give me a napkin and some water. Come and help me," he said to the girl.

Naïs dipped the corner of a napkin in some water and went down on her knees in front of Frédéric to rub the spot.

"Don't bother," said Mme Rostand. "That will do no good."

But the girl did not let go of her young master's trousers, which she went on rubbing with all the strength of her shapely arms, while he continued scolding her.

"I never saw such clumsiness. She must have brought it close to me on purpose to smash it. If she waited on us at Aix our china would soon be all in pieces," he grumbled.

These reproaches were so out of proportion to the gravity of the offense that Mme Rostand thought proper to try and appease her son as soon as Naïs had gone.

"What have you against the poor girl? One would think that you could not endure her. Be more gentle with her. She is an old playmate of yours, and she is not in the position of an ordinary servant here."

"Oh, she's a nuisance!" replied Frédéric, affecting a rough manner.

That evening at dusk, however, Naïs and Frédéric met in a shady spot at the end of the terrace. They had not yet spoken to one another alone. No one could hear them from the house. The pines filled the still air with a warm, resinous odor. Then Naïs asked in a whisper, in the familiar way of their childhood:

"Why did you scold me so, Frédéric? You were unkind."

Without replying he caught hold of her hands, drew her toward him and kissed her. She made no resistance but afterward went off, while he sat down on the parapet in order not to appear before his mother in his then excited state. Ten minutes afterward the girl was waiting at table with perfect and somewhat proud calmness.

Frédéric and Naïs made no appointments. Late one evening they found themselves together under an olive tree near the edge of the cliff. During dinner their eyes had several times exchanged glances. Then Naïs had gone home, and Frédéric had begun to roam about, possessed by a strange feeling. And, indeed, when after a while he came to the old olive tree he found her there, as if waiting for him. He sat down by her side and put his arm round her waist while she let her head fall upon his shoulder. For a moment they remained silent. The old olive tree with its gnarled limbs covered them with a roof of gray leaves. Before them stretched the sea, motionless beneath the twinkling stars. Marseilles, on the far side of the bay, was hidden by a cloud; on the left the revolving Planier light shone out every minute, piercing the gloom with a yellow ray which suddenly disappeared, and nothing could be softer or more tender than this light, constantly vanishing on the horizon and constantly returning.

"Is your father away?" asked Frédéric.

"I got out of the window," she said in her quiet voice.

They spoke no word of their love. That love came from afar, from the days of their infancy. The dawn was almost rising when they sought their rooms again.

CHAPTER III

LAND OF FIRE

WHAT a glorious month it was! Not one day of rain. The sky, invariably blue, displayed a satiny sheen, unflecked by any cloud. The sun rose a ruddy crystal and sank in a cloud of golden dust. Yet it was not hot, for the sea breeze came with the sun, and though it died away when he set, the nights were deliciously cool and balmy with the scent of aromatic plants diffusing the sweetness gathered during the day. The country is splendid. From both sides of the bay rocky arms jut out, while in the distance the islands seem to bound the horizon. In fine weather the sea appears to be nothing but a vast basin, a lake of an intense blue. In the distance, at the foot of the mountains, the houses of Marseilles climb up the low hills. When the atmosphere is clear one can see from L'Estaque the gray Joliette pier and the slender masts of the vessels in the port; beyond, houses peep out from among clumps of trees, and the chapel of Notre-Dame-de-la-Garde glitters white against the sky. The coast line winds about and takes broad sweeps before reaching L'Estaque, where manufactories throw out intermittent clouds of smoke. When the sun sinks below the horizon, the sea, almost black, looks as if it were slumbering between the two rocky promontories, whose whiteness is relieved by tinges of yellow and brown, pines, too, showing the dark green foliage against the reddish soil beyond. It is a vast panorama, a glimpse of the east, which departs, however, with the dazzling heat of day.

But L'Estaque has other sights besides the sea. The village, clinging to the mountainside, is traversed by roads which wind through a chaos of shattered rocks. The railway line between Marseilles and Lyons passes amid those masses, crosses bridges thrown over ravines and plunges under the cliffs themselves, remaining there for a distance of some four miles in what is called the tunnel of La Nerthe, the longest tunnel in France. Nothing can equal the savage grandeur of those gorges hollowed out among the hills, those narrow paths winding along at the foot of precipices, those barren mountains planted with pines, uprearing ramparts tinged as with rust and blood. Now and then a pass widens; a field of struggling olive trees fills the hollow of a valley; a lonely house shows its white frontage and closed shutters. Then come other rugged paths, impenetrable thickets, overturned rocks, dried-up torrents— all the surprises of a desert march. Over all, above the black fringe of pines, the sky stretches its expanse of silky blue.

Then there is the narrow line of coast between the rocks and the sea, the red soil pitted with immense holes, from which is taken the clay for tile-making, the chief industry of the district. Everywhere the ground is cracked and sundered, supporting with difficulty a few sickly trees and seemingly parched by a breath of burning passion. The roads are like beds of plaster, in which the traveler sinks to the ankles at every step, and flying clouds of dust powder the hedges at the least puff of wind. Little gray lizards sleep alongside the hot walls, which reverberate like ovens, while from the scorched grass rise whirring clouds of locusts. In the still and heavy air of the sleepy south there is no other sign of life than the grasshopper's monotonous song.

It was in this land of fire that Naïs and Frédéric loved one another for a month. It was as if all the heat of the sky had entered their veins. For the first week they were satisfied with their nightly meetings under the same olive tree on the edge of the cliff. There they tasted untold bliss. The cool night soothed their fever; they offered their burning cheeks and hands to the passing breeze, refreshing as a mountain spring. The sea broke with its slow, voluptuous dirge over the rocks at their feet; the penetrating odor of seaweed intoxicated them with passion.

Then leaning on one another's arms, they would watch across the bay the lights of Marseilles tingling the water at the mouth of the port with a reflection as of blood, the twinkling gaslights outlining the streets in many a graceful curve, while in the midst of all, above the town, it seemed as if there were a mass of sparkling flame. The garden on the Colline Bonaparte was plainly distinguishable by a double row of lights mounting heavenward. Those innumerable lights above the slumbering bay appeared to be illuminating some fairy town which the dawn would presently sweep away. And the sky, stretching over the black chaos of the horizon, also had its charm for them, a charm which alarmed and made them cling closer to one another. A rain of stars fell. On those clear Provençal nights the constellations resemble living flames. Shuddering beneath the vast space, they bowed their heads, turning their gaze on the solitary flicker of the Planier lighthouse, whose dancing scintillations stirred them, while their lips met again in a kiss.

But one night their eyes fell on the gigantic disk of the moon, glaring upon them with her yellow face. Out at sea a train of fire glittered, as if some enormous fish, some serpent from the depths, were trailing endless folds of golden scales, and then the glitter of Marseilles and the outlines of the gulf were obscured. As the moon rose the light increased; the shadows became more sharply defined. That heavenly witness was unwelcome to them. They feared they might be surprised if they remained so near La Blancarde. So when they next met they left the spot and walked into the shadowy open country. They found a meeting place in a deserted tile field; a ruined shed there concealed a pit in which two kilns remained still open. But the hovel saddened them; they preferred to have the open sky above their heads. So they explored the clay pits; they discovered delightful nooks, perfect little deserts, whence they could hear nothing but the barking of watchdogs. They prolonged their walks, wandering along the rocky coast in the direction of Niolon, following the course of the narrow gorges in search of distant grottoes and crevasses. For a fortnight they thus spent their nights. The moon had now disappeared; the sky had become dark again, but it seemed to them as if La Blancarde was too small to hold their love, as if they needed all the limitless expanse beyond it.

One night, as they were following a path above L'Estaque in order to gain the gorges of La Nerthe, they fancied they could hear a muffled step keeping pace with their own behind a plantation of pines stretching beside the road. They stopped in alarm.

"Do you hear that?" asked Frédéric.

"Yes; some stray dog," whispered Naïs.

And they continued on their way. But at the first bend in the road, after leaving the pines, they distinctly saw a dark object glide behind the rocks. It was certainly a human being, curiously shaped, looking, indeed, as if it were humpbacked. Naïs uttered an exclamation.

"Wait here," she said quickly.

And then she darted in pursuit of the shadow. Presently Frédéric heard the sound of rapid whispering. She returned, composed, but rather pale.

"What is it?" he asked.

"Nothing," she replied.

Then after a moment's silence she continued: "If you hear any steps don't be alarmed. It's Toine—you know, the hunchback. He wants to keep watch over us."

And, in fact, Frédéric was occasionally conscious of someone following them in the darkness. It was as if a protecting arm were stretched over them. More than once Naïs tried to drive Toine away, but the poor fellow merely asked to be her dog; he would not be seen; he would not be heard; why should he not be allowed to do as he pleased? From that time forward, if the lovers had listened attentively as they kissed in the lonely gorges, they would have caught the sound of smothered sobs behind them. It was Toine, their watchdog, weeping in his horny hands.

But at last those walks no longer sufficed them. They grew emboldened and took advantage of other opportunities to meet. Mme Rostand, who saw nothing, still blamed her son for being overrough toward his old playmate. Yet one day she almost surprised them kissing.

After dinner, when the evening was cool, Mme Rostand often liked to go for a walk. She then took her son's arm and went down to L'Estaque, telling Naïs to bring her shawl as a measure of precaution. They went all three of them to see the sardine fishers come in. Out at sea the lanterns danced, and soon the dark silhouettes of the boats could be discerned nearing the beach amid a muffled sound of oars. On good days joyous voices would ring out, and the women would hurry down, laden with baskets, while the three men who manned each boat set to work to empty the net, which, as it lay under the thwarts, looked like a broad, dark ribbon dotted with flashes of silver. The sardines, hanging by the gills to the meshes, still struggled and threw out a metallic luster. Then they fell into the baskets like a shower of crown pieces amid the pale light of the lanterns. Mme Rostand would often leave her son's arm to talk to the fishermen standing near a boat, interested by the sight, while Frédéric, standing at Naïs's side, outside the radius of light, clasped the girl's hands in a burst of passion. Meanwhile old Micoulin preserved stubborn silence. He went out fishing and came home to do a day's work, with ever the same deep look on his face. But at last his little gray eyes assumed an uneasy expression. He threw side glances at Naïs without saying a word. She seemed to him changed; there was something about her that he could not quite understand. One day she ventured to argue with him, and he thereupon gave her a blow which cut her lip.

That evening when Frédéric saw her mouth swollen he questioned her anxiously.

"It's nothing; only a blow my father gave me," she said.

Her tone was gloomy. And as the young man became angry and declared that he would see into it, "No, never mind," she said; "it's my business. There'll soon be an end to it."

She never told him of the beatings which she received. Only on the days when her father had treated her cruelly she kissed her lover with more ardor, as if to avenge herself on the old man.

Naïs had at first taken the most minute precautions in going to meet Frédéric, but at last rashness seized hold of her. Then, imagining from her father's manner that he suspected something, her prudence returned. She missed two appointments, as her mother told her that Micoulin did not sleep at night but got up and went about from one door to another. However, on the third day, seeing Frédéric's distress, the girl once more forgot all prudence. She went out at about eleven o'clock, resolving that she would not remain more than an hour absent, and she was in hopes that her father, being in his first sleep, would not hear her.

Frédéric was waiting for her under the olive trees. Without telling her fears she refused to go farther. They sat down in their usual place, looking at the sea and the glow of Marseilles. The Planier light was beaming. As Naïs watched it she fell asleep on Frédéric's shoulder. He did not move and, gradually yielding to fatigue himself, his own eyes closed.

No sound, only the chirrup of the grasshopper. The sea slept like the lovers. But suddenly a dark form came forth from the gloom and approached them. It was Micoulin who, awakened by the creaking of a window, had missed Naïs from her room. He had left the house, taking a small hatchet with him. When he saw a dark mass under the olive tree he grasped the handle of the implement. But the children did not stir; he was able to walk up to them, bend down and look in their faces. A slight exclamation escaped him as he recognized his young master. No, no, he could not kill him thus; the blood spilled on the ground would leave traces behind it and would cost him too dear. A peasant does not openly murder his master, for the master, even when he lies under the ground, is always the stronger. As Micoulin stood there, however, a look of savage determination came over his tanned face. At last he shook his head and went off stealthily, leaving the lovers asleep.

When Naïs returned to her room shortly before daybreak, much alarmed at having stayed away so long, she found her window just as she had left it. At breakfast Micoulin calmly watched her eat her bread. She felt safe; her father certainly knew nothing.

CHAPTER IV

PICNICKING

"AREN'T YOU coming out fishing any more, Monsieur Frédéric?" asked Micoulin one evening.

Mme Rostand was sitting on the terrace in the shade of the pines, embroidering a handkerchief, while her son, lying at her feet, was amusing himself by throwing pebbles.

"Not I," replied the young man. "I'm getting lazy."

"You are wrong," continued Micoulin. "The traps were full of fish yesterday. You can catch as many as you like just now. You'd like it. Come with me tomorrow morning."

He said this so good-humoredly that Frédéric, who thought of Naïs and did not want to fall out with the father, finally exclaimed: "Very well then. But you'll have to call me. I shall still be sound asleep at five o'clock."

Mme Rostand, feeling rather uneasy, had ceased working.

"Mind you be careful," she said. "I am always anxious when you are on the water."

Next morning Micoulin shouted to Frédéric in vain; the young man's window remained closed. Upon this he said to his daughter, with a savage irony which she did not detect: "You go. He'll hear you, perhaps."

Thus it was Naïs who woke Frédéric that morning. Ten minutes later the young man appeared, clad from head to foot in gray canvas. Old Micoulin was sitting on the parapet of the terrace, patiently waiting for him.

"It's cool; you'd better take a wrapper," he said.

Naïs went to fetch one, and afterward the two men descended the steep steps which led to the sea, while the girl, standing above, followed them with her eyes. At the bottom old Micoulin raised his head and looked at Naïs; there were deep creases at the corners of his mouth.

For the last five days the northeast wind, the mistral, had been blowing. On the previous day it had fallen at evening, but when the sun rose it returned, at first rather gently. At that early hour the sea, lashed by the sudden gusts, was of a deep mottled blue, and the white-crested waves, illumined by the first slanting rays, chased one another over the bosom of the deep. The sky was almost white and clear as crystal. In the distance Marseilles stood out with a distinctness which enabled one to count the windows in the fronts of the houses, while the rocks in the gulf were bathed in a delicate rosy haze.

"We shall have our work cut out to get back again," said Frédéric.

"Very likely," replied Micoulin.

He plied his oars silently, without turning his head. The young man looked for a moment at his bent back, noting his sunburned neck and red ears, from which little rings of gold were hanging. Then he leaned over the side of the boat, gazing into the depths. The sea became rougher, and big shadowy weeds floated by, looking like tufts of some drowned man's hair. This saddened and even alarmed Frédéric a little.

"I say, Micoulin," he remarked after a long silence, "the wind's getting stronger. Be careful; you know that I swim like a lump of lead."

"Yes, yes, I know," replied the old man in a dry voice.

Still he continued rowing in mechanical fashion. Then the boat began to pitch; the white foam on the crests of the waves turned into clouds of spray, which flew before the wind. Frédéric did not want to exhibit his alarm, but he felt very uncomfortable and would have given a great deal to have been on land again. At last he grew angry and exclaimed: "Where the devil have you stuck your traps? Are we bound for Algiers?"

But old Micoulin, without seeming to trouble himself, again replied: "We're all right; we're all right."

All at once he let go the oars, stood up in the boat and looked toward the shore, as if for certain guiding marks; there was still some five minutes' rowing to be accomplished before getting among the cork buoys which showed where the traps were placed. Once there, while Micoulin was drawing up the baskets, he remained for a few seconds with his face turned toward La Blancarde. Frédéric, following the direction of his eyes, distinctly saw a white form under the pines. It was Naïs, still leaning on the parapet.

"How many traps have you?" asked Frédéric.

"Thirty-five, and we mustn't stop here any longer than we can help," said Micoulin.

He laid hold of the buoy nearest to him and drew the first basket in. The depth was enormous; there was no end to the rope. At last the trap appeared with the large stone which had kept it at the bottom, and as soon as it left the water three fish began to leap about like birds in a cage. It seemed as if one could hear the beating of wings. In a second basket there was nothing, but in the third was found a somewhat rare capture—a small lobster, which flourished its tail violently. Frédéric was all attention now, forgetting his fears, leaning over the side of the boat and awaiting the baskets with beating heart. Whenever he heard a sound as of wings he felt like a sportsman who had just brought down his game. One by one, however, the baskets were drawn into the boat, the water, meantime, streaming around, and soon the whole thirty-five were secured. There were at least fifteen pounds of fish— a splendid catch for the Gulf of Marseilles, which from several causes, especially the extremely fine mesh of the nets which were used, had been yielding less and less fish for many years past.

"That's the lot," said Micoulin. "Now we can make for home."

He had carefully arranged his baskets in the stern, but when Frédéric saw him prepare to set the sail he remarked that with such a wind blowing it would be more prudent to row. The old man shrugged his shoulders. He knew what he was about. And before hoisting the sail he cast a last look in the direction of La Blancarde. Naïs's white dress was still there.

Then came the catastrophe, as sudden as a thunderbolt. Afterward, when Frédéric tried to think over what had happened, he remembered that all at once a gust had caught the sail and that all had then overturned. He could not call anything else to mind, save a feeling of intense cold and bitter agony. He owed his life to a miracle; he had fallen on the sail, which kept him afloat. Some fishermen, having seen the accident, hastened to his help and picked him up, as well as old Micoulin, who was already swimming toward the shore.

Mme Rostand was still asleep, and they concealed from her the danger which her son had incurred. At the foot of the terrace Frédéric and Micoulin, dripping with water, found Naïs, who had witnessed the scene.

"Devil take it!" cried the old man. "We'd taken up the traps and were coming home. Bad luck to it all!"

Naïs, who was deadly pale, looked fixedly at her father.

"Yes," she muttered, "it's bad luck. But when you sail in a wind like that you know what to expect."

Micoulin flew into a rage.

"What's that to do with you, lazybones? Can't you see Monsieur Frédéric's shivering? Help me get him indoors."

The young man escaped with a day in bed and told his mother that he had a headache. The next day he found Naïs very dispirited. She refused to meet him out of doors again, though one evening in the passage she kissed him passionately. She never told him of her suspicions, but from that day forward she watched over him. Then at the end of a week her fears began to diminish. Her father went about as usual; he even seemed kinder and beat her less often.

Every year the Rostands used to go to eat a bouillabaisse in a hollow of the rocks on the shore, in the direction of Niolon. Afterward, as partridges abounded among the hills, the gentlemen would organize a shooting party. That year Mme Rostand wanted to take Naïs to wait on them and refused to listen to Micoulin's remarks when the old savage attempted to raise some objection.

They set out early. The morning was a charming one. Lying like a mirror beneath the gleaming sun was the blue expanse of the sea; ripples appeared amid the currents, where the blue was tinged with violet, while in apparently stagnant spots the azure faded away into a milky transparency. You might have imagined the sea to be an immense piece of shot satin, whose changing colors grew more and more indistinct as the limpid horizon was reached. And over that slumbering lake the boat glided very softly.

The narrow beach on which they landed was at the mouth of a gorge, and they settled down on a strip of scorched grass which was to serve as a table.

How enjoyable that picnic was! First of all Micoulin set off alone in the boat to take up the baskets which he had set the day before. By the time he came back Naïs had gathered some thyme and lavender and enough dry wood to make a large fire. That day the old man was to make the bouilla-baisse, the classic fish soup, the secret of which the coast fishermen transmit from father to son. And a terrible bouillabaisse it was, with its strong doses of pepper and odor of crushed garlic. The Rostands were greatly interested in the preparation of the savory mess.

"Micoulin," said Mme Rostand, "do you think you will be as successful as last year?"

The old man seemed to be in excellent spirits. First of all he washed the fish in sea water, while Naïs took the large pan out of the boat. Soon all was in progress: the fish at the bottom of the vessel, just covered with some water, with some onion, oil, garlic, a handful of pepper and a tomato; then the whole was placed on the fire, a formidable fire, large enough to roast a sheep. Fishermen say that the goodness of bouillabaisse lies in the cooking: the pan must disappear amid the flames. Micoulin gravely cut some slices of bread into a salad bowl, and at the end of half an hour he poured the liquor on the slices, serving up the fish separately.

"Come along," he said. "It's not good unless it's hot."

Then the bouillabaisse was devoured with the usual jokes.

"I say, Micoulin, did you put any gunpowder in it?"

"It's very good, but it wants a throat of brass to swallow it."

Micoulin devoured his share tranquilly, swallowing a slice of bread at each mouthful and showing at the same time how flattered he felt at eating with his masters.

Having finished, they sat there waiting for the heat of the day to pass off. The glistening rocks covered with ruddy streaks threw grateful shadows around. Clumps of evergreen oaks showed somber foliage, while on the slopes the rows of pines ascended in regular lines, looking like little soldiers on the march. An oppressive silence filled the quivering air.

Mme Rostand had brought the endless embroidery, which was never seen to leave her hands. Naïs, seated at her side, seemed to be interested in the movements of her needle. But her eyes were really on her father. He was lying on his back a few paces away, enjoying a siesta. Then farther still, Frédéric also was sleeping beneath the protecting shade of his broad-brimmed straw hat.

At about four o'clock they awoke, and Micoulin declared that he knew of a covey of partridges at the bottom of a ravine. He had seen them three days previously, so Frédéric allowed himself to be tempted, and they both took their guns.

"Pray be careful," said Mme Rostand. "You might slip and hurt yourself."

"Yes, that does happen sometimes," said Micoulin quietly.

They then went off, and as they disappeared behind the rocks Naïs jumped up and followed them at a distance, muttering: "I'm going to see."

Instead of keeping to the pathway at the bottom of the gorge, she turned to the left among the bushes, hurrying along and avoiding the loose stones for fear of setting them rolling. At length, at a bend of the road, she espied Frédéric walking quickly, slightly bent and ready to lift his gun to his shoulder. As yet she saw nothing of her father, but presently she discovered him on the same slope as herself; he was crouching down, looking toward the gorge, and he seemed to be waiting for something. Twice he raised his gun. Supposing the partridges flew up between the two sportsmen, Micoulin and Frédéric might shoot one another. Naïs, gliding from bush to bush, anxiously took up a position behind the old man.

Some minutes passed. On the other side Frédéric had disappeared in a dip in the ground, but finally he reappeared and remained for an instant motionless. Then Micoulin, still crouching down, took a long aim at the young man. But with a kick Naïs knocked the barrel of his gun upward, and the charge went off in the air with a fearful report which brought down all the echoes of the gorge.

The old man sprang to his feet. On seeing Naïs he seized the gun by its smoking barrel, as if he meant to dash her to the earth with one blow. But the girl stood her ground, her cheeks as white as death, her eyes darting fire. He dared not strike her, and, trembling with rage, he could stammer out in dialect: "I'll kill him; never you fear!"

At the report of the gun the partridges had flown off, Frédéric winging two of them. And about six o'clock the Rostands returned to La Blancarde, old Micoulin rowing with his accustomed air of sullen, stubborn brutishness.

CHAPTER V

The Finding of the Body

September was drawing to an end. After a violent storm the air had become very cool. The days grew shorter, and Naïs refused to meet Frédéric out of doors at nighttime. However, as she reached the house every morning at six o'clock and Mme Rostand did not get up till nine, the lovers still had opportunities for converse.

It was now that Naïs showed the greatest affection for Frédéric. She would take hold of his neck, draw his face toward hers and look into it with a passion which filled her eyes with tears. It was as if she feared that she might never see him more. And she showered kisses upon him as if to protest and swear that she would guard him.

"What is the matter with Naïs?" Mme Rostand would often remark. "She changes every day."

Indeed, she was becoming thinner and quite pale. The fire in her eyes was dying away. She often remained for a long while silent and then would give a start, looking alarmed, like a girl awakening from a bad dream.

"You are ill, my child? You must take care of yourself," repeated her mistress.

But Naïs would smile and answer:

"Oh no, madame, I'm quite well and happy! I've never been so happy."

One morning as she was helping to count the linen, she ventured to ask a question.

"Are you going to stop late at La Blancarde this year?"

"Till the end of October," replied Mme Rostand.

Naïs stood still for a moment with fixed eyes; then she unconsciously said aloud: "Twenty days more."

A continual struggle was going on within her. She wished to keep Frédéric near her, and yet at the same time she was constantly tempted to cry out, "Go!"

He was lost to her; never would that season of love return; she had felt it from their first meeting. One night of gloomy despair she had even gone so far as to wonder whether she ought not to allow her father to kill Frédéric so that he might never love another, but the idea of seeing him dead—he, so delicate, so fair, more like a girl than herself—was unbearable to her, and the evil thought filled her with horror. No, she would save him, and he should never know of it. He might love her no longer, but she would be happy in the thought that he still lived.

She would often say to him, "Don't go to sea today; the weather will be rough." At other times she pressed him to leave La Blancarde: "You must be sick of being here; you won't love me any longer. Go to town for a few days."

These changes of humor surprised him. He thought her less handsome now that her face had become drawn, and, besides, his was a very fickle temperament. He began to pine for the eau de cologne and the rice powder of the beauties of Aix and Marseilles.

Meantime the old man's words were constantly ringing in Naïs's ears: "I'll kill him; I'll kill him!" In the middle of the night she would wake up, thinking that she had heard shots fired. She became timid and screamed whenever a stone rolled away from under her feet. When Frédéric was out of her sight she was always worrying about him, and what terrified her most was that from morning to night she still seemed to hear Micoulin repeating, "I'll kill him!" The old man, however, preserved stubborn silence; he never made any allusion to what had passed, either by word or gesture; but for her, his every look, his every movement, implied that he would kill his young master at the first opportunity he might have of doing so without being disturbed. And afterward he would deal with Naïs. In the meantime he kicked her about like some disobedient dog.

"Does your father still use you badly?" Frédéric asked the girl one morning.

"Yes," she replied; "he's going mad."

And after showing him her arms, which were black with bruises, she muttered these words, which she often whispered to herself: "It 'll soon be over; it 'll soon be over."

At the beginning of October she became more gloomy than ever. She was absent-minded, and one could often see her lips move as if she were talking to herself. On several occasions Frédéric perceived her standing on the cliff, seemingly examining the trees around her and measuring the depth of the abyss. A few days later he discovered her with Toine the hunchback, plucking figs on the farthest part of the estate. Toine used to come and help her whenever she had too much to do. He was under the fig tree, and Naïs, who had mounted on a thick branch, was joking with him, calling to him to open his mouth and then throwing down figs which burst upon his face. The poor fellow opened his mouth as he was bidden and closed his eyes in ecstasy, while his huge face expressed complete beatitude. Frédéric was certainly not jealous, but he could not refrain from taking Naïs to task.

"Toine would cut off his hand for us," she said curtly. "We mustn't ill-treat him; he may be useful later on."

The hunchback continued coming to La Blancarde every day. He worked on the cliff, where he was cutting a narrow canal to bring some water to the end of an experimental kitchen garden. Naïs used to go and watch him, and lively talk would ensue between them. He was so long over the task that old Micoulin finally called him a lazybones and kicked his legs, as he would have done his daughter's.

Rain fell on two successive days. Frédéric, who had to return to Aix the following week, determined that before leaving he would once more go out fishing with Micoulin. And seeing Naïs turn pale he laughed and replied that he should not choose a day when the mistral was blowing. Then as he was to leave so soon, the young girl consented to meet him once more. They met late at night on the terrace. The rain had cleansed the earth, and a strong odor rose from all the freshened vegetation. When that usually parched country is thoroughly soaked all its colors and odors become intensified: the red earth looks like blood; the pines are of an emerald green, the rocks of the whiteness of freshly washed linen. However, that night all that the lovers could detect was the enhanced perfume of the thyme and lavender bushes.

Old associations led them to the olive trees. Frédéric was walking toward one which had sheltered their first love meeting—it stood quite at the edge of the cliff—when Naïs, as if aroused from a reverie, caught hold of his arm, dragged him from the edge and said, trembling, "No, no, not there!"

"Why, what is the matter?" he asked.

She hesitated and finally remarked that after such a fall of rain the cliff was not safe. And she added: "Last winter there was a landslip here."

They sat down farther back under another olive tree. And at last Naïs convulsively burst into tears and would not say why she was crying. Afterward a frigid silence took possession of her, and when Frédéric joked her about her sadness and apathy in his company she murmured:

"No, don't say that. I love you too much. But I'm not in good health, and, besides, it's all over. You're going away."

He vainly tried to comfort her, telling her that he would come again from time to time and that next autumn he would spend two months there. But she shook her head; she knew very well that all was over now.

Their meeting ended in embarrassing silence. They gazed at the sea; Marseilles was glittering with gas lamps, but the Planier lighthouse showed only a solitary, mournful gleam, and gradually the horizon imparted to them some of its own melancholy. At three o'clock, when Frédéric quitted Naïs, kissing her, he felt her shudder.

He could not sleep when he got back into the house; he read till dawn and then, feeling feverish, he took up a position at the window. Just at that moment Micoulin was starting off to take up his traps. As the old man passed along the terrace he raised his head and asked Frédéric if he were coming with him that morning.

"No," replied Frédéric, "I've slept too badly. Tomorrow."

The old fellow went off with a slouching gait. He had to go down to his boat at the foot of the cliff, just under the olive tree where he had surprised his daughter. When he had disappeared Frédéric, on turning his head, was astonished to see Toine already at work; the hunchback was standing near the olive tree with a pickax in his hand, repairing the narrow channel which the rain had damaged. The air was cool; it was pleasant at the window. Frédéric went to make a cigarette, and as he lounged back to the casement a terrible crash—a roll of thunder, as it seemed—was suddenly heard. He rushed to the window. It was a landslip. He could only distinguish Toine, who was running for his life, flourishing his pickax, amid a cloud of red dust. At the edge of the abyss the old olive tree with its gnarled branches had pitched forward, crashing into the sea. A cloud of spray flew up, while a terrible cry rent the air. Then Frédéric saw Naïs leaning over the parapet, her stiffened hands clutching at the stonework, while her eyes peered into the depths below. There she stood, motionless and expectant, with her hands pressed to the low wall. Still she no doubt divined that somebody was looking at her, for she turned her head, saw Frédéric and cried: "My father! My father!"

An hour afterward they found Micoulin's mutilated body under the stones. Toine, almost crazy, related how he had almost been carried away himself, and everybody declared that it was wrong to carry a stream along the top of the cliff, on account of the infiltrations.

The old wife wept a great deal. As for Naïs, she followed her father to the cemetery with tearless eyes.

On the day after the catastrophe Mme Rostand had insisted upon returning to Aix. Frédéric was very pleased to leave, for the terrible drama had disturbed his peace of mind, and, moreover, in his opinion peasant girls with all their good looks were not equal to their town-bred sisters. He resumed his old mode of life. His mother, touched by his attentiveness to her at La Blancarde, gave him more liberty, so that he passed a very pleasant winter and fondly hoped that his life would always thus glide smoothly away.

M. Rostand had to go to La Blancarde at Easter and wished his son to accompany him, but the young man made various excuses. When the lawyer came back he said the next morning at breakfast: "Oh, by the way, Naïs is going to be married."

"Never!" cried Frédéric in amazement.

"And you'd never guess to whom," continued M. Rostand. "She gave me such good reasons, however."

The fact was Naïs was marrying Toine. In that way nothing would be changed at La Blancarde. Toine would still manage the property, as he had done since Micoulin's death.

The young man listened with an awkward smile. Presently he expressed the opinion that the arrangement was the best one possible for everybody concerned.

"Naïs has grown very old and plain," continued M. Rostand. "I didn't know her again. It is astonishing how quickly girls age on the coast, and she used to be quite pretty too."

"Yes, a feast of sunlight," said Frédéric composedly, and he quietly went on eating his cutlet.

MME NEIGEON

CHAPTER I

LIFE IN PARIS

EIGHT DAYS have gone by since my father, M. de Vaugelade, allowed me to leave Le Boquet, the mournful old château where I was born, in Lower Normandy. My father has strange ideas about the present times; he is a good half century behindhand. However, I am at last living in Paris, which I scarcely knew at all, having simply passed through it on two previous occasions. Fortunately I am not over awkward in my ways. Félix Budin, my old schoolfellow at the College of Caen, pretended, on seeing me here, that I was superb and that the *Parisiennes* would surely dote on me. This made me laugh. But when Félix had left I caught myself standing before a looking glass, contemplating my five feet six inches and smiling at my white teeth and black eyes. Then, however, I shrugged my shoulders, for I'm not conceited.

Yesterday for the first time in my life I spent an evening in a Parisian drawing room. Countess de P——, who is in some degree my aunt, had asked me to dinner. It was her last Saturday. She wanted to introduce me to M. Neigeon, a deputy for our constituency of Gommerville, who had just been appointed undersecretary of state and is on the highroad, so people say, to become a minister. My aunt, who is far more tolerant than my father, plainly declared to me that a young man of my age must not sulk with his country, even if its government were Republican. She wishes to get me an official appointment.

"I will undertake to talk to that obstinate old Vaugelade," she said; "leave everything to me, my dear George."

Precisely at seven o'clock I reached the countess's house. But it seems that people dine very late in Paris. The guests arrived one by one, and some had not yet put in an appearance when half-past seven struck. The countess informed me with an expression of distress that she had been unable to secure M. Neigeon's company; he was retained at Versailles by some parliamentary imbroglio. Nevertheless, she still hoped that he might look in for a moment duing the evening. As a stopgap she had invited another deputy of our department, "fat Gaucheraud," as we call him down there. I knew him already, as we had once gone shooting together.

This Gaucheraud is a short, jovial fellow, who has lately let his whiskers grow in the hope of thereby giving himself a serious appearance. He was born in Paris, where his father was a petty solicitor of small means, but down our way he has a rich and very influential uncle, whom he somehow prevailed upon to run him as candidate. I was not aware that he was married, but at table my aunt placed me beside a young fair-haired lady, who looked very pretty and shy and whom fat Gaucheraud called Berthe at the top of his voice.

We were all assembled at last. It was still daylight in the drawing room, which looks toward the west, when all at once we entered the dining room, which had its curtains drawn and was lit up by a chandelier and several lamps. The change seemed very singular, and as we took our seats some remarks were made about the way in which the last dinners of the winter season are saddened by the lingering twilight. My aunt detested it. And the conversation on the subject was kept up: how mournful, said somebody, did Paris look when you drove across it in the waning light on your way to an invitation. I said nothing myself, but I had not experienced any such impression in my cab, though it had jolted roughly over the paving stones for a half-hour. As a matter of fact, Paris, seen amid the first gleams of the gaslight, had filled me with a passionate desire to partake of all the enjoyment with which it would presently blaze.

By the time the entrees were served, people raised their voices and politics were discussed. I was surprised to hear my aunt expressing political opinions. However, the other ladies were all conversant with state affairs, called prominent men by their names, without any such prefix as "monsieur," and debated and passed judgment on everything and everybody. In front of me Gaucheraud was taking up an enormous amount of room and talking at the top of his voice while steadily eating and drinking. But all those political matters did not interest me; I did not even understand the true sense of many remarks, and so I ended by devoting all my attention to Mme Gaucheraud, Berthe, as I already called her in my own mind for brevity's sake. She was really very pretty. As she sat beside me her ear struck me as being particularly charming: a pretty little rounded ear it was, with light yellowish hair curling around it. She had one of those fair necks, covered behind with little wavy locks which quite upset one. Every now and then, when her shoulders moved, her dress body, which was cut very low, gaped a little, and I noticed a supple, feline undulation about her back. I did not admire her profile so much, as it was rather sharp. She talked politics with even greater eagerness than any of the others.

"Madame, may I pour you out some wine? Shall I pass you the salt, madame?" I asked, striving to be as polite as possible, forestalling her slightest desires and interpreting her every glance and gesture. She had given me a long look as we sat down to table, as if to judge me once and for all.

"Politics bore you, do they not?" she said to me at last. "They plague *me* to death. But then one has to talk about something, and nowadays in society politics are the only thing that people care for."

Then she darted off to another subject.

"Is Gommerville a pretty place?" she asked. "Last summer my husband wanted to take me to see his uncle there, but I felt frightened and pretended that I was ill."

"The country is very fertile," I replied; "there are some beautiful plains."

"Ah, good. Now I know the truth," she resumed with a laugh. "It is a frightful spot, eh? A perfectly flat country with fields following fields and ever the same fringes of poplar trees rising up at intervals."

I wanted to protest, but she had started off again, discussing some proposed law on secondary education with the guest seated on her right hand, a solemn-looking man with a white beard. At last, however, the conversation turned to theatricals. Whenever she leaned forward to answer a question asked from the other end of the table, the feline undulations of her neck filled me with emotion. At Le Boquet, amid the covert impatience of solitude, I had dreamed of a fair-haired beauty, but she was slow of gesture and had a noble face, and Berthe's mouselike mien and curly hair quite revolutionized my dream. Nevertheless, while the vegetables were being served I glided into some wild fancies. We were alone, she and I, and I kissed her on the neck, and she turned round and smiled at me; whereupon we started together for some very distant land. But the dessert was served, and at that moment she said to me in a whisper, "Pass me that dish of sweetmeats there in front of you."

It seemed to me that there was a caressing softness in her eyes, and the light pressure of her arm on the sleeve of my dress coat gave me a delightful thrill.

"I'm awfully fond of sweetmeats, aren't you?" she resumed as she nibbled at some candied fruit.

Those simple words stirred me to such a degree that I fancied myself in love with her. As I raised my eyes I noticed Gaucheraud, who had been looking at me while I whispered with his wife. He wore his usual gay expression and smiled in an encouraging manner. The idea of the husband smiling calmed me.

But the dinner was drawing to an end. It did not seem to me that a Paris dinner party sparkled with more wit than one at Caen. Berthe alone surprised me. My aunt having complained of the warmth, the company reverted to their first subject of conversation, discussing the spring receptions and finally opining that it was only at wintertime that one really dined well. Then we went off to the little drawing room to take coffee there.

By degrees a great many people arrived. The three drawing rooms and the dining room likewise became crowded. I had sought refuge in a corner, and as my aunt passed near me she said to me hurriedly: "Don't go away yet, George. His wife has arrived. He has promised to fetch her, and I will introduce you."

She was still talking of M. Neigeon, but I scarcely listened. I had heard two young men near me exchanging hasty remarks which filled me with emotion. They were standing on tiptoes at a door of the big drawing room, and at the moment when Félix Budin, my old schoolfellow at Caen, came in and bowed to Mme Gaucheraud, the shorter of the two asked the other: "Are they still on the same terms?"

"Yes," the taller one answered, "more so than ever. It will last till the winter now. I have never known her keep an admirer so long."

This did not cause me any particular pang, but I felt hurt in my self-esteem. Why had she told me in so soft a voice that she was fond of sweetmeats? I certainly had no intention of contending against Félix, yet I ended by persuading myself that those young men had slandered Mme Gaucheraud. I knew my aunt; she was a person of very rigid principles and would not suffer women of doubtful repute in her house. Gaucheraud, as it happened, had just sprung forward to greet Félix, whom he tapped in a friendly way on the shoulder while eying him affectionately.

"Ah, here you are," said Félix as soon as he discovered me. "I came on your account. Well, will you let me pilot you?"

We remained together in a recess formed by a doorway. I should greatly have liked to question him about Mme Gaucheraud, but I did not know how to do so in an offhand, indifferent way. While seeking a transition I questioned him about a number of other people for whom I cared nothing at all. He named them to me and gave precise particulars about each of them. He was, I should say, a Parisian by birth and had merely spent a couple of years at the college at Caen at the time when his father was prefect of the department of Calvados. I found him very free in his language, and a smile appeared on his lips when I asked him for information about some of the women present.

"Are you looking at Mme Neigeon?" he suddenly asked me.

To tell the truth, I was looking at Mme Gaucheraud. And so somewhat foolishly I answered: "Madame Neigeon—ah, where is she?"

"She's that dark woman yonder, near the chimney piece. She's talking with a fair woman in a low dress."

Near Mme Gaucheraud, indeed, there stood a lady whom I had not previously noticed and who was laughing gaily.

"Ah, so that's Madame Neigeon," I repeated.

Then I examined her. It was a great pity that she was dark, for she struck me as being charming, not quite so tall as Berthe, but with a magnificent crown of black hair. Her eyes were both bright and soft. Her little nose, her finely modeled mouth and her dimpled cheeks indicated a lively and yet thoughtful disposition. Such, at least, was my first impression. But my views became confused as I looked at her, for I soon saw her laughing more loudly and freely than even her friend.

"Do you know Neigeon?" Félix asked me.

"I? Not at all. My aunt is to introduce me to him."

"Oh, he's a nullity, a downright fool," Félix continued. "Political mediocrity in all its perfection—one of those stopgaps that are so useful in parliamentary government. As he does not possess two ideas of his own and every prime minister can, therefore, employ him, he figures in the most contradictory ministerial combinations."

"And his wife?" I asked.

"His wife? Well, you see her. She is charming. If you want to obtain anything from him pay court to his wife."

Félix affected some unwillingness to say anything further. But at last he gave me to understand that Mme Neigeon had made her husband's fortune and continued watching over the home with a view to its prosperity. All Paris attributed lovers to her.

"And the fair lady?" I suddenly inquired.

"The fair lady," Félix answered without the faintest show of feeling, "is Madame Gaucheraud."

"She is a respectable woman, isn't she?"

"Oh, no doubt she's respectable."

Félix assumed a serious demeanor but was unable to preserve it. His smile appeared once more, and I even fancied that I could detect on his features an expression of conceit, which annoyed me. The two women had doubtless noticed that we were occupying ourselves with them, for they forced their laughter. I remained alone, a lady having led Félix away, and I spent the evening comparing Mme Neigeon with Mme Gaucheraud, feeling at once hurt and attracted, failing to understand things aright and experiencing the anxiety of a man who fears lest he may be guilty of some act of foolishness in venturing into a sphere of which he has no knowledge.

"Neigeon hasn't come; what a nuisance he is!" exclaimed my aunt when she again found me in the same corner by the door. "But it's always like that. True, it is barely midnight as yet, and his wife is still waiting for him."

I went round through the dining room and took up a position at the other door of the salon. In this wise I found myself behind the two ladies I have mentioned. Just as I reached the spot I heard Berthe calling her friend Louise. That is a pretty name. Louise was not wearing a low dress. Under her heavy coils of hair I could only see a white strip of neck, but that glimpse of whiteness seemed to me for a moment to be far more fascinating than the exhibition which Berthe was making of her back. Then, however, I no longer knew what to think; they both seemed adorable, and in the perturbed state in which I found myself it appeared to me impossible to choose between them.

But my aunt was looking for me everywhere. It was already one o'clock.

"Have you changed doors?" she said. "Well, he won't come. Every evening that man Neigeon has to save France. At all events, I will introduce you to his wife before she leaves. And mind that you are amiable, for that is important."

Without awaiting my answer the countess placed me in front of Mme Neigeon, giving her my name and briefly acquainting her with my position. I felt rather awkward and could scarcely find a few words. Louise waited with that smile of hers on her face, and then, seeing that I remained embarrassed, she simply bowed. It seemed to me that Mme Gaucheraud was looking at me contemptuously. Both rose, however, and withdrew. In the antechamber, used as a cloakroom, a fit of wild merriment came over them. However, their free-and-easy, bold, masculine ways astonished nobody but me. As they passed the other men drew back and bowed to them with a commingling of extreme politeness and social good-fellowship which stupefied me.

Félix offered me a seat in his cab. But I escaped from him, for I wished to be alone, and I did not hail any driver, for it pleased me to go on foot through the silence and solitude of the streets. I felt feverish, just as one feels at the approach of some severe illness. Was a passion springing up within me? Like the travelers who pay tribute to new climes, I was about to be sorely tried by the atmosphere of Paris.

CHAPTER II

Louise

It was only this afternoon that I met those ladies again, this time at the Salon de Peinture, which, it so happened, opened today. I confess that I knew I should meet them there and that it would be very difficult for me to pronounce an opinion on the value of the three or four thousand paintings before which I promenaded for four successive hours. Félix had promised me yesterday that he would call for me about noon; we were to lunch at a restaurant in the Champs Elysées and then repair to the salon.

I have reflected a great deal since the countess's soiree took place, but I must own that reflection has not brought me much enlightenment. How strange a world is Parisian society, at once so polished and so corrupt! I am not a rigid moralist but, nonetheless, I feel embarrassed when I think of the fearful things that I heard men saying to one another in my aunt's drawing room. If one were to believe their muttered comments more than half the women present were disreputable. How was one to tell the truth amid all those assertions? I had at first thought that in spite of all my father had said on the subject my aunt really received a very questionable set. But Félix asserted that things were just the same in most Parisian drawing rooms. Ladies, even the most severely inclined among them, were compelled to show a great deal of tolerance lest they should find their houses forsaken. Then, my first feeling of revolt having calmed down, I simply felt an impulse to snatch at the facile pleasures placed within my reach.

For the last four days I had never awakened in my little flat in the Rue Laffitte without thinking of Louise and Berthe, as I familiarly called them. A singular phenomenon was at work within me; I ended by confounding them together. I was now certain that Félix was Berthe's lover, but this, instead of wounding my feelings, seemed a kind of encouragement, and though my thoughts and plans remained very vague, I was convinced that I had only to choose between Berthe and Louise to become the master of one or the other.

When we entered the first gallery of the fine-art show I was amazed at the great crowd that was stifling there.

"The devil," muttered Félix; "we are rather late. We shall have to use our elbows."

It was a very mixed throng of artists, bourgeois and society people. In the midst of overcoats badly brushed and frock coats black and gloomy, there were many light gowns, those spring Paris gowns which look so gay with their soft silk and their bright trimmings. And I was particularly delighted by the quiet assurance of the women, who cut through the thickest of the throng without even a thought of their trains, whose waves of lace always ended by effecting a passage. In this wise they went from one picture to another as if they were simply crossing their drawing rooms. Only *Parisiennes* can thus retain a goddesslike serenity in a public crush, as if the words they hear and the contact they have to put up with could not possibly reach and soil them. For a moment I watched one lady, who Félix told me was the Duchesse d'A——. She was accompanied by two daughters of from sixteen to eighteen years of age, and the three of them examined a Leda without so much as blinking, while a party of young painters behind them made merry over the picture with the greatest freedom of language.

But Félix turned into the left-hand galleries, a succession of large square rooms where the crowd was less compact. A white light fell from the glazed roof, a crude light softened by linen hangings. The dust raised by the tramping of the people set, as it were, some slight smoke above the sea of heads. The women needed to be very pretty to bear the effect of that light, that uniform tone, with which the paintings on the four surrounding walls contrasted violently. There one perceived an extraordinary medley of colors—reds, yellows and blues all clashing and running riot amid the bright gold of the picture frames. It was becoming very warm. Some bald-headed gentlemen with polished, glistening craniums puffed as they walked about, hat in hand. Every nose was raised upward. There was quite a crush in front of certain canvases. And one incessantly heard the tramping of feet over the floor boards, accompanied by a vague, endless clamor like the roaring of waves.

"Ah!" Félix suddenly remarked to me. "There's the big affair that folks talks so much about."

People stood, five rows deep, in contemplation before "the big affair." There were ladies with glasses, artists talking spitefully and a tall, lean gentleman taking notes. But I scarcely gave a glance in that direction, for in a neighboring room I had caught sight of two ladies leaning against the handrail and inquisitively examining a little picture on the line. At first there was but a flash of thick black tresses and a mass of fair fluffy hair showing under stylish hats. Then this vision vanished; a wave of the crowd, a sea of heads, hid both ladies from my view. But I could have sworn to them. After taking a few steps I again caught sight now of the fair hair, now of the black tresses, between the ever-moving heads in front of me. I said nothing to Félix; I contented myself with leading him into the next room, maneuvering in such wise that it might seem as if he were the first to recognize the ladies. Had he already noticed them, as I had done? I almost believed so, for he gave me a glance full of delicate irony.

"Ah, what a fortunate meeting!" he exclaimed as he bowed.

The ladies turned and smiled. I awaited the effect of this second interview; it was decisive. Mme Neigeon quite upset me with a mere glance of her black eyes, whereas I seemed to be simply meeting a friend again in the person of Mme Gaucheraud. This time then it was the lightning flash. *She*—Mme Neigeon—was wearing a small yellow hat trimmed with a branch of glycine, and her gown was of mauve silk with trimmings of straw-colored satin, the whole forming a very soft yet showy toilet. However, it was only later that I really scrutinized her. At the first moment she appeared to me in a blaze of light, as if she scattered sunbeams around her.

But Félix was talking. "Nothing remarkable, eh?" he said. "I have seen nothing yet."

"It is the same, *mon Dieu*, as it is every year," Berthe declared.

Then turning toward the wall, she added: "Look at this little painting which Louise discovered. The gown is so beautifully done! Madame de Rochetaillé wore one exactly like it at the ball at the Elysée."

"Yes," murmured Louise, "only the ruches fell squarewise over the *tablier*."

They again studied the little picture, which represented a lady standing before a boudoir mantelpiece, reading a letter. The painting seemed to me very commonplace, but somehow I felt full of sympathy for the painter.

"Why, where is he?" suddenly asked Berthe, as she looked around her. "He loses us at every dozen yards!"

She was speaking of her husband.

"Oh, Gaucheraud is over yonder," quietly exclaimed Félix, who could see everybody. "He is looking at that big Christ in sugar candy, hanging from a gingerbread cross."

In a peaceful, disinterested way the husband, with his hands behind him, was indeed making the rounds of the room on his own account. On catching sight of us he came up to shake hands and said in his jovial fashion: "There's a Crucifixion yonder which shows remarkable religious sentiment. Have you noticed it?"

The ladies, however, were walking on. We followed them with Gaucheraud. His presence authorized us to accompany them. We spoke of M. Neigeon, who would no doubt look in at the show if he could only escape early enough from a committee meeting at which he was to give the government's opinion on a very important question. Gaucheraud, meantime, took possession of me with many expressions of friendship. This embarrassed me, for it was necessary that I should answer him. Félix smiled and gently nudged my elbow, but I failed to understand him. For his part, profiting by the fact that I was keeping the fat man occupied, he walked on in front with the ladies. I only caught snatches of their conversation.

"So you are going to the Variétés this evening?"

"Yes, I have taken a corner box; the piece is said to be amusing. . . . I shall take you, Louise. Oh, I insist on it."

And farther on:

"So now the season is over. The opening of the salon is the final Parisian solemnity."

"But you forget the races!"

"Ah yes, I've an idea of going to the races at Maisons-Laffitte. It's a very pretty place, I'm told."

Meantime Gaucheraud was talking to me about Le Boquet, a superb estate, he said, the value of which had been more than doubled by my father. I could tell that he was bent on flattery. But I barely listened to him. I was stirred to the depths of my being each time that Louise's long train brushed against me as she suddenly stopped before some picture. Under her black hair her white neck looked as delicate as a child's. However, she retained her masculine ways, which somewhat annoyed me. A great many people bowed to her, and she laughed at them and attracted general attention by her outbursts of gaiety and the quick motions of her skirts. On two occasions she turned around and looked at me fixedly. I walked on as in a dream; I could not say how many hours I followed her in this fashion, dazed by Gaucheraud's chatter and the leagues of paintings which spread out on right and left. I only knew that toward the end we were all chewing dust and that for my own part I felt horribly fatigued, whereas the women bore up and smiled with all bravery.

At six o'clock Félix carried me off to dinner. And at dessert he suddenly exclaimed: "I've got to thank you."

"What for?" I asked him in great surprise.

"Why, for the delicacy you have shown in not paying court to Madame Gaucheraud. So you prefer dark women?"

I could not help flushing, but he hastily added: "Oh, I don't desire your confidence. You must have noticed that I abstained from intervening. In my opinion a man ought to make his apprenticeship in life alone."

He was no longer smiling but wore a serious, friendly air.

"So you think——" I began.

"I think nothing," he answered. "Do as you fancy. You will soon see how things turn out."

I regarded this remark as a piece of encouragement. Félix had reverted to his ironical tone, and lightly, as if jesting, he pretended that Gaucheraud would have liked to see me fall in love with his wife.

"Oh, you don't know the beggar! You didn't understand why he flung himself so eagerly on your neck. The fact is that his uncle's influence is declining in your district, and if he had to face another election he would be heartily glad of your father's support. Well, as you can understand, I felt frightened directly I saw that you might be useful to him, for he has used me up already."

"But that's abominable!" I exclaimed.

"Why abominable?" Félix resumed in so quiet a fashion that I could not tell whether he was in earnest or not. "When a woman is bound to have friends it is just as well that they should prove useful to the home."

On rising from table Félix talked of going to the Variétés. I had seen the piece there two days previously, but I dissembled and expressed a keen desire to become acquainted with it. And what a charming evening we spent. The ladies happened to be in a corner box, quite close to our stalls. On turning my head I could read on Louise's features the pleasure she took in the actors' jests. A couple of evenings previously I had found those jests idiotic. But they no longer offended me; I enjoyed them, since they seemed to foster a kind of complicity between Louise and myself. It was a very broad piece, and it was at the most questionable passages that she laughed the loudest. Whenever our eyes met amid the laughter she refrained from lowering them. I could not help thinking that the piece helped on my interests. Truth to tell, the whole house enjoyed itself; many women in the balcony stalls laughed outright, without even indulging in any fan play by way of hiding their blushes.

We went to pay our respects to the ladies during one of the entr'actes.

Gaucheraud had just gone out, so we were able to sit down. The box was very gloomy, and I could feel Louise near me. Her skirts were spread out, and at a sudden movement she made they quite covered my knees. It was entrancing to be thus near her. That contact seemed to me like a first secret avowal, which bound us one to the other.

CHAPTER III

A Bargain

Ten days have now gone by. Félix has disappeared, and I can devise no pretext that might bring me and Mme Neigeon together again. My only resource is to buy five or six daily papers in which I read her husband's name. He intervened lately in a serious debate in the Chamber and delivered a speech about which people are still talking. At any other time that speech would have bored me to death, but nowadays it interests me, because it seems as if I could distinguish Louise's white neck and black tresses behind all the verbose phraseology. I have even had a violent discussion about M. Neigeon—whose incapacity I defended—with a gentleman whom I scarcely know. The malicious attacks of the newspapers quite upset me. That man is an imbecile, no doubt, but then this only proves the superior intelligence of his wife, if indeed it be true, as people say, that she has been the good fairy to whom he owes his fortune.

During these ten days of vain impatience and fruitless rambles I have called quite five times on my aunt, ever in the hope of some piece of good luck, some unforeseen meeting. On the occasion of my last call I managed to displease the countess so seriously that it will be a long time before I shall dare to return to her house. She had taken it into her head to procure me an appointment in the diplomatic service by M. Neigeon's influence, and her stupefaction was intense when I refused the offer on account of my political opinions. The worst was that I accepted it originally, that is, before I had fallen in love with Louise, and had come to the conclusion that I could not decently accept any favors from her husband's hands.

My aunt, who had no notion of the motives of delicacy which actuated me, expressed profound astonishment at what she called my childish capriciousness. Did not many Legitimists, who were quite as scrupulous as myself, represent the republic abroad? she asked. Indeed, diplomacy was the refuge of the Legitimists. They filled the embassies and rendered useful service to the good cause by keeping possession of high positions which the Republicans envied them.

I was, for good reasons, greatly embarrassed as to how I might answer my aunt, and at last I sought a refuge in ridiculous rigidity of principles, whereupon my aunt ended by calling me a fool, for she felt all the more furious since she had already mentioned the affair to M. Neigeon. But no matter! At all events, Louise will never have cause to think that I court her simply in order to secure a berth from the government.

People would laugh at me if I were to relate through what a strange succession of feelings I have passed during the last ten days. At first I felt convinced that Louise had noticed the emotion with which she inspired me and that it was not displeasing to her. Thus conquest on my part seemed quite possible. But on reflection I began to doubt all this. Surely I must be a fool to think that a woman would throw herself at my head so openly and quickly. Mme Neigeon could have no thought of me. It was quite possible that she had already had lovers, but assuredly any intrigue in which she had engaged had been a far more intricate affair than this. There must be a great distance between such a woman as I had dreamed of, a creature of mere elementary passions and instincts, and an artful *Parisienne,* expert in concealment, such as Louise doubtless was.

Thus she seemed to escape me entirely. I no longer saw her; I no longer knew even if it were indeed true that I had spent five minutes with her in a gloomy box in a theater, feeling her palpitate beside me. And I became very wretched—to such a point, in fact, that for a moment I thought of hurrying back to Le Boquet and shutting myself up there.

But on the day before yesterday there come to me an idea which I was astonished at not having had before. It was to attend a sitting of the Chamber. Perhaps M. Neigeon would speak; perhaps his wife would be there. But it was written that I was not yet to set eyes upon that singular man. Though it had been decided that he should speak, he did not even put in an appearance. It was related that he had been detained by some committee business at the Senate. On the other hand, as I was sitting down in the rear of one of the galleries I experienced keen emotion, for I perceived Mme Gaucheraud in the front row of the gallery facing me. She saw me and looked at me with a smile. Louise, alas, was not with her. My delight fell. On leaving, however, I contrived to meet Mme Gaucheraud in a passage. She displayed a familiar manner. Félix had certainly spoken to her about me.

"Have you been absent from Paris?" she inquired.

I remained speechless, indignant at such a question. Absent? When I had been scouring the city so furiously!

"Well, one meets you nowhere!" she resumed. "The last reception at the Ministry was superb, and the horse show was marvelous."

Then noticing my expression of despair, she began to laugh.

"Well, till tomorrow," she said as she walked away. "We shall see you over yonder, shan't we?"

I answered "Yes" in a stupid fashion, never daring to ask a question for fear that I might again hear her laugh. She had turned around and looked at me with a malicious expression. "Come," she murmured in the discreet tone of a friend who had some pleasant surprise in store for one.

A wild impulse came upon me to run off after her and question her. But she had already turned into another passage, and I bitterly reproached myself with my foolish pride, which had prevented me from acknowledging my ignorance. I was certainly quite ready to go "yonder," but where might "yonder" be? The vagueness of the appointment tortured me, and at the same time I felt ashamed at not knowing what everybody else seemed to know. In the evening

I hastened to Félix' rooms with the view of skillfully extracting from him the information which I needed. But Félix was not at home. Then in my grief I plunged into the perusal of the newspapers, selecting those which gave the most society news and striving to guess, among the announcements for the morrow, what spot *le bon ton* would select as a meeting place. But my perplexity increased, for all sorts of functions were announced: an exhibition of paintings by some of the old masters, a charity bazaar at a big club, a musical mass at Sainte-Clotilde, a general rehearsal, two concerts, the veil taking of an aristocratic novice, without mentioning horse races in all sorts of directions. How could a new arrival in Paris, a provincial conscious of his shortcomings, hope to arrive at the truth amid such confusion? I understood perfectly well that the proper thing was to attend one of those functions, but which one was it? Oh heaven! Finally, at the risk of wandering about all day consumed with vain impatience if I were mistaken, I dared to make a choice. It occurred to me that I had heard the ladies speak of the races at Maisons-Laffitte, and, an inspiration coming to me, I resolved to repair thither. This decision taken, I began to feel calmer.

What a delightful stretch of country is that formed by the environs of Paris! I was not acquainted with Maisons-Laffitte, which charmed me with its houses so gay of aspect, built on a slope which borders the Seine. Now that we have reached the first days of May the apple trees, which are all white, look like big bouquets amid the tender greenery of poplar and elm.

At first, however, I quite lost my bearings between the walls and the quickset hedges, for I was unwilling to ask anybody the way. On seeing a great many people take the same train I had felt overjoyed, but the ladies were not there, and as I scanned the passers-by in Maisons-Laffitte itself my heart contracted. I was really losing myself alongside the Seine, beyond all the houses, when all at once keen emotion brought me to a standstill near a big tuft of nettles. A group of people, still some fifty yards away, was slowly coming toward me, and I recognized Louise and Berthe. Gaucheraud and Félix, those inseparables, followed them at a distance of a few paces. So I had guessed rightly! This filled me with pride. But my emotion was so great that I behaved like a nincompoop. I hid myself behind the tall clump of nettles, full of a nameless shame, dreading lest I should appear ridiculous. When Louise passed the hem of her skirt brushed against the bushes. However, I at once realized the folly of my first impulse. And so I made all haste to cut across the fields, and as the others reached a bend in the road I came up in the most natural manner possible—like a man, indeed, who, thinking himself alone, is yielding to the dreamy mood inspired by the open air.

"Oh, is it you!" cried Gaucheraud.

I bowed, affecting extreme surprise. We all raised exclamations and shook hands. But Félix laughed in his singular fashion, while Berthe positively winked at me, thereby establishing additional complicity between us. As we walked on I remained for a few seconds with her, behind the others.

"So you have come," she said to me gaily in an undertone.

And without giving me time to answer she began to jest, saying that I was very happy in still being so young. I felt that I had an ally in her; it seemed to me that she would have been well pleased to help me with her friend. Then as Félix turned round to inquire, "What are you laughing about?" she replied in all tranquillity: "Oh, Monsieur de Vaugelade has been telling me of his journey in the company of a whole family of English tourists."

Gaucheraud, however, had again taken Félix by the arm and was leading him off as if to avoid troubling my tête-à-tête with his wife. I remained between her and Louise and spent a most entrancing hour on the shady road which followed the banks of the Seine. Louise was wearing a light silk gown, and her sunshade with its pink lining steeped her face in a warm, shadowless glow. Here in the country there was more freedom than ever in her demeanor; she talked in a loud voice and looked me full in the face while replying to Berthe, who turned the conversation to rather venturesome subjects with a pertinacity which greatly struck me later on.

"Give Madame Neigeon your arm," she ended by saying to me. "You are certainly not gallant; you can surely see that she is tired."

I offered Louise my arm, and she leaned on it at once. Then Berthe having joined her husband and Félix, we two remained together more than forty paces behind. The road ascended the slope, and we walked very slowly. Down below flowed the Seine between meadows stretching out like carpets of green velvet. There was a long, slender island, too, intersected by two bridges, over which the trains rushed with a noise like distant thunder. Then across the water there was a vast cultivated plain stretching to Mont Valérien, whose gray buildings could be seen amid a dust of sunshine on the very fringe of the sky. But what affected me almost to tears was an odor of springtide spreading all around us as it rose from the herbage on either side of the road.

"Shall you soon go back to Le Boquet?" Louise asked me.

I was foolish enough to answer "No," for I did not foresee that she would add: "Ah, that's annoying, for next week we are going to Les Mûreaux, my husband's property, which is only some two leagues from your place, and my husband meant to ask you to call and see us there."

At this I began to stammer that my father might possibly recall me sooner than I had expected. It had seemed to me that I could feel her arm pressing my own. Was she giving me an assignation then? With the ideas that I had formed of this *Parisienne*, so free and coquettish in her ways, I at once built up a perfect romance: an intrigue in the country, a whole month of passion under the trees. Yes, it was doubtless thus; she found in me the qualities of a young squire and would grant me her love amid suitable surroundings.

"I have to scold you," she suddenly resumed, assuming an affectionate, almost maternal manner.

"How is that?" I murmured.

"Yes, your aunt has spoken to me about you. It seems that you will not accept anything from us. That is very discourteous. Why do you refuse?—tell me."

I blushed again; I was on the point of making a declaration, of exclaiming, "I refuse because I love you." But she made a gesture as if she understood my intention and wished me to remain silent. And then she added with a laugh: "If you are proud, if you wish to render service for service, we will willingly accept your protection over yonder. You know that a general councilor has to be elected. My husband is a candidate, but he fears defeat, which in our posi- tion would be very unpleasant. Will you help us?"

It was impossible to be more charming. That election story seemed to me to be a mere pretext devised by a clever woman to enable us to meet again in the country.

"But certainly I'll help you," I answered.

"And if you succeed in getting my husband returned it is understood that he in his turn will give you a helping hand."

"It is a bargain."

"Yes, a bargain."

She offered me her little hand, and I tapped it, as the custom goes, by way of sealing our agreement. We made merry together. It really seemed to me most delightful. We had passed the last of the trees; the sunlight streamed down on the crest of the hill, and we walked on, silent, amid the great heat. But of course that imbecile Gaucheraud must come to disturb that quivering silence under the flaming sky. He had heard us mention the General Council, and he gave me no more peace but began to tell me all about his uncle and to maneuver for an introduction to my father. At last we reached the race ground. They found the races superb. For my part, I stood all the time be- hind Louise, looking at her delicate neck. And how delightful was the return homeward after a sudden shower! Beneath the rain the greenery had become softer still; the leaves and the earth sent forth a delightful smell, the very scent of love. Louise half closed her eyes, as if tired and penetrated by all the voluptuousness of springtime.

"Remember our bargain," she said to me at the railway station as she entered her carriage which was waiting there. "At Les Mûreaux in a fortnight's time, eh?"

I pressed the hand she offered, and I fear that I must have been a little rough, as for the first time I saw her become grave, with two little creases as of dis- pleasure about her lips. But Berthe still seemed bent on encouraging me to be bold, and Félix retained his enigmatical smile, while Gaucheraud slapped me on the shoulder, exclaiming, "At Les Mûreaux in a fortnight, Monsieur de Vaugelade. We shall all be there."

The devil take him!

CHAPTER IV

NEWS

I HAVE JUST COME BACK from Les Mûreaux, and such contradictory ideas and impressions fill my mind that it is needful I should recapitulate the day I have spent with Louise in order to arrive at a clear opinion.

Although the estate of Les Mûreaux is only two leagues from Le Boquet, I knew little of that part of our district. Our own shooting is in the direction of Gommerville, and as a rather long round has to be made to cross the little Béage River, I had not gone there a dozen times in my life. Yet the slope is delightful with its climbing road edged by big walnut trees. Then after reaching the plateau you dip down again, and Les Mûreaux lies at the entry of a dale, whose slopes soon contract into a narrow gorge. The house, a square building of the seventeenth century, is of no great importance, but the grounds are magnificent with their broad lawns and the snatch of forestland at the far end—such a tangle of trees that the very paths are barred by the branches.

When I arrived on horseback two big dogs greeted me with a prolonged barking and jumping. At the end of the avenue I caught sight of a white spot. It was Louise in a light gown and a straw hat. She did not come down to meet me but remained motionless and smiling on the large flight of steps that leads to the hall. It was nine o'clock at the latest.

"Ah, how nice of you!" she called to me. "You, at all events, are an early riser. I am the only one up at the château, as you see."

I complimented her, saying that for a *Parisienne* she was really courageous. But she added with a laugh: "It is true that I have only been here five days. I would get up with the chickens the first mornings. Only as soon as the second week arrives I gradually relapse into my sluggardly ways and end by coming down at ten o'clock, the same as in Paris. This morning, however, I am still a countrywoman."

I had never seen her looking so charming. In her haste to leave her room she had negligently knotted her hair and slipped into the first morning wrap she found. And with her eyes still moist with sleep and her cheeks quite fresh she seemed a young girl again. Some little locks of hair were waving over her neck, and whenever her broad sleeves gaped I could see her bare arms as far as the elbows.

"Do you know where I was going?" she resumed. "Well, I was going to inspect a screen of convolvuli on that arbor yonder. It is marvelous, it seems, when the sun has not yet closed the flowers. The gardener told me of it, and as I missed the sight yesterday I don't want to do so today. You will come with me, won't you?"

I felt a great inclination to offer her my arm, but I understood in time that it would be ridiculous. She ran on like a schoolgirl enjoying a holiday. On reaching the arbor she gave a cry of admiration. From aloft hung quite a drapery of convolvuli, a shower of little bells, pearly with dew, and of delicate hues ranging from vivid rose color to violet and pale blue. The whole suggested one of those phantasies of exquisite grace and strangeness that one finds in Japanese albums.

"This is one's reward when one gets up early," said Louise merrily.

Then she sat down under the arbor, and on seeing that she drew back her skirts to make a little room, I ventured to place myself beside her. I was in a state of keen emotion, for the thought had come to me of bringing matters to a crisis by catching her round the waist and kissing her on the neck. I felt well enough that such roughness was better suited to a young lieutenant dealing with a housemaid, but I could think of nothing else. I don't know whether Louise understood what was passing in my mind, but though she did not get up her face assumed a very grave expression.

"First of all, shall we talk of our business?" she said.

There was a buzzing in my ears, but I tried to listen to her. It was dim and rather cold in the arbor. Sparks of golden sunshine came in here and there between the foliage of the convolvuli, and on Louise's white wrap they looked like golden flies, golden insects, settling there.

"Well, what is the position?" she asked me with the air of an accomplice.

I thereupon told her of the singular change which I had noticed at my father's. He, who for ten years had never ceased railing at the new state of things and had forbidden me to serve the republic, had now given me to understand, on the very evening of my return, that a young man of my age owed duty to his country. I suspected my aunt of having effected this conversion. Some women must have been set on him. Louise smiled as she listened, and she ended by saying: "I met Monsieur de Vaugelade three days ago at a neighboring château where I was making a call. We had a little conversation."

Then she quickly added: "You know that the election for the General Council will take place next Sunday. You must start on your campaign at once. With your father's help my husband's success will be certain."

"Is Monsieur Neigeon here?" I inquired after some slight hesitation.

"Yes, he arrived last night. But you won't see him this morning, for he has gone off in the direction of Gommerville to take *déjeuner* with a friend, a landowner who has a good deal of influence."

She rose, but I remained seated for yet another moment, deeply regretting that I had not kissed her on the neck, for never should I again find such a dim little nook and such an early propitious hour. It was too late now, and I understood so thoroughly that I should simply make her laugh by falling at her feet on the damp ground that I put off my declaration till a more favorable moment.

Besides, I had just perceived Gaucheraud's bulky silhouette at the end of the path. On seeing Louise and myself come out of the arbor he gave a little sneer. Then he expressed astonishment at our courage in rising so early. For his part, he had only just come down.

"And Berthe?" Louise asked him. "Did she sleep well?"

"Well, I really don't know," he answered; "I haven't seen her yet."

Then noticing my astonishment, he explained that his wife had a headache for the whole day whenever she was disturbed in the morning. And he added that they had long found it most convenient to have separate rooms, one for him and one for her. I must confess that this gave me food for thought. I recalled all manner of stories that I had heard and read of *Parisiennes* in country houses, and when I saw Berthe and my friend Félix come together out of the hall I could not help thinking that my surmises might be true.

I shook hands with Félix, and I can hardly account for it, but by the smile which Louise and Berthe exchanged while Gaucheraud stood by, quietly whistling, the idea occurred to me that Louise was not ignorant of the matter I have referred to. And more than ever now I regretted not having kissed her while we were in the dim little arbor.

We had *déjeuner* at eleven o'clock. After the meal Gaucheraud took himself off for his siesta. He had unbosomed himself to me, telling me that he feared he might not be successful at the next elections and that he proposed remaining three weeks in the district in the hope of gaining support. Thus after staying with his uncle he had desired to spend a few days at Les Mûreaux in order to show everybody that he was on the best of terms with the Neigeons, for this, in his opinion, might win him a good many votes. I understood that he was also extremely desirous of being invited to my father's. Unfortunately it seemed that I did not care for fair-haired women.

I spent a very gay afternoon with the ladies and Félix. Château life, with Parisian graces frolicking in the open air amid the sunshine of early summer, is really charming. The drawing room spreads out over the lawns. It is no longer the winter drawing room, where you are virtually cooped up, where the women in low dresses ply their fans while the men in black swallowtails stand up alongside the walls. It is a kind of holiday drawing room, with women in light garb scampering freely hither and thither, while the men in their short jackets show themselves amiable and natural: a setting aside, as it were, of society etiquette, a familiarity which banishes the boredom of the stereotyped conversation that one hears at the winter gatherings. Nevertheless, I must confess that the behavior of the ladies still surprised me, reared as I was in the provinces among pious folks. When we took coffee on the terrace after *déjeuner* Louise allowed herself a cigarette, and Berthe talked slang in the most natural manner possible. Later on they took themselves off amid a great rustling of skirts, and one heard them laughing in the distance and calling one another, full of a flightiness which greatly disturbed me. It is foolish to own it, but these manners, so novel to one like myself, made me hope that Louise would give me an early assignation. As for Félix, he quietly went on smoking cigarettes, but at times I caught him looking at me in his almost sarcastic way.

At half-past four I spoke of leaving. But Louise immediately protested: "No, no; you can't go yet. I shall keep you to dinner. My husband will certainly come back, and then you will see him. Really, now, I must introduce you to him."

I explained to her that my father was expecting me. I was compelled to be present at a dinner he was giving at Le Boquet, and with a laugh I continued: "It is an election dinner; I have got to work for you."

"Oh, in that case," she said, "make haste. And if you succeed, you know, come for your reward."

It seemed to me that she blushed as she spoke those words. Did she simply refer to the appointment in the diplomatic service which my father is urging me to accept? I thought I might attribute another meaning to her words, and no doubt I assumed a very conceited air, for all at once, for the second time, I saw her become very grave, with those little creases about the lips which gave her such an expression of proud displeasure.

But I had no time to reflect upon that sudden change of expression. As I was starting a little conveyance drew up before the house steps. I already imagined that the husband had returned. But there were only two children, a little girl about five and a little boy of four, in the vehicle, accompanied by a maid. They stretched out their arms and laughed, and as soon as they could spring to the ground they threw themselves among Louise's skirts. She kissed them on the hair.

"Whose pretty children are these?" I asked.

"Why, mine," she replied with an air of surprise.

Hers! I cannot express in words what a blow that simple answer dealt me. It seemed to me as if she were all at once escaping from me, as if those little beings with puny hands were digging an impassable abyss between her and me. What! She was a mother, and I had known nothing of it! I could not restrain the cry: "So you have children?"

"No doubt," she quietly responded. "They went to see their godmother, two leagues from here, this morning. Allow me to introduce them—Monsieur Lucien, Mademoiselle Marguerite."

The little ones smiled at me. I must have looked very stupid. No, I could not accustom myself to the idea of it. It upset all my notions. I went off with my head in a whirl, and even at this moment I don't know what to think. I see Louise in the arbor draped with convolvuli, and I see her kissing the hair of Lucien and Marguerite. Decidedly those *Parisiennes* are far too intricate for provincials like me. I must get to sleep. I will try to understand things tomorrow.

CHAPTER V

A LESSON

THIS IS THE FINISH of my adventure. Oh, what a lesson! But let me try to relate things calmly.

Last Sunday M. Neigeon was elected as general councilor. After the counting of the votes it became evident that without our support he would have failed. My father, who, for his part, has seen M. Neigeon, gave me to understand that a man of such utter mediocrity was not to be feared. Besides, it was a question of beating a radical candidate. However, after dinner in the evening the old Adam reappeared in my father, and he contented himself with saying to me:

"All that is not very clean business. But everybody repeated to me that I was working for you. Well, do what you think fit. For me the only course left is to take myself off, for I no longer understand things."

On the Monday and Tuesday I hesitated about going to Les Mûreaux. It seemed to me that it would be bad taste to go in search of thanks so quickly. The thought of the children no longer inconvenienced me. I had persuaded myself that there was very little motherliness about Louise. Besides, did not people say in our part of the country that the *Parisiennes* never allowed chil-

dren to interfere with their amusements but handed them over to the care of
servants, so as to enjoy perfect liberty themselves? So yesterday, Wednesday,
all my scruples disappeared. I was consumed with impatience and set off for
the battle at eight o'clock in the morning.

My plan was to reach Les Mûreaux as on the first occasion, at an early hour,
so as to find Louise alone. But when I dismounted from my horse a servant
told me that Madame had not yet left her room and made no offer to go and
warn her of my arrival. So I simply replied that I would wait.

And, indeed, I waited two long hours. I don't know how many times I made
the rounds of the flower beds. Every now and again I raised my eyes to the
first-floor windows, but the shutters remained closed. Tired, enervated by this
long promenade, I ended by sitting down in the bower of convolvuli. The sky
was overcast that morning, and the sunshine did not glide in golden dust between the foliage. It was almost night, indeed, amid the verdure. I reflected, resolving that I must risk everything. I was convinced that if I should again hesitate I should lose Louise forever. As soon as I should be alone with her I would
take hold of her hands and affect great emotion so as not to frighten her too
much, but afterward I would kiss her on the neck, as I had thought of doing
on the former occasion. I was for the tenth time perfecting my plan when all at
once Louise herself appeared before me.

"Where are you hiding?" she gaily called, looking for me in the dark arbor.
"Oh, you are here, are you? I have been hunting for you for the last ten
minutes. I must apologize for having kept you waiting."

Somewhat huskily I answered that there was nothing unpleasant in having
to wait when one's thoughts were of her.

"I warned you," she replied without paying attention to my silly compliment, "that I'm not a countrywoman for more than the first week. I've now
become a Parisian again and can no longer leave my bed."

She had remained at the entrance of the arbor, as if she did not wish to risk
herself amid the gloom falling from the foliage.

"Well, aren't you coming?" she ended by asking me. "We have to talk, you
know."

"But one is very comfortable here," I said in a quivering voice. "We can
talk on this bench."

She again hesitated, just for a second, then bravely replied: "Oh, as you like.
It is rather dark here; still we don't need to see our words."

Thereupon she sat down near me. I felt like fainting. So the fateful hour had
come! Yet another minute and I should take hold of her hands. She, however,
still perfectly at ease, continued chatting in her clear voice, in which there
was not the faintest sign of emotion.

"I won't thank you in ready-made phrases," she said. "You have given us
good help, without which we should have been beaten."

I was in no condition to interrupt her. I was trembling and exhorting myself to be brave.

"Besides, there is no need of words between us," she resumed. "We concluded
a bargain, you know."

She laughed as she said this, and her laugh suddenly emboldened me. I caught hold of her hands, and she did not withdraw them. I could feel them so little and so warm in my own. She surrendered them to me in a friendly, familiar way, while repeating: "Yes, that is so, isn't it? And now it is my turn to carry out my part of the agreement."

Thereupon I suddenly became audacious and rough, drawing her hands toward my lips. The gloom had increased; a cloud must have been passing over us, and the strong scent of all the plant life around us intoxicated me in that nest of foliage. But before my lips could reach her she freed herself with a nervous strength which I should never have suspected and in her turn caught me roughly by the wrists. And she held me like that without any show of anger, her voice remaining calm, though it assumed somewhat of a scolding tone.

"Come, no childishness," she said. "This is what I feared. Will you allow me to give you a lesson while I hold you here in this little corner?"

She showed the smiling severity of a mother reprimanding a boy.

"I understood you from the very first day. You had been told horrors about me, had you not? And so you conceived fancies which I forgive you, for you know nothing of our sphere of society. You landed in Paris with the ideas of this wolfish region, and perhaps you may say that it is in some measure my fault if you made a mistake. I ought to have stopped you, for you would have withdrawn at a word from me. That's true, and I did not speak that word; I let you go on, and you must regard me as an abominable coquette. Do you know, however, why I did not speak that word?"

I began to stammer. The strangeness of the scene paralyzed me with aston-ishment. She held my wrists yet more tightly and shook me while remaining so close to me that I could feel her breath on my face.

"I did not say it, because I felt interested in you and wished to give you this lesson. Young men fresh to the world form very erroneous and foolish ideas of women. You don't understand as yet, but you will reflect and guess. We women are very much slandered. Perhaps we do all that is needed to bring that about. Only, you see, there are some who are perfectly virtuous even among those who seem to be the wildest and most compromised. All that is a very delicate matter, but, I repeat, you will reflect and end by understanding."

"Let me go," I murmured in confusion.

"No, I will not let you go. Beg my pardon, if you wish me to do so."

In spite of her jesting tone I could feel that she was growing irritated; that tears of anger were rising to her eyes beneath the affront she had received from me. Within me was springing up a feeling of esteem, of genuine respect, for that woman who was at once so charming and so capable. Her amazonian grace in virtuously enduring her husband's imbecility, her blending of coquetry and rigor, her disdain for evil tittle-tattle and her skill in playing a man's part in the household amid seeming flightiness of conduct—all made her a very com-plex creature and filled me with admiration.

"*Pardon!*" I humbly said.

She released me. I at once rose to my feet while she remained quietly seated